# NORTH

P.F. Chisholm is an author and
journalist. She is a graduate of Oxford
University with a degree in History. Her
first novel, *A Shadow of Gulls*, published
when she was eighteen, won the David
Higham Award for Best First Novel.

Also by P.F. Chisholm

KNIVES IN THE SOUTH

*Comprising*

A Plague of Angels
A Murder of Crows
An Air of Treason

# GUNS
## IN THE
# NORTH
## P.F. CHISHOLM

*Comprising*

A FAMINE OF HORSES

A SEASON OF KNIVES

A SURFEIT OF GUNS

HEAD
ZEUS

First published as an omnibus edition in the UK
in 2017 by Head of Zeus, Ltd
This paperback edition first published in 2017
by Head of Zeus, Ltd

*A Famine of Horses* first edition 1994
*A Famine of Horses* Copyright © P.F. Chisholm, 1994

*A Season of Knives* first edition 1995
*A Season of Knives* Copyright © P.F. Chisholm, 1995

*A Surfeit of Guns* first edition 1996
*A Surfeit of Guns* Copyright © P.F. Chisholm, 1996

*Guns in the North* Copyright © P.F. Chisholm, 2017

9 7 5 3 1 2 4 6 8

A CIP catalogue record for this book is available from the British Library.

ISBN (PB) 9781786696120
ISBN (E) 9781786696168

Printed and bound in Germany by CPI Books GmbH

Head of Zeus Ltd
5–8 Hardwick St
London EC1R 4RG

WWW.HEADOFZEUS.COM

# CONTENTS

Introduction

# INTRODUCTION

Anyone who has read any history at all about the reign of Queen Elizabeth I has heard of at least one of Sir Robert Carey's exploits— he was the man who rode 400 miles in two days from London to Edinburgh to tell King James of Scotland that Elizabeth was dead and that he was finally King of England. Carey's affectionate and vivid description of the Queen in her last days is often quoted from his memoirs.

However, I first met Sir Robert Carey by name in the pages of George MacDonald Fraser's marvellous history of the Anglo-Scottish borders, *The Steel Bonnets*. GMF quoted Carey's description of the tricky situation he got himself into when he had just come to the Border as Deputy Warden, while chasing some men who had killed a churchman in Scotland.

'...about two o'clock in the morning I took horse in Carlisle, and not above twenty-five in my company, thinking to surprise the house on a sudden. Before I could surround the house, the two Scots were gotten into the strong tower, and I might see a boy riding from the house as fast as his horse would carry him, I little suspecting what it meant: but Thomas Carleton...told me that if I did not...prevent it, both myself and all my company would be either slain or taken prisoners.'

The nondescript William Carey, who had supplied the family name by marrying the ex-official mistress, quite clearly did not supply the family genes. Lord Hunsdon was very much Henry VIII's son—he was also, incidentally, Elizabeth's Lord Chamberlain and patron to one William Shakespeare.

Robert Carey was (probably) born in 1560, given the normal education of a gentleman from which he says he did not much benefit, went to France for polishing in his teens, and then served at Court for ten years as a well-connected but landless sprig of the aristocracy might be expected to do.

Then in 1592 something made him decide to switch to full-time soldiering. Perhaps he was bored. Perhaps the moneylenders were getting impatient.

Perhaps he had personal reasons for wanting to be in the north. At any rate, Carey accepted the offer from his brother-in-law, Lord Scrope, Warden of the English West March, to be his Deputy Warden.

This was irresistible to me. In anachronistic terms, here was this fancy-dressing, fancy-talking Court dude turning up in England's Wild West. The Anglo-Scottish Border at that time made Dodge City look like a health farm. It was the most chaotic part of the kingdom and was full of cattle-rustlers, murderers, arsonists, horse-thieves, kidnappers and general all-purpose outlaws. This was where they invented the word 'gang'—or the men 'ye gang oot wi'' —and also the word 'blackmail' which then simply meant protection money.

Carey was the Sheriff and Her Majesty's Marshal rolled into one—of course, I had to give him a pair of pistols or dags, but they only fired one shot at a time. He was expected to enforce the law with a handful of horsemen and very little official co-operation. About the only thing he had going for him was that he could hang men on his own authority if he caught them raiding—something he seems to have done remarkably rarely considering the rough justice normally meted out on the feud-happy Border.

Even more fascinating, he seems to have done extremely well— and here I rely on reports and letters written by men who hated his guts. By 1603 he had spent ten years on the Border in various capacities, and got it quiet enough so he could take a trip down to London to see how his cousin the Queen was doing. Unfortunately for him, Carey also seems to have been too busy doing his job to rake in the cash the way most Elizabethan office-holders did.

So when Carey made his famous ride, he was a man of 42 with a wife and three kids, no assets or resources, facing immediate redundancy and possible bankruptcy. As he puts it himself with disarming honesty, 'I could not but think in what a wretched estate I should be left...I did assure myself it was neither unjust nor unhonest for me to do for myself. ...Hereupon I wrote to the King of Scots.'

What Carey did after his ride will have to wait for future books—or you could read his memoirs, of course. As GMF says, 'Later generations of writers who had never heard of Carey found it necessary to invent him...for he was the living image of the gallant young Elizabethan.'

Based on a few portraits, I think he was quite good-looking—as he had to be to serve at Court at all, since Queen Elizabeth had firm views on the sort of human scenery she wanted around her. As he admits himself, he was a serious fashion victim. Nobody wears a satin doublet *and* a sash of pearls unless that's what they are, which is how he's peacocking it in one of his portraits. Most remarkable of all, he married for love not money—and was evidently thought very odd for it, since he was perpetually broke.

And that's it, the original man, an absolute charmer I have lifted practically undiluted from his own writings. The various stories I tell are mostly made up, though all are based on actual incidents in the history of the Borders. About half of the characters (and most of the bad guys) really lived and were often even worse than I have described. As I say in most of the historical talks I give, we like to think we're terribly violent and dangerous people but really we're a bunch of wusses. The murder rate has dropped to a tenth of what it was in the Middle Ages—and they didn't have automatic pistols. It took real work to kill somebody then.

And yes, I'm afraid I have fallen, hook, line and sinker, for the elegant and charming Sir Robert Carey. I hope you do too.

# A FAMINE OF HORSES

*To my grandmother, Dr Lila Veszy-Wagner,*

*who wrote historical novels in Hungarian*

# FOREWORD

There are few joys in life as sweet as discovering a new author—new in the sense of being hitherto unread. A friend put me onto the mysteries of Robert Crais. I became a fan of Dana Stabenow's Alaskan mysteries at the last Bouchercon Mystery Writers Convention. I found Janet Evanovich by lurking on an on-line mystery newsgroup. I began to read Laurence Shames after a fortuitous mention in a review of another writer's novel. And I owe the Poisoned Pen's Barbara Peters a huge debt for introducing me to P.F. Chisholm. I knew, of course, of her writing as Patricia Finney; writers of historical fiction sometimes seem like an endangered species and so we tend to keep track of one another.

But I was unaware that she was writing Elizabethan mysteries under the name P.F. Chisholm until Barbara brought it to my attention. Once I started to read *A Famine of Horses*, my own life came to a screeching halt while I plunged wholeheartedly into Robert Carey's. To me, it is an added bonus that he actually lived, an honest-to-God cousin and courtier of the Tudor Queen, Elizabeth. I can think of no more enjoyable way to learn history than to read one of Ms Chisholm's mysteries—just be prepared to let dinners burn and bills go unpaid while you're in Robert's world, a world that is seductive and occasionally savage and always mesmerizing. Dana is absolutely right when she says these are You-Are-There books. A Chisholm mystery is the next best thing to time travel, and perhaps even better when we consider 16th-century sanitation and flea-infested inns and wine so polluted that impurities had to be spat out before it could be safely swallowed. For those readers who are purists and believe a book will rise or fall upon the merits of the story

7

line, rest assured that a Chisholm mystery will provide enough suspense and plot twists to satisfy even the most critical of audiences. For those who find the journey more compelling than the final destination, a Chisholm novel will offer an unforgettable Elizabethan pilgrimage. And for those who just enjoy good writing, a neat turn of phrase, again Ms Chisholm delivers. Thanks to P.F. Chisholm, a door is opening upon the 16th century; I would urge you all to take advantage of the opportunity and cross over.

Sharon Kay Penman
sharonkaypenman.com

# A FAMINE OF HORSES

# SUNDAY, 18TH JUNE 1592, NOON

Henry Dodd let the water drip off the end of his nose as he stared at a trail in the long sodden grasses. It was simple enough: two horses, both burdened, though from a long slide mark by a little hump he thought the bigger of the two was carrying a pack rather than being ridden by a man who could have avoided it. The prints kept close enough for the one to be leading the other.

He looked up and squinted at the low hills north of the border where the Picts' Wall ran. They melted into the grey sky so it seemed there was no difference between the earth and the cloud and a lesser man might have made comparisons between them and the area of moss and waste between, where the purely theoretical change between England and Scotland took place.

Sergeant Henry Dodd, however, had no time for such fancyings. He was mortally certain that the two men, or possibly one and a packhorse, had been where they had no business to be, and he wanted to know why.

Blinking intently at the traces, he turned his horse and let her find her own path amongst tussocks and rabbit holes, following the trail before it was washed into mud.

Behind him his six patrolmen muttered into their chests and followed in sodden misery. They had been on their way home to Carlisle from a dull inspection of the fords on the River Sark when the Sergeant had seen the trail and taken it into his head to follow it. By the time they got to the guardroom, Lowther's men would have taken the best beer and the least stale loaves and if there was cheese or meat left, it would be a wonder.

Dodd crested a small rise and paused. Ahead of him three crows yarped in alarm and flapped into the sky from a little stand of gorse, to which the trail led directly.

'Sergeant...' began Red Sandy Dodd, nervously.

'We're still in England.'

'We could send some men out this afternoon...'

Dodd twisted in the saddle and looked gravely at his brother, who shrugged, smiled and subsided. The Sergeant turned and kicked his reluctant mare down the slope towards the gorse.

The others followed, sighing.

Beside the stand of gorse was a stone marked about by the prints of hooves where horses had stood. From there into the gorse there was a swathe of flattened and rubbed grass, stained here and there by smears of brown almost completely turned back to mud now. None of the horses wanted to approach, they neighed and sidled at the smell. The Sergeant's mare tipped her hip and snorted long and liquidly in warning.

Dodd leaned on his saddle crupper and nodded at the youngest of them.

'Right, Storey, go and fetch it out.'

Bessie's Andrew Storey had a pleasant round face with a few carefully nurtured brown whiskers about the upper lip and he looked denser than he was.

'In there, sir?'

You're struggling against fate, said the Sergeant's dour look.

'Ay,' he answered.

Dodd turned away to inspect the marks in the ground again. Bessie's Andrew looked at the gorse and knew his horse had more sense than to venture in. He slid down from his saddle, knocking his helmet from its hook as he went and muttered as it landed in a puddle.

'Bessie'll have your guts if yon man's got plague,' said Bangtail Graham cheerily. Dodd grunted at him.

Nobody else spoke as Storey squelched through the scrub, following the trail, pushing spines aside with his elbows and sidling through the gaps as best he could. His sword caught on a low branch and another spined branch whipped back as he let go of it and caught him round the back of the head. Still cursing he disappeared from sight.

'There's a body here, Sergeant,' he called at last.

'Is there now,' said Dodd in tones of sarcastic wonder. 'Whose?'

'I'm not sure, sir. The face...' There was a pause and a sound of swallowing. 'The face is pecked, sir.'

'Guess.'

'I dunno, sir. From the look of his jack, I'd say it might be a Graham.'

There was a general shifting in saddles. Dodd sighed deeply as Bangtail Graham came up beside him looking worried and intent. The other men looked covertly at the two of them from under their lashes.

'Which Graham?'

'Dunno, sir. He was shot in the back.'

More silence.

'Fetch him out then, man,' said Dodd gently, 'it's wet out here.'

## SUNDAY, 18TH JUNE 1592, NOON

Barnabus Cooke had bruises and blisters on his backside and was filled with loathing for his master. The rain fell without cease, as it had since they left Newcastle, the horses were sulky and unwilling, two of the packs had been so ill-stowed by the grooms at their last inn that they forever threatened to break loose. In the meantime the expensive brocade trim on his cloak (that his master had told him not to bring) was ruined, and his velvet doublet would need an hour of brushing if it was not to dry to a lumpish roughness and his ruff was a choking wad of soaked linen that he had not the heart to take off and squeeze dry.

His master came trotting up to ride beside him and smiled.

'Only another ten miles, Barnabus, and we'll be in Carlisle.'

Ten more miles, *only ten*, thought Barnabus in despair, what's sir's bum made of then, cured leather? 'Yes, Sir Robert,' he said. 'Any chance of a rest?'

'Not around here, Barnabus,' said Sir Robert Carey, looking about as if he was in some dubious alley in London. 'Best keep going and rest once we're inside the castle.'

Barnabus looked about as well, seeing nothing but disgusting empty green hills, close-packed small farms, coppices of trees, rain, sky, rain. No sign of civilisation except the miserable stone walls the barbarian northerners used in place of proper hedges, and the occasional ominous tower in the distance.

Behind him trailed the four garrison men from Berwick that Sir Robert's brother had sent to meet them at Newcastle, and behind them Barnabus's nephew Simon whose mother had terrorised him into taking her baby to learn him gentle ways. That was while he and Sir Robert had been at Court, serving Her Majesty Queen Elizabeth, eating palace food and standing about in anterooms and galleries while Barnabus raked in fees from the unwary who thought, mistakenly, that the Queen's favourite cousin might be able to put a good word in her ear. That was in the happy profitable time before the letter came for Sir Robert via the Carlisle Warden's messenger riding post. Barnabus had been sent out to buy black velvet and see if Mr Bullard would give Carey a bit more credit and make a new suit in two days flat.

To be fair Sir Robert had offered to get Barnabus a job with his friend the Earl of Cumberland if he didn't want to go into foreign northern parts. He'd even offered to pay some of the back wages he owed, but Barnabus Cooke had been too much of a fool to grab the offer and stay in London where he could understand what men said.

The four Berwick men were muttering incomprehensibly to each other again. One came cantering past Barnabus, spraying him with mud, to talk urgently to Sir Robert.

Barnabus hunched his back and shifted forwards a little to try and take the weight off the worst worn parts of him. Sir Robert was talking quickly with the soldier, his voice suddenly tinged with an ugly northern harshness, so Barnabus could no longer understand him either.

There were men with lances on one of the hills nearby, he could see that now. Sir Robert was staring at them, narrowing his eyes, peering north, then south.

Barnabus began to feel a little sick. Everyone was behaving exactly as if they were in Blackfriars coming out of a primero game and the alley was blocked by armed men.

There were eight lancers, to be precise.

Sir Robert was riding alongside him now.

'Have Simon come up behind me,' he said in a low voice. 'Where's your gun?'

Barnabus collected his scattered wits. 'In the...er...in the case, sir.'

'I told you to have it ready.'

'Well, but...it's raining, sir.'

'Is it loaded?'

Barnabus was offended. 'Of course.' He saw that Sir Robert already had his own dag out under his cloak, and was winding the lock with a little square key he carried on his belt. Suddenly Sir Robert's insistence on expensive modern wheel-lock guns without powderpans made sense—who could keep a powderpan dry in this weather?

'Sir,' ventured Barnabus, beginning to think, 'if it's footpads, I've my daggers.'

Sir Robert nodded. 'Good man,' he said. 'Go to the rear with Robson. If there are eight on the hill, there's another four behind us, somewhere. If they come up fast, kill them.'

'What, all four, sir?'

'As many as you can, Barnabus.'

'Right sir.'

Sir Robert turned his horse to go to the front, stopped.

'Aim for the faces, they'll be wearing padded jacks.'

'Yes sir.'

Heart thudding under his wrecked doublet, Barnabus slowed his horse until he was level with Simon, sent the boy up ahead and then nodded to the Berwick man who joined him.

'Spot of bother coming then, eh?' he said brightly, hoping the rain would disguise the fact that he was sweating.

The Berwick man frowned at him, shook his head. 'Ah wouldna like tae ride for Carlisle at this distance.'

'No,' said Barnabus with feeling, 'nor me.'

'It's aye the packs they'll be after.'

Barnabus made a face. The three pack ponies were trudging along under a remarkable quantity of clothes and gear, including,

Barnabus was sure from the weight, a certain amount of weaponry.

'Why didn't Sir John send more men?' asked Barnabus. 'Seeing it's his brother.'

There was a cold stare from the Berwick man.

'He didnae have more men to send.'

'Well,' said Barnabus desperately, 'we're still in England, ain't we? They can't be Scots, surely?'

The Berwick man rolled his eyes and did not deign to answer.

They rode along and the men with the lances paced with them. Sir Robert was casting increasingly anxious glances to the rear. At last, one of the broader of the strangers detached from the group and rode down through the scrub to stop beside a flowing pothole. Sir Robert held up his hand to stop his own procession and trotted forwards, smiling blithely. That was a thing the Court taught you, reflected Barnabus, drying his hands on his padded breeches and taking out one of his daggers covertly under his cloak. To paste a smile on your face and keep it there, no matter what.

The two men talked while Barnabus tried to see in two directions at once. Was that a movement behind a rock there, in the rain? The sticky squelching was only the rearmost pony shifting his feet, and that…no, it was a rabbit.

Out of the corner of his eye he saw Sir Robert laugh, lean forward and…thank God, shake the man's hand. Barnabus let his breath puff out once more, and resheathed his dagger with fingers that were trembling so much it took him three tries.

Sir Robert waved them on towards him, while the broad northerner did the same with his men. Snorting protestingly the pack ponies let themselves be led forward to pick between the pools and ridges, while the strangers came down from their hillock. Four more materialised from the south, but walking not galloping.

'My brother-in-law Lord Scrope,' said Sir Robert loudly, 'has very kindly sent Mr Thomas Carleton, Captain of Bewcastle, to escort us the last few miles into Carlisle, the country being somewhat unsettled since the death of his father.'

The Berwick men grunted and relaxed a little. Barnabus suddenly felt his gut congeal as he puzzled out the implications. Footpads were one thing, highwaymen were another thing, but a country where the Lord Warden of the West March had to send an escort for the area around his own city...What in God's name was Carey doing here?

'Welcome to Carlisle,' said the Captain of Bewcastle, looking like a beer barrel but sitting his horse as if he were born on it and ignoring the little rivers running down the curves of his helmet. 'I see the weather's kept nice for you.'

## SUNDAY, 18TH JUNE 1592, AFTERNOON

He'd been shot from behind, that was clear enough. There was a gaping hole in the chest and white ribs visible in the mess of red, mixed with tatters of shirt, doublet and leather jack with the padding quilted in the Graham pattern. The crows had not had time to wreck his face completely: there was no mistaking the long jaw and sallow skin of a Graham. No doubt the eyes would have been grey.

Red Sandy had ridden up behind Dodd to peer at the body.

'Devil take it,' he said. 'Is that...?'

'Ay,' said Bangtail, wiping his hands on the seat of his horse, looking upset and disgusted, 'it's Sweetmilk Geordie.'

'Oh Christ,' said somebody.

'Jock of the Peartree's youngest boy,' said Dodd heavily.

Bangtail nodded. 'He'll not be happy.'

Dodd blinked through the thinning rain at the grubby sky and wondered briefly what particular thing he had done was warranting this, in God's ineffable judgment. Storey was openly worried, while the other men were gathering closer and looking over their shoulders as if they were expecting a feud to explode immediately like a siege bomb. Which it would, of course, but in due time. Dodd coughed and shook his head at Archie Give-it-Them who had his hand on his swordhilt.

'Sim's Will Croser, I want your horse.'

Sim's Will was the next youngest to Storey and slid from his mount resignedly, grabbing his steel bonnet from the pommel and putting it on. As if he had shouted an order, the others all put on their own helmets. Dodd thought about it and decided to stay with his squelching cap. Why deliberately look more martial than you were?

Croser was taking his own cloak off, but Storey said, 'His cloak's in the gorse still.'

Sim's Will crashed into the gorse to fetch it, while Dodd walked all around the corpse and toed him. Dead and gone since yesterday, no doubt of it. The pale leather of the jack was stained black around the small hole in the back where the bullet went in.

Croser had returned and was laying the cloth on the ground. Storey and Bangtail moved the corpse onto it and bundled it up, a makeshift shroud. Bangtail tried to cross Sweetmilk's arms on what was left of his chest. The corpse was not co-operative so he made the Sign of the Cross on his own. Croser covered his horse's eyes and led him forwards, while Story and Bangtail huffed and heaved to get Sweetmilk slung over the animal's back before he knew what was happening. Sweetmilk fitted nicely, which helped. By the time the hobby's small but sharp brain had taken note of the blood and the weight and it had begun to hop and kick, Croser had wrapped his stirrup leathers round Sweetmilk Graham's wrists and ankles and after a couple of protesting whinnies, it quieted and stood looking offended at Croser.

'Lead your horse, Sim's Will,' said Dodd. 'Archie and Bangtail to the front, Archie goes ahead a way, Bessie's Andrew and myself with you, Red Sandy and Long George at the back. Anyone asks, it was a Bell we found.'

They paced on towards the ford of the Esk at Longtown, hoping they would meet no Grahams.

Longtown was quiet and the ford seemed clear of danger, though the water was higher than usual. Archie Give-it-Them splashed across, scrambled up the bank, and cantered on down the path. Dodd waited a minute, then gestured for the rest of them to go on. Then just as they were in the middle of the ford, Archie came galloping back on the opposite bank, with five fingers raised, and then a thumb pointing down, meaning he'd seen ten men ahead, and as Dodd made to draw his sword, five more came out of the bushes on foot. Bugger, thought Dodd.

'I'm the Sergeant of the Carlisle Guard,' he shouted. 'We're on Warden's business.'

Bangtail's horse was already out on the bank, but Sim's Will, Bessie's Andrew and Dodd were still in mid-stream because Sim's Will was having trouble leading his hobby through the high water. Bessie's Andrew stared open-mouthed at the lances surrounding them, stock still. Dodd swung about and brought his crop down on the laden animal's rump. It whinnied, pranced sideways and at last Croser hauled the snorting animal up the other bank. Dodd and Andrew Storey followed.

'Surely they wouldna dare...' stuttered Bessie's Andrew.

Well, at least, Dodd thought, feeling his pulse in his temples and wishing he'd put his helmet on while he had the chance, if they were planning to dare, they would have done it while we were still sloshing about in the Esk.

A long-faced, grey-eyed, grey-haired ruffian in a patched and mended jack and a dull blued steel helmet trotted forward, his two younger sons behind him. The third they had across Croser's hobby, of course. Surely nothing he'd done recently deserved this much trouble, Dodd though protestingly. Just in time he saw that the idiot lad Storey was reaching for his sword, and he spurred his horse up behind and cuffed the boy out of the saddle.

'If you want a fight, you can fight them alone,' he said.

Jock of the Peartree smiled. He had four teeth missing and one chipped and a nose that had been broken at least three times. Storey picked himself up out of the mud resentfully.

'Now then, Jock Graham,' said Dodd civilly.

'Is that one of mine ye have there, Sergeant Dodd?'

Dodd did not look at the corpse. 'It's one of the Bells, I think,' he said. 'We're taking him to Carlisle...'

'I'll have him.'

Dodd sucked his teeth and thought. He liked silence, and the little jinks of harness and the creaking noise made by men in leather jacks leaning forward with their spears only confirmed the blessedness of

19

it. Behind them the Esk was purling its way to the marshes about Rockcliffe castle and thence to the sea. There were hardly any men in the fields with the wet, most of them at the summerings anyway, a few women peering out of their huts further down the road. Jock folded his arms and narrowed his eyes impatiently. Dodd could see no reason for hurry, the man was dead after all.

'Well Jock,' he said at last, 'I'd need to ask the Warden's permission...'

'Now.'

Dodd sighed, his gloomy face lengthening with weariness.

'What makes you so interested in a Bell?'

'I'm nae interested in any dead Bell, nor you neither Sergeant, and ye know it. I think he's a Graham,' said Jock. 'That's good enough for me. I've five men out...'

'On a raid?'

'They were in Carlisle to buy horses.'

'Ah,' said Dodd agreeably, 'I see. Well, Jock, as you know, I'd like to oblige you, but I canna. If you had found him, that would be one thing. But we found him and that makes him Warden business for the moment.'

'If ye drop him accidental off the horse, and I come upon him, then I've found him, eh?' suggested Jock.

Dodd looked at his men. 'If it was myself and none other, then I'd oblige you, Jock.' He glared at Bangtail who seemed dangerously close to opening his mouth. If Jock of the Peartree knew for sure that his favourite son was dead, there was no telling what he might do...God help the man that killed Sweetmilk, Dodd thought, for nobody else will dare.

He leaned on the crupper again, calculating ways and means. They were about five miles from Carlisle which was over-far for a race as far as he was concerned, if he could avoid it, and nobody in their right senses wanted to mix it with the Graham surname. Storey might, but then Storey had family reasons.

Jock of the Peartree was speaking. 'What use d'ye have for a corpse in Carlisle?' he demanded. 'There's a man that'll foul no more bills and it's late to think of stretching a rope wi' him.'

'It's the law, Jock,' Sergeant Dodd explained, all sweet reason, with a trickle of either rain or sweat itching his back under his shirt. On the other hand they were at least talking, and it was probable even the Grahams might think twice about killing the Sergeant of the Carlisle Guard and his men. Possible at any rate. 'The law says there should be an inquest for him and an inquest there will be. If he's yours, ye can have him to bury in two days.'

As if that closed the conversation, Dodd clucked at his horse, waved the men on, and rode slowly past the Grahams. Collectively holding their breath and praying that the Grahams were not in a mood for a fight, the patrolmen followed after, with Croser's mare pecking irritably at the leading rein as she bore her cloak-wrapped burden. The prickling down Dodd's spine continued until he heard Jock of the Peartree shout, 'Two days, Henry Dodd, or I'll burn your wife from your land.'

Red Sandy winced, but Dodd merely looked back once and then continued. Bangtail Graham, who was Jock's nephew by marriage, had the grace to look embarrassed.

'It's his way of talking, sir…'

Dodd's face cracked open a little.

'God help your uncle if he goes up against my wife and her kin, Bangtail,' he said, before slouching deep into the saddle and seeming to fall asleep.


## SUNDAY, 18TH JUNE 1592, EVENING


They reached Carlisle as the rain slackened off a little and the day slumped towards evening. The cobbles were slippery and treacherous and none of the townsfolk were impressed by Dodd or his men, making way with very ill grace.

'What will we do with him?' asked Red Sandy as they passed through the gate by the uneven towers of the Citadel. 'We canna take him to Fenwick or any other undertaker, Jock will hear ye lied to him by morning.'

Most of the shopkeepers on English Street were too busy shutting up their shops to pay much attention to them.

'I never lied to him,' said Dodd. 'I said I thought it was a Bell. I canna help it if I made a mistake.'

Red Sandy grinned and waited.

'We'll take him to the castle and find a storeroom to put him in until the inquest.'

Once past the Captain's Tower into Carlisle keep, they found the courtyard and its rabble of huts full of disorderly folk. Lowther was back from an inspection of the Bewcastle waste, and the castle guard was being changed. Carleton and his men were in town as well. Dodd and his men threaded quietly through the confusion to the Queen Mary Tower, where he, Bessie's Andrew and Red Sandy hauled Sweetmilk awkwardly up the stairs and into one of the empty chambers that unexpectedly had tallow dips lit around the walls. They rolled the corpse onto the bed and covered it up with the counterpane.

'He'll ruin the bedcover...' muttered Bessie's Andrew, whose mother gave him a hard life.

'Aw shut your worriting, Andrew,' said Red Sandy. 'Any fool knows a corpse that cold doesna bleed and, besides, that counterpane's older than you are, or it should be, the state it's in.'

When they clattered down the stairs and out under the rusted portcullis, they found Bangtail and Long George waiting for them in great excitement.

'Ten new horses in the stables?' Not even Dodd could hide his blazing curiosity which he showed by rubbing his cheek with his knuckles. They hurried to the stables by the New Barracks to look at the beasts.

As expected, Lowther's men had made free with their rations and the ale had succumbed to the usual vinegar fly, so they went back through the Captain's Gate to the outer ward where Bessie Storey had her strictly illegal but long-tolerated alehouse hard by the crosswall.

An hour later, Dodd's belly was gratefully full of Bessie's incomparable stew and ale, and he was already hoarse with argument over the likely stamina of the six new horses and how a cross with one of his hobbies might turn out.

'See, you'd get the southern speed and a bit of extra bone...'
Red Sandy was explaining when he noticed Dodd had gone silent
and was trying to become invisible in the back of the booth. Red
Sandy looked at the door and saw a boy in Scrope's livery craning
his neck.

'Sergeant Dodd, Sergeant Dodd...' called the boy.

'He's here,' said Bessie's Andrew, waving, no doubt getting his
revenge for the gorse bush.

The boy came barging over through the press, neat work with
his elbows.

'Sergeant Dodd,' he squeaked, stopped and managed to drop
his voice. 'The Warden wants you, he wants you in the Keep, sir.'

'Now?' asked Dodd, wondering why he had paid good cash
to be Sergeant of the Warden's Guard and whether he could find
some fool to sell the office to and recover his money.

'He wants you to meet his new Deputy.'

'I already know Richard Lowther.'

'No sir.' The boy's face was alight with pleasure at knowing
something Dodd didn't. The conversations round about them
suddenly sputtered and died. 'It's not him.'

'What?' demanded Dodd, who had been straining himself to
be pleasant to Lowther in anticipation of his confirmation in the
Deputyship.

'I thought he was set to get it,' protested Red Sandy, concerned
about his own investment, 'I thought the old Lord promised him...'

The boy shook his head. 'It's not him.'

'Well who is it then?' demanded Bangtail.

Cunning disfigured the child's face. 'I dinna ken,' he said.

Dodd picked up his cap which had been steaming next to the
fire. 'Is it still raining outside?'

'Yes sir, but he wants...'

At the door, digging his cloak out of the steaming heap, Dodd
looked narrowly at the boy.

'Are you one of Bangtail's kin?'

'Second cousin, once removed, sir.'

'Graham?'

'Yes sir, Young Hutchin Graham.'

That was an ill to-name to be saddled with, thought Dodd, he'd be called Young Hutchin when he was seventy and bent like willow.

'Then you'll be Hutchin the Bastard's boy?'

'Yes sir.'

'You know who my Lord Scrope's new deputy is, don't you?'

'I might,' allowed Young Hutchin carefully.

They stepped away from Bessie's door and dodged to the covered way from the drawbridge to the Captain's Tower. The rain had slackened off to a fine mizzle and the dusk was stretching itself out above the clouds. The boy grinned.

'It's not one of the Warden's relatives.'

'Of course it is,' said Dodd. 'Why else would he make a mortal enemy of Richard Lowther?'

Young Hutchin shook his head and looked smug. Dodd sighed and gave him a penny. Perhaps he wouldn't make it to seventy.

'It's one of his wife's kin. He's just ridden up from London and the Queen's Court and the strange horses in the stable are...'

'Good Christ!' said Dodd disgustedly. 'It's a Carey. It's not Sir John is it? Say to me Scrope hasn't made John Carey Deputy Warden in the West March as well?'

'Oh no, sir, that one's still just Marshal of Berwick Castle. It's his youngest brother Robert.'

'Who?'

'Robert Carey. Sir Robert, I heard. Lady Scrope's his nearest sister in age and she thinks the world of him and he's no money and would like to be away from Court, so I heard, so she made my Lord offer him the place...They've put him in the Queen Mary Tower for the night, in the main bedchamber.'

'Ah.'

They were let in through the Captain's Gate at the shout of their usual password, crossed the yard and came to the stair to the door of the Keep where Scrope's apartments were. At the foot Dodd gave Young Hutchin another penny.

'Fetch your cousin Bangtail, my brother Red Sandy and Long George Ridley, oh and Archie Give-it-Them if he's sober and tell them to shift the baggage that's in the Queen Mary Tower into one of the feed huts for the night. Tell them to do it now, not when they've finished their quarts.'

'Ay sir. What is it?'

'A package,' said Dodd gravely. 'Go on, run.'

Dodd waited until the boy had disappeared through the Captain's Gate, reflecting that whoever Hutchin the Bastard's mother had been, she must have been uncommonly fine-looking for her looks and hair to survive two generations of Graham breeding so well. The lad had better never go near the Scottish King's Court with that tow head and blue eyes, not until he'd put on enough bone to defend himself.

He opened the heavy door and went into the big main room. Two of Scrope's attendants were there and a round ugly little man was huddled up on a stool by the fire in the vast fireplace finishing mulled ale from a leather tankard. Next to him was a soft-looking lad, sitting on a pile of rushes, dispiritedly oiling some harness and in the corner, four louts with Berwick stamped on their voices were arguing the toss over whether a shod horse went better than an unshod one in a race. The ferret-faced man on the stool slapped his knees, stood up and said something in what sounded like English, if spoken by a man with a head-cold and the hiccups. Dodd couldn't understand a word seeing it was some kind of southern talk, but the boy did and the two hurried out into the rain, the boy tripping on some of the harness straps.

At Scrope's impatient 'Enter' he pushed open the oak door with the mysterious axe-mark in it and went in. The air was full of woollen steam from the heavy cloak hanging by the fire and Scrope's hangings were given a courtly glamour by the fat wax candles all about the room. At least it was warm there.

Scrope, as usual, was sitting hunched like a heron in his carved chair by the desk while Richard Bell the clerk packed up papers behind him. Two other men looked up as he came in. Captain Carleton was standing, and a stranger was sitting at his ease on the cushioned bench.

'Good evening, Sergeant,' said Scrope, 'any news from the patrol?'

'The Sark fords are high for the time of year and I doubt anyone's been across them this summer, except perhaps the horse smuggler we've heard tell of,' said Dodd. 'We met Jock of the Peartree with fifteen men by the Esk ford at Longtown.'

'What was he doing there?' asked Scrope.

'Looking for lost cows?' suggested Thomas Carleton sarcastically. He had parked his bulky body in front of the fire, blocking most of the heat, and wore a face full of repressed amusement.

'He said he'd five men that had gone to Carlisle to buy horses.'

Carleton snorted. 'Good luck to them. We've a famine of horses hereabouts.'

'Was there anything else, my lord?' asked Dodd patiently.

'No…Yes. Sir Robert, may I present to you Henry Dodd, Sergeant of the Guard. Henry, this is my brother-in-law Sir Robert Carey, who will be my Deputy Warden.'

Dodd made a stiff-necked bow, Carey came to his feet, returned the courtesy, held out his hand and smiled. There was one who'd be expensive to put in livery, thought Dodd. He was taller by an inch or two than Dodd, who found himself in the unfamiliar position of looking up at someone. He took the proffered hand, which was long, white and nicely manicured, with three rings on it, and shook it.

'Sir Robert,' said Dodd non-committally.

'Apologies for hauling you up here on such a foul evening,' said Carey affably. 'Captain Carleton says he's too busy to take me for a tour of the area tomorrow, and I was hoping you would oblige?'

It was on the tip of Dodd's tongue to say that he had a lot less time than Carleton, and stay out of trouble, but then he reflected. After all, this was the Warden's brother-in-law, a courtier come riding up from London, and not just any courtier but one of Lord Hunsdon's boys. He might even be grateful for a friendly face. Perhaps if he got on well with this Court sprig, who seemingly was the new Deputy Warden, Dodd might snaffle a couple of the offices in the Deputy's gift to sell on. And Lowther was a miserable bastard in any case.

'No trouble, sir.'

'Dodd, is it? From Upper Tynedale.'

'My grandfather's land, sir. Mine comes to me from my wife, I've a tower and some acres not far from Gilsland.'

'Bell or Armstrong land?'

Dodd coughed. 'Ay sir,' he said stonily. 'English Armstrongs. And a few Dodds.' He hated nosiness, particularly from courtiers. Though Carey looked little like a courtier in his dark green woollen doublet and paned hose; just the lace on his collar and the jewels gave the game away.

There was a clatter of light boots on the stair and Scrope's lady came through the door in a hurry, her doublet bodice open at the neck and her satin apron awry. Scrope looked up and smiled fondly; she was a pleasing small creature with black ringlets making ciphers on her white skin. At the sight of Carey her face lit up like a beacon.

'Robin!' she shouted and ran into his arms like a girl. Carleton's lip curled at the sight, which had cost Richard Lowther at least fifty pounds and much credit. Carey grinned, kissed her, lifted her up and kissed her again. She giggled and batted him away.

'Was it a hard journey?' she asked. 'How is the Queen, did you meet John?'

'Yes, well enough, no,' said Carey methodically.

'Philadelphia...' began Scrope.

'I may greet my brother, I think,' said Lady Scrope haughtily. Carey whispered in her ear and she frowned, then picked up a work bag from near the fire, sat down on her stool and began rapidly stitching at a piece of white linen, her steel needle with its tail of black flashing hypnotically before Dodd's eyes. 'And I wanted to speak to him privately as well.'

'When we...'

'How much did you want?' asked Carey. Lady Scrope tutted at him.

'Not money,' she said primly. 'I do not always lose at primero, you know.'

'Oh no?' said Carey sceptically. 'I swear on my honour I have seen you draw to a flush with no points on three separate occasions.'

Dodd, who had heard some of the legends about Lady Scrope's gambling, hid a smile.

'My lord has been teaching me better play,' said Lady Scrope with dignity, a blatant lie as far as Dodd was concerned, since Lord Scrope was even worse than she was.

Carey raised his eyebrows severely.

'My lord,' said Dodd across the argument, 'I must have a private word...'

'Later, Sergeant, later,' said Scrope irritably. 'I have some business with Sir Robert, my dear...'

Philadelphia made three minute stitches and finished off the end, unfurled a new length from her bobbin, snipped, threaded and began stitching again. A blackworked peapod was taking shape like magic on the linen. 'Pray continue,' she said. 'My business can wait a little.'

Dodd decided he had been dismissed and turned to go, wondering what the disturbance downstairs might be. Carleton came with him. They were stopped by Carey's voice.

'Sergeant,' he called, 'shall I meet you at dawn in the yard tomorrow?'

Dodd thought about it and sighed. 'Ay sir.'

He reached for the door and nearly had it slammed in his face. There on the threshold stood Sir Richard Lowther, resplendent in tawny velvet and red gown, his greying hair further frosted with rain and murder in his face.

'What is this I hear,' he said, dangerously quiet into the instant silence, 'about the Deputyship?'

Scrope was on his feet, coming forward.

'Ah, Sir Richard,' he said, 'may I present to you Sir Robert Carey, my brother-in-law and...er...'

Dodd had backed into a corner, the better to watch the show. Philadelphia had stopped sewing and was also watching intently, Carleton was leaning against a wall, with a cynical grin on his face. Hands on hips, Lowther advanced towards Carey, who was standing, smiling unconcernedly.

'Sir Richard Lowther,' he said with a shallow Court bow. 'Pleased to make your acquaintance, sir.'

'Well I,' snarled Lowther, 'am not pleased to make yours, *sir*.'

Carey's eyebrows went up again. 'I'm sorry to hear that.'

Scrope coughed frantically, and wriggled his fingers together like knobbled worms. 'I am...er...appointing Sir Robert as my Deputy,' he said. 'The post is in my gift.'

'A bloody foreigner? A *southerner* to be Deputy Warden.'

'I was brought up in Berwick, my father Lord Hunsdon is East March Warden,' said Carey mildly.

'Oh Christ!' roared Lowther. 'One of *those* Careys. That's all we need. What's the old woman up to then, making the poor bloody Borders a sinecure for all her base-born cousins?'

Carey went white and drew his sword. Its long wickedly pointed blade caught the firelight and slid it up and down distractingly. Carleton blinked and stood upright, glanced at Dodd who was ready to move as well. One of those long modern rapiers, he thought professionally, fine for a duel but unreliable for a fight where men were wearing jacks. Would Lowther draw?

'I don't like the way you talk of my family and I don't like the way you talk of the Queen,' said Carey very coldly. 'Would you care to discuss the matter outside?'

Lowther looked a little surprised, under his rage. His own hand was on his swordhilt, he had not yet committed himself. In the silence that followed, Dodd reflected that it was always interesting to watch the way a man held a sword, providing he wasn't facing you at the time. Beyond the question of whether he knew how to use it, there was the way he stood, was he tense, had he killed before, how angry was he? Carey looked competent with his rapier and not at all a virgin in the way of bloodshed. Of one thing Dodd was morally certain, who had met both of them: his brother, Sir John, would not have drawn, his father would have drawn and struck.

'Gentlemen, gentlemen,' said Scrope, breaking out of his trance and moving between them, 'I will not have my men duelling. Sir Richard, if you have a quarrel with the way I appoint my officers, please take it up with Her Majesty. Sir Robert, you will put up your weapon.'

Carey hesitated a moment, then sheathed his sword. Lowther growled inarticulately, turned on his heel and stamped out of the room. They could hear his boots on the stairs and his bull-bellow as he passed through to the lower room.

All of them let out a breath, except for Carleton who looked disappointed.

'I should have warned you...' began Scrope apologetically, but Carey had sat himself carefully down on the bench again, clasped his hands and was looking at them abstractedly.

'Who controls the dispatches to London?' he asked, seemingly irrelevantly.

'That's Lowther's job,' Carleton answered him, 'fairly bought and paid for.'

Carey looked at Scrope regretfully. 'My lord, we have a problem.'

'Why?' asked Scrope pettishly, 'I made him know who was Warden here.'

Lady Scrope was sewing again. 'Robin means, my lord,' she said tactfully, 'that Sir Richard will be writing to my Lord Burghley and we can't stop his letter.'

Carey smiled fondly at his sister.

'Why should that matter?' Scrope demanded. 'I'm the Warden.'

'Fully confirmed, with your warrant?' asked Carey.

'Well...'

'Not yet,' said Philadelphia, raising her eyebrows exactly like her brother. 'There hasn't been time since the old lord died. It was less than a week ago, remember. He isn't even buried yet, he's still in the chapel, poor old soul.'

'No warrant?'

'I'm only Warden during pleasure anyway,' said Scrope. 'What would Burghley do...'

Being a man who often edited what he wanted to say, Dodd recognised the symptoms in someone else.

'Well, my lord,' said Carey after a deep breath, 'if you remember, it was the Earl of Essex who gave me my knighthood. He and Burghley...er...hate each other.'

'Oh,' said Scrope, beginning to understand, 'Court factions.'

'Of course, Robin is the Queen's favourite...' began Philadelphia.

'Heaven preserve me from that,' said Carey feelingly. 'No, she likes me, but Essex has the...er...honour at the moment. Even so, she would prefer me back at Court under her eye. This needs to be handled with care, my lord.'

'Surely I can appoint my own deputy,' said Scrope.

Carey and his sister exchanged glances. 'Of course. One thing

I must have settled tonight, my lord,' he said, 'is the question of men. The garrison men my brother lent me must go back to Berwick tomorrow, he's short-handed enough as it is. I need my own men here, appointed to me, paid by me and loyal to me.'

Too late Dodd realised that he should have left with Lowther, no matter how fascinated he was. He tried melting into the tapestry, but Carleton did for him, damn his guts.

'Sergeant Dodd here is the loyalest man I know,' boomed Carleton with an evil grin.

'Oh Ah could niver...'

'Rubbish, man, no deputy could wish for a better guard than you and your soldiers.'

'Excellent idea, Captain,' drivelled Scrope. 'Yes. Sergeant Dodd, you can transfer to Sir Robert's service until he releases you.'

Carey had spotted his reaction too, alas. Dodd coughed and did his best to look honest but thick.

And then how would Dodd deal with Richard Lowther's wrath? It was too much to cope with on top of Sweetmilk Graham's killing.

'Sir,' he said to Carey, 'I'd best get back to my men and explain to them.'

'Of course, Sergeant,' said Carey. 'How many of them are there?'

'Six, sir.'

'Six. Good.' Carey coughed a little. 'Well, I'll see you in the morning then, Sergeant. Good night.'

Dodd clumped down the stairs, shaking his head and hoping he wouldn't need to do any more thinking that night. Then Lowther stopped him in the lower room, looming by the fire, his broad handsome face like a rock carving on a tomb.

'Well, Sergeant?'

'Ay sir.'

'What did they say after I left?'

'Say, sir?'

Lowther's grey eyes narrowed.

'Of what did they speak when I was gone?' The words sprang out half-bitten.

Dodd thought for a while.

'Scrope turned me over to the new...to Sir Robert as sergeant of his guard, me and my men together.'

Lowther humphed to himself.

'You'll not forget where your true interests lie, Sergeant,' he said with heavy meaning.

Christ man, thought Dodd to himself, if you're here demanding blackrent off me, say so out clear, ye've not the talent for subtle hinting.

Aloud he said stolidly, 'No sir.'

'So what did they say?'

Dodd thought again. 'It was some chatter about Court factions and Carey said he wasna the Queen's favourite, the Earl of Essex was, and they'd need to be careful of you.'

Lowther humphed again. 'Was that all?'

Inspiration struck Dodd. 'All I understood, sir, seeing they were talking foreign.'

'What, southern English.'

'No, I can make that out usually: foreign, French maybe or Latin even. I don't know.'

Lowther looked sideways at him under his flourishing grey brows and Dodd stared into space. Lowther snapped his fingers at John Ogle, who bristled, but came towards them.

'Find me and the sergeant some beer,' he said, stepping over a snoring pile of sleuthdogs and sitting on one of the benches. At his gesture Dodd sat down next to him, itching to get back to the barracks and find out what his men had done with Sweetmilk. He gulped the beer when it came, from Scrope's brewhouse, not the garrison's, and not half bad.

'Scrope's mad,' said Lowther dourly. 'A bloody courtier, what does he know about the Border?'

He knew enough to identify immediately where most of Dodd's surname lived and that Gilsland was full of Armstrongs, Dodd thought, but said nothing and nodded.

'Still, that might not be so ill a thing...' muttered Lowther, thinking aloud. 'What do you make of him, Sergeant?'

Dodd forebore to point out that he had exchanged perhaps three sentences with the man, and shrugged.

'He's got very polished manners.'

'He might not be here long,' said Lowther pointedly. Dodd didn't reply because in his present mood he might have said something he would regret later. And Janet would have his guts if he lost his place before he had his investment back. Which on current showing might be well into the next century, assuming he lived that long.

'Keep an eye on him for me, will you Henry?' Lowther said, the firelight catching his pale prominent eyes and the broken veins on his cheeks and nose. To complete the effect, he made a face which might, if practised, have counted for a smile one day.

'Ay sir,' said Dodd woodenly.

'Good lad.' Lowther clapped him on the shoulder and headed purposefully across the room to the fire, threading between benches and trestle tables.

Dodd hurried out the door. At the dark foot of the stairs outside, he looked about him impatiently.

'Where have you put it then?' Dodd asked, thinking longingly of his bed.

Archie Give-it-Them coughed and the others looked sheepishly at each other. Dodd sighed again.

'Well?' he said.

'We tried, Sergeant,' said Bangtail Graham, 'but the new Deputy had a man on the door already and he wouldna let us in, but.'

There was a long moment of silence. Dodd thought of the thirty good English pounds he had given for the sergeant's post, which was a loan from Janet's father as an investment, and decided that if he lost his place he would ride to Berwick and take ship for the Low Countries.

'Good night,' he said, turned on his heel and walked off to the stables to think.

## SUNDAY, 18TH JUNE, NIGHT

Carey saw his sister up the stairs to the Warden's bedchamber, and she leant on his arm smiling and chattering so happily that he knew how hard it had been for her. Goodwife Biltock was pulling a warming pan out of the great bed.

'God's sake, this weather, June, who could believe it...' she was muttering as she turned and saw him. 'Oh now,' she flustered, dropping a curtsey, 'well, Robin, what a sight...'

Carey crossed the floor in three strides and picked her up to give her a smacking kiss on the cheek. She cuffed his ear.

'Put me down, bad child, put me...'

Carey put her down and handed her his handkerchief, while Philadelphia smiled and brought her to the stool by the fire until she could collect herself.

Carey was pouring her wine from the flagon on the plate chest, since women's tears had always had him come out in a sweat. He brought it to her and squatted down beside her.

'So it's true Scrope offered you the deputyship,' she said at last. 'I never thought...'

'...I could drag myself away from London?' Carey made a wry face. 'Nothing easier when I could feast my eyes on you Goodwife...'

'Pfff, get away, Robin, your tongue's been worn too smooth at Court. Well you're a sight for sore eyes and no mistake and I see you can find a clean handkerchief now which is more than I could say for you once. Will you stay do you think?'

Carey coughed. 'I don't know, Goodwife, it depends.'

'You take care for that Lowther fellow...'

'Nurse...' warned Philadelphia.

'I speak as I find, I'm sure. Where are you lying, Robin, is it warm and dry?'

'Nowhere better in the castle, it's in the Queen Mary Tower.'

'Hah, warm and dry, I doubt. They use the place as a store-room...'

'Do they?' said Carey, straightfaced.

'Oh they do, flour mostly, and I'll be struck dumb with amazement if the lummocks even thought to air the place, let alone light a fire, I'll go and...'

'No need, Nurse,' said Carey, 'I've a man in there already, and my own body servant will be seeing after making it comfortable, you're not to trouble yourself.'

'Well, have you eaten?'

'I had a bit with the men in the...'

'Oh in the Lord's name, old bread and last year's cheese, and the beer brewed by idiots, I'll go and fetch something out of my lord's kitchen, you stay there, Robin, and dry your hose...'

'Would you have it sent up to my chamber, Nurse. I'll be going to bed soon.'

Goodwife Biltock opened her mouth to argue, then smiled. 'There'll be enough for your servants too,' she said. 'Be sure you eat your share, I know you. Good night, Robin.' She reached over and ruffled his hair, heaved herself up and bustled out, rump swinging beneath a let out gown of Philadelphia's. She looked very fine in green velvet, though worn and of an old style. But then the Goodwife had always liked to look well, even when she was nursing Carey babies.

'Didn't you tell her?' Carey asked as he took her place on the stool.

'No one was sure you were coming until your messenger arrived this morning while we were all in church. I made Scrope send Carleton out. And I didn't want to disappoint her in case the Queen called you back before you got here.'

Philadelphia brought up the other stool and settled down facing him.

'Be very careful of Lowther, Robin, he's the reason...'

'...why I'm here. So I gathered.'

'I wish you had fought him, right there and then,' whispered Philadelphia, screwing up her fists on her apron and causing it to crumple.

'Philly...' Carey saw she meant it and changed what he had to say. 'It might have been a little messy. Have you ever seen a real sword fight?'

'No, but I've nursed enough sword cuts. I'd nurse Lowther too, I would, nurse him good and proper.'

Carey looked away from her vehemence. 'What was it you couldn't tell me in your letter?'

'Only that he has this March closed up tight in his fist. He has most of the lucrative offices and he takes the tenths of recovered cattle, not the Warden.'

Carey's lips moved in a soundless whistle.

'What's left? Just the thirds from fines.'

'What there are of them, we've had no justice out of Liddesdale for fourteen years. Sir John Carmichael...'

'He's still the Scots West March Warden?'

'For the moment, but the rumours are he wants to resign.'

'Wise man.'

'He's well enough, he's an honest decent gentleman, too good for this country. Did you ever meet him?'

'I think I did. Last time I was at King James's Court he was there, I remember.'

'He does his best, but the Maxwells and the Johnstones ignore him and the Armstrongs and Grahams...'

'Who will bind the wind?'

'Exactly. Old Lord Scrope held it together because towards the end he simply did what Lowther told him and let the rest go hang and Lowther kept the peace as far as it suited him.'

'Not far?'

'Well, it's remarkable how often people who offend him get raided and their houses burned.'

'Who by?'

'Grahams or Elliots mostly, but Nixons and Crosers too.'

Carey rubbed his bottom lip with his thumb. 'This is no restful sinecure I think,' he said.

'Did you think it would be?'

Carey laughed. 'Christ, no, or I'd never have come.'

'Don't swear, Robin, you're getting worse than Father.'

'He warned me that things were rotten here, but he didn't know the details.'

'How would he, staying warm in London with the Queen and messing about with players.'

'Why Philly, you sound bitter.'

She put her face in her hands.

'John does his best in the East March but...'

'He makes an ass of himself from time to time and the Berwick townsmen can't stand him, I know.'

'We need Father to run a good strong Warden's Raid,' said

his sister ferociously, 'burn all their towers down for them. Then they'd behave.'

Carey put his arm round her shoulders and held her tight.

'You don't need Father, you've got me, Philly my dear,' he said. 'Don't worry.'

'You won't let him make you leave?' She was blinking up at him with a frown.

Carey sucked wind through his teeth. 'If the Queen orders me back to Westminster, you know I have to go.'

'She won't, will she?'

'Not if we can forestall whatever Lowther writes to Burghley.'

'You could send a letter with the Berwick men and have John put it in his usual package to London.'

'Yes,' said Carey, thoughtfully, 'I'll do that.' He yawned. 'I'll do it in the morning before I go out with Dodd. There'll be no time later, I want to inspect my men before I call a paymuster for them. And I must go to bed, Philly, or I'll fall asleep here and you'll have to turf Nurse out of her trundle bed and put me in it.'

Philly grinned at him. 'Nonsense, she'd carry you down the stairs on her back and dump you with the other servants in the hall and then she'd give you a thick ear in the morning.'

'She would,' Carey said as he stood up, and kissed his sister on the forehead. 'Thank you for your good word to Scrope.'

'You don't mind that I made him send for you?'

'Sweetheart, you did me the best favour a sister could, you got me out of London and saved my life.'

'Oh?' said Philly naughtily, 'And who was she?'

'None of your business. Good night.'

## MONDAY, 19TH JUNE, MORNING

Dawn came to Carlisle with a feeble clearing of the sky and a wind to strip the skin and cause a dilemma over cloaks: wear one, be marginally warmer and risk having it ripped from your back by a gust, or leave it off and freeze. Dodd put on an extra shirt, a padded doublet and his better jack and decided to freeze.

Carey was already in the stableyard when he arrived, between two of the castle's rough-coated hobbies, checking girth straps and saddle leathers and passing a knowledgeable hand down the horses' legs. He had on a clean but worn buff jerkin, his well-cut suit of green wool trimmed with olive velvet and his small ruff was freshly starched. He looked repulsively sprightly.

'Do you never shoe your horses, Sergeant?' he asked as Dodd came into view.

Dodd considered an explanation and decided against it. 'No sir.' Carey patted a foreleg and lifted the foot to inspect the sturdy, well-grown hoof. He smiled quizzically and Dodd relented a little. 'Not hobbies, sir.'

'I like a sure-footed horse myself,' said Carey agreeably and mounted.

Privately deciding to send Red Sandy out to Gilsland to warn Janet of a possible raid by Jock of the Peartree if he hadn't found the dead man by the evening, Dodd cleared his throat.

'Different from London I doubt, sir.'

Carey was deep in thought. 'Hm? London? Yes. Have you ever been there?'

'No sir. I've been to Edinburgh though, carrying messages.'

'What did you think of the place?'

Dodd tried to be just. 'It had some fair houses. Too many...'

'Scots?'

'Er...people.'

Carey grinned. 'You wouldn't believe how many people there are in London. And every man jack of them with some complaint to bring as a petition to Her Majesty.'

'You've been at Court, sir?'

'Too much. However, the Queen likes me, so I do the best I can.'

Dodd struggled for a moment, then gave in. 'What's she like, the Queen?'

Carey raised an eyebrow. 'Well,' he said consideringly, 'a scurvy Scotsman might say she is a wild old bat who knows more of governorship and statecraft than the Privy Councils of both realms put together, but *I* say she is like Aurora in her beauty, her hair puts the sun in splendour to shame, her face holds the heavens within its compass and her glance is like the falling dew.'

'You say that do you, sir?'

'Certainly I do, frequently, and she laughs at me, tells me that I am her Robin Redbreast and I'm a naughty boy and too plainspoken for the Court.'

'Christ.'

'And then I kiss her hand and she bids me rise and tells me that my brother is being tedious again and my father should get up to Berwick and birch him well, and that poor fool of a boy Thomas Scrope apparently wants me for a deputy in the West March, which shows he has at least enough sense to cover his little fingernail, which surprised her, and what would I say to wasting my life on the windswept Borders chasing cattle-thieves.'

'What did you say, sir?' Dodd asked, fascinated. Carey's eyes danced.

'I groaned, covered my face, fell to my knees and besought her not to send me so far from her glorious countenance, although if it were not for the sorrow of leaving her august presence, I would rejoice in wind, borders and cattle-thieves, and if she be so hard of heart as to drive me away from the fountain of her delight, then I shall go and serve her with all my heart and soul and try and keep Scrope out of trouble.'

Despite himself, Dodd cracked a laugh. 'Is that how they speak at the Court?'

'If they want to keep out of the Tower, they do. I'm good at it and she likes my looks, so we get on well enough. And here I am, thank God.'

He looked around with the air of a man escaped from jail, before some memory, no doubt of Lowther, clouded him over.

'For the moment anyway. Burghley may convince her she wants me back at Court.'

Dodd grunted as they turned from the main trail, heading north, taking a wide sweep around the town, and passing the steady stream of folk going out from the city to work in their farms and market gardens.

They were almost back at the south gate when Carey said, 'Longtown would be a little far to go now, no doubt.'

Here it comes, thought Dodd, bracing himself. 'I could take you with some men.'

'I thought things were calmer in summer with the men up at the shielings.'

'Well they are, sir, but 'tisn't seemly for the Warden's Deputy to be out with no attendant but the Sergeant of the Guard.'

'Much going on near the Sark, at the moment? My lord Scrope said you were there yesterday.'

Was the man taunting him? 'I came on Jock of the Peartree at the Esk ford...'

'I know. Any of them get shot in the back?'

In a way it was better to have it out in the open, at least he would know the worst. As often happened to Dodd his mind came up with three dozen things to say, all of which sounded inside him full of the ring of excuses and blame-passing, and in the end he said nothing save a stolid 'No sir'.

Carey sighed. 'All right, Sergeant,' he said, 'I give in. Let's call vada and I'll see your prime. Tell me about my would-be bedfellow of last night.'

'I only put him there for lack of any other place...'

'Is there no undertaker in Carlisle?'

'Three,' said Dodd, 'but they would know him and...'

'Who is he...was he?'

Dodd told him. It seemed Carey had heard something of Jock Graham's reputation, for he was thoughtful.

'When's the inquest?'

Dodd sighed at the reminder of things he hadn't done yet. 'I'll try and fix it for tomorrow: there's no question of the verdict.'

'Any hint of the murderer?'

Dodd shrugged. 'Jock of the Peartree could likely tell you more about that. Who knows? Who cares?'

Carey gave him an odd look. 'I think murder is still against the law, isn't it?'

'Sweetmilk? He's already had three bills fouled against him in his absence for murder in Scotland and he was just gone eighteen. Only the Jedburgh hangman will be sorry he's dead.'

'And Jock of the Peartree, no doubt.'

'Oh the Grahams will be riding once they know who did it. We've no need to trouble ourselves about Sweetmilk's killer once the inquest's finished and Jock's got the body.'

'Why didn't you give him to Jock when you met yesterday?'

Dodd blinked. 'Well sir, I wanted the fee and I didnae want to be facing a grieving Jack and fifteen Grahams with only six of my own behind me.'

'Fair enough, Sergeant. I want a look at the place where you found the body—can you show me this afternoon?'

'Ay sir, but...'

'Excellent.' Carey urged his hobby up the cobbles to the castle gate and Dodd had to raise a canter to catch up with him again.

'Sir...'

'Yes, Sergeant. Oh I shall want to inspect the men at two hours before midday.'

'Inspect the men?'

'Yes. You and your six patrolmen. And I'd be grateful if you could put your heads together and make a list for me of any defensible men within ten miles of Carlisle who dislike Lowther and might come out to support me in a fight.'

'But sir...'

'Yes, Sergeant?'

'Sir, where's Sweetmilk's body?'

'You'll find him, Sergeant.'

# MONDAY, 19TH JUNE, MORNING

Having been given fair warning by Carey, Dodd mustered the men as soon as he rode into the castle, told them what would happen and further his reaction if they failed to show the Courtier how things were done properly on the border and his men scattered looking deeply worried.

Paperwork for the inquest attended to and his temper a little improved by a morning bite of bread and cheese, Dodd checked his tack, his weapons and his armour, and after a nasty scene with his occasional servant, John Ogle's boy, was in reasonable order by ten o'clock.

'Armstrong blood, sir.'

'How old?'

Archie's talents were not in his brain. 'Sir?'

'How old is the blood?'

Archie mumbled, 'I killed him in April.'

The snotty git, thought Dodd, to pick on poor Archie. Carey nodded for Archie to go back to his position in the line. He then stood with his left hand on his rapier hilt and his right fist on his hip and looked at them thoughtfully.

'Gentlemen,' said Carey at length, 'I have served in France with the Huguenots, and under Lord Howard of Effingham against the Spanish Armada. I have served at several sieges, I have fought in a number of battles, though I admit most of them were against foreigners and Frenchmen and suchlike rabble. I have commanded men on divers occasions over the past five years and I swear by Almighty God that I have never seen such a pitiful sight as you.' He paused to let the insult sink in.

'I was born in London but bred in Berwick,' he continued in tones of reproach. 'When I took horse to come north, a southerner friend of mine laughed and said I should find your lances would be rotten, your swords rusted, your guns better used as clubs and your armour filthy. And I told him I would fight him if he insulted Borderers again, that I was as sure of finding right fighting men here as any place in England—no, surer—and I come and what do I find?' He took a deep breath and blew it out again, shook his head, mounted his horse without touching the stirrups and rode over to where Dodd sat slumped in his saddle, wishing he was in the Netherlands.

'Sergeant, sit up,' said Carey very quietly. 'I find your men are a bloody disgrace which is less their fault than yours. You shall mend it, Sergeant, by this time tomorrow.'

He rode away, while Dodd wondered if it was worth thirty pounds to him to put his lance up Carey's arse. He had still not found Graham's body.

Carey came by while they were waiting for the blacksmith to get his fire hot enough for riveting and beckoned Dodd over.

'Who's in charge of the armoury?'

'Sir Richard Lowther…'

'Who's the armoury clerk?'

'Jemmy Atkinson.'

'Is he here?'

Dodd laughed shortly and Carey looked grim. 'As soon as you've finished, I want to roust out the armoury and see what sins we can find there.'

Dodd's mouth fell open. Sins? Sodom and Gomorrah came to mind, if he was talking about peculation in the armoury. 'We'll not have finished with your orders until this evening, sir,' he protested feebly.

'I want to see if your longbows are as mildewed as the rest of your weapons, assuming you have any longbows. The rest can wait.'

'But sir…'

'Yes, Sergeant.'

'It's locked.'

'So it is, Sergeant.'

The Lord Warden was there when they went to the armoury in a group, a little before dinnertime, walking up and down, winding his hands together and blinking worriedly at the Captain's Gate.

'Yes my lord,' said Carey briskly, inserting the crowbar in the lock.

'But Sir Richard…'

There was a cracking ugly noise as the lock broke and the door creaked open. Everyone peered inside.

Carey was the first to move. He went straight to the racks of calivers and arquebuses. Those near the door were rusted solid. Those further from the door…Dodd winced as Carey pulled one down and threw it out into the bright sunlight.

Bangtail whistled.

'Well, Atkinson's found a good woodcarver, that's sure,' he said.

More dummy weapons crashed onto the straw-covered cobbles, until there was a pile of them. They were beautifully made, carefully coloured with salts of iron and galls to look like metal. Occasionally Carey would grunt as he found another real weapon and put it on the rack nearest the door. Then he went to the gunpowder kegs and opened them, filled a pouch from each, and brought out the least filthy arquebus.

'Please note, gentlemen,' he said, taking a satchel from his perspiring servant, 'this is the right way to clean an arquebus so it may be fired.'

By the time he had done scraping and brushing and oiling, there was an audience gathered round of most of the men of the garrison. Behind him the Carlisle locksmith was working to replace the lock he had broken.

Carey made neat little piles of gunpowder on the ground and called for slowmatch. The boy he had brought with him came running up with a lighted coil. He blew on it and put it to the first pile, which burned sullenly.

'Sawdust,' said Carey.

In silence he went down the row of little mounds with his slowmatch. Lord Scrope had his hand over his mouth and was staring like a man at a nest of vipers in his bed. The last pile of gunpowder sputtered and popped grudgingly.

'Hm. Sloppy,' said Carey sarcastically, 'they must have missed this barrel.'

He loaded the arquebus with a half-charge, tamped down a paper wad and used his own fine-grain powder to put in the pan. He then fastened the arquebus carefully on the frame his servant had brought, aimed at the sky, and stepped back.

'Why...?' began Scrope.

'In Berwick my brother had two men with their hands and faces blown to rags after their guns exploded,' said Carey. The audience immediately moved out of range.

He leaned over to put the fire to the pan, jumped away. The good powder in the pan fizzed and the arquebus fired after a fashion. It did not exactly explode; only the barrel cracked. There was a sigh from the audience.

'What the devil is the meaning of this?' roared a voice from the rear of the crowd.

Carey folded his arms and waited as Lowther shouldered his way through, red-faced.

'How dare you, sir, how dare you interfere with my...'

His voice died away as he saw the pile of dummy weapons and the still feebly smouldering mounds of black powder.

'*Your* armoury?' enquired Carey politely.

Lowther looked from him to the Lord Warden who was glaring back at him.

'There is not one single defensible weapon in the place,' said Lord Scrope reproachfully, 'not one.'

'Who gave him authority to...'

'I did,' said Scrope. 'He wanted to check on his men's longbows as part of the preparations for my father's funeral.'

'I see no longbows.'

Lowther looked about him. Most of the men in the crowd were grinning; Dodd himself was hard put to it to stay stony-faced and the women at the back were whispering and giggling.

'Where's Mr Atkinson?' he asked at last.

'I've no idea,' said Carey, 'I was hoping you could enlighten us.'

Lowther said nothing and Carey turned away to speak to the locksmith.

'Finished?'

'Ay sir,' said the locksmith with pride, 'I did it just like yer honour said.'

Ceremoniously Carey paid him, shut the door to the armoury and locked it, put the key on his belt and gave the other to Scrope.

'Where's mine?' demanded Lowther.

The Carey eyebrows would have driven Dodd wild if he'd been Lowther, they were so expressive.

'The Deputy Warden keeps the key to the armoury,' he said blandly, 'along with the Warden. Though it hardly seems necessary to lock the place, seeing as there's nothing left to steal.'

Lowther turned on his heel and marched away. Most of the crowd heard the rumbling in their bellies and followed. Bangtail Graham and Red Sandy were talking together and Dodd joined them as Carey came towards him.

'How far is it to where you found the body?' Carey asked.

Dodd thought for a moment. 'About six miles to the Esk and then another two, maybe.'

'That's Solway field, isn't it, where the battle was?'

'You come on old skulls and helmets now and then,' Dodd allowed. 'It's aye rough ground.'

'We'll go tomorrow then, when we're more respectable, after the inquest.'

'Ay sir.'

'And now, while we're at the whited sepulchres, shall we have a look at the stables and the barracks?'

God, did the man never stop? Dodd's belly was growling heroically.

'Ay sir,' he said sullenly.

Carey smiled. 'After dinner.'

At least the stables were clean, which was a mercy because Carey poked about in a way that Lowther never had, digging deep into feed bins, lifting hooves for signs of footrot, tutting at the miserable stocks of hay and oats which was all they had left and agreeing that the harness was old but in reasonably good condition.

The barracks Carey pronounced as no worse than many he had seen and better than some. Even so, he had two of Scrope's women servants come in with brooms to sweep the ancient rushes from Dodd's section out into the courtyard so the jacks could be sponged and dried and oiled.

When Dodd asked him why on earth he cared about the huswifery of the barracks he told a long story about the Netherlands, how the Dutch seldom got the plague and that he was convinced it was because they kept foul airs out of their houses by cleaning them. Dodd had never heard such a ridiculous story, since everyone knew that plague was the sword of God's wrath, but he decided he could humour a man who would face down Richard Lowther so entertainingly.

The wind helped them to dry off the cleaned jacks and weaponry, and they worked on through the long evening and by torchlight after sunset, while Carey wandered by occasionally, making helpful suggestions and supplying harness oil. He also went down to Carlisle town and bought six longbows and quivers of arrows with his own money, which he announced he would see tried the next day.

At last, dog-tired, with sore hands, worrying over the Graham corpse which had not yet turned up, and beginning to hate Carey, Dodd went to his bed in the tiny chamber that was one of his perks as Sergeant. He would have to be up out of it again in about five hours, he knew.

When he pulled back the curtain, he stopped. A less dour man would have howled at the waxy face with the star-shaped peck in the right cheek that glared up at him from his pillow, but Dodd had no more indignation left in him. He was simply glad to have found the damned thing, rolled it off onto the floor and was asleep three minutes later. At least the bastard Courtier had wrapped it in its cloak again.

## Monday, 19th June, evening

Barnabus Cooke had seen his master in action in a new command before and so knew what to expect. By dint of making up to Goodwife Biltock, the only other southerner in the place, he had found an ancient desk in one of the storerooms, and acquired it. After cleaning and polishing and eviction of mice it went into Carey's second chamber in the Queen Mary Tower, followed by a high stool and a rickety little table. Richard Bell, Scrope's nervous elderly clerk, was astonished when he was asked for paper, pens and ink and had none to spare. In the end they made an expedition to the one stationer in town, where they bought paper and ink and some uncut goose feathers on credit.

'Barnabus, this is splendid. Thank God I can trust at least one of my men.'

Barnabus snorted and elaborately examined a shoulder seam that seemed on the point of parting. Carey got the message.

'How can I thank you?' he asked warily.

'You can pay me my back wages, sir.'

'God's blood, Barnabus, you know what...'

'I know the third chest is heavy, sir,' said Barnabus. 'And I know you had an argument with my Lord Hunsdon before you left London.'

'Aren't you afraid your savings might be stolen in this nest of thieves?'

'If I had any, I might be, sir. But there's a goldsmith in the town will give me a good rate on it and I know what you plan for tomorrow so if I might make so bold and strike while the iron's hot, as it were, I'd rather have what I'm owed now than wait another year...'

Carey winced. 'I still owe the tailors...'

'...far more money than you can pay, sir,' said Barnabus, putting down the cramoisie doublet and picking up the new black velvet one. 'However they're in London and...'

'...and you're here and can make my life miserable.'

'Yes sir,' said Barnabus blandly. 'That's about the size of it.'

Carey made a face, took his sword off, leaned it against the wall and went to the third chest. He opened it, scattered shirts and hose until it was empty, and then released the false bottom. Barnabus stared at the money with the blood draining from his face.

'Jesus Christ,' he said.

'How much do I owe you?'

'Thirty-eight pounds, ten shillings and fourpence, including the money I lent you last month,' Barnabus answered mechanically, still hypnotised by the gold and silver in front of him.

Carey counted the cash out, and handed it over.

'Wh...where did you get it all from, sir?'

'I robbed a goldsmith on Cheapside.'

Although he was fully capable of it, if necessary, Barnabus didn't find this funny. 'Lord Hunsdon...'

'My father gave me some but the Queen gave me the rest and if I lose it, she'll put me in the Tower. It's a loan, anyway,' said Carey sadly, 'and it took an hour of flattery to stop her charging me interest. So for God's sake, keep your mouth shut, Barnabus. If somebody robs me before I can use it and I go into the Tower, you're going into Little Ease and staying there.'

'Never, sir,' said Barnabus, recovering a bit now Carey had put the false bottom back in the chest. 'I'd be in Scotland, you know that.'

Carey said 'Ha!', went back to the desk and sat down. 'They'd rob you blind and send you back naked, that's what I know. Now then, my lord Scrope will be here in a little while when he's had supper with some of the arrangements for the old Lord's funeral which he wants me to organise. Any chance of a bite...'

As luck would have it, Simon came in at that moment with part of a raised pie, mutton collops, good bread from Scrope's kitchen and some cheese Lady Scrope herself had made, according to Goodwife Biltock, and some raspberry fool.

The talk of the funeral took twice as long as it needed to because Scrope would not keep to the point. Carey dealt with him patiently, sitting at his desk, writing lists and making notes like a clerk, until the question of horses came up.

'What do you mean, my lord, there are no horses? You mean, no black horses?'

Scrope was up off the chair that Biltock claimed Queen Mary had sat on and was pacing up and down the room, the flapping false sleeves on his gown guttering the rushlights.

'I mean, no horses, black, white or piebald. We've what there are in stables but the garrison will need them to form an honour guard, but apart from the six you brought, the horse merchants say they've never known mounts to be so hard to find and the price in Scotland is astonishing, sixty or seventy shillings for a poor scrawny nag, I heard, and whether it's Bothwell being in Lochmaben at the moment or what, I don't know, but horses there are none...'

'How many do we need?'

'Six heavy draught horses at least to pull the hearse and fifty more mounts for the procession and we can't use packponies so...'

'Where have they gone?'

'Scotland, I expect. I was hoping for black horses, of course, but any beasts not actually grey or piebald will do well enough, we could dye the coats...'

'What's the need for horses in Scotland, at the moment?'

Scrope blinked at him. 'I don't know. Probably the Maxwells are planning another strike at the Johnstones or the King is planning a Warden Raid at Jedburgh or Bothwell's planning something...'

'Bothwell?'

'He took Lochmaben last week, didn't you know?'

'No.'

'Did you ever meet him at King James's Court?'

'I did,' said Carey feelingly. 'Once. No, twice, the bastard fouled me at a football game in front of the King. What's he up to?'

Again Scrope shrugged. 'It's some Court faction matter in Scotland. I'm hoping Sir John Carmichael will let me know when he knows what's going on.'

'And the Earl of Bothwell's taken Lochmaben, you say? How the devil did he do that?'

'Nothing would surprise me about Bothwell. So he's got all the horses in the north.'

'Well no, the surnames have their herds of course, but they won't loan them out to us no matter what we offer and...'

'The surnames are refusing honest money? How much did you offer?'

'Twenty shillings a horse for the two days.'

Carey put his pen down. 'Aren't you worried about this, my lord?'

Lord Scrope flapped his bony hands. 'Philadelphia keeps telling me to be careful, but what can I do? It's all happening in Scotland and until my father's buried and the Queen sends my warrant, my hands are tied.'

'With respect, my lord...'

'Anyway, we simply must get this funeral organised, I will not have my father dishonoured with a miserable poor funeral. Lowther says he might be able to get horses.'

Barnabus winced, knowing how much his master disliked

clumsy manipulation, but Carey only took a deep breath.

'Well,' he said, 'I'll see what I can do.'

'I beg your pardon, my lord?'

'It's all over the castle.'

Barnabus prepared to duck, but Carey spoke quite quietly, counting off on his fingers in an oddly clerkish way.

'Well, I...'

'Tell me now, my lord. If my position is insecure I can do nothing at all to help you.'

There, thought Barnabus with satisfaction, if you want your father buried nicely, there you are.

'Do you think you can deal with Lowther?'

'Oh yes, my lord. I can deal with Lowther.'

'Right,' said Scrope, still twiddling. 'Yes. Right. I'll confirm you as my Deputy of course and I'll support you...'

'To the hilt, my lord. Otherwise, I go back to London.'

'Yes, to the hilt, of course, right.' As if he had only just noticed the compression of Carey's lips, Scrope began wandering to the door. Carey stopped him.

'My lord.'

'Er, yes?'

'I want my warrant before dawn tomorrow.'

'Good night, my lord.'

Scrope shut the door carefully and went on down the stairs. They heard his voice in the lower room and the creak of the heavy main door. Barnabus got ready.

'JESUS CHRIST GODDAMN IT TO HELL!' roared Carey, causing the shutters to rattle as he surged to his feet and kicked the little table across the room. The goblet hit the opposite wall but luckily was empty. Scrope's half full goblet rolled after it, bleeding wine, and Carey had the stool in his hand when Barnabus shouted, 'Sir, sir, we've only found the one stool, sir...'

He paused, blinked, put the stool down and slammed his fist on the desk instead.

'*Good God!*' he shouted slightly less loudly. '*That* lily-livered halfwitted pillock is Henry Scrope's son, I can't bloody believe it, JESUS GOD...'

Barnabus was mopping busily and examining the goblets, only one of which was dented, fortunately. He could take it to the goldsmith when he went tomorrow. What was left of the table would do for firewood. Simon, he noticed, was cowering in the corner by the bed while Carey paced and roared until he had worked his anger off. Those who doubted the rumours about Carey's grandfather being King Henry VIII on the wrong side of the blanket, and not the man who complaisantly married Mary Boleyn, should see him or his father in a temper, Barnabus thought, that would set them right.

He beckoned Simon over and sent the trembling lad out for some more wine. By the time he came back, Carey was calm again and looking wearily at the pile of papers Scrope had brought.

'God's truth,' was all he said, 'he's set it for Thursday and it's Monday now. How the devil does he think I can organise anything in two days...?'

## TUESDAY, 20TH JUNE, BEFORE DAWN

He stumbled out of the barracks to find the scurvy git standing there, flanked by his two body-servants holding torches, waiting patiently for his men to appear.

At least they were lined up quickly since turning out fully armed in the middle of the night was something they did regularly, even if nothing much generally came of it. Lowther had always liked to make a bit of a show of a hot trod.

Once they were there, Carey nodded.

'Not bad,' he allowed. 'I know the Earl of Essex's soldiers would still be scratching their backsides and wondering where their boots were. Now then.'

There followed a full hour of meticulous individual examination followed by shooting practice with the new longbows at the butts on the town racecourse. At the end of it Carey brought them back to the castle, stood in front of them and said simply, 'I find you satisfactory, gentlemen.'

Carey opened up the account book and squinted at the figures. He blinked, his lips moved as he calculated and his face took on an irritated cynical expression. Just then a short figure erupted from the Keep and ran across the yard, comically dressed in shirt, hose, pattens and a flying taffeta gown. He was already gabbling in a high-pitched squeak that it would be quite impossible for anyone without the right training in accounts and mathematics to understand the very precise and detailed figures it was his job to...

Carey shut the book and smiled down at him.

'What did you pay for your paymaster's job, Mr Atkinson?' he asked.

'Sir Richard had fifty pounds from me, sir,' said Atkinson, surprised into honesty.

'For the two offices, the Armoury and the Paymaster?'

'N-no, sir. Just the Paymaster clerkship.'

'And how long have you held this particular lucrative office?'

'Er...only four years and...'

'Then you have made back your investment at least tenfold and will suffer no loss if you lose it.'

'I...'

'You have lost it, Atkinson. Get out.'

There was a murmur of interest from the men, craning forward to hear this exchange.

'Silence in the ranks,' snapped Carey as he seated himself at the table and reopened the account books. 'Sergeant Dodd, you may call your men to muster for their pay.'

Goddamn him, Dodd thought, as the men cheered, and Red Sandy looked with morbid curiosity at him. On muster days it was Red Sandy's job to bring in three of their cousins to take the place of the patrolmen who had died and whose pay Dodd kept.

Blandly Carey began to call through the men's names and pay out as each stepped up in front of him. They didn't get all of their backpay, naturally, but they got six months' worth each which was better than they had ever done under old Scrope. Dodd was called last.

'Your pay, Sergeant,' said Carey, handing it over. Dodd took the money in silence and turned to go. 'Sergeant.'

He turned, waited for the axe to fall.

Carey pointed at the dead men's names. 'Faggots, I take it.'

Dodd's mind reverberated with excuses, sickness, wounds, dilatoriness. In the end he said, 'Yes sir.'

'Have you a reason for defrauding the Queen?'

Outrage almost made Dodd splutter. It was traditional for the sergeant to take the pay of men who died, how else could he live?

'Yes sir,' he said stonily.

'What's that?'

'Poverty.'

Carey smiled. 'I'm the youngest of seven sons, and the last time I was out of debt was in '89, the year I walked from London to Berwick in twelve days for a bet of two thousand pounds.'

Dodd said nothing. Did the bastard Courtier expect him to be impressed?

'I'm not one to go against tradition, Sergeant. You may keep two faggots at any time and no more. Do you understand?' He crossed out one of the names.

Oh God, Janet would have his guts. 'Yes sir.' He turned to go, but Carey stopped him.

'Sergeant, do you think you could give me that list of men I can call upon to fight by this evening?'

'Any particular surnames?'

'No, Sergeant, surname doesn't matter to me,' said Carey heretically. 'Dislike of Lowther and a willingness to fight is all I want.'

'Well sir...'

'I've asked Richard Bell to be your clerk if you need him.'

Carey grinned, shut the book and stood up.

'We've finished here. Don't drink it all at once, gentlemen, that's all I've got. Company dismissed.'

# Tuesday, 20th June, morning

The men left the castle in a rabble, jingling their purses and planning extensive wanderings among the town's alehouses that night. Naturally they decided to have a magnificent breakfast at Bessie Storey's and they marched into the common room in a bunch, called for quarts and steak for their meals. Oddly enough she seemed to be expecting them and as soon as the last order was in, Bessie's cousin Nancy Storey barred the door. Bessie herself shuttered the windows and rang her bell.

Janet Dodd, broad and resplendent in her red wool market gown, led the wives of Bangtail, Archie, Red Sandy and Long George into the common room. Grim determination on their faces, they split up and moved in on their husbands. At last Dodd cracked. He laughed and laughed until the tears were dripping in his beer, while Janet marched up to him, sat down beside him and held her hand out. Still snorting feebly, Dodd took five shillings beermoney out of his pay and gave the rest into her hard upturned palm.

'I hear he's a fine man, your new Deputy Warden,' she said smugly. All around them arose whining and protests, while Bessie stood by with a broad grin on her face, ready to calm marital discord with a cudgel. Her son Andrew had already given her his pay.

'You've met him?' said Dodd in astonishment.

'No, no, Lady Scrope sent her girl Joan with Young Hutchin yesterday to tell me what was afoot. I told the others.'

Privately deciding to tan Young Hutchin's arse for him next time they met, Henry drank his beer without comment.

Janet put hers down with a sigh of satisfaction. 'Lord, Bessie knows how to brew, I wish I had her skill. Is he married, the new Deputy?' she asked.

'No.'

She elbowed him in the ribs. 'Come on, Henry,' she said, 'what's the difference? By tomorrow you'd be in the same state, only you would have drunk and gambled the money and I would be after you with a broom handle.'

'That fine Courtier found out about my faggots.'

Janet made a face. 'I minded me that was what he was after, I even brought in three of my brothers, only I saw we couldna get them into the castle in time, so I sent them home. The Borders are very tickle at the moment, the Middle March was hit yesterday, but only four horses stolen and they lost a man because they hadna paid the Warden first. Did he leave you any faggots?'

'Two. He said that's all I'm to take the pay off.'

'It's not so bad, then. Dinna be so glum.'

'Ha. Yon Courtier had us cleaning ourselves like bloody Dutch housewives yesterday, you wouldna ken the barracks now, and even Archie's gun is gleaming bright,' Dodd said grudgingly.

Janet seemed to find this funny.

'I heard he took on that Turk Lowther too, and bought you new bows. Ay well, think upon it, Dodd. He has to make his mark which he's now done. He's paid you cash and where he got it, I don't know for I'm certain there's been no Queen's paychest come into the city for the last six months. Would Lowther have paid cash?'

Dodd laughed at the idea and started to unbend a little. 'How's the farm?'

'Mildred died.'

His good humour promptly dried up again. 'What was wrong with her?'

Janet looked worried. 'I had the knacker's man take her and he didn't know either. At least Shilling's well enough. What's this I hear about us getting raided?'

'Was that from Young Hutchin?'

'He said I might want to have some of my brothers to stay with me and a couple of men to go out to the summer pastures for a week or so, just in case. There's a lot of broken men about, he said.'

Mostly Hutchin's relations, but it was kindly of the boy, Dodd thought, deciding to let him live. Henry found himself close to wishing Lowther had got the deputyship after all. A comfortable if unprofitable life was now all back to front and looked likely to get worse and for lack of rest and unaccustomed labour he was falling asleep where he sat.

'At least we can afford to buy a new horse,' Janet said, after counting the money.

'Now there's a novel idea,' said Henry Dodd, blinking into his leather beaker. '*Buy* a horse with *money* instead of me having to ride about the countryside at dead of night with your brothers...?'

Janet grinned at him. 'I'll keep it to meself if you will.'

## TUESDAY, 20TH JUNE, MORNING

The inquest, such as it was, took half an hour. Scrope sat in his capacity as Warden at the courtroom in the town hall; Bangtail came forward, identified himself as Cuthbert Graham, known as Bangtail, identified the corpse as his second cousin by marriage George Graham, known as Sweetmilk, youngest son of John Graham of the Peartree. Dodd explained of his own knowing that the man had been shot in the back by person or persons unknown and Scrope adjourned the case to the next Warden's Day.

A black-haired ill-favoured man at the back of the court came forward to claim the body, and took a long hard stare at Dodd as he passed by. Dodd thought it was Francis Graham of Moat, one of Sweetmilk's cousins, and his nearest available relative that wasn't outlawed and at risk of arrest in England.

By the time the clouds had cleared and the sun shone down for the first time in a week, Carey, Dodd and all six of his men were out on the road to Longtown ford where the Esk began spreading itself like a blowzy wife on the way to Rockcliffe Marsh and the Solway Firth.

At the ford Carey stopped and looked around.

'This is where you met Jock?'

'Ay,' said Dodd, not relishing the moment, 'they had us neatly.'

Carey said nothing but chirruped to his horse, let him find his own way down into the water and splashed across and up the muddy bank. The rest of them followed. Unseasonable rain had washed away most of the traces, but there were still a few old prints in sheltered spots.

When Dodd gestured wordlessly at Sweetmilk's bushes Carey stopped, leaned on his crupper and looked all around him. A gust of wind nearly took his hat off, but he rammed it down again and slid from the saddle.

'Tell me the tale, Sergeant.'

Dodd told it and Carey followed his movements exactly, then beckoned for Bessie's Andrew and Bangtail to follow him into the gorse. Bangtail rolled his eyeballs but obeyed: it was remarkable how gold could sweeten a man's disposition. After a struggle with his worst nature, Sergeant Dodd also dismounted and followed them. The springy branch which had caught Bessie's Andrew nearly took his cap off and he swore.

'Wait a minute, Sergeant,' said Carey, examining the branch as if it was the first he'd ever seen. 'No,' he said, disappointed. 'Pity.'

In the centre was a flattened place and some broken branches.

'Tell me what you saw.'

Bessie's Andrew looked bewildered.

'I saw a corpse, sir.'

'Yes, but how did you see it? How was it lying?'

The lad swallowed. 'The crows had pecked it.'

Carey was patient with him. 'I know, but which way was it lying? Was it on its back, or...'

'On his side.'

'Which side?'

'God, I don't know, right side I think.'

'Then the right cheek was to the ground.'

'Ay.'

'Was it stiff?'

'Stiff as a board, sir.'

'Well, how did you get it on a horse to bring it back then?'

'Sir?'

'If the body was stiff, how did you put it over a horse? Did you have to break him...'

'Och no sir, nothing like that.'

'Then how...'

'It was bent over already,' snapped Dodd. 'Like this.' He showed the mad Courtier and the mad Courtier grinned like a Bedlamite.

'Would you say he'd been brought here on a horse?'

'Well, of course, he was, sir,' said Dodd. 'I told ye, I followed the tracks of two nags from the ford...'

'But he was dead when he was put on the horse and then brought here; not, for instance, alive when he came and dead when his killer left him?'

What was the man driving at? 'Ay sir. I'd say so, the tracks of one of the horses didn't look like a beast was being ridden, more a beast burdened.'

'Excellent. So he was killed somewhere else and dumped here, on an old battlefield in the hope that after a few months anyone who came on the bones would think they died fifty years ago.'

'I suppose so, sir,' said Dodd, who couldn't see any point in this expedition at all. 'There weren't any traces of blood or suchlike around about here either.'

Carey nodded. 'What did he have on him?'

Bessie's Andrew blushed. Dodd saw it and hoped Carey wouldn't. Unfortunately he did.

'So what did you take off him, Bessie's Andrew?' Carey asked ominously.

'Nothing sir, I...'

Carey folded his arms and waited. Dodd was glaring at Storey who looked terrified.

'Well, nothing much, sir...'

'What did you take off him?' Carey didn't raise his voice.

Bessie's Andrew muttered something.

'Speak up, boy,' growled Dodd.

'He...er...he had a ring.'

'A ring?' Carey's eyebrows were very sarcastic. Dodd wondered if it was the eyebrows that broke Bessie's Andrew's spirit.

'Well, he had three rings, gold and silver and one with a little ruby in it,' stammered the boy in a rush, 'and he had a purse with some Scots silver in it, about five shillings' worth and he had a dagger with a good hilt...'

'By God,' said Bangtail admiringly, 'that was quick work picking him clean, lad.'

Bessie's Andrew stared at the ground miserably. 'And that's all, sir.'

'*All?*'

Dodd was impressed for the first time. Bessie's Andrew's face twisted. 'He had a good jewel on his cap. No more, I swear it.'

Carey reached out and patted Storey's shoulder comfortingly.

'The Papists say that confession makes a man's soul easier in his body. Don't you feel better?'

'No sir. Me mam'll kill me.'

'Why?'

'I only gave her the rings sir, but I took a liking to the jewel and the dagger and the silver...'

'Of course you did,' said Carey softly. 'Now, Storey, look at me. Do I look like a man of my word?'

'Ay sir.'

'Then you believe me if I swear on my honour that if you ever rob a corpse while you're in my service, I will personally flog you.'

Bessie's Andrew went white. His large Adam's apple bobbed convulsively as he nodded.

'And,' Carey continued, 'if there's a second offence, I will hang you. For March treason. Do you understand?'

Bessie's Andrew squeaked something.

'What?'

'Y-yes sir.'

'Which applies to any man in my service whatsoever,' said Carey, glaring at Bangtail and then at Dodd. 'You'll see the men know that.'

'Yes sir,' said Dodd. 'When did you want to flog him?'

'It depends if he's told the truth this time and if he hands over what he took.'

Bessie's Andrew's face was the colour of mildewed parchment. 'But my mother...'

'Blame it on me.' Carey was inflexible.

'Och God...'

'You can bring me what you took after we get back. I might be merciful this time, since you were not, after all, in my service when you stole Sweetmilk's jewels.'

'What are you looking for, sir?' asked Bangtail. 'More gold?'

'That or bits of cloth. Anything that shouldn't be in a gorse bush.'

They all looked. It was Bessie's Andrew who found the only thing that Carey found interesting, which was a long shining thread of gold. Carey put it away in his belt pouch and they searched fruitlessly for a little while before struggling back out of the bushes again to find the men also wandering about, checking hopefully for plunder from the old battlefield. There was none of course, the field had been picked clean for fifty years by crows and men. And nobody had bothered to set a watch, which caused Carey to lecture them again.

# TUESDAY, 20TH JUNE, AFTERNOON

With Carey gone about some urgent business, Dodd rubbed down his own horse, saw the animals were properly watered, fed and clean, and then wandered, belly rumbling, down towards Bessie's again. Time enough to eat the garrison rations when he had no more money left. He was still in a bad temper and cursing Bessie's Andrew: if the ill-starred wean had behaved properly with his windfall and shared it with his sergeant, Dodd could have given Janet a little ring with a ruby in it which she would have liked. On the other hand, he might then have had to ask for it back…

He was sauntering along, thinking about that with his long dour face like the past week's weather, when he saw something that cheered him at once.

There, astride Shilling his old hobby, rode the splendid sight of his wife Janet, market pannier full of salt and string and a sugar loaf poking out the top, her eyes and the dagger at her waist daring any man to try robbing her. Unlike the Graham women, she felt no need of carrying a gun to keep her safe. Dodd liked his woman to look well and Janet was in her red dress with the black trim, a neat little ruff round her neck, and a fine false front to her petticoat made of part of the old Lord Scrope's court cloak, which the young lord had disdained since it was out of fashion, Philadelphia had accepted, her maid taken as a perk and Janet snapped up as a bargain the month before. Her white apron was of linen she had woven herself and was a credit to her. The red kirtle suited her high colour and the snapping pale blue eyes and Armstrong sandy hair. If her teeth were a little crooked and her hips broad enough to be fashionable without need of a bumroll (though she wore one of course) and her boots heavy and hobnailed, what of it? He put his hand to the horse's bridle and Shilling whickered at him and tried to find an apple in the front of his jerkin. Janet smiled at him.

'Now then wife,' said Dodd, grinning lecherously at her.

'I heard you were out on patrol.'

'We were looking at the place where we found a body.'

Janet frowned. 'Was that the body of Sweetmilk Graham you've not yet told me of?'

'It was.'

'Will Jock raid us, do you think?'

'Why should he?' demanded Dodd. 'It wasn't me that killed his son.'

Janet looked dubious. 'What about lying to him at the ford?'

Christ, how did she hear so much? 'He'll know it was because I was not inclined to a fight. And where are you off to?'

'To see my lover,' said Janet with a naughty look. Dodd growled. She slid from the horse and began leading the animal, holding her skirts high above the mud.

'How's the wheat?' Henry asked, walking beside her and enjoying the view.

Janet began to suck her bottom lip through a gap in her teeth and her brow knitted.

'Sick,' she said. 'We might get by with the oats and the barley if there's no more rain. I'll leave that field fallow next year.'

'But it's infield,' protested Dodd.

'Give it time to clean itself. I might run some pigs on it. The beans are doing poorly too.'

'What will you do to replace Mildred?'

'I've heard tell there's one for sale.'

'Not reived?'

Janet shrugged. 'Not branded, any road. That's why I want to buy him.'

'Buy,' said Dodd and shook his head.

Janet giggled. 'Will you want to come with me or would it go against your credit to be seen giving money for a beast?'

Dodd considered. Janet was almost as good a judge of horseflesh as he was himself, and knew most of the horses from round about and wasn't likely to be sold a stolen animal, at least not unknowingly. But she was only a woman. If it had been a cow...

'I'll come with you,' he said.

They turned down a small wynd leading to one of the many ruined churches of Carlisle: this one had a churchman in it, a book-a-bosom man who spent most of his time travelling about the country catching up with the weddings and christenings.

'Good afternoon, Reverend Turnbull,' said Janet politely, 'we've come about the horse.'

Now Dodd was no different from any other man. He may have had a longer and more ill-tempered face than most, but he could fall in love. He fell in love immediately, with the elegant long-legged creature that was tethered inside the porch of the church. The colour was unusual, a piebald black, the neck high and arched, the legs strong and firm, hooves as healthy as you could wish and best of all, he still had his stones.

Janet's face was bland. 'Where was he stolen?'

The Reverend Turnbull looked offended. 'Mrs Dodd, I would never try to sell you or the Sergeant a...stolen animal. I swear to you on my honour as a man of the cloth, that he was honestly bought. Besides, do you think an animal like that could be reived and the Sergeant not know about it?'

Dodd turned away so the churchman wouldn't see his face which he knew would be full of ardour. With a horse like that he could win the victor's bell at any race he chose to enter, he thought, and the fees he could charge at stud...

'Well?' said Janet.

'Eh?' Dodd had his hands on the horse's rump, running them down the beautiful muscles, feeling the tail which needed grooming to rid it of burrs.

'Have you heard of a horse like that being reived recently?'

'Reived...no, no, I'd have heard for sure. There now, there, I've no apples, I'm sorry...'

'Dodd,' growled Janet. Henry paid no attention.

'He's an English beast, surely,' he said. 'Never Scots, not looking like that, unless he's out of the King's stable.'

'Is he?'

'Is he what?'

'Is he out of the King's stable, Reverend?'

The churchman laughed fondly. 'No, no, he's an English horse, from Berwick, I know that from the man that sold him to me.'

Dodd took the reins and swung himself up onto the horse's back, rode in a tight circle before the church. He had a lovely gait, a mettlesome manner though he might have been short of horsefeed recently, and a mouth as soft as a lady's glove.

'Who was that?' asked Janet.

'Oh, a pedlar I know. He told me he came from further south than that, but he bought him in Berwick. I think he may have had some notion of crossing the border with him to sell to the Scots, but I convinced him he should not break the law and I bought him to sell on.'

Dodd slid from the horse's back again and patted his proud neck.

'Hm,' said Janet, took Henry Dodd's arm and moved him out of earshot. 'Henry Dodd, wake up. Yon animal must be stolen.'

'Not from here,' said Dodd, 'I'd know.'

'From Northumberland then.'

Dodd shook his head and smiled. 'Get a bill of sale on him and he's ours legally.'

'Oh, you...'

'Janet, he's beautiful, he'll run like the wind and his foals will be...'

'I know you in this state with a horse, you'd blather like a man possessed and pay three times the right price. If you promise me he isn't stolen from this March, I'll buy him, but you get away from here or the Reverend will see you've lost your heart.'

Henry smiled lopsidedly. 'I can't promise he's not reived, but I'm sure as I can be.'

'We may have trouble keeping hold of him, you know, once the Grahams and the Elliots know we've got him.'

Dodd shrugged. 'I'm not mad, Janet. I'll have him cover as many mares as I can in the time, then I'll enter him at the next race and sell him after to the Keeper of Hermitage or Lord Maxwell.'

Janet laughed. 'Against the law.'

Dodd had the grace to look embarrassed. 'Or the Captain of Bewcastle or the new Deputy or someone strong enough to hold him.'

Janet punched him gently in the ribs and kissed his cheek. 'He's a light thing to look upon, isn't he.'

Dodd forced himself to turn about, bid the churchman a gruff good day and walk away while Janet leapt hard-faced into the bargaining.

Afterwards, she took the horses by back routes to the castle so that fewer unscrupulous eyes would see the beauty, and tethered both in Bessie's yard. When she went in she found Henry, Red Sandy, Long George and Archie Give-it-Them all playing primero with a tall handsome chestnut-haired man she didn't know, who talked and laughed more than anyone she had ever met, and had skyblue eyes to melt your heart.

She sat down, watched the play which was tame, and waited to be noticed.

'Oh Janet,' said Dodd happily, drinking from his favourite leather mug. 'Sir Robert, this is my wife; wife, this is Sir Robert Carey, the new Deputy Warden.'

Janet rose to curtsey to him and instantly took to him when he too rose and made his bow in return, smiling and addressing her courteously as Mrs Dodd rather than Goodwife. That arrogant lump Lowther would have grunted at her and told her to fetch him another quart. Though she would hardly need to be introduced to him.

'Get me another quart, wife,' said Dodd, oiled enough to make a point of it. Janet smiled, thinking what babes men were, picked up the jug and went to where Bessie was tapping another barrel, with her bodice sleeves unlaced and laid over a stool, the sleeves of her smock pushed back.

'How are you, goodwife?' Janet asked politely.

Bessie shook her head, her lips pressed tight, from which Janet concluded that her Andrew was in trouble and she didn't want to talk about it.

The primero game was still in progress. Someone had dealt a new hand and Carey glanced at his, and called, 'Vada. I've a flush here.'

Everyone laid down his cards, but Red Sandy held the highest points and pulled in the pot, grumbling at Carey's sport-stopping flush.

Carey stood. 'Good night, gentlemen,' he said, 'you've cleaned me out.'

'You could stay and try and win it back,' said Red Sandy unsubtly.

Carey smiled. 'Another night, Sandy Dodd, I shall take you on and mend my fortunes, but not tonight. Thank you for your list, Sergeant.'

Janet watched him go, wondering how much his extremely well-cut dark cramoisie doublet and hose had cost him in London, and who had starched his ruff so nicely. He surely was a great deal easier on the eye than Lowther or Carleton. Archie had taken the pack and was shuffling the cards methodically, his tongue stuck out and his breath held in his effort not to drop them from his enormous hands.

'I'm for home,' she announced, 'I'll want to be there before nightfall with things as they are.'

Dodd followed her out where they ran smack into Bangtail coming from the midden. He smiled weakly at her and rejoined the game.

'There he is,' she said, pointing at where the beautiful horse was whickering and pulling at his tethering reins. Dodd went up and patted the silky neck, his face filled with happy dreams of golden bells and showers of silver. 'What shall we call him?'

Dodd had unhitched him and was walking him up and down again.

'He walks so nicely,' Janet said consideringly, with her head on one side, 'like your new Deputy Warden, somehow.'

Dodd grinned at the poetic fancy. 'There's his name. Courtier. How about it?'

'I like it,' said Janet approvingly, 'they'll know he's out of the common. Do you want to keep him with you in the castle or shall I take him back to Gilsland?'

Dodd hesitated. 'Lowther might spot him and take a fancy to him. Or the new Deputy. Better keep him in our tower. But will you be all right on the road back? It's a long way and I canna come with ye.'

'I willna be alone. My cousin Willie's Simon is here today, I heard. I'll offer him a good meal at Gilsland and a bed for the night if he'll bear me company.'

Dodd nodded approvingly. It would help if some thought the horse belonged to the Armstrongs rather than him.

Janet kissed him and then took the horses out of the yard. Dodd went back into Bessie's and set about losing the rest of his pay. He didn't succeed, if only because Bangtail had already gone. Archie Give-it-Them said he'd muttered something about an errand for his wife and Dodd was too pleased at the possibility of winning to wonder at it.

## WEDNESDAY, 21ST JUNE, 2 A.M.

That night Dodd dreamed he was about to be hanged for some crime he could not remember. He could hear the Reverend Turnbull intoning his neck-verse in a huckster's gabble.

'Have mercy upon me, oh God, according to thy loving kindness; according unto the multitude of thy tender mercies blot out my transgressions.

'Wash me thoroughly from my iniquity and cleanse me from my sin...'

He was just trying desperately to think of something to say as his last words when the drums leading him to the gigantic scaffold turned out to be a fist hammering on the door of his little chamber.

'Sergeant!' roared Carey's voice. 'Up and rouse out your men.'

Dodd was already hauling on his hose and shrugging on his doublet. He put on his second-best jack, the one Janet had spent hours reinforcing with bits of secondhand mail where ordinary steel plates would chafe. By the time his eyes were properly open he had laced himself up, buckled on his sword and found his helmet under the bed, and he was following Carey down the dark passage past the tackroom to the barracks door, as the Carlisle bell started ringing.

'Where's the raid?' he asked.

'A boy came in a quarter of an hour ago and he said the Grahams lifted ten head of cattle and three horses out of Lanercost at midnight.'

'How many reivers?'

'Between ten and twenty men, he thought.'

'Forty in all then,' said Dodd, and Carey nodded. He was already booted and spurred and his own jack seemed well-worn and serviceable. No way of telling the man's courage though when it came to it, Dodd thought, he wished he'd seen Carey in a fight before having to follow him on a hot trod. What was wrong with a cold trod, anyway, they had six days to follow in for it to be legal, and nobody blinked much at a day or two to spare? Which would be worse? A fire-eater or a man who was all bully and brag and no blows? His face settling into its customary sullenness, Dodd decided he was hoping for a coward who would follow the trod well back and discharge his duty without too much sweat. But seeing Carey's grin and the sparkle in his eyes, Dodd began to feel uneasy.

By the time the men had turned out and were in the castle yard, with sleepy hobbies snorting and stamping protestingly and blowing up their barrels to prevent their girths being fastened, another boy had ridden in with news of a herd of horses gone missing from Walter Ridley's fields and a farmhouse broken into on the way. Estimates of the Grahams' strength ranged from fifteen to forty men and Dodd nodded.

'Where are the Elliots?' he asked.

Carey turned to the most recent arrival, a lad of about twelve on his father's fastest pony, his face flushed with the ride and the excitement.

'We didna see them,' he said.

'The Grahams don't always ride with the Elliots, though Sergeant?' Carey asked, raising his voice to be heard above the clanging of the bell.

'Not always,' Dodd allowed. 'Usually. It could be Johnstones or even Nixons or Scotch Armstrongs. Tom's Watt Ridley,' he called to the other boy, 'did your uncle say aught about the Scots?'

'Only he hadna seen none,' said Tom's Watt, helpfully. 'It was all Grahams.'

Dodd sucked his teeth.

'Are these out of Liddesdale, Tom's Watt?'

'Oh ay.'

Red Sandy came bustling up, with his steel bonnet in his hands and a crossbow under his arm, followed by his two sleuthhounds. The two dogs were bouncing around him, panting and leaping up with their paws and making the odd excited strangulated squeaks of dogs that have been taught not to give tongue.

'No sign of Bangtail,' he said, 'no sign of Richard Lowther either. The Warden says Sir Robert's to lead the whole castle guard.'

Carey nodded and looked pleased. If he had any worries about it they didn't show.

'Sergeant, if you were the Graham leader, where would you be taking the animals?' asked Carey.

'Into Liddesdale across the Bewcastle Waste,' said Dodd instantly. 'There's plenty of nice valleys in the dale with pens for holding booty in, no better hiding hole.'

'I take it we don't want to be pursuing them directly into Liddesdale?' said Carey.

Dodd winced while Red Sandy looked appalled.

'No sir.'

'Name me a meeting place within two miles of the mouth of Liddesdale.'

Dodd named the Longtownmoor meeting stone which was a mile from Netherby, held by an unfortunate Milburn who paid blackrent to everyone.

Carey smiled at Tom's Watt, drew him aside, spoke for a time and gave him a ring from his hand before drawing his gloves on. Dodd mounted up and trotted between his men to see all of them were properly equipped. The few who owned calivers had left them behind because of the rain. Dodd himself took the burning peat turf on the end of his lance that signified a hot trod. The horn he was supposed to blow in warning if they had to cross over into Scotland was at his belt.

'Sergeant, do you know the Bewcastle Waste well?'

Dodd considered. 'Ay sir. Well enough.' Red Sandy snorted at this modesty.

'Up here by me, then. I know it not at all and am in your hands.'

With the Carlisle bell still clanging irregularly into the night behind them, they walked their horses through the town, glared at by cats interrupted in their own reiving. Once through the gates they came to a canter northwards, the darkness about them sparsely sequined with signal beacons.

They picked up a trail of several dozen cattle a little to the south of Lanercost, the hounds lolloping and panting along and giving no tongue as they had been trained. At least Carey seemed in no hurry to close with the Grahams. As soon as he could the Graham leader dodged into the Waste, and as the sky greyed and the rain fell again, Dodd was threading through the bogs and scrub with Carey uncharacteristically quiet beside him. He rode well enough, Dodd allowed grudgingly, perhaps a little too straight in the saddle for endurance, a little too reluctant to let his mount judge her own pace.

Always Carey wanted to be round to the east of them and the strategy seemed to be working for the Grahams let themselves be herded westwards rather than northwards. Dawn was theoretical rather than real as they wove in and out of ditches and up hills, while the Grahams doubled back and crossed water to try and lose the hounds, all of it cruelly rough country. By the time it was full morning, Carey at last had lost some of his bounce, and began to take on the experienced loosebacked slouch of Dodd and his men.

By the sourness of his expression, Henry Dodd's men could tell he was enjoying himself, countering every Graham turn and ruse, and reading the man's mind ahead of himself, until he lifted his head, turned while Carey urged his hobby through another little stream, and nodded with supreme satisfaction.

'There they are, sir.'

Ahead of them they could make out against the grey wet curtains drooling out of the clouds, the lances and lowing of the raiding party.

'Where are we?' Carey asked, a little breathless.

'One mile south of the meeting stone,' said Henry and nodded to the right. 'Liddesdale's that way sir.'

'No sign of Elliots or Armstrongs.'

'Doesna mean there are none,' said Dodd, hoping his various cousins by marriage might remember who he was if they were there.

'What are they doing now?'

'Rounding up the cattle again, sir, ready to take them into the Debateable Land.'

'How long will it take them?'

'Five minutes.'

Carey scraped his thumb on his lower lip where his nicely trimmed courtier's goatee was invading upland pastures. Like all of them Carey was caked in mud and the slogging through the Waste seemed to have dulled even his enthusiasm for movement. They had come about in a broad anticlockwise arc.

'What do you think of them, Sergeant?'

Dodd blinked into the rain and considered.

'They're slow, sir.' A thought came to him unbidden but he suppressed it. As Lowther had said to him many times, it wasn't his job to think.

'Could be the cattle.'

'No, see, sir, I could have had the cattle into Scotland by now.'

Carey raised an aristocratic eyebrow.

'Are they waiting for us?'

'Might be,' said Dodd reluctantly, 'I don't know. They might be waiting for us.'

'So the betting is they've got someone to back them hiding in the valley?'

'Ay sir.'

'Where have they set the ambush?'

'I'm not sure, sir,' said Dodd cautiously.

Carey smiled. 'As an expert, speaking from your past experience.'

Dodd sucked his teeth again, thought and pronounced his opinion. By the end of his explanation, Carey had begun to look worried. He peered over his shoulder at the miserable pale sun where it was struggling against the clouds and squinted at the western horizon. For a moment it almost seemed to Dodd that he was listening. Far away came the peewits of green plover disturbed by the reivers. Carey urged his tired horse to a fast canter up a slight knoll, stood in his stirrups, looked all around, and came trotting back cheerfully again.

'Let's have them then,' he said.

'Now sir?'

'Yes, Sergeant.' He stood in his stirrups again. 'Gentlemen,' he said at large to the men, 'we're taking back the cattle. With God's help, we have friends on the other side of the Grahams who will come and join the fun.' He didn't mention the possibility that the Grahams might have friends too.

There was the clatter and creak of harness as men tightened the straps on their helmets, loosened their swords, gripped their lances. None except Carey had firearms but Carey's were a beautiful pair of dags with a Tower gunsmith's mark on them, ready shotted and wound.

'Nineteen of us?' said Dodd.

'Twenty,' said Carey quietly, letting his horse back and snort nervously as he took one gun in each hand. Bloody show-off, thought Dodd, I hope the recoil breaks his wrist.

'There's twenty-five of them at least from their trail,' Red Sandy said reasonably, 'and ten others and the Elliots unaccounted for... We could likely come to some arrangement...'

Carey's eyes narrowed. 'Now we come to it,' he said, 'do I have grey hair? Is my face red? Do I look like Richard Lowther to you?'

'No sir, but...'

'Which is it to be? Do I shout come on, or do I shout go on and shoot the first coward who hesitates?'

Red Sandy flushed. ''Tis only business...'

'No, it's theft.' Carey's lip curled. 'Christ, I knew you were dishonest and I knew you were sloppy. God as my witness, I never thought you were scared...'

Red Sandy darkened to ruby. He backed his horse into the group of men, put his lance in rest.

'All right,' said Carey, taking a deep breath, 'let's have the bastards.' He spurred his horse to the gallop. Dodd thought of Lowther's gratitude and then decided he didn't care and kicked his hobby till it ran and caught up to Carey in a shower of mud. There were horsemen on the Longtownmoor.

'Elliots?' he yelled, pointing at them.

Carey laughed. 'Who knows?' he shouted back.

They had been spotted. Carey put a gun under his arm, winded his own horn three times, dropped it and took the gun again. The strange horsemen shimmered and shifted down the slope in the distance. The raiders put a shot in among the cattle to scatter them and bent low over their horses' necks as they rode hard for Liddesdale. They seemed to think the other group were their friends the Elliots. In the last few seconds Dodd saw the Grahams suddenly haul their horses up short. At that moment, Dodd, Carey and the men were amongst them. Carey shot one Graham in the face, misfired with his other dag from the wet. Ducking a lance, he thrust his guns back in the saddle case and drew his sword which was the long slender article that Dodd had seen him draw on Lowther. He wielded it more with his forearm than his shoulder. Unexpectedly, he managed to run at least one man through under the arm with it: the blade flickered in and out again like a needle. Dodd with his broadsword was mournfully and methodically cutting and kicking his way through the press of men, and Archie Give-it-Them successfully ran a Graham through the thigh with his lance, which broke off.

By which time Thomas Carleton and a number of Musgraves and Fenwicks had surrounded the mêlée and when the Elliots came swarming out of the valley a few seconds later, the reivers had all either run or surrendered, except for the three of them that were dead and one badly wounded. Seeing the situation, the Elliots swung round and rode away back into Liddesdale again as fast as they could, with a few Carletons whooping dangerously after them.

Dodd came upon Carey wiping sweat and rain off his face with a handkerchief while he stood by his horse to let it catch its breath. He was glaring disgustedly at his pretty rapier which had broken off on somebody's jack.

'Five prisoners,' Dodd reported, 'Young Jock Graham, Young Wattie, Sim's Sim, Henharrow Geordie and...er...Ekie Graham.' Pray that Carey didn't know Ekie Graham was Bangtail's half-brother.

'Where are the horses?' demanded Carey.

'Well, they're here, sir...'

'Not the ones we rode, Sergeant, the ones they stole. It's all cattle here.'

Dodd looked about. 'Ahh,' he groaned. Carey's lips were pressed tight together as he strode over to where the prisoners were being tied in a line by Long George and Captain Carleton's younger brother.

'You,' he snapped to Young Jock, who was the tallest and the spottiest and had the best jack and helmet, 'where's your father?'

Young Jock grinned impudently. 'Wouldn't you like to know, eh, Courtier?'

Long George slapped him across the face. 'Speak civil to the Deputy Warden,' he said.

Young Jock spat on the ground. Carey looked at him narrow-eyed for a moment, suddenly not seeming angry any more. He turned to Red Sandy who was bustling up with ropes over his shoulder.

'Take a list of the Fenwicks, Musgraves and Carletons that helped us,' said Carey, 'see they get their share for backing a hot trod.'

Long George was amused. 'Och sir, Captain Carleton'll see to that, never fear.'

Captain Carleton was overseeing the gathering up of the Graham weapons and horses. His voice boomed over the moor, saying that the wounded man could bide there until his friends came back for him.

'The prisoners, sir? Shall I find some trees?' asked Red Sandy. 'Trees?'

'To hang them on.' Dodd gestured with his thumb. 'We caught them red-hand on a lawful hot trod, we have the right.'

He sent the prisoners off with ten men and with the remaining nine he set about recapturing the cattle. These were long experienced in being raided and had settled down out of their stampede to munch at what fodder they could find.

Dodd and his men urged their weary horses round about the cattle to gather them again, with the dogs darting and nipping among the legs to help them. It took a while, but they had the cattle running in a stream southwards when Dodd cantered up to the Deputy Warden and asked if he wanted them brought through the Waste again.

'No,' said Carey, 'we'll bring them through Lanercost valley and through the pass, and not too fast or the milch cows will take sick.'

Dodd privately objected to being told something he had known before he was eight, but only turned his horse and yipped angrily at an enterprising calf.

# WEDNESDAY, 21ST JUNE, 2 A.M.

At the same time as Dodd was hearing his neck-verse in his dream, Janet Dodd was shaken awake by one of her women, a young cousin by the name of Rowan Armstrong.

'Mistress, mistress,' she hissed, 'Topped Hobbie's ridden in, there's reivers coming.'

Janet was instantly awake. She pulled her stays over her head and her petticoat, while Rowan fumbled her kirtle off the chest. 'How far?'

'A few miles away. He could hear them but not see them. I told him to fetch up Geordie.'

'Good girl.' A horn sounded from the barnekin, loud and urgent. Janet disappeared in the midst of her kirtle, reappeared, her fingers flying among the lacings. She went to the narrow window, opened the shutter and leaned out into the muggy darkness—cloud and no moon, a fine soaking rain. 'Did Topped Hobbie say who it was coming?'

'He thought it was Grahams, but he doesn't know. He thought he heard Jock of the Peartree's voice, mistress.'

Janet pulled her lip through the gap in her teeth. 'You go and wake the other maids, get yourself dressed and booted, then go help them bring in the cattle and the sheep nearby.'

'What about the horses, mistress?'

'Shilling and Courtier are both in the lower room of the tower already.'

The horn stopped blowing, there were torches being lit in the barnekin. She peered out into the blackness as she pulled on her boots. 'Geordie,' she shrieked.

'Yes, Janet.' Her brother's voice sounded strained.

'Is the beacon lit?'

'As soon as we can get the kindling to catch, Janet. There are other beacons alight already, the March is up.'

'Are the men in harness?'

'They will be. We'll ride out and fight them in...'

'You will not. You will bring in every beast we have and bar the gate, then get on the wall with your bows.'

'We canna catch them all in the time.'

'Bring in what you can.'

'But if he fires us...'

'Every roof is wet through. Do as I say.'

Janet ran down the stairs with her skirts hitched over her belt, out the door of the tower and into the barnekin which was already filling with desperately lowing cows, two half-panicked horses and frightened women trying to control over-excited children. Janet ran out of the gate and climbed on a stone to direct the running traffic of cattle, horses, men, boys, chickens, pigs, children, and, she would have sworn, rats as well. They could hear hooves; she waited as long as she dared, then shook her head.

'Come in, Geordie and Simon and Little Robert, leave the rest!' she yelled. 'Come on in.'

Her cousin and her brother came galloping out of the mirk on their own horses, and Willie's Simon had an arrow in his arm. Janet waited on them as the hooves and the shouting grew louder, slid through the narrow gate last of all, helped Geordie shut it and bar it and barricade it with settles from the hall, as a couple of arrows thudded into the wood. There was whooping and the flicker of torches on the other side.

'I thought he was already in,' said Geordie as he took the crossbow and began winding it up. Willie's Simon slid awkwardly from his horse and walked away.

'He's not in the tower,' Janet said, frowning. 'He must be outside still, God help him, I hope he has the sense to lay low.'

There was loud shouting outside and the noise of a scuffle. Janet looked about for a ladder to the fighting platform, and then motioned Geordie to go up it first.

'Janet...' he began to protest.

'Shut up.' He obeyed, climbed the ladder and stayed crouched like the other men on the platform, while she climbed up behind and squatted beside him. She peered cautiously over the pointed wooden stakes.

On the hill something was burning: no doubt it was Clem Pringle's farm, since it was traditional to set light to it. The stones that made the walls were set hard as rock together from repeated firings.

There were some men riding about, some torches set in the earth to give them light, two torches in two roofs, trying stubbornly to spread through the sodden turves. A little further off she could hear protesting lowing and whistles.

'Jock!' she shouted, 'Jock of the Peartree!'

An arrow on fire sped over the wall, nearly setting her hair ablaze and she squatted lower, crawled further along.

'I want to talk to you, Jock.' Before the next arrow could come, she moved again. Somebody put the other one out.

'Where's my horse?' came a shout from the other side.

'If you can see him, shoot him,' Janet whispered to Geordie.

'Steady Janet, do we want a feud with the Grahams?'

'You fool, we're already at feud with them.'

'Oh Christ.'

'Don't blaspheme in my house.'

'But you...'

'Shut up. *Jock!*' she roared.

'Janet Dodd, I have Little Robert here and I want my horse back. In fact, I want all your horses.'

'What?' She peeped over the palisade and there he was in the torchlight, the young fool, fifteen years old and no sense, kneeling in the mud with four Graham lances at his throat and back, and blood purling down his face from a slice on the head.

'I bought him fair and square,' she shouted. 'If I'd known he was yours I wouldna touch him on the end of a lance. But I bought and paid for him.'

'What did you pay?'

'Five English pounds.'

'I dinna believe you, Janet, no one would sell my Caspar for so little, he's the cream of Scotland. Your man Sergeant Dodd took him off my son when he shot him dead from behind.'

'He'd nothing to do with it, you know that.'

'I don't, Janet. Sweetmilk's dead, your man had the body and lied to me about it. Who else would kill Sweetmilk, he was the gentlest wean I ever had.'

God give me strength and patience, Janet thought, remembering Sweetmilk in a brawl at the last Warden's Day. 'Jock, would you keep hold of a horse from a man you'd murdered like that?'

There was silence on the other side.

After a while Janet stood up. 'Give me Little Robert back, Jock.'

Jock's voice was mocking. 'I'll let you buy him off me with all the mounts you have in there and for a sign what a patient man I am, I'll not even take the kine.'

Janet closed her eyes so as not to see Little Robert trying not to wriggle when the lancepoints poked him as their wielders' horses moved.

'I canna give you Shilling,' she said. 'He's sick with what killed Mildred.'

'Fair enough. Ye've five mounts to give me then: my Caspar, and the nags your two brothers were riding and the two from the Pringles. Do it now or I'll use this one for pricking practice.'

Down in the barnekin Willie's Simon was staring up at her, his arm bandaged and in a sling. She nodded at him. Anger in every inch of his back, he went to the tiny postern door in the base of the tower and led out their beautiful Courtier, which Jock called Caspar. The other horses were still out in the courtyard.

Janet beckoned Simon up onto the fighting platform and waited until all the crossbows were wound up. Rowan had one as well: she was a good shot and Janet told her to pick out Jock and keep her bow aimed at him.

'Send Little Robert forward,' she shouted, 'and you all fall back ten paces.'

Down on the ground, everyone was watching as she peeked through a shot-hole while the horses stamped and snorted and pulled at their halters.

At a prodding from Jock's lance, Little Robert got unsteadily to his feet and staggered forwards. Janet had Clemmie Pringle, Kat's vast husband and Wide Mary on either side of the gate, ready to shut it if there should be treachery. She opened it, then smacked each horse hard on the rump and shrieked. The horses broke forwards through the gate, snorting and panicking.

'Run, Little Robert!' she yelled.

He ran, dodging to and fro and between Caspar and Sim's Redmane, a lance stuck in the mud behind him, he tripled his speed and fell into Janet's arms as the gate shut behind him. There was nothing wrong with him bar his headwound, a little rough handling and stark fear, so she passed him to Clemmie Pringle to take to Kat, and climbed the ladder again.

There was confusion as the Grahams caught their booty and then the sound of hooves riding off. 'Stay where you are,' she snarled, when Geordie began to unwind his crossbow. 'How do we know this isn't some trick?'

'Why would they trick us, Janet?' Geordie asked reasonably. 'They've got what they came for.'

'Henry'll be fit to be tied,' said a voice in the background.

Janet pretended she hadn't heard. 'We'll wait until morning and then we'll out that little fire and see the damage and I'll take Shilling to Carlisle.'

'The March is up,' said Geordie, 'Lowther's on the trod already if they didna pay him for this. Why go to...'

'Did ye not hear what I told you? There's a new Deputy there and I've business with one of Dodd's men.'

'God help him,' muttered one of the other men.

## WEDNESDAY, 21ST JUNE, 9 A.M.

Lady Philadelphia Scrope was glaring worriedly at her embroidery hoop as she sat on a padded stool in the Queen Mary Tower and finished a rampant blackwork bee. She heard her brother's boots coming heavily up the stairs, tripping once. There was a pause at the door before he opened it and came in.

Almost laughing with relief at the sight of him, she put down her work and ran to hug him. He was rank with sweat, horse and human, and the oddly bitter scents of sodden leather and iron, he was spattered from head to foot with mud and blood, but none of it fresh enough to be his, thank God. The only thing not some shade of brown on him, other than the grubby rag of his collar, was his face which was white with weariness.

'You caught them,' she said joyfully. 'You caught the reivers.'

Robin's swordbelt clattered onto a chest and the pieces of rapier fell out.

He swatted at her feebly.

'For God's sake, Philly, I can do it myself. And where's Barnabus?'

'He had to go a message.' The room was beginning to steam up.

'Christ, who sent my own bloody servant off...'

'And anyway, he told me himself he's not much of a hand with armour and suchlike, you never took him to the Netherlands with you remember. I'm much better at it than he is.'

'I can't afford to lend you any more...'

Resisting the impulse to punch him, Philadelphia sat him on the stool, which made him wince satisfactorily, and hauled off his left boot.

'Be quiet,' she said. 'Behind the screen is my lord's own hip bath with hot water in it. The cold is in the ewer next to it, don't knock it over. There's a towel and a fresh shirt airing on a hook by the chest, and your other suit, the good cramoisie, and your other boots and—come on, Robert, *pull* will you?—a fresh pair of hose. Don't worry about the leaves in the water, they're lovage, they'll soothe your saddle burns...' She put the boots down near the door.

'How do you know I've got saddle burns?'

'And on the table by the bath is a posset...'

'I hate possets.'

'Which you will drink and a mess of eggs on sippets of toast with herbs in, which I made myself...'

'Which I must eat?'

'Which you will eat or I'll wave your shirt out the window like the mother on a wedding morning. My lord wants to hear the whole tale when you've finished. Leave your soiled linen on the floor as you usually do and I'll send Barnabus as soon as he's back.'

'Why the cramoisie suit?'

She hid a pert little grin. 'For a good and sufficient reason which I will tell you as soon as you've finished with the Warden. Don't forget to comb your hair.'

She dodged his attempt to stop her and cross-examine her about whatever female plot she was working, humphed at him like a mother of five and then her skirts swished through the door and she was gone.

Wondering what she meant about his shirt, he pulled the clammy thing off and found its lower half spotted with fresh blood in a dozen places. Shuddering he hobbled to the screen, holding up his hose with one hand and feeling the damage tenderly with the other.

## WEDNESDAY, 21ST JUNE, 10 A.M.

It was unjust, thought Dodd, after Carey had supervised the penning of their fees in the little fold within the Carlisle castle walls, the feeding, watering and rubbing down of their tired hobbies, and the feeding, watering and congratulating of the men and gone wearily to the Queen Mary Tower. What was unjust was that he had servants to help him clean up after fighting, whereas John Ogle's boy who was supposed to look after Dodd's needs had disappeared to Carlisle town. Dodd was reduced to a quick scour under the barracks pump which got the worst off; he left his jack to Bessie's Andrew and received with sour silence Bangtail's explanations of the whorehouse he'd been in when the summons came to go out on the hot trod.

He thought he'd done well for himself until he saw the blasted Courtier, hair combed, sweet-smelling as a maid on her wedding morning, and spruce in a fresh ruff and a fine London suit the colour of a summer pudding, with one of Scrope's spare swords on his belt. It was enough to make a man puke.

Captains Carleton and Dick Musgrave, and the bad penny Sir Richard Lowther, were all present at the meeting in the Warden's council chamber. Carey told the tale of the raid and the capture of five Grahams red-handed with a fine blend of modesty and fact-improving. It was not a long tale; shorter by far than the reports Lowther generally gave, in which he explained why the trods he led always, for some excellent reason, just missed catching the reivers.

'What will you do with your fees?' asked Lowther.

'We might kill the older cow to salt down, but the other two we'll sell to buy powder and guns,' said Carey.

'And the Grahams?' asked Scrope.

'We can keep them until the next Day of Truce,' said Carey. 'Then I can swear of my own knowing that they were raiders and hang them where their deaths will do most good.'

Scrope nodded at the sense of this. 'That's why you didn't hang them on the spot.'

'Yes, my lord,' said Carey. 'I also wanted to talk to them.'

'Oh?' asked Lowther. 'Why?'

'Horses,' answered Carey. 'I'm concerned about horses. Not just the ones we lack for your father's funeral, my lord, but the fact that we seem to have a general famine of horses.'

'I heard there was a horse plague in Scotland,' said Lowther.

'Did you?' said Carey. 'I've not heard of it. Where is it worst?'

Lowther shrugged. 'I don't know. It would account for the lack of horses...'

'It would,' said Carey slowly, 'but what concerns me is that the Grahams might be reiving horses for a different reason.'

'Why?' Scrope's fingers were at their anxious self-knitting again.

'For a large-scale long-range raid at the next opportunity,' said Carey. 'If they want to ride deep into England, they'll need remounts, especially for the return when they'll be driving spoil and at risk of meeting us.'

Lowther's eyes had gone so small they almost disappeared under his grey eyebrows.

'What happened this raid...' Carey shook his head. 'They used the cattle as bait, knowing we'd follow, with Elliots to spring the trap just outside Liddesdale. Luckily Captain Carleton was there...'

'No luck about it,' growled Carleton, deep in his chest, 'I got your message.' Lowther glared at him.

'...so we caught them. But meanwhile the main band of Grahams were winnowing the border of horses and taking them off north to Liddesdale. From the preliminary complaints, I'd say they had enough for a journey of a hundred miles or more and back again, depending on how many reivers there are.'

'When would this happen?' asked Scrope.

'Well, they won't want the horses for long because feeding that many animals could beggar them for their winter horsefeed. And further, the perfect date would be one when all the gentlemen of the March will be otherwise engaged.' He said the last couple of words with a great deal of emphasis and looked at Scrope.

'Oh Lord,' said the Warden with deep dismay. 'You mean on the day of my father's funeral?'

'Yes, my lord. I would also point out that the preparations are not ready, even if we had the horses for the bier.'

'I thought you were supposed to be arranging it,' sneered Lowther. Carey did not rise to this.

'I have been a little busy, Sir Richard.'

'Yes, yes, quite,' said Scrope. 'Are you saying that you want me to postpone the funeral?'

'Yes, my lord. For a few days only. Hold it on Sunday rather than tomorrow. If you made a proclamation at the Market Cross this noon and sent fast messengers to the gentlemen expected for the service warning them to be ready for a long-range raid...'

'On the evidence of the theft of a few nags?' protested Lowther. 'It's hardly conclusive that they'd be trying any such thing. And this is the wrong time of year.'

'It looks bad to me,' grunted Carleton.

'What about the body?' continued Lowther. 'Won't it start to stink?'

Scrope was offended. 'My revered father's corpse has been embalmed of course, a few days should do no harm.'

'And I'd rather postpone the funeral unnecessarily than have to explain to the Queen why we allowed the broken men of the Debateable Land to foray deep into England,' said Carey sincerely.

Lowther, who had never met her, rolled his eyes but Scrope, who had, was nodding anxiously.

'I think you're right, Sir Robert, we'll postpone the funeral until Sunday. I'll see to the proclamations and messages. Will you make any other arrangements necessary, and deal with the complaints from this raid.'

'Yes, my lord.'

The meeting broke up and Carleton caught up with Carey as he hurried to the door.

'Here's your ring back, Sir Robert. Now, I'm sending a message to my cousin that keeps a stud in Northumberland—he has some draft horses with good dark coats he'd be willing to lend us for a fee. They'll be here by Saturday.'

'Oh ay? What about this long-range raid?'

Carey shrugged. 'There's little I can do about that save be ready for them if they come. Though I'd give a lot to know where they're gathering.'

'If it's Bothwell planning it, they'll be riding from Lochmaben.'

Carleton nodded. 'I heard that the Grahams were blaming Dodd for the murder, poor man.'

'You don't think he did it either?'

'God, no,' Carleton laughed. 'Any man of any sense that had a Graham corpse on his hands like that would take him down to the Rockcliffe marshes and throw him in the deepest bog he could find, not take him up to the old battlefield and try and hide him in a gorse bush.' Carleton shook his head, his broad face full of mirth. 'Me, I'd leave him on Elliot or Armstrong land and let them take the heat. Dodd's no jewel, but he's not mad.'

As they went down the stair, Carey put his hand to his head as he remembered something.

'By the way, Captain, you've a right to a part of our fee for helping the trod, haven't you?'

Carleton clapped a massive paw on Carey's shoulder.

'Lad,' he said, 'watching you and Dodd and the garrison mixing it with those Grahams was almost worth the fee to me. Pay me a quarter of whatever you make on the heifer and the younger cow. I haven't enjoyed myself so much for months, and you won me a pound off my brother.'

'Oh?' smiled Carey. 'What did you bet on?'

'Whether you'd dare attack, what else?'

Carey laughed. 'At least it wasn't on whether I'd fall off my horse.'

Carleton's face was full of pleasure. 'Nay, Sir Robert, I won that bet the day before yesterday.'

# WEDNESDAY, 21ST JUNE, 10 A.M.

Philadelphia Scrope was waiting impatiently for the men to stop blathering and come out of the council room at the back of the keep. She stopped Robert, who was looking very fine, if a bit baggy under the eyes, and took him mysteriously by the arm.

'All right, Philly,' said her brother resignedly, 'what's the surprise?'

'Come with me.'

'Philly, I've about a hundred things to do and at least fifty letters to write and Richard Bell promised me he could only be my clerk this morning, so...'

'It'll take no more than ten minutes.'

Carey sighed and suffered himself to be led. They went out through the Captain's gate and down the covered way a little to Bessie's handsome inn and through the arch to the courtyard.

Behind them three of Dodd's men came tumbling out of the inn's common room, teasing a fourth for missing out on his share of the trod fee. The men headed for the drawbridge gate shouting crude jokes about the origins of Bangtail's nickname and how they would improve it, looking very pleased with themselves. Carey watched them go approvingly and when Philly pulled impatiently on his arm, he turned the way she was pointing him.

A tall woman in a fine woollen riding habit of dark moss green and a lace-edged ruff was standing with her back to him, talking to a sandy-haired young man with broad shoulders and a terrible collection of spots, pockmarks and freckles. Carey stopped dead when he saw them.

'Philadelphia...' he growled.

She grinned naughtily at him and went over to the woman. 'Lady Widdrington,' she said, 'how splendid to see you.'

They embraced, and Lady Elizabeth Widdrington saw Carey over Philly's shoulder. Philly could feel the indrawn breath and had a good view of the blush creeping up from under Lady

Widdrington's ruff to colour her rather long face to a surprising semblance of beauty.

Lady Elizabeth curtseyed to Robert, who automatically swept her an elegant court bow. He paused, took breath to speak, then paused again. Philadelphia decided to take a hand.

'There, Robin,' she said blandly, 'you can go back to your dull old papers now.'

Lady Widdrington was the first to recover her senses.

'Sir Robert,' she said formally, 'I believe I should congratulate you on your Deputyship. I hope you don't miss London and the Court.'

He made a little bow and laughed with delight.

'Only you,' he said, instincts reasserting themselves, 'could have brought me here so quickly to the land of cattle-thieves. I'd hoped I could find an excuse to chase a few raiders into Northumberland and catch them dramatically on your doorstep...'

'And if necessary you would have paid them to go that way,' said Lady Widdrington drily. Carey laughed again.

'Absolutely.'

'Of course, I'm only here for my Lord Scrope's funeral. Your sister invited me.'

Philly managed to look both smug and shocked. 'It was Sir Henry I invited.'

'In the certainty that his gout would prevent him coming,' said Robert. 'Honestly, Philadelphia, your plots are transparent.'

'Who cares so long as they work,' said Philly. 'Will you come to dinner, Lady Widdrington. I'm hoping my brother remembered to bring some new madrigal sheets with him, and if he didn't I'll make him listen to one of our border minstrels instead.'

'No, please, save me,' said Robert. 'I brought the madrigals and they're well beyond my voice so good luck to you.'

'You're invited too, Robin,' said Philly inflexibly. 'We need a tenor. Now...'

What she was about to suggest next nobody ever found out. There was a sudden shouting and commotion further down the street, near the drawbridge gate.

A woman had come riding in at a gallop, sandy red hair flying. She hauled her horse back on his haunches when she saw Dodd's men staring at her from the gate. Then she leaped from the saddle and caught one of them by the front of his jack. She let fly with a punch and booted him in the groin for good measure. The man tried to defend himself, hurt his hand on her stays, got another boot in his kneecap, and rolled away. He ran limping up the street with the woman in full pursuit, her homespun skirts kilted up in her belt, and Carey saw it was Bangtail Graham and that his enemy was Janet Dodd.

Automatically he stepped out of the courtyard into the street. 'What the...?'

Bangtail ran behind Carey and dodged another punch.

'It wasna me, it wasna me...' he was shouting, 'I only told my brother...'

Janet Dodd sneered at him as she circled round. 'Get out from behind that man, Bangtail, you bastard, you lily-livered git, you've lost me five horses, a house and half a field of grain trampled...'

'Mrs Dodd, Mrs Dodd...' Carey tried to remonstrate.

'I've no quarrel with you Deputy but if ye protect yon treacherous blabbermouthed...'

'What's he done?'

Behind Janet, Carey could see Sergeant Dodd sprinting down from the Castle yard.

Bangtail unwisely made a break for it from behind Carey's broad back, and Janet was on him. Philly, Lady Widdrington and Young Henry Widdrington watched with open-mouthed curiosity. Bangtail tried his best, even marked Janet's cheek, but he was borne down and kicked again before Dodd came up behind his wife and grabbed her round the middle, swung her about like a dancer in the volta, dodged a fist, and roared in her ear, 'Goddamn it wife, what's wrong?'

'He sold us to Jock of the Peartree,' she shouted. 'That filthy bastard Graham told Jock...'

'I never...' protested Bangtail.

'What? What happened?' Dodd was shaking his wife's shoulders. 'Are you saying Jock raided us last night?'

'Five horses,' shrieked Janet, 'five horses, Clem Pringle's house burned again, half the barley trampled into the mud, poor Margaret miscarrying her bairn with the fright, Willie's Simon with an arrow in his arm because yon strilpit nyaff couldna keep his mouth shut…'

'Jock of the Peartree did this?'

Carey watched with interest. Dodd perpetually looked as if he had lost a shilling and found a penny, but he was beginning to suspect that that often denoted good humour. Now the long jaw and surly face were darkening and the thin mouth whitening with rage.

'I talked to him from the wall,' Janet said catching her breath. 'Courtier's his horse, he called him Caspar. You said you'd know if he was reived from this country, you said you'd know…Stay there, Bangtail, or I'll gut you…'

'You never gave him Courtier,' shouted Dodd.

'I had nae choice, he caught Little Robert and ransomed him for all the horses except poor Shilling,' Janet wailed. 'He said Courtier was his and he said he was proof you'd killed Sweetmilk…'

'Jock of the Peartree has *Courtier*…?'

'Oh Christ,' muttered Carey under his breath, having listened to Dodd boast about the beautiful stallion most of the way back to Carlisle that morning.

'Wake up, Dodd, wake up. It's not just the horse, it's the Grahams thinking you were the one who murdered Sweetmilk. Ye think it's bad now? What will ye do when they come and burn the tower and us all in our beds…?'

Looking at his Sergeant, Carey could already hear the hooves thundering and the lances clattering. Dodd's face was now completely white.

'Mrs Dodd, Sergeant,' Carey appealed, stepping between them with his hands out and his most courtly appeasing smile on his face. He managed to have got between both Dodds and Bangtail who was nursing a bleeding nose and his groin and looking terrified. 'Please. If you've been raided…'

'What business is it of yours?' demanded Dodd. 'I'll have my own justice. Janet, did you send to your father?'

'I did and I also…'

By this time a small audience had formed, including Elizabeth, Philly and Henry Widdrington, plus Scrope himself, glimpsed like a nervous crane fly beyond the crowd.

'If you will come into the castle,' hissed Carey, 'we'll see what we can...'

'Keep yer long neb out of my affairs, Courtier,' snarled Dodd.

Carey was tired: in particular he was very weary of Dodd's sullenness. Without any of the usual warning signs his patience suddenly snapped. He drew his borrowed sword, stepped up close to Dodd and put the point against the man's belly.

There was a moment of shocked silence. Scrope winced and began backing away. Out of the corner of his eye, Carey saw Janet's hand go to the hilt of her knife.

'Now,' he said very softly. 'Firstly, Sergeant, you will address me as sir if you wish to speak to me. Secondly, this ugly street brawl will stop. Thirdly, you will come into my office now, with me, where we will consider what is to be done. And fourthly, Dodd, if you tell me this is not my affair once more, I'll run you through. Mrs Dodd unless you want to be a widow, you'll put up your weapon.'

For a moment the whole thing held in the balance, and then Janet said, 'What *is* your interest, Sir Robert?'

'If the Sergeant of the Warden's Guard is raided by any man, Scots, English or Debateable, that makes it my affair. I will not have it.'

'You'll lead the trod?'

'I will.'

Janet smiled, which was in some ways more frightening than her rage.

'*If* there's a trod,' added Carey.

'What does the Warden say?'

Scrope was trying to become invisible at the entrance to a wynd. Carey glared at him.

'Oh I agree,' said Scrope, rearranging his gown. 'Absolutely. Can't have the Sergeant raided. It's an insult to the Wardenry.'

Thank you Thomas, thought Carey, watching Dodd intently. Dodd was still tense, but seemed to be thinking. He nodded. Carey put his sword away and the audience began to wander off on important appointments, since the thrilling prospect of a fight between the Warden's Deputy, the Sergeant and his wife seemed to have faded. Philly was speaking in a low tactful voice to the Widdringtons and leading them into Bessie's. God damn the luck, that Elizabeth should have had to see such a brawl.

'Now please, come up to my chamber,' he said to the Dodds. 'No need to broadcast to Jock what trouble he's in.' Not very subtle flattery, but it worked well enough.

Both Dodds nodded at that and they all walked docilely towards the castle. Missing someone important, Carey fell back a little and spotted Bangtail limping down an alley. He darted after the man, grabbed his collar and twisted his arm up his back, propelled him along in front. Bangtail gibbered excuses.

'Silence,' hissed Carey, 'or I'll break your arm.'

'But I never…'

'I'll give you to Janet Dodd.'

'Yes sir.'

Scrope disappeared, muttering about arrangements for the funeral. Carey barged Bangtail up the stairs of the Queen Mary Tower, followed by the Dodds. Once into his second chamber, he ordered Richard Bell the clerk out, pulled up a stool for Janet to sit on, kicked the door to the stairs shut, dropped Bangtail in a heap on the floor and then sat at his desk. The others stood looking at each other.

'Barnabus!' Carey roared.

The servant's ferret-like face poked nervously round the door.

'Fetch wine and four goblets. Send Young Hutchin to bring in Mrs Dodd's horse and have him rubbed down and settled with some fodder in the stables.'

It was interesting to watch how they waited. Janet ignored the proffered seat and stood with her arms folded and her hip cocked and her long wiry ginger hair adrift from its pins down her back with a colour on her cheeks that the Court ladies spent hours in front of their mirrors to achieve. Dodd simply stood in a lanky slouch, his fingers tapping occasionally on his belt buckle. Bangtail had the sense to stay where he'd been dropped, pinching his nose to stop the blood.

Barnabus came in with the wine and four silver goblets from

Carey's own silver chest. He had a napkin over his arm and at Carey's imperceptible nod he poured, bowed and removed himself.

Carey rose, passed around the goblets as if he were hosting a dinner party in London. Bangtail took his with considerable surprise and some gratitude.

'Sergeant Dodd, Mrs Dodd, Mr Graham,' said Carey formally. Bangtail blinked, seemed to get the message and scrambled to his feet. He quailed at Janet's glare but remained standing. 'I give you the return of the Sergeant's horses and confusion to Jock of the Peartree.'

'Ay,' muttered Dodd. Bangtail coughed, Janet said nothing. They all drank.

Carey seated himself once more, cleared some bills of complaint away and looked up again.

'We will never again have a scene like that in public.' Janet took breath to speak but Carey simply carried on. 'I don't care if King James is hammering over the border with the entire Scots lordship at his back and Bangtail is to blame, it will not happen again. Is that understood?'

Dodd nodded, Janet simply pursed her lips.

'Please, Mrs Dodd, be seated.' She sat. 'Now give me the story.'

He heard the tale in silence, turned to Bangtail.

'Mr Graham. You were not with us on the hot trod as your duty was, where were you?'

'I was sick,' Bangtail said full of aggrievement, 'I was sick in my bed with an ague...'

Bangtail reddened and looked at the floor.

'Somebody told the Graham family who had this horse Sweetmilk rode,' said Carey reasonably. 'Who else knew you had the animal, Sergeant?'

Dodd counted off on his fingers. 'Me, my wife, the lousy git that sold him to her—Reverend Turnbull—anyone who was in Bessie's courtyard last night.'

'You saw Courtier,' said Janet accusingly to Bangtail, 'you came in from the midden while I was talking to Dodd.'

'Ay,' growled Dodd, 'and then you were off somewhere in an almighty hurry. Ye left the game.'

'But I didna, I swear it on my oath...' Janet looked as if she was about to interrupt. Carey glared at her and she contained herself. Bangtail was waving his arms and clearly winding himself up for a magnificent weaving together of diverse falsehoods.

'Bangtail Cuthbert Graham,' said Carey very quietly, 'I take very seriously any man who forswears himself to me. I don't care who else you lie to, but not to me. Do you understand?'

'Ay sir,' mumbled Bangtail.

'Now, I ask you again and for the last time. Did you tell anyone of the Sergeant's new horse?'

Bangtail's boot toe scraped in the rushes and kicked a flowerhead into the fireplace.

'I might...I might have mentioned it by accident to Ekie last night—that's my half-brother—I think I was talking of...of well, fine horseflesh and where you could get it and I might have said the Sergeant's wife had a stallion that was as fine as the King of Scotland's own. And that's all.'

Dodd remained ominously silent, while Janet simply snorted. Carey let the silence run for a bit. Bangtail flushed, looked at the floor, squashed a stray rush with his other boot toe, coughed and added, 'I might have said I thought it was Jock's new stallion, Caspar, but I asked him not to tell.'

Janet let out a single derisory 'Ha!' and subsided again.

'How many men would we need to take your horses back from Jock of the Peartree?' Carey asked Dodd. The Sergeant considered for a minute, his considerable military sense at last beginning to work.

'It's well too late to stop him reaching Liddesdale, especially with only horses to drive,' he said mournfully. 'And to pry him out of Liddesdale with the notice he's had—I wouldna like to try it with less than a thousand men, sir.'

Privately Carey thought that was optimistic. 'Bangtail, how many men can your uncle have in the saddle by this afternoon?'

Bangtail looked shifty. 'I don't know...'

'I think you do know, Bangtail,' Carey said with quiet venom, 'and I'm waiting to hear it from you if you want to keep your neck the length it is now.'

'What would you hang me for, sir?' demanded Bangtail. 'I never did...'

'March treason, what else?' said Carey, smiling unpleasantly. 'For bringing in raiders.'

'Oh.' Bangtail thought for a little longer. 'By this afternoon he'd have 800 men or so, plus however many Elliots felt like turning out, and another 300 in the morning, if he calls in the Debateable Land broken men or the Johnstones. If Old Wat Scott of Harden comes in for him, well, it's another 500 at least and...'

'Going into Liddesdale on a foray with Jock warned and his kinship behind him...' Carey shook his head.

'I can bring in a hundred Dodds myself,' said Henry, 'and Janet's brothers and father can call on another two hundred, all English Armstrongs. And Kinmont Willie would listen to her, he's an uncle and he likes her and he can have a thousand men in the saddle by morning if he wants...'

'Are ye saying it's too hard to go and fetch Courtier back from Jock of the Peartree?' asked Janet. Carey felt his temper rise again, she was near as dammit giving him the lie. He took a breath and held it, let it out again.

'No, Mrs Dodd. I am saying that to go into Liddesdale bald-headed and crying for vengeance is simply stupid, since Jock will have laid an ambush and called out every man he could last night in the hope that you and the Sergeant would do precisely what you wanted to do. He'll cut all your kin to pieces, take prisoners for ransom and go off laughing to run Dodd's horse at the next race he can.'

They exchanged glances and looked at the floor.

'So there's nothing ye can do,' said Janet.

'On the contrary, since your husband is my man, there is a great deal I can and will do. In fact, I give you my word on it. You'll have your horses back.'

They took the hint. 'Thank you, sir,' said Janet. Dodd grunted assent, and Carey ushered them to the door. 'Send someone to Janet's father and your brothers, Sergeant, we don't want them wasting their time.'

'Ay sir.'

'But I thought...'

'Bangtail,' said Carey, full of regret, 'if you were capable of thought, you wouldn't *be* here. What possessed you? Never mind. You stay here under lock and key until we get the Sergeant's horses back.'

'In jail, sir?' Bangtail protested.

'In jail.'

'I'll give ye my parole.'

Carey shook his head. 'I'd like to take it, but I daren't.'

'Och sir, don't put me in the jail, it's...'

'If I have any more bloody rubbish from you, Bangtail, I'll chain you as well. Now come on. And cheer up, I expect it'll only be for a couple of days.'

## WEDNESDAY, 21ST JUNE, 11 A.M.

The castle dungeon was extremely damp after all the rain and stank as badly as most jails. Carey shoved Bangtail into the last empty cell, slammed the door and peered through the Judas hole. Bangtail was sitting on the bare bench, chewing nervously on one of his nails.

One of Lowther's men, whom Carey vaguely remembered was a Fenwick, came in carrying a bag full of loaves of bread and a small cheese. Behind him Young Hutchin was staggering under a firkin of ale. Both of them looked surprised to see him there, so he leaned against a wall and watched as they cut up the cheese and threw the food into each cell.

'Hey,' shouted Young Jock Graham, 'where's the butter, man? Lowther promised...'

'Shut up,' growled Fenwick, 'the Deputy's here.'

'Well, I want to talk to him.'

'It isna...'

'I want to talk to Young Jock too,' said Carey agreeably. 'Let me in.'

'Who're ye?' he demanded. 'Where's Lowther?'

'I'm the new Deputy Warden,' said Carey. 'I'm also the man that captured you and didn't hang you on the spot. You should thank me.'

Young Jock grunted ungratefully and sank his teeth into the cheese. Three weevils popped their heads out and wriggled and he spat them into the straw and stamped on them, then swallowed the rest.

'What d'ye want?'

'I want,' said Carey thoughtfully, 'a full account of where your father has taken the horses he reived last night and also what he's planning to do with them.'

Young Jock stared at him as if he was mad. At that moment, Young Hutchin knocked and came through the door with a leather mug full of ale, which Young Jock took and gulped down.

'Now then, Young Hutchin.' Jock was picking absent-mindedly at his ear.

'I'm sorry to see you here, Jock,' said the boy. 'Can I get you anything else?'

'Ay, you can find me the keys and a nice sharp dagger.' Young Jock examined his fingernail for trophies.

Hutchin smiled and left while Carey hummed a little tune.

'What are ye waiting for, Courtier?' Jock was delving at his ear again.

'I'm waiting for you to tell me what I asked.'

Young Jock spat messily near Carey's boots.

'You can wait there until you die, ye bastard, I'm telling you nothing.'

'It could save your neck.'

'Go to the devil, Courtier, my neck's safe enough.'

Young Jock set himself to eating and Carey nodded, banged on the door to be let out and watched carefully while Fenwick locked it after him.

On his way out, he paused to shout through the Judas hole at Bangtail.

'I want to know what's going on, Bangtail, and you'll tell me.'

'I willna,' said Bangtail feebly.

'You surely will,' said Carey ominously. 'One way or another, with the use of your legs or without them.'

# WEDNESDAY, 21ST JUNE, 11 A.M.

When she came down the steps of the Queen Mary Tower, Janet was met by Lady Scrope and a gentlewoman she didn't know. She was intending to see after poor old Shilling who had run like a hero all the way to Carlisle and might need comforting, but when she curtseyed to the ladies, she found her hand taken and the Warden's wife was speaking to her gently.

'Mrs Dodd,' said Philadelphia, 'I'm sorry to hear of the raid, is there anything I can do to help?'

Janet flushed a little. 'Well,' she said, 'the new Deputy has promised he'll get my horses back but whether he will or not...'

Lady Scrope grimaced a little. 'Knowing my brother, he'll half kill himself to do it if he promised to. Who was it sold you the beast that belonged to Sweetmilk?'

'Reverend Turnbull, may God rot his bowels.'

'That's the book-a-bosom man isn't it?'

Janet nodded. Lady Scrope exchanged glances with the other woman. A certain amount of mischief appeared on Lady Scrope's pointed little face.

'Shall we go and speak to him, then?'

'It's very kind of you to take so much trouble, Lady Scrope,' she began, 'but I think I can...'

'Hush, Mrs Dodd,' said Lady Scrope. 'We only want to give Sir Robert what help we can to get back your horses.'

'And this needs doing quickly because when Reverend Turnbull hears what happened, he'll be out of Carlisle as fast as his legs will run,' added Lady Widdrington. 'Ah, look,' she said kindly, 'he's heard already, I think. Is that him, Mrs Dodd?'

The Reverend Turnbull was at that moment shutting the door to the little priest's house next to the church, wearing a pack on his back and carrying a stout walking stick. Janet nodded.

The Reverend Thomas Turnbull had had very little to do with real ladies in a not always reverend past, but he knew them when he saw them. With the Warden's wife on one side, and a tall long-nosed lady on the other, he found himself accompanied into his church and sat down on one of the porch benches. It wasn't that he didn't think of running nor that he couldn't perhaps have outrun them—ladies seldom or never ran, so far as he knew, and their petticoats would have tripped them up—it was that he didn't somehow feel he could do it with the Warden's wife holding his arm confidingly under hers and the tall one glinting down at him with a pair of piercing and intelligent grey eyes.

When he sat down the third woman, whom he recognised with a sinking feeling as Janet Dodd, helpfully took his walking stick and laid it on the ground near her foot. Lady Scrope sat down next to him, still trapping his arm, while the tall one continued to pin his soul to the back of his head with her eyes. Janet Dodd crossed her arms and tipped her hip threateningly.

'I'm s-sorry, Mrs Dodd,' he stammered at once, deciding immediate surrender would save time, 'I had no idea the horse would cause you such trouble. I'd have cut my throat before I sold it to you if I'd known, truly I would...'

'Well, tell us who you bought the horse from and we'll forgive you,' said Lady Scrope gently.

'And tell the truth,' added the tall woman.

Reverend Turnbull bridled a little as he sat. 'Madam,' he said with as much dignity as he could muster, 'I am a man of the cloth and...'

'As capable of lying as any other man,' snorted the tall woman.

'Now Lady Widdrington,' said Philadelphia Scrope reprovingly, 'I'm sure the Reverend will tell us the truth. You will, won't you?' she said winningly to him. 'I'll get into trouble with my brother if I give him the wrong information.'

'And so will you,' added Lady Widdrington ominously to the Reverend.

Turnbull shook his head. 'I bought the beast from a cadger

named Swanders and I'd no reason to think him reived at all. He said he was from Fairburn's stud in Northumberland and had been sold because of an unchancy temper and...'

'Why didn't they geld him then?' enquired Lady Widdrington.

Turnbull coughed. 'I didna think to ask, your ladyship, I admit it, I was a trusting fool but the Good Book teaches us that it's better to trust than to be ower suspicious.'

'Does it?' said Lady Widdrington with interest. 'Where does it say that?'

Turnbull's mind was blank. He could barely make out the words of the marriage service and much of the Bible was a wasteland to him.

Lady Scrope got him off the spot.

'Do you know where this man Swanders may be?'

Without question he was halfway back to Berwick by this time, no doubt laughing at Turnbull as he went.

'I dinna ken, your ladyship, I wish I did and that's the truth.'

'Oh, ay,' muttered Janet.

'What did you pay for the horse?'

'Er...four pounds English,' lied Turnbull. 'See, I didna expect to make much profit and it was all to go to the repair of the church roof, which lets in the weather something terrible.'

'Oh be quiet,' growled Janet Dodd. 'You know you paid two pounds for the creature and so do we.'

How did they know, wondered Turnbull, when God had made them poor foolish women? How dare they show such disrespect to a man of the cloth?

'Well, it doesn't matter now,' said Lady Scrope soothingly. 'You can give what's left of your three pounds profit back to Janet Dodd and then claim the money off Swanders the next time you see him.'

Turnbull's mouth fell open with dismay.

'B-but it's all spent,' he protested.

'Is it now?' said Lady Widdrington. 'And what exactly did you spend it on?'

A happy night at Madam Hetherington's bawdy house, among other things, but Turnbull couldn't bring himself to say so. He muttered the first thing that came into his mind.

'Charity?' said Lady Widdrington. 'Well, that's very Godly of you. Mrs Dodd, when do you think your husband and some of his patrol would be ready to come and talk to Reverend Turnbull?'

'Oh, I can run and fetch him now,' said Mrs Dodd, turning to go, 'I'm sure if the lads pick him up and shake him something will fall out.'

'Och Chri...well, I might have some of it about me.'

The ladies turned their backs obligingly as Turnbull unstrapped the pouch from his thigh and the bright silver rolled out in the crusting mud. Lady Widdrington scooped up most of it and gave the money to Janet Dodd.

'You can owe the rest, Mr Turnbull,' she said, 'I wouldn't want you to be travelling the Border completely empty-handed.'

'No. I thank you,' said Turnbull feebly.

'Good day, then. I expect you'll want to be out of Carlisle before Sergeant Dodd tracks you down,' said Lady Widdrington and added formally, 'God go with you.'

'Ay, well, good day, ladies.'

Turnbull trudged up the wynd feeling as if he had already walked ten miles and wondering how one started proceedings against witches. He thought he heard the sound of laughter behind him but decided he must have been mistaken.

'You know what I find so odd?' said Lady Scrope after a while. They were gathered in a private room of the Bear and Ragged Staff, near the drawbridge gate of the castle. The windows of their private room overlooked the moat so they could watch the pleasant sight of the fish who were a thrifty source of food to anyone that could catch them and were therefore as cunning as foxes.

'What?' asked Lady Widdrington as she cautiously drank the beverage sold to her as wine.

'Why didn't this man Swanders go to Thomas the Merchant Hetherington? Or if he did, why didn't Thomas the Merchant buy such a beautiful piece of horseflesh as this Courtier was supposed to be?'

'Ay,' said Janet slowly, 'now that is odd.'

'He'll have known we'd have paid good money for the animal,'

Lady Scrope went on. 'Seven or eight pounds, likely enough, if he was good; God knows we've been searching out decent horses ever since the old Lord got sick.'

Lady Widdrington put down her goblet. 'Shall we ask him?'

## WEDNESDAY, 21ST JUNE, 12 NOON

Thomas the Merchant Hetherington happened to be completing his accounts for some important clients when his servant came in to announce that the Ladies Scrope and Widdrington would like to see him. He was honoured and a little puzzled. He was a man who could see a way to make money at anything: the kind of man who bought up and forestalled barley when there was going to be a bad harvest, who paid cash down in advance for the entire shearing of the West March sheep and then joyfully twisted the cods of the Lancashire woolbuyers who came to do business with him and him alone because there was nobody else. However, stay laces and pots of red lead for improving ladies' appearances he left strictly to the common cadgers and pedlars, since they were small, retail items and invariably low profit. He dabbled in horses but only because he loved them.

The ladies came in and he bowed low.

'How may I serve you, your ladyships?' he said in a voice as unctuous as he could make it.

'We are here on the same errand,' said Lady Scrope, 'in search of good horses.'

You and me both, thought Thomas the Merchant.

'We heard that Mrs Dodd had bought a beautiful animal from the Reverend Turnbull and we were wondering if you knew where it came from?' said Lady Scrope blithely. Lady Widdrington frowned at her across the room.

'Surely,' said Thomas the Merchant with a warm smile, 'this

is really a matter I should discuss with your husband, my lady Scrope, since...'

'Of course,' said Lady Scrope, nodding vigorously, 'I would never dream of buying a horse without his advice and permission.' Lady Widdrington made what sounded like a repressed snort.

'But I do so want to help him find the right horses for his father's funeral and he's so busy with other matters, I thought I could save him a little time.'

'But it's just been postponed to Sunday.'

'We'll still need horses.'

Suddenly Thomas the Merchant was alert. He was as sensitive and shy of trouble as a fallow deer and could sense it on the wind in much the same way. He looked from Lady Scrope to Lady Widdrington and back again. Damn me, if Janet Dodd isn't outside, waiting on them, he thought suddenly.

Thomas the Merchant normally backed his hunches, to great effect, but that was only because he meticulously checked on them first. He turned from the high desk he used standing up, as if he were a mere clerk which was what he had been twenty years before.

'It's a little close in here, mesdames,' he said, to cover the move. As he opened the little diamond-paned window, he looked down in the street, and there, of course, was Sergeant Dodd's wild-looking Armstrong wife.

'Alas,' he said smoothly, 'I canna help ye ladies. I know nothing of Turnbull's horse save that he bought him, perhaps unwisely, from Swanders the Pedlar.'

'Do you know where Swanders got it?'

'Presumably,' said Thomas the Merchant, steepling his fingers and smiling kindly at their womanly obtuseness, 'presumably he stole it from the Grahams, or so it seems.'

'He might have another source of horses.'

'He might,' allowed Thomas the Merchant, 'but I doubt it.'

'Why?' asked Lady Widdrington suddenly.

'Er...'

'Why do you doubt it, you seem very sure.'

Thomas the Merchant was nettled. 'Because, madam, I ken

'verra well where every single nag in this March was born, raised, and who it was sold to and stolen from, I make it my business to know.'

'Do you?' said Lady Widdrington kindly. 'Then you knew when Swanders showed you the animal in question that he belonged to Sweetmilk Graham. Why didn't you buy him to give back to the Grahams—surely they'd like that?'

Thomas the Merchant moved with dignity to the door and opened it.

'I verra much regret that some ill-affected fellow has been telling you ladies the old scandal about the Grahams and myself, but that was tried and I was cleared of the charge at the last but one Warden's Day.'

'Oh,' said Lady Widdrington, not moving, 'and what scandal was that? I live in Northumberland and I'm not familiar with the gossip in this town.'

Give ye two days and ye'll know the lot, madam, Thomas the Merchant thought to himself, but didn't say.

'He was accused of collecting blackmail money for the Grahams,' explained Lady Scrope.

Thomas the Merchant found himself being examined at leisure by Lady Widdrington's steely grey eyes. He examined her in return. Her face was too long and her chin too pronounced for beauty but she was a striking-looking woman, with soft pale brown hair showing under her white cap and feathered hat. He disliked tall women, being a little on the short side himself.

'I fear I canna give you ladies the information you're seeking,' he said humbly, 'as I have not the faintest idea what you're talking about. If ye will excuse me now, I have a great deal to do.'

Lady Scrope moved to the door, but Lady Widdrington stayed still for a moment. Then she smiled suddenly, not a particularly sweet smile.

# WEDNESDAY, 21ST JUNE, AFTERNOON

Barnabus brought his master bread and cheese to eat immediately after he came out of the castle jail. Carey, to his surprise, gave him the afternoon off. While Carey and Richard Bell disappeared into the Queen Mary Tower to attack the tottering pile of papers and the arrangements for the postponed funeral, Barnabus hung around the castle twiddling his thumbs. He found a young lad with shining fair hair sitting in the stables, polishing some horse tack and borrowed him from the stablemaster to act as his guide. Then Young Hutchin and he wandered down to the market place.

At noon the town crier made the announcement at the Market Cross that his lordship, Henry Lord Scrope, quondam Warden of this March, would be buried on Sunday and not the next day which caused Young Hutchin to blink and raise his eyebrows.

'He's lying in state at the cathedral,' explained Young Hutchin slowly and carefully so Barnabus could understand him, 'so anybody that wants can be sure the old bugger's dead as a doorpost and not as sweet.'

'Not much liked hereabouts, eh?' asked Barnabus, munching on a flat pennyloaf (referred to by Hutchin as a stottiecake) with salt herring in it, since it was a fishday. Young Hutchin grinned and shook his head, but didn't add any information.

'Well.' Barnabus patted his belly as he finished. 'Now what shall we do?'

'I could show you round about the town, Mr Cooke,' said Young Hutchin, 'so ye can find your way.'

'Lead on.'

No one who knew his way around London town could be in the least confused by Carlisle which was barely a village by comparison. They wandered down Castle Street and looked at the cathedral, which was in a little better condition than St Paul's, and examined what was left of the abbey. English Street was where the best shops were and Barnabus had been there before to buy paper and ink for his master with Richard Bell and also to visit the goldsmith's. Young Hutchin's eyes shone as he peered through the thick bars of the goldsmith's grille and counted the rather poor silver plate and gold jewellery displayed there. Barnabus wondered if the goldsmith also dealt in receiving stolen goods, as some of his London colleagues did, but Young Hutchin, when asked, explained virtuously that he knew nothing of such sinfulness.

They examined the glowering two towers of the citadel, with their cannon, defending the road called Botchergate which led to Newcastle and ultimately to London. Then they retraced their steps and bore right up Scotch Street which was a poorer place altogether, though well-supplied with ale houses, horse dealers and smiths.

All about them flowed the townsfolk, greatly thinned in their numbers by the men who had gone out to work the fields round about. The women kept many of the shops, particularly the fish and butcher's shops, and some of the fish they were selling actually looked and smelled quite fresh. Barnabus remembered they were only a few miles from Solway and no doubt there were fishermen who went out to harvest the Irish sea. Perhaps Wednesdays and Fridays would not be such a trial here as they were in London, where the trotting trains from Tilbury and East Anglia could not bring in the fish any quicker than two days old.

They were passing by a wynd with the strong smell of herring saltworks coming from it when Barnabus said to Young Hutchin, 'Where would I go to...er...find a woman?'

Young Hutchin grinned cynically. 'Depends on the woman, master,' he said. 'What kind of woman was ye thinking of?'

Barnabus coughed. Well, Devil take it, he'd just been paid and what else was there to spend his money on? There was no bear- or bull-baiting in this backwater and there certainly wasn't a theatre. 'I was thinking of a...helpful sort of woman,' he said. 'The kind that might take pity on a poor southerner far from home.'

Young Hutchin nodded in perfect comprehension. 'Ay, well there's two bawdy houses, ye ken, but neither of them have lassies that are much in the way of beauty if ye're used to London ways...'

'Are they poxed?' asked Barnabus.

Young Hutchin raised his eyebrows and for a second he looked astonishingly like Carey, who could be no relation.

'Now, master, how would I know such a thing, being only a poor lad meself.'

'You might have heard where the nearest of them is, so I can go and inspect them myself,' said Barnabus, gravely.

'Nay, master, I'm too innocent for...'

Barnabus sighed and produced a groat. 'I could likely find the place myself,' he said, 'or ask someone else?'

Young Hutchin took the groat smoothly and led the way down the nearest wynd.

Barnabus liked the boy's technique. For instance, he was perfectly well aware that he was being led on a deliberately twisting and complex route so he would have difficulty finding the place again and that Young Hutchin had tipped the wink to one of the lads sitting in the street minding his family's pigs that he was bringing in custom. He didn't mind in the least, it made him feel nicely at home, though every time he looked up he saw a nasty unsmoky sky and almost every wynd off Scotch Street eventually ended in red brick wall.

Down one of the culs-de-sac they came on a brightly painted house with red lattices, a painted wooden sign of a rainbow and a girl sitting on the step. She stood up and smiled at him, leaned over so her large breasts could press enticingly over the top of her stays, and in a reek of cheap perfume, said, 'Can I help you, sir?'

His breath coming short, on account of being away from the stews of Southwark for so long, Barnabus nodded. To Young Hutchin he said, 'You stay here, my son, we wouldn't want your innocence being corrupted, would we?'

'What, wait here in the street?' asked Young Hutchin with dismay.

'I'd never shirk my responsibilities to you, my son,' he added preachily, 'and you're not getting corrupted on my money today. Besides, if you stay outside and give me a list of everyone who comes in and goes out while I'm there, you could earn yourself enough for two women in the one bed.'

That caused Young Hutchin to brighten considerably and he settled down on the step as Barnabus went in. He was met by a grey-haired woman of formidable expression, dressed in a tawny velvet kirtle with a damask forepart and embroidery on her stomacher, her hair covered by a cap and a long-crowned hat in the Scottish fashion, with a pheasant's feather. Her ruff was edged with lace and starched with yellow starch and altogether she was as magnificent a woman as complete flouting of the sumptuary laws could make her. London work, as well, Barnabus estimated, his eyes narrowing, it seemed Hutchin had brought him to the most expensive place in town. No matter. Barnabus regarded money invested on good whores as money well spent. No doubt the Scots went to the other bawdy house, wherever that was, since he could hear none of their accents which he was just beginning to be able to tell from an English Borders accent.

'Welcome to this house,' said the woman in a clear southern voice, somewhere in London, Barnabus judged in surprise. 'How may I serve you, sir?'

The common room where the whores paraded was nicely floored with fresh rushes and had a fireplace, though no fire since the weather had turned warm and muggy. There was a man there, no doubt acting as security against anyone who tried to leave without paying, a young, clever-faced man, with a weather-beaten face, black ringlets and long fingers. There was something familiar about him but Barnabus couldn't place the resemblance. He was throwing dice idly and Barnabus watched how he scooped up the ivories and tossed them and hid a smile to himself. It seemed coney-catchers were another universal thing. It was enough to bring tears to his eyes.

'Shall we have a game, sir?' asked the man in friendly fashion. 'To pass the time until the whores are ready?'

Barnabus swallowed a laugh. 'Well,' he said, 'I've only a little bit more than the price of a woman here, but I'll keep you company.'

He sat down, took the wine he was brought and sipped it cautiously, and waited for the other man to make the first throw.

'I'm Barnabus Cooke,' he explained, 'servant to Sir Robert Carey, the new Deputy.' Since they almost certainly knew that already, he didn't see any reason not to confirm it.

'I'm Daniel Swanders,' said the man, 'pedlar by trade, but I'm waiting about here for a while until whatever's happening in Scotland has finished happening.'

Barnabus nodded pleasantly, betraying no interest at all. He calculated they'd give him about twenty minutes to win some money before the whores arrived and then after he'd finished with a woman, Daniel Swanders would have a friend arrive, and he'd be brought into some plot to cheat the friend at dice since he was such a good player. Barnabus felt a warm pleasant feeling lift his heart nearly as much as the prospect of seeing to some womanflesh; it was almost like being back in London again.

Two hours later, comfortable and easy in his skin with only a tiny niggling doubt chewing in the hole at the back of his mind where he'd locked up his conscience, Barnabus Cooke walked out of the Carlisle bawdy house, known as the Rainbow, about two pounds richer than when he came in. Daniel Swanders was still inside, examining his four identical dice with great puzzlement, since they seemed to have betrayed him for the first time in his life, and his friend was trying to be jovial with Barnabus and offering to see him home. Barnabus, who had last fallen for that game when he was twelve years old, loosened his knife and explained to the importunate friend that he already had a guide to see him back to the castle and his master was expecting him to wait at dinner.

As they walked back up the wynd, past the courtyards redolent with herring and mackerel drying on the racks, Barnabus said quietly to Young Hutchin, 'Can you use a knife?'

Young Hutchin looked insulted. 'Ay, master, of course I can.'

'Good,' said Barnabus. 'Now, we're being followed by a large co from near the bawdy house, ain't we?'

Hutchin stopped to kick a stone, dribbled it round a post in the street and back again. Good, Barnabus thought, liking the boy's style.

'You know 'im, don't you,' said Barnabus, as usual losing his careful Court voice in the excitement.

'I might. I dinna ken his name, but,' said Hutchin.

My eye, thought Barnabus, it's probably your own brother.

'Now then,' said Barnabus as he stopped to examine a cooking pot hanging on an awning for sale, 'I don't want to 'urt 'im, I just want to 'ave a little talk wiv 'im, see?' Young Hutchin looked bewildered and Barnabus got a grip on his tongue and repeated himself more clearly. Young Hutchin nodded nervously. 'This is what's going to 'appen. I'm going down that alley there to take a piss, and you carry on and give 'im whatever signal you've arranged between yourselves.' Young Hutchin's mouth opened to protest his utter innocence but he wasn't able to stop his fair skin colouring up. Barnabus had often given thanks that he wasn't liable to blushing with his sallow complexion. The pockmarks helped as well.

'Don't worry,' he reassured the boy, 'I was doing your job down in London before you was born. Now, as soon as you see him go in after me, you follow and put your knife against his back first opportunity you get.'

'I canna...' began Young Hutchin indignantly. The large man was standing by another shop, staring elaborately at the sky. Barnabus hid a grin.

'I'm not asking you to knife the bugger, did I say that? No, so don't jump to conclusions, I want you to prick him enough to let him know you're there and tell him to stop what he's doing.'

'But...'

'Listen, son. If you don't want to do it, just say so now and you can hop along up the castle and we'll say no more about it. But if you want to learn something from a real craftsman, you do as I say and I'll pay you for it too out of my dice winnings.'

Hutchin's mouth dropped open. 'You *won* the dice game?' he gasped.

''Course I did, I told you, I'm a craftsman. Well, what do you say?'

'I'll help ye,' said Young Hutchin.

'Just one thing to bear in mind, my son. I don't want to kill this man, but I will if I have to, and the thing that'll make me have to kill him is you buggering me about, you got that? And if you do that, son, I'll find you and I'll teach you better manners, you got that?'

'Yes, master,' said Young Hutchin in a subdued tone.

'Never mind,' said Barnabus kindly, 'you're doing your best, don't worry, it gets easier as you know more.'

Arthur Musgrave saw his quarry disappearing down a wynd that was almost blocked out by the heavy buildings straining towards each other overhead. He'd had the all clear from Young Hutchin. He hurried after the plump ferret-faced southerner, taking out his cudgel as he went, hoping this would square it with Madam Hetherington who was enraged at him and Danny losing the bawdy house stake. He paused to take his bearings, wondered where the bastard Londoner had got to and felt a heavy weight thump down on his shoulders from above. The lights went out.

Fighting his way clear of the cloak, he got his head free only to find somebody's knee crunching into his nose. He lost his temper and managed to grab the Londoner by the doublet front and bash him against the wattle and daub wall of one of the houses, making a man-shaped dent in the plaster. Suddenly he felt the cold prickle of a knife at his back and stopped still.

Somebody's fist smashed into his gut three or four times and he toppled onto his face, mewing and fighting to breathe. The cloak went over his head again, his belt was undone with unbelievable speed and then wrapped around his body and arms at the bend of the elbow and buckled tight, all before he'd even managed to breathe once. So he lay there, choked with muddy cloak, waiting for the worst and found himself being lifted upright.

It was the bastard bloody southerner again, with that mangling of consonants and dropping of aitches which made him impossible to understand.

'I don't want your purse because I know there's nothing in it and I don't want your life yet,' repeated Barnabus patiently, 'I want to know who's the King of Carlisle.'

'What?'

The would-be footpad tangled up in Barnabus's cloak couldn't show the bewilderment he felt, but Young Hutchin's face said it all.

'Bloody hell,' said Barnabus, 'are you telling me there isn't one? Isn't there anybody collecting rent off the thieves here to keep them safe from the law?'

Young Hutchin snorted with laughter. 'No, master, generally it's the thieves that collect the rent from the lawful folk.'

'If ye mean surnames, mine's Musgrave, and my father's cousin to Captain Musgrave, so if ye…'

'Shut up,' said Barnabus, kicking him. 'Young Hutchin, are you saying that none of the thieves and beggars in Carlisle are properly organised?'

Young Hutchin nodded. 'There's never been enough of them in the city,' he explained. 'Outside, well, I suppose every man takes a hand in a bit of cattle-lifting and horse-thieving now and again, even the Warden or the Captain of Bewcastle.'

'Especially the Captain of Bewcastle,' muttered Arthur Musgrave, who hated all Carletons.

'Who do you work for then?' demanded Barnabus of Arthur. 'Your father?'

Arthur Musgrave's father was humiliated by Arthur's inability to get on with horses and had kicked him out of the house five years before. 'No,' said Arthur, 'it's Madam Hetherington's stake you've got there.'

'*The* madam?'

'Ay.'

Barnabus nodded. It stood to reason, of course, seeing she was a southerner. Well, that changed his plans a bit.

'All right, on yer feet,' he said, giving Arthur Musgrave a heft and leading back into Scotch Street. A few people glanced at them but didn't feel inclined to interfere. It gave Barnabus great satisfaction to navigate his way back to the Rainbow without Hutchin's help, and yell for Madam Hetherington.

A moment later she appeared on the top step with a primed caliver and lit slowmatch in her hand. Barnabus grinned at her and toed Arthur forwards until he landed on the bottom step, and lay there, feebly struggling.

'I've got no argument with you, Madam,' he said cheerily. 'And just to show what a generous sort of man I am, here's half of your stake back.' He took out the twenty shillings he'd earned and tossed the half-full leather purse onto the step at her feet.

Madam Hetherington's eyes narrowed and the gun did not move. 'Why?' she demanded.

'Well, I've charged you the money for the useful lesson in diceplay I gave your lads...'

'No, why did you come back?'

Barnabus's smile went from ear to ear of his narrow face. 'I want to be a friend, not a coney,' he said, 'I know you won't try this on me again, but I'd like to be welcome here to join the girls if I want.'

Madam Hetherington finally smiled. 'I welcome anyone with the money to pay me.'

'Seriously,' said Barnabus.

'And I would be willing to pay for more lessons in diceplay.'

Barnabus twinkled his fingers together. 'Delighted to oblige, I'm sure, mistress.'

## WEDNESDAY, 21ST JUNE, LATE AFTERNOON

'I refuse to believe that streams can chase you round the countryside,' she said.

'On my honour they did,' said Robin, picking up a date stuffed with marzipan and nibbling it, 'and what's more the hills followed us too, so the ones we struggled up on the way north turned themselves round and we had to struggle up them again on the way back south.' He winced slightly, put the date down and ate a piece of cheese instead.

'Did you find you were being adopted by a herd of brambles and gorse bushes as well?' asked young Henry Widdrington. 'When I go out on a hot trod, I'd swear they follow me as lovingly as if I was their mother. Then when I fall off my horse one of them rushes forward bravely to break my fall.'

Listening to the laughter, Philadelphia felt a little wistful. She loved giving dinner parties and the pity of it was, there were so few people she could invite in Carlisle; most of them were dull merchants or tedious coarse creatures like Thomas Carleton who would keep beginning tales of conquests at Madam Hetherington's and then remember where he was and fall silent at the best bit. It was a pity she had no pretty well-bred girl she could bring in to make up the numbers for Henry Widdrington, but she was used to there being an oversupply of men. After all, very few ladies would want to live in the West March and those that were bred to it were poor dinner party material. London was so much more fun. Somehow her husband's 3,700 pounds per annum from his estates wasn't the compensation her father had told her it would be.

'And all this on account of one horse stolen from the Grahams?' asked Elizabeth Widdrington.

'I don't think so,' said Robin, 'I think it was a long-planned raid for remounts and where they're planning to go with them, I wish I knew.'

They had sat down at 2.30, fashionably late, and when Lord Scrope had said grace, her guests had flatteringly spent most of the first twenty minutes eating and occasionally asking each other to pass the salt. She was particularly fond of the salt cellar, being newly inherited from the old lord, a massive silver bowl with ancient figures in armour on it and some elaborate crosses, but she would have to check on the kitchen supplies of salt to see what had happened there.

Elizabeth Widdrington caught her eye questioningly and she nodded with a smile that she should broach their expedition of the morning.

'Did you know that Janet Dodd bought the horse from that little priest, Reverend Turnbull?' asked Elizabeth casually.

'Damn,' said Carey. 'I'm sorry, Philly,' he added at his sister's automatic frown, 'I meant to go and question the man about where he got the nag but it clean slipped my mind and I expect he's halfway to Berwick by now...'

'We went and asked him a few questions,' offered Elizabeth. 'And yes, he was on his way, but he very kindly stayed for us and told us what we wanted to know.'

Robert's face lit up. '*You* talked to him?'

'Wasn't that a little dangerous?' asked Henry Widdrington with a frown.

'Oh never fear, Henry, I went with Lady Scrope and Mrs Dodd,' Elizabeth said, hiding a smile at her stepson's concern. 'He was very helpful.'

'I'm sure he was,' murmured Robert, 'poor man. I would have been.'

'He told us he'd bought the horse from a pedlar called Swanders and...'

'Good God!' said Robert. 'Sorry Philly, are you saying that Daniel Swanders is in Carlisle now?'

'I don't know.' Elizabeth took a French biscuit and broke it in half. 'Do you know him?'

'Yes, yes I do. He's a Berwick man though, deals in anything small and portable or that has four legs and can walk. My brother almost hanged him once for bringing in of Scots raiders only he got enough respectable men to swear for him and got away with it.'

'How did he do that?' asked Henry naïvely.

'He bribed them, Henry,' said his stepmother. 'Most of them do that can.'

'The thing was, Janet was surprised that he didn't go straight to Thomas the Merchant to sell such a good animal since Thomas has been our agent to find decent horseflesh and would know we'd want him,' added Philadelphia.

'Good point,' said Carey, 'and why didn't he?'

'We went to speak to Thomas the Merchant as well,' said Elizabeth, biting elegantly into her half biscuit, 'and I'm certain he lied in his teeth to us.'

'Did he now?' said Robert with an answering smile. 'That was bad of him.'

'I do object to it,' Elizabeth agreed.

God help Thomas the Merchant for offending Elizabeth Widdrington, Philadelphia thought at the look in Carey's eyes.

'What he *said* was that he didn't know what we were talking about and he'd been cleared of the accusation that he collects blackrent for the Grahams,' added Elizabeth, finishing the biscuit and brushing her fingers. 'He gave me the impression that he was a mite too big for his boots as well.'

'Hm.'

'It's only important because the Grahams think it important,' said Philly, resisting the impulse to shake her obtuse husband, 'and because it was apparently the horse that Sweetmilk was riding when he was murdered.'

'Which makes me even more interested to know why Swanders happened to have it,' said Carey.

'Yes,' said Scrope, standing up and wandering restlessly to the virginal kept under cover in the corner of the room, 'but why does anyone care that Sweetmilk was murdered? Apart from the hangman, that is?'

'Well, my lord,' said Carey with a patience Philly hadn't seen in him before, 'firstly the Grahams seem to believe that it was Sergeant Dodd did the killing because he had the horse, or his wife did. Secondly because of the way the killing was done.'

'Shot wasn't he?'

'Yes. But from behind.'

'Best way to do it, I've always thought, especially dealing with a Graham.'

Carey coughed. 'Well, my lord, I'd agree, except that I had a chance to look at the body and the back was black with powder burns and further, the body wasn't robbed.'

Scrope began to press the keys gently, listening for sour notes. He found one and began hunting for the tuning key.

'Is that important?'

'It means he was shot from very close behind him, which argues that he knew his murderer and didn't mind him being there. And then whoever did it wasn't interested in theft, which cuts out practically anyone on the borders.'

'That or he was afraid the jewels would be recognised,' added Elizabeth Widdrington.

'Killed Sweetmilk?' asked Henry Widdrington, picking up one of the sheets and squinting at it.

'Not Swanders. He doesn't own a dag. A knife in the ribs would be more his mark. Can you take the bass part?'

Henry Widdrington whistled at the music. 'I can try.'

Elizabeth had already taken the alto sheet. At least Robert had had the sense not to buy the four-way sheets which had the different parts printed as if on a four-sided box, thought Philly—they were almost impossible to make out.

Robert carried the complete song to Scrope, who was still fiddling with the fah string and humming to himself.

'Ah, mm, yes. Yes I see, dear me, they get more intricate every year, look at this bit...Philly, you mustn't let your throat tighten on the higher notes, you know, or it will come out like cats.'

Robert laughed. 'It usually comes out like cats anyway,' he said, 'but it's all the rage at Court at the moment, God help...I'm sorry, Philly.'

Robert had a good tenor voice which went well with Philadelphia's high true but weak soprano. Elizabeth Widdrington had a powerful alto, but was out of practice at sight-reading and Henry Widdrington, with his still unformed bass, had a tendency to lose his place and blush furiously under his spots. Scrope, who had an extraordinary reach on any keyboard and could sight-read anything first time, though his voice was appalling, took each of them through twice separately, rapping with his toe to give the time. At last they all took deep breaths, waited on Lord Scrope's signal and launched into 'When Philomela Lost Her Love'. After three collapses and Philadelphia's helpless attack of giggles when she got lost amongst the fa-la-las they managed to work through to the end and stood looking at each other with satisfaction. Then they sang it again with gusto and the beautiful intertwining medley of voices briefly turned the grim old Carlisle keep into an antechamber of Westminster.

## THURSDAY, 22ND JUNE, BEFORE DAWN

Sitting on the bench, rubbing his sandy eyes, and trying to convince himself that the walls were not really coming towards him, Bangtail ventured to call out to his half-brother Ekie, in whom the Graham blood had run true and who was certain sure to hang, if only for the various bills against him that had been fouled in his absence.

'Ekie?' he asked, 'Ekie, are ye there?'

'God Almighty,' growled Ekie, 'the bastard Courtier's shut his goddamned screeching at last and now you wake me up. What is it, Bangtail?'

'What should I say, Ekie?'

'Eh?'

'Shut up,' yelled somebody else, 'some of us want to sleep.'

'I mean when the Deputy comes to question me, should I tell him about Netherby and the Earl?'

'Jesus Christ, I don't care. Tell the git what you want, it willna make no odds.'

'I think he thinks the horses are for a foray into England.'

There was a moment's silence and then somebody snorted with laughter, Young Jock's voice by the depth of it.

'Does he now? Well, let the man think what he likes.'

The others laughed.

'He'll want to know,' persisted Bangtail.

Ekie sighed. 'Bangtail,' he said, 'a' your brains are in yer balls. D'ye think *we* know where the Earl of Bothwell's planning to raid? D'ye think he'd tell us when he knows fine half of the men he's got would sell him out sooner than fart? All anybody kens is it's a long way to ride and there's fighting and treasure at the end.'

'Oh,' said Bangtail sadly.

'Tell him ye don't know where we're going and leave it at that and let him plump up the watches and guard all the fords and passes and tire himself out while we do the Earl of Bothwell's business, whatever it is.'

Young Jock Graham didn't know Carey very well, of that Bangtail was sure, but he didn't dare ask any more and lay down on the pallet again. After a lot of scratching he slept.

He woke blearily when the door clattered and crashed open and Carey came in, followed by Dodd with a lantern. Jesus, wasn't sunrise early enough for them, it was still black as pitch outside. Bangtail was too tired and miserable to protest when Dodd picked him up by the scruff of his jerkin's neck and propelled him through the door so hard he banged his head painfully on the opposite door. He kept his feet and heard the protests from the other prisoners.

'Go back to sleep,' said Carey, 'I only want to talk to my friend Bangtail here.'

There was a great deal of unsympathetic laughter.

'Tell him nothing, Bangtail,' said Ekie.

'You got your pinniwinks on you, Courtier, you'll need them for Bangtail,' said Young Jock.

'Ay,' said Ekie, 'but I know where I'd put them, I'd crack his nuts for him, that's what I'd do...'

'Shut up,' yelled Bangtail, beginning to shake as Dodd clapped his wrists in manacles and Carey motioned him out the thrice-barred door behind the Sergeant.

They wound up in Carey's own office chamber where his servant, looking as heavy-eyed as Bangtail felt, was just on his way to fetch some morning bread and ale from the buttery. Carey sat at his desk and looked sadly at Bangtail.

'What the devil are pinniwinks?' he asked.

Bangtail's mouth was too dry to answer so Dodd said grimly, 'Thumbscrews.'

It was impossible to say what Carey thought of thumbscrews by looking at his face. Bangtail supposed it was too much to hope that the Courtier was one of those eccentric folk who disapproved of torture.

'Are there any in the castle?' asked Carey casually.

Dodd sucked his teeth. 'I dinna ken,' he said, 'there might be. There's the Boot somewhere in the armoury.'

Please God, thought Bangtail incoherently, don't let them give me the Boot, oh please God...

'Good,' said Carey. 'In fact I think I tripped on the frame when I was in there, though the wedges and the mallet were missing.'

'We can have the carpenter find ye some,' said Dodd helpfully. 'Do ye want me to go and ask him, sir?'

Oh God, oh God, oh God, thought Bangtail, wondering if they could see his legs shaking.

'No,' said Carey slowly, 'no need to waken the man just yet. There's plenty of time, after all.'

'Ay sir.'

'And it's possible we may not need them?' At last he looked at Bangtail, his eyebrows making a question.

'N-no sir,' Bangtail managed to say.

'What can you tell me, Bangtail?'

I'm a Graham, he thought desperately, we're tough and stubborn folk...Oh God, oh God, oh God...

'Wh-what do ye want to know, sir?'

'Tell me what you did after you saw the horse Janet Dodd bought.'

'W-well, sir, I knew it was Caspar right away, though somebody had put a few extra white patches on him so he looked piebald, but ye could niver mistake the face of the animal, it were so noble and his legs and his...Anyway, I was in a state, so I did the first thing I thought of which was to ride to Netherby tower to tell... er...to tell Ekie.'

'Why not go directly to Jock?'

'I wasn't sure I should do it, sir, I knew what might happen, I wanted to talk to Ekie first, but Ekie said I should tell him since Sweetmilk was riding Caspar when he disappeared. He was allus the favourite, you know, sir, best dressed, best mounted.'

'Was Young Jock or any of the others jealous of him?'

'Well they might have been, sir, but Sweetmilk is...was so sweet-natured, ye couldna help liking him even if he did talk too much. So I talked to Jock of the Peartree and he thanked me and said he'd remember me if we ever met in a fight and I went back to Carlisle but the gate was shut. I was sleeping outside in a bush, but then the bell rang and ye all went riding out on the hot trod so I slipped in behind ye and went to Madam Hetherington's.'

Bangtail tried to spread his hands to show he'd finished but the manacles stopped him.

'Well?' said Carey, swallowing, drinking and dabbing his moustache and beard with a napkin like the pansified southerner he was.

'Well, sir?'

'Shall I fetch the Boot?' asked Dodd.

Carey sighed. 'I hate to cripple a strong well-made pair of legs like his, but...'

'Wh-what else do you want, sir, please, I...'

119

'What's going on at Netherby?'

'S-sir?'

'Who's there, why do they want horses?'

Bangtail gulped and tried to think. Carey watched him patiently, his usually humorous face unreadable.

Dodd growled. 'You're with us, or agin us, Bangtail.'

What would Ekie do to him? Was it even a secret who was at Netherby? Anyway, what could the bastard Courtier do about it?

'Th-the Earl of Bothwell.'

There was a flicker of something on Carey's face. Dodd made an mmphmm noise in his throat.

'Who else?' demanded Carey.

'Och, his own followers of course, like Jock Hepburn and Geordie Irwin of Bonshaw, and there's Johnstone and Old Wat of Harden and a fair few broken men from Liddesdale and the Debateable Land like Skinabake Armstrong and his lot.'

'And what does he want all these men and horses for?' enquired Carey softly from behind his fingers.

Bangtail's face twisted in despair. 'I dinna ken, Deputy, I wish to God I did and that's the truth, but nobody knows except the Earl himself and his man Hepburn and Old Wat, and not me that's certain and I'd tell ye if I knew it, I swear to God I would, but I dinna and if ye put me in the Boot I'll know no more…Oh God.'

He put his face in his hands and tried not to cry. 'Ekie said none of them know, but he could be lying…'

'If *you're* lying to me, Bangtail…' said Carey menacingly.

'Och no, sir, I'm not lying, I got no reason to, I'm not in the rode, see ye, and it's no gain to me whatever they do, though I heard tell that Captain Musgrave's helping out with a few remounts for Young Jock and Long Nebbed Robert, on a share, ye know, but that's all I know and I tellt ye the truth, as God's my judge…'

'All right,' said Carey, 'no need to take the Lord's name in vain any more.'

'It's not in vain, sir,' said Bangtail, shocked, 'I dinna swear sir, not falsely, my word's as good as any other man's in the March.'

'I thought there was a complete dispensation for that on swearing to the Warden or his men.'

Bangtail blinked. 'Eh?'

'He means,' translated Dodd, 'that he knows fine ye'll swear your oath till you're blue in the face to the Warden but it doesna count in men's minds if ye go and break it the next day. Not the way it would if ye swore to Jock of the Peartree or some other man that was your equal.'

'Well, it's not false, I swear by God and the Holy Bible, I told you all I know and that's that,' said Bangtail sullenly. 'If ye dinna believe me, then ye can fetch in the Boot and go to hell.'

Surprisingly Carey smiled. 'Well said, Bangtail.' He nodded to Dodd, who grabbed Bangtail's arm and led him to the door.

'Will ye let me go?' he asked hopefully.

'Not yet, Bangtail,' said Carey, the bastard Courtier, while his bastard servant finished what was left of his bread and sausage and the ale, God damn him. 'When I've checked your story. Not that I don't believe you, but you could be mistaken, and you don't know the most important thing. Perhaps you could find out for me?'

'In jail?'

'Where else? I can hardly lodge Young Jock and Ekie in the town, they'd be out of the place in an hour.'

'I doubt they know, sir,' said Bangtail. 'And they willna tell me if they see me come back…er…'

'Untouched, as it were,' said Carey. 'We can arrange that.'

'Well no, sir, I didna mean…'

'No hard feelings, Bangtail,' said Sergeant Dodd as he pushed Bangtail down the stairs and punched him on the face, 'I wouldna want you under suspicion from Ekie.'

# THURSDAY, 22ND JUNE, 10 A.M.

Thomas the Merchant had been seriously considering a quiet trip to his newly bought manor in Cumberland, but he knew a man in a hurry when he saw one and so he let the finely ruffed green-suited gentleman and his servant come sweeping into his study and called his own servant to fetch wine.

'How may I serve you, sir?' he asked.

The gentleman smiled. 'Do you know me, Mr Hetherington?'

'I have not had the pleasure...'

'I am the new Deputy Warden.'

'Ah,' said Thomas the Merchant, smiling in perfect under-standing, 'I see.'

'I am in search of some help.'

'Of course,' murmured Thomas the Merchant, pulling his ledger from the shelf, the one that gave details of his interests in the Carlisle garrisons. 'I am delighted to see you, sir. Who was it recommended you to see me? Captain Carleton or Sir Richard?'

Carey opened his mouth to answer and then shut it again, wondering if Thomas the Merchant was carrying on the same conversation he was. Barnabus solicitously pulled up a gracefully carved chair that was standing by the wall and he sat down in it.

The two of them looked at each other for a moment. 'Well,' said Thomas the Merchant, dusting his fingers, 'as you know, I have always been very generous when it comes to the gentlemen who protect us from the Scots.'

Carey's eyebrows went up but he said nothing, which made Thomas the Merchant a little uneasy. Thomas's servant entered with the wine, served it out and made his bows. Carey drank cautiously, then drank again looking pleased and surprised.

Let's get on with it, thought Thomas, surprised that the conversation was taking so long. 'Have you a sum in mind, sir?'

'For what?' asked the Courtier. Behind him his servant was looking nervous.

'For your...er...pension, of course,' said Thomas, astonished at such obtuseness. 'I must warn you that business has been very bad this year and I cannot afford to pay you as much as I paid Lowther while the old lord was sick. Shall we say three pounds a week, English?'

'For me?' asked Carey slowly.

Thomas sighed. 'And of course, for your servant, I can offer one pound a week—really sir, I can afford no more.' Thomas was hoping wildly that Lowther hadn't told him the truth about what he was really getting from Thomas the Merchant.

He noticed that Carey's fingers had gone bone white on the metal of the goblet. Well, happiness took people differently, perhaps Thomas had made the mistake of offering too much. Alas, too late now. Carey's servant had backed into a corner next to the door and was looking terrified. Good, thought Thomas, that's the way to deal with serving men, keep them in fear of you and then they have no time to be plotting rebellion or...

'Have I understood you correctly, Mr Hetherington?' asked Carey in a soft, almost breathless voice. 'Are you offering me a free gift of 156 pounds per annum?'

Thomas the Merchant beamed. This one would last about three minutes; what possessed the Queen to send someone so naïve into the cockpit of her kingdom?

'Well, nothing in this life is free, sir, except the Grace of God,' he said. 'I naturally hope to gain your...er...goodwill, perhaps even your friendship.'

'And on the right occasions a little blindness, perhaps even the occasional tip-off.'

Did he have to spell it out so baldly? 'Yes,' said Thomas, embarrassed at such crassness, 'of course.'

'Naturally, although of course the matter is in confidence.'

Carey longed to bring his fist down on Thomas's desk hard enough to make the windows rattle and the ledger hop in the air like a scared goat. He didn't do it, though he knew Barnabus was tensed ready for him to roar. The insult of it! How dare the man? How dare he even *think* of buying the Queen's cousin for less than ten pounds a week? And how dare he do it with such arrogant presumption, as if he were discussing no more than a business partnership.

'Mr Hetherington,' he began, and then changed his mind. He was up off his chair and had crossed the room to Thomas the Merchant's desk and swept the ledger out from under his long thin nose before the Merchant could do more than take in a gasp of surprise. Carey flipped quickly through the pages, squinting at the crabbed Secretary hand, lighted on a few names and laughed. 'I'd be in noble company, I see. I wonder, does Her Majesty know you have the Wardens of the West and Middle Marches in your pay?'

'Er...?' began Thomas the Merchant.

It was tempting to throw the ledger in the greasy skinny man's face and march out, but Carey saw a better way of continuing to call his own tune. He shut the ledger and tapped it.

'I want information, Mr Hetherington, much more than I want money. And it's not my way to enter into this kind of...business arrangement.' His servant made a desperate little whimper. 'And so, I'll thank you to tell me all you know about the horse that Janet Dodd bought, the one that came from Jock of the Peartree's stable. To begin with.'

'Er...' Thomas the Merchant was staring wildly at Carey as if at a chimaera, which indeed Robert Carey was, thought Barnabus bitterly, being the only man ever at Court capable of turning down a bribe.

Carey leaned over him threateningly. Thomas the Merchant made a feeble swipe for his ledger, but Carey skimmed it across the room to Barnabus who scrambled and caught it.

'Now then,' said Carey with his hand suggestively on the hilt of his sword, 'let's hear the tale.'

Thomas the Merchant sat down on his high stool again and blinked at the fine set of plate he displayed every day on the chest in his room.

'A cadger brought the horse to me,' he admitted at last, 'and I refused him because I had...er...seen him before, ridden by Sweetmilk. I wanted no trouble with the Grahams...'

'I thought they were clients of yours.'

'Sir!' protested Thomas. 'The accusation was found clean six months ago and...'

'Never mind. When did you see the horse being ridden by Sweetmilk?'

'Oh. Er...on Saturday.'

'Where?'

'Where what? Oh, ay sir, he was riding out the gate on the nag.'

'Who with?'

Thomas the Merchant was sweating, gazing sincerely into Carey's eyes. 'Alone.'

'And when was the horse offered to you?'

'On Sunday. Naturally I refused to do business on the Sabbath.'

'Naturally,' agreed Carey drily. 'But you were suspicious?'

Thomas the Merchant smiled. 'A little,' he admitted. 'It was a coincidence. I wanted nothing to do with any criminal proceedings.'

'Of course.'

Carey moved to the door, motioned his servant to give him the precious ledger and walked out of the door—simply took it in his hand and walked out of the door. Thomas the Merchant was appalled at such high-handedness.

'Sir, sir,' he protested, rushing after him, 'my ledger, I must have it...'

'No, no, Mr Hetherington,' said Carey, with a smile and a familiar patting of the calfskin binding, 'I'm taking your ledger as a pledge for your good behaviour, as my hostage, Mr Hetherington.'

'But...'

The rat-faced servant barred his passage.

'I wouldn't if I was you, sir,' said Barnabus, sympathetically. 'I know, he's a little high-handed at times. It comes of being so closely related to Her Majesty, you know. His father is her half-brother, or so they say.'

Thomas wasn't interested in Carey's ancestry.

'My ledger...What shall I do...'

'Amazing how memory can serve you, sir, if you let it. I'd bet good money that if you sat down and rewrote it, you'd end up with exactly the same ledger.'

'But...'

'Also, I might as well warn you, Sir Robert is wary of taking regular money, but he might be persuaded to accept a gift.' The servant grinned widely, showing a very black set of teeth. 'I can usually convince him if I set my mind to it.'

This Thomas understood. He nodded sadly. 'But my ledger...'

'Well, you've lost it for the moment, sir, you might as well...'

Carey poked his head back round the door.

'I forgot to ask. What was the name of the pedlar you didn't buy the horse from?'

'Daniel Swanders.'

Carey's face lit up.

'Splendid. At least that's the truth,' he said. 'Do you know where he is?'

'No sir.'

'Let me know if you find out. Goodbye to you.'

## THURSDAY, 22ND JUNE, 11 A.M.

Barnabus had run back to the castle, stored the ledger in Carey's lock-up chest, and run back again to find Carey drinking ale at a small boozing den on the corner of Scotch Street.

'You know the establishment, do you?' said Carey, nodding at Barnabus to sit down and refresh himself.

'Of course, sir.'

Carey smiled. 'Tell me about it.'

'There's a backdoor leading into a courtyard and then into another alley and it's backed onto the castle wall. Madam Hetherington...'

'Good God, another one?'

'Yes sir, I believe she's a distant cousin.'

'Go on.'

'Madam Hetherington is from London and it's a very well-ordered house: she has six girls, one Irish, two Scots, one French and two English...'

'Pox?'

'Not as far as I could see.' Carey grunted and drank. 'It's expensive, a shilling a room, not including food or drink or clean sheets...'

Carey was surprised. 'She provides clean sheets, does she?'

'Only if you pay for it,' said Barnabus, who hadn't bothered. 'There's a man called Arthur Musgrave acts as her henchman and this man Daniel Swanders...'

'Late of Berwick town...'

'...was playing dice there when I went yesterday.'

'Any good?'

'He had a couple of bales of crooked dice, a highman and a lowman and one with a bristle on the pip, but he hasn't the way of using them properly yet. I was going to give him lessons.'

Carey laughed. 'I'm sure you'll make a fine teacher.'

'Well, it offends me, sir. I like to see a craft practised well and he was trying but it was no good. Madam Hetherington says she'll pay me for the teaching, if you take my meaning, sir.'

'I have no intention of offending Madam Hetherington,' said Carey. 'She might well object to me arresting someone in her house. On the other hand, I want a quiet chat with Swanders.'

Suddenly he leaned forward.

'This is what we'll do.'


## THURSDAY, 22ND JUNE, NOON


Daniel Swanders had only just crawled blearily out of a tangle of blankets next to the fire in the kitchen of Madam Hetherington's. The girls were all at their meal at the big table, laughing and chatting and making occasional snide comments to each other. The curling tongs were heating up on the hearth and a couple of pints of ointment, guaranteed to help a man's prowess, were being strained into little pots by Madam Hetherington's cook. The smell was awful: rendered lard and lavender, rosemary and pepper.

'Good morning, ladies,' he yawned as he pulled on his jerkin and shambled to the table. 'Any room for a little one?'

The girls shoved up for him, packing their petticoat-covered bumrolls together and making an enchanting sight with their hair pinned roughly and their breasts pushed up by their corsets. Two of them were magnificent that way and with typical female perversity, Madam Hetherington insisted that they wore high-necked smocks, the better to entice the customer into wanting to undress them.

'This is Barnabus Cooke, Daniel,' she said. 'Are you listening?'

'Yes mistress,' said Daniel humbly. 'I'm sorry, I was only admiring Maria.'

'Maria, cover yourself, you're not working now. I want you to pay attention to what Barnabus teaches you, since he's a master craftsman at this game.'

'Yes mistress.'

Barnabus Cooke gave him a considering look and then said, 'Madam Hetherington, I'm happy to teach Swanders some of my secrets but they're worthless if everyone knows them, so...'

'Of course,' agreed Madam Hetherington, 'you may use the private banqueting room at the back, no one is using it.'

Arthur Musgrave came struggling in with his arms full of fire-wood and glowered at Barnabus who smiled back and raised his hat.

'I was going to suggest the courtyard, but the private room is even better,' he said. 'Come on, Daniel.'

The smell of roast beef and wine always clung to the walls of the private room which occasionally saw some very strange behaviour. Barnabus carefully cleared the rushes away from the floor at one end of the big table and then went to the glass-paned window and opened it.

'Well, here we are,' he said loudly, breathing deeply. 'Let's begin with the basics of palming dice. After all, it's no good using highmen if you can't swap them for lowmen when your opponent is playing, is it?

'This is called Find the Lady,' said Barnabus wisely, 'and it's not much good for catching coneys in London now, since even the coneys have heard of it, but you might find it worthwhile here or in Scotland. The idea is they bet on where the Lady—the die—is going to end up. See it's all done with the fingers, like that. All right? Now you try.'

Daniel tried and found it much harder than he had thought at first and very different from the way he usually palmed dice. For ten minutes he moved the beakers and tried to shift the dice without being spotted by Barnabus's beady eye, and although Barnabus said he was improving, he felt a little the way he had when his father had first begun teaching him the ways of persuading people to buy. There was so much to learn, so little time, and so many men who were better at it than him, he became quite depressed. Though that could have been the effect of living with so many beautiful girls and no money to pay them.

He was trying again to move a die from his sleeve to the table and back again without being spotted, when he heard the sound of someone at the window. He turned to look and saw to his horror that Robert Carey was sitting on the sill with one knee drawn up, ready to jump down.

Barnabus had drawn a knife, but Daniel was in too much of a panic to be afraid of it. He simply fell backwards off the bench, scattering dice in all directions, rolled, headed for the door. By some miracle, he got through it first, slammed it, tried to lock it, dropped the key in his haste and ran up the stairs to the bedrooms, with Carey hot on his heels.

It was Maria's room they barged into, and she already had her first client of the day. Daniel dodged, tried to hide behind the bed, but Carey skidded to a halt and stared.

'What the Devil...' wailed the man on the bed, whose shirt had tangled round his armpits as Maria worked on him. He sat up, throwing Maria aside and tried desperately to pull down his shirt.

Carey had turned his back.

'I'm very sorry, my lord,' he said in a strangled voice, 'I was chasing a horse-thief...I had no idea.'

Barnabus, who had seen Burghley's hunchbacked son Robert Cecil in circumstances too wonderful to tell and was not at all concerned, went behind the bed like a ferret and hauled out Daniel, with a knife at his neck.

'You've caused a lot of trouble, you,' he hissed into Daniel's ear as he twisted Daniel's arm behind him very painfully. 'That's the Lord Warden of the West March you've offended. What did you think you was doing, running like that, we only wanted a little chat. Guilty conscience, that's what it is. Come on.'

'For God's sake,' said Thomas Lord Scrope, then realising he looked worse standing up than he did in bed, he sat down again and pulled the covers up to hide his embarrassment. 'Robin. You won't tell Philly, please. I know she's your sister, but…'

Carey still had his back turned, but his fists were clenched. At last he turned with a perfectly calm expression on his face.

'Don't worry, my lord,' he said, 'I would never do anything to hurt her.'

Scrope winced and looked at the floor. 'She's a good woman,' he said lamely, 'she'd never…well, you know. I'm only flesh and blood…'

Carey had got a proper grip on himself. 'I think we should both forget that this happened, my lord,' he said.

Scrope's face was full of relief. 'Er…yes, forget it, absolutely right, of course.'

Barnabus was at the door with Daniel, not being too careful with his knife point either. Daniel squawked and struggled as he nearly lost his earlobe but the pain from his arm stopped him. Carey took a step closer to the bed.

'One thing, though, my lord,' he said very quietly.

'Er, yes, Robin,' said Scrope vaguely. He was being distracted by Maria's busy fingers under the covers, Daniel saw jealously.

'If you pox my sister, I will personally see to it that you never have the opportunity again. Do you understand me?'

'Well…er…'

'I'll make a woman of you, my lord, is that clear?'

Thomas Lord Scrope quivered and shrank back under the bedclothes.

Carey didn't wait to see his reaction, but waved Barnabus on and walked out of the room, shutting the door very carefully behind him.

They processed down the passage, where they met Madam Hetherington, with her dag.

'What do you think you're doing?' she demanded. 'And who are you?'

'I am the Deputy Warden of the West March and I am arresting your man Daniel Swanders, for horse theft and murder.'

'He's not my man, he's only staying here,' said Madam Hetherington quickly.

'So we are absolutely clear, madam, I have…ahem…checked the matter with the Lord Warden, who is in agreement. I apologise for the disruption to your establishment, but I had hoped to take him quietly out of the courtyard, without bothering you at all. Circumstances…'

Madam Hetherington's eyes narrowed. 'Are you taking him to the castle, sir?'

'Not yet. I would like to use your private room, if that's possible.'

Madam Hetherington nodded curtly, led the way down the passage and handed him the key to the room.

Carey was staring into space, his face working oddly. Barnabus wondered if there was going to be an explosion, and there was. It was Carey roaring with laughter.

'Oh Barnabus, did you see his face…Jesus, I nearly died.'

'I think so did he, sir,' said Barnabus primly. 'Very unhealthy for any man, that sort of shock.' Carey creased up again.

'Oh…oh…God, I must stop this, it's a very serious matter… with his shirt up and his prick all covered with lard…' Carey bent over and howled.

Daniel had picked himself up off the floor, felt his ear where blood was oozing and rubbed his arm and shoulder. He smiled at them uncertainly, took two of the dice from the floor near his feet and tossed them from hand to hand.

Carey was recovering himself, wiping his eyes with his hand-kerchief, blowing his nose and coughing. 'Oh Lord, oh Lord, I wish I could tell Philly. No, Barnabus, I know I can't, but…All right. Enough. To business.'

Carey hitched the padding of his trunkhose onto the table and stared down its length at him. Daniel sat on the bench and continued to juggle, staring back guilelessly.

The silence suddenly became very thick, a little decorated round the edges by sounds of chatter from the kitchen and the creaking of beds upstairs.

'Get on, Robin,' Daniel said at last, 'ye know me. I take it, you're saying was it me killed Sweetmilk Graham and stole his horse? You know I'd never be mad enough to do such a thing.'

Carey sighed. Barnabus had at first stared at his impudence in using Carey's nickname, then narrowed his eyes suspiciously.

'Danny,' said Carey, 'I don't know you. I knew you five years ago, but how do I know what you might have done since then? I've fought in three separate wars since then, and what I couldn't have done in 1587, I might well be capable of now given reason enough. So tell me what happened. And please, Daniel, tell me the truth.'

Daniel Swanders had been travelling on foot across the little nook of a border that lay north and west of the Solway firth, around the site of the Battle of Solway Moss. It was the Saturday, and he was on his way back to Carlisle from some successful business conducted with both the Maxwells and the Johnstones, involving horses, which it was forbidden to export to Scotland, and whisky which was heavily taxed. Thomas the Merchant trusted no one with the whisky which would follow later as part of a pack train, so Daniel was travelling light.

He thought he was very lucky at about sunset, when he saw two horses in the distance, lightly tethered to the root of a gorse bush and no one guarding them.

He came up on them cautiously, using the cover, watching to see if a guard should appear. Both of them looked tired, as if they had been ridden hard for a while. One was an ordinary hobby, a sturdy short beast with shaggy coat, no different from any of the others that rode the borders, but the other horse was another matter altogether. He was a beautiful tall animal, with a graceful neck and a noble head, a black coat with a white blaze on his forehead and two white socks and every line of him proclaimed speed, endurance and even intelligence. He was a horse any lord would covet. He was also a stallion, which meant he must have a sweet nature and that meant that his worth at stud was enough to give a man heart failure.

Daniel wrestled with his conscience for at least four seconds, before conscience won out over caution. It would have been a crime to leave the animal behind him and not even try to steal him.

There was still no sign of any owner or rider, so Daniel simply walked up to the beautiful creature, untied him, offered him an apple from his pack, let himself be smelled and inspected, and then jumped on his back. The stallion hopped a little, then snorted and turned his head eagerly north, so Daniel let him have his head, went to a trot.

A yell from behind made him turn in the saddle. A tall man was struggling out of the gorse bush: he was in his doublet, and he had his fighting jack in one hand and a cloth in the other which he was waving.

Daniel didn't wait to see any more, put his heels to the horse's flank and galloped away.

'He's a beauty, he's the Lord God's own delight to ride, you know, Robin, so fast and so smooth,' said Daniel, waving his arms in horse-shaped gestures at Carey and Barnabus. 'I had him hammering over rough country and I could have been in my bed at home, oh he'll bear away a few bells in his time, that horse, mark my words.'

Daniel brought the horse round in a wide circle, coming only a few miles short of Netherby tower at one point, before he got on the southern road to Carlisle. All the time he was nervous, in case the horse's rightful owner came after him on the hobby, but he needn't have worried. Nobody chased him and he rode happily to Carlisle. He got there too late to get in before the gate was shut, so he stayed the night in one of the little inns that made up part of the overspill at the southern gate, beside the River Calder, and then first thing on the Sunday morning he went proudly to Thomas the Merchant to sell him the horse.

'I couldna hope to keep him,' Daniel said sadly, 'not having a tower of my own nor a surname to back me, but oh it broke my heart...'

Much to Daniel's surprise, Thomas the Merchant went white when he saw the animal and refused point blank to have anything to do with him. This Daniel had not expected, but when he asked if the horse belonged to some important man on the border, Thomas the Merchant simply shook his head and bade him be gone.

'So then I thought I'd see the Reverend Turnbull who's a book-a-bosom man that sometimes travels with me, and ask his advice, him being educated and all. And I thought it might be best to be rid of the horse, in case it belonged to old Wat of Harden or Cessford or some unchancy bastard like that.'

'Jock of the Peartree,' said Carey.

'Ay, I know it now,' agreed Daniel ruefully, 'and Turnbull said he couldna offer what the beast was worth, but he could offer me two pounds English because it was all he had, and then he'd sell it on for me and split the profit. So I agreed and then because I was nearly sure the horse was owned by some headman of a riding surname, I decided it might be healthier to wait a while in Carlisle, here, until the fuss was over with.'

Carey looked at him gravely for a long time, so long that Daniel became nervous.

'Well, what more do you want?' he demanded. 'That's what happened, it's God's truth, that's all. And I've admitted to horse-stealing, what more do you want?'

'I'm not quite certain what the legal position is when you steal a horse from the thief that stole it,' said Carey, 'but you haven't told me the most important thing.'

'What's that?' Daniel was wary.

'Who you saw in the gorse bush?'

Daniel threw up his hands, palms upwards. 'If I'd known him, I'd tell you, of course I would, especially when the bastard must have done a murder for the beast. But I didnae know him, I'd never seen him before. And he didna look like a Borderer, forbye.'

'Why not?'

Daniel shrugged. 'Too glossy, too elegant, with his pretty doublet with the gold thread in it, looking like some sodomite of a courtier, is what he looked like, saving your presence, sir.' He grinned disrespectfully at Carey, who looked stern.

'Could you recognise him again?'

Daniel winced a little. 'Well, I only left Berwick a couple of weeks ago.'

'And why did you leave?'

'Er…well…your brother's very hot against horse-smuggling

at the moment and he's never liked me. I'd had a couple of nasty frights so I thought I'd go where it was a mite calmer.'

'And you came *here*, to the *West March*.'

Daniel coughed. 'You know what I mean.'

'How did you know Thomas the Merchant?'

'I didn't. I had a letter of introduction from Mr Fairburn in Northumberland, and this was the first job I did for him.'

'Do you know anything of Netherby castle and what they're doing there?'

Daniel shook his head. 'No, I've never been there.'

'Have you ever met Jock of the Peartree, Old Wat of Harden or the Earl of Bothwell?'

'No, never, thank God, and I hope I never do.'

Carey was stroking his neat court beard thoughtfully. 'Do you know anything of the reason why the Earl of Bothwell might want a couple of hundred horses at the moment?'

Daniel shook his head.

Carey beckoned Barnabus over into a corner with him, while Daniel continued to play with Barnabus's dice. He'd pocketed a couple of them, Barnabus noticed.

'I'm very worried,' Carey said, 'I want to know three things: what the Earl of Bothwell is up to...'

'I thought the Earl wanted to keep the Queen sweet at the moment, sir.'

'Barnabus, the man's mad. He'd probably think he could charm her round.'

'And could he, sir?'

'Who knows? If I understood that well how Her Majesty's mind works, I'd be rich. He's got good legs, he might. He surely thinks so, anyway.'

Barnabus nodded. 'And the other things, sir?'

'The other problem is Dodd's horses. I gave my word on it that he'd get them back, and I'll lay all Westminster to a Scotsman's purse the nags are eating their heads off at Netherby right now. And I don't like the sound of Jock of the Peartree believing Dodd was the man that killed Sweetmilk, so I want to find out who really did it.'

'What are you planning, sir?' asked Barnabus warily, knowing the symptoms of old.

Carey grinned at him, confirming all his fears. 'It seems the answers to all of my riddles lie at Netherby and so...'

'Oh no sir, we're not going to Netherby tower?'

'You're not, I am.'

'Sir...'

'Shh. Listen. I'll borrow Daniel's clothes and his pack and you can shave off my beard and brown my face and hands and then...'

'Sir, sir, 'ow do you know you can trust 'im, 'e's a thief and he's a northerner and...'

'He's a relative of mine. Also, we'll have his clothes and we'll give him to Madam Hetherington to keep safe for us.'

'What do you mean, sir, relative? What sort?'

'Ask my father.'

'Oho, it's like that is it?'

'It's like that, and if you gossip about it, I'll skin you.'

'But look sir,' he said conscientiously trying again, 'why couldn't you send Swanders in there instead of you, if you need a spy so bad, I mean, if they topple to you, you're done for, ain't you? Daniel...'

'It'd be worse for him. They'd likely hang him if they thought he was a spy, but they might not kill me. Anyway, I want to know who killed Sweetmilk Graham so I can bring him to justice and get Jock of the Peartree off Dodd's back. There's the makings of a very nasty feud there, when they've finished with their raid.'

'What about the Earl of Bothwell, you said yourself 'e's mad and I've heard tell 'e's a witch besides, won't 'e know who you are?'

Carey shook his head. 'I doubt it. It's four years since I was at King James's Court and he met me with a number of other gentlemen. There was the football match, but I don't see why he'd remember that either. I've got unfinished business with him anyway.'

'What sort of unfinished business?'

'He practically broke my shin bone taking the ball off me.'

'Sir, you can't...'

'Oh shut up, Barnabus, I know you mean well, but my mind's made up.'

'Well can I come with you...'

'Absolutely not. What would Daniel Swanders the pedlar be doing with a servant from London—you'd stick out like a sore thumb.'

'So would you, sir, you don't sound like...'

'Ah was brought up in Berwick, Barnabus,' said Carey, switching to a nearly incomprehensible Northumberland accent, 'an' I rode a couple of raids meself when I were a lad.'

'Oh bloody hell, sir.'

'Don't swear,' said Carey primly, 'Lady Scrope doesn't like it. Now you run out and find an apothecary; buy some walnut juice and borrow shaving tackle from Madam Hetherington on your way back. I'll talk to Daniel.'

Barnabus left the bawdy house at a dead run and sprinted through an alleyway into English Street, heading for the castle. Once there he quartered the place looking for Lady Widdrington and found her at last in the kitchen supervising the making of sweetmeats for the funeral feast. He panted out his tale to her, she took it all in and frowned.

'He's mad,' she said.

'Yes ma'am,' said Barnabus disloyally. 'Ma'am, will you come and talk him out of it...'

Barnabus sprinted back down Castle Street and English Street, bought the walnut juice at one of the apothecaries, made a quick detour to an armourers in Scotch Street and came panting and blowing into Madam Hetherington's an hour after he left.

When he'd recovered a little, he found Carey and Daniel Swanders drinking and eating an excellent dinner of baked chicken and a bag pudding, reminiscing in harsh Northumbrian voices about some escapade they had both been involved in as boys.

'What kept you, Barnabus?' asked Carey, switching back to his normal way of speaking, 'I was starting to get worried.'

It was so odd to hear him: one minute he was a northerner to the life and the next minute he was as understandable as any of the Queen's courtiers. Barnabus sat down to what was left of the meal and got his composure back.

'I couldn't tell you weren't a Northumbrian myself, sir,' he said, 'but what about a native, couldn't he tell?'

Daniel shook his head. 'No, it's wonderful how he can do it, I wouldna ken if I didna ken, you follow.'

Carey looked complacent.

'I was telling Daniel earlier, there's a little man in my father's company of players, what's his name, can never remember what it is, said I could have been a player if I'd been born in a lower station of life. He had me read to him endlessly in my Northumbrian voice, so he could get the sound of it for some play he was working on, which I told him was too conscientious for the London mob, best get some pretty boys in petticoats and a good thundering battle for the end and he'd do well enough. My father thinks the world of him, God knows why, dullest man I ever met.'

'Can you do any accent, sir?' Barnabus asked, fascinated.

Carey swallowed what he was eating and smiled. 'If I've heard it for a few days, yes. It's a gift like singing, makes it easier to learn French or Italian too. It's all in the rhythm. My father's little player prosed to me for an hour about it, and I'd have kicked him out, only Father had told me to be polite to him. He was odd that way: he used to track down foreigners, Welshmen, Cornishmen, Yorkshiremen and pay them by the hour to read to him and talk to him, just so he could catch the rhythm of their voices. Wasted effort, I called it, but he seemed to think it was important.'

'What are you going to do, sir?'

'Today? I'll change clothes with Daniel here, you shave my beard and brown my face a bit…'

'I bought some hair dye too, sir,' said Barnabus. While sprinting around Carlisle he had realised that the harder he argued against one of his master's schemes, the more determined Carey became. He had decided to leave any dissuading to Lady Widdrington. 'After all, they might have heard that Swanders is a black-haired man.'

'True enough, well done. We'll do all that and when it's dry and I look the part, we'll leave Carlisle and go north. Daniel stays here with Madam Hetherington and I've promised to pay her enough so she'll let him have one of her girls for the night, the sinful git.' Daniel smiled slyly. 'You wait for me outside Carlisle in one of the inns and when I come back tomorrow morning, we'll decide what to do.'

It broke Barnabus's heart to shave Carey's lovely trim little beard and then brown his skin with the walnut juice. Dyeing Carey's hair took longer than they expected, what with having to ask Madam Hetherington for a basin and two ewers and waiting for the water to be heated. To his horror, Barnabus found some nits and would have had at them with a fine-toothed comb, but Carey told him to leave them since no one would believe a cadger that hadn't a few headlice.

'You'll look a sight for the old lord's funeral.'

'Oh, the brown comes off your skin with lemon juice,' said Carey, 'and I can hide my hair under my hat. Nobody will notice, they'll all be too busy worrying what they look like themselves.'

While Carey waited bare-chested for his hair and skin to dry, Daniel explained his price system and he memorised the commonest items, laughing heartily when Daniel explained what some of them had really cost him, in case he needed to bargain down.

Barnabus had drawn the curtains while Carey and Daniel Swanders stripped off and swapped clothes. Daniel and he were almost exactly of a size, with Daniel perhaps an inch or two shorter. Swanders tried on Carey's doublet and posed in front of the mirror they'd had brought in while Carey laughed at him and told him the Queen would love him until she found out he couldn't dance, sang like a crow and had stolen all her jewels.

By this time Carey was scratching a little in Daniel's coarse hemp shirt, and putting on his worn homespun woollen hose and greasy leather jerkin. He pulled Daniel's blue statute cap down over his ears, looked at himself in the mirror and laughed again.

'I got you these sir,' said Barnabus diffidently, taking out the knives he had bought. 'See here, this one goes behind your neck, this one's on your belt and this one's in your sleeve. The two hidden ones are for throwing...'

'I'm not the dead shot you are, Barnabus...'

'It don't matter, sir, aim for the body and if they stick in anywhere they'll distract 'im long enough for you to make a run for it. Which you will do, won't you, sir, if they rumble you.'

'Not if I can help it, since they'll have horses and I won't.'

'Aren't you even going to ride?'

'Well Daniel hasn't any horses, and I can't ride one of my own, it would be spotted as coming from the south and somebody would ask questions. I can't ride anything from the Castle stables because of the brands. And I don't want to buy another horse, even if there were any to be had, which there aren't.'

Barnabus sighed unhappily. 'Can I wait for you a mile or two outside, then sir, with a horse in case you need to...'

'Barnabus, Barnabus, I appreciate your concern, I really do, but you'd get caught. Bothwell will have riders all around the place watching in case anybody tries to steal all his stolen horses back from him and you'd be caught and then they'd beat you up and I'd have to tell them the story to stop them and it would all be very embarrassing. You stay in Carlisle until I get back, do you understand?'

'Yes sir,' said Barnabus mutinously, thinking bleakly of having to face Carey's father with an explanation of how his youngest son happened to wind up kicking in the wind by his neck from Netherby's gatehouse.

'Right,' said Carey, 'here's my purse with my rings in it, you arrange things with Madam Hetherington and pay her whatever she asks for looking after Daniel, and then you go back to the castle and tell everybody I'm sick in bed...'

'Can't I even come a little way with you?'

'Oh all right, if you must, you can meet me in the alleyway.'

Carey took Daniel's pack, winced a little at its weight, then opened the window and climbed out into the little courtyard.

Barnabus went unhappily to negotiate with Madam Hetherington.

# Thursday 22nd June, late afternoon

Even Barnabus had to admit, walking through Carlisle, that Carey made an uncommonly convincing pedlar. He even flirted with one of the girls selling meat pies and had her shrieking at an incomprehensible Northumbrian joke.

It took some argument to get Carey, afire with impatience to put his head in the noose, to pause for a beer at the Golden Bell. As soon as they entered the common room, a tall figure in fine grey wool, piped with murrey, snapped her fingers at Barnabus and beckoned them over.

'What the...' hissed Carey. 'God's blood, you told her, you sneaking little bastard, I'll tan your backside for you...'

'Well, Danny,' said Barnabus, deliberately insolent, 'I don't know what good getting in a fight with me would do you, but if that's what you want, I'm game.'

Carey growled at him. Lady Widdrington had lifted her head haughtily and was beckoning again.

'I think there's business to be done with the lady, mate,' said Barnabus. 'Ain't you going to find out what it is?'

In fact, Barnabus nearly gave himself a rupture trying not to laugh as he watched his elegant master slouch over to Lady Widdrington, haul off his statute cap and make an ugly-looking bow. In a minute he had his pack off his back and had opened the top and was delving in the depths. She apparently wanted a thimble, and when he pulled out five in a little packet, she examined them carefully and asked if he was mad.

Barnabus loafed over with the beer, so as not to miss the fun.

His face hidden by digging in the pack, Carey was muttering his reasons for sneaking into Netherby to Lady Widdrington, who listened with regal calmness.

'I see why you want to do it,' she said, to Barnabus's shocked disappointment, 'but have you thought it through?'

'I think so, ma'am,' said Carey, producing a card wound with stay laces.

'Do you? Well, I don't. What's your excuse for going to Netherby? Why are you there at all? To sell Bothwell broidery silks and some pretty ribbons for his hair?'

This nonplussed Carey, who had been so charmed at the idea of getting into Netherby, he had not in fact thought it through. Lady Widdrington examined the laces and talked rapidly out of the side of her mouth.

'In the stables are three northern horses, with Fairburn brands on them, and also the Widdrington mark which might not be known here. They are my horses which I am lending to you as cover. You take them into Netherby and offer them to Bothwell and if he's as anxious for remounts as you say he is, then he'll be delighted. We'll work out a way of getting them back later.'

Carey opened his mouth to argue, stopped, thought, then nodded intently.

'Now you'll have trouble getting out in the morning, because if the raid is due in the next couple of days, I expect Bothwell will simply close up the castle and let no one out for any reason. He may be mad but he isn't stupid. So if you find it hard to get out, put all of this powder...' She put down a twist of paper next to some lace bobbins, '...into your wine or beer and it'll give you all the symptoms of a man with the first stages of the plague—fever, headache, sneezing, and if you complain of pains in your neck, groin and armpits that should frighten the life out of them.'

'It isn't...er...plague...?'

'No, Robin, it's poison, a very mild one and you'll feel very ill too, but that will help convince them. They'll kick you out of Netherby themselves and then you'll have to do the best you can. If I haven't heard from you by late afternoon tomorrow, I'll tell Scrope and we'll come and get you out.'

'Elizabeth, my dear...'

'One of the hardest things to disguise in a voice is endearment,' interrupted Elizabeth Widdrington frostily. 'This is a lunatic scheme, but if your heart is set on it, well...And I most certainly will not pay five pence for stay laces Daniel Swanders may have paid a penny for at the most, what can he be thinking of? I'll take this thimble though.'

She picked up a small ivory thimble and paid for it, and then watched impassively as Carey thanked her with extravagant obsequity and started shoving his things back in the pack.

'Go carefully with those silk stockings, they fray and they're your stock in trade, remember. I'll leave, and Barnabus will go for the horses, while you stay here. Barnabus will walk them up to the gate with me and then he'll go on round the walls and wait for you at Eden bridge. You follow when you've drunk your beer.'

Carey was smiling fondly at her. Many men might have resented her high-handedness, but he was used to managing women. He thought she never looked handsomer than when she was taking charge of something.

'Is there anything else I can do to help?' she asked.

'I wish I could kiss you,' said Carey. That put colour in the lady's cheeks. It was a good thing the light was so bad, no doubt to assist the diceplayers in the corner. Barnabus would have been over there to investigate if Lady Widdrington hadn't included him in her plan.

'It would be unseemly,' said Lady Widdrington sternly. 'If any cadger...I'd have my steward throw him out.'

'No steward here, my lady,' said Carey with a wicked grin, caught her hand and bent over it with a kiss. 'Now you'd better slap me.'

She was a quick-thinking woman, thought Barnabus approvingly, because she didn't slap him, she boxed his ears as she would any servant who behaved like that. One of the innkeeper's large sons came looming over with a cudgel in his hand.

'Is he bothering ye, ma'am?' he asked.

'Yes, he is,' said Lady Widdrington coldly, wiping her hand with her napkin, 'but I think he's drunk. You'd better throw him out.'

'Tut, and it's only the afternoon too,' said the innkeeper's son primly.

It did Barnabus's heart good to see his master frogmarched to the door and kicked into the mud outside, where he landed on his face. For good measure, Barnabus picked up the pack, stuffed the rest of the gear inside along with the twist of paper, and slung it after him.

'And stay out,' he ordered sternly. 'That'll learn you better manners wiv her ladyship.'

Knowing Carey, he turned away quickly, but he wasn't quick enough to avoid the clot of mud that hit his back. Not such a bad shot as all that, he thought, though of course knives were a different matter.

He went back to Lady Widdrington, who was drinking a tot of whisky on the house, to settle her nerves after her nasty experience, with the landlord making excuses and promising that the drunken sot would never be allowed to darken his respectable door again. Lady Widdrington nodded and generously said that she couldn't possibly hold it against him since the man had no doubt been drinking all day somewhere else and had been the best her servant could find.

Once the landlord had subsided and gone back to his less prestigious but more valuable customers, Barnabus attended on her assiduously, and murmured the story of Carey's visit to Thomas the Merchant.

'I think he was in too much of a hurry, ma'am,' he said. 'I think Thomas hadn't told us the half of what he knew, but once he heard the name Swanders confirmed, of course sir had to be off.'

'He is like that,' agreed Lady Widdrington. 'Straight into the thick of it at top speed. Well, he's done it before and never a scratch on him, so God must be watching over him.'

'Ma'am,' said Barnabus slowly, 'I don't want to pry, but...er... why didn't you stop him?'

'Stop Robin Carey when he's got the bit between his teeth?' She smiled at him. 'Could you?'

'Well no, ma'am, though I tried. But I thought...'

'I wouldn't back the Queen herself against him, once he's in that state. In fact she couldn't stop him running off to fight the Armada though she threatened him with the Tower. So if I can't prevent him, I can help him to do whatever mad scheme he's hatched more efficiently.' She let out a little sigh and clasped her hands together. They were not very ladylike hands, being large, square and strong, though they were as white and neat as lemon juice and buffing could make them.

'I see, ma'am,' said Barnabus sympathetically, who did indeed see. 'Do you think he'll manage it?'

She folded her lips consideringly as he refilled her larger goblet with wine, mopped a tiny spill with a cloth. Eventually, Barnabus thought, her long nose and determined chin would begin to curl towards each other as she got old and her teeth fell out.

'I don't know, Barnabus,' she said at last, her voice firm and quiet. 'At worst they might shoot him or hang him, or even torture him if they take it into their heads he might tell them something they want to know. At best they might ransom him, if he can overcome his pride long enough to tell them who he is. I'm sure Scrope will buy him free if he has to.'

Barnabus, who remembered the scene at the bawdy house, wasn't so sure, but didn't feel inclined to say so. He bowed to her and she smiled radiantly at him.

'And of course, he might even succeed. After all, he has unexpectedness on his side. I think he will if God watches over him as He always has so far.'

That was good enough for Barnabus and he smiled back.

'Come along,' said Lady Widdrington. 'You'd best get those horses for me. They're in the end stable, if Young Hutchin got it right, the bay, the dapple mare and the chestnut.'

She walked to the door with her back straight as an arquebusier's ramrod.


# THURSDAY 22ND JUNE, LATE AFTERNOON


Young Hutchin had had a very trying day. Somehow he had lost track of the new Deputy in the morning, which had annoyed Richard Lowther very much indeed. In the afternoon, he hung around the stables on the grounds that if Carey was planning to go anywhere, he'd need a mount, and as his own horses were all there, he hadn't gone yet. Even though the stable master set him to the eternal chore of harness cleaning, it had been well worth it. Elizabeth Widdrington had come sweeping in and ordered him to put halters on two of her own animals and the oldest saddle and bridle in the place on the third.

He followed her obediently out of the castle, wondering what on earth was going on, while she went to the Golden Bell in the little squabble of huts outside the Carlisle citadel gate. When she dismissed him, he followed his instinct and skulked around near the inn doorway, to be rewarded by the sight of Barnabus Cooke and another much taller man going in. Peering through one of the windows, he saw them all talking to each other and then, when the stranger kissed the lady's hand, he recognised the way of moving rather than the face and realised with shock that he was looking at the Deputy Warden in disguise. Moments later he had to dodge back behind the stable yard gateway, as Carey made his undignified exit.

Filled with relief and the glorious certainty that Lowther would reward him well, he hung about the stable block until Barnabus Cooke came for the horses and then followed him cautiously well back, dodging into doorways and booths every few moments. He had a healthy respect for Barnabus.

However, Barnabus was preoccupied and didn't seem to notice him. He went round outside the walls with the horses, past the racecourse and up to the Eden bridge, where he tethered them to a stone and sat down to wait.

Young Hutchin hid behind a dry stone wall and waited. In a few minutes a cadger with the long bouncy stride of the Deputy Warden came walking past him, still wiping mud off his face and jerkin. As Carey came close to Barnabus, Young Hutchin trailed him behind the wall, hardly daring to breathe.

'One peep out of you, Barnabus, and you're a dead man,' warned Carey as he swung his pack from his back and began strapping it onto one of the horses. In tactful silence Barnabus helped him, but at last, as Carey swung up into the saddle he held a stirrup and asked, 'Sir, what'll you do if they torture you?'

Carey looked down at him with his eyebrows up. His face looked very odd without its goatee beard. At least he didn't have a receding chin like Lord Scrope.

'I see no earthly reason why they should, Barnabus,' he said, 'but if they do I expect I'll tell them who I am and they'll have a good laugh at my expense.'

'Will Scrope ransom you?'

Carey laughed. 'Eventually. Or I'll escape.'

'Be careful, sir. Do you think you'll get there in time?'

'Oh Lord, Barnabus, it's only ten miles. Even you could ride ten miles before sunset if you didn't fall off too often.'

'Well sir, if you ride like that, with your hand on your hip so prettily and your back so straight, they'll know you're fake before you're close enough for them to see the walnut juice.'

Carey had the grace to look embarrassed, put his hand down and slouched a bit.

'Better?' he asked.

'I suppose. Sir.'

'Well, then, off you go, Barnabus, and tell them all I'm sick or something.'

'What should I say to Sergeant Dodd?'

Carey thought for a moment. 'I don't think he's in it with them, whatever it is, but you could wait until after sunset. Use your judgement, Barnabus.'

'All right, sir.'

'See you tomorrow, God willing.'

'Amen,' said Barnabus fervently as Carey chirruped to the horses he was leading and clopped his way over the flimsy bridge northwards.

Young Hutchin waited for a long while after Barnabus had set off back to Carlisle. He was in a quandary. Should he run across country to Netherby and warn his Uncle Jock what was going on, or should he go back into the castle and tell Richard Lowther as he'd been paid to. In the end he decided to go to Lowther, because if Carey happened to catch him on the way, then nobody would know what the Deputy Warden was up to until it was too late. Also it wasn't nearly so far to run.

Lowther's bushy eyebrows almost met over his nose.

'He's going to Netherby dressed as a pedlar? Good God, why?'

Young Hutchin shrugged. 'He's mad, but he could...'

'I know what he could do, lad, none better. Ay. You did right coming to me.'

'What are you going to do, sir?'

'None of your business, Young Hutchin. Here's some drink money for you, and a job well done. Off you go, don't spend it all at once and if I catch you in the bawdy house again I'll leather you and send you back to your father.'

Heart glowing at the bright silver in his hand, Young Hutchin ran off, leaving Richard Lowther very thoughtful as he sat down at his cousin's table again.

## THURSDAY, 22ND JUNE, EVENING

As Carey rode out of the Cleughfoot Wood and into sight of Netherby tower, with the pretty little stonebuilt farmhouse nearby, he knew perfectly well he was being paced by two men who had spotted him not far from Longtown. As he slowed his horse to an ambling walk, they came in close behind him but didn't stop him.

In the horse paddock outside Netherby tower was a most remarkable press of horses, with Grahams and Johnstones bringing in bales of hay for their fodder, and feeding them oats and horse nuts besides, which must have cost a fortune at that time of year.

Outside the paddock was a kicking yelling scrum of men, in their shirts and hose. Carey paused to watch. There was some nasty work going on in the centre of that mêlée. Suddenly, from the middle of them a wild figure burst, dribbling the ball in front of him. As the scrum broke apart leaving a couple of fist fights, he wove between two large Grahams bearing down on him, dodged back and faked neatly as a Johnstone poked a foot in front of him. For a moment it seemed he would be caught, but he elbowed the fourth defender out of his way as he pounded on alone to the open goal made by two piles of doublets at the far end of the field.

The man in goal looked horrified, dodged back and forth, fell for a lovely feint and dived in the wrong direction as the Earl of Bothwell kicked the ball straight into goal.

Some of the players cheered; the others looked sulky. Carey dismounted and led his horses forward to the edge of the field and watched as an argument developed over whether it was a fair goal or not.

'Who's winning?' he asked the massive black-bearded ruffian who was watching with his arms folded and a deep frown on his face.

'The Earl's men,' said the man.

'Do ye not think it would be better if ye had to have a defender or two between you and the goal when you played the ball?'

'What for?'

'It might make it more interesting, and ye'd have less motive for fouls.'

'More motive for fights after, though,' commented the broad man after some thought, 'as if it were nae bad enough now.'

The Earl was shouting at the leader of the opposing team.

'And who're ye?' demanded the black-bearded man, swinging round to look at him.

'Daniel Swanders, at your service,' said Carey, taking off his cap.

'What're ye doing here?'

'I heard ye were after horses. Are you the laird?'

'Nay, lad, that's Wattie Graham there, with the red face shouting at the Earl. I'm Walter Scott of Harden. Ye're not from this country.'

'No, master, I'm from Berwick.'

'Ay, thought so. The horses yourn?'

'Ay master.'

'Mphm.'

Francis Stuart, Earl of Bothwell, was a large handsome man with brown hair and a long face never at rest, its features oddly blurred by the continual succession of emotions crossing it, like weather. He was in a good mood from winning the football match and after slapping Wattie Graham on the back and promising him a rematch, he spotted Carey and came striding over to inspect him.

Carey tensed a little: it wasn't very likely the Earl would recognise him, he thought, having met the man only once, officially, and the Earl being the kind who is usually so wrapped up in his own importance that anyone not immediately useful to him is nothing more than a fleshly ghost. But still, Bothwell was the only one there who knew Carey at all.

Carey doffed his cap and made a clumsy bow and repeated his story about the horses. He found himself being looked up and down in silence for a moment.

'What's the price on them?' asked Bothwell, his guttural Scottish bringing back memories of King James's Court that Carey would have preferred to forget. At least he could understand it, once his ear was in, and it made it easier for him to slip into the Berwick manner of speaking that southerners thought of as Scottish in their ignorance.

'Well, sir, I thought...'

Bothwell laughed. 'Makes no matter what ye think, man, I havnae got it. So now.'

That was no surprise. Carey smiled ingratiatingly. 'Sir, I thought I could lend them to ye, for the raid, and then get them back with a little extra for the trouble after. As an investment, see.'

Bothwell's eyes narrowed suspiciously. 'What do ye know of the raid?'

'Nothing, your honour, nothing. Only I canna see why ye would be collecting horses for fun.'

Bothwell barked with laughter. 'And the pack?'

Carey coughed. 'Well, I'm a pedlar by trade, sir, I thought ye might let me open it and offer what I have to your ladies.'

'And yourself?'

'Myself, sir?'

'You look a sturdy man, yourself, can you back a horse, hold a lance?'

Carey hesitated. What would Daniel say? He decided on cunning. 'I can ride as well as any man, but it's no' my trade, see.'

'There's more than cows where I'm riding, ye could come well out of it.'

'Well sir...'

'Tell me later,' said the Earl generously and clapped Carey's shoulder. 'Put your horses in the paddock with the others. If ye ride with us, ye've got your own remounts and I'll see ye have a jack and a lance. If ye dinna, ye must bide here till we come back, if ye follow me?'

'Ay sir.'

There was a clanging of a bell from the castle and Carey trotted his horses over to the paddock, then joined the general rush of football players and watchers and horse tenders into the barnekin and so up the rickety wooden steps to the main room of the keep.

Crammed up tight on a bench at a greasy trestle table between a man with only one ear and another Scott, who was one of Old Wat's younger sons, Carey knew perfectly well that no one trusted him. With the number of outlaws around, it was a wonder anyone could trust enough to put their heads down to eat. Broad wooden platters lined the tables filled with porridge garnished with bacon and peas. Carey reached behind him for his pack and pulled out Daniel's wooden bowl and spoon, drew his knife and wiped it on his hose, which only made it greasier.

The braying of a trumpet behind him almost made him jump out of his skin. He craned his head round to see the dinner procession of servants in their blue caps, bearing steaming dishes: he caught the smell of cock-a-leekie and a roasted kid and even some bread. Odd to see all that food go by and know none of it was for him. It was a hard job for the servants to pass between the packed benches and up to the high table where the Earl sat, with his cronies on one side of him and Wattie Graham of Netherby on his right, then Old Walter Scott of Harden, each of them flanked by his eldest sons and the young laird of Johnstone. There didn't seem to be a woman in the place, though Carey couldn't blame their menfolk if they wanted them out of sight.

As the procession reached the high table and the chief men were served, the Earl stood up and threw half a breadroll at a nervous-looking priest in the corner.

'Say a grace for us, Reverend,' he shouted.

The Reverend stood up and gabbled some Latin, which was in fact a part of the old wedding service, if Carey's feeble classical knowledge served him right. Everyone shouted Amen, bent their heads and began shovelling food into their guts as if they were half starved.

There was indeed a shortage of food: Carey was slow to help himself and wound up with watery porridge, a few bits of leek and kale and a minute piece of bacon that had hidden under a lump of oatmeal. He gulped the skimpy portion down, and hoped it wouldn't give him the bellyache.

At the high table the Earl of Bothwell was laughing at some joke told by the man beside him; a man, Carey saw with narrowed eyes, who wore a gold threaded brocade doublet and a snowy white falling band in the French style. Unfortunately, about five of the men around Bothwell, including Wattie Graham, had some gold thread in their doublets, being well able to afford finery on their ill-gotten gains.

'Where are ye from?' demanded the earless man beside him. Carey trotted out his story again and the man nodded.

'One-Lug Johnstone,' he explained with his mouth full. 'And that's Old Wat's Clemmie Scott.'

The man on the other side, who had been digging his elbows into Carey's ribs as he struggled with a tough piece of bacon, nodded politely.

'Old Scrope's dead,' began Carey.

'Ay, so I heard, Devil keep him. His son's the Warden now, I heard tell. How's Lowther?'

'The Warden's got a new Deputy,' said Carey.

'Not Lowther?' One-Lug found that very funny and beckoned over two friends of his who'd been playing football. 'Listen to this, Jemmie, the man's saying Lowther's not Deputy Warden.'

'Who is it then?' demanded Jemmie.

Carey coughed. 'Some courtier the Queen's sent up from London,' he said modestly, 'they say he willna last the year out.'

'Nor the month.' All three of them were hysterical with laughter at the idea. 'Och save me,' said One-Lug, in what he thought was a London accent, 'Please don't stick that lance in me, Mr Graham, it hurts.'

'A cow?' added Jemmie. 'Why, what on earth's a cow?'

'Och, my lord Warden, the rude men have stolen my horses...'

Carey laughed with them until Old Wat's Clemmie finished chewing on his lump of bacon, swallowed what he could, spat out what he couldn't onto the floor and grunted, 'He faced down Sergeant Dodd at the castle yesterday, I saw him.'

Ice trickling down his spine, Carey looked as interested as he could.

'What with, a cannon?' asked One-Lug.

'A sword. Mind you, it was to stop Dodd going out after his horses, when Jock of the Peartree was all set to catch him at the Strength of Liddesdale, lying out in the cold wood all night for nothing, thanks to the damned Courtier. They say he's a sodomite...'

'Ye canna be a courtier without ye sell your bum,' agreed Jemmie wisely. 'He must have annoyed the old Queen something powerful.'

'If ye ask me,' said Old Wat's Clemmie, 'he was short of money to pay his tailor's bills, if ye looked at him with his great fat hose and his little doublet, ye never saw such a pretty suit.'

'Ye canna pay a London tailor with a cow.'

'What do ye know about it, the Edinburgh tailors take horses.'

While the argument raged across him, Carey scraped the last of the porridge off his bowl with his finger and put it away in his pack. He looked around the room idly and froze still.

Bothwell was talking to one of the lesser Grahams who had acted as servants to bring in the meal, gesturing in Carey's direction. The boy came struggling down to Carey just as he was helping to clear the trestle tables. The middle of the floor was being swept clean of rushes and sprinkled with sand.

Bothwell had moved: he had the laird's own carved armchair, was drinking wine from a goblet and beside him sat a sinewy grey-bearded man with a broken nose. The Graham boy who had come for Carey threaded past the men who were now rearranging the benches ready for the evening's entertainment, which was a cockfight. Carey saw the combatants being brought in, still in their cages, crowing defiance and fluttering aggressively and concluded that at least one of them had been got at.

Remembering Bothwell's vanity, when he came up onto the

153

dais, he bobbed his knee to the Earl and stood holding his cap and successfully looking scared.

'There's the man, Jock,' said Bothwell, 'he must have left Carlisle but a few hours gone.'

Jock of the Peartree spent a good minute examining Carey, who smiled ingratiatingly and hoped the walnut juice wouldn't dissolve in his sweat. The keep was infernally hot with all the bodies packed into it.

'I heard,' said Jock of the Peartree in a very level voice, 'that you was the man sold Sergeant Dodd's wife Sweetmilk's horse.'

With a swooping in his gut, Carey remembered that she had in fact bought it from the Reverend Turnbull and that some sort of Reverend had said grace. He wanted to turn and look for him but didn't. In any case, he didn't know what Turnbull looked like.

'No, master,' he said, bringing his voice down from a squeak, 'I didnae.'

'That's the word,' said Jock. 'You say you know nothing about it?'

'Nowt, sir.'

Jock watched him at his leisure for a while. Carey thought frantically. Surely to God, if Turnbull was here, he wouldn't have admitted to his part in the trafficking in that thrice-damned nag. Had he? Had he bought his own safety by selling them an intruder? Turnbull was the book-a-bosom priest Daniel sometimes travelled with, he must have known Carey wasn't Daniel Swanders...Why should he? Carey had given the name only to Wat of Harden... Don't speculate, ask.

'Sir, who was it said it was me had the animal?'

Jock and the Earl exchanged glances. 'That was the word in Carlisle, last we heard,' said the Earl. 'Do ye tell me on your honour that you never had the horse?'

'Never clapped eyes on him, on my honour, my lord,' said Carey, only slightly mendaciously.

Jock snorted slightly. 'Do ye know aught ye could tell us about Sweetmilk's killing?' he asked.

'No sir,' said Carey, 'but it wasnae Sergeant Dodd.'

'How do ye know that?'

'If what I've heard is right, sir, he wouldna make such a bodge of it.'

The Earl laughed. 'Any other news out of Carlisle?'

'Er…they postponed the funeral of the old lord.'

'I know that. They think we're riding into England,' said Bothwell.

'Are ye not?' asked Carey guilelessly, heart hammering again.

Bothwell smiled, a little coldly. 'That's for me to know and you to learn in due course, Daniel.'

'Yes sir.'

'Are you riding with us, Daniel?'

No help for it. 'Yes sir, though I'm not a right fighting man if I'm honest with ye.'

Bothwell clapped him on the shoulder again and grinned: he had remarkably good, even teeth and it gave his smile an odd glaring quality. Carey smiled back.

'If ye want custom, wait about a bit and Wattie Graham will take you to see the women, they're all agog for whatever's in your pack.'

Wattie Graham was as good as his word: as the betting round the makeshift cockpit reached manic proportions, Carey followed the laird up the winding stair to the next floor, where his womenfolk were hiding from the untrustworthy men down below.

There was a crowd of them, perhaps ten or eleven, and a bewildering number of Jeans and Marys with an occasional Maud and one Susan, sitting on little stools at a trestle table eating their own meal, which looked even worse than the one still rattling about Carey's stomach. There was no sign of even a speck of bacon in it.

Wattie's wife, Alison Graham, came to meet them at the door. Her broad, lined face lit up at sight of him and she took his hand in her own small rough one and led him into the feminine billow of skirts and aprons.

Surrounded by them, Carey opened the pack, laid out what it contained in the way Daniel had shown him and gave tongue like a London stallman.

'Ribbons, silks, beads and bracelets, laces, creams, garters and needles, what d'ye lack ladies, come buy.'

They giggled and elbowed each other. Mrs Graham fingered the ribbons and another girl picked up a packet of hairpins.

'How much for these?' she asked, and Carey told her.

It was bedlam for a while after that, as Carey told prices, held bargaining sessions over quantities of needles and some perfumed soap direct from Castile, as he insisted, although he knew perfectly well it was boiled up in York, and so did they.

At the end of the hour he had made Daniel a profit of about five shillings, and despite a throbbing head and a dry throat, he was feeling well pleased with himself.

Mrs Graham brought him a goblet of sour wine well watered, which he drank gratefully and then told him to sit down and he'd shortly get better fare than he would downstairs.

'Unless you want to go and watch the cockfighting?' said another girl, Jeanie Scott, extremely pregnant and glowing with it.

Carey grinned and decided to risk it. 'Nay, mistress,' he said, 'I laid my bets before I came up.'

'Don't you want to see which wins?'

'I know which cock'll win,' said Carey, 'it's the one that wasna given beer beforehand to slow him down.'

They all laughed knowingly at that. 'What's the news from Carlisle?' asked Alison Graham.

'I wasna there but ten days,' said Carey, 'I don't know the doings yet.'

'Is it right Jock of the Peartree raided the Dodds?' asked Jeanie Scott.

'Och, you know he did,' said another woman impatiently. 'He was a' full of it when he came back.'

'I heard Janet Dodd say her Cousin Willie's Simon had an arrow in his arm during the raid,' ventured Carey. 'And a woman called Margaret lost her bairn with the excitement.'

Jeanie Scott tutted sadly. 'That would be Margaret Pringle, Clem Pringle's sister, poor lass. I hope she's not poorly with it. D'ye know how she fares, cadger?'

Carey shook his head.

'How's Young Jock?' asked another girl, a thin, small pale creature, with a startling head of burnished gold hair. One of her wrists was tightly bandaged.

'He's in the jail at Carlisle,' said Carey cautiously.

'They havena chained him?'

'Not that I know.'

Mary seemed on the brink of tears, which surprised Carey. 'I couldna bear it to lose another brother...Will the Warden hang Young Jock, d'ye think?'

Carey shrugged. 'He was caught with the red hand, Mistress, the Deputy could have hanged him on the spot.'

'Ay, you listen to him,' said Alison stoutly, 'and dinna concern yourself; Lowther'll see him well enough, mark my words, it's only a matter of waiting.'

'But after Sweetmilk...' began Mary, and the tears started trickling down her face. From the red rims round her eyes it looked something she did often.

Alison rolled her eyes. 'Now Mary, Sweetmilk's dead and gone and that's the end of it. He's with God now and your dad'll get his revenge once he finds the man that did the killing.'

Mary only cried harder and put her head on Susan's shoulder.

'Is she Sweetmilk's betrothed?' asked Carey privately of Jeanie Scott, fetching out a hanky from his pack that was edged with lace and handing it to Mary. Service at Court had made it almost a reflex with him, when he saw a woman crying, although naturally what he really wanted to do was to cut and run.

Jeanie didn't look sympathetic. 'No, she's Sweetmilk's sister and what she's in such a taking about, I'm sure I dinna ken.'

It was Mary who had bought a packet of extra-long staylaces as Carey was sure Mrs Graham had noticed. She was mopping her eyes again: Carey saw her fingernails were bitten down to the quick.

'It's a sad thing to lose a brother,' added Jeanie briskly, 'but God knows, it's worse to lose a wean, and she's a fancy man here too, if I'm any judge.'

'Is she not married yet?' added Carey in surprise.

'Nay, she's only sixteen, she's but a flighty maid with her head full of stories. Jock has her betrothed to an Elliot but she doesna want him. She'll change her tune in time.'

'Better to marry than burn, the preachers say,' said Carey meaningfully.

Jeanie Scott eyed him. 'Ay,' she said at last, 'that's the way of it.'

'Do you know who killed Sweetmilk?'

Jeanie shrugged and patted her stomach. 'Save for the way it was done, it could have been a Storey or a Bell or a Maxwell or anyone that found him with cows that didna belong to him.'

'Hey, pedlar,' sang out another Mary, 'how much for the whalebone?'

There was a little more selling and then the girl called Susan came in with a large wobbling junket, sweetened with rosewater and honey. They served it to him, laughing at his expression and told him a fine figure of a man like himself needed better feeding than what they were getting downstairs and it would settle his stomach nicely. Three of them had messages for friends in Carlisle, Jeanie Scott wanted him to tell the midwife Mrs Croser that the babe was head down at last, and a fifth wanted to know what a roll of green velvet would cost and if he could get it for her from Edinburgh next time he went. Carey promised he would find out from Thomas the Merchant, which seemed to please them.

At last with his pack a good bit lighter than before and his purse considerably heavier, Carey went to the door. Mrs Graham followed him with a roll of cloth.

'Here,' she said, 'ye dinna want to jingle among that lot downstairs, roll your money in this.'

He did as she suggested and behind the door, he slipped it down inside his shirt and tied it round his waist. At the bottom of the stairs he found Wattie Graham, frowning.

'Ye took your time.'

Carey shrugged. 'I canna rush the ladies when they canna make up their minds,' he said reasonably. 'Who won the cockfight?'

'The Duke of Guise, Old Wat of Harden's best cock,' said Wattie Graham dourly, 'and if ye ask me, it was fixed.'

Carey went over to One-Lug and Jemmie to collect his winnings, and then agreed to join a game of primero with them. As soon as he took the cards in his hands, he knew they had been marked with pin pricks on the back and had to hide a smile. With a quick shuffle, he had the system worked out, and it was one that the London card-sharps had abandoned five years before.

It was quite pleasant to let himself slip into a card-playing frame of mind, finding a clearer colder self as he watched the cards and the play and calculated the odds according to the Italian book he had read ten years before and which had saved his life. At Court it could sometimes be far more dangerous to win than to lose: he won steadily but had never taken more than he lost off the Earl of Leicester, nor from his successor at Court, the Earl of Essex. Sir Walter Raleigh was a different matter: he had spotted Carey's careful odds playing at once and had insisted on learning it from him.

Carey ended the evening by paying back to Old Wat's Clemmie and One-Lug and Jemmie exactly what he had won off them at the cockfight, which made them feel they were somehow one up on him. There was music as well: a scrawny old man with a plaited beard took up a little harp like the ones they had in Ireland and strummed and sang a whining ugly song about a fight of some sort. There followed a scurrilous and probably truthful ballad about Scrope and his personal habits and a wistful lament for Sweetmilk Graham that had Jock of the Peartree dabbing his eyes and nodding and sighing.

It hardly seemed possible for the number of men they had fed there to be able to sleep, even after some of them had been set to watch the horses and guard the Longtown ford. And to Carey's frustration, there was still no word on where the raid was headed. But there was no help for it, and so with his pack pillowing his head and a thread from it wound round his thumb, his dagger in his hand and Daniel's thin greasy cloak wrapped round him, he lay down to sleep, with One-Lug's boots by his head and Jemmie's backside wedging him into the wall. Which hardly seemed a coincidence, though if they were watching him they were doing it in their sleep. For a long time he was too tight-strung to shut his eyes as he lay in the smoky darkness listening to an orchestra of snores and grunts and farting. In the end, even he slept.

# Friday 23rd June, before dawn

All her life Elizabeth Widdrington had risen well before dawn to dress herself and pray in the quiet pale time before the world sprang to life. It calmed her and gave her space to breathe before she must plunge into managing her husband's house and lands and nursing her husband himself. It was a precious thing to be able to speak to God without interruption by maidservants wanting to know if the linen should be washed despite the rain and menservants needing the tools out of the lockup.

Of course, sometimes she was hard put to it to keep her mind on her prayers: Philadelphia's brother would keep marching into her thoughts. It had been a long time since her lawfully arranged husband Sir Henry had been well enough for the marriage bed and sometimes she despaired of ever having children. At twenty-eight she was getting on for childbearing...And there was the memory of Robert Carey again, courteously determined, blue eyes smoky and intent, whispering his desire to her in the little garden at the palace, while the rain of that stormy summer fell and the whole land held its breath and waited for the Armada. And afterwards... No, she wouldn't think of it.

She rose and started to dress. On this particular morning she was in one of the little apartments in the Carlisle Keep, since Lady Scrope refused to hear of her lodging in the town. As always she padded silently about in her shift, not needing a tiring woman since her stays laced unfashionably at the front, and once she was into her grey-woollen gown and her ruff tied at her neck, she crept out through Philadelphia and Thomas Scrope's chamber with her boots in her hand. The two of them were invisible behind the curtains of their bed and the maidservant snoring at a high pitch by the wall. None of them woke as she opened the heavy door and went down the stair.

It was a little more difficult to pick her way amongst the servants asleep in the rushes in the main room, but she managed it with no more than a few grunts and a feeble grope after her by one of the men. She was on the point of opening the heavy main door, when she heard stealthy footsteps and whispered conversation, and the rattle of keys.

She froze, then as she heard them open the iron door to the jail and go in directly beneath her, she pulled on her boots, opened the door a little, to peer out.

Sir Richard Lowther was emerging from under the wooden steps that led to the door she was hiding behind. At his back were five tousled bearded men—no, six. The last she knew was Bangtail Graham and the others must be the raiders Sir Robert Carey had captured the day before yesterday.

Lowther beckoned them to stand around him.

'He's gone to Netherby,' he explained, 'dressed as a pedlar, by name Daniel Swanders. Now you'd know him again, wouldn't you Young Jock.'

'Oh ay,' said Young Jock, 'I'd know him.'

'I can't spare you more than one horse, so Young Jock will have to ride and the rest will have to follow, but...'

Elizabeth Widdrington opened the door, walked out onto the steps and stopped, looking down at them.

Richard Lowther looked up at her, not at all worried.

'Good morning, Sir Richard,' she said.

'Good morning, Lady Widdrington,' he said.

'What are you doing?'

'These men have got bail, Lady Widdrington,' he said, 'I'm letting them go home to their families.'

'Bail?' she asked archly.

'My lord Scrope agreed it last night.'

Damn the man for his vagueness. Even when he was sick, Scrope's father would have wanted to know the reason for Lowther's interest.

'They've given their words of honour they'll come when their bills are called at the next Day of Truce, and they cost the castle six pence a day each to guard and feed.'

'Is the gate open yet?'

'Not yet. Soon enough.'

No, she was not going to let him give one of their precious horses to Jock of the Peartree's sons. Let the raiders walk to Netherby on their own two feet that God gave them.

She came down the steps as the whole group of them went to stand by the gate and wait for it to open. At least Lowther hadn't the authority to open it before time. As they passed her she stopped Bangtail.

'Where's the Sergeant?' she demanded.

'He has a little chamber by the barracks door,' said Bangtail, 'Why did ye want him, missus? Can I help?'

'I doubt it, but you could wait and see if I have a message for you if you want to earn yourself a little drinkmoney.'

'Ay missus.'

Elizabeth hurried across the yard to the bright new barracks building and opened up the door to find Janet Dodd standing in the passage in her kirtle with her stays half laced, head down as she brushed her red hair.

'Janet, where's your husband?'

'In there,' said Janet, surprised at seeing a gentlewoman up so early. 'Why, what's the matter, my lady?'

'Would you go in and see if he's decent. I must speak to both of you at once.'

'Yes ma'am.'

Janet peeked round the door, turned to Elizabeth.

'He's dressed and drinking his beer, and if I were you, I'd wait until he comes out, he's ay like a bear in the morning.'

'I'm sorry, this is very urgent.'

From behind the door that led to the main part of the barracks came the hawking and moaning of the garrison waking up. Brooking no argument, Elizabeth gestured Janet ahead of her into the tiny chamber and followed herself.

Dodd was sitting on the little sagging bed with his chin on his hand, drinking miserably.

'Goddamn it, woman, can ye never find better than sour…Oh, sorry, ma'am.' To be fair to him, Dodd pulled at the open front of his doublet and made to stand up, but Elizabeth shook her head, shut the door firmly behind her.

162

'Lowther's freeing the men you and Sir Robert caught the day before yesterday. They'll be out at the gate as soon as it opens.'

Dodd looked cynical. 'That's no surprise, he's well in with the Grahams and wants to stay that way. Why? What do you care?'

Elizabeth charitably ignored his insolence. 'I care because Robert Carey went to Netherby last night in disguise as a pedlar.'

That woke him up. He sat bolt upright. 'Good Chri...why?'

'Didn't Barnabus tell you last night? To see about getting your horses back and finding the man that really did kill Sweetmilk. And also to know where Bothwell is planning to raid.'

'The man's mad,' said Dodd definitely.

'I never thought he'd do that when he gave his word,' said Janet, clearly appalled. 'They'll half-kill him if they find out.'

'Which they will do as soon as Young Jock and his men get to Netherby.'

'Who else knows of this?' asked Janet.

'Myself and Robert's servant Barnabus Cooke, who's still abed as far as I know. And Lowther, somehow.'

'Cooke's a Londoner,' said Dodd. 'Canna ride better than a hog in breeches. What's to be done?'

'Stop Lowther.'

Dodd sucked his teeth. 'I dinna see why he should pay me any mind, but I'll try for ye, my lady. Good God almighty...Sorry ma'am. Disguised as a pedlar, would ye credit it?'

Elizabeth left them there with Janet doing up Dodd's laces and finding his cap, while she hurried back to the keep, threaded through the wakening servants and ran up the stairs to the Scropes' chamber.

It took her five minutes to shake the maidservant awake and the maid took another five to waken Philadelphia, who climbed tottering out of the high bed and blinked at Elizabeth.

'Wh-what's wrong?' she asked. 'Is it a raid?'

'No, it's your brother.'

'What's he done?'

Elizabeth told her, including what Lowther was up to. Philly's eyes widened, her hand went to her mouth.

'But the Earl will hang him.'

'Robin didn't think so.'

'He doesn't know the Earl of Bothwell, he's a wicked Godless man and cruel with it. Thomas, Thomas, wake up.'

'I'm awake,' came Scrope's tetchy voice from behind the curtains. 'What's that mad brother of yours done?'

Elizabeth fidgeted about the room while Philadelphia explained. The two voices rose and fell, one irritable, one pleading. At last Scrope poked his head out of the curtains, causing his nightcap to fall off.

'I said they could have bail and I'm not going back on it,' he snarled. 'Lowther can let them out but they're not to have horses.'

'But Robin...' wailed Philly.

'Your precious Robin can look after himself. He should have thought of it before. Man's mad, going into Netherby dressed as a servant...'

'A pedlar...'

'I don't care if he went dressed as the bloody Queen of France, I'm not getting him out of some schoolboy scrape.'

There was a thump as Scrope flounced back onto the pillows.

'Anyway,' came the reedy voice, 'I'm unwell. I think I have an ague.'

Philadelphia scrambled out of bed again, leaving the curtains drawn, and fluttered about the chamber, trying to get dressed while she crumpled up her little face and bewailed her husband. Elizabeth waited for a moment, then decided there was no help to be got there, made an impatient 'Tchah!' noise, and went down the stairs again.

Out in the courtyard she found Dodd having a shouting match with Lowther by the gate, watched by a group of highly amused Grahams.

'Ye canna let them out and have him taken, he's the Deputy Warden,' he was shouting.

'I can and I will,' growled Lowther, 'And what's more, *I'm* rightfully the Deputy Warden, not that upstart Londoner, or I will be by the end of today, I think.'

'That's telling him,' laughed Young Jock. 'Do ye want the man roasted a bit for impudence before we hang him?'

'No,' said Lowther, 'hang him up first, then roast him, don't take any chances with the young pup.'

'Jesus Christ, at least ransom him, we need to know where the raid's going...'

'Shut your mouth, Sergeant Dodd,' said Lowther, 'I know where the raid's headed and so does Captain Musgrave.'

'Bothwell could be lying to ye...'

Lowther smiled slowly. 'He's not lying, not with what it is he's hoping to steal.'

'And what's that?' put in Elizabeth. 'If you really do know, which I doubt.'

Lowther laughed at her rudely. 'I'm not telling ye, all women are blabbermouths and ladies nae different. If ye were my wife I'd tan your hide for asking what's men's business and none of yours.'

Lady Widdrington paled and her lips tightened. She looked as if she was swallowing a great many large words with great effort.

Young Jock, Ekie and all the Grahams were helpless with laughter. Dodd stepped towards them with his fist raised, but Lowther got in his way, still grinning.

'These are out on bail now, Sergeant,' he said, 'and as Deputy Warden I forbid you to leave the castle today. Do you understand me?'


# FRIDAY, 23RD JUNE, BEFORE DAWN


Carey awoke out of too little sleep, knowing someone was stealing his pillow. He knew before he was properly awake that he couldn't allow that: gripped it tighter, rolled and pushed himself onto his feet with his back to the wall and his dagger ready.

'Ah well,' said Jemmie's voice, 'it was worth a try. Don't stick me, pedlar, I was only wondering.'

Carey showed his teeth and waited until Jemmie had backed

off. One-Lug lifted himself up on an elbow and cursed both of them, then lay down and went back to sleep. Old Wat's Clemmie hadn't even stirred.

With the inside of his mouth as full of muck as a badly run stables and his head pounding, Carey thought of trying for another hour's sleep, but decided against it. Instead he picked his way across the crammed bodies, scratching his face where the newly shaved beard was coming back and his body where the fleas had savaged him. Once outside there was blessed fresh clean air, only a little tainted with the staggering quantities of manure produced by the men and horses packed into Netherby, and the stars rioting across the sky, with just a little paleness at the eastern edge.

Carey wished he could wash his face, but couldn't find water, so wandered towards the cow byres set against the barnekin wall where there were lights and movement.

Sleepy women were trudging about there with pails and stools. Alison Graham was standing by the big milk churns and she nodded curtly at him as he slouched towards her.

'Ye're up early,' she said to him. 'Any of the other men up and doing, eh cadger?'

'One of them tried to steal my pack, but no,' said Carey ruefully. 'Any water about fit to drink?'

She gestured at some buckets standing by for the cows and he went and dunked his head, drank enough to clear out his mouth.

'Is Mary with you?' he asked, 'Mary Graham?'

'In with Bluebell at the moment, why?'

'I wanted to ask her about Sweetmilk.'

'Why?'

'In case I heard anything, in my travels. I do, you know.'

Alison Graham looked him up and down suspiciously. 'If ye're trying...'

'God curse me if I lie, missus, I only want to talk to her.'

After a moment she nodded. As she took the buckets from the girl bringing them over on a yoke, lifted and poured them without visible effort, she said, 'She only has to squeal and the crows'll be feeding on you by midday.'

Carey nodded, did his best to look harmless and went into the byre where Bluebell and two other cows were ready to be milked. Following the sound of retching, he came on Mary in the corner, being helplessly sick on an empty stomach. She had her fist clenched on a lace she wore about her neck. Carey watched silently for a moment, knowing perfectly well what was wrong since he had seen the malady before. At last Mary stopped, spat, and sat down on her stool, with her head rested against the cow's flank. As if nothing had happened she started milking away with her sleeves rolled up and the muscles in her white arms catching light off the lantern on the hook above as she worked, though she favoured her bandaged wrist.

She jumped when he coughed.

'Can I sit and talk with ye, missus,' he asked gently.

She shrugged and carried on. Carey squatted down with his back to the wall. They watched the milk spurt in white streams, the round sweet smell of it mixing with the smell of hay from the cow's breath.

'When's the babe due?' asked Carey after a while, deciding to bet his shirt on a guess.

Mary Graham gave a little sigh and closed her eyes.

'What babe?' she asked. Squersh, squersh, went the milk and the cow chewed contentedly on her fodder.

Carey said nothing for a while. 'I wish ye could help me, for then I might help you,' he said at last. 'It's a Christmas baby, is it no'?'

She shrugged, turned her face away from him. Her head was bare like most of the maids in the north, and the straight red-gold hair knotted up tightly with wisps falling into her face as she worked.

'What did Sweetmilk say?'

That opened the dyke. Her fingers paused in their rhythm, her shoulders went up then down, and he saw water that was not sweat dripping off her chin.

'He said...' she whispered, 'he said he'd kill the father.'

'Did he know who the father was?'

No answer.

'Can ye tell me?'

'Why should I, if I didna tell my brother and my own father doesnae ken yet.'

'Was it one of Bothwell's men?'

There was a telltale little gasp. 'How did ye know?'

'If it was one of the men from about here, ye could marry him and if he was married already he could take the bairn for you.'

'I may lose it yet.'

Carey said nothing. Privately he believed that only women who longed for babes ever lost them: the more embarrassing a child was likely to be, the more certain its survival. Unless the mother went to a witch, but he thought this girl not ruthless enough for that. And not brave enough.

'They say pennyroyal mint will shift it. Do you have any about you, cadger?'

'No,' said Carey, coldly. Mary Graham sneered at him and went on with the other two teats. The cow shifted experimentally and tipped her hoof. Mary banged unmercifully on the leg and the cow lowed in protest.

'Would you marry the father if he asked?' pressed Carey, hoping she wouldn't slap him.

She didn't quite: she scowled at him and turned her shoulder to him.

'Not if he was the Earl himself,' she whispered fiercely.

Carey nodded. That at least removed the prime suspect, but it confirmed that she must know who killed Sweetmilk. Not that she was likely to tell, even if her father beat her which he no doubt would. Poor lass.

He let her finish milking the cow and when she rose from her stool and rubbed her back, he too rose to go.

'Make yourself useful, pedlar,' she said to him, 'take this over to Mistress Graham for me.'

Embarrassed into women's work, Carey took the buckets and carried them out of the byre. Without a yoke to take the surprising weight and steady them he slopped some of the milk and Alison Graham sniffed at him, lifted each one and poured it out and sent him back to swill the buckets with water and take them in to Mary again. He knew perfectly well she'd tell him nothing more and he wasn't her servant, so when he had done as he was bid, he walked out into the dawn again and yawned and stretched.

'What will you do about Mary's bairn?' he asked Mrs Graham when she snorted at him like an irritable horse.

'Why? Are you offering for her hand?' demanded the mistress. 'She'll take it if ye do.'

'Er...no...'

'Then leave her alone. She's enough to contend with.'

'Yes missus,' said Carey meekly.


# FRIDAY, 23RD JUNE, DAWN


Dodd was sitting glumly in the cell recently vacated by Bangtail, looking at the neat pile of turds in the corner. He had worn out his fury kicking the stout door and now his toes were sore as well as his stomach and his face and he hadn't had breakfast.

The rattle of keys did not make him look up, since he expected it was Lowther come to gloat.

'Wake up, Dodd,' snapped his wife's voice, 'unless ye want to bide there until your hanging.'

'Lowther's put one of his men at the gate,' said Lady Widdrington, 'but Lady Scrope tells me there's another way out of the castle, some secret passage to the Tile Tower.'

This was the first Dodd had heard of it, but he supposed it wasn't the kind of thing generally bandied around. Lady Widdrington put a purse into his hand, and when he got into the passage, he found his wife had piled his jack and sword and helmet into a corner. He drank the ale from the bottle she handed him and gave her a kiss.

'We haven't much time,' said Lady Scrope. 'My husband says he's got an ague and won't do anything, and Lowther's got the whole castle locked up tight.'

'It's too late to stop the Grahams getting to Netherby even on foot,' said Dodd gloomily.

Janet was helping him into his jack, Lady Widdrington handed him his helmet and sword, even Lady Scrope was helping with the lacings. It was an extraordinary situation to be in.

'I know that,' said Lady Widdrington impatiently. 'All we can do now is stop Bothwell from hanging him when he finds out.'

'How can we do that?' asked Dodd. 'He's an unchancy bastard to meddle with, that Earl and I dinna...'

They seemingly had a plan. Surrounding him with their skirts and selves, and with one of Lady Scrope's velvet cloaks over his head, they simply walked him quickly round to the empty inside of the keep, through the servants' quarters and to the place in the wall where the well was enclosed, supplying independent water to all the keep. Janet unbolted and pulled down the shutter.

'Through there,' said Lady Scrope.

'What?' asked Dodd, appalled.

'If you climb through the gap,' said Lady Scrope brightly, 'and feel about with your feet, you'll find the rungs of a ladder set into the wall. Climb down until you find another hole in the wall on the opposite side. That's the entrance to the tunnel that goes to the Tile Tower.'

Dodd peered through the hole, which was black and smelled very wet and mouldy.

'Christ Jesus,' he said. To his surprise, no one told him not to swear. He would have thought there would be a chorus.

'When you get to the Tile Tower,' continued Elizabeth Widdrington coldly, 'it's up to you how you get out of the city, but I doubt Lowther knows of this since it's knowledge passed from Warden to Warden. So he'll expect you to try for the gate. I'll have Bangtail try and make the attempt, and no doubt he'll wind up in here which will serve him right.'

'What for?'

'For existing,' said Janet.

Dodd wasn't sure if it had been Bangtail who punched him in the kidneys when he was arguing with the Grahams about being locked up in his own jail, but wasn't inclined to give anybody the benefit of the doubt.

'What then?' he asked. 'If it's too late to warn Carey to be out of Netherby and Scrope willna move, what can I do?'

They told him. He hated the sound of it, but he had to agree there didn't seem anything else to be done. Lady Widdrington gave him one of Carey's rings in case he needed to produce proof. Janet produced a rope which she passed around his middle and then kissed his face.

'God keep you, husband,' she said.

'Bloody hell,' said Dodd, blinking at the hole he was supposed to climb through. Would his shoulders go, or would he be left stuck and kicking? He poked his head through, eased his shoulders, and found that with some wriggling, they fitted. Some bits of stone slipped and fell: there was an awfully long wait, it seemed, before the splash. The place was pitch black. He spread his arms wide, feeling about, and sure enough there were rungs in the wall a little to the side.

Pulling back with long streaks of mould on his back and chest, he found a lantern being lit by Elizabeth Widdrington. As he was about to snarl he couldn't be expected to do anything without light, he was nonplussed by this. They really expected him to do it.

Oh God, what would they do if he refused? He looked at their soft white faces, set like saints' faces in an unreformed church, and decided he didn't want to find out. And besides, he wouldn't put it past Janet to go herself, she was in such a rage and what she would say to him afterwards, he hated to think. A short life and a miserable one, whatever I do, thought Henry Dodd glumly.

He brought up a stool, climbed on it, poked his shoulders through again and felt for the rungs of the ladder. The first one he found and tested for its strength, promptly came out of the wall at one side.

'The mortar's rotten,' he said, thinking maybe he could survive Janet's fury.

'Get on with it,' hissed Lady Widdrington, 'someone's coming.'

It was all very well for her, she wasn't risking her neck in some horrible deep well…The second rung seemed firm enough to take his weight. He swallowed hard, got a grip on it with both hands and heaved himself through the little hole, the sword on his belt catching and scraping.

171

Almost at once, Lady Widdrington put the lantern on the ledge and fitted the shutter back in the hole. He heard the bolts going home as he hung by his hands from the top rung. That was when he thought of taking off his jack, sword and helmet and lowering them down on the rope, but it was too late to do it. Scrabbling desperately with his toes for one below him, he thought that all except the top rungs had fallen out, but at last he found a foothold and could distribute his weight.

He passed the end of the rope round the top rung and felt down gingerly for the next rung. That one held, he went down a little further, gasping a bit with fear. The rung after that was rotten but the three below it were firm enough.

It might have taken him two minutes or half an hour to climb down to the little ledge he could dimly see in the light of the lantern above. He couldn't bring it with him, he didn't have the hands. Once on the ledge he got his breath back and looked about. There were some rotten wooden boards propped up against the wall, and then he saw the opening of the tunnel on the other side, just as Lady Widdrington had said.

It wasn't badly planned, he thought to distract himself as he inched round the ledge towards it. Any besiegers who found the passage would have to reverse what he was doing to get in and it would be a simple matter for the defenders to drop things down on them from above and knock them off. And the ledge was deliberately made too narrow to stand and use a bow. God, it was narrow, and the well was still too deep to see the water. And then, if the garrison wanted to use the passage to make a foray, or get food, they would have control of the well shaft and they could put down planks across the yawning hold so it wasn't so dangerous.

Dodd crouched down by the opening, put his head into it and banged his nose on something metal. Cursing and feeling with his hand, he discovered an iron grille, firmly set in the rock.

'Oh Christ, it's been blocked up...'

Sense told him otherwise. If the passage was to be blocked up, they would have done it properly with bricks and mortar; this was a defence. Which meant it could be lifted, perhaps like a portcullis.

The light from the lantern high above him was guttering, but he couldn't bring himself to climb and fetch it and trim the wick. Somewhere by the opening there had to be a... His hand fell onto a lever, and he pulled it down. It was stuck.

'Come on,' he muttered, wrenching at it. At last it creaked and groaned and the iron grille lifted a little. Just like a portcullis. Sweating freely and feeling sick from the smell of mould, Dodd pulled at the lever again, heard a crunching of gears as the ratchet within the mechanism caught its teeth, and the iron grille lifted up a little higher, and then suddenly something worked and it pulled right out of the way. There were long sharp spikes along the bottom.

Terrified of being spitted like an animal in a trap, Dodd looked around for something to wedge it with, pulled one of the rotten planks towards him and jammed it in the groove.

The passage was tiny and slimy and horrible. He didn't want to go in. On the other hand, he couldn't climb back up either.

'Carey, you bastard,' he moaned, pushed his sword in its scabbard in front, put his head in and scraped his shoulders through. There was an ominous creak and whine from the iron gate. Dodd whimpered and crawled forwards on his elbows as fast as he could, heard the rattle and cracking as the rusty chain broke and the wood splintered, and brought his feet up under him just in time, scraping a long hole in his hose and grazing his knees. The iron grille slammed into the holes behind him, and he wanted to be sick.

He didn't, it was too unpleasant a thought, having to crawl through it. The passage was bad enough as it was, slimy and stinking of rats and excrement, with little spines of limestone sticking up and hurting his hands and spines of limestone hanging down to bang his head. Why the hell was he doing this for Carey, he didn't even like the man, what the devil did he care...

The passage opened out a bit after a few yards of eeling along on his belly, so he could crawl on hands and knees, feeling ahead of himself with his sword, in terror that the roof might have fallen in. There was one place where some stones had fallen down, but he managed to slither through there as well, to find a puddle on the other side.

He splashed through that, crawled for another age, cursing

173

Carey, Lowther and both Scropes comprehensively, and then the point of his sword rammed into solid stone blocking the way. Not knowing whether his eyes were open or shut, except by the way his sweat was stinging them, he felt the stones. Masonry, tightly packed. He must be at the Tile Tower by now, surely. And surely to God, there was a way out. He felt around, found a small slimy drain that was producing a stink to fell an ox. He thought he must suffocate from it and his head was starting to spin.

The wall in front of him stayed obstinately immovable. Dodd pushed and heaved with his neck muscles cramping and his knees giving him hell, almost weeping with frustration. He finally lay down flat to rest, and happened to look upwards.

Either something was wrong with his eyes or there was a tiny squeeze of daylight up there. Above him was no tunnel roof, only a shaft and beside him, now he had calmed down, he could feel some more metal rungs. He sniffed. He thought at last that he knew where he was: this was the garderobe shaft for the Tile Tower, which was one of the lookout towers on the north wall of Carlisle. It was still in use, clearly, by sentries. God, no wonder the tunnel stank and what exactly was it he'd crawled through...

'Bastard, bastard, bastard,' he muttered in a litany of ill-usage, as he strapped his sword on again and set himself to climb. The rungs were slippery but they seemed firmer than the ones in the well. At last he found the light coming from a little window above a small stone platform. At that point, he could get his bearings. He was in the outer wall where it was at its thickest, seven or eight yards thick, he thought and couldn't remember. There must be a way to the outside, or why bother with a passage?

Now afraid of twisting his ankle when he had ten miles to run, Dodd lowered himself down on his arms and fingers, dropped into the soft earth and brambles of the ditch and then sat there for five minutes, gasping and shuddering and swearing all sorts of desperate reformations if God would never make him do that again. At last, with his knees killing him and his legs still rubbery, he scrambled up the other side of the ditch and walked across the rough grass to the river.

Once he got to the Eden he mopped off some of the green streaks and filth that covered him from head to foot. There were a few curious stares from some of the women washing linen at the rapids, but none of them saw fit to comment. Then he set off along the old Roman road at a fast jog trot, past the banks and ditch of the old Pict's Wall, heading for Brampton nine miles away where Janet's father lived with his kin, the first of the men on Carey's list of those who disliked Lowther. Nobody enjoyed paying blackrent for protection against raiders Lowther brought in himself, but some resented it more than others. Will the Tod Armstrong, Janet's father, had bent his ear often enough on the subject, God knew.

The day was hot for the first time in weeks, and Dodd thought seriously about hiding his jack in a bush and coming back for it later. In the end he simply couldn't bring himself to do it and risk losing an old friend.

As he loped along, he kept watching for horses though he knew there was less than no hope of finding a loose horse to steal this close to the marauders denned up at Netherby. Most of the men were at the shielings anyway, so not even cows were visible, and the womenfolk hard at work in the fields and gardens near their houses. Some of them unbent their backs to look at him, a couple recognised him, but as they could hear no tolling of the Carlisle bell, they were puzzled to know what to do and simply stood watching. He ignored the ones who called out.

Perhaps his father-in-law would take pity on him and lend him a horse to carry him the further seven miles to Gilsland where he could rouse out his own surname.

God help Carey if he's had the bad taste to get himself hanged before I can bring help to Netherby, was all Dodd could think, as he pounded along the rutted gravel of the Roman road. I'll hunt him down and beat his brains out in Hell itself.

She was talking again.

'What do you want me to do?' he asked, not sure he had heard it right.

'You and I are going to Thomas the Merchant and we're going to get the full story he's hiding about what he knows of Sweetmilk. And then, depending on what we find, you might go straight to Netherby to tell Jock of the Peartree of it.'

Henry choked on a lump of cheese. 'But I haven't got a pass to go into Scotland.'

'You will by the time you need one, Philadelphia Scrope is seeing to it. Now come along.'

Thomas the Merchant had a very fine wooden town house on English Street, solidly built of Irish timber and the walls coloured faint pink with a bull's blood wash. Elizabeth Widdrington swept in, with the top of her high-crowned hat brushing the door lintel and servants scattering behind her like chaff. Henry knew his job for this kind of thing, at least, having collected rents with his stepmother in the past. When an ugly man his own height dared to bar their path, he drew his sword, put it on the man's chest and walked straight on so he had the choice of giving way or being spitted. The man gave way.

At the end of the hallway stood a middle-aged slightly built merchant in rich black brocade, trimmed with citron velvet and green braid, clasping his hands nervously.

'Lady Widdrington, Lady Widdrington, what is the meaning of this…'

Henry set his face in an ugly scowl and advanced on the man with his sword. Occasionally he was grateful for the spots and pockmarks that ruined his face for the girls, because they made him look so much more unsavoury than he knew he really was.

'Thomas Hetherington,' said Elizabeth in tones that would have skewered a wild boar, 'you will tell me what you know about the killing of Sweetmilk Graham and what happened to his horse and you will do it *this instant*! Sit down.'

'How dare you come breaking into my house and threatening my servants, I have never been so slighted...'

'Then it's about time you were,' said Elizabeth. 'By God, I have had enough of your patronage and your shilly-shallying and this time you shall tell me what I ask and you shall tell the truth or I will destroy you and everything you own.'

Thomas the Merchant's face went putty-coloured. 'This is unseemly,' he said, and Henry had to give him credit for courage. 'Madam, I must ask you to leave or I shall call...'

'Oh?' asked Elizabeth, 'and whom, pray, shall you call? The Warden? He's in bed. The Grahams? They're busy. However, I am here and I will have no arguments, do you understand?'

'I'll sue, I'll...'

Elizabeth smiled very unpleasantly. 'Nothing would please me more than to meet you in Westminster Hall. In the meantime, tell me what I ask, God damn you, or I'LL LOSE MY TEMPER.'

Henry thought it was wonderful how his God-fearing stepmother could swear when she was angry, but he kept his face straight and his sword ready. She had another advantage, in that she was tall and when she shouted her voice deepened, rather than becoming shrill. Personally, he would have told her everything he knew, down to the place he'd buried his gold, if he was Thomas.

Thomas the Merchant had the sense to sit down. Elizabeth pulled up a heavy chair and sat down opposite him.

'I may have the body of a weak and feeble woman,' she said, quoting the Queen whom she greatly admired, 'but I have the heart and stomach of a lord, by God, and I'll have your heart and stomach out in the light of day if I must, Thomas the Merchant, and swear you tried to rape me. So. Tell me about Sweetmilk.'

# Friday, 23rd June, morning

The man in charge of caring for the horses was called Jock Hepburn, a by-blow cousin of Bothwell's, who claimed to have Mary Queen of Scots' second husband the fourth Earl of Bothwell for his father. He explained this to Carey and the sixteen other men who had been set to do the work, told them to call him 'sir' or 'your honour' since he was noble and they weren't, and then sat on the paddock fence, played with the rings on his long noble fingers and shouted orders all morning.

Some surname men were in the paddock too, seeing after favourite animals, but since most of the horses were stolen, the work fell to Carey and his fellows. At least it gave him the chance to mark out Dodd's horses, which he did by the brands. They were standing together, heads down, as horses often did when they were miserable.

Once the feed and water had been brought in, Hepburn took it into his head that the horses needed grooming, since most of them still had mud caked in their coats from when they were reived. In fact, Carey thought, as he worked away with a straw wisp and a brush at the warm rough coat in front of him, Hepburn was perfectly right, but he could have called in some of the idlers playing football in the next field to help: at this rate they'd be at it all day. He was getting a headache and his arms were tiring from unaccustomed work. If Dodd could see me now, he'd surely die laughing, thought Carey grimly as he scrubbed at the hobby's legs, and there's still been no word from Bothwell where we're supposed to be going.

The next horse he went to seemed very skittish, prancing with his front hooves, away from Carey. Carey chucked and gentled the animal, saw a tremor when he put his hoof to the ground. After much backing and shying, he'd calmed the horse enough so he could lift up his leg. What he saw there was thoroughly nasty: white growths and an inflamed reddened frog, and the other forehoof was quite as bad.

Without even thinking, Carey led the horse gently to the side of the paddock, took a halter off the fence and slipped it over the twitching nervous head.

'There now, there now,' he murmured. 'We'll have it sorted, there now, poor fellow...'

Somebody thumped him between the shoulder blades, hard enough to knock him down. Carey rolled over in the mud, came to his feet with his hand clutching the void at his left hip where his sword should have been.

Jock Hepburn was standing there, flushed and angry.

'Where do ye think ye're going with that horse?'

'He's got footrot and he needs to see a farrier,' said Carey, in no mood for an argument.

Jock Hepburn stepped up close and slapped him backhanded. 'Sir,' he said. 'Ye call me sir, ye insolent bastard.'

Carey hadn't taken a blow like that since he was a boy. He started forwards with his fists bunched, saw Hepburn back up hurriedly and reach for his sword. He stopped. Rage was making a roaring in his ears and his breath come short, he was about to call the man out there and then, when he caught sight of the Earl of Bothwell hurrying over from his football game and remembered where he was and what he was supposed to be doing.

'What's going on?' demanded the Earl.

'This man was trying to steal a horse.'

Bothwell's eyes narrowed. 'I said I'd hang anyone that tried to reive one of our horses and I meant it.' He paused impressively. 'What d'ye have to say for yourself?'

Carey took a deep breath and relaxed his fists. His face was stinging, one of Hepburn's rings had cut his cheek, and his headache was settling in properly.

'Only I'd steal a horse that could run if I was going to,' he said, his throat so tight with the effort not to shout he could barely whisper. Bothwell's eyes narrowed at his tone. 'My lord,' he managed to say, adding, 'This one couldna go two miles, his footrot's that bad.'

The Earl lifted one of the horse's feet, prodded the sore frog hard enough to make the beast dance and snort.

'Ay,' he said at last, 'it's true enough. Take the nag up to the tower and ask Jock of the Peartree if he'll take a look. With a good scouring he might be well enough for a pack tomorrow night.'

'Ay sir,' said Carey, taking hold of the bridle. The Earl stopped him with a heavy hand on his shoulder.

'Ye've too high a stomach on ye for a pedlar, Daniel,' said Bothwell shrewdly. 'What was ye before, at Berwick?'

For a moment Carey couldn't think what to say.

'I've no objection to outlaws, ye know,' said Bothwell, and smiled, 'I am one myself, after all.'

Carey's mind was working furiously. He managed a sheepish grin. 'Ah, it wasnae the fighting, sir,' he said, 'it was the women.'

Bothwell laughed explosively. 'There y'are, Jock,' he said to Hepburn, who was looking offended, 'dinnae be sa hard on the man, ye've a few fathers after ye and all.'

'Husbands, sir,' said Carey, 'it was husbands.' That tickled Bothwell greatly.

He clucked at the horse and led him on to the paddock gate.

'Hey, Daniel,' called Bothwell, 'stay away from Alison Graham or Wattie'll be after ye with the gelding shears.' Carey smiled wanly and lifted his hand to his forehead, leaving the Earl still howling at his own wit.

Carey's back prickled with Hepburn's eyes glaring at him. He tried to slouch a bit more while he went over soft ground to save the horse's feet.

Once at the tower, he tethered the horse at the wall and asked for Jock of the Peartree of one of the boys running past playing wolf-and-sheep.

Jock was inside the main downstairs room with Wattie Graham his brother and Old Wat of Harden who was spread into three men's space on the bench. They were squinting at a sketch map drawn in charcoal. Carey tried to get a look at it, but didn't dare come close enough.

'Master Jock,' he said to all of them with his cap in his hand, 'the Earl said, would ye look at this horse outside, he's got the footrot.'

Jock, very fine in a red velvet doublet, stood up and stretched.

'Ay,' he said, 'where's the nag?'

Wattie Graham was rolling up the map and Harden stood, scraped back the bench. 'It a' makes my head swim,' he complained, 'I dinna like going so far out of mine own country.'

The two of them went ahead through the door, ambling on towards the gate. Carey went ahead of Jock to lead him to the horse, when he saw a commotion outside by the football field. There was a little group of men gesticulating, the Earl at the centre, some of them pointing towards the tower. Screwing up his eyes, Carey saw a lanky frame topped with black hair, and a hand going up characteristically to twiddle in his ear.

Realisation dawned. It was Young Jock, Ekie—all the reivers he had taken red-handed two days before. They were shouting, waving their arms. His own name floated over to him, poking familiarly out of the shouting. Wattie Graham and Wat of Harden were looking at the fuss, turning to look back at him as the shouting reached their ears.

All the world turned cold and clear for Carey. The thought of the horse still tethered to a ring in the wall flickered through his mind, to be dismissed at once. As he had said himself, there was no point stealing a horse that couldn't run.

'Laddie, ye're in my...' Jock began behind him.

Carey half turned, drove his elbow into Jock's stomach. Jock, who had eaten a much better breakfast than Carey, went 'oof' and sat down. Carey backed into the tower, slammed the door, bolted and barred it, then kicked Jock of the Peartree over again as he struggled wheezing to his feet.

Carey had his dagger in his hand, but decided against using it and put it back. Instead he kicked Jock deliberately in the groin and when he hunched over with his eyes bugging, Carey turned him on his stomach, put a knee in his back, undid Jock's own belt and strapped his arms together behind him before Jock's eyes had uncrossed.

Grabbing a bottle of ale off a table as he went, Carey propelled Jock in front of him by the neck of his jerkin. Behind him there was a thundering on the door.

Carey dropped Jock on the floor and put a bench on top of him, then shoved one of the tables up against the door. Somebody let off a gun outside, and splinters flew from a shot hole, followed by shrieking.

'Halfwits,' muttered Carey, looking about for weapons. There were no firearms but there was a longbow with a couple of quivers of arrows hanging on the wall by the door, so he grabbed them gratefully, picked up the struggling Jock and clamped his arm round the man's neck.

Bothwell was shouting orders, Scott of Harden was shouting orders, Wattie Graham was shouting at them not to burn his bloody tower. There was a double thud of shoulders against the iron-bound door, which had been designed to withstand battering rams.

Jock was going blue, so Carey let him breathe for a moment.

'Now Jock,' he said, 'I'm sorry to do this to you, but you're my hostage.'

Jock struggled feebly at the indignity, so Carey cut off his air again and half-dragged him up the spiral stair to the next floor. An iron barred gate was pegged open there, so Carey unpegged it one-handed and it clanged shut, having been recently oiled. He didn't have the key to the lock but he managed to jam it with a chest standing in the corner.

Jock was thrashing about under his arm again, so Carey squeezed until the man's eyes crossed. He could hear a lot more shouting outside. It seemed Wattie Graham was still objecting to his door being bashed in.

'I don't want to kill you,' he said reasonably, panting a little as he hauled Jock up the next flight of stairs and past the next iron gate.

Something moved in the corner of his eye: he ducked his head and held his hostage up as a shield and the swinging bolt of wood landed on Jock's skull not Carey's. Carey dropped him and the longbow, dived sideways, glimpsed Alison Graham in a whirl of skirts with a club in one hand and a dagger in the other, her eyes wild.

He charged into her with his shoulder, knocked her against the wall so the breath came out of her, still got a glancing blow about the head with the club and pricked in his arm by the dagger, tried a knee in her groin to no effect and then punched her stomach and bruised his knuckles on her whalebone stays. Christ, where weren't women naturally armoured? No help for it. He punched her on the mouth, and she finally went down, bleeding badly. Please God, he hadn't killed her. No, she was breathing. One of her teeth looked crooked, which was fine since he'd taken the skin off his knuckles on them. He found the bunch of keys on her belt, ripped them off, picked her up under the armpits—Jesus, the weight of her—and hauled her into the linen room where she had been at some wifely pursuit. He locked the door on her, turned back to Jock and found him still googly-eyed from Mrs Graham's blow.

Gasping for breath he shut the gate, tried six of the massive bunch of keys and at last found the one that locked it. He turned and looked for the final flight of stairs up to the roof. There was no staircase, spiral or otherwise, just a ladder at the end of a passage. He could think of only one possible way he could get Jock and himself up there. He choked Jock off again to make sure, trapped his head with a bench from one of the rooms, climbed the ladder and heaved the trapdoor up. Blinking at the sunlight on the roof, he put down the longbow which was miraculously unbroken, the bottle and the two quivers, only half of whose arrows had fallen out. Then he went down the ladder again, heard a deep ominous boom from all the way downstairs. Clearly Bothwell had prevailed on Wattie Graham to let his tower be broken into. Carey picked up Jock by the front of his red velvet doublet. At least he was still stunned.

A treacherous voice inside said perhaps he didn't need Jock of the Peartree on top of his other troubles, and another voice said it was too late now and he might as well be hanged for a sheep.

'Right,' he said more to himself for encouragement, than to Jock who couldn't hear yet, 'you're coming with me.'

He slid Jock up to a sitting position, got hold of his shoulders and hefted Jock onto his back with his legs hanging down in front. There was about thirteen stone of solid muscle and bone to the man and it took two heaves for Carey to stagger to his feet. The ladder looked as if it stretched halfway to the moon.

He climbed one tread at a time, gasping through his teeth, with the sweat making a marsh of his shirt. Halfway up, Jock came to and started to struggle and swear: they swayed dangerously and the ladder creaked.

'STAY STILL!' roared Carey. 'Or I'll dump you on your head.'

Jock threshed once more, then saw how far they were from the floor and stayed still. Carey went the rest of the way up the ladder, heaved Jock onto the roof.

He kicked Jock in the stomach again to slow him down, turned, pulled up the ladder with his abused arm muscles shrieking at him, heaved the trapdoor into its hole and bolted it, then sat with his back against the parapet and waited until he had stopped crowing for breath and the spots had gone from his vision.

Jock glared at him, sprawled like a trussed chicken on the roof flags, bleeding from his nose and a nasty lump on his head.

'That's better,' said Carey and coughed. He didn't think he'd ruptured anything, which was a miracle. His heartbeat seemed to be slowing at last. 'Now we can talk, Jock.'

## FRIDAY, 23RD JUNE, LATE MORNING

It so happened that Will the Tod Armstrong was out in the horse paddock of his tower with a young horse that he was breaking on the lungeing rein. His youngest grandson was watching admiringly from the gate. Dodd came at a fast jog trot to the fence, ducked under it and walked up close to his father-in-law, who took one look at his battered sweaty face and became serious.

'Is Janet all right?' he asked at once. 'Where's the raid?'

Never mind Janet, Dodd thought, what about me, I'm half dead of thirst.

'Sit down, rest yourself. What happened to your horse? Did ye come on foot from Carlisle, ay well, ye're young. Little Will, run down to the house and bring back some beer for your uncle. No, you may not ride the horse, use your legs.'

Both Dodd's calves chose that moment to start cramping. He swore and tried rubbing them.

'Walk about a bit,' advised Will the Tod, 'I mind I ran twenty miles to fetch Kinmont's father once when I was a lad, and if ye stop too suddenly, ye cramp.'

Twenty miles, was it? thought Dodd bitterly, ay it would be. Nine and a half miles over rough country and mostly uphill in much less than two hours, and Will the Tod will have done twice that in half the time in his youth.

'Well, what's the news?'

Dodd told him. Will the Tod found the whole thing hilariously funny. His broad red face under its grey-streaked bush of red hair shone with the joke, he slapped his knee, he slapped Dodd's back, he slapped the fence.

'Ye ran from Carlisle to save the *Deputy Warden*?' hooted Will the Tod. 'Jesus save me. Why didn't ye run to fetch *his* dad? There's a man that has a quick way with a tower.'

'He never burnt yours,' Dodd pointed out. There were still bitter memories on the border of Lord Hunsdon's reprisals after the Rising of the Northern Earls.

'Only because I paid him.'

'He could have taken the money and still burnt you out.'

'Ay well, that's true. So his boy's in trouble, eh?'

Dodd explained, as patiently as he could, that he was.

'What do ye expect me to do about it?'

Dodd suggested, still patiently, that if he could really put sixty men in the saddle at an hour's notice as he'd boasted the last time they met, then he might give the Deputy Warden cause to be grateful to him. Not to mention pleasing his daughter Janet, who was in such a taking about the blasted man, it might have worried a husband less trusting than himself.

'Oh ay, call out my men for the Deputy Warden.' Will the Tod found that funny too. Dodd, who had blisters on both his feet and his shoulders, not to mention the damage he'd taken struggling through the secret passage, failed to see the joke. He waited for the bellowing stupid laugh to stop and then said, 'Well, sir, if ye've come over to loving Richard Lowther in your old age, I'll be on my way to the Dodds at Gilsland.'

Will the Tod's laugh stopped in mid-chuckle. He glowered at his son-in-law.

'Lowther's the man the old lord Warden would have made Deputy Warden. Carey's the young Lord Scrope's friend,' explained Dodd through his teeth. 'Carey may be a fool of a courtier who's too big for his boots, but he's not Lowther. According to Janet he snuck into Netherby to try and steal back our reived horses because he knew a proper hot trod would be cut to pieces. Now Lowther's let out some raiders Carey took that can identify him to Bothwell, who'll likely string him up.'

At least Will the Tod was listening. He nodded and Dodd continued.

'Lowther doesna want to lose his hold over the West March and Carey's bent on taking the power from him. If he can get Carey killed it'll clear the way for him and we'll have him back in the saddle, taking blackrent off us, favouring his kin and bringing in the Grahams and the Johnstones and the Elliots every time any one of us dares to make a squeak about it. There'll be nae chance of justice in this March with Carey gone, believe me. But as it seems ye've made your peace with the Lowthers...'

Will the Tod's face darkened. 'Make peace with the Lowthers? Never!' he growled. 'You're saying, if I bring out my men and save Carey's skin as you ask, we'll stop Richard Lowther from becoming Deputy Warden under the new lord?'

'Ay sir,' said Dodd, 'that's what I've been saying. For the moment, anyway, seeing how well Lowther's dug in.'

Will the Tod clapped Dodd on his back. 'I like you, Henry,' he said expansively, 'ye think well.'

'It's your daughter's plan,' Dodd muttered.

'Of course it is, but you've the sense to see the sense in it.'

And I did all the bloody running and crawling through shit pipes, Dodd thought, but didn't say. Will the Tod stared into space for a moment, and then rubbed his hands together.

'Off ye go, Dodd,' he said, 'up to the tower and ring the bell. I'll have a horse saddled up for you when ye come back.'

Run up there, thought Dodd, despairingly.

'Get on, lad, we havenae got all day. Ye dinna want to get to Netherby and find your man swinging in the breeze.'

It was hard going up to the tower now he'd lost the rhythm, but he wasn't going to give Will the Tod any opportunity to tell him more tales of notable runs by Will the Tod in his youth. It half killed him but he gasped his way up the bank, almost fell through the door, found the rope to the bell and started ringing it.

Perhaps he rang it for longer than he need have done, but when he came back down the hill to the house where Will the Tod normally lived, he saw the sight that still lifted his heart no matter how often it happened: the men were coming in at the run from the fields, the women were rushing from their work to the horse paddock to round up the horses—thank God Will the Tod had not been raided by the Grahams, even if he wasn't respectable enough to lend horses to Scrope—and some of the boys were already coming out of the stables with the saddles and bridles, the jacks and helmets.

Will the Tod was standing on a high mounting stone, his thumbs in his broad belt, yelling orders as his family ran purposefully past him in all directions. His second wife, the pretty, nervous little creature whose name Dodd could never remember, came running up with a large ugly gelding snorting behind her and then Will the Tod was in the saddle, closely followed by his five sons, two of his sons-in-law, four nearly grown grandsons, and fifteen assorted cousins already riding in with their families from their own farms nearby.

Henry was brought a large Roman-nosed mare he remembered as having an evil temper at odds with her name, which was Rosy, and he mounted up with relief. If God had meant men to run around the countryside he wouldn't have provided them with horses.

'Off you go then, Henry,' shouted Will the Tod, waving his lance. 'Rouse out the Dodds.'

Dodd brought Rosy up alongside Will the Tod, who was letting his mount sidestep and paw the air and roaring with laughter at his surname crowding up around him, all asking where was the raid and whose cows were gone, and how big was it, to be out in daylight? Rosy tried to nip Will the Tod's leg.

'Wait,' Dodd said, hauling on the reins, 'we've got Netherby to crack. Where will we meet?'

'Longtownmoor meeting stone,' said Will the Tod, 'where we always meet when we're hitting Liddesdale, ye know that Henry. Shall I send to Kinmont?'

'Send to anybody ye can think of that would like to see Lowther's nose rubbed in the shite.'

'Och God, there'd be no room for them all. I'll just send to the ones that werena burnt out of house and home by your young Deputy's father in '69, eh?'

Dodd nodded impatiently, set his heels to the horse's flank, and headed on up the road for Gilsland after a sharp tussle with Rosy's contrariness, which he won. Behind him Will the Tod stood up in his stirrups and addressed his immediate surname in a bellow. Dodd knew when he explained the Deputy Warden's problem because the laughter rolled after him over the hill like the breaker of a sea.

It occurred to him that perhaps Carey would have preferred to hang rather than be rescued from Bothwell's clutches in quite this way.

## FRIDAY, 23RD JUNE, NOON

Netherby tower was roofed with stone against fire and had a narrow fighting parapet running round it behind the battlements. In the south-east corner was the beacon, a large blackened metal basket raised up on a ten-foot pole with a pile of firewood faggots under tarpaulin at the base. Carey cleared the wood away and tied Jock of the Peartree to the pole in a sitting position, using the rope binding the faggots. The firewood he piled as makeshift barricades across the parapet by the trapdoor.

Every so often he would poke his head over the wall and shoot an arrow at the men with the battering ram, so they'd run for cover. Way down below him, he could see Bothwell, his brocade doublet shining in the sun, foreshortened like a chessman, waving his arms and shouting more orders. He popped his head over and dropped one of the stones kept ready for sieges, close enough to the Earl to make him dive for cover.

Arrows came sailing over and clattered harmlessly onto the roof. That roof could have done with some attention, Carey thought, much of the mortar around the stones was cracked and rotten. On a sudden inspiration, he heaved up a couple of the loosest stones and dragged them over to the trapdoor, piled them on top.

'Who the hell are ye?' demanded Jock.

Carey told him.

Jock mulled it over for a bit, then growled: 'Ye'll never get out of this.'

'I don't know. I've got you as a hostage. You're an important man,' said Carey, sitting down again and taking a sip of beer from the leather bottle. He wasn't too worried about thirst since there was a full rainwater butt at the north-western corner, set there to put out besiegers' fires. On the other hand, his belly was cramping him.

Jock spat. 'D'ye think the Earl willna shoot to save my skin?'

'No,' said Carey agreeably, 'I think with the mood he's in, he'd perfectly happily shoot through you to get me, but Wattie's your brother...'

'They must be aye sentimental in the south,' sniffed Jock, 'Wattie'd shoot as well.'

'Well, I suppose, so would John,' admitted Carey, thinking of his pompous whingeing elder brother in a similar situation. 'Still, he might hesitate. His aim might be off. He might even talk to me, negotiate some arrangement.'

'Are ye hoping for ransom?' demanded Jock of the Peartree.

'No. I hadn't thought about it.'

Jock laughed shortly.

'There's no other way ye'll get off this tower still breathing, lad, so ye'd best think about it now and right hard.'

It was in fact perfectly true that Carey had no idea how he was going to get off the top of Netherby tower in one piece. When he came to Netherby he had had a vague plan that involved stealing the Dodd and Widdrington horses quietly early in the morning as soon as he knew where Bothwell was planning to raid and making off back to Carlisle as fast as one of them could carry him. Once that was no longer possible, thanks to Lowther's machinations, he had simply reacted according to instinct.

'What do you think I'm worth on the hoof?' Carey asked after a pause.

'Everyone knows Scrope's a rich man. A thousand pounds, perhaps,' said Jock consideringly. Carey whistled.

'He might not pay that much.'

Jock clearly regarded this as a feeble attempt at bargaining.

'Well, if ye're Lord Hunsdon's son, he'll stump up for you. Of course, first ye've got to get yon Earl to talk civilly to ye, and that might take a while.'

'He is very upset. What are my chances?'

'It's always possible,' Jock allowed, 'a one-legged donkey with spavins could win the Carlisle horserace, but I wouldnae put my shirt on it.'

'I think you're a bit of an optimist, Jock,' said Carey drily.

Jock laughed again, then winced. 'Ye could loosen my arms a bit,' he suggested, 'I canna feel my hands.'

Carey leaned over cautiously and felt one of the hands. It was a little swollen, but not too bad.

'No,' he said, 'I've got too much respect for you, Jock. I don't want to waste all the care I had of you if you take it in your head to jump off the top of the tower.'

'I think it's you'll be making the jump from a high place in the end.'

'No,' said Carey, leaning his head back and feeling very tired, 'he won't hang me.' Jock looked dubious. 'That'd be too quick for Bothwell.'

Jock grunted. 'I never said he'd hang you first. That'd be after he'd skelped and roasted you. And I'll be first in with the whip, believe me.'

Carey had his eyes half-shut. 'Oh, I believe you, Jock. And yet, you know, one reason I came here was so I could find out who killed Sweetmilk.'

Jock's face changed. The long craggy canyons in it deepened, the mouth lengthened, and his chin fell on his chest.

'Poor Sweetmilk,' he said, 'he was such a bonny wee bairn, running after me and laughing.' Jock's chin quivered, then hardened again. 'Anyway, what do ye care, Deputy, he's one less Graham you've got to chase over the Bewcastle waste.'

Carey thought of trying to explain the idea of an impartial law enforcement officer, as interested in the wanton killing of Grahams as in cattle raids and suchlike, but decided it would take too long.

'I don't want you blaming Dodd,' he said at last, 'and I'm puzzled about it.'

'What's to puzzle about, the lad was shot in the back.'

Carey shook his head. 'You wouldn't be interested, it was only a theory of mine.'

## FRIDAY, 23RD JUNE, EARLY AFTERNOON

Jock was watching the bottle as Carey drank from it, too stiff-necked to admit he needed a drink. Carey found one of the rags for lighting the beacon, went to the rainbutt to wet it and came back to Jock. He held the bottle for Jock to drink, then mopped the dried blood off Jock's face with the rag. Jock tolerated this in grim silence. On a thought Carey went back to the rainbutt, found two buckets there, filled both of them and brought them to where he was sitting with Jock.

'Does Netherby have any long ladders about?' he asked.

'I hope so.'

Carey peered over the parapet again, saw somebody with an arquebus taking aim and ducked down just in time. The crack sounded in the distance, but the bullet didn't even splinter the wall. He picked up one of the buckets and poured it over the side, producing a yell of anger from below, then went and refilled it.

The next time the men with the battering ram from the log pile backed up, Carey shot at them with one of their own arrows. Three more came sailing over the wall, before Bothwell yelled for them to stop.

'Why did you do this?' asked Jock.

'A number of reasons,' Carey said. 'Firstly, I wanted to know what Bothwell needed all the horses in the West March for.'

'Och, that's easy. I'll tell you, since you're going nae further with it. We're running a big raid deep into Scotland, to Falkland Palace, to lift the King and hold him to ransom for a big pot of gold. It's about two hundred miles, so we've all needed remounts.'

Carey breathed cautiously. 'Right,' he said, 'you're kidnapping King James.'

'Ay,' said Jock. 'Bothwell says he's worth the Kingdom if we can get him.'

'Right,' said Carey again. 'Of course, Bothwell tried before at Holyrood and he didn't manage it. That's why he's an outlaw.'

'He didna have us with him.'

'No. Don't you think somebody might notice, a big pack of Border raiders riding into Scotland like that? Don't you think they might take it into their heads to warn the King?'

'Not if we ride fast enough and keep to the waste ground.'

'And there are the horses, of course.'

'Eh? Oh ay, we've got enough horses now. We'll be off tomorrow.'

'Is that so?' Carey's voice was carefully casual. 'No, I didn't mean the little nags you've been reiving. I meant the King's horses. But I suppose you're not interested in them.'

'No,' said Jock, 'we're not. It's the King we're reiving.'

'Right.'

'What theory?' demanded Jock.

'Eh?'

'What theory were ye talking about before? Your theory concerning Sweetmilk.'

'You wouldn't be interested.'

'How the Devil do you know that if ye won't tell me what it is?'

Carey peeked over again, saw Bothwell, shot at him, missed and ducked down again as two more arquebuses cracked down below.

'I suppose the nearest cannon are in Carlisle?'

'Of course they are,' said Jock, 'unless your friend Lowther's bringing one up here.'

'No, he wouldn't have any powder for it.'

'Is that a fact?'

'You know it as well as I do. In fact, I'll bet the powder they're shooting at us with is Carlisle's finest.'

Jock grunted. 'It's no' very good quality,' he complained, 'and he charges something shocking for it. What theory?'

Carey sat down facing Jock, with his knees drawn up, examined the skinned knuckles on his right hand and flexed them. He hated punching people in the face, it always hurt your hand so much.

'Did you ever hear of a man called Sir Francis Walsingham, Jock?'

Jock nodded. 'Ay, the Queen's Secretary. Sir John Forster in the Middle March did him a good turn, oh, ten, twelve years ago.'

'I know. He's dead now, but I was on an embassy with him to Scotland in the summer of '83, it was the first time I went to King James's Court.'

'What did you think of it?'

'It was well enough so long as I kept my arse to the wall and a table between me and the King.'

Jock laughed. 'Took a fancy to ye, did he?'

Carey coughed and looked down. 'You could say that.'

'Jesus, man, what are ye doing here? Your fortune's made.'

Carey shook his head. 'I couldn't do it. In fact I damn near puked in his lap when I finally worked out what it was he wanted.'

Jock found that very funny. 'What did Sir Francis think of it?'

'He was a strange man, you know, Jock. I've met my fair share of puritans, and most of them are hypocrites, but he was not. He was an utterly upright man. He worked night and day to keep the Queen safe, though he hated the thought of obeying a woman...'

'Small blame to him,' said Jock, 'it's unnatural.'

Carey thought of the iron grip most border women seemed to have on their menfolk, but didn't say anything. He peered over the parapet and saw Bothwell and Wattie and the other men gathered together talking, while Old Wat of Harden walked up and down. To keep them on their toes he shot a couple of arrows at them. They scattered and dived for cover satisfactorily.

'When I told him what the King wanted from me, he saw to it that I was never alone with him again without it seeming he was doing it, if you follow. And I never knew him to take a bribe.'

'What, never?'

'Never. When he died his estate was gone and he was deep in debt.'

'Why was he at Court then, if he didna take bribes?'

Carey shrugged. 'To serve the Queen, he said, because she was the best hope for the True Religion against Papistry. To his mind it was immoral to take money for giving her advice he knew was bad, and immoral to take money for giving advice he would give anyway.'

'What's your point?'

'He always told me that truth belonged to God, it was sacred. Every lie, every injustice was an offence to God because it was an offence against truth. The stock of truth in this life is limited like gold, and every time you can dig out a little more of it from the mud and the clay of lies, you bring a little more of God's Grace into the world.'

'It's a fine poetical sentiment,' said Jock consideringly, 'but aye impractical.'

'He believed also, that like gold, truth was incorruptible and would always leave traces. And if you were prepared to dig and scrape a bit, you could find out the truth of anything.'

'What's this got to do with Sweetmilk?'

'Somebody murdered him and got away with it. To me, that's an offence against justice.'

'Justice, truth. What are we doing up here, lad, we should be in church.'

Carey ignored him. 'It happened I got a good look at his body and I went to see the place where Dodd found it. It was all very odd.'

'Why?'

'The shooting for a start. There were powder burns all over the back of his jack, no sign of a struggle. That gives you a bit of truth right there.'

Jock swallowed and blinked at the sky. 'Why?' he rasped. 'It was a quick death, so?'

Carey shook his head. 'It was more than that. The dag that killed him must have been right up behind him, close, perhaps less than a foot away. Would you let your enemy get so close to you with a loaded dag?'

Jock thought about it. 'I wouldnae,' he said finally, 'if he's that close, you've a chance of knocking it away or hitting him before the gun can fire, and if he's waving a dag at ye, it's worth a try because he's going to kill ye anyway.'

'Precisely,' said Carey pedantically, 'no gun ever fires instantly: if it's got a powder pan, the flash has to go down into the gun, if it's got a lock, the mechanism has to unwind to make the sparks. Sweetmilk knew that as well as anybody.'

Jock nodded slowly. 'Ye're saying, he let whoever killed him come up close because he wasnae an enemy, he was a friend.'

'Exactly. Or at least someone he knew and had no reason to fear right then.'

Jock nodded again. 'Go on, Courtier.'

Carey peered over the parapet again and saw men hurrying about with lighted torches and faggots of wood. He shot at them, and got one through the leg. He stayed there with his bow, wishing he was a better shot, peering over the parapet and trying to think himself into Bothwell's mind.

'He'd been robbed by the time we got the body.'

'Yes, that was one of Dodd's men. I have the jewels and rings in Carlisle and I'll send them back to you when I can.' He coughed. 'If I can.'

'Wasna robbed, eh? He was wearing some good stuff.'

'I know. So why was he killed? It wasn't a fight, it wasn't to steal his jewels, or even his horse.'

'Ah, the horse. I should have known the beauty would be trouble.'

'There's a reason why I don't think he was killed for the horse, but I'll come to it. The next point is where the killer left the body. Solway Moss, in a gorse bush.'

'Maybe that's where he was killed?'

Whatever else he was, Jock was not stupid. 'The man didna know of a better place or couldna reach it in the time,' he said. 'He's a stranger to this country.'

'And Daniel Swanders saw someone when he stole Caspar,' said Carey. 'He saw a man in a rich doublet, cleaning a jack, and what's more, the man didn't chase after him either so Caspar wasn't the reason for the...'

'A rich doublet,' repeated Jock.

'So,' said Carey, counting off on his fingers in a way he had picked up wholesale from Walsingham, 'we have signs and portents of the murderer. He was well-known to Sweetmilk so he could get up close behind him with a loaded dag, he was rich, he was a stranger to these parts...'

'Good God Almighty,' said Jock, putting his head back against the wooden post, 'I've been sitting down to eat with my son's killer for this past week.'

'It has to be, doesn't it?' said Carey. 'It has to be the Earl or one of his men.'

'But why...?'

'I don't know,' said Carey, but he couldn't hide the expression on his face well enough for Jock.

'Ye do know.'

'I don't.'

'Ay, ye do,' said Jock, 'and ye'll tell it me, if you've gone this far.' He laughed mirthlessly. 'Who knows, it could even get you out of this alive.'

'Don't lie to me, Jock.'

'Well, it could get you a quicker death, any road. Come on.'

'Whoever killed Sweetmilk is the father of your daughter Mary's bairn.'

'Her *what*?' Jock's eyes were glaring with fury and he struggled against the ropes holding him. 'WHAT did you say?'

'Your daughter Mary is expecting a babe around Christmas time. Bothwell, or one of his men, is the father.' Jock's face was swollen, he seemed to be choking. Carey, who knew perfectly well he was talking for his life, but was a natural gambler, carried on remorselessly. 'My thinking is that Sweetmilk found out what had happened to his sister, and challenged the man to a duel. They went off away from Carlisle to fight it out, so Mary wouldn't be shamed by it, and while they were on their way, the man came up behind Sweetmilk when he wasn't expecting it, and shot him. Then he abandoned him at the only place he could think of and came back.'

There were tears flowing down Jock's crusty face. 'God damn him, God damn him to hell, poor Sweetmilk, I'll skelp the little bitch, I'll...'

'You'll marry her off quickly is what you'll do. I think she might have been forced.'

'What do you know about it?'

'I've talked to her and I don't think she was willing.' Carey, knowing what he did of the Queen's maids of honour, thought she'd probably been perfectly willing at the time, but felt sorry for her. 'At best, he persuaded her against her better judgement. At worst he raped her.'

'God, so that's what's been ailing her. Why didn't she tell me when Sweetmilk was killed?'

'Afraid of you. Afraid of the man, perhaps he threatened her. Perhaps she still had a liking for him. Who knows?'

Jock shook his head, snorted violently against his running nose. 'How can I find the man?'

'Well, I've done a lot of the work,' said Carey reasonably, 'I've narrowed it down from most of the population of the March to Bothwell or one of his men. And I hate to admit it, but I don't think it was Bothwell either.'

'Why not?'

'Mary said she wouldn't marry the father *if* he was the Earl himself, so I think he wasn't. It's not that Bothwell wouldn't do it, but I don't think he did on this occasion. So you've got three or four possible murderers to choose from.'

'I suppose it would be wasteful to shoot all of them and be done with it,' said Jock thoughtfully. 'And it might be a little tickle to do at that. So, how do I find out which one to kill?'

'Who was at Netherby on the Saturday? Who did Sweetmilk ride out with? Who came back?'

'Ah,' said Jock, wriggling his shoulders against the wood. 'Let me think.' If his arms were cramping him, he didn't say anything about it, and Carey wouldn't have risked untying him anyway. He was a grizzled old bastard and tough as doornails, he could suffer.

Carey's belly started rumbling again. It was dinner time and nothing to eat but raw pigeon squabs from the little dovecote on the south-western corner. Well, he wasn't that hungry yet. Or perhaps he could light a little fire with the materials for the beacon and roast them.

There was a stealthy clatter on the other side of the roof. Jock didn't seem to have heard, but Carey knew if he'd been a horse, his ears would have swivelled.

He picked up one of the long hardwood poles used for poking the beacon and crept round to the opposite parapet. When he peered over, he saw that the ladder they were trying to use was too short, but that the man climbing it had a caliver under his arm, with the slowmatch lit.

'Halfwits,' said Carey again, under his breath, 'haven't any of you heard of Pythagoras?'

Very carefully, while the man was still halfway up, he reached with his pole over the wall, hooked it into the top rung of the ladder and pushed. There was a scream, a bang from the caliver, a loud crash and clatter. Carey went back to where Jock was and offered him some water, which Jock drank. Neither of them commented on the ladder.

'Ye canna win,' said Jock, 'ye canna hold out indefinitely. Sooner or later ye must sleep.'

'Oh, it'll be quicker than that,' said Carey, 'sooner or later they'll work out how to do it.'

'And how's that?' demanded Jock.

Carey shook his head. 'Besieging's a science, and I'm not going to give you lessons.'

'You mean they'll burn ye out.'

'Us. They'll burn us out. It's probably only Wattie's objections that's stopping them now.'

Jock turned his face away. 'What's making ye so cheerful? It's only a matter of time before you die.'

Carey couldn't really explain it. He knew perfectly well he'd got himself into a ridiculous situation; that his scheme for finding out what was going on in Netherby had perhaps not been one of his best, and that while Elizabeth might be wondering where he'd got to, there was very little she could do for him. Somehow, with the sun shining down on him and the sight he had of Liddesdale valley glowering to the north, sitting talking to a trussed-up Jock of the Peartree was almost pleasant.

'Well,' he said after he'd wandered round the parapet looking for activity down below and seeing nothing, which would have worried him if he'd been a worrying man, 'maybe we can narrow it down even more. Tell me what happened here on Saturday.'

'Now then. A couple of the women went down to Carlisle to buy oatmeal, but they were back by noon. That was when Mary fell and hurt her hand. And I'd sent Sweetmilk, and Bothwell sent two of his men, Jock Hepburn and Geordie Irwin of Bonshaw, to Carlisle to see if they could scout out who had horses and where they were, and buy a few if they saw some cheap. Sweetmilk was in a taking with something that morning, but he wouldna tell me what it was, so I thought it was some girl or other—it usually is, was.' Jock swallowed. 'I said he should take Caspar, which the Earl of Bothwell had brought to me as a fee, in case Scrope was interested in buying him and also to...er...so people could admire him, ye know. So they'd send me their mares.'

Jock wriggled again. 'That's the last time I saw him alive.'

'So it's Geordie Irwin of Bonshaw, or Jock Hepburn. Or the Earl.'

'Unless he met somebody at Carlisle, of course. I mind that the Affleck boy, not Robert, he's dead, but his younger brother, Ian, he didn't come here until early Sunday.'

'Well it couldn't be him, could it, if I'm right about Mary.'

'Oh ay. So it's Geordie Irwin or Jock Hepburn.'

'Well?'

'Well what?'

'Which do you think it is?'

'Och, lad, it could be any of them, they're a' bastards. And I'm not convinced it wasna the Earl; he's allus had an eye for women that one, and Mary's a bonny little girl. He wasnae in Netherby on the Saturday either, and I dinna ken where he was.'

'What's he got against King James?' asked Carey after a moment.

'The Earl?' Jock laughed shortly. 'I think he had a similar problem wi' the King to yours. Only he took it harder.'

'And what are his plans if he captures the King?'

'Och, I think it's the Earl of Bothwell for Lord Chancellor and Chamberlain, and Chancellor Robert Melville and his brother for the block. After that...' Jock shrugged as far as he could. 'I dinna think he knows himself.'

'Do you think he will—capture the King, I mean?'

Jock looked at him thoughtfully. 'Why? What do ye care?'

'Curious. Come on now, I can hardly warn his perverted Majesty from here, can I?'

'I think he's got a verra good chance of it, with us and with...' Jock shook his head. '...with his other advantages.'

An inside job, thought Carey instantly, there are men at the Scottish Court who will help the Earl. Lord above, what am I supposed to do about this? What can I do?

'And of course there are the horses,' said Carey, pursuing a line he had started earlier.

'Ay, ye mentioned them. What horses?'

'Falkland Palace is a hunting lodge. I've been there, the stables are enormous.'

'Oh ay?' Jock was pretending indifference, but Carey knew how passionate the Borderers were for horseflesh.

'The King keeps most of his horses there so they're ready for him to ride when he takes a fancy to go hunting.'

'What are they like then?'

'Well,' said Carey consideringly, 'Caspar wouldn't stand out among them.'

'No?' Jock didn't believe him.

Carey shook his head. 'King James is very particular about his mounts and he has them brought in from France by sea. They're the best horses in Scotland, and perhaps even England too.'

'Oh?' Jock was struggling with himself internally. Pride lost and curiosity won out. 'How many are there?'

'About six hundred.'

'*What?*'

'It could be more.'

'What's the King want with six hundred horses?'

'Not all of them are his, a lot belong to the people at Court. But that's the nearest number, I'd say.'

'Jesus,' said Jock, and Carey could almost see the thoughts whirling past each other in his brain. Clearly Bothwell had neglected to mention the living treasure trove at Falkland: far more valuable than gold to Borderers, because horses could run. Jock coughed and shifted his legs a little. 'Would ye happen to know if they're heavily guarded?'

'Not very heavily.'

Jock was suspicious again. 'Why not? Are they hobbled?'

'No, they're not hobbled. In fact, during the summer most of them are out in the horse paddocks round about the Palace.'

'Not inside a barnekin?'

'There'd be no room for a herd that size.'

'Why aren't they guarded?'

'Jock,' said Carey sadly, 'you wouldn't understand if I tried to explain to you what a law-abiding country is like, so I won't try. They're not guarded because no one thereabouts is likely to steal them.'

Jock snorted disbelievingly.

'Does Bothwell know about these horses?'

'Of course he does, he's been at Court, same as I have. I expect he didn't want you distracted from King James.'

'No,' said Jock, a little uncertainly, 'he's nothing to worry about anyway. We're going to reive the King out from under the noses of his bad counsellors.'

'Of course,' said Carey, 'and I know you don't care about a charge of High Treason…'

Jock's eyes narrowed.

'Well, that's what it is, isn't it?' said Carey. 'You live on the

Scottish side of the line. If you go out in arms against the King, it's High Treason.'

'We're rescuing him from bad counsellors,' insisted Jock.

'He's agreed to be rescued, has he? Rescued by Bothwell, I mean, whom he hates because he thinks the Earl's King of the Scottish Witches. He knows all about this scheme, does he?'

'Are ye trying to turn me against the raid?'

Carey leaned forward. 'Listen Jock,' he said, making sure he stayed out of head-butting distance, 'I don't give a turd what you do. If you want to make an enemy of the King—who has a very long memory, by the way, and has been kidnapped before—that's entirely your affair. If the raid goes wrong somehow, and the King comes out to Jedburgh with blood in his eye and an army behind him to hunt down the Grahams and wipe them off the face of the earth, that's nothing but good news to me, alive or dead. If you want to pass up the chance of reiving six hundred of the best horses in Scotland in favour of Bothwell's lunatic scheme, I'm not the one to stop you. I just hate to see a man put his head in a noose without knowing the full story.'

Jock grunted. There was silence from him, so Carey made another circuit of the parapet. Below he could see smoke and flames licking from near the door. He took the bow from his shoulder, nocked an arrow and waited. Sure enough, six men holding bucklers over their heads appeared from one of the sheds nearby with a battering ram between them, and charged at the door. He shot off four arrows, but they bounced off the shields and after two attempts there was a splintering crash and a chorus of cheers as the door finally gave way.

He went back to Jock, who was staring into space, looking very thoughtful.

'They're into the tower,' said Carey. Jock said nothing. Thuds and bangs and a screech of metal below, feet pounding up the stairs, another outburst of clanging and crashing.

In his mind's eye Carey could see the scene one floor below. They'd have released Alison Graham and yes, there was wailing and Wattie yelling threats up through the trapdoor.

He'd been calm before, talking to Jock to keep his mind off what was happening. Now his mouth was dry again and his stomach clenched into a knot. He was no longer hungry.

'Carey,' said Jock.

'Hm?' His eye had caught movement over on the hills to the east, a glitter of spears, movement of men. Had the Grahams brought in more of their men to help retake Netherby?

'Do ye think the Earl knew what happened with Sweetmilk?'

Carey shrugged. 'I've no idea. He might, he might not. Whichever it is, he won't have told you, you know that.'

Jock nodded.

'Would ye agree to be ransomed?'

'I thought you said there'd be no chance...'

'I'll pledge for ye. Well?'

Carey laughed, a little desperately. 'I've never been ransomed before, but yes.'

'He'll likely chain ye up in the dungeon until your family's paid up. It's no' a very nice place.'

Carey licked his lips. The whole thing was a disaster. Then he shrugged. 'Better than hanging though.'

'Untie me then,' said Jock. Carey hesitated. 'Come on, man, ye havenae got all day.'

Men with bucklers over their head were trotting in and out of the tower carrying turves and faggots of wood.

Carey undid the ropes holding Jock to the beacon post, but left his hands strapped behind him. He drew his dagger and put it to Jock's neck, then let Jock go over to the trapdoor.

'Ye're still alive,' said the Earl's voice.

'Ay, of course I'm still alive, if I was dead, I wouldna be speaking to ye, now would I?' snarled Jock.

'What a diplomat,' muttered Carey.

'Shut up, ye. *Bothwell.*'

'What do you want, Jock?'

'The Deputy Warden will surrender himself to me if ye'll ransom him after the raid and he'll not talk about it after.' Jock glowered at Carey, daring him to disagree. Carey felt his shoulders sag, but nodded.

'How much?'

'A thousand pounds, English.'

'No.'

'And why the hell not?'

'I'll have him in half an hour anyway, why should I negotiate? You're getting soft, Jock.'

Jock made a face, shrugged his shoulders. Carey hadn't really expected Bothwell to say yes, but his stomach squeezed itself up tighter under his breastbone. He tried to avoid wondering what Bothwell would do to him before he was hanged. Maybe not. Maybe the Earl would ransom him anyway.

'He's worth more alive than dead, Bothwell,' said Jock.

'I'll be rich enough after the raid,' said Bothwell, 'and so will ye, if ye can live through the next hour.'

There were a couple of echoing cracks from below as Bothwell tried to shoot the trapdoor away.

'It's nae good,' shouted Jock, 'he's put stones over the hole. Have ye got gunpowder?'

'Jock!' said Carey protestingly.

'My arms are killing me, Carey, let's get this bloody farce over with.'

'I'm in no hurry.'

There was a sound of crackling and tendrils of smoke started coming up through the cracks around the trapdoor and the holes in the roof. There were more of them than he'd thought, Carey noted, and the smoke was thick and black. Bothwell was using damp turves on top of the dry wood.

'Eh, Wattie must be in a rare mood,' said Jock, 'and Alison. She'd never let him burn us out if ye hadnae hit her.'

'I know,' said Carey.


## FRIDAY, 23RD JUNE, AFTERNOON


Dodd had split his force into three to come at Netherby from the south west, the south east and the east. Will the Tod took the road north from Longtown that passed beside the river Esk, his son Geordie came in from Dodd's tower at Gilsland with the Dodds but joined up with his own surname and went through Slackbraes wood and Cleughfoot Wood. The Dodds went over Slealandsburn and Oakshaw Hill and also passed through the eastern part of the Cleughfoot Wood that cupped itself around Netherby. They rode well spread out and caught four of the men that Bothwell had stationed to watch.

At Longtownmoor stone, Geordie, Will the Tod and Henry Dodd had agreed that as they didn't know exactly how many men Bothwell had or where they were, their best plan was to hit hard and fast, drive off his horses, capture Bothwell himself if they could and if they couldn't, to trap him in Netherby tower with as few of his men as possible and then negotiate.

The daylight made things difficult for them, experienced night raiders though they all were, since they would be visible further off and they had no torches to signal the onset with. After some argument, they agreed on horncalls when they were ready, which would warn Bothwell, but might confuse him as well, or so they hoped. It might make him think the Carlisle garrison had come out to rescue the Deputy Warden.

And so, being the last to get into position because of having to go over the hill, Dodd put his horn to his lips as soon as he sighted the tower through the trees, and then all three of the groups of men broke from the woods and galloped over fields and barley crops straight up to Netherby tower.

It seemed that Bothwell was distracted, though unfortunately most of his men were already in the barnekin. Geordie and his men got into the horsepaddocks where the vast numbers of horses were—Jesus, there must have been a couple of hundred at least—broke down the fences and drove the horses off into the wood, leaving two men dead behind them.

Will the Tod and Henry rode hard for the barnekin, aiming for the gate. Complete confusion broke out round the tower. Some of the Grahams turned away from what they were doing and shot at them with arquebuses, a couple of the women managed to free the gates. Six men ran outside to help shut the big main gate: there was a sharp fight with ten more who came out with lances to hold them off and then the gate was shut and barred and most of the Grahams outside either surrendered or legged it northwards for Liddesdale and the Debateable Land.

Dodd let them go, he was looking all about him. 'Can ye see the Deputy?' he yelled. 'Check the trees, where is he? Where's Bothwell?'

'DODD!' came a happy roar that was unmistakably Carey's voice—at least he could still shout. Where the devil was it coming from?

'DODD, I'M UP HERE ON THE ROOF.'

By God, so he was. Dodd squinted, shaded his eyes from the sun and saw a smutty wild figure waving his arms from the top of Netherby tower where the smoke was billowing in great black clouds. Some Graham down in the barnekin shot at him with a caliver at a hopeless range and he ducked down. In a moment he was up again.

Dodd sat back in the saddle and grinned.

'Och,' he said to Will the Tod who was beside him, 'they've got him treed.'

'That him?' asked Will the Tod curiously. 'Are ye sure?'

'Ay,' said Dodd, 'he doesnae normally look like that, he's generally a very smart man, almost a dandy. But ay, that's him, and he's given 'em a run for their money, if I'm any judge.'

'Wattie Graham must be ay annoyed at having to burn his own tower.'

'And he's got Jock of the Peartree.'

Will the Tod's face was split in the broadest of grins. 'Ay, it's a grand thought, Jock made a hostage by the Deputy Warden of Carlisle. That's worth the bother by itself. He's his father's son, true enough.'

'I thought ye didn't take to Lord Hunsdon.'

'Oh, I wouldna say that, he never burned me and he did burn a few of my enemies when I pointed them out to him. I've got nothing against the Careys, me.'

'Good,' said Dodd, 'but now we have to get the Deputy down from the tower.'

'It's a tickle situation, Henry. What's your plan?'

'Talk to Bothwell.'

'And if Bothwell willna talk?'

Dodd shrugged. 'Avenge Carey and give him a decent burial.'

'It'd be a pity.'

'Ay.'

'So now. I'm the English Armstrong headman, Henry, so I think it's fitting if I do the talking.'

Dodd opened his mouth to argue and then thought better of it. He nodded. Will the Tod looked pleased with himself.

'Hey, BOTHWELL!' he roared. 'Show your face, I want to talk to ye.'


# Friday, 23rd June, afternoon


Jock coughed hackingly. 'When will ye surrender?' he asked. Carey had hustled him back to the beacon post and tied him to it again. Hammering came from below—they must have brought in lances or long poles. Carey backed away from the trapdoor, behind the angle of the roof and his barricade of firewood. He counted out his arrows—he had five left—and laid them in a row in front of him, set his bow before him and waited. Counting the knives still in their scabbards on his wrist and at the back of his neck, he had seven shots at whoever poked his head through the trapdoor, before it was hand to hand.

'Why should I surrender if Bothwell won't ransom me?'

'Och, I'll protect ye, lad. Ye've talked me round wi' that smooth courtier's tongue of yours, I'll not let Bothwell harm ye, nor Wattie. Ye've my word on it.'

'Well,' said Carey, tempted against his will. A drift of smoke caught him and he coughed.

'Ye'll get us both killed. Ah can save ye, if ye let me lift up the trapdoor and talk to Bothwell. Ye can keep an arrow pointed at my back if ye like. There's no need to die.'

That was when Carey and Jock both heard the sound of horns, of hoofbeats, shouting, fighting, the creak and double thud of the barnekin gate. Carey ran to the eastern parapet, peered over, batting furiously at the smoke, and there was Sergeant Dodd, filthy, armed and triumphant, with something like eighty men about him. Carey shouted, waved his arms, shouted again. He'd never have thought he could be so delighted to see that miserable sullen bastard of a Sergeant.

Jock of the Peartree brought him back to reality.

'So the garrison's out,' he said dourly. 'It makes nae odds to ye, ye bloody fool. Bothwell's still going to have ye either by breaking in the trapdoor or he'll wait until the smoke kills ye. Me, I'd wait.'

Carey was coughing again: the smoke reeked and was making his eyes stream. He fanned the air uselessly.

'Us, Jock, you too. Still,' he said between hacks, 'we can negotiate a bit better because if he kills me, he'll have to fight Dodd and I don't think he wants to with his big raid due tomorrow. So why don't you try talking to him again, Jock?'

'Nay, I tried my best, it's a waste of breath now. Let Dodd and that fat Armstrong father-in-law of his do all the hard work.'

'Oh the hell with it,' he said, 'Jock, will you swear not to play me false if I let you free?'

'Ay,' wheezed Jock, 'I swear.'

Carey hesitated a moment longer, then went to him, cut the ropes that bound him and undid the belt still holding Jock's arms behind him. Jock whined a little with the pain of returning circulation, brought his arms round very slowly and flexed them. He turned to Carey.

'That was kindly of ye, Courtier,' said Jock grudgingly. 'Ah wouldnae have done that for ye in this situation.'

'No,' coughed Carey, 'I'm too soft, that's my problem. Get on the other side of the roof until it's over.'

'Ay,' Jock muttered, moving away, 'y'are soft an' all.'

There was a heavy thump on the trapdoor. Carey watched through tears and coughing. They must have lit a fire right under it, they weren't about to waste gunpowder when fire would work as well even if it was slower. Once the wood was burned through, the weight of the flagstones would...

Something hit him like a mallet in the stomach. It was a block of stone off the roof, shrewdly thrown by Jock, and it took every wisp of air out of him. He tottered, tried to keep his feet, tried to draw his dagger, but Jock moved in, caught him briskly, steadied him, and kneed him hard in the balls.

He landed bruisingly on the hot parapet, agony flaring white in his eyes and no breath even to mew with pain; he tried but failed to puke. Locked in a private battle with what felt like a black spear in his groin, lancing up to his chest, he dimly heard Jock pushing his feeble barricade of firewood aside. There was a scraping sound as Jock pulled the flagstones off the trapdoor, and cursing because the metal and wood were hot, shot the bolts.

Carey was beginning to be able to uncurl when Jock kicked him in the head, grabbed the back of his doublet and some hair and dragged him over the stones, behind the angle of the roof.

'Bothwell,' shouted Jock, busily tying Carey's wrists behind him with the ropes that had just been cut off his own arms, 'I've got him. D'ye hear me? The trapdoor's open, ye can come up.'

'It could be a trick,' came Bothwell's voice. 'Carey, what are you up to?'

'He's surrendering unconditionally,' said Jock. 'In fact, I dinna think he can talk at the moment, he seems verra preoccupied.'

'What happened?'

'Och, he's a courtier, wi' notions of honour and such, he only went and untied me arms.'

There was a lot of unkind laughter down below. Carey would have felt betrayed, but as Jock was giving him a scientific kicking while he spoke, he found he couldn't think of anything except how to roll up tighter. There were sounds of hissing as water was poured over the fire, cautious scraping sounds of a ladder being brought.

Jock took a fistful of Carey's hair and hauled his head back. 'This is for the good of your soul, Courtier. Ah'm teaching ye not to beat up your elders...'

Carey blinked away the water springing out of his eyes and, out of pure stupid temper, spat in Jock's face.

'Och, Courtier, Courtier...' said Jock regretfully, 'ye're a hard man to teach.' He banged Carey's face a couple of times on the stone and the ugly world and Jock's ugly face went black.

Carey came to, still cross-eyed and dizzy, and tried to puke again. Jock had sauntered over to the parapet. He was peering out at the barnekin and horse paddock between fading drifts of smoke, still coughing. Carey must have made some sort of moaning noise, because Jock turned to him.

Privately Carey thought he'd had a great deal worse than Jock, but he couldn't see any point in arguing and it was too much effort anyway.

'Thought so,' said Jock with satisfaction, still gazing outwards at something he could see over the parapet. 'Thank God Sergeant Dodd knows what he's at.'

One of Carey's eyes was swelling shut and he could do no more than dully wonder through his multifarious pains why Jock had picked up the bow and the remaining arrows and had nocked one on the string. He was still where Jock had hauled him, out of sight of the trapdoor, uncomfortably half-curled, half-sprawled on the roofstones, his head jammed against the parapet wall and his knees pulled up. His hands had already gone numb. A tentative movement of his shoulders to try and free his head got him kicked again, so he stayed where he was. Then the trapdoor moved, shifted, was hefted out of the way.

The head and shoulders that appeared through the hole were Bothwell's, and he was holding a dag with the match ready lit. He and Jock looked at each other for a moment.

'Now,' said Jock, 'ye're going to talk to Sergeant Dodd, my lord Earl, and in exchange for the men he caught and all our horses which he's rounded up and has started on their way back south and for him agreeing to take himself and his men off again, we'll give him his precious Deputy Warden. Onless ye want to give up on yer raid altogether, because if ye dinna agree then I'm out of it and so are all my kin.'

'Why Jock? What do you care about one of Hunsdon's boys? Has he got a knife at your back?'

Jock laughed. 'Ye know me better than that, Bothwell. Nay, he's down here on the floor by my feet, feeling right sorry for himself.'

Carey had tried to wriggle out of range while Jock was busy, so Jock gave him another kick in the back, but the arrow pointed at Bothwell's heart remained rock-steady. Bothwell blinked through the final wisps of smoke, finally spotted Carey, who had decided to play dead for the moment despite the heat of the stones, and laughed heartily.

'Untie him and let me shoot his right hand off, so he never troubles us again.'

Jock hesitated. 'I'd let ye, my lord,' he said, 'but he didna kill me when he had the chance and I said I wouldna let you harm him.'

'Ye've harmed him yerself, it looks like.'

'That's different.'

'He wanted to use you as a hostage.'

'Nay, I'm no' a good hostage and he knows it. He is, though,' grinned Jock. 'Are ye fixed on fighting Sergeant Dodd and his men, Bothwell, or would ye rather save the powder for our raid?'

'What did you tell him about it?'

'Jesus, my lord, what do ye take me for, I told him nothing of it,' said Jock sincerely. 'We've been talking of family matters. It's been verra interesting, eh Courtier?' Jock kicked Carey in the ribs again and smiled blithely at Bothwell.

## Friday, 23rd June, afternoon

At last Bothwell climbed up to the fighting platform behind the sharpened logs of the Netherby barnekin and shouted for Sergeant Dodd. Dodd had glimpsed activity at the top of the tower and was wondering irritably if Carey had managed to get himself killed at the last minute.

'I'm the headman...' began Will the Tod.

'Shh,' said Dodd, 'he thinks I've brought the Carlisle garrison too.'

'But ye havna. Lowther...'

'Let him think it. Ay my lord,' yelled Dodd, 'what d'ye want?'

'We've got your Deputy Warden prisoner, Sergeant,' said Bothwell.

'Is he still alive?'

Bothwell grinned. 'Ay. He's not very happy, but he's still alive. Tell me why I shouldnae cut his throat and be done with it.'

'Prove he's alive first,' said Dodd, his voice hard with suspicion, 'I've nae interest in his corpse.'

Bothwell nodded, leaned down and gave some orders. Two men appeared behind the pointed logs: Dodd recognised a battered Jock of the Peartree with his knife at the neck of an even more battered Robert Carey.

Dodd relaxed a little. Why on earth hadn't they killed him when they caught him? Ah well, who could fathom the way the mad Earl's mind worked.

'What will ye give me for him?' shouted Bothwell.

'He's only the one man,' yelled Will the Tod in return, 'and he's no' very valuable.'

'Shut up,' hissed Dodd, 'he's the Deputy Warden and...'

'Och, Henry,' said Will the Tod, not at all offended, 'Janet's right, ye know nothing of bargaining.' He raised his voice again. 'If ye give him to us, we might consider going away and leaving ye in peace.'

Dodd couldn't quite make out expressions at that distance, but he rather thought that one of Carey's eyebrows had gone travelling upwards again.

'What about my horses?' demanded Bothwell.

'What horses?' asked Will the Tod sweetly.

'Don't try my patience, Armstrong, ye ken very well which horses.'

'D'ye mean the few nags that belong to ye, or d'ye mean all the peaceable innocent men's horses ye've reived in the past week?'

'I mean all the horses in the God damned paddock,' shouted Bothwell, 'or I'll send him out to you in pieces.'

'Och, my lord,' said Will the Tod, enjoying himself hugely, 'we're only discussing it, there's nae need to be offensive.'

Dodd rolled his eyes.

Jock of the Peartree leaned over the barnekin wall.

'We'll let ye keep the Dodd horses I took and that's all.'

Will the Tod turned to Dodd. 'Do ye like the terms, Henry?'

'Get on with it.'

'Ts. Young men have nae patience. Your Courtier's got Jock on his side, he'll do well enough.'

'He's what?'

'Ay,' shouted Will the Tod, 'that's good enough for us. We'll gi' ye back all the horses bar the ones that belong to Sergeant Dodd here and we'll go home when we've got our man and we'll no' fight ye unless ye come after us.'

Geordie brought back the huge herd of horses from the eaves of Cleughfoot Wood, separated out those with Dodd brands, and put the rest back in the paddock. The captured Grahams they left tied to the paddock fence.

They waited. At last the gate opened and Carey was shoved through on foot, limping, weaponless, black with smoke, the left side of his face swollen up, his back straight and his expression unreadable.

Understanding perfectly from the way he walked that somebody —Jock, no doubt—must have been using the Deputy's privates for football practice, Dodd led up a nice quiet soft-paced mare, and held her while Carey set himself, fastened his teeth on his lip, and mounted up very very carefully.

'Can ye ride, sir?' Dodd asked solicitously.

Carey lowered himself down in the saddle like a maiden sitting for the first time on her wedding morning, took a deep breath, held it and nodded. Dodd was sorry to see that the bounce seemed to have quite gone out of him.

He was still every inch the Courtier: once the group of them were out of sight of Netherby, it was very touching the way he took the trouble to thank all of Dodd's surname and Janet's relatives too, Armstrongs though they were. Dodd stayed at his back, feeling a bit as he did when one of his younger brothers had got himself a belting when they were lads: privately, he thought it was funny, but he saw no reason why anybody should add to the man's discomfort by smirking or commenting. So he glowered over Carey's torn and battered shoulder, and not one of his kin disgraced him by cracking a smile.

To keep Carey's mind off things as they rode back to Carlisle, Dodd told him the epic tale of his own arrest, escape from jail and journey through the secret passage, followed by his run to Brampton, very generously only slightly editing the ladies' part in the story. At least Carey was impressed.

'You did it in a jack and helmet, too?' he said, his voice still hoarse with the smoke. 'I doubt there's a man in the south that could do the like.'

Dodd's long face continued to look as mournful as a hound with the bellyache, but inwardly he was reluctantly flattered. He said, on a friendly impulse, 'I'm sorry your plan went awry, Cour...sir. It might have worked wi'out Lowther to spike yer guns for ye.'

'Oh but, Sergeant,' said Carey, wincing and closing his eyes as the horse he was riding pecked at a pothole, 'it did work, it worked beautifully. It only went wrong at the very last minute. You watch, you'll see how it all worked out.'

He's still mad, thought Dodd dourly, no longer sorry for him.

## FRIDAY, 23RD JUNE, EVENING

Barnabus Cooke was waiting in the Carlisle courtyard when Dodd brought Carey home. Clearly, Lowther had heard what had happened and seemed to think it a good idea to be present, which Barnabus thought was probably a serious mistake. The Lord Warden himself seemed embarrassed at his inaction and he was wandering about in the courtyard too. With the women also there, it was a regular little welcoming party and Barnabus rather thought Carey would have preferred not to see any of them.

However he smiled wanly as he came in, dismounted slowly and carefully, and then held onto the saddle to steady himself.

'Are you wounded anywhere, sir?' Barnabus asked, clicking his fingers imperiously at Hutchin Graham to lead the horses away.

Carey shook his head. Dodd came up behind Carey looking as miserable as if he had not just rescued his Deputy Warden. Then Carey spotted Lowther, standing by the barracks door with his arms folded and a look of deep satisfaction all over his face at Carey's condition. The Deputy Warden was in a lamentable state: Daniel Swanders's jerkin and shirt were in tatters and blackened with soot, and Carey couldn't even see out of his left eye, which was on the side of his face that was puffed out like a cushion.

The other eye narrowed and its eyebrow went up. This will be interesting, thought Barnabus, and settled back a little to watch the fireworks.

'How are you, Robin?' asked Scrope, breaking the tension between them. 'What happened, why did you do it? It was very...'

Carey took a deep breath and put his fingers up to rub between his eyebrows. 'Thank you, my lord, I'm a lot better than I expect you think I deserve to be.'

Scrope coloured. He couldn't seem to look at Carey straight.

'Well, it might have worked...' began Scrope generously.

'Ha!' said Lowther.

Carey ignored him elaborately. 'Of course it might if you didn't have a traitor claiming to be your Deputy,' he said smoothly. 'Very unfortunate that he chose to let out the Grahams who could identify me just when I happened to be at Netherby. But I expect he thought he was doing the best he could for his employer.'

Scrope looked puzzled and Carey didn't bother to enlighten him. He turned to go to his chambers in the Queen Mary Tower and found his path blocked by Lowther.

'Are ye calling me a traitor?'

Carey blinked at him and smiled his most superior and supercilious smile. It wasn't quite as effective as usual in driving men wild, because only half his face was working properly, but the veins on Lowther's nose throbbed all the same.

'Yes, I am, Lowther,' he said, 'March traitor, in that you bring in raiders, and traitor to your Queen in that you failed to inform her of important information in your possession. Why, surely you don't mind, do you?'

'We'll see what Burghley has to say about this escapade,' huffed

Lowther, still not ready to call Carey out to his face.

Carey smiled even more, which must have hurt. 'That's right,' he said softly, 'you dig your own grave and lie in it, Sir Richard. Didn't you know that Burghley and his son support King James's succession to the throne after Her Majesty dies? I'm sure my lord Burghley will be fascinated to hear how you tried to stop me discovering Bothwell's plans to raid Falkland Palace and capture the King of Scotland. So will King James. Please save me the trouble and do it yourself.'

Lowther's mouth was open. Carey very gently put out a finger and pushed past him. 'Now, I've had a long hard day and I'm tired. If you'll excuse me, I'm going to bed. Good night ladies, good night my lord.'

Lovely, Barnabus thought, trotting after his master, that'll puzzle him, and you kept your temper as well, you're learning fast, ain't you?

'Oh bloody hell,' said Carey, pulling on his night shirt and dressing gown, and sitting down on the side of the bed.

It was Dodd, poking his head round the door. 'Sorry to disturb ye sir, but I've spoken to Lady Widdrington and she wants to see you tomorrow and she also says her stepson Henry's waiting at Bessie's to take a message to Chancellor Melville and he has a passport from Scrope so he can go at once.'

Carey blinked as he caught up with all this. 'Excellent,' he croaked at last. 'Wait a minute.' He hobbled over to his desk in the next room, wrote a few lines, signed it, and folded and sealed it.

'Tell Henry to take the long way round and on no account go anywhere near Liddesdale. The verbal message is that Bothwell's got at least two hundred men with remounts, mostly Grahams, and I think there's someone working for Bothwell amongst the courtiers inside the palace.'

When Dodd had gone, Barnabus said tactfully, 'Shouldn't you warn him about King James's...er...habits, sir?'

Carey laughed, stopped with a wince and sat down on the bed again. 'Not Henry: he's far too spotty for His Majesty's tastes. And Melville's known him since he was a boy, he'll look after him.'

'Seems like you've saved the King's life, if he gets through.'

'Hmf. Knowing the King he won't pay a blind bit of attention. But I've drawn the raid's sting anyway and he'll never understand how.'

'Why's that, sir?' asked Barnabus, wondering if he should call in a surgeon to strap Carey's ribs which were black and blue and looked very much as if they might be cracked.

Carey smiled. 'I told Jock of the Peartree about the horses in Falkland Palace. By now he's told all his brothers and nephews and cousins and they'll have lost interest entirely in King James.'

He lifted his feet onto the bed, dropped the cloth on the floor. 'And I've almost solved the problem of Sweetmilk's murderer and I've made friends with Jock of the Peartree, if you can call it that, and I've...'

He snored richly. Barnabus tucked him up and drew the bed curtains. He'd send for the surgeon tomorrow, when Carey would be in a terrible mood, and he'd get Lady Scrope to bring him and Lady Widdrington could continue to organise the funeral which she was doing with her usual briskness.

Simon had made friends with some of the other lads in the castle and reported that Young Hutchin seemed remarkably rich in silver at the moment, which information Barnabus would decide whether to pass on to Carey in the morning.


## SATURDAY, 24TH JUNE, MORNING

Carey woke up late at seven o'clock with a ravenous hunger and ribs that twinged monstrously every time he moved or breathed. Someone had pulled his bedcurtains to let the sun in and left a tray laden with fried collops of ham, grilled eggs, bread, and a flagon of mild beer, which made his mouth water so much he almost drooled as he pulled it towards him.

Ten minutes later it was all gone, despite the way his jaw hurt when he chewed. But his belly was packed tight and his sore face and body receded slightly in significance. Then somebody knocked on the door.

'Enter,' said Carey, thinking it was Barnabus. The door opened, and Philadelphia came flying in, her clothes in their usual tumble no matter what the attentions of her tiring woman, and threw herself into his arms, never mind that he was still in his nightshirt and dressing gown.

'I thought they'd hang you, oh Robin, Robin, I was so afraid they'd hang you...'

'So was I,' said Carey gruffly, 'but they didn't, so why weep about it?'

'They hurt you...' She was touching his face and he reared back.

'That was Jock of the Peartree,' said Carey, 'and he's just as sore this morning as I am. Well almost.' He handed her his handkerchief from under the pillow and Philly blew her nose, composed herself and flipped bewilderingly into scolding him.

'I hope you're thoroughly embarrassed, Dodd having to come to the rescue like that? Did you hear how he got out of Carlisle through the secret passage nobody knows about except the Warden?'

'Yes. Twice.'

She wasn't going to leave him in peace, blast her. Carey grabbed his clothes off the chest where they were laid out, shut the bedcurtains and started dressing. Philadelphia continued.

'Well please don't do it again. It was awful waiting here with Lowther keeping the gate with his men and threatening Red Sandy with flogging there and then if he tried anything. You won't do it again, will you, Robin?'

Carey was coughing again. He cursed. There was still smoke in his lungs and it nearly killed him every time he did that. 'I don't think anyone in these parts will trust strange pedlars any more. I've probably ruined their trade. Is Red Sandy all right?'

'Scrope made Lowther leave your men alone if they promised to stay in the castle.'

'Good, I'm glad they tried.'

'How could you do something so dangerous? Scrope said you were mad and he wouldn't get you out of a schoolboy prank.'

'I'll bet,' muttered Carey to himself.

'What?'

'I said, did he?'

'Yes, he did. I'm still not speaking to him. Stupid man, pretending he had an ague, I hate him. And I hate you too, for worrying us like that.'

Carey drew back the curtains again and climbed out of bed to pull on his boots, saying, 'You're allowed to hate your brother but you're not supposed to hate your husband, Philly.'

'Well, don't give me some romantic nonsense about learning to love him, either. In any case, that's not what I married him for.'

'Of course not,' said Carey, 'you're not a peasant. But you are supposed to respect and obey him, Philly.'

'Pah!' She tossed her head and her curly black hair partially escaped from its white cap and fell down her neck. 'I've brought some people to see you and first you're going to have a surgeon.'

'Oh no, Philly, I don't need a surgeon...'

She ignored him and led the man in, a stocky, thickset thug called Mr Little, with hair growing luxuriantly out of his nostrils and up his arms, who prodded and grunted, strapped Carey's ribs, declared that neither his skull nor his nose were cracked, but his cheekbone probably was, which Carey knew already, and let him eight ounces of blood from his left arm to balance up his humours. He offered to put in a clyster to guard against infection and was offended when Carey told him curtly to go and ask Barnabus for his fee.

'Bloody surgeons,' he muttered, as he carefully pulled on his shirt and doublet again. He took a quick look down his hose at the damage there, winced at the sight and wondered if he'd ever be the man he was. God knew, the ride back to Carlisle had been Hell, Purgatory and the Spanish Inquisition rolled into one, and every step he took was a punishment. He simply hadn't had the courage to let the surgeon examine his balls.

Somebody else knocked on the door. Damn it, the place was like the Queen's antechamber in Westminster, with all the bloody traffic in it.

'What the hell do you want?' he roared, then coughed when his ribs caught him.

Lady Widdrington marched in, trailing an unwilling but resplendently dressed Thomas the Merchant Hetherington. Behind her, obviously primed, Barnabus shut the door and no doubt stationed himself outside to repel interruptions and, naturally, cram his ear against the panelling.

When she first married her elderly crook of a husband, Elizabeth Widdrington had not known the meaning of the word 'tact'. He had taught it to her, with the aid of his belt, on several occasions. When her rage had subsided she had decided to learn subtlety and dissimulation, no matter how hard it came to her, since it seemed that was what God wanted.

She still wanted to fold him into her arms and kiss his poor face, but she knew how that would drive him away. So she put one hand out to touch his arm and said, 'Thank God you're alive, Sir Robert.'

He looked at the floor. She had, after all, tried to dissuade him. No doubt he was waiting for her to tell him she'd told him so.

'Thank you,' he managed to say.

'Are you still interested in Sweetmilk?'

Carey looked up. 'I beg your pardon?'

'Do you still want to know who killed him? If you've found out already, I won't waste any more of your time. But if you haven't, Thomas the Merchant has a tale he'd like to tell you.'

Good, that distracted him, he'd always liked puzzles and challenges. There went that silly eyebrow of his, ridiculous the effect it had on her.

Carey led the way through to the room he used as an office and sat down behind his desk.

'Well?' he said to Thomas the Merchant, pointedly not offering a seat.

Thomas the Merchant harrumphed, clasped his hands under his belly.

'Early on the Saturday,' he began, harrumphed again.

'Yes.'

'Jock Hepburn and Mary Graham came to me wanting rings. They were handfasting one another in secret.' Thomas looked distasteful at this evidence of sin, seemed to consider commenting

220

on it, but changed his mind at Carey's expression. He went on quickly in his resentful drone. 'While they were here, Sweetmilk came in wanting horses and caught them. He was verra put out. He called Jock Hepburn a bastard that had dishonoured his sister, and Hepburn struck him on his face, so he threw down his glove. Hepburn picked it up, but Mary Graham was clinging to Sweetmilk and begging him not to kill her man. He only threw her down and walked out with Hepburn.'

Carey's good eye was narrowed with interest. 'How were they armed?'

'They werena clad for business. Sweetmilk had his best jack and nae lance and Hepburn was very fine in a French brocade, three pounds the ell, I'd say, and a jack as well, but foreign make. Nice rings too.'

'I know,' said Carey. 'Their arms?'

Thomas the Merchant pulled the corners of his mouth down in thought. 'Swords, daggers, the usual.'

'Who had a gun?'

'Neither of them.'

'Did you look out into the street?'

'I did. Hepburn and Sweetmilk were riding down tae the gate together, with Mary chasing after them on her pony still crying to Sweetmilk not to do it.'

'She didn't think Hepburn would win?'

Thomas smiled broadly. 'Och, no, he's a bonny man, but Sweetmilk had the experience. I was betting on him meself.'

'Think hard, Mr Hetherington. Did any man there have a firearm?'

'Nay, neither of them had more than swords.'

'Thank you, Mr Hetherington. I want you to make a proper statement for Richard Bell to take down and I'll be calling you as a witness against Hepburn at the next Warden's Day.'

'Sir...'

'Quiet. Off you go.'

Thomas the Merchant went, but Elizabeth Widdrington stayed for a moment.

'Will you try and arrest Jock Hepburn?'

'Yes,' said Carey. 'It might have to wait until after Bothwell's raid and we can lift him quietly without too much trouble, but yes.'

'Why? He only killed a Graham, an outlaw.'

'Sweetmilk wasn't an outlaw, yet. He wasn't killed in a fair fight, he was murdered so Jock Hepburn could avoid a fight.'

'Why...' Elizabeth paused, 'why did you take so much trouble over it?'

Carey looked down at his hands. 'Do you know what justice is?' he asked at last, in an oddly remote voice. 'Justice is an accident, really. It's law that's important. Do you know what the rule of law is?'

'I think so. When people obey the laws so there's peace...'

Carey was shaking his head. 'No. It's the transfer of the duty of revenge to the Queen. It's the officers of the Crown avenging a man's murder, not the man's father or the family. Without law what you have is feud, tangling between themselves, and murder repaying murder down the generations. As we have here. But if the Queen's Officers can be relied on to take revenge for a killing, then the feuding must stop because if you feud against the Queen, it's high treason. That's all. That's all that happens in a law-abiding country: the dead man's family know that the Crown will carry their feud for them. Without it you have bloody chaos.'

It was strange to hear anyone talk so intensely of such a dusty subject as law; and yet there was a fire and passion in Carey's words as if the rule of law was infinitely precious to him.

'All we can do to stop the borderers killing each other is give them the promise of justice—which is the accidental result when the Crown hangs the man who did the killing,' he said, watching his linked fingers. They were still empty of rings and looked oddly bare. 'You see, if it was only a bloodfeud, anyone of the right surname would do. But with the law, it should be the man that did the killing, and that's justice. Not just to take vengeance but to take vengeance on the right man.'

'So you'll make out a bill for Sweetmilk Graham and go through all the trouble of trying Hepburn and producing witnesses and finding him guilty...

'And then hanging him, when a word to Jock of the Peartree would produce the same result a lot more easily. But that wouldn't be justice, you see, that would only be more feuding, more private revenge which has nothing to do with justice or law or anything else. Justice requires that the man have a trial and face his accusers.'

'But you think Jock Hepburn did it.'

'Who else was there?' said Carey. Elizabeth opened her mouth to speak, took a breath, and then paused. 'But at least at a trial he could argue against my suspicions.'

'It's a complicated thing, this law,' Elizabeth said, trying to speak lightly. 'Do you think you'll be able to explain it to Jock of the Peartree?'

Carey smiled lopsidedly. 'No, never in a thousand years.'

It was so hard to sit there and not move nearer, not hold her hands out to him. Why was it so hard, even after all this time? After all they had first met in '87 when he was on that difficult and dangerous embassy to King James, and again in the Armada year when she had been at Court with Philadelphia. They had played at all the light, silly, sweet confections of loverlike convention, half joking, half deadly serious.

He looked awful, but despite the brown walnut stain and clownish bruising, there was something in his blue eyes and the way he smiled that had the power to hypnotise her, make her forget all her faith in God and hard-held virtue, everything. When she had read sceptically the verses about the romantic disease of love poured out by the sonneteers, she had never believed it was such a dangerous uncomfortable beast. But she had been wrong. She looked at the floor so as not to be caught, flushed and struggled. No, she thought harshly, I'm a married woman and unfaithfulness is breaking a vow I made in God's presence. That's all. And now I have to go, so I can think straight.

She stood up. Carey stood as well, moved towards her.

'Thank you,' he said gently, 'I know what you did for me.'

No, she couldn't stand it, in another moment she would burst into tears and tell him how she had paced the castle through the day in terror of his death and let him kiss her and then it would be too late to stop. He wanted to kiss her, any fool could see he needed less than half an excuse to reach out and catch her to him...her face as flushed as a girl's, she hung her head, muttered something half-gracious, and fled through the door.

Behind her Carey stared after her, reddening with frustration. Then he yelled, 'GOD DAMN IT!' and threw his stool at the wall.

## SATURDAY, 24TH JUNE, LATE AFTERNOON

Lemons, Barnabus thought, lemons, the walnut juice stain comes off with lemons, no problem there, Barnabus, all you need to do is find some lemons. It appeared, however, that there were none in Carlisle. The few lemons that had made the long journey from Spain and the south of France, to wind up in the market as slightly wizened specimens, had been snapped up by Lady Scrope the previous week to make syllabubs. Food prices had gone sky high all over Carlisle, what with the unreliable harvest weather, and the arrival of dozens of gentlemen and attendants from all over the March. Thomas the Merchant had bought up most of the spices in Carlisle the night Henry Lord Scrope died and had made a very hard bargain with Lady Scrope.

The boys scattered, talking intently. Barnabus went to Carey's chamber where he finished polishing Carey's best boots and checked the starching and sewing of the new ruff his master was to wear at the funeral. The new black velvet suit was hanging up ready for wear and very fine Carey would look in it too, even if he wasn't ever likely to pay for it. It was quite plain with only a little black braid over the seams and the panes of the hose decorated with brocade. Barnabus would have liked there to be a bit of slashing and a lining of tawny taffeta, but Carey had forbidden it and insisted on cramoisie red silk lining as being more suitable. Eight months in Paris as a youth of nineteen had given Carey very decided ideas about clothes, which ten years of service at Court had confirmed.

Barnabus was just about to make sure that his own best suit of fine dark blue wool was in a reasonable state, when there was a hammering on the door. He opened it to find Goodwife Biltock, bright red with heat and rage, standing there holding Young Hutchin Graham by his right arm twisted up behind his back and his left ear.

'What is the meaning of this, Mr Cooke?' she demanded, sweeping into the room past him.

'Er...'

'Why would this young scoundrel want to steal lemons from the kitchen, eh?'

Barnabus knew his mouth was opening and shutting. Goodwife Biltock shoved Young Hutchin into the corner, where he sat rubbing his ear and looking embarrassed. The Goodwife squared up to Barnabus, her broad face on a level with his chest, and shook her finger under his nose.

'Sixpence a lemon,' she snapped, 'I'll sixpence a lemon you, you thieving clapperdudgeon...'

Barnabus backed away. 'Goodwife, Goodwife...'

'Send boys out to steal from the kitchens would you...'

'Goodwife, I only said if they could find lemons, I would pay sixpence for them. It's to take the walnut stain off Sir Robert's face and hands, that's all.'

As he'd hoped it would, that slowed her down.

'Ah,' she said. 'Well, fair enough. I can't spare you any lemons, but I can give you verjuice which has the same quality of sourness.' She turned to Hutchin Graham. 'You, boy!' she barked, 'I've got an errand for you, come with me.'

As she herded Hutchin out of the door ahead of her she glowered at Barnabus.

'Mind your manners, Mr Cooke,' she said, 'I know you and where you're from.' Barnabus could think of nothing to do except bow. If anything her frown became fiercer. 'I'll send this thief back to you with the verjuice. My advice is to beat him well.'

'Thank you Goodwife Biltock,' said Barnabus faintly.

When Hutchin got back with the little flask of verjuice, Carey had returned from inspecting his men along with Captain Carleton. Barnabus was serving them with what remained of the good wine they had brought north with them: Carleton had parked his bulk on Carey's chair next to the fireplace and Carey was sitting on the bed telling the full tale of his adventures at Netherby. Carleton held his sides and bellowed with laughter when he heard how Carey had been foolish enough to free Jock of the Peartree on his word not to attack and Carey looked wry.

'Well,' he said, 'I'll know better next time, but it might have saved my life at that. Now then Young Hutchin, what have you got there?'

'Verjuice, sir. From Goodwife Biltock.'

'That was kind of her with all she has to do. Give her my thanks and best regards.'

Hutchin looked hesitant.

'I'm supposed to give him a beating, sir,' said Barnabus helpfully.

'Good lord, why? What's he done?'

'Tried to steal some of the Goodwife's lemons.'

There were volumes of the comprehension in Carey's battered face, but all he said was, 'Well, that was very devoted of you, Hutchin, but much more dangerous than simply lifting a few head of cattle. We'll remit the beating for now because I want you to take part in the funeral procession tomorrow.'

Young Hutchin, who had been looking sullen, stood up straighter.

'We need a groom to ride the lead horse pulling the funeral bier. You'll have a mourning livery and it'll be your job to be sure the horses are calm and go the right way. Can you do it?'

Hutchin was looking for the catch. 'Is that all, sir?'

Carey nodded. 'Your fee will be the livery: it's a suit of fine black wool which I think will fit you well, and a new linen shirt. We can't arrange for new boots but your own don't look too bad if you give them a polish, and you'll have a black velvet bonnet with a feather.'

Hutchin thought carefully.

'Ay sir, I'll do it.'

'Excellent. Be here two hours before dawn and Barnabus will see you properly kitted out.'

Astonishingly, Hutchin smiled, took off his cap and made quite a presentable bow. He turned to go.

'Oh, and Hutchin.'

'Ay sir?'

'Your Uncle Richard Graham of Brackenhill is coming, so he'll be behind you in the procession.'

Hutchin smiled even wider before clattering off down the stairs. Carleton looked quizzically at Carey.

'That young devil is chief of the boys in Carlisle,' said Carey in answer to his unspoken question. 'If they're planning some bright trick for the funeral, he'll either be in the thick of it or know who is and now he'll see to it that they don't do it.'

Carleton nodded. 'Ay, there's sense in that.'

'Which is also why I got Scrope to invite the Armstrong and Graham headmen.'

Carleton smiled. 'Well, it's worth a try, any road.'

Dodd arrived looking harassed, and Barnabus served him with the last of their wine. He sniffed suspiciously at it, then drank.

There was further tying up of endless loose ends to be done: petty details that somehow always slipped your notice until the last minute. It had invariably been like that when Carey was taking part in an Accession Day Tilt: you thought you'd got everything sorted out and then a hundred things suddenly rose up the night before and sneered at you.

It was getting on towards sunset and Barnabus could see that Carey was tired. However, it seemed he had one further important piece of business to transact.

'Couriers?' asked Dodd.

'The regular service to London from Carlisle. The weak link is the man who rides from Carlisle to Newcastle, before he hands it on to my brother's courier to take the rest of the way.'

'Why do you want him stopped?' demanded Carleton suspiciously.

'I want to know what Lowther's saying about me, since he apparently controls the March's correspondence.'

'Oh ay,' agreed Carleton, 'I see.'

'And I don't want him stopped. I just want his dispatch bag... borrowed, so I can read the letters.'

'There are ways of opening dispatch bags without breaking the seals.'

'Are there?' asked Carleton. 'What are they?'

'Well, you could unpick the stitching at the bottom and take the papers out that way.'

'Nay sir,' said Dodd, who had carried them on occasion and done his best to satisfy his curiosity, 'they're double, and the outer one's oiled canvas.'

'Damn,' said Carey, 'I suppose Walsingham will have advised him how to do it. Well, that leaves Richard Bell.'

'The little clerk,' grunted Carleton. 'Ye could threaten him, I suppose.'

Bell was quite a scrawny specimen, but he was also tall and gangling rather than small. However, Barnabus had noticed that fighting men invariably referred to clerks as 'little'.

Carey shook his head. 'That would send him straight to Lowther or Scrope. Can he be bought?'

'I dinna ken,' said Dodd, 'nobody's tried.'

'Are you joking?' demanded Carey, clearly shocked. 'Are you seriously telling me that nobody's even tried bribing him for the dispatches?'

Dodd shook his head. 'I suppose we wouldn't know if they had, but if he's been bribed he's very canny about it, his gown's ten years old at least.'

'He'll have had livery for the funeral, though?'

Carleton shook his head as well. 'He's not been invited into the procession.'

'Why not? He served the old Lord Scrope for years?'

Dodd and Carleton exchanged embarrassed glances. It seemed that Richard Bell had been left out.

'Well,' said Carleton, shifting in the chair, 'ye hardly ever notice him, he's that quiet, I suppose they forgot.'

Carey was genuinely appalled. 'Well, that's simply not good enough. Where would he be now, do you think?'

'Scrope's office,' suggested Carleton.

'I'll go and talk to him, if you'll excuse me, gentlemen.'

Dodd and Carleton took their leave. Carey picked up his hat and headed for the door, then turned to Barnabus.

'I've an errand for you, Barnabus.'

'Yes sir?'

'I want you to go down to Madam Hetherington's and find Daniel Swanders. Tell him I lost his pack and wouldn't advise him to go to Netherby to get it back for a while until things have cooled down there. If he doesn't mind the risk, he might try in a month or so. In the meantime, here's three pounds English for him to buy new stocks and the five shillings I made while I was doing his job with the ladies at Netherby.'

'What about his clothes, sir?'

'Oh Lord, I think Goodwife Biltock burned those. He'd better keep the suit he's got on: he'll get a much better class of customer with it.'

'Sir...' Barnabus, who had had his eye on that suit for Simon when he finished growing, since it was entirely the wrong size and shape for himself, was very aggrieved. 'It's worth more than the pack by itself.'

'Considerably more,' agreed Carey.

'You'll only have three left.'

'Don't fuss,' snapped Carey, 'I can get something made up in wool when Scrope pays me. Now go and do as I say, and get back here before the gate shuts.'

'Yes sir,' said Barnabus, sadly.

'I'll see to the walnut stain myself. I suppose the hair colour will just have to grow out.'

'Yes sir,' said Barnabus, 'unless you want to go blond.' Carey gave him the piercing blue stare that told him he was pushing it. He added hurriedly, 'If you let me cut your hair short, it'll be quicker.'

'In the morning.'

They went down the stairs together and Carey hurried over to the keep.

## SATURDAY, 24TH JUNE, EVENING

Carey found Richard Bell still standing at his high desk, his pen dipping in the ink bottle and whispering across the paper in front of him in the hypnotic dance of a clerk, with a triple candlestick beside him to light his way through the thickets of letters.

Carey stood and waited quietly until Bell carefully cleaned his pen on a rag, put it down and stretched and rubbed his fingers with a sigh. He caught sight of Carey and blinked at him.

'I'm sorry, sir, I didna see ye.'

Bell was as thin as a portrait of Death and yet didn't look unhealthy or consumptive: it seemed natural to him. His shoulders were a little rounded, his eyes blinked against the flicker of the candles. He and Scrope made a matched pair, in fact, although Scrope was better built and looked stronger and might even run to fat in a few years.

'How can I help you, sir?'

'Mr Bell, I heard something that astonished me a moment ago, and I hope you can clarify it for me.'

'Yes sir?'

'I heard that you were not to be a part of the funeral procession.'

Bell said nothing and looked at the floor. Carey stepped a little closer.

'Is it true?' Bell nodded. 'Did you refuse a place…?'

'No sir,' said Bell, then looked up shyly. 'I have been very busy with the arrangements, and I suppose it…er…slipped the Lord Warden's mind.'

'If you were offered a place, would you accept?'

'Yes sir, of course, I would…I would be honoured.'

Carey smiled. 'How are you with horses, Mr Bell?'

Bell looked confused. 'Not bad, I like them. I've carried dispatches in the past, when they were particularly urgent and the man had already gone.'

'No problems walking a couple of miles?'

Bell smiled. 'No sir. I'm not as weak as I look.'

'Excellent. Let me talk to Scrope and see what I can do. I'm sorry you seem to have been passed over, Mr Bell.'

Bell studied the paper before him.

'Sir Richard...' he muttered. Carey raised an eyebrow. 'Sir Richard Lowther said he would see to it,' Bell explained.

'I'm sure he meant to,' said Carey generously, 'but I expect it slipped his mind with all the press of business. Don't worry, Mr Bell, I'll see my brother-in-law now and talk to him about it.'

## SUNDAY, 25TH JUNE, 2 A.M.

Carey wandered through the noise and spied the erect figure of Elizabeth Widdrington going into the castle kitchens which leaned up against the walls of the keep. He followed her, ducking automatically past strings of garlic and onions and the hams that were to be served later, and found her by the long table in the kitchen watching as two of the scullery boys heaved kid carcasses onto the empty spits by the vast fire. The baker was already pulling bread from the oven next to the fire, slamming in batches of penny loaves at a terrible rate. Half the produce of Carlisle market was heaped up in baskets by the larder door waiting to be turned into sallets and pot-herbs while Goodwife Biltock stood by the cauldrons hanging on the brackets over the flames, stirring mightily, her face verging on purple and her hair escaping from her cap in grey strings.

The small round greasy creature Carey knew as the Carlisle cook was sitting on a stool watching stale bread being turned to crumbs by two kitchen girls. He was the idlest man Carey had ever met outside the Court, rarely out of his bed before eight, but it seemed Lady Widdrington had impressed him with the importance of the occasion...Terrorised was perhaps a better word to describe the way he looked at her.

Carey turned to go, but Elizabeth caught sight of him and

came bustling over, wiping her hands on her clean white apron, and smiling.

'How are you, Sir Robert?' she asked. 'Is Lady Scrope up yet?'

'I don't know,' Carey admitted, 'I can wake them if you like.'

She nodded. 'Scrope's body-servant has the new livery for the boy and a decent gown for Bell. Any luck with the wine?'

Carey shook his head. 'If Barnabus can't find any, nobody can. I expect Bothwell had all the good vintages in Carlisle.'

'Can't be helped. I don't suppose anybody will notice and there's plenty of beer and ale. I'll soon need two strong men to help me carry the raised pies into the hall.'

She gestured at the table along one wall where three enormous pies, complete with battlements, stood waiting.

'They're a little greasy, so don't send anyone who's wearing his mourning livery.'

'What happened to the sweetmeats?'

'They're in Philadelphia's stillroom, drying out. They can wait though: the less time they spend in the open for flies and boys to get to them, the better. How are your ribs?'

'Well enough...' began Carey, but Goodwife Biltock came up to him with a mug of ale, looking stern.

'You're as pale as a sheet,' she scolded, 'and bags to hide a pig in under your eye. Drink that, it's spiced and has medicine in it.'

'What sort of medicine?' Carey demanded suspiciously.

'Something to prevent a fever. Let me see your face.'

She reached up, took his face between her rough hands and turned it to the light from the fire.

'Jesus,' she said, 'you look a sight. I wish I could have got to your face with a few leeches when that was done...'

'Goodwife...' began Carey.

'And an axe for the man that did it to you.'

'I don't...'

'Drink your ale.'

He drank.

'What do you think, Lady Widdrington? Will Lady Scrope...?'

'I'm sure,' said Elizabeth, still smiling at him. 'Anyway, it can't be helped and most of Carlisle knows what happened.'

'We don't want anyone laughing.'

'They won't.'

'When did you last wash behind your ears, Robin?'

For God's sake, he didn't have to take this any more. 'Last night,' said Carey repressively, 'with your verjuice. It's the best I can do without lemons. I'll go and wake the Scropes if they're not up already, my lady.'

As he left Goodwife Biltock tutted and said 'Temper! Temper!' but he pretended to be deaf and carried on out the door, up the stairs and through the hall where trestle tables were set up and Scrope's steward was shouting at a girl who had dropped a large tablecloth in the rushes. She put her apron over her head and howled as Carey slid by, climbed the stairs to the Scrope private apartments. He hid a grin as he knocked: it seemed the preparations for elaborate ceremonial were identical wherever you went. He almost felt homesick for Westminster.

Scrope was already awake and Philadelphia was in her smock and fur-trimmed dressing gown with her hair full of curling papers, her back eloquently turned to her husband.

'Philadelphia, my dear,' said Scrope nervously. Philadelphia sniffed. Carey was irresistibly reminded of a kitten sulking at being refused a second helping of cream, or no, hardly that, perhaps at having her tail trodden on. 'Your brother's here.' Scrope rolled his eyes eloquently at Carey who tried to look sympathetic. Philadelphia came over and kissed him on his good cheek.

'Robin, you're here, that's splendid,' she said. 'How is Elizabeth doing?'

'I wish we had her supplying the English troops in the Netherlands,' said Carey gallantly, and then balked because Philadelphia was leading him to her dressing table. 'What...?'

'Now don't fuss, didn't Elizabeth say why I wanted you?'

'No, she...What the devil are you doing? No, I don't want to sit there, I have seven men to...'

'Oh hush, Robin, this won't take a moment.' Philadelphia pushed her stool up behind his knees so he sat automatically in front of the mirror. She chewed meditatively on her lip and then darted forward and picked up a little glass pot.

'What the blazes...'

She started dabbing the cream onto his bruised cheek. Carey caught her wrist.

'Philadelphia, what are you doing?'

'I'm going to cover up all the black bruising so you don't look like a Court jester, now let go.'

'I'm not wearing bloody face-paint at a funeral...'

'Yes, you are. Come on, Robin, did you never wear anything at Court?'

'I most certainly did not, who do you think I am, the Earl of bloody Oxford? I never heard anything so ridiculous in my... Ouch!'

'Don't move then. Honestly, I've seen horses easier to deal with than you. Nobody will know if you let me...'

'Goddamn it,' growled Carey, looking round for moral support. Scrope had disappeared into his little dressing room.

'There now. A bit of red lead, I think, just a bit...Your skin's hard to match, Robin, it's lucky you're not a woman. At least you got most of the walnut juice off, what did you use?'

'Verjuice, but...'

'Oh.'

'I can't do it round your eye because it'll get sore. We'd better set it...'

She picked up a feather pad and dabbed it in powder, brushed it over his face. He sneezed.

'Now,' said Philadelphia with satisfaction. 'Don't touch your face, don't rub your eyes, and when Barnabus cuts your hair, put a towel round your head so you don't get clippings on it, but I think you'll do. And be careful if you change your shirt as well. There, lovely. You look as if you've been in a fight, but you don't look as if you lost it any more.'

'Philly, I...'

'That's all right, you don't have to thank me. Now I expect you've got a great deal to do,' she added with emphasis, 'I certainly have.'

Barnabus had the sense not to make any comments when Carey climbed back up the stairs of the Queen Mary Tower to his room. Carey conscientiously protected his face with a towel while Barnabus snipped at his curls.

Once the sky began lightening he examined his face very carefully in the mirror while Barnabus was tying his doublet points and there was no denying the fact that he looked a great deal less like someone who had recently been given a kicking by an expert. His skin felt stiff and odd and he wondered how people like Oxford and even Essex stood it day after day. The Queen wore triple the thickness but women were used to it, he supposed, as he put on his rings.

He complimented Barnabus on his boots which were gleaming and slipped on a pair of wooden pattens to keep them decent until he could mount his horse. He had forgotten to give orders about his sword, but Barnabus had seen to it anyway, and it was glittering and polished. He left the lace-edged ruff off until after he had eaten the breakfast of bread and beer Simon brought him, knowing the magnetic attraction white linen had for crumbs and brown stains, and once that was on and his hat on his head, he was ready. Looking in the mirror again brought a private unadmitted lift to his heart. Not even the Queen could find fault with his elegance, though no doubt she would shriek and throw slippers at the smell of verjuice disguised with perfume. Otherwise he could have attended her in the Privy Chamber with no worries at all.

When he ventured out into the courtyard again the chaos had given place to a semblance of order. There was a row of men pissing against one of the stable walls, and Dodd and Carleton were already mounted. Simon ran to the row of horses, brought out Carey's best horse, Thunder, and led him over. Carey thought about it, joined the row of men to relieve himself, refastened himself carefully because one of his recurring nightmares while serving at Court had been attending the Queen with his codpiece untied, then went over to his horse, slipped off the pattens and mounted up carefully. Dodd lifted his cap to him, replaced it with his helmet and followed him as he rode down the short row of his own six men.

Carey went all round them in silence, eyes narrowed, while the horses shifted nervously and their riders did their best to stare stolidly ahead.

Bell was also waiting, watching out of the side of his eyes as he held Henry Lord Scrope's old horse. It had been the work of two minutes to make the younger Scrope thoroughly ashamed of forgetting Richard Bell and secure him the position of honour, leading the riderless charger behind the bier. Carey approved of the fact that Bell had groomed the animal himself. He came round in front of the men again.

'Archie Give-it-Them,' he said gently.

'Ay sir,' said Archie nervously. Somebody had put him under the pump: his hair was still wet.

'Dogs get tangled up in them, horses take a dislike to each other, people fall off their horses, women faint, children make rude remarks. With luck we won't find a nightsoil wagon with a broken axle barring our path as we did at an Accession Day parade I took part in once.' Most of them sniggered at that. 'It doesn't matter. If it concerns you directly, sort it out quietly. If it doesn't, ignore it and try not to laugh. If some idiot child gets himself trampled, and his mother is having blue screaming hysterics in the middle of the road, Red Sandy, Bangtail and Long George are to clear the path and join the tail end if they can.'

He smiled and caught young Simon's eye: he was carrying the big drum. 'Let me hear you give the double-pace beat, Simon.'

Simon blushed, dropped a drumstick, picked it up and banged a couple of times.

'Can you count?' asked Carey patiently. The sun was up, the Carlisle gate was open, the crowd of mourners, some of them drunk, were putting on their gowns, and the draught horses were hitched to the empty bier. In about two minutes the Carlisle bell would start tolling.

'Y-yes sir,' said Simon.

'Try again. Count one, two, one, two.'

'One, t-two, one, two...'

'Bang on the one.' Simon did so. 'Better, much better.'

Two more boys with drums came running up and looked at him. One of them had his cap over his ear. Carey sighed.

'Can you remember that, Simon?'

Over in the corner Lowther was trying to shine the trumpeter's instrument with his hankerchief.

'Don't think of anything else. Say it to yourself: bang, two, bang, two.'

'A-ay sir.'

'And keep it slow. We're not going into battle.'

That got a laugh. High overhead the bell at the top of the keep made its upswing and came down with a deep solid note. Normally sounded in the middle of the night when raiders came over the border, it was eerie to hear it in the morning. The trumpeter snatched back his trumpet, made an accidental raspberry and began blowing an abysmally untuneful fanfare.

As they waited their turn to go out the gate, Carey nodded to himself. Dodd had done as he asked, though he suspected wheels within wheels, since one of Lowther's men had a burst lip and Dodd had fresh grazes on his knuckles. His men were clearly smarter than Lowther's and while he doubted anyone except himself really noticed that, still it pleased him...Oh Lord, he'd forgotten to put on his gloves.

Somebody waved a wooden rattle right by Thunder's head. Carey used the whip to stop the crow-hopping which jarred him painfully, and caught Lowther's face turned over his shoulder expectantly. Damn, the man was a complete pillock.

Once at the cathedral, they filled up the battered old building from the back. The churchyard was packed just as tight, with puffing blowing horses investigating each other's necks and four of Lowther's men set to guard them and keep the lesser Borderers from temptation to the sin of horsetheft.

Within, Carey stood, hat in hand, grave reverence on his face, long practice filtering out the mendacious eulogy of the bishop while his mind wandered where it would. There was Philadelphia behind her husband in the front pew, pert and handsome in black with her ruff slightly askew. For all the rehearsed wailing of the paid mourners, there was not a wet eye in the house. Old Scrope had been respected, but not loved, particularly not by his eldest son whom he regarded, rightly, as a fool. His younger son, a solid, pleasant man, had had less expected of him and earned less of his father's impatience: he at least looked sad.

The cathedral choir managed the psalms well, if a little sharp, and the pall bearers succeeded in not dropping the coffin, now closed. In the rush to mount up again outside and form the procession once more, Carey was braced for disaster, but it all went astonishingly smoothly.

They were halfway down the road to the citadel when Carey suddenly knew that something was going on behind him. There was an odd yowling and the crowd was laughing at the bier.

'Straighten your face, Dodd,' he hissed, 'don't let Lowther know we've spotted it. We're supposed to fall off when we mount up after the burial.'

'God rot the bastard...'

'Shut up. This is what we do...'

At the graveside he listened as the words of the burial service were intoned by the bishop, dropping like pebbles of mortality before them. The coffin was lowered into the grave, Scrope and his brother scooped earth on top of it.

Carey backed away from the grave immediately, followed quietly by his men. At the edge of the graveyard were the horses with their reins looped around the fence posts. Choosing their mounts carefully, Carey had his men in the saddle, lined up just outside the gate in two rows, with their helmets off. As they left the burial, Scrope and the gentlemen of the March would pass between them. He kept his own head covered. When Scrope went by, he took his hat off and bowed gravely in the saddle. Scrope beamed with pleasure.

Carey looked through the lychgate to see Lowther furiously trying to stop his men from mounting.

'The Lord hath delivered him into my hands,' he intoned piously to Dodd opposite him, who snorted. In the graveyard there was a sequence of thuds, yells and complaint as eight of Lowther's men discovered what had happened to the girthstraps of the horses that were left. Thunder was there, over by the fence, neighing at him reproachfully while the lad who had taken him slid slowly sideways into the mud.

'Tch,' said Dodd, 'nae discipline.'

'Now follow.'

The gentlemen's horses were on the other side of the gate, with

grooms waiting to help the ladies into the saddle. There was a
flurry of mounting. As the cavalcade rode off back up English
Street to the waiting funeral feast, Carey and his men followed
meekly, leaving confusion behind them.

## SUNDAY, 25TH JUNE, NOON

Carlisle Castle was packed with gentlemen and attendants: the
common folk got their meat and bread and ale in the barracks,
while the gentlemen and their ladies filled the hall of the keep and
attacked the carved beef, mutton, kid, venison and pork with gusto.
In the centre of the main table was Philadelphia's artistic subtlety
of a marzipan peel tower under siege, only made more realistic by
patching here and there where kitchen boys' fingers had explored it.

The various headmen of riding surnames south of the Border
were shouting and talking: lines of tension sprang when the
heads of two families at deadly feud happened to cross each
other's paths, and Richard Graham of Brackenhill and William
Armstrong of Mangerton were moving among the throngs, not
overtly unwelcome, but watched covertly wherever they went.
There was, of course, an official truce until sunset the following
day to let everyone get fairly home.

Scrope came up to Carey busily.

'Robin,' he said, clearing his throat and hunching his shoulders
under his black silk gown, 'that was well done at the churchyard,
quite a compliment, eh? Whose idea was it?'

'Mine, my lord.'

Scrope looked sideways at him and smiled nervously. 'Well,
thank you. Very graceful. Er...Lowther seems to think there was
some kind of mischief, but I'm not clear what.'

Does he indeed, thought Carey, who had felt honour was
satisfied by swapping the horses and hadn't planned to make any
more of it.

'Yes, my lord,' he said blandly, 'despite Lowther's guard on the horses outside the church, somehow our girthstraps were half-slit.'

'Oh dear. Very difficult for you. Any idea who did it?'

'No my lord,' lied Carey. 'Perhaps Lowther had a better notion. It was his men who were supposed to be guarding the beasts, after all.'

'Ah. Whose girths, exactly?'

'Mine and those of my men.'

'Ah. Oh.' Scrope sidled a bit, then reached past Carey's elbow to grab a sweetmeat off a tray as it went by. The boy holding it skidded to a halt, and stood waiting respectfully, one cheek bulging. 'Wonderful comfits Philadelphia made, do try one.'

'No thanks, my lord. My teeth won't stand it.'

Scrope was full of sympathy. 'Dear me, was it Jock…'

Carey smiled. 'No, they survived Jock well enough. It was the Queen feeding me sugar plums and suckets every time she thought I looked peaky that ruined them.'

Scrope laughed and then caught sight of someone over Carey's shoulder, hurried away to speak to another gentleman.

Carey spoke to everyone once, even passed the time of day with Mangerton and Brackenhill. Armstrong of Mangerton was a tall quiet man whose carroty head had faded into grey. Graham of Brackenhill could not have been anything except a Graham, with his long face and grey eyes, though he was twice the width of Jock of the Peartree his brother.

'Brought your pack, eh, pedlar?' he asked and guffawed.

'It's still in Netherby,' said Carey equably. 'Would you go and fetch it for me, Mr Graham?'

Graham laughed louder. 'God's truth, Sir Robert,' he said, wiping his eyes and munching a heroic piece of game pie. 'Ah niver laughed so much in my life when I heard what ye did tae Jock. Wattie still hasnae forgiven ye for the damage to his peel tower. Bit of a tradition in your family, eh, damaging peel towers?'

'I hope so,' said Carey with a little edge, 'I'd like to think I could be as good as my father at it if I had to.'

Graham of Brackenhill stopped laughing. 'Ay, he burnt mine an' all in '69. Took fifteen kine and four horses too. But it's a good variation, eh, having us break 'em down ourselves?'

Carey smiled at him. 'You may speak truer than you know.'

'Eh?'

'If I had my way, I'd make you cast down every tower in the March.'

'Nae doubt ye would, but we canna do that with the Scots ower the border. Even the Queen must ken that.'

'Have you thought, Mr Graham,' said Carey softly, 'of what will happen when the Queen dies, as she must eventually, God save her?'

Clearly he hadn't. Carey left him with the thought and decided he needed some fresh air. The London fashion for drinking tobacco smoke hadn't travelled this far north yet, but still the air in the keep was thick enough to stick a pike in it.

Out in the castle yard you might have thought it was a wedding, not a funeral, with the folk milling about and the queue for beer at the buttery. By the castle gate was a table, guarded by four men, piled high with weapons.

On an impulse, Carey wandered over to it. There was a hideous array of death-dealing tools, most of them well-worn and extremely clean and sharp. In a neat pile over to one side was a collection of dags and calivers.

'Whose are these?' he asked one of the men guarding the table, a Milburn if memory served him.

'What, the guns, sir?'

'Yes.'

'They're the women's weapons, sir. Brackenhill's women. All of them carry firearms when they're in Carlisle.'

'Good God, why?'

'The Grahams dinnae like their women to be raped, so it seems,' said the man and grinned.

'But the recoil would knock them over.'

The man shrugged. 'Most of them are broad enough.'

Carey was staring open-mouthed at the weapons, with his mind spinning. Somebody took his arm and drew him to one side. It was Elizabeth Widdrington.

'Mary Graham had hurt her wrist,' he said, seeing the pattern of it all fall into place. 'She was there when Sweetmilk challenged Hepburn. Mary Graham shot Sweetmilk?'

Elizabeth nodded. 'To save her lover.'

'Who then sent her back to Netherby so he could get rid of the body on Solway Moss.'

'And would have nothing more to do with her.'

'When did you know?'

'When I heard Thomas the Merchant's tale. Sweetmilk would never have let Hepburn get up behind him, but Mary...'

'Why didn't you tell me?'

Elizabeth flushed. 'I wasn't sure. I didn't know the Graham women carried dags. I might have made a mistake—all I had was guesswork.'

Carey nodded. 'And you felt sorry for her?'

Elizabeth didn't answer. Then she added firmly, 'And sorry for Jock of the Peartree too. He's lost a son, why take his daughter?'

Carey stared at her. 'For justice. Because she killed her brother.'

To his astonishment, her face twisted into a sneer. 'Oh yes, justice,' she said. 'I'd forgotten. She's sixteen, she's with child, she's a fool who lost her heart to a man, and we must put her on trial and bring witnesses and get her to confess, and then when her babe's born, we must hang her.'

'Yes,' said Carey simply.

Elizabeth turned, walked away from him.

## SUNDAY, 25TH JUNE, EVENING

Carey went upstairs to the cubbyhole next to Scrope's office used by Richard Bell. One of the boys had come to him in the afternoon asking if he would care to do so, and he went, wondering if Bell meant to thank him.

Richard Bell was, as usual, writing when he came in. He wiped his pen and put it down at once, and came over holding some papers.

Feeling tired and very sore, Carey leaned against the wall by the closed door, took the papers with his eyebrows raised, and skimmed through the Secretary script still used by Bell.

'Lowther's letters,' he said neutrally when he'd finished.

'Ay sir.'

'Not very flattering, are they?'

'No sir. I have a second…er…draft of the letter referring to you.'

Carey took that one, glanced at it, read it carefully and smiled.

'Very subtly done, Mr Bell,' he said, 'Burghley will make the same response to this as he would to the other if he disagreed with it.' He waited.

Bell looked down at his desk. 'Sir Robert,' he said, 'I will be frank with you. I served the old lord faithfully and I will serve his son in the same way. If the lord Warden writes a letter like that to my lord Burghley, you will never see it and nor will I…er… improve it as I have with this. However, Lowther is not my lord and…I would rather be your friend than his.'

'I already regard you as a friend, Mr Bell,' said Carey, his heart lifting. Surely it couldn't be as easy as this, surely the man would want money?

Bell smiled at him, a remarkably sweet smile for such a skull-like face.

'May I have the other letters back, then sir?'

Carey handed them over, keeping the one that described, in withering terms, his doings of the Friday. Before his eyes, Richard Bell put the three letters into the dispatch bag and sealed it.

'May I keep this?' he asked, waving the paper.

'I hope you'll burn it.'

'Naturally, I will,' said Carey, 'but I want to be sure I've understood it properly.'

Bell shrugged. 'These are the only letters dictated by Sir Richard,' he said, pointing to the dispatch bag. 'That one in your hand must be a libellous forgery.'

Carey tucked the paper into the front of his doublet and grinned.

'Of course it is,' he agreed. 'I'm in your debt, Mr Bell.'

'No sir,' said Bell, as he put the dispatch bag on a hook, 'I regard this as fair exchange.'

'Well, good night Mr Bell.'

'Good night, Sir Robert.'

Even when he slept at last, Elizabeth Widdrington haunted his dreams with her hand bandaged and her gun smoking.

## Saturday, 1st July, morning

The week had passed with breathless quiet, since all the worst raiders among the Armstrongs and Grahams were busy deep in Scotland and the hay harvest was in full swing. After the hurry of the days before the funeral, Carey took life easy for a while and spent some of the time, once he felt more comfortable on a horse, riding out across the rough hills and learning how they lay. He even got in some hunting with dogs, since all the falcons were still in moult, though they returned empty-handed.

It was Young Hutchin Graham who came to Carey as he stood in the castle yard at dawn on the Saturday following Scrope's funeral, and muttered that if he chose to ride up to the ford at Longtown, he might find some horses. This confirmed everything Carey had heard about Young Hutchin from Barnabus, but he only narrowed his eyes and said, 'Anything else?'

'Ay,' said Young Hutchin, 'if ye go alone, there might be someone to meet ye there.'

'Will that someone be alone as well?'

'Ay. He gives ye his word on it.'

'I'll be armed.'

Young Hutchin grinned. 'So will he.'

Probably I shouldn't do it, Carey thought, as he shotted both his guns and put them in their carrying case, probably it would be wise to have Dodd and the men follow at a distance.

Longtown was alive with horses, most of them too tired and

footsore to do more than crop the grass ravenously. He rode through them and found Jock of the Peartree sitting in a tree by the ford, with the Widdrington nags tethered to the next bush.

'Good day to you, Jock,' he said.

'Now then, Courtier.'

'How was the raid?'

'Och, it was beautiful,' said Jock, showing the gaps in his teeth. 'The horses...Ye told naught but the truth, I never saw such magnificent animals before.'

'How many of them did you get?'

'I'm not sure. About five hundred, give or take a few.'

'And the King?'

'He's well enough. He was a wee bit upset when we banged his door in and he still canna understand it how the sixty men he had with him in the house managed to drive off two hundred Borderers. He thinks it was God saved him, though Chancellor Melville did his best when ye sent him word.'

'Is that all, a wee bit upset?'

'Well, he's verra upset, to tell ye the truth. I hear he's on his way to Jedburgh with three thousand men to do some justice.'

'And Bothwell?'

'Gone north to the Highlands. He's worn out his welcome here and he knows it.'

They looked at each other in silence for a moment, Carey wondering if he dared ask.

'Ay,' said Jock, 'I dinna like his way of doing things. About Sweetmilk.'

'Yes.'

'I know who killed him.'

'Oh?' said Carey carefully. 'Did...er...did Mary tell you?'

Jock spat. 'Not a peep out of her and I broke a stick thrashing her.'

'Then how do you know?'

Jock stared off into the distance, one hand on the bough beside him.

'All the time we were conversing on top of Netherby tower there was something about your face that was troubling me, Courtier.

245

I didna mind me what it was until we'd let ye go and then it came to me. It was the cut on your cheek.'

Carey had forgotten all about it, though he put his finger to the scar now. 'What about it?'

'I spent a full night before he was buried, looking at my Sweetmilk's poor dead face,' said Jock, 'and it was sorrowful what the crows had done to it, but none of the peckmarks had bled. Except one, the one on his cheek, like yours, that had bled, ay and clotted too. It was the same shape, ye mind, like a star, made by a fancy ring.'

Jock's mouth worked. 'I asked the Earl if anyone hit ye while ye were at Netherby playing at pedlars. He said it was Jock Hepburn that struck you for not calling him sir. Nobody else until I got to work on ye. And Hepburn had a ring like a star, with emeralds on it.'

'Had?' asked Carey, feeling hollow and tired.

'Ay, had,' said Jock, 'I asked him, he admitted he hit Sweetmilk, he admitted Sweetmilk called him out. He denied shooting my son in the back, but he lied.'

'Did he have a trial?' demanded Carey, his voice shaking with a sudden surprising rage. 'Did he get a chance at justice?'

'Justice? There ye go again, Courtier, you're ower impractical. What justice did he give my Sweetmilk? If he'd killed him honourably in a duel, ay well, it would have been sorrowful, but what he did… He's had all the justice he deserves.'

It was on the tip of Carey's tongue to tell Jock the truth about his daughter, but somehow the words stuck there. The silence broken by horse noises was all around him while he tried to decide: would justice truly be served by her hanging? Would Jock even believe him? Mary's death would bring back neither Sweetmilk nor Hepburn. Perhaps Elizabeth was right; he remembered her anger, which had puzzled him. At last he said, 'Where is Hepburn now?'

'His soul's in hell, but ye'll find his body where he left Sweetmilk's, if you've a mind to go fetch it. I wouldnae bother, myself. It's no' very pretty, ye follow.'

'You could have waited, Jock,' said Carey tightly, 'I was planning to arrest the murderer. You could have waited for a trial and proper justice.'

Jock shrugged. 'Why?' he asked. 'Ye're begrudging an old man healing his heart? Besides Hepburn could likely buy his way clear—who cares about the killing of a reiver? This way Sweetmilk can rest quiet.'

'Very neat,' said Carey bitterly.

He turned his horse away to return to Dodd and start the long wearisome job of rounding up the horses, sorting them out by brand and knowledge, and take them back to their rightful owners. Jock called after him, 'I'm in debt to ye, Courtier. I'll mind ye if we meet in a fight and if ye need aid from the Grahams, ye've only to call on me.'

Carey turned back.

'God forbid,' he said, 'that I should ever need help from the likes of you.'

Jock was not offended. 'Ay, perhaps He will. But if He doesna, my offer stands. Good day to ye, Courtier.'

# A SEASON OF KNIVES

*To Melanie, with many thanks*

# FOREWORD

## P.F. CHISHOLM WRITES YOU-ARE-THERE! BOOKS.

A You-Are-THERE! book is a book that can make you feel the nap of Sir Robert Carey's black velvet doublet beneath your fingertips. A You-Are-THERE! book can make you smell the sewer in the streets of Elizabethan Carlisle. A You-Are-THERE! book can make you taste the ale at Bessie Storey's alehouse outside the Captain's Gate at Berwick garrison, and a You-Are-THERE! book can make you hear the arquebuses firing at Netherby tower. A You-Are-THERE! book can make you feel like you're ready to pack up and move THERE, if only you had a time machine.

THERE, in the case of P.F. Chisholm, is the nebulous and ever-changing border between Scotland and England in 1592, the thirty-fourth year of the reign of Good Queen Bess, five years after the Spanish Armada, fifty-one years after Henry VIII beheaded his last queen. Reivers with a high disregard for the allegiance or for that matter, the nationality of their victims roved freely back and forth across this border during this time, pillaging, plundering, assaulting and killing as they went.

Into this scene of mayhem and murder gallops Sir Robert Carey, the central figure of the mystery novels by P.F. Chisholm.

Sir Robert is the Deputy Warden of the West March, and his duty is to enforce the peace on the Border. Since everyone on the English side is first cousin once removed to everyone on the Scottish side, it is frequently difficult to tell his men which way to shoot. The first in the series, *A Famine of Horses*, begins with Sir Robert's first day on the job and the murder of Sweetmilk Geordie Graham. In *A Season of Knives* Sir Robert is framed and tried for the murder of paymaster Jemmy Atkinson. On night patrol in *A Surfeit of Guns*, he uncovers a plot to smuggle arms across the Border.

Sir Robert is as delightful a character as any who ever thrust and parried his way into the pages of a work of fiction, in this century or out of it. He is handsome, intelligent, charming, capable, as quick with a laugh as he is with a sword. He puts the buckle into swash. He puts the court into courtier; in fact, his men's nickname for him is the Courtier.

The ensemble surrounding him is equally engaging. There is Sergeant Henry Dodd, Sir Robert's second-in-command, who does 'his best to look honest but thick.' There is Lord Scrope, Sir Robert's brother-in law and feckless superior, who sits 'hunched like a heron in his carved chair.' There is Philadelphia, Sir Robert's sister, 'a pleasing small creature with black ringlets making ciphers on her white skin.' There is Barnabus Cooke, Sir Robert's manservant, who thinks longingly of the time when he 'raked in fees from the unwary who thought, mistakenly, that the Queen's favourite cousin might be able to put a good work in her ear.' And there is the Lady Elizabeth Widdrington, Sir Robert's love and the wife of another man, who is 'hard put to it to keep her mind on her prayers: Philadelphia's brother would keep marching into her thoughts.' There is hand-to-hilt combat with villains rejoicing in names like Jock of the Peartree, and brushes with royalty in the appearance of King James of Scotland, who's a little in love with Sir Robert himself.

And who can blame him? Sir Robert is imminently lovable, and these books are a rollicking, roistering revelation of a time long gone, recaptured for us in vivid and intense detail in this series.

What is a You-Are-THERE! book?

It's a book by P.F. Chisholm.

Dana Stabenow
stabenow.com

# A SEASON OF KNIVES

# Sunday, 2nd July 1592, evening

If he had been doing his duty as a husband and a father, Long George Little would not have been in Carlisle town at all that evening. All the other men of his troop were out on their family farms, frantically trying to get the hay made while the good weather lasted. Some of them were also taking delivery of very tall handsome-looking horses recently raided by their less respectable relatives from the King of Scotland's stables.

Long George hated haymaking. It wasn't his fault, he reflected gloomily, as he came out of the alehouse by the castle wall and ambled down through the orchards and into Castlegate Street in the warm and shining dusk. There was something in hay which disagreed with him. It was fine while the grass was growing, and he could even mow with impunity, but put him in a hayfield among neat rows of drying grass, and within minutes he was wheezing and sneezing, his eyes had swollen, his nose was running and his chest felt tight. His wife refused to believe in these summer colds. It stood to reason, she would snap, that you got colds in the cold weather, not the hot. That was logic. It didn't matter; whatever the logic of it, haymaking made him ill and if he started pitchforking the hay onto a wagon, he would also come up in a bright red rash that made his life a misery for another week at least.

On the other hand, his wife was going to make his life a misery as well because there were two fields to mow, and none of the children were old enough to do more than bind and stack. Without her man the whole weight of it fell on her alone since she had no brothers and Long George's family were busy with their own fields.

Long George didn't even want to leave the town. His nose was running already: if he went out into the countryside, it wouldn't be as awful as if he were haymaking, but it would be bad enough. Life was unfair. He didn't want to be a bad husband...

He paused, his hair prickling upright on the back of his neck. Perhaps unwisely he had been taking a shortcut through an alleyway called St. Alban's vennel between Fisher Street and Scotch Street. The thatched rooves hung over, within an easy arm's reach of each other and although it was light enough outside, in the alley night had already fallen. A tabby cat was watching with interest from a yard wall.

And he could smell sweat and leather and just make out the ominous shapes of three men hiding in various doorways.

Long George drew his dagger and picked up a half-brick, began backing away. His heart was pounding and he wished he had on better protection than a leather jerkin and his blue wool statute cap. He took a glance over his shoulder to check if there was someone coming up behind him, tensed himself ready to make a dash for Fisher Street.

'Andy Nixon, is that you?' came a low growl.

'No. No, it's not. It's me, Long George Little.'

'Och,' said someone else in a mixture of relief and disgust. Long George recognised the voice and let his breath out again.

His brother detached himself from the shadows and came towards him. He had a cloth wrapped round the bottom half of his face.

'What's going on?' Long George asked.

The cat blinked and sat up. The smell of an imminent fight faded as the three other men came out of their hiding places and joined Long George. Their voices growled and muttered for a while, arguing at first and then gradually came to some agreement. Long George grinned and wiped his nose triumphantly on his shirt sleeve. All four of them went back into hiding, with Long George putting his knife away and climbing over the cat's wall, to hide behind the rainbarrel there.

On a warm Sunday night, a little the worse for drink, Andy Nixon was in a good mood as he turned into St. Alban's vennel, thinking of his bed and the various jobs he had to do in the morning. He still had bits of hay in his hair from his usual Sunday-night tryst with his mistress and the smug warmth that came from making the two of them happy. He savoured the memory of her again as he ambled along the alley, picking his way instinctively between the small piles of dung left by a neighbour's pig and the old broken henhouse quietly rotting against a wall, replaying the feel of his woman's thighs entwined with his own and...

Two heavy shadows jumped out behind him, grabbed for his arms. Andy tried to dodge them, managed to punch one on the nose and knock him over, swung about and tried to run back into Fisher Street.

Another shape vaulted the wall and got in his way as he ran, both of them went over, wrestling against the henhouse and breaking it. Andy tried a headbutt and missed, almost got free from the other man's grip and then felt his arms caught again and locked painfully behind him. He took breath to yell but one of the attackers clamped a large horny palm over his mouth.

'We've a message for ye fra Mr Jemmy Atkinson, Andy,' said the muffled voice. 'Ye're to leave his wife alone. Understand?'

Andy's eyes widened as he realised what was coming. He heaved convulsively, throwing one man into the wall and almost getting away, but by then the one whose nose was bleeding had picked himself up, waiting his moment, and punched Andy vengefully several times in the stomach.

Andy doubled over and fought to breathe, but before he could, somebody else drove the toe of a boot deep into his groin and he toppled over into a black pit of pain. More pain exploded in his right hand as someone trod on it; he put his arms up to protect his head and his knees up to protect his stomach. He was walled in by boots that thudded into his back and shins and pounded his bones to jelly and faded the world into a distant island in a sea of hurt.

From far away he realised one of the men was pulling the others off, spoiling their fun. He could just make out the words of the man who had given him the reason for the beating.

'He isnae supposed to be deid,' snarled the man. 'So leave off when I tell ye. Ay, and ye, for God's sake, what d'ye think ye're doin' wi' a rock? Mr Atkinson said to warn him, no' kill him.'

There were mutinous grumbles and whining. Somebody felt inside the front of his jerkin.

'An' he's no' to be robbed,' came the imperious voice. 'Get off, will ye.'

They caught their breaths while he lay there in a heap, gradually coming back to the sickening pain all through his body, and trying not to moan in case they started again. There was a sound of them brushing each other down.

'Mind,' said another, lighter voice, 'it wasnae a fair fight, four on one.'

'It wasnae meant to be,' grunted the man giving the orders. 'Did ye mind the lad in the wrestling at the last Day of Truce?'

'Ay. I won a shilling, thanks to him.'

'Well, that's thirty-one shillings he's earned ye,' said a third, cheerful voice. 'And Pennycook's one rent-collector the less for a bit.'

They laughed and gave him a couple more kicks in the back for luck as they passed by, going on to Scotch Street.

Andy Nixon lay still for a long long time, waves of blackness passing through him every so often and moving the stars round the heavens above him. He waited between them for the simple act of breathing to hurt a bit less and nursed his swelling right hand, sick with anger and humiliation and fear for Kate Atkinson, his mistress. The cat jumped down and sniffed curiously at his ear, but then trotted silently off and left him in peace.

A serving girl had lit the wax candles in the Mayor of Carlisle's dining room, although the long dusk was still burning in the west. The combination of lights fell about the card players, complicating the shadows and flattering the ladies outrageously. Sir Robert Carey, the new Deputy Warden of the English West March, had glanced at his own four cards, known immediately that he had the makings of a chorus and put them down again with an instinctive caution he had learned at Queen Elizabeth's Court. He looked around idly.

His sister Philadelphia, Lady Scrope, was as pert and tousled as ever in black velvet and burgundy taffeta. She was frowning at her cards. Laboriously she totted up her primero points, while her husband watched her, his gaunt, beaky, under-chinned face quite softened for that moment. Even the Lord Warden of the English

West March could lose his heart to a woman and it was right that the woman was his wife. Unfortunately, his wife did not return the sentiment.

To Carey's left sat Sir Richard Lowther, his enemy and rival for the Deputy Wardenship. Sir Richard was glowering at his cards as if they were reivers he planned to hang, but might be persuaded to let go for a bribe.

Nothing interesting would happen for a while, Carey thought, and let his attention wander again. Two of the players in the second game at the other end of the table were not very well known to him. There was Edward Aglionby, the Mayor, who had invited them to the card party and whose house this was. He was a handsome solidly built man with fine wavy grey hair under his hat and a grave pleasant manner. There was a local merchant, John Leigh, like Aglionby a Carlisle draper and grocer. He was not paying proper attention to his cards and had lost heavily. Now he was blinking at them again, but clearly not seeing them. Then there was Young Henry Widdrington, heir to the headship of one of the major English East March surnames, painfully spotted. And the one Carey knew so well, who had methodically been taking John Leigh's money off him all evening, was sitting upright and alert on the bench beside him, with the rose-tinted light from the window falling just so on her face and making her beautiful.

She isn't beautiful, Carey thought to himself while he waited for his sister to finish counting under her breath. Not even the most maddened poet in the world could say Elizabeth Widdrington was like Cynthia or Diana or Thetis or whoever. She had a long nose and an extremely determined chin and there was no question but that age would make her even beakier. Her hair was a wavy brown, her eyes were the blue-grey of a steel helmet and her mouth would never ever be a rosebud. Wisely she didn't put red lead on it to make it something it wasn't.

She felt the warmth of his stare, looked up, caught his eyes and coloured. He smiled, and her cheeks became rosy and her eyes sparkled. It delighted him privately that she blushed when she saw him, more prized in her because otherwise she was distressingly self-possessed. He wondered idly where the blush started and how far down it went and from there went on to his perennial speculations about what he would see when he finally lifted her smock over her head and...

'Honestly, Robin, you should pay attention to the game.' He looked round to see his sister grinning at him naughtily. Young Henry Widdrington on Elizabeth's right was gazing elaborately into space so as not to see the byplay between his young step-mother and Carey. What little skin that could be seen between his outrageous collection of spots was redder than Elizabeth's. He had folded.

Elizabeth was watching him and he looked steadily back at her. Her eyes were still sparkling and she lifted her chin, her mouth curving. Carey moved his padded hose on the bench, the ruff round his neck suddenly feeling tight and uncomfortable. Lord, Lord, her husband, Sir Henry, was a lucky man. Damn the old villain for marrying her; damn Carey's own father for arranging the match; and damn Elizabeth too for being a great deal more high-principled than most of the married women he had met at Court.

'Er...' said Scrope, and pushed his stake into the middle. Philly exchanged three cards—what on earth does she think she's doing, Carey wondered briefly, as he dropped one card on the table for replacement. Lowther exchanged two, glanced at the cards, and his bushy grey eyebrows almost met in the effort to look disappointed. His fingers started drumming on his thigh. Scrope took two cards, squinted and humphed.

Carey got his new card which was a bit of a long shot, looked at it and relaxed. Most of the time he played strictly on the odds but every so often he gambled wildly on an unlikely hand, just to keep people guessing. On this occasion his gamble had suddenly turned into a much better bet. He was holding all of the fives—a chorus, with a point score of sixty. There were only three hands that could better it: a chorus of aces, sixes or sevens. Naturally it was possible somebody had one—he hadn't seen any aces, sixes or sevens discarded. The next stage in the game was the vying; it was a peculiarity of primero that you must announce how many points you held in your hand and while you could exaggerate your score, you couldn't understate it.

'As I have sixty points I think I'll raise you,' said Scrope, with his habitual nervous smile. Philadelphia looked annoyed and folded.

'Have you indeed?' sniffed Lowther. 'I've seventy-two and I'll see you and raise you.'

Carey smiled lazily. 'Eighty-four,' he said, as he often did, and raised the both of them. As they had all folded on the last deal, there were now about three pounds in the pot. Philly tutted under her breath and frowned, while Scrope looked from him to Lowther and back again, trying to read their minds. It was Lowther that Scrope was really worried about, Carey noted with interest; obviously Lowther's overbid was likely to mean something.

After a lot of hesitation, Scrope folded as well. Lowther glowered at Carey who looked back, still smiling. He scratched the itch on his cheekbone of the glorious green and yellow remnants of a black eye he had got a week before. A prominent local reiver had given it to him, along with many other grazes and bruises and a couple of cracked ribs, but the fault lay entirely with Sir Richard Lowther, who had once been Deputy Warden of the West March and intended to be so again, soon. Carey found that baiting Lowther had added greatly to his enjoyment of the evening; otherwise the play was too slow for him and too inept.

For ten years he had attended at Court and occasionally played cards with his cousin and aunt, the Queen; tense high-stake sessions lasting past midnight, sometimes with the Earl of Leicester, before his death; more recently with the magnificent and prickly Sir Walter Raleigh and Carey's own patron the Earl of Essex. Nothing could be more different from Carlisle. The hot faintly honeyed smell of expensive beeswax candles had brought it all back to him. At Court there were also occasional yawns from dozing maids-in-waiting and men-at-arms, the rustle of silk and velvet around the table, and the soft clatter of the Queen's pearl-ropes as she moved to bet. To his surprise he felt wistful for it: the brilliant colours and decorous smells, the sense of finding the edge of himself, every nerve stretched with the necessity for being witty as well as playing cleverly. The Queen was an excellent player with a good memory for the cards and absolute intolerance of hesitation or ineptitude. She expected to win much of the time but she also despised cheating to make sure she would and could spot it better than many coney-catchers in the City. Carey generally found it took five or six sessions with less dangerous courtiers in order to finance one evening playing the Queen.

He brought himself back to the present because Lowther had raised him again by two pounds, so he thought of his bed and of the walk back to the castle postern gate with Elizabeth.

'Well, Sir Richard,' he mused. 'What should I do?'

'You could try folding,' suggested Sir Richard.

Carey shook his head. Sir Richard had misunderstood the reasons why he had folded most of his hands in the first part of the evening; he had been betting only on the odds and very cautiously at that, in order to build himself up. Carey was flat broke again, needed to buy a new suit and pay for a new sword, and had borrowed three pounds off his own servant Barnabus in order to join the game.

'I'll have to hurry you, I'm afraid, Robin,' said Scrope's reedy voice.

Suppressing his instant irritation at Scrope's use of his nickname, which he preferred to restrict to relatives and women, Carey nodded and continued to pretend indecision.

'I have a number of letters which need urgent attention,' Scrope continued in an injured tone. 'And a message from the King of Scotland too.'

That was portentously spoken. Quite happy to let Lowther's tension build, Carey looked up at his brother-in-law and raised an eyebrow.

'What does His Majesty want, my lord?' he asked.

'Well, as you know, he's bringing an army of three thousand men into Jedburgh soon to try and hunt down the Earl of Bothwell,' said Scrope, looking at his fingernails. 'He's asked me to hold a muster for the defensible gentlemen of the March, to support him if he needs it during his justice raid.'

From the other end of the table Young Henry Widdrington whistled. 'Won't three thousand men be enough?' he asked naïvely.

Lowther barked a laugh. 'Not if he's going into Liddesdale after the Earl.'

'Mm,' said Carey casually. 'Of course, he'll be disappointed. The Earl's not there.'

'Oh?' That took Scrope's attention from his fingers. 'Where is he? Not in England, I hope?'

Carey shook his head. 'I understand he's gone north to the Highlands.'

'And how d'ye know that, Sir Robert?' rumbled Lowther.

'I have my sources,' said Carey blandly.

Carey had been distracted by Elizabeth again. The other card game seemed to have finished for the moment. They were drinking spiced beer brought by John Leigh's ugly little Scottish whippet of a servant and Elizabeth was listening gravely to some involved story from John Leigh while she counted her money. One of the two footmen standing by the door yawned suddenly and looked embarrassed.

'Half of the horses are in England at any rate,' said Philadelphia. 'Thirlwall Castle's captain had to go off in an awful hurry and I'm sure it's because his steward told him he had the chance of some superb horseflesh while the going was good. It's quite lucky really, because it means Lady Widdrington can stay with him on her way home.' She stopped. 'Oh, no, she can't,' she contradicted herself. 'The packtrain's due. Isn't it, Mr Aglionby?'

The Mayor smiled tightly across at her.

'Well, Lady Scrope, we try not tae gossip about the packtrains too much.'

There was a movement over by the window where Mrs Aglionby was sitting stitching at a frame underneath a candle. The woman was sitting up and looking worried.

Philadelphia's expression became very sweet and innocent which Carey knew from experience meant that the Mayor had annoyed her.

'I'm sure we're all friends here,' she said. 'And your dear wife told me she thought I would be able to get some black velvet to mend my old bodice by Saturday.'

The dear wife shut her eyes and bit her lip. Aglionby cast a single glance at her before he answered Philadelphia.

'Ay,' said the Mayor, just as sweetly. 'There's nae doubt we'll have a piece in the warehouse for ye when we've turned it out, and a pleasure to make a gift of it to the Warden's Lady.'

'How very kind,' said Philadelphia. 'So Lady Widdrington will be able to stay at Thirlwall?'

'I dinna ken, alas, my lady,' said the Mayor through his fixed smile.

Carey glanced under the table to be sure of his aim and then kicked his sister hard on the shin.

'Quite right, Mr Aglionby,' he said to cover her yelp and to have an excuse to move his own legs right out of her way. 'It must be a constant struggle to stop the local surnames from disrupting commerce.'

'Ay,' said the Mayor heavily. 'It is.'

Carey was glaring gimlet-eyed at his sister who was glaring back. Get the point, Philly, he was thinking; you weren't this thick-headed in London, but then you were drinking less. With King James expected in the area and prices already high in Carlisle, the old Roman road from Newcastle is probably choked with plodding ponies, heavy-laden with temptation.

'Are you going to bet, Sir Robert?' demanded Lowther, losing patience at last.

Elizabeth was giving back half her winnings to John Leigh and receiving his note of debt in return.

'Sir Robert?' said Lowther with emphasis.

Carey smiled sunnily at him. 'Sir Richard,' he said and pushed every penny in front of him into the middle of the table. A very pregnant silence fell.

'I'm raising you,' he explained, unnecessarily. 'Er...' he waved a negligent hand, causing the engraved garnet ring he had once won off the Queen to flash in the candlelight, '...however much that is.'

The others round the table abruptly remembered their jaw muscles and shut their mouths, with the exception of Philadelphia who solemnly studied the embroidery of her petticoat's false front. She had forgotten her annoyance and her face was suspiciously pink. Carey prayed she wouldn't explode into excited giggles as she had a couple times at Court. The Queen found it charming, but he didn't because it gave the game away.

Young Henry Widdrington came over, helpfully pulled the pile of coins towards him and counted them out and there was silence while he did it. The other players watched. Elizabeth took in the scene, looked amused and whispered into Aglionby's ear. He glanced at her astutely and shook his head, so she whispered to John Leigh and got a nod. Carey felt light-headed with that glorious cold fizzing in the pit of the stomach which could be found only at the gaming tables and in the moment of charging into battle. Elizabeth had seen him play at the peak of his abilities at Court when she was there with Philadelphia in the Armada year and she knew what she was about when she placed her side-bet. Carey hoped Lowther hadn't noticed. He hadn't. He was watching Henry count Carey's winnings of the evening, quite a lot of it originally his money.

'Twenty-one pounds fifteen shillings and sixpence,' announced Henry with a slight quaver in his voice.

'All of it?' queried Scrope.

'Yes, my lord,' said Carey simply.

Everybody was looking at Lowther. He checked his cards again—surely he must know what his points were by now, Carey thought. He was scowling heavily.

'What did you say your points were?' he asked again.

'Eighty-four,' said Carey. It was the point-score of the highest possible hand in primero: four sevens, each worth twenty-one points.

'You always say that.'

'No, I don't. Not always. Are you going to see me?'

Oh, it was agony to watch him. His hand came up to rub his moustache. The sensible thing for him to do, of course, and what Carey himself would infallibly have done, was to fold gracefully. Unless he actually had a chorus of aces, sixes or sevens.

'Well?' asked Scrope tetchily. 'I must get back to my bed before midnight, Sir Richard, if I'm putting out a muster in the morning.'

Carey felt the outlines of his new goatee beard which was just at the itchy stage, tapped his fingers on his teeth and hummed a little tune. He had decided to shave it in the morning because it was a different colour from his hair at the moment. Lowther had started to sweat. Couldn't he afford to play? Then he should learn to do it better, thought Carey unsympathetically, who had never been able to afford bad card-playing in his life. Philadelphia had got a grip on herself and was beckoning over John Leigh's servant.

'Jock Burn,' she said, 'is there any spiced beer left?'

'Ainly the wine, my lady,' said Burn after checking the flagons.

'Oh well, I suppose it'll have to do,' said Philadelphia, holding out her goblet imperiously.

Jock Burn came over into the pool of silence that had formed around them and poured for Philadelphia and then for everybody else. He was a dour enough man, and strictly should not have been employed south of the Border at all, since he was a Scot. It was a law everybody flouted since the Scots would work for half the cost of an English servant.

John Leigh was watching the play anxiously, with occasional glances at the window.

'Sir Richard?' whined Scrope again.

'My Lord Warden,' reproved Carey gently. 'Take all the time you want, Sir Richard,' he added generously to Lowther.

Lowther made a strangulated noise.

'Will ye accept my note of debt, Sir Robert?' he asked in the tone of a man telling a tooth-drawer to do his job.

'Of course,' beamed Carey.

Lowther snapped his fingers irritably at Jock Burn who came over with paper and pens. Lowther scribbled for a moment and then added the note to the pot along with the remnants of his cash.

Carey reached across, picked it up, checked it, nodded and put it back.

'Just making sure you haven't raised me,' he explained to Lowther, who seemed close to explosion.

'Get on with it.'

'You first, Sir Richard,' Carey said courteously, wondering for a single icy moment whether Lowther had fooled him.

Lowther laid down a chorus of kings, with a total point score of forty.

Carey laid down his own hand showing sixty points. Everyone, including Philadelphia, sighed and Lowther let out a high little whine. Thought you had me there, did you, you old pillock, Carey thought with savage satisfaction as he scooped in his large pile of cash. There was actually too much to fit in his purse, but Jock Burn was at his elbow with a velvet bag, supplied like magic from under his sister's kirtle. Elizabeth Widdrington was also receiving a sum of money from John Leigh and smiling triumphantly across at him. Carey smiled back, wanting to laugh.

'Well,' said Philadelphia almost truthfully, 'this has been a very exciting evening.' She was standing up, shaking out her petticoats and farthingale and smoothing down the back of her kirtle where it had rumpled. Lady Widdrington was doing the same as she rose from her own padded stool. 'Mr Mayor, Mrs Aglionby, thank you so much for a delightful dinner and some splendid play.' Tactfully, Philadelphia did not mention the wine which had been terrible. Carey had left all of his, although Philadelphia had finished hers, he noticed. Philly was curtseying to Aglionby and his wife, who curtseyed back in mute distress.

'Ah, yes, indeed,' said Scrope benignly. 'Most excellent. Greatly enjoyed myself.'

Edward Aglionby bowed to both of them and then slightly less deeply to Carey and Lowther. Carey returned the courtesy; Lowther hadn't noticed since he was staring into space looking very green above his ruff.

It seemed John Leigh was in a hurry to go and had already made his bows while Philadelphia was speaking and left the room, followed by Jock Burn.

Down the stairs and into the darkened street where two yawning, blinking servants were waiting for them with torches to see them back into the Castle. The main gate had long shut but of course Scrope had the key to the postern gate. Carey looked around in irritation.

'Where's my man Barnabus?' he demanded of the oldest torchman.

'Ah dinna ken, sir,' came the answer. 'When we were having our dinners in the kitchen, he said he knew a place he could get better fare and went off, sir.'

'Blast him,' said Carey, who had the ingrained caution about walking around with a large sum of money acquired by anyone who had lived in London for any time at all. 'Oh, well. We should look dangerous enough.'

Lowther said goodnight to Scrope and departed to his home, and the rest of them set off up the side of the market place, past the stocks and into Castle Street. The town was empty so close to midnight, even in summer when the sky never really darkened down to black but hung above, a canopy of deepest royal blue, studded with stars.

All about them the scent of haymaking thrust its way across the usual town smells of horse dung and kitchen refuse and the butchers' shambles on their right. Carey breathed deep and happily before offering Lady Widdrington his arm.

'You truly like Carlisle, don't you, Sir Robert?' she said.

He paused, looked at her and put his own hand on her firm square one.

'My lady,' he said. 'I have won enough money to pay for my new sword and buy me a suit; I have infuriated Sir Richard Lowther; I am away from London and best, best of all, I have your arm in mine.'

She smiled quickly and then looked down.

'It would take very little more to make me the happiest man in England,' he hinted delicately and found himself skewered by a grey glare.

This was sensible; Lowther had almost succeeded in getting Carey killed the week before, although Scrope had insisted on an insincere reconciliation. Lowther had been Deputy Warden under the old Lord Warden and had run the March pretty much as he liked. After the Warden's death, he had confidently expected old Scrope's son Thomas to make him Deputy Warden in turn and had been very displeased to find that Scrope had asked his brother-in-law to do the job instead. The five hundred pounds per year that the office was worth was only the beginning of the financial loss this had caused Lowther, never mind the set-down to his prestige and power.

'I can't help it,' said Carey trying to look contrite and failing. 'He's so eminently teasable. Blast and damn Barnabus! I was looking forward to returning the money I borrowed off him so

Lowther could see that even if he didn't have a better hand, he only had to raise me again and I'd have had to fold.'

Elizabeth snorted, trying not to laugh.

\* \* \*

Unlike London, Carlisle was dead at night, most of the crime taking place outside its walls rather than inside. And with the hay harvest even the reivers were working hard. If there was a footpad in Carlisle with more practical experience than Barnabus, then Barnabus thought it would be interesting to meet him. He was like a cat at night, automatically silent and stealthy, even when seriously over-oiled and not actively looking for trouble.

It so happened that he took a shortcut through St Alban's vennel between Scotch Street and Fisher Street and tripped on a soft bundle that moaned.

Knowing one of the nastier games played in London, he drew his dagger and looked carefully all about him. There were no bulky shadows lurking that he could see. He bent down again and squinted at the man at his feet, whistled softly.

'You bin done over good and proper, ain't you?' he said.

As Carey said later, if Barnabus had ever in his life paid attention to the Gospel on the Sundays when he had to attend church, he might have behaved differently. As it was, he did at least see the door the beaten man was feebly trying to crawl through, and he lifted the latch and pushed it open, even hefted the man through it. Unfortunately, that was an excuse for him to find the man's purse on his belt and quietly cut it.

Leaving whoever it was in a heap on the other side of his door, Barnabus turned on his heel and hurried back to Madam Hetherington's bawdy-house.

\* \* \*

'What story did John Leigh tell you that persuaded you to let him have his money back?' Carey asked Elizabeth conversationally as they walked slowly back to the Castle.

'Oh, a tediously long tale about roof mending and the cost of litigation. He has to pay the thatchers in the morning and a barrister in London is bleeding him dry over a suit in Chancery for some property of his wife's.'

'What's the property?'

'I really can't remember the details, Robin, but I think it's the house next door to his own in Carlisle, which was apparently supposed to be inherited by his wife and instead was somehow wrongly inherited by her half-brother. He wants it because he has five children and another on the way. Also, it's prime property and he could expand his business conveniently into the shop-front on the ground floor.'

'What did you say to him?' Carey led her around a large soft patch where the market beasts were usually tethered near the Cathedral. Ahead of them walked Young Henry Widdrington, being very tactful; before him were Lord and Lady Scrope, and at the tail and head of the little procession, the two torchbearers.'

'I said there was no substitute for overseeing litigation personally and that when Michaelmas Term begins he should post down to London and deal with it himself.'

'Have you been in Westminster Hall?'

'You know I was, Robert. In 1588 I dealt with that problem over the chantry lands Sir Henry was supposed to get from the man who murdered his brother.'

'What happened?'

'We won.'

Carey hid a smile.

'That must have been when I was ill,' he said.

'No, you were convalescing by then, but you weren't very interested.'

This time he had to laugh a little. 'I could have been a barrister, you know.'

Elizabeth turned her face to him and looked disbelieving, the Castle looming behind her shoulder.

'It's true. Father suggested it to me; he said he'd pay for me to go to one of the Inns of Court if I wanted and he would find me a good pupil-master. After that I would be on my own, naturally.'

'They say it's a good way to office at court,' Elizabeth said neutrally.

'Besides,' added Elizabeth, 'put you in Westminster with some jowelly lawyer insinuating that you must be either insane or lying, while his father-in-law the judge agrees with him, and your sword would be out in a moment.'

'Nonsense,' said Carey, quite offended. 'I can orate, if I must. It's the studying law that would have been hopeless. The only Latin I ever learned was Catullus and that was because my brother told me what it meant. *Vivamus, mea Lesbia, atque amemus...*'

'Good Lord,' said Elizabeth, curiously. 'Are you trying to impress me with Latin poetry? I'm not the Queen, I know hardly any Latin.'

'Yes,' said Carey truculently. 'Why not? I even remember what it means. "*Let us live and love, my...Elizabeth...And judge the jealous rumours of old men worth but a penny*".'

That was a little too apposite, given the age of Sir Henry Widdrington. Elizabeth turned away and sniffed briefly. Carey touched her hand with his to draw her attention, and went on insistently. Damn it, the beatings his tutor had inflicted in his youth to try and drive at least one declension into his head must be good for something! Besides, this was a crib he had learned by heart for some much-feared lesson long ago, and miraculously it had stuck, perhaps because it was scandalous. And God knew he was no hand at making up stuff like that for himself; he had learned not to embarrass himself that way before he was twenty. Other men's plumage would do for him. He smiled and recited softly, like the very gentlest passage of a madrigal.

'"*The sun may set and return again, but when our brief light is doused, we sleep in endless night. So give me a thousand kisses, and then a hundred more, and a thousand yet again, and a further hundred, and then when we have kissed so many thousand times, let us tumble them together, that neither we nor evil jealousy may ever tell, how very many were our kisses*".'

She was watching him steadily with those clear grey eyes, and as they walked, Carey leaned over and down a little, and kissed her lips.

'One,' he said and smiled for sheer delight at the taste of her, for all it had been quite a decorous kiss. Her chin trembled for a moment before she set it firmly.

'Did the Queen's maids-in-waiting find your Latin impressive?' she asked. The harshness of the words was a little tempered by the softness in her voice. He couldn't take offence; why should he? He wanted her in his bed that night, he was determined on it and she knew it.

'Of course not,' he laughed. 'There are far better Latinists than me about the Queen. Hundreds of them. I expect her laundress knows more than I do.'

'Card-players?'

'No. There, I'm the best.'

Again the dubious snort. He found it charming. But, as he had to admit, he found everything about her unreasonably charming.

'Why did you leave?'

'To be closer to you.'

'I don't think so,' said Elizabeth Widdrington with that same hard grey stare. 'I think you were bored.'

He gestured with his free hand. 'That too, of course. But I could have gone back to the Netherlands. I could have gone to Ireland...'

'What?'

'Well, no; perhaps not Ireland—but France. I could have wangled a place with the King of Navarre. I know the man and he likes me.'

'Oh, don't be silly, Robin. This is all very flattering, but you're here on the Border because it's closer to the King of Scots, and you know Burghley and his son want King James on the Queen's throne when she dies.'

For a moment he examined her face quite seriously. As a younger man he might have been annoyed at her unwomanly astuteness; now he thought how refreshing she was after the greedy empty-headed girls of the Court.

They had passed the orchards and the sweet smell of the Castle's physic garden, and had come, very unhelpfully, to the postern in the main gate which Scrope was trying to unlock. Young Henry

Widdrington took his leave of them and ambled off to his lodgings. Carey drew Elizabeth aside a little.

'Are you offended with me, my heart?' he asked softly. 'There's no need to try and create a quarrel. I love you. If you don't love me, say so now, and I will leave you in peace.'

Elizabeth frowned and looked down. 'I am...I am only offended because...I'm married.'

'To an old bully with the gout.'

'It's easy to despise the old when you're young and healthy.'

'I'm not that young and I...'

'Robin, even if I were a widow you would be mad to marry me.' Her voice had taken a metallic tinge as she cut across his words. 'No friend of yours would let you. I've no more than four hundred pounds in jointure; Young Henry gets the land and houses when his father dies. You should marry some rich lady of the Court and settle your fortunes properly.'

It would have hurt less if she had slapped him. They were the last to go through the postern gate, so Carey shut and locked it and threw the keys to Lord Scrope, who dropped them.

'I'm sorry you think so little of me,' Carey managed to say to Elizabeth, without sounding as bad as he felt.

'Be sensible. I think very well of you, too well to think you'd let yourself be carried away by romantic nonsense.' She hadn't been looking at him, but now she did. 'How much do you owe?' He didn't answer because he wasn't quite sure himself. 'Thousands, I'll be bound. You're neither rich enough nor poor enough to marry for love, and it's a very fickle foundation for a proper marriage anyway. You've been at Court listening to silly poets vapouring about their goddesses for too long.'

Now they were facing each other, suddenly turned to adversaries, wasting a still summer night designed for dalliance. Elizabeth no longer had her arm in his.

For a moment Carey couldn't think of anything to say, since she was completely right about his finances, and what she said was no more than what all his friends and his father had told him often. He didn't care.

'You haven't told me you don't love me,' he said stubbornly.

'That's got nothing to do with anything,' she said. 'I'm married. Not to you, but to a...a rightful husband called Sir Henry Widdrington. That's the beginning and end of it.'

She turned away, to follow the Scropes up to the Keep. Carey thought of his bed, with its musty curtains and its expanse of emptiness, and put his hand on her arm to hold her, turn her to him and kiss her until he relit the passion in her...She slapped his hand away and hissed, 'Will you stop?'

She picked up her skirts and ran.

Carey went blindly after her through the covered way, through the Captain's gate and under the starclad night to the Queen Mary Tower. He climbed the stairs feeling heavy and tired, found his bedchamber dark and empty. He lit a rush-dip from the one lighting the stair, poured himself some wine and sat looking at the pewter tankard for a long time. He had never seen tears on Elizabeth Widdrington's face before.

\* \* \*

At the Red Bull, Jemmy Atkinson counted out the money in front of the men he had employed to beat up his wife's lover. Billy Little's brother Long George had somehow come into the matter as well. Never mind, they weren't asking any more for him.

'You told him, Sergeant?'

'Ay,' said Ill-Willit Daniel Nixon.

Atkinson's thin lips pursed with satisfaction.

'Mr Atkinson?' said Long George. 'What happens if Andy Nixon remembers who we are and sues for assault and battery?'

'You didn't let him get a look at you?'

'Not much of one. But he heard Sergeant Nixon's voice at least.'

'Don't worry,' said Atkinson. 'All of this has been arranged through Sir Richard Lowther. If there's a court case Sir Richard will be your good lord and see to the jury, and Nixon knows he'll not get off so lightly next time.'

They looked at each other and nodded, but Long George was still frowning worriedly. He wiped his runny nose on his sleeve again.

'Well, but, master,' he said, 'Sir Richard's not Deputy Warden any more.'

Atkinson's face grew pinched and mean. The actual Deputy Warden, Sir Robert Carey, had wanted to sack him from his office as Armoury Clerk on discovering that most of the weapons in the Carlisle armoury had disappeared, to be replaced with wooden dummies. The Warden had been Atkinson's good lord on that occasion, protesting that they didn't have anyone else in Carlisle capable of dealing with the armoury. Carey had in fact sacked Atkinson from his other, even more lucrative, office of Paymaster to the Garrison, after somehow getting hold of and reading the garrison account books.

'I have every confidence in Sir Richard's ability to send that nosy long-shanked prick of a courtier running back to London crying for his mother,' he said venomously.

'Mm,' said Long George. He started to say something and then thought better of it.

'And in addition no one else will be witnesses, will they?'

'No,' said Ill-Willit Daniel.

Long George and his brother stayed in the common room until late, playing dice for pennies with their new-gotten wealth. Atkinson too seemed to be waiting for something, and sat drinking in solitary splendour. At last Billy touched Long George's arm and he turned to see Lowther advancing towards Atkinson. Long George stayed still and hoped he'd be invisible.

## SUNDAY, 2ND JULY 1592, MIDNIGHT

Solomon Musgrave was a big fat man with one arm and no teeth; he had lost an arm in action under Lord Hunsdon during the Rising of the Northern Earls, and so he had a permanent position in the Carlisle garrison despite being useless for fighting. He generally kept the gate and slept happily through the day, living as nocturnally as the Castle cats. He was usually the first to see the beacons that told of reivers over the Border and had the job of waking the bellringer who lived permanently up at the keep. Occasionally he bribed one of the boys to do his job, but as a general rule he liked it. It was peaceful in the night and his eyes were so adjusted to darkness that he found daylight often too bright for him and hard-edged.

And he saw a great deal. To his private satisfaction, he knew more about what happened in the Castle than anyone else. He had watched the new Deputy try and coax his ladylove to bed and receive his setdown. He had heard the Scropes in their usual arguments as their yawning maid and manservant got them undressed and he knew that Young Hutchin Graham was doing his best to bed one of the scullery maids, with no success whatever.

He stood at his sentrypost, admiring the stars as they wheeled across the sky, and heard somebody approaching the barred main gate.

Solomon Musgrave tilted his halberd against the stone quietly and leaned over the battlements. There was a hiccup and a loud belch, followed by the noise of puking. The words that floated up to him were too slurred and distorted for understanding, though he recognised the voice and grinned.

Looking across at the Queen Mary Tower, which still had the shutters on the window open, he saw the faint light of a rush-dip still burning. The lusty and fire-eating young Deputy could wait all night for his servant. Barnabus Cooke had had a skinful: more than a skinful. Singing floated up in the silence, something mucky about a Hatter's Daughter of Islington, wherever that was, and then more swearing.

'Shut that noise,' he called down. 'Folks wantae sleep.'

'Lemme in,' came the answer. 'C'mon, or I'll sing.'

Solomon Musgrave grinned. 'Ye can sleep there or find a bed. Ah dinnae care which, but if ye sing I'll spear ye like a fish.'

There was another loud belch. 'Come on,' whined the Londoner below, 'I've...got to shee to hish honour Sir Robert Carey inna morning.'

'Then I'll do his honour a right favour and keep ye out. Ye'd fell him with yer breath the way ye are, I can smell it from here. Go to sleep.'

'He'll beat me if I'm abess...abs...not there,' came the pathetic bleat.

'And nae more than ye deserve,' said Solomon Musgrave primly. 'Shame on ye, to be so drunk. Go to sleep.'

*'She was only a 'atter's dooooorter an' she...'*

Quietly Solomon went along the sentry walk, picked a slim javelin from its sheaf, went back and listened to the adventures of the Hatter's Daughter for a few seconds until he was sure of his aim, then threw. There was a satisfying whipchunk sound, and the vibration of the wooden shaft. The caterwauling stopped. After a moment, Barnabus's voice came again.

'Wotcher do that for?'

'I said I would.'

'You could've killed me.'

'Ay. Next time I willnae miss. Go to sleep.'

There was more sullen muttering and cursing, then shuffling and rustling sounds. Solomon Musgrave squinted down and saw that, from the look of it, Barnabus had picked up the javelin, rolled himself up in his cloak with his back against the wood of the door, pulled his hat over his eyes and gone to sleep. A noise that combined the music of a pigpen and the regularity of a sawpit rolled up towards him.

Solomon Musgrave sighed. 'Ah wish Ah'd known the man sounded better drunk and awake.'

Feeling sorry for the Deputy who presumably shared a room with that awful noise, he went back to his contemplation of the heavens.

## MONDAY, 3RD JULY 1592, EARLY MORNING

'I'll fetch your father his porridge,' said Kate Atkinson. 'And then I'll come and show you a new stitch.' She sighed. She needed more help in the house, but her husband refused to allow her to waste his money on idle girls so she could sit by a window and plot like his bitch of a half-sister.

'I done this one almost straight,' said little Mary proudly. 'Look.'

Kate Atkinson looked and agreed that it was much straighter than the one above and in a little while all her stitching would be completely straight. The child wasn't likely to be a beauty, with her mousy hair and sallow complexion, but she would have a good dowry and unimpeachable skills in housewifery; she should make a good enough match.

Suppressing the knowledge that her own marriage had been a good enough match according to her mother, Mrs Atkinson took the bowl of porridge, sprinkled salt on it, laid it on a tray with a mug of small ale and steeled herself to the unpleasantness that awaited her upstairs. He had been drinking half the night. She knew he had; she had woken in the dark to the pungent smell of beer and the lolling body of James half shoving her out of bed. The watch-light had burned down wastefully and he hadn't even drawn the curtains to keep out the dangerous bad airs of the summer. She muttered to herself about it as she climbed the stairs carefully.

It was a long time before she came down again, and when she did she was as white as linen. Her hands shook as she found her husband's black bottle of aqua vitae in the lock-up cupboard and took a couple of painful swallows.

Ten minutes later, Mary Atkinson trotted self-importantly through the broad streets of Carlisle, carefully lifting her kirtle away from the little midden heaps all around. Mrs Leigh their next-door neighbour waved to her and asked how she was, and she explained that she was very well as her mam had told her to do, before trotting on. She avoided the courtyard with the Fierce Pig in it and said hallo to three cats and a friendly dog, which took a little time. She also waved to Susie Talyer but couldn't stop to skip with her because she was taking a Message.

She was picturing herself walking up St Alban's vennel to Mr Nixon's door and banging on it and explaining her Message, when she was very disappointed to see Mr Nixon coming down the street towards her. He looked funny; his mouth was all swollen, his eyes were bruised and he was walking with a limp and his arm in a sling. It was sad she wouldn't be able to knock on his door now, but she could still take her Message and she liked him, so she squealed his name and when he looked, she ran straight for him and cannoned into his legs.

Mr Nixon made an odd little squeak-grunting noise and held onto her tightly.

'Don't do that!' he growled at her.

Her face crumpled and puckered and tears started into her eyes.

Mr Nixon sighed, let go of her arms and patted her head.

'There,' he said awkwardly and rather hoarsely. 'Dinna cry, Mary my sweet, I'm not angry at ye, only ye hurt ma legs which is sore this morning.'

She might get a penny off him to quiet her, so she cried all the harder.

'Is yer father in?' he asked her cautiously, without taking proper notice of her tears.

A bit surprised that her magic power hadn't worked this time, she nodded and gulped. 'But me mam said for ye to come anyway, she said ye mun come right now and never mind what ye're at, she said she needs ye bad.'

Mr Nixon's face looked very odd and he stood still for a long while. He looked angry and afraid at the same time.

'Me dad's still asleep,' she said helpfully. 'He wouldna wake when mam yelled for him. She said he'd drunk too much last night.'

'Did he, by God?' said Mr Nixon in a nasty voice. He put his left hand on his dagger hilt and made the lift and drop move-ment that even Mary knew was the prelude to a fight. She took the arm that wasn't in a sling and started pulling him after her.

'Ye must come, Mr Nixon, please,' she said. 'Me mam's very upset, her face is as white as her apron, it is so, and she wouldna show me the new stitch like she promised, so please come.'

Mr Nixon's face took on a new set of lines under the bruising, his lips went all thin and into a straight line.

'Ay,' he said. 'I will.'

'I did it, mam,' she said plaintively. 'I did the Message.'

Her mam looked at her vaguely as if not seeing her. 'Go help Julia with the buttermaking,' she said, as if Mary had not just delivered an important message for her. Mary was thinking about crying again, but Mr Nixon did a sort of smile for her and nodded. 'I'll give ye the money for a penny bun if ye go off like a good lass now,' he said, so she held out her hand and after a pause he put the penny in it and she trotted off to the scullery where the paddle in the milk was finally beginning to make the *plunk plunk* noises that heralded butter. Perhaps she could get some buttermilk to drink as well.

Kate Atkinson blinked at Andy Nixon for several seconds after her daughter had gone. Her mind seemed not to be working properly, or at least it was some while behind what her eyes saw. She didn't look as if Atkinson had beaten her, or he had kept away from her face if he had. She frowned suddenly.

'Andy, what happened to your face... and your arm?' she asked.

'What d'ye think, Kate?'

'I...don't know.'

'Och, work it out, woman.'

'Did something fall on you?'

Andy Nixon managed a mirthless smile. 'In a manner of speaking. Four men, if ye want to know.'

'What?'

'Your husband paid four men to beat me last night.'

It seemed impossible but her face grew whiter. Both hands went to her mouth.

'Oh,' she said.

'Ay,' agreed Andy. 'Ah was comin' to tell ye we canna go on; I willnae come to see ye any more. Not for a while, any road. I'm going back to my father.'

Well, he hadn't expected her to like it, but whatever he had expected it wasn't a peculiar high-pitched little laugh.

She saw it frightened him, so she swallowed hard and took a deep breath.

'Come and see him,' she said, taking his good arm and leading him to the stairs.

'Kate, are ye mad? I dinna wantae see him. After what he had done to me last night, I willna be responsible for what I...'

'Oh, shut yer clamour and come wi' me,' snapped Kate. 'Ye'll understand when ye see him.'

He did indeed. While Mary had done her message, Kate had already stripped the sheets off the bed, but left her husband half wrapped in the worst-stained blanket. Dead bodies were nothing new to Andy Nixon, but he had never before seen anyone grinning so nastily from his throat, with all severed tubes and the like showing as if he were a slaughtered pig.

Kate bolted the door behind him as he took in the scene. It was all too much for his aching head and aching body. He sat down on the clothes chest beside a tray of cold porridge, and put his face in his hand.

'Oh, good Christ,' he croaked.

'Ay,' she said. 'What am I to do?'

'What happened?' he asked eventually, with a horrible cold suspicion fully formed in his heart. Atkinson had boasted of what he had done to his wife's lover and his wife had taken a knife and...

'Why? D'ye think I did it?' Kate's voice was shaking. 'I left him as alive as you are, and after I'd milked the cow and skimmed the cream for Julia and made the porridge and seen to the children and sent them off to school, I came back and this is what I saw. And...and the blood all over everywhere.'

He was still staring at her and for all his trying, she saw the doubt in his eyes. Her hands clenched into her apron.

'As God is my witness,' she said, very low and intense. 'I did not kill my husband.'

'Ay,' he said, still not able to deal with it. Kate laughed that high silly noise again.

'I was going to ask ye if ye'd done it yourself,' she said.

Andy's mouth fell open and he felt sick. He hadn't thought of that, but there was no denying the fact that he had wanted the little bastard dead as well.

'But I didna,' he said.

'No more did I,' she told him.

The two of them stared at each other while each could see the other wondering and wondering. Finally, Kate Atkinson made a helpless gesture and turned back to the corpse.

'Well, he's dead now. What's to be done?'

'I…I suppose I'd best get Sir Richard Lowther, and tell Fenwick to come for the body and…'

She whirled back to face him with her fists clenched. 'For God's sake, Andy, think!' she hissed at him. 'Who d'ye think they'll say did it? You and me, for sure. You think the women round about here havenae seen us? Well, they have and they'll delight in making sure Lowther knows the lot, and the Warden too. They won't know how it was done for sure, but they'll know I was in the house and that ye would likely be angry with him. What do ye think will happen? We're not reivers, ye're only Mr Pennycook's rent collector and I'm just a woman. You'll hang and I'll burn.'

'Burn?' he said stupidly.

'Ay. Burn. For petty treason. If you kill a man, Andy Nixon, and ye're caught, that's murder and you'll hang for it. If a woman kills her husband, that's no' just murder, it's petty treason. They hang, draw and quarter you for high treason and they burn ye for petty treason. So now.'

Andy Nixon was not a bad man, but neither was he a very clever one. He was broad and strong and quick in a fight, and he could withstand injuries that would have put a weaker man in bed, which was the only reason he could walk at all that morning. But thinking was not what he was paid to do by Mr Pennycook and, generally speaking, he left that to his betters. He gazed at the corpse and his mind was utterly blank.

'Well?' asked Kate Atkinson. 'We canna leave him there. What shall we do?'

'I don't know.' He blinked and bit the hard skin of his knuckles. 'I could likely say it was me did it, and ye knew nothing of it and then I'd hang but ye wouldna burn,' he offered as the best he could come up with.

Kate Atkinson looked at him for a moment with her mouth open. He shrugged and tried to smile.

'I canna think of anything else,' he explained sadly. 'I don't know what to do.'

She suddenly put her arms round him and held him tight. He put his good arm about her shoulders and felt the juddering as she wept into his shoulder, but she was holding him too hard and it hurt his bruises, so he whispered, 'Mind me ribs, Kate. I'm not feeling myself this morning.'

She lifted her head up and wiped her tears with her apron. 'You're Mr Pennycook's man,' she said, still sniffling. 'Would he be a good lord to ye, d'ye think?'

'He's no' bad to work for,' Andy allowed, trying to think it out. 'And he's rich and he has men to do his bidding.'

'Would he turn you over to the Warden?'

'I dinna think so.'

'Could we buy him?'

'Oh ay,' said Andy. 'He's always ready to be bought, is Mr Pennycook.'

'Well, I'll pay him a blackrent of five pounds in silver plate, if he'll find a way out.'

Andy nodded. 'He might listen at that. And five pounds would keep him quiet in hopes of getting more. It's worth trying.'

'Good,' she said, and patted at the shoulder of his jerkin with her apron to dry the wet there. She used one of the keys from the bunch at her belt to open the small plate chest under the bed and gave him a couple of chased silver goblets to use as a sweetener. 'Off you go to Mr Pennycook then, Andy, and say nothing to anyone...'

'Do you take me for a fool?' he demanded, and she managed to smile at him demurely.

'No, Andy.'

Just for a moment he felt a stab of happiness, because if they could only slip clear of the noose and the stake, she was a widow now and he could marry her at last. No more skulking about in the cowshed. He forgot about his ribs and put his good hand on her shoulder, pulled her close and hurt his mouth kissing her.

'There now, sweetheart. Pennycook will see us right. Dinna fret, Kate.'

## Monday, 3rd July 1592, dawn

Barnabus Cooke awoke from a dreamless sleep into the belief that someone was beating him over the head with a padded club and kicking him in the ribs. The first was untrue, the second was true. It was Solomon Musgrave waking him into the worst hangover he had had since... Well, since his last hangover.

'Laddie,' said Solomon patiently, 'ye're blocking the gate.'

'Urrr...' said Barnabus self-pityingly, rolled onto his hands and knees and stayed there for a moment with his head about to fall off, his tongue furred with something that tasted of pig manure, and his stomach roiling. He was collecting the courage to stand. His clothes were all damp with dew, as was his cloak, and he had tangled himself up with a javelin.

'Wha...what 'appened?'

'Some enemy o' yourn must have poured too much beer and aquavita down your poor neck,' said Solomon drily.

The soft mother-of-pearl light in the sky was stabbing his eyes, his body ached, he needed to piss, and he was shaking.

'Oh God.'

'Ay,' said Solomon. 'That'll be him. Will ye get out of my way, Barnabus, or shall I kick ye again?'

'Give me a minute, will you?'

'Ye see, laddie, I would, but there's a powerful number of people waiting for the gates to open and it's no' my place to keep them waiting, so...'

Solomon's foot drew back and Barnabus scuttled out of range, hurting his hands and knees on the cobbles and stones. He reached the corner of the wall and used it to climb himself to his feet, then stood there swaying while Solomon completed his duties.

'Ye'd best go see after your master,' suggested Solomon kindly. 'Ah heard him roaring for ye a minute or two back, now.'

Very carefully and gently Barnabus walked to the Queen Mary Tower. He was still climbing the stairs like an old man, one tread at a time, when he was almost knocked flying by Carey trotting down them. Carey was one of those appalling people who wake refreshed and ready for anything every morning about an hour before everyone else, and then bounce around whistling happily, avoiding death only because they move faster than the people who want to kill them. This morning he wasn't whistling and was looking very bad-tempered, but otherwise he was his usual horribly active self.

Barnabus flailed helplessly on the step until Carey's long hand caught his doublet-front and steadied him.

'Where the devil were you last night...?' Carey began, and then caught the reek of Barnabus's breath. He looked critically at his shaking, swallowing, pockmarked servant and shook his head. 'By rights I should give you a thrashing,' he said conversationally, 'for drunkenness, venery and abscondment.'

'Wha...'

'And it's evident I don't work you hard enough.'

'But, sir...'

'*Shut up!*' Barnabus winced, though Carey hadn't shouted very loudly. 'What the bloody hell do you think you are? If I had wanted some idle beer-sodden fool without the wits of a caterpillar, who hasn't even the sense to be where he's ordered to be, when he's ordered to be there, I could have hired me some brainless wonder from the Court. Couldn't I?'

'Sir.' Briefly Barnabus wondered if a thrashing would be half as painful as Carey's loud voice in the confines of the stairwell, and then decided it would. Definitely. He swallowed hard. Puking on Carey's boots would not be a tactful thing to do, even if he hadn't much left in his stomach to do it with.

'I...er...I think I slept by the gate, sir.'

'Passed out there?'

'No, I...'

'Get upstairs. I want my chambers immaculate; I want my clothes in order; I want my jack and fighting hose ready to wear, and I want my spare boots cleaned.'

'Yes, sir,' said Barnabus despairingly. 'I'm not very well, sir. I'm sorry sir...'

'And,' added Carey venomously, using Barnabus's doublet-front to pull him nose to nose, 'if I find you snoring in bed when I come back, I'll bloody well kick you out of it. Understand?'

Barnabus nodded, scurried past, up the stairs and through the door. Carey scowled and was heading for the stables when his sister caught sight of him.

'Robin,' she called. 'Robin, can I talk to you for a moment?'

Carey wanted only to get in the saddle and ride out of the city so he could be away from crowds of people and do some thinking. He pretended not to hear.

'Robin! I know you heard me.'

He stopped and sighed. 'What can I do for you, Philadelphia?' he asked politely. Philly came up to him looking very businesslike in a claret-coloured wool kirtle and bodice of black velvet, a lace-trimmed linen apron skewed halfway under her arm. She wrinkled her brow at him.

'What's wrong with you this morning?' she demanded, clearly in no very good temper herself. 'You didn't drink enough to have a hangover, and you wrung Lowther dry as well. Why aren't you happy?'

He wasn't going to answer that question, which he saw too late was as good as a complete exposition to his sister.

'Oh,' she said, a little regretfully. 'I see. I hoped Elizabeth might...Well, serve you right. I've got a great big bruise on my shin. You'll be wanting something to take your mind off things. Come with me.'

'Why?'

'I want you to help me...do some persuading. You used to be fairly persuasive, as I recall.'

Carey harrumphed, which almost made his sister grin despite her sore leg and sorer head, because it was so exactly the noise their father made.

Perhaps because he had a long list of muster-letters to write to gentlemen of the county, and a teetering pile of complaints from Scotland about the recent large raid on Falkland Palace, Carey went along with her meekly enough, until she took him round the back of the Keep into the scurry of sheds and old buildings there. Finally he protested.

'What am I doing?' repeated Philadelphia with fine rhetoric.

'Why, nothing, Robin. Except assisting my husband in his duties,' she said over her shoulder as she stalked ahead of him through the cool dim dairy to the cheese store at the back. Out of a corner she got a cheese that was never of her making, being stamped with a large C. Carey recognised it at once.

'That one's got weevils in it,' he told her helpfully. 'All the Castle ration cheeses have weevils, or worse. Why don't you…'

She glared at him, hauled it onto the cutting board and gave him a knife.

'You cut it, then. I want about half a pound.'

'But, Philly…'

'Go on, if you want to find out what I'm doing. I hate the way they wriggle even after you've cut their heads off.'

Carey did too, but he manfully cut the required piece and lifted it gingerly onto a platter. Philadelphia arranged nasturtium leaves and dill around it and looked about for somebody to carry it. One of her maidens hurried past in the passage, carrying a newly scoured butterchurn.

'Nelly,' she shouted. The girl was a round-faced doe-eyed creature with a wonderful crop of spots and the faint cheesy odour of all dairymaids. She blenched at the sight of what she was supposed to hold.

'Don't drop it,' Philly ordered the horrified girl, as she swept into the wet larder by the Castle wall. She went purposefully to a barrel of salt beef in the corner of the room, this one with a no less ominous JP for James Pennycook on it, and used the tongs to fish up a piece of meat that managed to be as hard as wood and still stank, with a decorative light green sheen. Slicing it with great effort and her breath held, she arranged the whole on another platter, with some loaves of gritty bread and a dish of rancid butter, grabbed Carey's youngest servant Simon Barnet as he wandered past still rubbing straw off his hose, and had him form a procession up to the Keep. She herself took a pewter jug, dived into the buttery, and filled it from the ale barrel that was shunned by anyone with a nose.

'Robin,' she said brightly as they walked back to the draughty Keep. 'Do you remember what you were telling me the other day about victualling contracts?'

'Er...yes.'

'Good,' she said, tweaking Simon's blue cap straight. 'I'll go first. Then Simon and Nelly, then you, Robin. Then agree with everything I say and back me up.'

'Philadelphia...' began Scrope in a strained voice as the combined smells hit him.

'Yes, my lord?' said Philadelphia sweetly, turning back.

'My lady, we can't serve this to our guests...'

Her face crumpled with concern. 'Oh my lord, I'm so sorry. It's their own supplies. I thought they'd be interested to see the quality of them. But if the food's too rotten to eat, I'll go down and fetch something better...'

Carey coughed with the effort of keeping a straight face. Four pairs of male eyes were glaring at his sister.

'Madam,' intoned Michael Kerr, Pennycook's factor and son-in-law, 'surely these gentlemen should not be expected to eat the same food as the common soldiers of the garrison?'

'No?' asked Philadelphia, greatly surprised. 'Why not? It costs as much as our own food from our estates. More, in fact. And my brother eats it, don't you, Sir Robert?'

'Yes, yes, I do.' Carey had his face under control now. 'When it's edible.'

'Ye eat with the men?' asked Pennycook, disbelievingly. 'But Ah thocht ye were the Deputy Warden.'

'It's good practice for a Captain to do so sometimes,' said Carey blandly. 'That way, he and his men get to know each other better, which is important in a fight.'

This was certainly true, as far as it went. However, he generally ate with them at one of the many Carlisle inns, not in the Keep hall where this rubbish was served up to those of the garrison who had spent or gambled all their pay.

Scrope was watching hypnotised as a maggot broke from the safety of the cheese and began exploring the rest of the platter. No doubt it was in search of its friends still hiding in the meat. Perhaps they could have a little party...Get a grip on yourself, man, Carey told himself, as he sat down beside Michael Kerr and drew his eating knife to cut the bread. Simon came rushing back with the goblets and plates, laid them out and Philadelphia served them all from the jug, curtseyed again and swept from the room, followed by Simon and Nelly.

Carey was enjoying the row of stunned expressions. Lord Scrope had been told often enough about the appalling quality of the garrison rations and he had in fact carried out a short inspection. But clearly it had taken the sight of the muck laid out on plates ready to eat to bring home to him just how badly he and the Queen were being cheated.

The junior clerk swallowed stickily. With a flourish straight from the Queen's Court, Carey offered the platter to James Pennycook, who flinched back.

Scrope coughed. 'I think we're in agreement then, gentlemen,' he said lamely. 'The old contract is renewed for the following year. I'll have Bell draw up the notice...'

'Excuse me, my lord,' said Carey very politely. 'I was wondering if you'd had a chance to sort out the question of wastage?'

'Wastage?'

'Yes, my lord. When I was in the Netherlands...'

'My brother-in-law has served with the Earl of Essex in the Low Countries,' explained Scrope. 'He's an experienced soldier.'

'The Earl of Essex, eh?' said Pennycook. 'Is he the Queen's minion...er...favourite?'

'Yes,' said Carey pleasantly. 'I received my knighthood from him. The Queen was very put out; she said she had wanted to knight me herself since I'm her cousin.'

There, you Scotch bastard, he thought. Chew on that.

'Do have some of this meat, sir,' he added. Pennycook smiled feebly, held up his hand and Carey, deliberately misinterpreting, gave him two generous slices. Oh dear, he'd got some severed weevils as well.

'While I was fighting the Spaniards, I learned a great deal,' he continued, taking some of the food onto his own plate. No help for it, he had to do it, thanks to Philadelphia. 'Particularly from Sir Roger Williams, a most reverent and experienced soldier.' They weren't really listening; they were watching him cut a slice of cheese that was veined with blue mould, tap out the foreigners. 'He always got on very well with his purveyors.' He ate the cheese while the men who had supplied it watched in fascination, realising to their dismay that if he ate their food, common courtesy dictated that they must too. There was an acrid musty tang to the cheese, not too bad, really, he thought to himself. It was actually better than the frightful stuff they'd eaten on board ship when fighting the Armada. He swallowed and continued. 'The contracts were generous—as yours are—but always included a clause stipulating that any food that was unfit to eat was sent back to the purveyors and its price subtracted from the next payment.'

'That's a good idea,' said Scrope, with an air of pleased surprise. Pennycook picked up a piece of bread, nibbled on it. Carey could hear his teeth grating on the grit, sand, sawdust, ground bones and God knew what else these thieves adulterated the flour with. Pennycook put it down. Michael Kerr had eaten a piece of cheese and was blinking unhappily at the crock of butter. The junior clerk looked at the meat and wisely decided to nibble on some bread. Thank the Lord, Philadelphia hadn't seen fit to offer them any of the salt herring as well; Carey had recognised the barrels as ones that had been condemned as unfit for the English fleet in the Armada year, four years ago.

Scrope put down his knife with a bright smile. 'You'd have no objection to a clause like that in our agreement, would you, gentlemen?'

Carey thought about braving the meat, but decided to stick with the cheese since the bellyache you got from that rarely killed you.

'But the food we supply is of the verra highest quality,' protested Pennycook automatically, falling straight into the trap. Michael Kerr choked on his ale.

'Of course it is,' said Carey smoothly. 'I'm sure that, as with Sir Roger, we will hardly need to use the wastage clause. The Queen will approve as well. She was very concerned at some of the troubles my brother has had with his victuallers in Berwick. Can I offer you some cheese, Mr Pennycook?' Mr Pennycook, who was, as

Carey knew, one of the victuallers to the Berwick garrison, shut his eyes, shook his head.

'That's settled then,' said Scrope, who sometimes behaved as if he were not quite so foolish as he looked. 'We'll include the clause in the new agreement. A splendid idea, Sir Robert; thank you.'

Pennycook and his men glowered at him in unison and he favoured them with a particularly sweet smile.

'Ehm,' said Pennycook, his voice rather higher than normal. 'This is all verra weel, Sir Robert, my Lord Warden, but we canna go about putting in new clauses to the victualling contracts wi' nae mair than a wave of a hand...The advocates to draft it will cost a fair sum, d'ye not think?'

Mr Pennycook had small brown watery eyes and a pale bony face gone very waxy. There was a pause while he seemed to be struggling for words. 'Sir Robert?' he said, drawing his rich brocade gown tight about him. 'Surely ye canna be threatening me wi' legal action?'

'Threatening you, Mr Pennycook?' Carey laughed artificially. 'Nothing could be further from my mind. I was only agreeing that while we're briefing lawyers to draw up the new wastage clauses in the victualling contracts, we should get our money's worth and have them look at the contracts as a whole as well. Wasn't that what you said?'

Mr Pennycook had in fact paid good money to the young lord Scrope's father and Sir Richard Lowther to keep the contracts unexamined. He made a little rattle in his throat.

'After all,' Carey added confidingly, 'clerical errors do creep in, don't they, what with copying and recopying.'

For a horrible moment Mr Pennycook wondered if this strange creature had actually read the contracts, and then decided it was impossible. Nobody except a lawyer could understand a word of them. He fixed on high indignation as the only possible escape.

'And now ye're dooting ma word.'

'Far from it, Mr Pennycook,' Carey said affably. 'Why would I do that? Have some more ale.'

'I'll not sit here and be insulted,' Pennycook said, rising to his feet with dignity. 'Good day to ye, my Lord Warden, Deputy.' He fixed the thoughtful Michael Kerr with a glare and said, 'Are ye with me, Michael?'

Kerr stood, made his own bows and followed Pennycook from the chamber in a rush of dark brocade and velvet. Scrope sat staring at the green meat before him and frowned worriedly.

'Was that wise, Robin?' he asked and began twiddling his knife in and out of his spidery fingers. 'Our stores are nearly empty.'

'Well, my lord,' Carey said. 'Sir Roger told me that until the contract's signed, you have them at a disadvantage. They need you more than you need them. Pennycook has warehouses full of food that no one can sell anywhere else, bought dirt cheap, and harvests paid for in advance. If his contract is not renewed, then he's a ruined man.'

'Hm. I never thought of that. So you think he'll come round?'

'Definitely.'

'There isn't more in this, is there, Robin?'

I wish you wouldn't call me by that name, Carey thought, but shrugged.

'What do you mean?'

'You're not after the victualling contract yourself, are you? Or for somebody you...heh...know?'

Carey made a little shake of his head. He hadn't in fact thought of it that way, but it was an interesting idea. Everyone knew victualling contracts were pure gold...

'I don't know, my lord,' he said honestly. 'But it's a thought, isn't it?'

Scrope beamed at him. 'Get Simon to clear this dreadful rubbish away,' he said. 'I'm not at all hungry.'


## MONDAY, 3RD JULY 1592, MORNING


Pennycook walked speedily away from the Castle, trailing his factor and junior clerk, collected two further henchmen at the gate and went to his house.

'How much d'ye think the new Deputy Warden wants?' Pennycook asked Michael Kerr as they sat with spiced wine and wafers to settle their stomachs. Michael was his son-in-law and he valued the young man's advice.

Kerr shook his head. 'I don't think it's so simple as that,' he said. 'I heard Thomas the Merchant offered him the usual pension and he turned it down flat.'

Pennycook half choked on his wine. 'Eh? But he's a courtier, is he no'?'

Michael Kerr shrugged. 'He is, but that's what I heard.'

'Good...Heavens.'

'Perhaps it's Lord Scrope putting him up to it. Perhaps he's turning the screw on the price.'

Pennycook sat back in the carved chair, looking relieved. 'Ay,' he said. 'That must be it. He'll get the difference between what the Queen pays and what we ask, and he'll have put his Deputy up to the game...I dinna like this talk of lawyers, though.'

'Well, you started it,' Kerr pointed out. He was pacing up and down, looking very worried. 'I wish ye hadnae. That young Deputy's mad...'

'Don't trouble your head, Michael. It's Lord Scrope.'

'No, but...' Michael Kerr was rethinking his own theory. 'It must have been a surprise to him, when he saw the...the...er, vittles brought in. I saw his face. He's not that good an actor, and he was angry wi' his little wife as well. No. It's the Deputy. And I know what he's up to.'

'What?'

'See, if it was just a bribe he was after, he would have come to you privately and said, this is what I'll do unless...And you would have argued a bit and then paid it. This was too public. If he suddenly changed his tune, him or Scrope, and says the vittles is fine, well, it's an embarrassment.'

'So?' asked Pennycook warily.

Michael Kerr drank some wine.

'He's after the victualling contract himself,' Kerr said grimly.

'Or he's doing it for some big London merchant.'

Pennycook screwed up his face in horror. 'But they canna supply from London…'

'Or in Newcastle or where he grew up in Berwick. Anyway, they only back him. He insists on the wastage clauses and that gives him the way out of renewing. Then Scrope will give him the contract and then…'

He didn't have to explain it. The two of them were as deep in the business as they could be. There were ships already on their way from further down the coast and packtrains from Scotland, all of which would need paying soon—and with what, if not the Queen's money?

Pennycook's face was a bony mask and Kerr felt sick.

A servingman knocked at the door and then slid round it.

'Mr Pennycook, sir,' he said, cap in hand, 'Andy Nixon's waiting downstairs. He's desperate to see ye, sir.'

'What does he want?'

'Willna say, sir. Only he has to see ye now.'

\* \* \*

Elizabeth Widdrington regretted having to leave Carlisle, in a way, but in another way it was a relief to have the decision taken from her. She would have liked to give her poor horses more rest—after all they had been from Netherby to Falkland Palace and back in a week—but she would take the journey to Widdrington very gently and spend four days on it, rather than the two it had taken her coming the other way.

She sighed, signalled for her menservants to carry the packs down from her chamber in the Keep, and followed after them hoping she would find the two men-at-arms Scrope was lending her, but not Philadelphia's persistent brother.

Like them, he was waiting for her at the stables. She paused by the muck heap before he saw her, and watched him for a while. It was likely to be her last good stare at him, so she took her time. Cramoisie wool for his suit was a dangerous colour for him, but this was the right shade of purple red: his hose were paned and padded but not foolishly so, and made his long legs very elegant; his doublet had a slight peascod belly for fashion's sake, the kind a man could only get away with if his own stomach was as flat as a pancake. The fit was perfect across his broad shoulders. It was trimmed with black braid and had a row of carved jet buttons down the front that caught the light. She found it horrifying to think what the buttons alone might have cost, never mind the London tailoring that shrieked from every line of his clothes. He was wearing a plain linen collar on his shirt, rather than a ruff.

She smiled a little. There was no question he was vain, but she couldn't help forgiving him for it. He had evidently changed his mind about regrowing his little Court beard because he had shaved that morning. His hair was still dyed black though showing dark chestnut at the roots. She had saved his face quite consciously for last, his long mobile face with that jutting Tudor nose, his blue eyes which could make her laugh only by dancing and quirking an eyebrow…Oh, for goodness' sake, he was only flesh and blood and she was mooning like a lovelorn girl.

She ignored those tediously sensible thoughts and stayed where she was, watching. At the moment he was talking to one of the grooms; now he went and greeted his charger, a large black beautiful creature completely out of place among the scrawny tough little hobbies. He smiled, patted the shining arched neck affectionately, gave him some salt from his hand. It hurt her deep inside her chest—where her heart was, she assumed—to see the casualness of that affection. If only he knew it, she valued that in him far more than his unconcealed passion for her. Passion, she believed, could only be fleeting, no matter what silly poets might say, but kindness…That was built into a man, or it wasn't. She had never seen her husband show kindness to any creature: from his horses, his dogs, his servants, his son, his wife, from all of them he simply expected obedience, in exchange for not beating them or humiliating them.

And that memory brought her back to earth with a vengeance. She took a deep breath, let it out again to quell any foolish tremors, and forced herself to march forwards.

Her grooms had prepared the horses. Young Henry was there checking hooves and legs. Carey turned to face her, one long hand still at his favourite horse's neck. He bowed to her, she curtseyed. Young Henry straightened up, patted the hobby's neck and shook his head.

'I'm not happy, ma'am,' he said to her in his surprisingly deep voice. 'They're still not recovered.'

'Why the haste, my lady?' asked Carey.

For a moment there was a flood of words in her mouth, battering at her teeth to be let out. Because if I stay in Carlisle much longer, Robin, you'll have me in your bed and that would not only mean ruin for both of us, it would be a wicked sin in the face of God. The words were so bright in the forefront of her mind, for a second she thought she had said them, but his expression didn't change the way it would have. She swallowed hard and the nonsense subsided. For answer, because her throat wasn't working properly, she took a letter from her sleeve and gave it to him.

Carey took it; his eyes narrowed at the seal. He opened it, and read it. The blue stare scanned the curt lines from her husband, and then lifted to hers.

'I see,' he said. 'You told him what you had done to help me at Netherby. Was that wise, my lady?'

A week before she had lent him the Widdrington horses to provide cover for his masquerade as a pedlar, knowing full well it would take a miracle if she was to see them again. Although the miracle had happened, wrought by Carey somehow, still...

'It would have been foolish to do anything else,' she said coldly, 'since his friend Lowther would have told him the full tale, with embellishments. At least this way, I cannot be accused of dishonesty.'

'Yes,' he said.

'But you understand, I simply cannot stay here against my husband's clear orders.'

'You told him the horses would be overtired?'

'At the time I wrote to him, I didn't know whether I would get them back.'

'I wish you would stay a day or two more,' he said. 'I could give you a proper escort then, when my men come back from haymaking.'

'We have our own hay to get in,' Elizabeth said. 'That's partly why he's...angry. And the reivers will be busy too.'

'Not the broken men,' said Carey. 'They can steal what others mow and stack.'

Elizabeth shrugged. There was no help for it and she saw no point in putting it off. 'I'm sure my husband's name will be some protection,' she said.

'Not in this March. In the East March, certainly, the Middle March perhaps, but not...'

'Sir Robert, there is simply nothing to discuss. I must start for home today. Are the horses ready, Henry?'

'Yes,' he said. 'As ready as they'll be without a couple of days' more rest.'

She clicked her fingers at one of the grooms, and he led her horse up to the mounting block. He would have offered her his arm to mount, but Carey was there first. The flourish he gave the simple act of helping her into the saddle could have been meant for the Queen of England, and she knew perfectly well he did it that way on purpose.

'Do you never ride pillion?' Carey asked, smiling up at her.

'I prefer to make my own mistakes,' she told him severely and he smiled wider. 'Goodbye Sir Robert,' she managed to say, without the least wobble in her voice, and felt quite proud of herself for doing it.

Young Henry was in the saddle as were the other four men, all of them wearing their jacks and carrying lances. Henry's jack betrayed him by its new pale leather. Nominally, Young Henry was in command as her husband's heir and those who wished to think it true, could do so. Elizabeth nodded at him, checked that her hat was well pinned to her cap and hair, and let him take the lead out of the stable yard.

She had already embraced Philadelphia and exchanged courtesies with Lord Scrope, though the two of them were in the main castle yard to see her off. She rode with her back so straight that her horse skittered sideways uneasily, catching the desperation she was cramming down tight inside herself. She breathed deeply, took the mare in hand and forced her to behave herself.

She simply would not—she refused to—look over her shoulder, though she knew that Carey was there, staring at her departing back as she passed the gate and started down through Castlegate on the long road for Newcastle.

\* \* \*

About fifteen minutes later, the large handsome charger was trotting down English Street as well. When he was through Botchergate and past the Citadel, Carey put his heels in. The sheer pleasure of feeling the power in Thunder, as he made the transition faultlessly to a gallop, almost broke his dark mood. The sun was shining bright and the meadows round about were alive with men and women and carts, the women raking the golden hay into piles, the men flinging them up onto the tops of the wagons where boys and girls raked it all into shape. Every so often, a cart would rumble along the ruts to a barn or haystack and the same activity would start again in reverse. The pace seemed very hectic and Carey wondered why as he galloped past, given the warmth of the day and the clear harebell blue of the sky with a few clouds floating in from the west.

He caught up with them quickly and reined in, let Thunder get over his customary side-stepping and pawing as he came back to a sedate walk.

The look Elizabeth Widdrington gave him was not what he would have wished. Carey swept his hat off and bowed low in the saddle to her and tried to smile. He found that the steadiness of her grey glare was making him feel like a schoolboy in the middle of an escapade and for a moment he felt awkward. Then he had to grin.

'Do tell me the joke, Sir Robert,' Elizabeth said frostily.

He waved an arm expansively. 'I was thinking that only the Queen and yourself can take me back to my schooldays so easily.'

Elizabeth faced forwards and said, 'Humph.'

'Thunder needed exercise,' Carey explained innocently. 'I

thought I'd bring him along the Roman road for a while.'

She said 'humph' again. Thunder snorted and tried to speed up to go past, but Carey hauled him back. Young Henry Widdrington was pretending he hadn't noticed Carey's arrival but the wide neck at the base of his helmet was bright red and not from the sun.

'Have I offended you again, my lady?' he asked Elizabeth.

'Do you understand the meaning of the word *discretion*?' she asked very haughtily. Never mind, at least she was talking to him.

'No, my lady,' he said. 'Please explain it to me.'

'Oh, for goodness' sake, you're making a public exhibition of yourself. What do you expect me to do? Welcome you with a kiss?'

'That would be nice,' he said wistfully and wondered if she would slap him. She didn't, but it looked like a near thing.

'Haven't you got anything better to do than make a nuisance of yourself?' Elizabeth asked in tones that would have withered a tree. Lord, he liked looking at her when she was in a temper.

'Yes, I have,' he said. 'I have piles of tedious papers to deal with and Scrope won't let me have Bell to be my clerk today, so I have to write all the damn letters myself.'

'It sounds as if you had best get back to work then.'

'On the other hand, the sun is shining and Thunder...'

'Needed exercise. So you said. You haven't raised a sweat on him yet, so we'll move aside for you and you can give him a good run. Then you can get back to your papers.'

'To hell with the papers,' Carey said conversationally, 'I wanted to ride with you for a while.'

'Why do you insist on making this so difficult for me?' she asked, and for a moment he felt guilty. Only for a moment, though.

'How am I making it difficult?' he asked, deliberately obtuse. 'I'm not in your way. I'm riding alongside in a perfectly proper manner. I thought you might like to be entertained with some conversation for a little of your long journey.'

'I really don't want to talk,' she said, looking straight between her mare's ears.

'Then I shall ride beside you in silence, my lady.'

'Hmf.'

He did manage to stay silent for several miles, so they could hear the shouts from the hayfields. They got stuck for a while behind a haywagon screeling along behind two yoke of oxen, so Carey trotted ahead and asked the driver to stop while they squeezed past at a wider place. With the road clear ahead of them he let Thunder have a run and then came back to the Widdringtons. Young Henry looked as if he was trying to decide whether to say anything to the scandalous Deputy Warden but, as Carey knew, Young Henry was a likeable young man and far more sympathetic to his stepmother than he was to his unpleasant father. On the other hand, he took his responsibilities as heir very seriously.

Carey took Thunder alongside Henry and tipped his hat in courtesy. Henry bent his head a little and flushed.

'How badly tired are the horses, Mr Widdrington?' he asked and Young Henry frowned.

'We shouldn't be travelling at all, Sir Robert,' he said. 'If none of the horses goes lame, it'll be a miracle. We should have rested for two more days.'

'I quite agree,' Carey said. 'Did you explain this to Lady Widdrington?'

'Yes,' said Henry unhappily. 'I did, and she said my father had ordered us home and so home we would go.'

'It's a pity none of the horses went lame in Carlisle,' said Carey innocently. Young Henry looked at him sideways and then quietly swore.

'I never thought of that,' he admitted.

'Nor did I until this minute,' Carey said candidly. 'Never mind, we'll know better next time.'

'And she would spot it,' Henry added.

'Of course she would. But what could she do about it?'

Young Henry sighed.

'I daren't try it now,' he said. 'She'd know.'

'I'm not happy about you travelling at the moment, with the Debateable Land so stirred up,' Carey went on. 'I wish you could stay in Carlisle.'

'If I turned back to the Castle now, I wouldn't put it past her to carry on by herself. And my cousins would obey her, I think, not me. So might the Castle men.'

Carey looked at the two large Widdrington menservants critically. He knew the other two slightly, both Carlislers and often used for dispatches. They would take Lady Widdrington to Newcastle and then wait there for the next dispatch bag from Burghley down in London.

'Well, they look dangerous enough to keep off any chancers,' he admitted. 'And so do you. But what happens if a horse goes lame while you're in the middle of some waste?'

'Have you heard anything, Sir Robert?'

'No. But I'm not happy.'

Henry looked at him with his jaw set square. 'There could be another reason for that,' he said after a moment.

'Well, there is,' said Carey lightly. 'But I'm making allowances for selfishness and I'm still not happy.'

Henry gestured with his lance. 'Go and talk to Lady Widdrington. You know my opinion; I'd willingly turn back to Carlisle and stay there, but my lady...'

'Your father's letter was certainly very...peremptory.'

Henry set his jaw again and suddenly looked like the man he would be in a few years' time. Then he swallowed and broke the illusion of maturity.

'I wish you were a reiver, Sir Robert,' he burst out. 'I wish you could sweep down on us with all your men and carry her back to your peel tower.'

Then he shut his lips very firmly and looked as if he expected Carey to laugh at him for his romantic notions.

'I won't deny the thought had crossed my mind,' Carey said slowly. 'But why do *you* wish that? Is she so unhappy with Sir Henry?'

Henry had the peculiar expression of someone who is longing to explain a great deal but can't bring himself to the necessary disloyalty.

'What's she going back to, and why is she in such a hurry about it?' Carey hadn't meant to sound so peremptory but his heart had gone cold.

Young Henry stared ahead for a few moments longer and then said, in a rush, 'Well, Sir Robert, you know if someone has to have a tooth pulled, they're either one way or the other. Some people put it off for as long as possible, and others get it over with as quick as possible.'

For a moment Carey didn't understand. 'But she…Oh.'

Even Henry's spots were glowing red and he looked quite wretched.

'It's his right,' he mumbled. 'And he's a very suspicious man. It took him a long time to…to calm down when she came back from Court. And now…'

Carey understood perfectly. His voice became remote.

'Is he likely to kill her?'

'Well…'

'Widdrington, I want to know what she's facing.'

'Well…I don't think he'd kill her. You see, he needs her to nurse him when he's having one of his attacks of the gravel in his bladder.'

'Couldn't he marry again?'

'I don't think any of the families near us would give him one of their daughters. And none of the widows would take him either,' Henry explained damningly. 'He had to send all the way to Cornwall to get her, remember.'

With some part of his mind, Carey planned to have a great many words with his father the next time they met. But for Lord Hunsdon, Elizabeth would never have married Sir Henry. On the other hand, then they might never have met.

'How did your mother die?' Carey demanded, too angry to be tactful.

Young Henry said nothing, which was much worse than an answer. Carey took a deep breath, looked back over his shoulder at Elizabeth riding sedately along. Her face was perfectly normal, though she still looked thoroughly annoyed.

Certainly Philadelphia could have no idea. It hadn't really occurred to him, although he had no quarrel with a man exercising proper authority over his wife. Obviously, what Young Henry was alluding to was more than that. Coldness trickled down his spine as he wondered if Sir Henry had the brainsickness he knew that Walsingham's inquisitor Topcliffe certainly had. He couldn't ask Young Henry, he wouldn't understand.

Henry was speaking again, in a low mumble.

'What?' he asked.

'I was saying, my father might make her do penance if she's…
er…if he thinks she's committed adultery.'

'What, spend Sunday standing outside the church in a white
sheet with a candle?'

Henry nodded. Carey looked over his shoulder again. Elizabeth
was watching him now, so he turned back in case she saw his face.
Considering her pride, he suspected she would prefer to be beaten.

Young Henry was screwing up his face as if he was trying to find
the courage to ask something insolent. Carey knew immediately
what that was and pre-empted it.

'Your stepmother, Mr Widdrington,' he said coldly and clearly,
'is the most virtuous woman I have ever met. I won't deny I've been
laying siege to her with every…every device I have, and I have got
nowhere. Nowhere at all.'

Despite the beetroot colour of Henry's face he seemed happier.
He nodded.

'But I suppose, given Sir Henry's nature, he isn't likely to believe
it, even without Lowther to poison the well for us.'

Henry nodded again. Carey rode along for a moment.

'Christ, what a bloody mess.'

Abruptly he swung Thunder away from Henry's horse and put
his heels in again. Thunder exploded straight into a gallop, catching
his rider's mood. Carey let him have his head, though he got no
pleasure from it now, and then brought him to a stop under a shady
tree where he dismounted and walked Thunder up and down to let
him cool more slowly, and waited for the Widdringtons. He stood
watching them as they came up and cursed himself for being so
obtuse, for thinking he was playing a game with Elizabeth when
she was in fact gambling with her life. She reined in beside him
and he came to her stirrup and looked up at her.

'My lady,' he said gently, 'I'll leave you here.'

'What were you talking about with Henry?'

He also wondered how much she knew of what was in his mind,
but she wasn't a witch, only a woman.

'We were agreeing with each other about the dangers of

303

travelling in this March with horses that need more rest,' he lied bluntly. It wasn't a lie. He was worried about it.

'We shall be well enough,' said Elizabeth sedately. 'Thank you for your concern, Sir Robert.'

'Good day to you, Lady Widdrington,' said Carey, uncovering to her as they continued past. 'God speed.'

\* \* \*

Barnabus knew better than to say anything to his master when Carey slammed into his chambers with a face as dark as ditchwater and went straight to the smaller room he used as an office. He sat down at the desk, opened the penner and took out pens and ink. Summer sunlight like honey streamed in through the window and he looked up at it once and sighed, then drew paper towards him and dipped his pen.

Somewhere around noon they had a visitor. James Pennycook and his son-in-law knocked tentatively at the door and, after wine had been brought, Barnabus and Michael Kerr were told to leave and shut the door.

'What's Mr Pennycook after?' Barnabus asked Kerr as they sat on the stairs, waiting to be called back. Michael Kerr fiddled with one of the tassels on his purse, looked up at the arched roof and said, 'Och, it's the usual. Mr Pennycook wants to know his price.'

'What for?'

'For not interfering with the victualling contracts.'

Barnabus sucked his teeth. 'What a pity Mr Pennycook didn't send you to me first,' he said meaningfully.

Kerr looked knowing. 'Oh,' he said. 'Expensive, is he?'

'Very,' said Barnabus. 'And very unpredictable. He's got to be approached just right, has Sir Robert.'

The low muttering inside had stopped suddenly. Barnabus braced himself.

'Barnabu-u-us,' came the roar.

Barnabus opened the door and went in. Mr Pennycook was standing in the middle of the floor, looking pinched about the nostrils.

Carey was by the fireplace with his back turned.

'Barnabus, escort Mr Pennycook to the gate, if you please.'

'Yessir,' said Barnabus briskly and came forward. 'This way sir,' he said confidingly. 'Best to leave now.'

'But...' said Pennycook.

'Good day to you, Mr Pennycook,' said Carey curtly and walked through into his office, where he sat down.

Barnabus sighed heavily at more riches unnecessarily thrown away—after all, it wasn't as if Carey had yet seen a penny of his legendary five hundred pounds per annum.

'See,' he said to Michael Kerr, as he led the two of them down the stairs again. 'He's a bit touchy, is my master.'

Barnabus finished polishing Carey's helmet and sword, his boots and other tack, then gathered up yesterday's shirt and moved to the door. He suddenly thought of something and coughed. What was the betting Carey hadn't eaten all day? Perhaps some vittles might mend his mood.

Barnabus coughed again gently and when that got no response said, 'Sir, shall I bring up something to eat?'

'What?' The voice was irritable. Carey was recutting the nib of his pen which had worn down.

'Food sir. For you, sir?'

Carey waved a hand dismissively. 'I'm not hungry. Get me some beer.'

'Yes sir,' said Barnabus, confirmed in his suspicions.

The shirt went into the Castle laundry with the other linen and Barnabus wandered to the kitchens where the idle little cook had his domain. He had gathered together a tray of bread, cheese, raised oxtongue pie, sallet and pickle and was going to the buttery for beer, when a boy stopped him in the corridor.

It was Young Hutchin Graham, his boots and jerkin dusty and his blond hair plastered to his head with sweat.

'Mr Cooke,' said Young Hutchin in an urgent hiss. 'I wantae speak to the Deputy.'

'Well, you can't,' said Barnabus pompously. 'He's very busy.'

'I must, it's verra important.'

'What's wrong?'

Young Hutchin looked furtive and unhappy and then shook his head. 'Ah'll tell it to the Deputy and naebody else.'

'You can give me the message and I will ask the Deputy if he wants...'

'Mr Cooke, Ah can tell ye, he'll wantae hear what I have to say, but I'll say it to him only.'

Barnabus looked shrewdly at the boy's anxious face and could see no more dishonesty than usual in the long-lashed blue eyes.

'Very well,' he said. 'Come up to the Queen Mary Tower with me and you can...'

'Nay, I'll not go there. Ask him if he'll please come down here so I'm not seen wi' him.'

Barnabus gave Hutchin a very hard stare and then shrugged.

'I'll pass it on, my son, but I doubt he'll...'

Young Hutchin bit his lip and then whispered, 'It's concernin' Lady Widdrington.'

'Hm,' said Barnabus. 'I'll tell him.'

In fact he let Carey eat what he wanted of the food he'd brought before he mentioned Young Hutchin's anxiety. Carey was preoccupied and it took Lady Widdrington's name to get him to leave his careful list-making and go down the stairs and across the yard to the buttery beside the keep, Barnabus following behind him out of plain nosiness.

Once in privacy by the huge casks of beer and the ample sweet smell of the malt, Young Hutchin gabbled out his tale.

Young Hutchin had seen Mick the Crow Salkeld at dawn in the Castle stables, taking one of the hobbies and asking about the best route to Netherby that avoided the road. When somebody wanted to know why he was sneaking into the Debateable Land, he had tapped his nose and said something about Lady Widdrington.

'What did he say?' demanded Carey.

'Ah dinna like to repeat it, sir, it were...rude,' answered Hutchin primly. 'It were along the lines o' my uncle...er...takin' your place, so to speak.'

Carey breathed deeply through his nose for a moment and then nodded. 'Go on.'

Young Hutchin had been greatly taken with Lady Widdrington,

so he had decided to go to Netherby himself and see what was up.

'Ah dinna trust Uncle Wattie, see,' explained his treacherous nephew. 'It's costing him a fortune to mend Netherby an' there isnae a man he's met since it happened that isnae jestin' ower the way ye pulled the wool over his eyes and got the better of him.'

Carey's eyes had narrowed down to slits.

'You didn't run all the way there and back again? It's ten miles.'

Young Hutchin coloured. 'Nay sir. Ah ran a couple of miles to the further horse paddock and...er...borrowed a hobby and a remount. I brung 'em back too,' he added with proud rectitude.

Carey nodded.

'So, anyway, sir, I got to Netherby an' it were full up wi' me cousins and the like, and Skinabake Armstrong and his gang. Ah couldnae get close enough to hear what Mick the Crow's message was, but half an hour after he arrived he was back on the road south again and the place was boiling out like an overturned beeskep.'

'Which way did they go?'

'South east. Across the Bewcastle Waste, sir.'

'How many?'

Young Hutchin squinted at the roofbeams and thought hard. 'By my guess he'd have fifty men or thereabouts, fra the look of them.'

'Armed?'

'Oh aye, sir. Well armed.'

'Who was leading them?'

'My Uncle Wattie, sir, nae mistaking it. Only, Ah wouldnae tell ye if it were nobbut a raid, but my thinking is that Mick's tellt Wattie which way my Lady Widdrington's gone an' he's intending to lift her and ransome her to ye. He'll have heard by now how she helped ye.'

Carey said nothing for a moment and looked as if he was thinking furiously, which surprised Barnabus who had expected immediate fireworks. He was thinking regretfully about all the hard cleaning work he had put in on Carey's fighting harness which would now no doubt be wasted.

'Barnabus,' said Carey eventually. 'I know you're there, skulking in the corner. Go and find Long George and Bessie's Andrew and tell them to come to my chambers in an hour. Young Hutchin,

307

thank you for telling me this. I'm indebted to you. Only I'd like to know why you did it.'

Young Hutchin went pink about the ears.

'It wasnae for ye, sir,' he said gruffly. 'Only, I like the Lady, see.'

Carey looked shrewdly at Young Hutchin for a moment, causing further reddening around the ears, and then smiled.

'All the better,' he said. 'That's a perfectly honourable reason.'

Barnabus came hurrying back to the Queen Mary Tower from his errand and was surprised to see Carey still wearing his ordinary clothes. He would have expected the Deputy to be in helmet and harness and chafing to ride to rescue his beloved, knowing the man. Carey grinned at his obvious shock.

'Barnabus, think,' he said. 'I've got no men around here; they're all at the haymaking and even if they weren't, seven certainly is not enough to match fifty riders. And we don't know for sure what's going on.'

'But if Wattie Graham's after Lady Widdrington, shouldn't we get after 'im, sir...?'

'You're a bit rash, Barnabus.' Barnabus blinked at this outrageous instance of a kettle calling a brass warming-pan black. 'I said, think. Nothing's going to happen to her today because unless she's been extraordinarily unlucky, she'll be into Thirlwall Castle by now.'

'Ain't you going to send a message? Or talk to the Warden?'

'No, I'm going to talk to Lowther first, he's due to take the patrol tonight.'

Barnabus trotted after Carey as he strode out of the Castle and into the town where Sir Richard had a small town house on Abbey Street.

## MONDAY, 3RD JULY 1592, AFTERNOON

Carey was magnificently languid as he was ushered into the Lowther house and bowed to the dumpling-faced nervous creature who was Lady Lowther. Sir Richard came out and his face hardened with suspicion. After a few exchanges of airy courtesy, Sir Richard growled, 'What can I do for you, Sir Robert?'

'I would like to take your patrol out tonight.'

'Eh?'

'I've heard a rumour about where some of the King of Scotland's horses are being kept and I'd like to investigate. Unfortunately, most of my men are out making hay and as it's your patrol night tonight, I thought I'd ask you.'

He smiled guilelessly, looking remarkably dense for one so intelligent. Barnabus wondered uneasily what elaborate lunacy he was maturing now.

Lowther grunted with suspicion. Barnabus watched him considering the suggestion. Discourteous as ever, Lowther hadn't even offered his master anything to drink, but Carey was standing there playing with his rings as if he hadn't noticed, looking benignly enthusiastic.

Carey reached into his belt pouch and took out a folded sheet of paper. 'I could...er...give you this back,' he offered. It was Lowther's note of debt for fifteen pounds.

Uh oh, thought Barnabus, he's overdone it. Lowther will want to know why he's so eager to take somebody else's patrol.

Lowther did want to know. 'That's very handsome of ye, Sir Robert,' he said. 'Why are ye willing to say goodbye to so much money for such a minor thing?'

Carey smiled. 'King James is offering a large reward for his horses,' he explained. 'If I can find those horses and bring them in, I might make ten times that, besides pleasing the King.'

'Ah.' Lowther's expression lightened slowly. This he understood, and he was only too happy to tear up his large losses at primero. 'I'll speak to Sergeant Nixon then.'

He reached for the paper but Carey put it away again.

'You can have it when I get back,' he said.

Aggravatingly, when they returned to the Queen Mary Tower, Barnabus was sent to find Young Hutchin and make sure he stayed near the stables where Carey could find him, though out of sight.

Carey arrived a little later with Long George and Bessie's

Andrew, all three of them wearing their helmets and jacks. Long George's pink-rimmed eyes were looking amused and Bessie's Andrew was swallowing nervously and biting his fingernails, whereas Carey was humming something complicated and irritating about springtime and birds going hey dingalingaling.

'Barnabus,' he said as he passed by. 'Don't try and wander off; I want your help as well.'

'Yes, sir,' said Barnabus resignedly, making sure he had his dagger and the throwing knife behind his neck. The one he usually kept up his left sleeve was currently in pledge with Lisa at the bawdy-house. Then he climbed up one side of a box partition and sat on top of it with his legs dangling.

All the men bunched up in a disorderly rabble and stood picking their teeth while Lowther made a short speech explaining that Sir Robert Carey would take them out in search of some of King James's horses and they were to render to him all the assistance they would to himself, etcetera and so on. Touching, Barnabus called it. Then Lowther departed, quite pleased with himself, while Carey looked them over. Considering the state of them, Barnabus wondered what he would say, but all he did was to ask, 'Where are your bows, gentlemen?'

They looked at each other. Sergeant Nixon spoke up.

'We havenae got none.'

'Ah,' said Carey. 'Well, I want you to get some. I assume you can use them? Good. Sergeant Nixon, take your men down to the armourer's in Scotch Street and buy them all bows and a dozen arrows each.'

He tossed Sergeant Nixon three pounds to pay for them and nodded at him to be off.

This seemed to thaw even Ill-Willit Daniel's heart. He touched his hand to his helmet as he led his troop back out of the stables. Carey watched them pass and then said, 'Mick the Crow.'

'Ay, sir,' answered the one with greasy black hair hanging out under his steel cap, a sallow skin and a lamentable jack.

'I've got another errand for you, Mick; wait here a moment.'

'Ay, sir.'

They waited, while Barnabus learned from Carey's humming

that springtime was also the only pretty ring time. The excited chatter of Lowther's troop faded in the direction of the gate and out of earshot.

'Well, Mick,' Carey said in a friendly fashion, and nodded meaningfully at Long George and Bessie's Andrew. Long George had moved behind Mick the Crow, examining a hobby's forehoof. Now he whisked about and put his long arm round Mick the Crow's neck. Bessie's Andrew was slower but managed to catch Mick's right arm before it reached his sword and twist it behind his back. Mick kicked wildly at Carey, so Barnabus leaned down from his perch and put his dagger point under Mick's nose. Mick squinted at it and took breath to yell.

''Course you could get along wivout a nose, mate,' said Barnabus conversationally. 'But it wouldn't arf 'urt your chances wiv women.'

'Eh?' gasped Mick the Crow. 'What the hell are ye doin'? Lemme go...'

Carey leaned forward and pulled Mick's sword out of its sheath, looked at it distastefully and dropped it in the straw. The dagger went the same way. Carey handed Bessie's Andrew some halter rope and he and Long George tied Mick's hands behind him.

'What the...what's goin' on...'

'Shut up,' said Barnabus. 'Think of your nose, mate.'

'But I...Ouch!'

'Oh. Sorry.'

Carey pointed at Mick the Crow's chest. 'You're under arrest, Mick the Crow Salkeld,' he said. 'For March treason.'

'What? Wha' are ye talkin' about...?'

'Question is, which March is the treason in?'

'You'll swing for his one,' said Long George regretfully. Mick the Crow was beginning to look worried. He licked some blood off his moustache. March treason was the catch-all charge: if you couldn't think what else to hang a man for, you hanged him for 'bringing in of raiders'—helping raiders to cross the Border.

'Ah've done nothin'...'

'Shut up,' said Carey. 'All I want to know from you is where the Grahams are setting their ambush. They'll have to lift her before she reaches Tynedale, because there are too many surnames there at feud with the Grahams to risk it. So where are they doing it?'

Mick's eyes bulged. He croaked a couple of times.

'My guess is by the Wall somewhere, because they can hide behind it, but I want to know the exact place.'

Mick the Crow was a good rider and a bonny fighter, but he hadn't the brains for a traitor, Barnabus decided. His brow knitted and his lips moved as he tried to catch up.

'Look,' Barnabus whispered to Mick from his perch on top of the partition. 'I know you're wondering how he knows so much, but you'd be much better off wondering how you're going to stop him making you look forward to your hanging. Right? I mean, he learned a lot from Walsingham's boys, you know.'

'That's enough, Barnabus.' Carey's voice was curt.

'Yessir,' cringed Barnabus, enjoying himself greatly.

'Also, Mick, I want to know who they're planning to hit on their way back to make the trip worthwhile.'

'But I dinna ken that, sir. How could I? All I did was, I took the message, that's all.'

'What message?'

Carey had pulled his dagger from the sheath hanging from his belt at the small of his back. It was a fashionable London duelling poignard, nine inches long, with a pretty jewelled hilt and an eye-wateringly sharp point, and he was using it to clean his nails. Mick the Crow watched him and licked his lips.

'Ahh…he said Wattie could fetch himself a good ransom if he would foray out to the Roman Wall and catch…er…'

'Catch whom?'

'Er…Lady Widdrington, sir.'

Carey trimmed his thumbnail carefully and then fixed Mick the Crow with a blue considering stare. He tossed the poignard up in the air while Barnabus winced a little. As far as he was concerned, showing off with blades like that was a good way to get religious-looking holes in your palms.

'Who sent you?'

Mick licked his lips again. 'Er…who, sir?'

'Yes,' said Carey with dangerous patience. 'Who sent you?'

Mick's face twisted in panic. 'I canna say, sir.'

'Why not?'

'Ah...' Inspiration struck him. 'I didna ken who he was, sir. It were dark.'

'You took a message into the Debateable Land, for a man you don't know?'

'Ay, sir. He give me a shilling for it.'

There was an awful pause while Carey considered this. Mick was shaking like a mouse in a cat's mouth.

'Give me the message,' Carey said at last.

Mick shook harder. 'It was writing and Wattie burnt it.'

'What was in it?'

'I dinna ken, sir. I canna read.'

Carey was tossing the dagger again. 'You carried a letter to Netherby for a man you don't know.'

'Ay, sir.' Mick the Crow was sweating.

Carey squinted at him in the light from the open top door and the poignard flashed and slapped hilt-first back in his hand. 'If it makes you feel happier, I'll regard any obscenity dealing with my Lady Widdrington as being of other authorship.'

Mick's eyes bulged again with bewilderment.

'He's saying, he won't kill you for being rude about the lady; he'll kill the man what sent you,' translated Barnabus helpfully.

'But I canna tell ye what was in it, I dinna...' There was a rising note of panic in Mick's voice.

'You knew they were planning to take Lady Widdrington,' snapped Carey.

'Ay, sir, he let it slip an'...an' they could call in on Archibald Bell by the way, sir, for he hasnae paid his blackrent. That's all. As God's my witness.'

Carey stared coldly at the shaking sweating creature before him, and his mouth made a small twitch of distaste.

'You're very frightened of this man, aren't you, Mick? The one you don't know.'

'Ay, sir,' said Mick hoarsely, licking blood off his lip again. 'I'm a married man, see ye, and I've three small weans.'

'It seems to me,' said Carey remotely, 'that entirely too many of you are married men. Will you tell the Lord Warden what you've just told me?'

Mick closed his eyes and moaned softly. 'They're ainly little, sir,' he said pleadingly.

Carey sighed and put his poignard back in its sheath.

'Would it help if I put you in gaol for refusing to tell me the man's name?'

Mick opened his eyes again.

'Oh, ay,' he said pathetically. 'It would so. Only not the Licking-stone cell, please, sir. It's sae dark in there.'

'Come along,' said Carey sadly. 'We'll do it before I see the Warden.'

\* \* \*

The really damnable nuisance of it, Carey thought, as he rode out of Carlisle with Sergeant Nixon and the others (except for Mick the Crow) in a bunch behind him, was that this wasn't even the raiding season. July was one of the few times of year when you could be fairly secure from raiding because the nights were too short and too light and any sensible man with a square foot of meadow was out getting his hay in. There was never enough hay for the number of horses on the borders, although the hobbies could get by on about half of what Thunder needed to survive. The Borderers sent cattle skins and salt beef and cheeses south and north to pay for the horsefeed they needed, but it was expensive bringing it in, so whatever you could grow was pure profit. Despite what he had said, even reivers made hay because while cows, sheep and horses had legs and could run, haystacks did not. All this activity in high summer was most irregular.

After deep consideration and with some worry, he had sent Young Hutchin Graham on a fast pony out ahead of him on the road with a letter for Captain Carleton in Thirlwall, telling him on no account to let Lady Widdrington out of the gates the next morning. He thought it very unlikely the boy would get through in time to stop her, assuming—which was highly unlikely—Hutchin's

Uncle Wattie hadn't put fore riders in place around the castle to guard against such things. At least if the Grahams caught Young Hutchin, they wouldn't kill him as they might Long George and certainly would Bessie's Andrew Storey, with whose surname they had a feud. Young Hutchin could say convincingly that he had no idea what was in the letter he was carrying since he couldn't read and would probably end up at Wattie's side during the raid. That might even give Carey a card to play if everything went horribly wrong. He would have liked to send Long George off with a letter for the Middle March Warden, Sir John Forster, since the raid was actually due to happen on his ground, but he didn't dare. Firstly, Long George was more than likely to end with his throat slit, and secondly, Carey didn't like the thought of being alone on the road with Sergeant Nixon and his thugs and no one to guard his back but Bessie's Andrew.

The situation was actually worse for him than it would have been for Lowther or Carleton because he didn't know the ground well enough. He was beginning to get a rough shape of it in his mind from his hunting expeditions of the previous week, but nothing like the detailed knowledge of someone born there. He knew the land round Berwick far better from living there as a boy; in Carlisle he was a foreigner. As a result he didn't know what route Wattie Graham would take from Netherby, nor where he would lie up for the night, nor where on the old road he might be planning to take Lady Widdrington.

Take Lady Widdrington. Damn it, how dare they! How dare Graham try to salve his wounded pride with a raid of fifty riders against one woman and five men? God damn them all for bloody cowards, if he could catch them red-handed he'd string them up on the nearest trees, by God he would, and to hell with giving them a fair trial...

He pulled his mind back from that train of thought, simply because he knew that if he followed it he would end up too enraged to think straight.

Sergeant Nixon was riding beside him with an ingratiating expression on his face. Carey looked sideways at him; he was a strongly built ugly man with bulging cheeks like a water-rat's and a long pointed nose, and the blackest beard on a pale face Carey had ever seen. He was not a man you would willingly buy a horse from, nor anything else, and the surly competence in the way he rode and carried his lance implied that you would be wise not to fight him. Which made him probably near enough to Lowther's ideal of a henchman.

'Did you want to ask something, Sergeant?'

'Ay, sir.' Unlike Sergeant Dodd's miserable drone, Sergeant Nixon's voice was the most attractive part of him. 'I was wonderin' how ye got word of the twenty horses ye say are at Brampton.'

'Ah,' said Carey opaquely. 'Now, that would be telling, wouldn't it, Sergeant?' He had in fact deduced it from the fact that nobody at Brampton had rendered a complaint about horses reived from them. He wasn't sure there were twenty there, but it was as many as he thought their pasturage could stand.

'Would we be getting any of your fee, sir?'

'You might.'

'Only we heard ye'd paid Dodd and his men their backwages...'

And you thought I might be a soft touch, Carey thought but didn't say. 'Perhaps you had better talk to Sir Richard Lowther about that.'

Sergeant Nixon sniffed. 'Ay, sir.'

Sunset was coming, a slow beacon setting light to half the sky and turning the clouds to purple. There were still people working in the fields, which astonished Carey. He asked the Sergeant about it.

'Well, sir,' said Nixon, seeming surprised. 'It's going to rain soon; can ye not feel it hanging in the air?'

Now he mentioned it, the air was sultry and heavy and the warmth was oppressive. Carey had only his shirt on under his padded jack but was still feeling sticky. He sniffed the air. If it rained Wattie Graham's trail would be a great deal harder to follow back...But then Lady Widdrington might even stay at Thirlwall for an extra day...No, she wouldn't; he was fooling himself.

'Yonder's the road to Brampton,' said Nixon after a long straight canter.

'I know, Sergeant,' said Carey. 'We're going to Gilsland first.'

'Why?'

Carey stared at him for a while. Eventually Nixon got the message and coughed.

'Why, sir?'

'Because I want to talk to Dodd about something.'

Sergeant Nixon was frowning heavily, but then he shrugged. There was no love lost between him and Dodd, but neither were they enemies and nor were their families at feud.

Even so, Carey nodded at Long George and Bessie's Andrew. Long George let his horse fall behind until he was at the rear of the men, while Bessie's Andrew came up to Carey's left shoulder and looked thoroughly nervous. God help me if Sergeant Nixon gets suspicious, Carey thought, then dismissed the thought from his mind. Sergeant Nixon wouldn't get suspicious, that was all there was to it.

As Carey's body swung rhythmically with the horse's stride, he turned over and over in his mind the various loose combinations of ideas he was trying to form into a sensible plan. Scrope had been willing enough to let him try and deal with Wattie Graham's raid, but was as hamstrung by lack of men as he was himself. He had barely ten men in the place and all of them were needed. He hadn't even let Carey send off his clerk, Richard Bell, with a message to Forster because, as he pointed out, the Bells were yet another surname at feud with the Grahams and he didn't want to lose the one man in the West March who had a thorough grasp of March Law. He had promised to send for a few of the gentlemen to the south of Carlisle, but had opined that they were unlikely to be reliable in a fight against the Grahams.

'Most of 'em pay blackrent to Richard Graham of Brackenhill,' Scrope had said, looking tired. 'None of them want any trouble with that family.' Brackenhill was the acknowledged Graham headman and wealthy enough to arm most of his own men with guns.

What I need in this Godforsaken country is at least a hundred men I can trust and some decent ordnance, Carey thought bitterly. And pigs will fly before the Queen gives me the money to find them.

# Monday, 3rd July 1592, evening

Sergeant Henry Dodd nodded at his brother Red Sandy, and the laden cart creaked off towards their main hay barn. The two small English Armstrongs, cousins of Janet, who had been helping him load, sat quietly together on top. One of the sandy heads was nodding.

'Lizzy,' called Dodd, and a freckled face under a mucky white cap peeked over. 'Stop your brother from sleeping or he'll fall off.'

'Ay, Mr Dodd,' she said, hiding a yawn. 'Will ye be wanting us back again?'

He did really, but hadn't the heart. 'No, sweeting, get to your bed.'

Red Sandy touched up the oxen and the cart creaked away, a plaintive yell floating from the top as Lizzy obediently pinched her brother to wake him up.

The sun was down and there was another field to get in, but after that, it was done. Janet was coming towards him across the stubbly meadow with bits of hay stuck to her cap and a large earthenware jug on her hip. She smiled at him, and the back of his throat, which felt as if it had glazed over with the haydust stuck to it, opened a little involuntarily in anticipation. He put his hands behind the collar of his working shirt and eased the hemp cloth off the sunburn he'd collected a few days before while mowing this same field. He resisted the urge to have a go at the itchy bits of skin that were coming off because if he started scratching, all the little bits of dust that had got inside his clothes and stuck to his skin would start itching too and drive him insane.

Janet arrived where he stood leaning on his pitchfork, gave him the leather quart mug she had in her other hand and filled it with mild beer. He croaked his thanks, put it to his lips, tilted his head and forgot to swallow for a while. It almost hurt, it felt so good. He finished two-thirds of it before he came up for air.

'Ahhh,' he said, and leered at her. Janet had untied her smock and loosened the laces of her old blue bodice to free her arms for raking and there was a fine deep valley there, just begging for exploration. Not in a stubbly field though, and they were both too old and respectable now to bundle about in the haystack, but a marriage bed would do fine, later, if he wasn't too tired. And if he was, well, there was the morning too before he had to set off for Carlisle. She leered back at him and took breath to say something that never was said.

'Och, God damn him to hell,' moaned Dodd, seeing movement, men on horseback breasting the hill in the distance over her shoulder, and instantly recognising the man in the fancy morion helmet at the head of the patrol riding towards them along the Roman road. 'God rot his bloody bowels...'

'Eh?' said Janet, startled. She turned to look in the same direction as her husband, and her eyes narrowed.

'But those are Lowther's men he's with.'

Dodd knew with awful clarity exactly what the thrice-damned Deputy Warden was doing out at Gilsland with Lowther's Sergeant and Lowther's bunch of hard bargains. Full of wordless ill-usage, he picked up his pitchfork and drove it tines first into the ground, narrowly missing his own foot.

'Make yerself decent, woman,' he growled unfairly at his wife, who had only been behaving as a good wife should to her hardworking husband. She gave him a glint of a stare and he handed her what was left of his beer by way of apology. Still, she tied her old smock again, pulled up her bodice lacings and the curves of her breasts went back into their secret armour.

Dodd folded his arms and waited for the Deputy to come to him. There was some satisfaction in the thought that he must be hot wearing a jack and morion in this weather, followed by a gloomier memory of just how miserable a jack could be in summer.

Carey left Lowther's men at the wall and came trotting over.

'Good evening, Sergeant. How's the haymaking?'

The bloody Courtier had probably been sitting on his arse all afternoon, unlike Dodd, who could only bring himself to grunt.

'Well enow.'

'Have you finished yet?'

Resisting the urge to snarl that if he was finished he wouldna be standing in a field like a lummock, he'd be at table stuffing his face, Dodd gestured in the direction of a long triangle of land which still had its neat rows of gold. Carey's face clouded over.

'Ah,' he said.

'What's the trouble, Sir Robert?' asked Janet. 'Is it a raid?'

Carey sighed and slid from his horse. 'In a manner of speaking, Mrs Dodd,' he said. 'I'm sorry to trouble you when you're so busy, Sergeant; if I had any other choice I wouldn't be here.'

Dodd grunted again, only slightly mollified, jerked his pitchfork out of the ground, straightened the bent tine with his clog heel, put it on his shoulder and set off for the last field. Janet picked his abandoned jerkin off the ground, and her own rake, and went with him. The Courtier went too, leading his horse.

As they went he talked, and in Dodd's mind a picture formed of what was happening. At the end of it, he commented, 'Wattie Graham must be fair annoyed to be risking a foray into the Middle March and so close to Tynedale. Who put him up to it?'

'I've no idea, though I could guess.'

'Well, ye canna take fifty assorted Grahams and broken men with that lot over there.'

Carey half-smiled. 'I'm aware of it, Sergeant.'

'What's she...what's Lady Widdrington worth at ransom, then?'

'I haven't the faintest idea and I have no intention of paying it in any case.'

'No,' agreed Dodd. 'That'd be for her husband to do.'

'Dodd,' said Carey with a certain amount of effort, 'I am not going to allow her to be taken.'

That's what being at Court and listening to all them poets did for you, Dodd thought savagely; it rotted your brain.

'I dinna ken what ye can do about it, sir,' said Dodd, looking about for the other cart which should have finished and come back by now. Oh yes, there it was, being driven by Willie's Simon with his bandaged arm. Janet had already set down her jug and his jerkin and started in on the furthest row to pile it up. Two of the other girls came down off the wall where they had been waiting and drinking, and started on two other rows. The cart creaked in at the gate and lined up, ready for him. Normally Willie's Simon would have been helping Dodd pitch the hay, but the wound from an arrow in his arm ten days before was still not healed enough so Dodd had it all to do himself. Janet raked ferociously, muttering under her breath; Dodd knew she was calculating how much more food Sergeant Nixon and the others would require, when she was already feeding too many mouths.

'How long would this normally take?' Carey asked fatuously, waving at the field.

'I'd leave it till the morrow, but it looks like rain,' said Dodd, driving his pitchfork into a bundle and twisting to lift and throw. 'It'll be fair dark by the time we finish.'

'How many pitchforks have you got?'

What was the Courtier blethering about now?

'Four. Three over by the barn.'

Carey waved his arm at the men still sitting like puddings and letting their hobbies crop wildflowers from the wall's base.

'Sergeant *Nixon*,' he roared. '*Over here!*'

Nixon came trotting over, looking very wary.

'Send a man over to Sergeant Dodd's barn and fetch the spare pitchforks.'

Nixon's face became mutinous. 'We're on patrol,' he said. 'We didnae come here to help wi' Sergeant Dodd's...'

Carey didn't appear to have heard him.

'I will pay an extra sixpence to each man that gives a hand with a pitchfork,' he said. 'You can draw straws to decide which will be the lucky ones. The others can help rake if they want sixpence too.'

'I done my own fields yesterday...' whined Sergeant Nixon and then seemed to forget what he was going to say when Carey glared at him.

'Nixon, either you can do what you're told or you can go back to Carlisle, with no sixpence for a little bit of extra sweat and no chance of what's at Brampton.'

Dodd pricked up his ears at that and exchanged glances with Janet. Sergeant Nixon's mouth tightened, he turned his hobby and cantered sullenly off to his men. A chorus of whines and moans rose from them and then stopped, presumably at news of the sixpence which was a full day's pay for haymaking.

'Right,' Carey said to Dodd. 'I want your professional advice and I want men, and I can see I'll get neither if you're worrying about your hay.'

Carey took his morion off, scratched his hair and put the helmet down carefully on the wall. His sword belt he laid down beside it, followed by his knife-belt, then he slid his shoulders out of his jack, revealing a darned but very fine linen shirt. Janet was staring at him open-mouthed as he hung his armour over a stone, turned and grinned at Dodd who was just beginning to suspect what the madman had in mind.

'I'm afraid I'd be a danger to man and beast with a pitchfork,' he said. 'But I know how to pack a cart, so I'll do that.'

He turned and jumped up onto the empty cart, took the small rake lying in it.

Dodd made a short rattle in his throat. Carey was rolling up his sleeves.

'Barnabus will want to kill me,' he muttered to himself. 'What's the problem, Sergeant?'

What Dodd wanted to say was that he had never in all his life heard of a Courtier to the Queen helping to load a haywagon like a child. In fact his mouth was open to say it but no words came out.

Janet was better with her tongue. She came over to the cart and looked up at him severely.

'Sir,' she said. 'It's not fitting. You're the Queen's cousin.'

Carey raised his eyebrows at her. 'Yes,' he said down his nose. 'I am. That's why I can do what I bloody well choose.'

Sergeant Nixon and the Lowther cousin, who were looking after the horses, leaned on their saddle horns and openly gawked at the insanity of the Deputy Warden. Carey was telling the truth; he coped perfectly well with the forkfuls of hay being tossed up to him and didn't trample it down too much. Nor did he fall off when Willie's Simon was too busy staring to warn him when the oxen moved on along the rows. In fact, the lunatic looked as if he was enjoying himself. Certainly he was whistling something irritating.

Dodd shook his head to clear it and bent to his work. After

a while he began to see the funny side, and his ribs almost burst with the effort not to laugh. The last field was cleared in record time with so many helpers, and as Willie's Simon goaded the oxen through the gate, Carey slotted his rake in behind the seat and jumped down.

'What's the joke, Sergeant?' he asked as he came over, brushing bits of hay off himself.

Dodd snorted and put his pitchfork on his shoulder to follow the cart back behind the barnekin wall.

'Only I was thinkin' I'd be willin' to take ye on for the harvest, sir, if ye was free,' he said grudgingly while Carey hefted up his jack and put it back on again.

'Thank you, Sergeant,' said Carey deadpan. 'I'll certainly consider your offer.'

\* \* \*

Janet had already gone back to their peel tower ready to welcome them in with the best beer and lead them to their suppers. The trestle tables were packed tight with friends and neighbours in the hall of the tower and Dodd presided over the lot of them at the head of the top table. He had offered the place to Carey but Carey had courteously refused and sat at his right instead. Once Dodd had swallowed enough pudding to quiet his empty stomach, he banged mugs with Carey and laughed again.

'I'll have to ride wi' ye against the Grahams now,' he said, not feeling as miserable about it as he might otherwise have done.

'Yes,' answered Carey equably. 'I know.' He finished his beer and sighed. 'God, that's good.'

He lifted his mug in salute to Janet who tilted her neck to him in acknowledgement. Dodd poured himself some more before the Courtier could finish the lot.

Janet always served the strongest beer for this supper, unless you included what she gave to the harvesters after the last sheaf was in, which could knock you over. She was sitting at the next table which was packed with local girls who had been helping with the raking and the stacking. Word had evidently gone round about

323

the Courtier. Many of them were wearing ribbons in their hair and craning their necks to stare at the Deputy Warden. At least half had forgotten to tighten their bodice lacings which offered a very pleasing view. Dodd saw that Carey was human enough to be admiring it. After all, it was very distracting.

'So what would you advise, Sergeant?' Carey asked after a moment's thoughtful pause.

'I'd advise not mixing it wi' them,' said Dodd, wiping beer off his mouth and digging into his food again. 'Wi' the Grahams, I mean,' he clarified round a lump of beef, and Carey grinned perfect understanding. 'But what would be the use?'

'Come on, Dodd,' said Carey. 'Be reasonable. I can't let Wattie Graham lift Lady Widdrington. I couldn't hold my head up again in this March.'

'Ay, he's puttin' a bit of a brave on ye,' agreed Dodd. 'The cheeky bastard.' He snorted again at the memory of the elegant Deputy sweating on his hay cart. That would be something to think of on his deathbed, he decided; it would cheer him up no end. 'Well, sir, if it was me running the rode, and I had the start that he's got, I'd steer well clear of Bewcastle itself and lie up by Hen Hill or Blackshaws in the forest for tonight. I'd give it till the sun was up to let the lady get well on her way, then I'd cross the Irthing above the gorge and use the rough ground and the Giant's Wall as cover until I got to the Faery Fort at Chesterholm, and I'd nip her out there.'

'Right,' said Carey. 'Now, how many men do you think we could scrape up overnight?'

'If we ring the bell...'

'No, I don't want to do that; he might hear it. I want to stop Wattie quietly if I can.'

'Quietly,' repeated Dodd. 'Well, it doesnae make so much odds because we've got the night. Have ye not tried to warn Captain Carleton what's afoot?'

'Of course I have,' Carey said. 'But I'm not betting on my messenger getting through. It would only be sensible for Wattie to send some men out to Thirlwall Castle overnight to keep an eye on what's going on and make sure Carleton hasn't convinced

Lady Widdrington to let him send some men with her.'

'Ay,' nodded the Sergeant. 'Ye're right. I'd do it.'

'So would I.'

'Well, then, it's nobbut a couple of miles to Thirlwall. We get the men together, we deal with Wattie's lads and we warn the Castle what's afoot. Then we escort her along the road to Hexham.'

'Of course, there's the possibility that Captain Carleton's in on it as well.'

Dodd thought of the barrel-shaped Captain with the loud laugh, and decided it wasn't so unlikely as all that.

'And if Wattie's loose on Thirlwall Common with fifty men, there will be a pitched battle when he hits us on the road, with us at a disadvantage. We don't know he'll be at Chesterholm; there must be other places.'

'What's wrong wi' a pitched battle?' Dodd wanted to know, made confident by the beer. 'Bloody murdering Grahams.'

'With a woman in the middle of it.'

'So?' said Dodd, wondering if they were talking about the same Lady Widdrington. 'She'd likely grab a pike and do for Wattie Graham herself.'

Carey sighed. 'Listen, Henry. I've no quarrel with a pitched battle, I just like to choose my own ground. And getting to the Castle isn't simply a case of dealing with some lads. You know what the ground around it is like; it's horribly steep, there are earthworks everywhere. You could hold off an army if you placed your men right, that's why they built it there. I can't even be sure Wattie's got no more than fifty riders. I only know what left Netherby, not what he might have picked up along the way.'

'Ay,' allowed Dodd, beginning to wonder if Carey had some other pressing reason for not wanting to meet Lady Widdrington face to face.

'And there's the question of authority,' Carey added with a sigh. 'Once Wattie's over the Irthing and into the Middle March he's supposedly out of my jurisdiction and into Sir John Forster's. I don't want to start up any inter-Wardenry feuding if I can help it and Sir John's known to be difficult.'

Dodd nodded, appreciating the Deputy Warden's talents at

understatement. Sir John Forster was irascible, deeply corrupt, as old as the century and far into his dotage. Unfortunately, he also seemed to be indestructible.

'Anyway,' Carey went on, 'I want to teach Wattie a lesson. Who the hell does he think he is, running a raid that size across the March at haymaking?'

'Well,' said Dodd slowly after some more thought and a lot of cheese. 'We could surely come up with twenty or thirty good men from hereabouts, especially if we went to Archibald Bell and warned him, and in any case the Bells are always willing to give the Grahams a bloody nose when they can. That's all, I'm afraid, sir. Ye could get double the number inside the hour at a different time of year, but...'

'I know, I know. It'll have to do. All the more reason not to tangle with Wattie on the road.'

Dodd was thinking hard and sucking his teeth. 'We should be able to get over to north of the road and maybe shadow them, but it'll be a long ride and hard country, and the horses will be tired and...'

Carey shook his head. He swallowed one of Janet's eyewatering pickled onions half-chewed and drank some beer.

'No,' he said. 'I'm not prancing about in Sir John Forster's March with a mixed bunch of...of men, if I can help it. I want to stop Wattie quick and clean before he goes near Lady Widdrington. In fact I want to ambush him on the way and send him back to Netherby with his tail between his legs.'

Dodd's heart started to warm to the Courtier a bit more. It seemed he had some sense after all.

'Hm,' he said. 'Ay.'

'What about when he's crossing the Irthing? Where will he do that? There can't be more than a couple of places, it's too steep.'

A horrible thought struck him. 'By God,' growled Dodd, 'he'll be in among my own shielings as well. I've forty head of cattle at the summering up there, and nobbut a man and a boy to guard them. If that bastard bloody Graham...'

'Absolutely,' said Carey cheerfully. 'I agree, we must stop them there.' He was making messy puddles with his finger on the table.

'Is this what the country looks like?' he asked. Dodd squinted at the puddles and wondered what he was jabbering about. Carey explained patiently. 'If this was the Irthing and that was the bog...'

'Och,' said Dodd, having difficulty converting his instinctive knowledge of the land into a picture. 'Ah. Maybe,' he allowed cautiously.

With the aid of some bits of bread, Carey explained what he wanted to do, and Dodd put in his notions to which Carey listened gravely. Although Dodd was being deprived of the dancing and the singing in order to go and fetch out the Bells, he didn't mind as much as he would have thought. It was a pity really, that Carey had had the misfortune to be born on the right side of such a very high-class blanket; he had the makings of a decent reiver in him.


## Tuesday, 4th July 1592, dawn


The first he knew was when one of Skinabake's broken men yelped and clutched his leg. Wattie Graham looked at the place and at first refused to believe what his eyes told him, that there was a feathered arrow shaft sticking out of it. Another arrow zipped by his nose and a third stuck in the hindquarters of one of the horses in the ford who promptly went berserk, reared up, stood kicking on its head and then crashed through the press of other horses and up the bank. Its rider was in the water, spitting mud and weed and looking astonished.

Wattie grabbed for his gun out of its case, pulled out the small ramrod, tried charging it, but more arrows were flying from the low hill. Men who had been lying down in the bracken on the slope were standing, shooting at them. They were at too great a range to do much damage, but the panic they were causing among the horses was bad enough. The cattle in the field lowed unhappily. Some of the broken men who had already come across trampled back down into the ford, trying to run away, and added to the thrashing, shouting, swearing confusion.

Wattie fumbled and dropped his ramrod, cursed, slammed the gun back in its case and drew his sword.

'Come on, ye fools, get on out of the water,' he roared. A few of them managed to do what he ordered and bunched around him looking scared, while the men on the hill continued to shoot judiciously. There was the sound of hooves from their right, men and horses boiling like bees from the little shieling, more men swinging themselves up onto their horses' bare backs from where they had been hiding in amongst the cattle, joining with the riders pounding down from the shieling.

Wattie swung round to face the threat, saw lances, hobbies, and at the head of them a long man in a morion pointing a dag straight for his chest. Unthinkingly, he slid sideways clinging to his horse's neck and actually heard the crack as the bullet passed through where he had been. Then the men hit them, and he found himself cutting and slicing against the press of bodies; it was all Bells at first, Archibald Bell at their head roaring something obscene about blackrent. He glimpsed Sergeant Dodd in there, riding bareback, with a face like a winter's day and blood on his sword, and then it was the man with the fancy morion battering at him with a bright new broadsword, and he recognised Sir Robert Carey.

'Shame on you, Wattie,' roared the Courtier. 'Attacking a defenceless woman.'

Somebody backed a horse between them, and Wattie managed to collect himself. Half his men had scrambled back across the ford; he could see a few horses' rumps galloping away in the distance. More broke from the right as they worked their way to the edges.

'Skinabake!' he yelled in a sudden breathing space, catching sight of the Armstrong reiver. 'Back across the ford; we'll have them if they follow.'

He felt something behind him, ducked; steel whistled over his shoulder and nicked his hobby which promptly squealed and tried to run away. He managed to turn about to face his attacker and found Carey must have been pursuing him because there he was again, sword in one hand, dag in the other and its wheel-lock spinning sparks. He froze, staring at death like a rabbit. It misfired.

He swung his sword down on Carey, hoping he would be distracted by his gun, but the bastard Deputy parried and slashed sideways, still shouting something incomprehensible.

Another plunging riderless horse banged into the other side of Wattie, bruising his leg against his own mount. Carey was coping with another rider on his other side, crossed swords a couple of times and knocked that man out of the saddle. Wattie disentangled himself from the terror-crazed nag, just in time to face the Deputy as he turned again and came after Wattie.

'Liddesdale, to me!' yelled Wattie, standing up in his stirrups. When as many as could were around him he launched his horse down the bank again, through the water, up the other side and turned about, breathing hard.

Let them follow us and we'll have them the way they had us, he thought, but Dodd and Archibald Bell were wise to that and so were the others with them, too wise to try crossing a ford opposed. Only the lunatic Deputy Warden seemed eager to try, but Dodd caught his horse's bridle and snarled at him and he seemed to calm down.

The two sides stared at each other, those of the Grahams who had bows stringing them frantically on their stirrups and awkwardly nocking arrows. It was very hard to use a longbow on horseback, but it could be done if you twisted sideways and leaned over a little. The bowmen on the hill came jogging across and lined up facing them over the water.

Wattie looked about at his men. A number of them were bleeding somewhere, there were five still shapes over on the other bank and three men surrounded. A couple of the ones who had fallen off during the mêlée in the water were climbing out again as fast as they could, cursing. Several horses were down, others galloping away squealing.

Skinabake came up beside him, shaking his head.

'We're out of it,' he said without preamble.

'Ay,' said Wattie heavily, knowing a lost cause when he saw it. He shook his fist impotently at the Deputy Warden. 'Ye'll regret this, Carey,' he shouted. 'I'm no' forgetting this.'

'Ah, go home and cry, Wattie,' sneered the Courtier. 'I'll give you a long neck one of these days, you bloody coward.'

Wattie's neck swelled and his eyes almost bugged out of his head. He took a firm grip on his sword, kicked his horse forward to the water.

Skinabake got in his way and the hobby was anyway not inclined to go near the blood-tinged water.

'Come on, Wattie,' said Skinabake, highly amused. 'Put a lance through him some other time.'

Wattie was shaking with rage. 'Did you hear...' he sputtered. 'Did ye hear what he called me?'

'Och,' said Skinabake negligently, in a voice that carried. 'He only said it to bring ye back in range of the bowmen there.'

Carey's head went up. He had heard, as he was meant to. But Dodd had already shifted his horse in front of the Deputy Warden's nag and had changed grip on his lance to bar his path.

Wattie spat over his shoulder, and began riding away north west, his men lightly gathered around him, the ones who had lost their mounts running at their friends' stirrups. Skinabake's outlaws were already breaking northwards for the Debateable Land.

Behind them, the heavy-laden packtrain owned by Edward Aglionby paced north west along the road, miraculously unmolested.

# Tuesday, 4th July 1592, morning

The roofbeams of the Carlisle Castle stables vibrated with the already legendary Carey roar.

'*He's what?*'

Bangtail winced and stepped back a few paces. All the horses stamped and shifted and some of them neighed protestingly. Dodd had to hold the headstall of the hobby he was rubbing down, to stop himself being knocked over.

'He...he's in the dungeon, sir,' Bangtail repeated. 'Lowther put him there on a charge of murder.'

Carey advanced on him, still in his sodden jack and wet morion. His fists were clenched tight and two spots of colour flamed below the incipient bags under his eyes.

'It wasna me, sir,' yelled Bangtail, dodging behind one of the stall posts. 'It was Lowther.'

Carey seemed to catch himself and stop. He breathed deeply, carefully unfisted his hands and folded them across his chest.

'Start at the beginning, Bangtail, and tell me exactly what happened.'

'Ay, well. It were Atkinson, ye see, sir, Jemmy Atkinson, the Armoury clerk, that used to be paymaster until you...'

'I think I remember him.'

'Well, what I heard was, he was found deid this morning, in an alley, with his gizzard slit, see ye, and so his wife sent for Lowther because he's known to be Lowther's man.'

'Clear so far.'

'An' Lowther's up to the Castle in a fearful bate just afore ye come in, sir, and I'd just arrived, see, and he says, it's bound to be ye that did him in, because ye didna want him fer armoury clerk, but ye werena there and nor was Dodd, so then he says, ye must have set the thief that serves ye on to dae it, and so he's gone up to the Queen Mary Tower and haled yer man out and thrown him in the dungeon and he's making a complaint out against ye now, forbye.'

'Is that it, that's the full tale?'

'Ay, sir, so far as I know.'

'Well then, thank you for coming to tell me of it so promptly.'

Bangtail smiled. 'We drew straws for it, sir, an' I got the short one.'

Carey coughed. 'Where's Lowther now?'

'He's still in with the Lord Warden.'

'Is he, by God! Well, go and keep an eye on him and try and see he doesn't find out that I'm back yet. Go on, off with you.'

'Ay, sir.'

As Bangtail trotted off on his mission, Dodd wondered what the Deputy Warden would do. For a moment as his colour faded he looked tired and thoughtful, and to be sure, his position was bad. Dodd knew that it wasn't so much the question of whether or not Barnabus had actually slit Atkinson's throat, it was whether Lowther could get the bill fouled against him and so hang him. Barnabus might even decide to turn Queen's evidence to save his own neck and say that Carey had ordered him to do the killing. In London or in Berwick, Dodd didn't doubt that Carey could muster enough influence to clear himself of such an accusation, but they were in Carlisle where his only important relative was Lord Scrope. And Lord Scrope was notoriously easy to persuade if got at right. It was unlikely but not completely beyond the bounds of possibility that Lowther might see Carey swing for the death of Atkinson, despite the Queen's liking for him, whether he had anything to do with it or not. Or no: as a nobleman, he would face the axe. At best, with his servant hanged for murder, the blow to his prestige meant Carey would have very little chance of commanding obedience in the March.

Carey set his back against the loose-box wall, one leg bent, took his helmet off and with his eyes shut, rubbed the red marks left by the leather padding and the chin strap.

'What'll ye do, sir?' asked Dodd morbidly, wondering if he should begin making overtures to Lowther. No, it would be a waste of time.

'Hm? See Barnabus first.'

Carey didn't have the keys to the inner door, but he gave Dodd his helmet, pulled aside the Judas hole and called softly, 'Barnabus. Wake up.'

There were a couple of grunts and an adenoidal 'Yes, sir.'

Carey was silent for a moment as his lantern light hit Barnabus's face. 'Did Lowther do that to you?'

A long liquid sniff. 'Yes, sir. It's a good one, isn't it?'

'Any particular reason, or was it just high spirits?'

Another sniff. 'Yes, sir. He wanted me to confess to killing Atkinson.'

'And did you?'

The sniff that followed was offended. 'No, sir. I'm not that stupid. Even if I dun it, which I din't, I'd never say I did, would I?'

'Was that all he wanted from you?'

'Er...no, sir.'

'Well?'

'He wanted me to say you'd ordered it and forced me to do it, sir.'

Carey nodded. He didn't look surprised. Evidently he had thought along the same lines as Dodd.

'I din't admit that either, sir.'

'I'm glad to hear it.' Carey's voice was dry.

'What do you want me to do, sir?'

'Where were you last night?'

There was an apologetic cough. 'Well, you wasn't 'ere sir, so...'

'You were at Madam Hetherington's?'

'Er...yessir.'

'All night?'

'After I'd been in Bessie's for a bit, I was there till this morning when the Castle gate opened and I come in. So I'd be here to serve you when you finished your patrol,' he added virtuously.

'Would Madam Hetherington testify that you were with her?'

'I dunno, sir. She might.' And then, complacently, 'Maria will, though.'

'Unfortunately a notorious French whore is not the best of alibi witnesses.'

'Well, if I'd known I'd need one, I'd've got a better one, wouldn't I, sir?'

Carey treated that impudence with a measured pause that said he was making allowances, but would not make them indefinitely.

'Did anybody else see you at Madam Hetherington's?'

'I don't think so, sir, that'd speak for me...Oh, bloody hell, it's started again.'

'Try pinching the bridge of your nose, see if that stops it.'

'I can't, sir. It's broken.'

Carey was silent for a moment. 'I'm sorry, I can't get you out yet, Barnabus,' he said. 'I haven't the authority. It probably wouldn't be a good idea anyway.'

'I know that, sir. Lowther's on the up and up, in'e?'

'For the moment.'

'You'll be able to sort it, though, won't you, sir? I mean, the juries round here won't be any more expensive than London ones, will they?'

Eh? thought Dodd. Carey had winced.

'Barnabus,' he asked gently. 'You didn't do it, did you?'

Barnabus's voice was an outraged adenoidal whine. 'Sir! You know me better'n that!'

'I seem to recall a fight at the Cock tavern...'

'That was different. I never done nuffing like this, sir, never, not that I haven't 'ad offers, mind, I just never would. 'S stupid. There's better ways of doing it than slittin' 'is throat in an alley. Besides, it's wrong.'

'Quite.'

'So what do you want me to do, sir?'

'Keep your mouth shut. That's all. Are you cold?'

'Yes, sir, freezing. I bin in Clink afore now, of course, but this ain't what I'm used to and Lowther's bastards took me jerkin and doublet off lookin' to see if I had a bloody knife, which they didn't find, I might add.'

'I'll get my sister to bring you some clothes and food.'

'Yes sir,' said Barnabus gloomily.

Dodd trailed after him as Carey marched from the dungeon, rounded the side of the Keep and was pounced on by his sister. She had her cap on crooked, her ruff under one ear, and her damask apron sideways, with a bundle of Barnabus's clothes under her arm. She took one look at her brother and said, 'You've heard then, Robin.'

'I have. How did you stop Lowther searching my office?'

Her heart-shaped face became very forbidding. 'Simon threw the key for your office in the fire and said you had it with you. I got there just after and when he wouldn't go I drew my dagger on him and told him I'd stick him if he moved a step nearer, and he believed me.'

Carey embraced her, but she pushed him off.

'What are you going to do about it, Robin?' she said. 'Lowther's out for your blood. He's telling everyone that Barnabus did it and he's half got Scrope believing you ordered him to.'

'How? I wasn't even here.'

'Well, that hardly matters, does it? Anyway, Lowther found

one of Barnabus's knives and a glove of yours by the corpse.'

'*What*?'

'Don't shout, Robin, and don't grab me like that, you're all wet and muddy.'

'Jesus Christ.'

'Don't swear. It doesn't help. And I would get out of the Castle, if I were you. My lord might even have signed a warrant for your arrest by now.'

Carey was staring at her as if unable to believe what he was hearing.

'How do you know all this?'

Philadelphia lowered her eyes demurely. 'Lowther has a very carrying voice,' she said.

Carey smiled faintly at her tone. Then he shook his head.

'Well, my sweet, if he does issue a warrant for me, block it any way you can.'

Philly scowled ferociously. 'I'll steal it if I have to, silly man. Where are you going?'

Carey chucked her under the chin. 'If I don't tell you, then you can tell the truth to your husband if he asks.'

'I wish you'd take your jack off; it's sodden.'

'I haven't got time.'

'And you haven't even got a hat...'

Dodd gave Carey the morion he'd been carrying, which Carey put on.

'Better?'

Philly's brow wrinkled. 'No, you look tired.'

'At least if I have to ride for the Debateable Land, I'll be properly dressed,' Carey said with a crooked smile.

Philly swallowed very hard. 'Do you really think it'll be all right? I mean, the Queen's an awfully long way away.'

'Yes. God looks after me always, remember?'

Philly snorted. 'Hmf. He didn't look after Jemmy Atkinson very well, did he?'

'Philly, you're being heretical. Anyway, Jemmy Atkinson was a bad corrupt man and I'm not.' He kissed her bunched-up forehead and tried unsuccessfully to straighten her cap which had been pinned on crooked. She batted him off and marched away across the courtyard.

Dodd kept on at Carey's heels as he lengthened his stride to pass through the Castle gate and down the covered way, his hands clasped behind his back and his head thrust forward.

'Where are we going, sir?'

'Hm? You still there, Sergeant?'

'Ay, sir.'

'It might be better for you if you got back to the Castle.'

Dodd considered this. 'Nay, sir,' he said. 'If Lowther's gonnae foul a bill against me, I'd rather it was in my absence.'

'Why should he?'

Dodd was surprised to hear Carey being so naïve. 'He reckons I'm one o' yourn now.'

'Ah. Of course.'

'Any road, I've always had a fancy to live in the Debateable Land.'

'Have you? I haven't.'

'Oh, it's no' sae bad, sir. Skinabake Armstrong, that's my brother-in-law, Janet's half-brother...'

'You're related to Skinabake Armstrong?'

'Oh ay, sir. Or Janet is.'

'Why didn't you say?'

'Och, sir. If I told ye all the reivers I'm related to through Janet, we'd be all day about it. Besides, what difference does it make?'

'Was that why you wouldn't let me fight Wattie Graham at the ford?'

'Ay, of course. I know Skinabake. He'd ha' put a lance in yer back the minute ye was busy with Wattie. I know him, he's no' a very nice man. That's why he likes it in the Debateable Land. He says he'd never live anywhere else, even if he wasnae at the horn in both countries.'

'Lowther might not include you in his feud.'

'Only if I turned Queen's evidence and swore ye ordered Barnabus to dae it, sir.'

'Ah. Well, let's see what we can do to prove I didn't order it and Barnabus didn't do it.'

'Ye didnae, did ye, sir?'

'I beg your pardon?'

'Well, he wasnae what ye could call a good armoury clerk and Scrope wouldnae let ye sack him, if ye see...'

Carey had stopped and he was an odd greyish colour. 'If you think I'm stupid enough to set my own servant on to cut someone's throat for me...'

'I wouldna hold it against ye, sir. I've known others do the like.'

'Who?'

'Lowther for one.'

'When?'

Dodd shrugged. 'When somebody didna pay him blackrent and give him cheek when he went round to collect. He had some of the Grahams drop by and kill the man. It's no' so unusual, ye ken.'

Carey took one of those deep breaths that signalled he was holding on to his anger. Then he laughed and carried on walking.

'Christ's guts, Dodd, I'm a bloody innocent in this place. Will you believe me if I give ye my word that, aside from a couple of hangings, I never killed nobody in my life without it was me holding the weapon?'

Dodd nodded gravely, noting with interest how Carey's voice had changed to pure Berwick.

'Ay,' he said. 'I know ye're a man of your word, Courtier. Ye're a bloody hen's tooth in Carlisle and no mistake.'

# TUESDAY, 4TH JULY 1592, LATE MORNING

The hen's tooth had several lines of inquiry in mind and was in a fever of impatience to follow all of them. Carey knew he had to be able to present an alternative theory to Scrope. After some thought, he sent Dodd to Bessie's to find out what he could of Barnabus's movements the night before, while he himself went to the two-storey house by the market that had belonged to Atkinson.

He knocked at the door, poked his head round it into the ground-floor living room. She was surrounded by her gossips: one was making bread and milk for the children by the fire, while two others held her hands and talked in low voices.

'What d'ye want, Deputy?' demanded the largest of Mrs Atkinson's gossips, looming up before him.

'I want to find out who cut Mr Atkinson's throat,' said Carey, politely taking off his morion and putting it on a bench as he came in. His head was crammed against the ceiling beams even without it on.

'Oh, ay?' said another, a middle-aged woman with a withered hand. 'From what I heard, ye should be asking yerself the question.'

Carey looked at her in silence for a while, without anger. He had spent much of the night before with Dodd riding about Gilsland, calling individually on the local Bell and Musgrave headmen. They had mustered two hours before dawn in order to catch Wattie when he crossed the Irthing. Perhaps he had slept for two hours in total. His thinking was slower than usual, that was all, but the women read threat into his lack of reaction. They all fell silent as well and the one who had spoken shrank back.

'Who are you, goodwife?' he asked.

'I am Mrs Maggie Mulcaster, Mrs Atkinson's sister,' she said stoutly.

'Well, you heard wrong, Mrs Mulcaster,' he said mildly. 'Who did you hear it from?'

'Lowther,' she admitted.

'You should know better than to trust a man that kills anyone who won't pay him blackrent.'

The women muttered between each other and Mrs Atkinson stood up, curtseyed and wiped her hands in her apron.

'What can I do for you, sir?' she asked, civilly enough.

'My condolences for your loss, Mrs Atkinson. Will you be good enough to tell me when you last saw your husband?'

She wiped her hands in her apron again. 'I...I saw him yesterday morning. He went out about the middle of the morning, to deal with some business, he said, and that's the last I saw of him.'

'Weren't you worried when he didn't come home last night?'

She looked studiously at the fresh rushes on the floor. 'He often stays out all night. I didn't think anything of it, and then the man came to…to tell me this morning.'

A well-built girl, fresh-faced and cheerful with red hair streaming down her back, came in carrying a large empty basket.

'I've put them back out again, mistress, but them sheets will take all week to dry with the way the sky…Oh.'

The girl looked at Carey and her mouth dropped open.

'It's all right, Julia,' said Mrs Atkinson. 'Go and see after Mary and the boys.'

'Oh, she's well enough,' said Julia, putting the basket down and picking up the empty pewter mugs. 'She's rolling dough for me in the scullery and the boys are feeding Clover.'

'Did you want to know anything else, sir?' demanded Mrs Mulcaster.

'Has anyone here seen Mr Atkinson since yesterday morning?'

They all looked at each other and shook their heads.

'Can you tell me which undertaker…'

There was a spasm in Mrs Atkinson's face, but she controlled herself.

'Fenwick,' she said shortly, naming the most expensive undertaker in Carlisle, and then stood there waiting.

Carey sighed. He hadn't expected to be very welcome. 'Thank you for your help, goodwives,' he said, picked up his morion and went out. The buzz of talk followed him out as he instantly became the prime subject of conversation.

\*\*\*

Mr Fenwick was one of the most prosperous traders in Carlisle, with a large house on English Street facing the gardens where the old Greyfriars monastery had been. He had a long yard out the back where he kept two different hearses, grew funeral flowers and ran a joinery business on the side for when business was slack. It seldom was. He himself was a large comfortably plump man, balding under his velvet hat, who wore black brocades of impressive richness and had a deep pleasant voice.

'Well, Sir Robert,' he said thoughtfully, after Carey had been seated in his sitting room and brought wine to drink. 'I hadn't expected to see ye. What can I do for you?'

'I want to see Mr Atkinson's body.'

'Ah.' There was a pause while Mr Fenwick's chins dropped onto his snowy ruff and he clasped his hands across his stomach. 'May I ask why, sir?'

Carey at first wasn't sure why. It had been an instinctive feeling that he should look at the corpse he was being accused of making. He wasn't sure how to deal with Fenwick either and in the end decided on honesty.

'You know how I'm placed here,' he said. 'My servant is falsely accused of killing the man and I am wrongly under suspicion for ordering him to do it. I am trying to understand what actually happened.'

'How will viewing the corpse help you?'

'I don't know, Mr Fenwick. I don't even know if it will. I haven't got a warrant with me, I am simply asking this as a favour.'

Fenwick had soft brown eyes which suddenly looked very shrewd.

'We are in the midst of preparing him for his funeral,' he said. 'If you are willing...'

'Of course.'

Fenwick stood and motioned Carey to follow him. There was a shed in the brightly blossoming garden where bodies could be laid out if there were not room for them at home or while they were waiting for an inquest. Atkinson lay there in his shirt and hose, while a slender woman sewed the gaping wound on his neck with white thread. Carey was not particularly squeamish but he looked away from that: it was ugly the way the needle pulled and tugged at the edges of flesh and no blood came.

'Where did you bring him from?' Carey asked. 'Where was he killed?'

'He was found,' said Fenwick carefully, 'in Frank's vennel, off Botchergate.'

'Found?' Carey lifted his eyebrows. Fenwick hesitated.

'There wasna hardly any blood about,' he said. 'In fact, there was none; my litter was hardly marked. He had his clothes on but not his boots. It was...' Fenwick stopped suddenly.

Carey turned to him urgently. 'Please, Mr Fenwick,' he said. 'I know you must be experienced in these things. If anything struck you as odd about Mr Atkinson, please will you tell me?'

Fenwick hesitated again, searching Carey's face. Whatever it was he found there, he nodded and led the way quietly back to his sitting room.

'Well, Sir Robert,' he said. 'The whole thing was odd and no mistake. The distribution of blood for one...None in the alley. None on the outside of his clothes, but his shirt soaked with it. No boots to his feet, but his feet not broken to take them off. I have collected men's mortal remains in many different circumstances and, yes, these were odd.'

'Are you saying that Atkinson was not killed where he lay?'

'It is not my place to say such things,' Fenwick remarked heavily. 'I can only speak of what I saw. I saw too little blood in the alley...'

'Yes, but it rained,' Carey objected. 'Couldn't the blood have been washed away?'

'The rain came on after we brought the body within. There was no rain last night.'

Carey nodded. He had been out in it and his jack was clammy from it, but there had indeed been no rain until after dawn.

Fenwick was silent again. He looked sympathetically at Carey who caught the look and found it didn't irritate him as it would normally. He stood up and found his morion.

'If you think of any other odd thing, will you let me know, Mr Fenwick?' he asked.

Fenwick nodded, and came to show him out. 'Frank's vennel?' Carey asked, to be sure.

'Ay.' The undertaker sighed. 'Poor fellow. Nobody seems sorry to see him go.'

Carey found the alley without much trouble and walked up and down, not knowing at all what he was looking for. Certainly Fenwick was right, there was no blood to speak of in the mud. The mark of where the body had lain could be seen, and the scuff marks of Lowther and his men, sightseers and Fenwick's men as well. The wheels of Fenwick's handcart were clearly printed in the soft combination of rush sweepings and animal dung that floored the alley, though they had turned into little runnels with the rain.

Carey stared at them for a long time, trying to make his brain work, and then cursed softly. He walked out of the alley and back along up English Street.

\* \* \*

Mrs John Leigh had three serving girls to help her in the house, and a boy and a man to serve in the draper's shop on the ground floor. Of her children, two were boys and old enough to go to the City grammar school by the Cathedral; the other three were girls, two of whom trotted around in their little kirtles and caps getting into fights, skipping rope in their yard and occasionally getting in her way when they decided to be helpful. The youngest girl was fourteen months old, not long out of swaddling clothes and with no more sense than a puppy. She was in her baby-walker at the moment, a round sausage of cloth tied about her head to cushion it when she fell over or bumped herself and currently her favourite game was making her wheeled wooden babywalker go as fast as it could over the expensive rush-matting until it rammed into one of the walls. All the new oak panelling was dented along the bottom where the babywalker had bashed it. Each time she made an earsplitting crash she crowed 'Waaarrrgh', and the noise went through Mrs Leigh's head like an awl. It was worse than the steady hammering from the men working on the roof now the rain had stopped. She had come into the small room over the shop at the front of the house to rest and do some sewing. However, rest was impossible. She was in too great a state of tension and there was too much noise in the children's room next door where Jeanie the wetnurse was with the baby. Why didn't the silly girl take the baby into the garden?

Somebody knocked at the street door. One of the lazy creatures finally went down the stairs and opened it. There was a mutter of voices and a man's boots on the stair. The girl came fluttering into the sitting room where Mrs Leigh had her feet up, followed by the long-legged new Deputy Warden. He was so tall he had to keep his head tilted to be clear of the ceiling beams. Evidently he had just come in from the Border since he was in his damp leather jack and carrying his helmet. Mrs Leigh hadn't seen him before, but had heard a great deal about him from those who had. None of them had lied and Mrs Leigh wistfully wished she were not in the last month of pregnancy and wearing her oldest English-cut gown. He bowed to her, saw her shifting her swollen feet to the floor to stand up and return the courtesy, and waved a long hand at her.

'Please, Mrs Leigh, don't tire yourself. May I ask you a few questions about the tragic murder that happened this morning?'

Mrs Leigh went pale and her hand flew to her mouth.

'Murder? This morning?' she trembled.

'Of Mr Atkinson,' Carey told her kindly. 'Had you not heard? I'm sorry, I would have...'

'N...no, no. I...well. Poor James.'

'He was found in an alley with his throat slit this morning,' Carey explained.

'In an...alley,' repeated Mrs Leigh, still white-faced and shaking. 'I...I...what a terrible thing. He...he was my half-brother.'

'I'm sorry indeed.' Carey was serious. 'I had forgotten that. If this distresses you too much, I can return at another time...'

'No. I would...like to help. What did you wish to know?'

There was the squeak and rattle of wheels in the next room, followed by a crash and a delighted 'Waauuugh!'

Carey turned his head at the noise. 'What's that?'

Mrs Leigh winced. Her headache was much worse. 'My daughter. She likes crashing her babywalker into walls...'

Carey grinned. 'According to my mother, I had a habit of diving out of mine, preferably into the fire.'

Mrs Leigh smiled back at him wanly. 'It is...very wearing, but she screams if we prevent her.'

'I won't keep you, Mrs Leigh; I can see you need your rest. All I wanted to ask you was whether you had happened to see Mr Atkinson leave his house yesterday morning on business. Nobody else seems to have done so.'

'No, I didn't.'

'Can you tell me anything else about the Atkinsons?'

Mrs Leigh lifted her head and sniffed. 'I have nothing to do with either of them.'

'But you are neighbours and kin.'

'He is...was my youngest half-brother. Unfortunately he made a bad marriage. We have not spoken for several years. I did not wish to have anything to do with him or...her.'

'Why not?'

Mrs Leigh's small pink mouth pouched in at the corners in disapproval.

'Mrs Atkinson is a disgrace to the family.'

Carey's eyebrows went up and he waited.

'She is...er...she is fraudulently preventing me from inheriting her house which was clearly intended to be mine and she is also a wicked unchaste woman.'

'Oh?'

Mrs Leigh looked prim. 'It's too disgraceful to repeat.'

'That's a pity. Any little information, no matter how... disgraceful, might help me clear my servant.'

Squeak, squeak, rattle, rattle, crash! 'Waaauuugh!'

Mrs Leigh stayed silent looking out of the little diamond-paned window beside her. She had a baby's nightshirt on her lap and was stitching at it desultorily.

'My husband, you know,' she said, 'is John Leigh, brother to Henry Leigh who holds Rockcliffe Castle for my Lord Scrope.'

'I know,' said Carey. 'I was playing cards with him the other night—at the same card party, I mean, not actually with him.'

'Yes,' said Mrs Leigh distantly, obviously not knowing or not wishing to think about John Leigh's losses. 'He is a prominent citizen and has a position to maintain. We are impossibly crowded in this house, what with the children and the servants, and the warehouse and showroom downstairs. My aunt always intended me to have the house next door, though she leased it to...my half-brother out of charity. Perhaps *he* would have let us have the house, but *she* has taken wicked advantage and the case is in Chancery at the moment.'

Carey tutted sympathetically. 'Legal disputes are very wearing,' he said. 'I have one rumbling along myself with one of my brothers.'

'And very expensive,' agreed Mrs Leigh. 'What the barrister charges is...criminal.'

Carey nodded with a straight face. Sometimes he wished he had become a lawyer, but he soon came to his senses again.

'I hope he's a good one?' he said.

'Very good, I understand,' said Mrs Leigh unhappily. 'Or he should be. Unfortunately, that woman has managed to get the services of a young man who has just become the judge's son-in-law.'

'Oh dear.'

Mrs Leigh nodded at him. 'It seems very hard. We are not unreasonable. We even offered the Atkinsons another house, a better house, that we own on Scotch Street, but she will not see reason. And she keeps a cow in her yard.'

'Oh,' said Carey, not knowing if he was supposed to be shocked about something so normal.

'That's where she meets her lover,' said Mrs Leigh.

'Ah...?'

'In the cow byre. He creeps in from the garden backing on behind, she goes out in the morning and evening and that's where they meet, the dirty sinful... Anyway, she disgraces the whole street.'

'Do her other neighbours know about this?'

'Of course they do. It's common knowledge she's got no use for her rightful husband and wants to marry Andy Nixon.'

Carey blinked a little at the venom in Mrs Leigh's voice. 'Are you saying that Mrs Atkinson might have killed her own husband?'

Mrs Leigh looked away. 'I would not wish to lay such accusations against anyone,' she said primly. 'However, it's a fact that she has a lover.'

'Is it, by God?' said Carey thoughtfully. 'Well, well.'

Squeak, rattle, rattle, crash...*crash!* 'Waah! Waah! *Mama!*'

'She's fallen over,' Carey explained helpfully. Mrs Leigh wearily moved her sore feet to the floor and started the rocking movements that would get her out of her chair. The Deputy Warden offered her his arm which she took gratefully.

'I'll see to her,' she said. 'The idiot girls are useless besoms. Did you want to know anything else, Sir Robert?'

He was looking satisfactorily thoughtful and absent-mindedly helped her to the door.

'I may do later,' he said. 'May I come back some time, Mrs Leigh?'

She smiled at him. 'Of course, Sir Robert,' she said. 'Whatever I can do to help.'

He smiled in return and clattered down the narrow stairs, leaning back and ducking his head to avoid the low ceiling beams. He went through the shop where Jock Burn was serving. Mrs Leigh longed to shout down and send the man for her husband so she could talk to him, but she couldn't yet. She waddled off to see after her smallest daughter who was still screeching.

\*\*\*

Carey was deep in thought as he walked up Castlegate towards Bessie's alehouse, at last noticing properly how clammy and uncomfortable his jack was. The outer leather was beginning to dry, but the inner padding still squelched whenever he moved his arms. He was supposed to be out on patrol tonight as well and he refused to think about going to bed for a nap as he had planned. He simply didn't have the time if he wanted to find out as much as he could before the trail went cold. Also, he was putting off going back to his chambers in the Castle. He didn't know what he might find there, whether Scrope would believe Lowther against him or give him the benefit of the doubt. The whole thing was ridiculous, but still very dangerous. He didn't seriously think Scrope would dare to execute him on such a trumped-up charge, for all Philadelphia's worries. But he might well find himself in gaol with no ability to help Barnabus, while evil tales galloped down the roads to London and the Queen. The whole thing could ruin him, in which case he might as well be dead, because if he went back to London with no prospect of office and no hope of favour from the Queen, his creditors would certainly put him in the Fleet prison for his mountainous debts. And there he would rot.

He paused to look unseeingly at one of the shops, a cobbler's, with a bright striped awning over the counter to keep the rain off the samples of leather and made shoes displayed there.

He heard his own voice out of the past, assuring Scrope that he could deal with Lowther when they had been talking the day after he arrived. Evidently he had seriously underestimated the man and his influence. That had been stupid of him.

'Can I help you, sir?' asked the man behind the counter hopefully.

'Er...no. Thank you.'

He left the shop behind him and carried on to where Bessie's alehouse squatted, unofficial but tolerated, by the wall of the Castle, feeling a thousand years old and heavier than a cannon. For a moment he thought about simply going into the inn courtyard, fetching a horse out of Bessie's stables and heading north for the Debateable Land. Jock of the Peartree would receive him, might even take him in; they had come to an odd sort of understanding at the top of Netherby tower, despite the old reiver's deplorable character. He had his sword and his harness, he could hire out as one of the many broken men of the area...

It was a fantasy. It wasn't that he was too brave to do it, rather the reverse: he was afraid to turn his back on everything he knew, on his cousin the Queen, on his sister...And furthermore he was feeling too tired, he'd probably fall asleep on his horse and wander into a bog.

Bessie's was packed, with no sign of Dodd or anyone else of Carey's troop. As he stood in the doorway, peering into the smoky shadows, Carey knew that every eye in the place was on him and that conversations were stopping in each direction. He smiled faintly and shouldered his way through the throng to the bar.

'A quart of double-double,' he said to Bessie, who looked at him slitty-eyed. 'On the slate.'

She snorted. 'I want your bill paid, Sir Robert,' she said. 'It's getting on for eleven shillings now.'

'Och, for the love of God,' boomed a rasping voice beside him. 'Give the man a drink, woman, he needs it. Put in on my tab if ye must.'

Bessie snorted again, flounced off to draw the beer. Carey turned to see Will the Tod Armstrong beaming up at him, his girth clearing three struggling would-be drinkers away from the bar. The beer slammed down beside him. Carey picked up the tankard and swallowed. It went down a treat; he'd forgotten how long it was since he'd put anything in his belly, and his headache and weariness started to recede.

'Thank you, Mr Armstrong.'

'And we'll have another quart in the booth over there when ye've a minute, Bessie,' Will the Tod added to Bessie's departing back as she went to mark up the English Armstrong's heroically long slate. 'Now then, Deputy, ye come along wi' me, we'll see ye right.'

Carey was borne along in Will the Tod's wake by sheer force of personality, to the booth where Dodd was sitting with a large jug in front of him and a plate of bread and cheese. Carey found his mouth watering at the sight.

Carey lifted his pewter mug to Will the Tod as he slid in beside Dodd, and put his morion down on the bench beside him.

'Thanks for coming to my rescue yet again, Will.'

Will the Tod laughed. 'Ay, I like to see my friends treated well. Now then. What's all this I hear about you and Jemmy Atkinson?'

Carey shrugged. 'It seems the whole of Carlisle believes I told Barnabus to slit his throat.'

'And did ye?'

The headache came back with full force. 'Mr Armstrong, I could have had him hanged for March treason last week, if I'd wanted...'

'Ay, but that were last week. What about this week?'

'God damn it, if you think I'm...'

'Now there's no need to get in a bate, Deputy. Did ye or did ye no'? I know ye didna do it yersen, for ye were riding about the Middle March with a pack of Bells and Musgraves givin' Wattie Graham and Skinabake a good leatherin', but did ye set any other man on to it?'

'For the last time, Armstrong, and on my word of honour, I had nothing to do with Atkinson's murder.'

'Well, no need to bang on the table neither; if ye gi' me your word, that's good enough. Might Barnabus have done it by himself, thinking ye might want it but wi'out asking?'

'No. He knows I'd hand him over to be hanged.'

Will the Tod's eyebrows went up to where his bristling red hair flopped over his forehead.

'Ay, well enough,' he conceded. 'Well enough.'

'And you, Will. Why are you in town?'

'Och, that's easy. I came to warn Henry here.'

'What about?'

Will the Tod harrumphed and took a long pull at his beer. Dodd spoke up.

'King James is coming to Dumfries on a justice raid,' he explained. 'He's looking for the horses that were reived from him last week.'

'I knew he was coming,' said Carey. 'But what's it got to do with you, Sergeant?'

Dodd was suddenly very thirsty as well.

'Nothing, Deputy, nothing,' boomed Will the Tod. 'Only a matter of public interest, that's all.'

Nancy Storey, who was known by the nickname of Bessie's Wife, came over with a jug on her hip and her fair hair loose down her neck. All the northern girls wore their hair loose and uncovered until they married, and it was a delightful sight, Carey thought appreciatively. On the other hand, there were rumours that Bessie had been seen to kiss her on the mouth when tipsy, hence her nickname.

'I'll have some bread and cheese too, Nancy,' Carey said to her.

She lifted her fair eyebrows. 'Who's paying?'

'It's encouraging to see how opposed Bessie's household is to murder,' Carey said sardonically as Nancy swayed her hips through the crowd.

Will the Tod quivered with laughter. 'Nay, Deputy,' he said. 'If she were worried by such trifles, she'd have nae customers. It's your position she's worriting about: if ye're no' the Deputy Warden any more, what are ye and where's yer money to come from? Ye've no family hereabouts, bar your sister, and no land and no men neither, bar the garrison men that have been given to ye and can be taken off ye again. So if ye're a broken man, how will ye pay your debts? And if ye go back to London, why should ye pay them at all? That's her concern.'

Carey grunted. There was nothing wrong with Bessie's assessment of his situation, unfortunately. He had to remind himself that to a Borderer, a broken man was simply a man without a master. He didn't like the sound of it; he had always thought of himself as the Queen's man first, and the Earl of Essex's second. But it was true at the moment: if Scrope took his office away, that was what he would be—broken.

'How did you do with your enquiries, Sergeant?' he asked. 'Did Bessie see him in here last night?'

'I only just got here,' said Dodd mournfully, swallowing his last piece of cheese. 'Ye can but ask. Hey, Nancy?'

Nancy put a wooden platter in front of Carey with the heel of a loaf and some cheese on it, with a couple of pickled onions rolling about beside the little crock of butter.

'Ay, what is it, Sergeant Dodd?'

Carey pulled out his eating knife and started engulfing the food. He wondered privately why Sergeant Dodd could not simply do as he had been told. What had he been doing all morning if he had only just got here?

'Did ye see Barnabus in here last night?'

She sniffed and tossed her head. 'I did. He was here all evening playing dice.'

'Where did he go when you closed?'

'Out the door with the rest of them.'

'Do you know where he was headed?'

'It's none o' my affair. Now if you'll excuse me, sir, we're that busy...'

'Thank you, Goodwife.'

Dodd and Will the Tod exchanged glances.

'Ah know how ye can solve yer troubles, Deputy,' said Will the Tod as he finished his second quart.

'How?'

'Find Solomon the gateguard and get him to say he saw Barnabus coming in for the night.'

'Barnabus says he was at Madam Hetherington's.'

Will the Tod guffawed. 'Ye could speak to the women, I suppose,' he said. 'For a' the good that'll do ye.'

'No doubt they'll lie,' said Dodd.

Carey looked at him properly for the first time. Dodd's long dour face was always hard to read, but at the moment he looked happy. That meant he was uncommonly pleased with himself.

'What have you been doing, Sergeant?' he asked. 'Before you came here, I mean.'

Dodd sniffed. 'I was looking for Simon Barnet.'

'Why?' asked Carey.

Dodd gave another sniff and drank some more beer. He looked as if he was having one of his perennial internal struggles. At about thirty-two years Dodd was the same age as Carey himself, although he looked older, and he had spent most of that time hiding a surprising intelligence. Whatever was going on under the miserable carapace would decide whether Dodd grunted something noncommittal or whether he actually explained what he was up to. Carey had already learned from experience not to interfere with his thought processes, and so he waited as patiently as he could.

'Ye see, sir,' Dodd began, 'begging your pardon, but I didna think what Barnabus was at last night was so important.'

Carey didn't like being told his orders were unimportant but he kept his mouth shut.

'Ye see,' Dodd said again, staring at the lees in his mug, 'I thought it stood to reason, if he'd had a good alibi for last night he would have said so to us. And he'd have said so earlier, and not even Lowther would have put him in the dungeon.'

'Go on.'

'So he hadnae got none or couldnae remember. So then I thought of what your lady sister said and I wondered, sir.'

'What Philadelphia said?'

'Ay sir. Lady Scrope.'

Carey tried to remember. Come to think of it, there had been something...

'She said they found Barnabus's dagger and one of my gloves by the corpse.'

'Ay, sir. That was it. So that set me to wondering. How they got the dagger—well, if Barnabus was at Madam Hetherington's it's no mystery, but how did the murderer lay hands on one o' your gloves?'

Carey laughed. 'By God, how did I miss that? Excellent, Dodd, of course.'

'Ay,' said Dodd smugly, 'so I said, the one to ask is Simon Barnet. But I havena found him.'

'Damn.'

'No bother, sir; the lads are in town now and I've set them to searching for him. He'll turn up. And then,' Dodd said ominously, 'we'll ask him.'

They had finished eating by the time Bangtail Graham and Red Sandy Dodd arrived, looking about for them. Red Sandy went straight up to Carey and handed him a piece of paper. Carey looked at it with awful foreboding; it was an official-looking letter sealed by Scrope's signet ring. He put it down by his trencher and finished his beer, his heart beating hard. The seal was in the nature of a Rubicon: once opened…He thought about it.

'Now why would the Warden do that?' asked Will the Tod's voice, fascinated.

'Hm?' Carey asked.

'Send for ye by letter? He only has to tell Red Sandy to tell ye…'

'Och,' said Dodd. 'It's quite friendly, really.'

Carey had worked it out but was a little surprised that Dodd had.

'See,' explained Dodd patronisingly to his father-in-law. 'If he's made a warrant out for Sir Robert, an' he tells him by letter, he's covered but Sir Robert can still…er…get away and no one the wiser. Or not, as he chooses.'

'Trouble is,' Carey said, putting his tankard down again with a decisive tap, 'where the hell would I go?'

'The Netherlands?' suggested Will the Tod, with all the impersonal ingenuity of one who was quite secure in his position. 'There's always room for right fighting men there.'

'Or Ireland?' put in Dodd with ghoulish interest.

Carey shuddered slightly. He had heard descriptions of

that particular hellhole from Sir Walter Raleigh, one of those unfortunate enough to have served there, of malarial bogs and half-savage but extremely intelligent and ferocious Wild Irish.

'Not if I can help it,' he said to the both of them as he picked up the letter and used his eating knife to break the seal.

Aggravatingly, Scrope had not seen fit to be clear when he wrote. All it said was, 'Sir Robert, I require to speak to you immediately. Please come up to the Keep at your earliest convenience.'

'Where are ye going, sir?' asked Dodd.

'Up to the Castle,' Carey answered, putting his helmet on.

Dodd gave a dour nod. 'I'll keep asking for ye,' he said as if it were a foregone conclusion that Carey would end up in the Lickingstone cell next to Barnabus.

Red Sandy came with him, not precisely as an escort, more likely out of nosiness.

'Will ye be taking the patrol tonight, sir?' he asked.

Carey had forgotten all about it and looked up at the sky. It was promising rain.

'I don't know yet,' he said. 'I hope so.'

'Ay,' said Red Sandy happily. 'Who d'ye think killed Atkinson, then?'

## TUESDAY, 4TH JULY 1592, EARLY AFTERNOON

Scrope and Lowther were waiting for him in the sitting room on the top floor of the Keep that Scrope was also using as his office, where Carey had first met both Dodd and Lowther. As Carey put his hand to the axe-marked door, he heard Lowther's voice growling dubiously, 'He'll never come.'

That was enough to make him pause. Carey eavesdropped shamelessly, having learnt the skill at Court and been grateful for it on several occasions.

'I don't know, Sir Richard,' came Scrope's reedy voice. 'I hear what you say, but I still don't believe it.'

'What more do you need, my lord?'

'I admit, the evidence is...er...damning, but you see, you've ignored one very important factor.'

'Which is?'

'Character. It doesn't make any sense, you see. I know the Careys. I can't claim to know Sir Robert as well as I know my lady wife, but...er...nothing I've seen from him since he got here has changed my mind.'

This was fascinating. Carey held his breath, wondering what would come next. Lowther grumbled something inaudible.

'Of course, I understand your point of view, Sir Richard, but even so...They're all extremely arrogant, of course, despite being upstarts. The cousinship with the Queen is the reason for their prominence, that and...er...my Lord Hunsdon's paternity.'

'I heard there was a bastardy in there somewhere,' said Lowther who was obviously not well up on Court gossip.

'Ah, well,' said Scrope. Being of an ancient family himself, he found lineage in men, horses or hounds deeply interesting. 'Y' see, Mary Boleyn, Lord Hunsdon's mother, was Anne Boleyn's older sister and thus Her Majesty's aunt.'

'Ay,' said Lowther. 'He's her cousin. I know that.'

'But also...' said Scrope's voice, rising with extra scholarly interest, 'Mary Boleyn was King Henry VIII's official mistress *before* Anne Boleyn...er...came to Court. She was married off to William Carey in a bit of a hurry.'

'Oh ay?' said Lowther, catching the implication.

'Yes,' said Scrope gleefully. 'And she called her first son, her rather...er...*premature* first son, Henry. And the King let her. You see? You've never met Carey's father, then?'

'I have,' said Lowther. 'Twenty years ago at the Rising of the Northern Earls. But he was a younger man. Loud, I recall, and a bonny fighter too, the way he did for Lord Dacre.'

'The resemblance to his...er...natural father has become more marked as he got older,' agreed Scrope. 'But you can see the Tudor blood coming out in my Lord Hunsdon's sons, and indeed in Sir Robert—arrogance, vanity, impatience and terrible tempers—but generally speaking they do not arrange for their servants to cut the throats of functionaries. It isn't their...style.'

Carey, who had been listening with rising irritation to this catalogue, nodded sourly. He supposed there was a little truth in it; he knew well enough he had a short temper, after all. He wasn't arrogant, though. Look at the way he had helped Dodd with his haymaking. As for vanity—what the Devil did Scrope think he was on about? Just because Carey knew the importance of a smart turnout and Scrope looked like an expensive haystack...

Lowther was saying something dubious about there being a villain in every family.

'True, true,' said Scrope. 'But although I wouldn't put multiple murder in some berserk rage past Sir Robert, I would put backstreet assassination.'

Carey decided he had heard enough. Berserk rage, indeed! He went down the stairs quietly and came up them again, gave a cough as he did so and pushed the door open.

Lowther had one fist on his hip and the other on his sword hilt, with a scowl on his face as threatening as the sky outside. Scrope was also wearing a sword and his velvet official gown and pompous anxiety in every bony inch of him.

If he hadn't been listening to Scrope's opinion of his faults, Carey would have felt sorry for the man. As it was, he had decided that there was no point shilly-shallying; it would only confuse the overbred nitwit. He advanced on Lord Scrope, who was behind a table he used as a spare desk, undoing his sword belt as he came. Then he bowed deeply and laid it with a clatter of buckles on the table in front of the Warden.

'I assume I am under arrest, my lord,' he said quietly, and waited.

Lowther snorted, and Scrope looked down at Carey's new sword with alarm. It had only been properly blooded that morning, Carey thought, a hundred years ago or so. Scrope would know nothing about that, of course.

'Well...er...not so fast, Sir Robert,' faltered Scrope. 'I...er... must ask you some questions, but...er...'

'My servant is in the Castle dungeon on a charge of murder,' Carey interrupted. 'I understand from him and...others...that I am suspected of ordering him to kill Mr Atkinson.'

'You deny it, of course,' scoffed Lowther.

Carey looked at him. 'Of course,' he said evenly.

Scrope sat down behind the table, but did not invite Carey to be seated. 'If you don't mind, Sir Robert,' he said, 'I must ask you to account for your actions since yesterday afternoon.'

With an effort Carey thought back. He told the story baldly. He had learned from a good source of a large Graham raid out of Netherby, threatening Archibald Bell and also Lady Widdrington who would be vulnerable on the Stanegate road.

'I take it that Mick the Crow is still in the Gatehouse gaol,' Carey commented at this point. 'I put him there because he wouldn't tell me the name of the man that sent the letter to Wattie.'

Lowther's heavy face was unmoved.

'He's not there now.'

'Did you release him, Sir Richard?' asked Carey innocently.

'Ay, I did. There was no charge and no need to keep him when he's wanted at home for haymaking.'

'There was a charge. It was a charge of March treason for bringing in raiders.'

'Pah,' said Sir Richard. 'He'd done nothing; I let him go.'

'Do continue,' said Scrope.

As a younger man, Carey would have argued about this but now he only gave Sir Richard a hard stare before telling how he had asked to borrow Lowther's patrol and had done so.

'Speaking of which, ye offered me my note of debt back, did ye not?' said Lowther offensively.

Silently Carey took the paper out of his belt pouch and handed it over. It was no loss, he reflected, since it was very unlikely Lowther was the kind who worried overmuch about paying his gambling debts. Lowther took it, squinted at it and tore it in pieces.

'Ye said you knew where to find some of King James's horses,' he accused. 'Well, did ye find 'em?'

'No,' admitted Carey. 'I didn't.'

'Hah,' said Lowther, rather theatrically, Carey thought.

'Go on,' put in Scrope.

'I'm fairly sure the horses were there, my lord,' he added. 'But obviously the people holding them got word I was on my way and hid them.'

It suddenly struck him how that could have happened and he mentally cursed himself for a fool as he continued, 'I didn't want to take Lowther's men into a fight against the Grahams...'

'And why not?' Lowther had the infernal impudence to demand.

'Because, Sir Richard, I didn't trust them,' Carey said as insolently as he dared. Lowther's bushy eyebrows were already almost meeting; he couldn't scowl any more deeply. 'So I went to my own Sergeant Dodd at Gilsland and he helped me call out the Bells and Musgraves. With their help, we met Wattie Graham and Skinabake Armstrong at the Irthing ford early this morning and put them to flight.'

'Well done,' said Scrope. 'It seems you have had a busy time of it.'

'Yes, my lord.'

'Doesna mean nothing,' said Lowther. 'It only shows he was anxious to be out of Carlisle last night. He could have given his order any time in the past week.'

Carey was itching to punch the evil old bastard, but he kept reminding himself that this was no time to lose his temper. He had had a swordmaster once, a big dark heavy man with wonderful lightness of foot, who deliberately goaded him into a fury, then disarmed him and knocked him on his arse in the mud to demonstrate how temper could undo him. Occasionally he remembered the lesson in time.

'On the evidence of a knife owned by your servant and a glove owned by yerself that I found by the body.'

'How frightfully convenient for you,' Carey drawled. 'Did you have much trouble stealing one of my gloves?'

'Are you suggesting that *I put them there*?' roared Lowther, the veins standing out on his neck.

'Really, Sir Robert...' began Scrope.

'With respect, my lord,' Carey said through his teeth, 'I'm sorry to find you have such a low opinion of my intelligence.'

'How dare ye, sir? I never was so insulted in all my...'

'For God's sake, Sir Richard,' Carey shouted back at him,

temper finally gone. 'What kind of fool do you think I am? Leave one of my *gloves* beside a *corpse*? Why not simply sign my name on his face and leave it at that? Or didn't you think of it when you watched them cutting his throat, you old traitor?'

That did it. Lowther drew his sword and put himself between Carey and the table where his own weapon lay. Carey backed hurriedly into a fighting crouch, pulling his poignard from its sheath behind his back and his little eating knife from the one by his belt pouch.

'Gentlemen, gentlemen...' said Scrope, jumping to his feet. 'Sir Richard, I insist you put up your weapon...'

Lowther ignored him. 'Call me traitor, would ye, you ignorant puppy...?' he hissed. 'Ye prancing courtier, ye...You had his throat cut and ye know it, because the poor wee clerk was an obstacle to ye and ye couldnae see another way to it...'

Carey circled, part of him vividly aware Lowther was trying to put him in one of the corners of the room. That same part was looking at Lowther's stance and the very experienced way he held his sword, and furthermore its length compared to a poignard, and not liking what it saw. Surely Scrope would do something. He did.

'Sir Richard,' he wailed. 'I will not have my officers duelling...'

'He's ignoring you, my lord,' Carey said. 'You'd better...'

'Your officers,' snarled Lowther sideways to Scrope, but not taking his eyes off Carey. '*I'm* the Deputy Warden in this March. What was good enough for yer father is good enough for ye, boy, and don't you forget it.'

Of course, thought the part of Carey that was getting ready to fight for his life, I'm wearing a jack and morion and he isn't; that's something, isn't it?

'Put your sword away, Sir Richard,' pleaded Scrope. 'I order you to stop.'

Don't order him, you fucking fool, Carey thought; make him. Your father would have killed him just for drawing a blade in a council chamber.

There was a faint creak of hinges behind Carey. He didn't dare turn his head to look. Then came a long clearing of somebody's throat.

'Sir Robert,' said Sergeant Dodd's doleful moan. 'We've found Simon Barnet for ye. If ye're busy, we can come back.'

Much of the murderous rage went out of Lowther's face to be replaced by something resembling embarrassment. Carey straightened a little, moved sideways so he could look at both Lowther and the door. Dodd was wearing his most stolid expression, but he had his still sheathed sword in his hand, ready to throw to Carey. By God, Carey thought affectionately, I was in luck the day Scrope put you under my command.

To Carey's surprise, the presence of Dodd alone tipped the scales for Lowther. Belatedly, he realised what he was doing, put his weapon back in its sheath and folded his arms.

Carey put his own blades away meekly enough, not sure what he felt nor why he was shaking. Was it anger or fear or relief? All of them, probably. He wondered a little at the shake since it never happened after he had been in a proper fight. Dodd rebuckled his sword belt, still looking dismal.

'We are...ahem...somewhat busy,' Scrope said to Dodd. 'Why have you brought the boy here?'

'Because he has a tale to tell I thought ye might wish to hear, my lord,' said Dodd.

'What on earth could a boy...'

'It's a tale about a glove, sir,' said Dodd. 'Which was found by Atkinson's corpse, sir.'

Scrope sat down again. 'Oh,' he said. 'Well, bring him in then.'

Simon Barnet came into view, an unremarkable snub-nosed lad of twelve with brown curly hair and brown eyes. He looked dusty and miserable, as if he had been hiding in a loft somewhere. There were muddy tear stains down his face, but he didn't look as if Dodd had beaten him.

Lowther drew a deep breath and glowered.

'Hiding behind a boy...' he muttered disdainfully. Carey chose not to hear him.

'Well, Sir Robert,' Scrope said. 'What does your boy have to say?'

'I haven't the faintest idea, my lord,' said Carey. 'I haven't seen him since...When did I see you last, Simon?'

'Yesterday morning, sir.'

'Ah.'

'Get on with it,' said Lowther.

Carey looked at him again and smiled. 'I think you should question him, Sir Richard, not me. That way you can't accuse me of coaching him to lie.'

Simon Barnet looked very scared and moved closer to Carey, like a chick to a mother hen.

'It's all right,' Carey said to him. 'Tell the truth, so my lord Warden can hear you.'

'Ay sir,' said Simon, still rolling his eyes at Lowther. Lowther advanced on him and he shrank back.

'Please don't threaten him with your sword, Sir Richard,' Carey put in. 'It wouldn't be fair. He's only young.'

Lowther gave Carey the kind of stare usually seen during the arrangements for a duel, and harrumphed at Simon Barnet.

'How much is Sir Robert paying you to say this?' he demanded.

'Er...p...paying me, sir? As his s...servant?'

'Perhaps, Sir Richard, we should hear the tale before we go around accusing people of lying,' suggested Carey icily.

'Ah, yes, er...quite. Be fair, Sir Richard.'

'What tale have ye brought, then?'

Simon Barnet stared wretchedly at Dodd, took his cap off, squeezed it, stared at the floor, stretched the cap out. 'Sergeant Dodd said I wouldnae be beaten for it,' he said in a small thin voice.

'I said I would ask the Deputy to go easy on ye. I made no promises.'

Carey sighed. The boy wasn't a fool either. 'There'll be no beating provided you tell the truth,' he said.

'A...ay sir.' Simon Barnet sighed wretchedly and continued to stare at the floor while he mumbled out his sorry tale. He had been approached by a man the day before. No, he had never seen the man before. The man asked him if he was servant to the new Deputy Warden. Simon had said he was. The man had said, he wasn't. Simon had said he was. The man had said, he bet anything Simon couldn't get hold of one of the Deputy Warden's gloves for him. Simon had taken the bet, which was large, and waited until Carey had gone out with Sergeant Nixon and Barnabus had gone down to Bessie's. He had lifted Carey's oldest glove, taken it to the man behind the stables and the man had laughed and said it could have come from anyone.

'I said it were London work.' Simon was aggrieved. 'He said he didna believe me, and then he said he would ask yer honour himself, and pretend he'd found it, but because I had an honest face he paid my bet anyway. And he went off wi' it.'

Carey sighed and shook his head. 'You're Barnabus Cooke's nephew, and you fell for that?'

Simon compressed his lips and scraped his boot toe in a circle round his other foot.

There was a silence as Simon came to the end of his story. Carey was frowning in puzzlement, and Lowther's expression remained grim.

'You may have to swear to that story in court, on the Holy Bible,' Scrope said. 'Will you do it, Simon?'

'Oh yes sir,' said Simon. 'Of course I will.'

'Do you know what swearing on the Bible means?' demanded Lowther. Simon turned to him. He had gained some courage from confession and managed to face Lowther squarely.

'Yes sir,' he said. 'It means if I swear and lie I'll go to hell.'

'Would you recognise this man if you saw him again?' Carey asked.

'I think so, sir.'

'What did he look like?'

'Well, big and wide.'

'Was he a gentleman?'

'No sir. He had a leather jack on and an arm in a sling and his face was bruised, sir.'

'No name?'

'No sir. He's not one of the garrison. I've not seen him about the Keep.'

'If you spot him again, Simon, try and make sure he doesn't see you. If you can, find out his name and come and tell me or Sergeant Dodd, understand?'

Simon nodded. 'Can I go now, sir? Only I havena eaten nothing today.'

He was at the age when one missed meal was a serious thing and two threatened instant starvation. Carey nodded.

'You're to stay in the Castle. Don't leave it for any reason.'

'Ay sir.'

'What did you do with the money?'

Simon looked even more woebegone. 'Och, sir. Ian Ogle had most of it off me at dice.'

Carey was careful not to laugh. 'Some advice for you, Simon,' he said. 'When you get a windfall, pay your debts first, then gamble with what's left.'

'Ay sir,' said Simon, who wasn't listening. 'May I go now, sir? They'll be ringing the bell...'

Carey looked at Scrope who nodded. Dodd was still there, busily pretending to be a piece of furniture.

'My lord,' Carey said intently. 'I'm beginning to have an idea of what's been happening. Will you hear me out?'

Scrope was squinting unhappily between his two hands at something on the table before him, underneath Carey's sword.

'Go on, Sir Robert,' he said.

Carey paced up to the table and back again. 'We have the corpse of Mr Atkinson, whose throat was cut, and which was found in Frank's vennel, off Botchergate. I've seen the corpse, I've talked to Mr Fenwick the undertaker and also to Mrs Atkinson and her neighbour Mrs Leigh.'

Lowther looked sour, but kept his mouth shut.

'Now then, firstly Fenwick's suspicious about it and he's seen more dead bodies than most. There was no blood in the alley where the corpse was found and although Atkinson's shirt was soaked, his clothes were unmarked on the outside and he had no boots on. That argues he must have had his throat cut when he was wearing only his shirt, and his killers then dressed him in his clothes. They couldn't get his boots on because his feet had stiffened by then. Somebody brought something heavy into Frank's vennel last night. There are clear tracks of a handcart in the alley, I've seen them.'

'It could have been there for another reason,' objected Lowther. 'Or Fenwick could have brought it to take the body away.'

'It could,' agreed Carey. 'But it's suspicious, especially as Fenwick used a litter; he told me so. Next, there's a knife and glove from Barnabus and myself. Respectfully, my lord, would you be so careless? Do you really think I would be? Would Barnabus? Anybody at all? The knife could have been lifted from Barnabus in Bessie's yesterday evening while he was drunk or at Madam Hetherington's which was where he went after Bessie closed for the night. As for my glove...You've heard Simon Barnet's story.'

'He could have made it up,' said Lowther.

'No,' said Scrope positively. 'The boy's not...er...enterprising enough. If it were Young Hutchin Graham standing there with that tale, I wouldn't believe a word of it, but I think Simon was speaking the truth.'

'So?' demanded Lowther. 'What are ye getting at, Sir Robert?'

You can't be that obtuse, Carey thought, but he answered evenly enough. 'Atkinson was not killed in the alley but somewhere else.'

'Where?'

'I don't know where, Sir Richard, since I didn't do it. But somewhere else in Carlisle his throat was cut. I expect, unless whoever did it was clever enough to choose a butcher's shambles for it, there will have been a great deal of blood about the place. No doubt, if you could find the blood, you could find the killers. Whoever killed him then put his clothes on, wrapped him in something, piled him on a handcart and trundled him into the alley where they dumped him. Then, to make it look as if it was Barnabus and I that did it, they left what they thought would be clinching evidence. Which means I would very much like to talk to this mysterious man who made the bet with Simon Barnet.'

Lowther growled something completely inaudible. He looked from Scrope to Carey and back to Scrope again.

'Ye'll not do it? He's convinced you with that smooth courtier's tongue of his, hasn't he?'

Scrope frowned. 'If you recall, I had my doubts from the beginning,' he said. 'I'm certainly not...er...going to take any rash

363

steps simply because you want to believe that your political rival would kill your man.'

This time Carey heard what Lowther said about brothers-in-law needing to stick together. It annoyed him, but he held his peace. Scrope heard as well and was more angered.

'I think you had better go, Sir Richard,' he said, sounding more genuinely the Lord Warden than Carey had heard him before. 'I may be related to Sir Robert, but if necessary I would arrest him, try him and execute him on a foul bill. I'll have no favourites here as my father did.'

Lowther was even more surprised than Carey at the determination in Scrope's voice. He looked down, put his fist on his hip again, took a breath to speak. Evidently he thought better of whatever he had been about to say because he let it out again and marched out of the room. Scrope picked up the paper he had been glancing at, folded it sideways and tore it into pieces. Carey's heart turned over to see how very close he had been to ruin. He smiled and was about to make some comment to Scrope about Lowther being a bad loser and to ask if Barnabus could have bail, when his brother-in-law fixed him with a fishy look.

'I may be satisfied you didn't do this, Sir Robert,' said Scrope. 'But I'm not at all satisfied about Barnabus. I may as well...er... tell you that I'm setting the Coroner's inquest for Thursday, since, thanks to the muster, we'll be able to empanel a good jury that will have some hope of not being entirely under Lowther's thumb. Oh, and there's a problem of jurisdiction here; whether I should... er...sit, or whether it should be the Carlisle Coroner. After all, Atkinson was a townsman and was killed in the town. We will have to see. You did manage to write the muster letters before haring off after Wattie Graham?'

'Yes, my lord,' said Carey virtuously. 'Barnabus should have taken them to Richard Bell yesterday evening.'

Scrope seemed surprised by this.

'Oh...er...good. I'm glad to...see you're not neglecting your paperwork. I want a report about this Graham raid, by the way.'

'Yes, my lord. Ah...my lord, about Barnabus...'

'No, certainly not, he can't have bail. It's a capital charge.'

'No, I realise that. But could he not be locked up in the gaol under the Warden's Lodgings rather than the Lickingstone cell?'

'Ah.' Scrope seemed more co-operative. 'Don't see why not. I'll talk to Barker and have him moved.'

'Thank you, my lord.'

'It's supposed to be your patrol tonight.'

'Yes, my lord.'

'Are you going to take it?'

Carey hesitated. 'I think so, my lord. Unless you want me to stay in Carlisle.'

'I'd prefer it if you didn't go too far away.'

'No, my lord. I give you my word I'll be at the inquest.'

'See if you can find some of King James's horses. I'm getting letters every day from his courtiers about them.'

'Yes, my lord.' Carey waited politely.

'Er...yes, well, that's all then, Sir Robert. Oh, and you'd better take this back.' Scrope gestured at the weapon before him.

Carey picked his sword up again, bowed and left the room, feeling puzzled on top of his perennial annoyance with his brother-in-law. How was it that Scrope could be such a dithering idiot one moment and then the next moment act like the old Lord Scrope in his heyday? Dodd followed him quietly down the stairs, for which Carey was grateful. Halfway down it hit him that he had been wearing his jack and helmet all day and he was going to be up much of the night. The energy that had kept him going up to now suddenly deserted him and weariness fell on him like a cloak. He sat down heavily on a bench in the gloomy Keep hall, took his helmet off and rubbed his aching forehead, wishing he had time for a nap. His eyes were feeling sandy.

A heavily pregnant lymer bitch spotted him and came over to plump herself at his feet. Absent-mindedly he reached down to rub her stomach and she panted happily.

'Do you know whether it's true that Mrs Atkinson had a lover?' he asked Dodd. The Sergeant sucked his teeth noncommittally.

'Janet could likely answer the question better. They're old friends.'

'Oh.' One more complication to add to the many surrounding him. 'Do you think Lowther did it?'

Dodd looked taken aback. 'I couldna say, sir,' he answered cautiously.

'It's all right, Sergeant, I won't hold you to it. I thought he might have, but when I let it slip out in front of the Warden, he was in such a rage it could have been genuine. I'm just interested to know what you think. Sit down and tell me.'

Sergeant Dodd sat down on the bench facing Carey and leaned his elbows on the trestle table behind him. He looked up at the roof with its dusty martial banners and grinned suddenly.

'What's so funny?'

The bitch was restless. She rolled herself back onto her legs and put her muzzle on Carey's leg, dribbling a little.

'Only, I recall Lowther telling me more than once that I wasna paid to think.'

'More fool him, then. Come on. I'm not paying you extra to think, by the way; I expect that as part of your ordinary duties. Anyway, I can't afford it.'

Dodd smiled again. Two in ten minutes, Carey thought, what is the world coming to?

'An' that's another thing I cannae understand, sir. There ye are, ye're wearing more money in ironware on yer belts than I see from one year's end to the next and ye say ye cannae afford this or that. Then ye go throwing money around: three pounds for Sergeant Nixon to buy bows; sixpence each for them to help with my haymaking.'

'Oh.' For the first time in his life it occurred to Carey to wonder if the way he spent money might have something to do with his debts.

'It makes me curious, sir,' said Dodd, quite loquacious now he'd been asked for his opinion. 'I thought all courtiers were rolling in money. Are ye not rich?'

Carey could not be offended with him, his curiosity was so naked. Instead he sighed again.

'Dodd, do you recall me telling you that the last time I was out of debt was in '89 after I walked from London to Berwick in twelve days for a bet of two thousand pounds?'

'Ay sir. I remember. You were taking one of my faggots off me.'

'Oh yes,' said Carey. 'That reminds me, we haven't recruited anybody for that place yet, have we?'

'No sir,' said Dodd, dourly.

'I expect I'll get round to it. Well, that was the last time I paid my various creditors. Since then…I'm a younger son, Dodd, as you are yourself. I get nothing from my father except the occasional loan and a good lecture. I've got no land and no assets at all, except my relatives and the people I know in London and Berwick.'

'How d'ye live at Court, sir?'

'The Queen likes me and she gives me money occasionally. Sometimes I can help someone get an office, or they believe I can.'

'Is that all? I heard it was very expensive, living at Court.'

'Oh Lord, Dodd, it is, it is. It's crippling.'

'So ye must have some means of earning money, sir; it stands to reason.'

'I'll tell you if you promise not to tell anyone else.'

'Ay. My word on it.'

'Gambling.'

'Eh?'

'I gamble. I play cards. Not dice, and I don't bet on bears or dogs. Just cards.'

Dodd was fascinated. 'Can ye win enough that way, sir?'

'Yes, usually. There are plenty of people with more money than sense at Court, and a lot of them want to play me because I'm the Queen's cousin and they're snobs and want to boast about it, or they've heard I'm…good, and they want to beat me.'

'And you get enough that way, sir?'

'Yes. I paid Sergeant Nixon out of my winnings on Sunday night. Most of it was originally Lowther's money anyway.'

Dodd laughed, an odd suppressed creaking noise. 'No wonder he's out for your blood.'

'He would be anyway.'

'No, but see, sir, he's used to winning against your sister and my lord Scrope.'

'Of course he is. They're both appalling players.'

'How about horses, sir? D'ye ever bet on them?'

'What, tournaments and suchlike? Yes, on myself to win, to try and cover the cost of it.'

'Nay, racing.'

'No. Cards are more reliable.'

'That's where I lose my money,' confided Dodd. 'At cards too, but on the horses as well. Will ye teach me to play, sir?'

Carey looked at him, astonished that the stiff-necked Sergeant could admit that he needed to learn. But then the only other person who had done that had been the famously proud Sir Walter Raleigh.

'I expect so, I learnt it myself from a book. I'm afraid I don't play seriously with you and the men, though, because you can't afford to lose enough.'

'Och, I'm happy to hear it. Take yer living off Lowther by all means. So why did ye leave London, sir, if ye could support yourself at play?'

'Well, unless you cheat, which I don't unless somebody's trying to cheat me, it's still fairly precarious. You can always have a run of bad luck. And things were getting a little... tense.'

Dodd had the tact not to ask directly. 'Ye felt like a change?'

'Ay,' said Dodd. 'Ye couldna keep on as Deputy then.'

'Quite.'

'Seems like ye'll need to marry money or land, sir, like I did.'

Carey sighed again, cracked his knuckles. 'That's what everybody keeps telling me.'

But ye've lost your heart to Lady Widdrington, who's married to someone else and not likely to inherit much either, thought Dodd sympathetically, though he didn't say it.

'So what do you think about who murdered Atkinson?' Carey asked abruptly, obviously forcing his mind away from depressing thoughts and back to puzzles.

Dodd hesitated a moment longer and then answered slowly.

'All I can say is, by my thinking there's two kinds of murder. There's the kind that happens in a right temper when ye go after a man that insulted you with a rock in yer hand and beat out his brains. Or there's the kind where ye think about it beforehand and then do it when he's not expecting ye. That's the kind of murder that happened to Atkinson.'

'Yes. Throat cut. I couldn't see any signs on him that he'd fought at all.'

'He wouldn't know how any road. What about the man that got your glove off of Simon Barnet?'

Carey nodded, scratching the lymer bitch around her ears. She moaned with pleasure and rubbed her chin on his leg. A couple of the Keep servants came in and began laying the tables ready for the second of the two meals they served daily.

'Either the murderer or his servant.'

'Arm in a sling and bruised face. Shouldna be too hard to find if he's in Carlisle still.'

'If.' Carey yawned jaw-crackingly. 'It's no good Sergeant, I've simply got to get some rest or I'll fall asleep in the saddle tonight.'

'Did ye not sleep well last night, then?' Dodd asked solicitously. Once they had returned from talking to the Bell and Musgrave headmen, he had given Carey the best bed and he himself had taken Rowan's truckle bed with his wife. After waking her up for his marital rights, he had slept like the dead until Carey woke him in the dark before dawn.

'Not really,' Carey admitted, not intending to explain that Dodd and his wife had kept him awake for the first half hour and then sea-green envy and a miserable worried longing for Elizabeth had wound him up too tight to do much more than doze after that. He came to his feet and the lymer bitch gazed up at him hopefully so he bent down and patted her broad yellow flank. 'I'll snatch an hour now before it's time to gather the men together.'

'Ay sir,' said Dodd cheerily. 'I'll have a wander round the town and see if I canna find this man wi' his arm in a sling for ye.'

Carey nodded, put his helmet under his arm and walked out of the Keep door, down the steps and across to the Queen Mary Tower where he was lodging. There was no Barnabus in his bedchamber to help him, and Simon Barnet was doubtless about to start stuffing his face with poor-quality boiled salt beef and bread across in the Keep's hall. The yellow lymer bitch had followed him all the way across and up the stairs and he hadn't the heart to throw her out.

He put his helmet and swordbelt on the top of his jackstand, wearily took his jack off, hung it up. He hadn't the energy to struggle with his riding boots, so he drew the curtains of his bed to keep out the sunlight and threw himself full length on it as he was. The big lymer bitch whined a couple of times and lumbered up on to the bed next to him. Ancient strapping creaked alarmingly under their combined weights.

'Oh, for God's sake,' Carey moaned, and tried to push her off, but she licked his face lovingly, turned round a couple of times and settled down against his stomach. He shoved her a couple of times, but she became a warm furry lump of immovability. If he wanted her off his bed, he knew he would have to get up and haul her off by the collar and he couldn't be bothered. 'You are not the kind of woman I want in my bed,' he told her severely and she yawned and panted and licked at his nose, so he held her muzzle with his hand and told her severely to be still. She put her nose down between her paws and watched him with her soulful brown eyes until his own eyes blurred and he pitched into sleep.

\*\*\*

Dodd stepped out into the sunlit courtyard and walked whistling out through the Captain's Gate and the covered way into the town. He couldn't have explained why, but the discovery that Carey the elegant courtier was only one step ahead of a warrant for debt in London made him like the man much more. Carey had the indefinable assets of birth and influence and the Queen's favour; Dodd had a good solid tower, a hundred pounds' worth of land at lease, and kin who would follow him if he asked them.

For a while Dodd quartered the town and then changed direction and went back to Bessie's. There, as he had expected, he found the rest of his men. He explained his quest to them and they were happy to join in.

Eventually Bangtail came hurrying up, trailing a boy whom Dodd recognised as Ian Ogle, the steward's young son.

'Tell him,' Bangtail encouraged the lad, who squinted up at

Dodd and wanted to know what was in it for him.

Feeling inspired, Dodd resisted the impulse to shake the information out of the boy, and instead handed over a penny. Ian Ogle squinted at it ungratefully.

'Ay,' he said. 'He were in here yesterday askin' which lad was it served the Deputy Warden, so I tellt him. Why'd ye want to know?'

'Who was?'

'Who was what?'

'Who was asking which lad…?'

'Andy Nixon, Mr Pennycook's rent-collector,' said Ian Ogle with a contemptuous sneer. 'And he'd had an argument he lost with somebody, by my reckoning.'

'Andy Nixon,' breathed Dodd, who knew more about Mrs Atkinson's private life from Janet than he had let on to Carey.

'Ay.'

'Have you seen him today?'

'No.'

'Well then, be off wi' ye. By God, Andy Nixon. I wouldnae have thought it.'

By the time Carey woke up to the sound of the yellow lymer bitch's echoing snores, the light filtering through his curtains was as yellow as her coat. He got up, feeling irritable and aching, mainly the effect of being stupid enough to sleep in his hose and boots, but there was no point in taking them off now.

Dodd knocked on the door just as Carey drank the remains of the beer in the jug and wished Barnabus was around to bring him food. He would have to talk to Scrope about finding another servant to look after him while Barnabus was in gaol.

Dodd's face was unrecognisable because it had a broad grin on it. That faded when he saw the frowstiness of the Deputy.

'I wouldna recommend sleeping in your boots,' he said helpfully.

'Thank you, Dodd.'

Carey scratched his hair, smoothed it down again, put on his morion and finished buckling his swordbelt.

'Well, we've got his name, sir,' said Dodd, full of happiness and bonhomie.

'Eh?'

'The man that bribed Simon Barnet for your glove. We know his name.'

That woke him up properly. 'Do you, by God?'

'Ay, sir. His name's Andy Nixon.'

Where had he heard that name before? He remembered the extremely pregnant Mrs Leigh with her nasty particles of gossip.

'Andy Nixon?'

'Ay. Mr Pennycook's rent-collector.'

That fitted. That all fitted nicely into place. Carey's jaw set. 'He's Mrs Atkinson's lover, isn't he?'

Dodd sighed regretfully. 'Ay sir. They was childhood sweethearts, but Kate Coldale's mother wouldna let her marry a man wi' no land and no prospects, seeing she had a good dowry in property, and she was married off to Jemmy Atkinson instead. But I canna see Kate...'

Dodd was looking at Carey with peculiar directness. Go on, thought Dodd, tell me you've never at least toyed with the notion of shooting Sir Henry Widdrington, tell me you haven't.

Carey's voice did trail off and he looked at the floor. Up again. 'It's a crime,' he said more quietly. 'It has to be a crime. If it wasn't, none of us could sleep easy in our beds.'

'Depends how ye treat yer wife, though, sir,' said Dodd with all the smugness of the happily married. 'And what her lover thinks of it and what kind of a man he is.'

Carey studiously ignored the personal implications of all this.

'You think Andy Nixon's capable of slitting Atkinson's throat?'

'Oh ay, sir. Andy Nixon wouldnae do the job he does if he couldnae use a blade.'

'And Mrs Atkinson? Do you think she knew?'

Dodd shrugged. 'I dinna ken sir.'

'Well, let's go and find out.'

'We need a warrant, sir...'

'I'll get the bloody warrant,' Carey growled. 'Fetch the men.'

Kate Atkinson was just about to lock up her house for the night when there came an almighty hammering on her door. She opened it and was faced with a waking nightmare: the tall Deputy Warden with a piece of paper in his hand that gave him the right to search her house, and behind him six men to do

372

it. At the tail of them all was Janet Armstrong's bad-tempered husband looking very uneasy.

They tramped their muddy boots up the stairs and into her bedroom; she hadn't been sleeping on her marriage bed, but on the truckle bed beside it, as she told them. Two of them went out into the back yard and started gingerly raking through her midden heap. She didn't go with them but sat on the window seat in the downstairs living room and looked at her clenched fists. When little Mary started to wail because she was frightened by the high comb of the Deputy's helmet, she did nothing because there was really nothing comforting she could say to her. Occasionally wisps of thought would gust through her mind. I should have gone to Lowther. I should never have told Andy. What can I say?

'Mrs Atkinson,' came a powerful voice from upstairs. 'Will you come here, please?'

She went and found the Deputy Warden and Henry Dodd staring at the mattress of her marriage bed. They had stripped the clean sheet off it and turned it up the other way again. The Deputy reached down a long glittering hand, prodded the large brown stain. It was still a little sticky, and he sniffed his fingers.

'Where are the other sheets to this bed?' he demanded.

'Downstairs, in the yard,' she said. 'Hanging out to dry.'

'And the blankets?'

'The same.'

'The hangings?'

'Ay.'

'Did all the blood come off?'

She looked down at her apron, which was greasy, and twisted her hands together.

'This is blood. You won't tell me, I hope, that you've been killing a chicken in your marriage bed?'

If he was making a joke, she didn't find it funny.

'Mrs Atkinson, look at me.' The Deputy's voice had an impersonal sound: not angry at all, which surprised her for Lowther would have been bellowing at her by now. She looked at him and oh, the bonny blue eyes he had; it was hard to concentrate, the way they looked into you.

'Mrs Atkinson, did you murder your husband?'

At least she could answer that question honestly and yet she didn't. She said nothing.

'Do you know who did?'

She shook her head.

The blue eyes narrowed; a little surprise, a lot of cynicism, more contempt.

'I think you do know.'

'I dinna, sir.'

Janet Armstrong's husband was staring at her in plain astonishment. Also suspicion. She must seem like every married man's nightmare, she supposed, as they were hers.

'I think either you or your lover Andy Nixon slit your husband's throat. You and he then conspired to dump the body in an alley and lay the blame on me, for whatever reason, though heaven knows I've done nothing against you that I know of.' The Deputy's voice was heavy with authority.

Yes, that was the sin of it, to lay the blame on an innocent man. But Pennycook had said somebody had to be blamed, and it might as well be the upstart southerner who was interfering with business and had no kin around Carlisle to back him up.

'We...er...' She stopped speaking. How could she possibly explain? She didn't even know for certain that Andy Nixon hadn't done it. And she had helped to dump the body. Which made her guilty of something, she supposed. She couldn't speak for the number of things she needed to say.

'You know what happens if ye refuse to plead, Kate,' said Dodd anxiously. 'Ye must answer.'

At least she was able to speak to him, if not to the terrifying Deputy. 'Ay,' she whispered. 'Pressing to death. Well, I didna kill my husband and nor did I plot with anybody to kill him. I dinna ken how he came to be dead. So now.' There, it was done. When they found her guilty, she would burn.

Carey took a deep breath. 'I'm afraid I must arrest you, Mrs Atkinson, for the crime of petty treason.' he said formally. 'Come with us.'

374

'No, wait.'

'What for?'

'The children,' she said wildly. 'I must get someone in to see after the children.'

'Oh,' said the Deputy with the surprise of the bachelor. 'Yes, I suppose you must.'

The next half hour passed in more chaos than the worst night terrors, Mary howling as her mother tried to explain, and the boys' faces white and scared; this was a terrible thing for them on top of their father's death. The Deputy Warden and his men stood around like lumps, getting in her way while she tried to sort things out. Of course, she couldn't go to her sister-in-law, Mrs Leigh next door, so Sergeant Dodd accompanied her to her sister, Maggie Mulcaster over the road, who came bustling across, full of excited goodwill. Telling her what was happening was akin to using the Carlisle town crier, but it couldn't be helped. Julia had gone home but she would go across to Mrs Mulcaster as well when she arrived in the morning to find the house shut. She could get in at the wynd to milk the cow and deal with the cream put to rise for today in the tiny dairy. Kate had to leave the plate-chest where it was under the bed and hope no one would find it. She closed and bolted the shutters. While they were all downstairs two of the men came in triumphantly from the midden heap, carrying sticky clumps of rushes that she had swept out of the bedroom, dropping bits of them on the new clean rushes.

At last they were organised, and Maggie herded the crying children across to her house in their shirts, carrying their day clothes in a bag over her arm. She paused to give Kate Atkinson's shoulders a squeeze and then hurried away.

'I can come with ye now, sir,' she said, noticing that the Deputy was at least looking less triumphant, though still severe. Henry Dodd was upset, which he should be. Perhaps Janet could help her?

'Take your cloak, Mrs Atkinson,' said the Deputy, snagging it off its peg and handing it to her. 'It's cold in the gaol.'

That nearly did for her. She choked and bit her knuckle, but swallowed her tears. How to save Andy, that was the question now, since it seemed she was a dead woman. No doubt God was punishing her for her sin of adultery, though she had thought her dead baby of last year punishment enough. Clearly it was only a warning. Unseeing, she tied the cloak and put its hood up. Everyone would know from Maggie, but she wanted to hide her face all the same. The Deputy asked for the key to the house and locked the door.

Dodd nodded to the other men of the guard who were staring at her in shock as if she had suddenly grown a viper's head, and they surrounded her. It was kindly of them, she thought, hiding her like that, since she was not likely to run away from them, but she almost had to run to keep up with them as they tramped her into the Castle gate, through the righthand door and up the tiny stairs into the upper of the two prison rooms there.

\* \* \*

Mrs Atkinson refused point-blank to tell Carey where Andy Nixon lodged, but it didn't matter because Sergeant Ill-Willit Daniel Nixon was willing to say where he was. His landlady answered the door to their knocking and said distractedly that he had gone, taken his baggage and left an hour earlier and she didn't know where, and the rent not paid.

Running Sergeant Nixon to earth again took time since he had gone to an alehouse in Fisher Street where he could drink in peace, as he put it. It cost a sixpence from Carey, but he finally admitted that while Andy was likely headed for the Debateable Land, as any sensible man would be, he might stay until nightfall at his father's farm a couple of miles out of Carlisle where he could get horses and food. Nay, he wouldna simply leg it there, not in his condition. Oh ay, he had cousins aplenty in the Debateable Land; once he got in they'd never winkle him out, and good luck to him. No, Sergeant Nixon would not come with them to help; Dodd knew the place well enough. Who the hell cared if somebody cut Atkinson's throat, it was no loss to man nor beast...

Carey and his men took horse and galloped from Carlisle, heading for a long low farmhouse with a surrounding brushwood fence, the walls made of stone halfway and wattle and daub the rest. It was close enough to Carlisle not to need its own peel tower, though there was a place on the next hill that was likely the Nixons' refuge if necessary.

The Deputy Warden spoke to Andy Nixon's father at the gate, a broad grizzled man with the habitual worried expression of someone who had to pay blackrent to Thomas Carleton as well as to the Grahams. John Nixon took the Deputy's warrant and looked at it upside down, which was lucky since it only referred to Mrs Atkinson's house.

'He's not here,' said John Nixon. 'He's gone to the Debateable Land.'

Carey peered over the gate at a saddled and bridled hobby standing at a hitching post, a remount already tethered behind it.

'I must make sure,' said Carey charmingly. 'You won't object, will you, Mr Nixon?'

Carey had given Dodd one of his wheellock dags, ready wound, with orders not to point it unless necessary. The other men he had already told to station themselves all about the fence, in case Andy tried making a break for it.

At this point Carey simply walked past John Nixon and into the small yard, stood with one hand negligently on his swordhilt and his other dag under his arm and looked around.

'Sergeant,' he said.

'Ay sir.'

'You and Red Sandy start searching the way I told you.'

'Ay sir.'

Carey settled himself with his back to the wall of the house, perched on the edge of a water trough, watching John Nixon's face. As Dodd and Red Sandy trampled noisily around the farm and outbuildings, Carey quietly sat and watched, privately laying a bet with himself. Dodd had left the pigpen till last and sure enough as he went in, there was a flicker of John Nixon's eyelids.

Carey stood upright, took the dag in his gauntleted hand and put it behind his back. Seconds later there came a lot of shouting from the stye, and a crunching sound. Dodd came reeling out to land in the mud. Andy Nixon charged past him, grabbed the dag out of his unresisting hand, vaulted two sows and the fence and then slowed. He advanced on Carey pointing the gun squarely at his chest. Carey smiled.

'Well, Andy Nixon,' he said, 'I must arrest you in the name of the Queen for the murder of Jemmy Atkinson.'

'I didna do it,' said Nixon, still advancing. 'Now get out of my way.'

Carey brought his gun out and levelled it at Nixon. 'This dag is loaded. That one is not. Do you think the Sergeant would let you get your hands on a loaded gun so easily? Shame on you, Andy.'

He and Dodd had spent ten minutes discussing ways of arresting Andy Nixon without having to fight him, something Dodd was keen to avoid. It was the best they could come up with.

Andy growled inarticulately and threw the useless dag at Carey's face. He jerked back, fired and missed at pointblank range, shooting one of the unfortunate pigs instead. It went berserk, charging round its pen and biting anything that got in its way, which included Dodd who was just trying to get to his feet.

Carey stayed upright, dropped his gun, pulled out his sword.

'Carlisle garrison to me!' he roared, and Andy Nixon looked over his shoulder to see Bangtail Graham and Long George crowding the gate, their lances ready. However, he could see that wave them though they might, neither of them were anxious to come and help. Andy drew his sword awkwardly, then transferred it to his left hand. Carey drew his poignard lefthanded and advanced on the man, his blades en garde before him: Dodd had been very insistent about the importance of not getting to close-quarters with Andy Nixon. On the other hand, Carey wanted him alive to confess, be tried and hanged, a scruple that Dodd clearly thought insane.

Dodd had managed to struggle stinking out of the pigpen and was menacing Andy's father with his sword, in case he got excited. The wounded pig continued to buck round the pen squealing like a human child.

Andy Nixon and Carey moved around each other, Carey trying to keep himself between Nixon and the horses. Nixon, who was desperate, moved in swinging his sword awkwardly. Carey parried with his two crossed blades and tried a quick underarm stab with the poignard, but Nixon skipped backwards too fast. Not in fact lefthanded, then, but holding his sword in his left hand because his right was hurt somehow. Simon Barnet had said something about his hand in a sling. And his face wasn't only smudged with pig dirt but also badly bruised about the cheeks and jaw. It was a square young-looking face on a square barrel-chested body, solid all through and very determined. Now after the fizzing excitement of anticipation Carey felt that cold narrowing down of focus, the hard beat of his heart and the strange sensation of everything being very slow and crystal clear, which was there whenever he fought. He liked it. That feeling was one reason why he had come to the north.

Andy Nixon's face tightened, the betraying flicker. Carey waited for him, caught the rhythm of his attack, slipped sideways and struck backhanded with his sword at Nixon's. Metal screeched as the blades slid past each other, he flicked his wrist, and Andy's sword was on the ground. Andy stared at it, panting slightly.

'Now, Andy,' Carey said reprovingly. 'Why don't you...?'

Andy cannoned into him frontally from low down and Carey was knocked backwards onto the ground practically under the hobbies' hooves. He had dropped his sword with the shock. The horses skittered nervously backwards and forwards, hooves coming and going, distractingly enormous right next to his face, while Carey found himself held down by immensely strong shoulders. He could have used his poignard, which he still had, but he wanted Andy Nixon alive, and anyway, Andy was holding his left wrist down. There was something flawed in that grip; Carey couldn't move the rest of him—where the hell was Dodd?—but he twisted his arm, jerked up on his elbow, reversed the poignard and managed to hit Andy across the head with the pommel.

He didn't even notice, except to land a punch on Carey's face which sent stars whirling through the sky. The horrible weight came off Carey's shoulders; Andy Nixon was getting into the saddle of one of the hobbies. Carey gasped some air into his lungs, heaved himself up still blind, grabbed Nixon's foot and shoved him up and off the horses's back on the other side. Nixon landed with a crunch on the ground. Carey ducked under the horse's head to grab him and was met with a kick like a mule which he saw coming just in time to turn and take it on his hip instead of his crotch. The force of it knocked him back and into the hobby which whinnied and swung about until stopped by the tether. Somehow he had dropped the poignard. Andy was on his feet again, rocking, gasping for breath, but up. Jesus, the man wasn't human, what was he made of—and where the bloody *hell* was Dodd? Carey dimly heard a sound of cheering...Cheering? Were his troop of useless scum enjoying this?

More enraged by that thought than by anything Andy Nixon had done, Carey forgot all about not coming to close-quarters with Nixon and launched himself at him. There was a confused moment, during which his legs and Andy's seemed to become mysteriously tangled, and then the ground was leaping up; he had landed bruisingly on his stomach and Andy was about to break his arm backwards over his shoulder. Carey kicked and bucked, there was a second when he thought he might get free at the cost of dislocating his arm and then there was a brisk movement above him, a dull thud and Nixon was keeling over with a sigh. Carey lay for a moment, cawing for breath, and then levered himself up off the ground with his hands, came to his knees. Dodd was there, a large rock in one hand, offering him the other. He took it and climbed back onto his feet. He stood for a moment while he concentrated on breathing and felt his wrenched arm and his incompletely healed ribs. Then he looked at Nixon who was lying there, bleeding from a graze on his head.

'Where the...hell...were you... Sergeant?' he rasped.

Bangtail and Archie Give-it-Them came forward with care, picked up the floppy Andy Nixon and tied his hands before him as fast as they could. Then they hefted him up over the lead hobby's saddle just as he began to mutter and connected his bound hands with a rope under the horse's belly to his feet.

Sergeant Dodd was grinning inanely. 'Och, I thought ye were making such a bonny fight of it wi' Nixon, ya didna need my help.'

If he had had the energy he would have punched Henry Dodd.

'B...bonny fight...' he got out. 'The...bastard...nearly broke my arm.'

'Ay,' said Dodd, not at all abashed. 'Ye did verra well, sir. Andy Nixon won the wrestling last summer for a' Cumberland, knocked Archie Give-it-Them out cold, and beat three Scots after.'

Carey sat on the edge of the water trough and spat some blood out. Nixon's punch to his face had cut the inside of his mouth against his teeth.

'The...the bastard nearly...broke my arm,' he said to Dodd again, still unable to believe such perfidy.

'Ay,' said Dodd. 'He beat ye right enough. I've won half a crown off Bangtail and...'

'Wait a minute. You...you bet on me to lose?'

'Ay sir. It were a safe bet.'

'Jesus Christ! I am going to kill you, Dodd.'

'In that state? I wouldna bet on it, sir,' said Dodd with great good humour.

Carey shook his head to clear it and picked up his morion whose chin strap had broken at some stage in the fight. He looked round at his men who were settling bets and nodding approvingly at him, then saw John Nixon who was being held by Red Sandy and Long George.

'Mr Nixon,' he croaked. 'I'm arresting your son Andrew on the charge of conspiracy and premeditated murder. If I have any trouble on the way home, I'll cut his head off. Understand?

John Nixon nodded.

Weapons were scattered all over the yard. Dodd had already retrieved both of his valuable Tower armoury dags; Carey himself picked up his sword and poignard, sheathed them, went over to Dodd to take his guns and reeled at the smell.

'Do something about the pigshit, Dodd,' he said drily. Dodd went to the water trough, picked up a bucket and poured the water over himself, which helped a little.

They mounted up. Red Sandy took the reins of the hobby carrying Andy Nixon because Long George was in the middle of a sneezing fit, and they started back to Carlisle. At the Eden bridge Carey told Dodd to begin the patrol and wait for him at the Gelt ford. He led the hobby himself as he turned the horses in towards Carlisle town with the sun dying in fire behind the Castle and the clouds. He had Archie Give-it-Them Musgrave on the other side to help if Nixon should get free.

Andy Nixon was conscious again, turning his face sideways to keep his graze away from the horse's flank and wriggling occasionally when the horse jerked. He had already been sick, there were traces of it on the horse's belly. Carey supposed the head-down position, the motion and the smell would make you sick, come to think of it. Good. Serve the bastard right. Not a scratch on him after fighting fifty-odd Grahams and outlaws that morning—and then he went to arrest one rent-collector and ended up feeling as if he had been run over by a cart and nursed by the Spanish Inquisition. His whole shoulder was aching with pulled muscles, his ribs were griping him again, his hip was sore though his jack had softened some of the force of the kick, and his face was bruised which made him talk out of one side of his mouth. He doubted there was an inch of his body which didn't have some complaint and he sincerely hoped Nixon was feeling much worse.

Nixon croaked something inaudible.

'What was that?' Carey asked.

Nixon lifted his head and yelled, 'I didna do it.'

Carey rode along in silence for a moment, thinking. 'I'm disappointed in you, Nixon,' he said flatly. 'I wouldn't have thought you were the kind of man that would let a woman face burning alone.'

The head flopped to hang downwards again. 'Ah Christ,' came a muffled groan.

There was no more chat until they got back into Carlisle and tethered their horses at the Keep. Carey had to keep fighting the illusion caused by taking an afternoon nap, that in fact he had fought the Grahams the day before.

A young man called William Barker was keeping the dungeons for Scrope, deputy to his grandfather who was officially the Gaoler. He stared with surprise as they rode into the inner yard and Archie Give-it-Them heaved Andy Nixon down from the horse.

'Fetch the irons, Barker,' Carey said.

The youth fetched them out of the little locker. Carey put them on Nixon's wrists before he cut the ropes binding him. Nixon's eyes looked like a cow at the slaughter. When he cut the rope, Carey saw the puffiness of Nixon's right hand.

'What happened there?' he asked.

Nixon's lip lifted. 'Some whore's get trod on it in an alley, Sunday night,' he said. He looked down and shifted his feet; Archie was putting leg irons round his boots.

Carey took the keys from Barker in the passage by the wine cellar, opened up the heavy door to the outer dungeon and Nixon shuffled clankingly inside, sat down on the stone bench. He looked at Carey hopelessly.

'Where's Kate?' he asked.

'In the Gatehouse prison,' Carey said as he swung the door shut and locked it. 'You can't see her.'

Leaving Barker in charge, Carey and Archie Give-it-Them changed horses and hurried back to the gate which was just closing. They cantered out of Carlisle and over the Eden bridge to catch up with Dodd for the patrol. Carey squinted up at the sky as he rode. The roof of clouds had an ugly grey bulbous look and the sun's last rays squeezed under its lower fringes.

'More rain, Archie,' he said conversationally.

'Ye'll not be sleepin' in yer boots again,' nagged Dodd's voice from the door. He was standing there, stinking only slightly now, holding a trencher of bread and cheese and a jug of beer and looking embarrassed.

'Er...no, Sergeant,' said Carey, starting to undo his laces slowly.

'Ay,' said Dodd dubiously. 'Well, I brung ye some vittles, seeing ye dinna have the sense of a child that way.'

'Well, I...'

'Nobbut a fool sleeps in his boots if he doesnae have to,' continued Dodd in an aggressively sulky tone. 'And even a fool will eat occasionally.'

He put the food on the largest chest, came over and helped Carey take off his armour, shook it and hung it on the jackstand to drip. The feeling of lightness and freedom that came with the sudden removal from his body of about fifty pounds' weight of iron plates and leather padding, almost made Carey's head spin. With the dour expression that said he was a free man doing favours,

Dodd helped Carey pull off his riding boots, always a two-man job if they fitted properly. Then he lit a couple of tapers off the watch-light, went to the bed and started to draw the still shut curtains aside.

'Och,' he said in a strangled tone of voice.

Carey was pulling off his smelly dank shirt streaked with brown from his wet jack. He went to look at what Dodd had found. Could it be worse than the corpse of Sweetmilk Graham which had welcomed him to Carlisle a couple of weeks ago?

It could. The yellow lymer bitch who had been his bedfellow earlier lifted her head and growled softly in her throat. She had pupped on the bed; there were three yellow naked ratlings squirming in the curve of her belly.

Carey looked at her and blinked. 'Oh God,' he sighed.

'Shall I have her off there?' asked Dodd, obviously working hard not to laugh.

Carey had to smile. It was funny, in a perverse sort of way.

'No. Leave her.'

He turned to put on his fresh shirt and then paused, looked again, having difficulty focusing his eyes. The bitch was whining softly, nosing at her tail end. Her flanks heaved, but nothing happened.

'There's something wrong here,' he said.

Dodd frowned and looked closer. 'Ay,' he said. 'She's havin' difficulty.'

He put out his hand to touch her and the bitch snapped at him warningly. Carey came close and tried as well, but she only sniffed at him and whined heartrendingly.

'There, there,' he muttered. 'It's all right, sweeting.'

Dodd brought a lit taper and put it on the watch-light shelf in the bedhead.

'Bring me another taper, an unlit one,' Carey said, kneeling down and peering at the bitch's rear end. That was another counterpane ruined, he thought absently—would Philadelphia have a replacement?

He could see something in her birth passage, but another heaving effort from the bitch moved it no further out. Dodd gave him the unlit taper and had a cautious look.

'It's stuck,' he said.

Carey nodded. He had seen what you did when that happened because he had spent a great deal of his boyhood in Berwick earning beatings for running away from his tutor to play with his father's hunting dogs in the kennels.

'Shall I fetch the kennelman?' Dodd asked.

Carey was using the tallow from the taper to grease his fingers. He yawned and shook his head to try and wake himself up a bit more.

'I'll have a try. She looks as if she's been straining for hours,' he said. 'Would you hold her head in case she snaps at me?'

Dodd did as he was asked. Carey lifted her tail and gently put his fingers in. The pup had a big head which was the reason for the trouble. Very carefully, he slid his fingers round the head, waited for the next straining heave from the bitch, and pulled. For a moment his fingers were being crushed and then the pup's nose came free and straight, and the little body shot out onto the bed. The bitch panted and sighed and licked Dodd's hand, then turned and started licking the puppy. It looked dead. Carey felt in its mouth, cleared out the bits of caul and the pup hiccuped and started to breathe. Its mother carried on licking it firmly while Carey had another feel in her birth passage.

'I think that was the last one,' he said, standing up and wiping his hands on his mucky shirt which he dropped in the rushes. 'Bring the taper out and shut the curtains for her; she can stay there and I'll have the truckle bed.'

Dodd had shut the curtains; now he went and brought the food to Carey.

'Eat,' he said.

'I'm not hungry.'

'Ay, well, I canna make ye,' said Dodd, putting the trencher on the chest again. 'Never mind. I'll see ye in the morning, sir, and we can talk to Andy Nixon. Good night.'

Dodd walked to the door looking mightily offended.

'Er...Dodd,' said Carey, ashamed of himself. 'Thank you.'

'Iphm.' Dodd nodded and clattered down the stairs.

# WEDNESDAY, 5TH JULY 1592, DAWN

When the light in his chamber began to change with dawn, Carey's eyes opened and he looked straight up at the ceiling beams, instead of the tester of a four-post bed. His legs were sticking unrestfully over the end of a musty straw mattress. For a moment he was confused, wondering if he was at Court or on progress, and then he remembered the dreamlike incident of the puppies. Although he could hear the shouts of the stable boys as they began work, the bedchamber was quiet. How peculiar to be the only person sleeping in it. He got up, scratching at a lot of new flea bites, yawned jaw-crackingly, finished the beer from last night and padded across the rushes in his bare feet to have a look between the bedcurtains at the bitch. She was fast asleep with her tumble of four puppies, the biggest one lying on his back with his paws in the air. As Carey watched he whined and twitched.

'You're mine,' Carey told him. 'As rent.'

'Eh, sir?' came a boy's voice from the door. It was Ian Ogle, the steward's eldest son, standing with a tray and looking alarmed.

'It's all right,' Carey said to the boy. 'Where's Simon Barnet?'

'He's coming, sir, only I was up before and he asked me.'

'Well, go and get him; I want him to help me dress.'

'Ay sir.'

Simon, when he arrived, had to be told what to do, which was irritating since he had watched his uncle attend Carey so many times before. It appeared he had paid no attention, and he fumbled maddeningly with the points at the back of Carey's green velvet doublet until Carey pushed him away with a growl and did them up himself. Neither the doublet nor the wide padded green brocade Venetians were quite fashionable, being a year and a half old, but as they hadn't been paid for yet, Carey felt obliged to wear them. When they were finished, Carey gave him a long list of things to do which included taking his shirt to the laundry and his leather fighting breeches to be brushed, finding sponges and cloths to dry and clean his jack and polish his helmet after he'd taken it to the armoury for a new chinstrap, and further bringing the kennelman in to inspect the bitch and her puppies and also making sure there was food and water for her.

Carey listened patiently while Simon falteringly repeated his list. 'Simon,' he said gently. 'You weren't paying attention. What would you do if I asked you to take a message for me? You'd forget it. You missed out cleaning my jack and morion, which is one of your jobs anyway.'

'Sorry, sir,' said Simon, still looking longingly at the rising sunlight outside.

'Go through it again.'

Screwing up his face with the effort, Simon managed to repeat it correctly.

'That's better. Off you go then.'

He picked up his pen, wondered self-pityingly how much longer Richard Bell would take to find him a suitable clerk to be his secretary, and began writing his report.

He was halfway into his second paragraph when someone lumbered into the bedchamber and sneezed fruitily. He looked up in irritation. Long George was peering behind Carey's bed curtains at the lymer bitch.

'What the devil do you want?' Carey snapped.

Long George leapt back guiltily and touched his forelock, wiped his streaming nose on his sleeve, then took his blue statute cap off his round head and plumped it back and forth in his hands.

'Well?' growled Carey, who hated being interrupted when he had settled down to paperwork—simply because he longed for an excuse to stop.

'Er...see, sir,' said Long George. 'Only I heard ye arrested Andy Nixon yesterday for killing of Jemmy Atkinson.'

'Yes?'

'I thought I'd best tell ye what we were at on Sunday night, see,' explained Long George.

'And what was that?'

'Ah...well, we give Andy Nixon the hiding of his life that very night round about midnight.' Long George sneezed again, apologetically.

'We?'

'Ay, sir. Me, my brother Billy Little, Sergeant Ill-Willit Daniel Nixon and Mick the Crow Salkeld. Y'see, Jemmy Atkinson paid my brother and his mates to gi' him a beating and warn him away from Kate Atkinson, an' I spotted them and joined in.'

'Where was this?'

'In the alley by his lodgings, St Alban's vennel; ye ken, the wynd that's a shortcut between Fisher Street and Scotch Street.'

'Did he know who paid for the beating?'

Long George nodded and sniffed vigorously. 'Ay, sir. Ill-Willit Daniel tellt him and he wis to stay away from Kate or he'd get worse.'

Carey put his pen down. 'Well, that certainly is interesting, Long George. When did Jemmy Atkinson pay you off?'

'Right after, sir, at the Red Bull.'

'Who else was there?'

'Naebody but us. Lowther looked in for a couple of minutes, but he went off again.'

'Lowther?'

'Ay, sir.'

'What did he want?'

Long George shrugged and snortled again. 'I dinna ken, sir.'

'Did he quarrel with Atkinson?'

'Nay, 'twas all smiles. He gave Mick the Crow a message.'

'Hm.'

'So ye see, sir, mightn't that have made Andy Nixon want to take revenge on Atkinson?'

'It might. Was that when he hurt his hand?'

'Ay, I think I trod on it, sir, unintentionally.'

'Of course.'

'I thought I'd tell ye sir, in case there was a reward.' Long George's watery pink eyes peered at him hopefully.

Carey sighed. 'Long George,' he asked. 'Do you realise you have just admitted to assault, battery and riot?'

Long George's face with its inadequate frill of beard looked shifty. 'Er...well, we were working for Mr Atkinson,' he said.

'It's still against the law to beat people up.'

This was a novel idea to Long George. 'Oh,' he said, and thought. 'I wouldna like to speak to it in a court of law, sir, if y'see what I...'

'Never mind. Thank you for coming, Long George. It's useful information.'

Long George nodded, glanced fascinated at the bitch and her puppies, who were suckling enthusiastically, crammed his hat back over his ears and clattered down the stairs, sneezing as he went.

Carey stood and peered out of the slit window down into the yard. There was Long George greeting Bangtail and Archie Give-it-Them who were waiting for him. And yes, as expected, Bangtail was clearly settling a bet with Archie.

Shaking his head, Carey returned to the duties which he really hated and dipped his pen again.

By the time he had finished the report Simon Barnet had come back with the kennelman and two bowls for the bitch's food and water.

The kennelman's face was bright red with emotion. 'I wis looking for her all night,' he said, his broad hand on the lymer dog's head. 'How did ye come by her, sir?'

'She followed me up here and pupped while I was out on patrol. She can stay there for the moment until she's ready to move down to the kennels again. Had a bit of trouble with the last one but we sorted it out.'

'Ay,' said the kennelman gently rubbing the bitch's ears. 'Ye're a stupid woman, Buttercup, and no mistake.' He nodded confidingly to Carey. 'She allus pups in somewhere strange. Last time it were the bakery and the time afore that she were in the tackroom. And there's a beautiful big pupping kennel all ready strawed for her, but she's a liking for luxury, this old girl...'

They set out the bowls for her on the rushes and she drank long and deep before jumping onto the bed and flopping herself down by her squirming blind little pups again. They squeaked and latched on greedily.

'Do you think he'd give me the big one?' Carey asked.

'Why not, sir? I'll ask him.'

Carey picked up the report and decided he could do some more letters later. He also took up a purse fat with money from his winnings of the Sunday and decanted some coins into his belt-pouch. The rest he put back in his heavy locked chest.

Carey took Simon Barnet with him to see Andy Nixon in the dungeons, by which time Dodd had finally woken and appeared, scratching and yawning and foul-tempered for some reason. It passed Carey's understanding how anyone could oversleep past dawn unless they were ill or injured. They all went under the Keep steps and through the ironbound door.

Carey lifted Simon Barnet up to look through the Judas hole in the dungeon door. The boy stared gravely for a while until his eyes had adjusted to the small light from the lantern in his hands and nodded.

'Ay.'

'Is that the man that wanted my glove?' Carey asked, putting him down again.

'Ay, it's him, sir.'

'When? What time of day did he come to you?'

'Afternoon, sir, on Monday.'

'You're sure? I may want you to testify and swear on the Bible that it's him. Can you do that?'

'Ay. My word on it,' said Simon with dignity.

They went to check on Barnabus in the lower of the two gatehouse cells, looking through the barred window.

'At least Scrope had him moved,' Carey muttered.

'I don't like the look of you, Barnabus. Are you all right?'

'Don't feel very well, to tell you the truth, sir.'

It smelled bad, and the floor was slimy although Barnabus had been careful to do his business as near to the drain as he could get. Carey frowned.

'Who chained you?' he demanded.

Barnabus looked dolefully at the chain from his ankles to the wall.

'Sir Richard Lowther.'

'I might have guessed. When did he do it?'

'Yesterday, after they moved me from the 'ole.'

Just after I had that argument with him, Carey thought, biting down hard on his anger; damn him. Barnabus was sitting on the wooden bench bolted to the wall which was the only other furniture of the cell, with his arms wrapped around his body.

'I'm working on getting you out but you must tell me everything you can. For a start, can you think of any reason why Andy Nixon might hate you enough to try and get you hanged for a murder he did?'

'I dunno, sir. Never met him.'

'All right, what about Sunday night?'

'Sunday night, sir?'

'Yes. Where were you at midnight on Sunday when you should have been lighting me home?'

'Oh well...er...' Barnabus looked shifty.

'How did you manage to get so stinking drunk you passed out by the gate until morning?'

'I...er...'

'You didn't rob someone, did you?'

Barnabus coughed and looked very shifty. Carey stared at him until he shrugged. 'In a manner of speaking, sir.'

'All right, what happened?'

'Well, I was coming back to you when I tripped on a...well, somebody who'd bin in a fight and got the worst of it, I'd say.'

'Where?'

'Down the alley between Scotch Street and Fisher Street.'

'And so you robbed him?'

'No, sir. First I helped him in his door, then I robbed him.'

Carey put his hands to his head. 'Barnabus, I have *told* you about footpadding...'

'I didn't footpad 'im, sir; 'e was already done over. I just...'

'You just bloody robbed a man who was lying there helpless. For God's sake, Barnabus, where's your Christian charity?'

'I was drunk, sir. It seemed like a good idea...'

'How much did you get?'

'Half a crown sir, and some pennies.'

'Well, you could hang for that half a crown, you silly bugger. You robbed Andy Nixon and I would imagine that's the reason why he went to the trouble of incriminating you.'

'Yes sir.'

'Which has indirectly caused me an immense amount of aggravation.'

'Yes, sir. I'm sorry, sir.'

'You damn well deserve to be in here, and that's the truth.'

Barnabus looked about him and evidently found this a bit hard, but he decided to say nothing, which was wise of him, Dodd thought, considering Carey's expression of disgust. At that moment there was a complicated rattle of keys and the gaoler let Lady Scrope into the cell. She looked around, sniffed and shouted over her shoulder, 'Mr Barker, bring a bucket and spade in here.'

Dodd helpfully moved out of the cell so there was room for Barker who came in eventually with a bucket and spade borrowed from the stables.

'Pick that up and take it out of here,' said Lady Scrope, pointing imperiously at the turds by the drain.

'That, my lady?' said the youth unhappily.

'Yes, that. It's causing bad airs. Quickest way to get gaol fever in a place, which you could catch as well, William Barker, and die of, what's more. So clean it up.'

'Me, my lady?'

Lady Scrope put her basket down on the wooden bench next to Barnabus and her hands on the bumroll padding out her hips.

'I'm not going to do it and nor is my brother. Barnabus can't because he's been chained. So that leaves you or Sergeant Dodd to fight it out between you, and personally, I'm backing Dodd.'

Dodd put his head round the door and fixed Barker with a glare that settled the matter. Mumbling that it wasnae his job and an insult forbye, Barker used the spade and bucket and slumped out of the door.

'I'll stand guard while you put that on the midden heap,' said Dodd, wondering briefly if this were some complex way of breaking Barnabus out of jail. No, why be so elaborate about it? If he was going to defy all of Scrope's authority and the law of the land into the bargain, the Deputy Warden could simply unlock the doors.

Philadelphia turned to Barnabus and briskly examined his eyes, mouth and ears, felt his forehead and wrist and demanded that he undo his doublet buttons and lift his shirt so she could inspect the bruises on his body.

Carey whistled with sympathy and muttered something about bringing a suit for assault against Lowther on Barnabus's behalf.

That made Carey look depressed and thoughtful for a moment. His sister took the cloth off her basket and brought out a couple of black leather bottles. Barnabus rolled his eyes as she poured two horn cupfuls of what looked like bogwater.

'Don't look so worried, Barnabus,' Philadelphia added. 'My lord Warden has already refused Lowther permission to put you to the question so nothing else is going to happen to you.' Barnabus swallowed stickily. 'Now what else is wrong with you?' she demanded, putting her hand on his forehead again. 'You're running a fever. Have you got a headache?'

'No, my lady,' croaked Barnabus. 'I'm sore, but...'

'Stick your tongue out.'

Barnabus did and Philadelphia squinted at it critically. 'Hm,' she said. 'Have you been vomiting or purging, or passing blood in your water?'

Barnabus hesitated and looked at Carey.

'Not blood, my lady.'

Philadelphia frowned. 'What then?'

'Er...nothing.'

'Barnabus,' growled Carey. 'If you've...'

'Shut up, please, Robin,' said Philadelphia to her brother. 'Now please don't play me for a fool, Barnabus. You're not well and you have to tell me everything that ails you. I'm worried you might be coming down with a gaol fever.'

Remembering the gaol fever he had caught on board ship after he had gone to fight the Armada in 1588, which had almost killed him, Carey looked carefully at Barnabus again, then shook his head.

'No. You see, Philly, he's been in gaol before.'

'Born there,' said Barnabus with some satisfaction. 'It can't be gaol fever, my lady. I've had both kinds and it's like the smallpox; you don't get it twice.'

393

'Well then, what's the matter with your water?'

'Er...' Barnabus looked at the ground. 'I'm pissing green, my lady. And...er...it hurts.'

There was a penetrating silence. 'I expect it's because of Lowther...' Carey began.

'Unless Lowther's a worse man than I take him for, that's not Lowther. That's the clap.'

Neither Carey nor Barnabus knew where to look, while Dodd by the door listened in fascination.

'It's that bawdy house, isn't it? Madam Hetherington's? The one Scrope sneaks off to occasionally?'

Both Barnabus and Carey made an extraordinary strangulated noise.

'And I suppose you've got a dose too, have you, Robin?' demanded Philadelphia in withering tones.

'No, I haven't,' said Carey with great emphasis. 'For God's sake, Philly...'

'Don't swear. Well, Barnabus, there is nothing whatever anybody can do for the clap, no matter what they say, except let nature take its course. You should drink as much mild beer as you can and eat plenty of garlic to clean your blood. You'll have to give him lighter duties until he's better, Robin. Anyway, he should rest for today and I think his nose may need resetting eventually. Drink this.'

Barnabus meekly drank down one cup of bogwater and looked relieved when the other cup turned out to be a lotion to put on his nose and face. Carey recognised the smell as the same stuff Philadelphia had been painting him with all the previous week. As far as he could tell it had done him no harm.

Baker came back from the midden and at Philadelphia's bidding, put the bucket inside the cell where Barnabus could reach it and use it. Carey snapped his fingers for the bunch of keys he carried, took it and unlocked the chains around Barnabus's ankles.

'Thank you, sir,' said Barnabus, rubbing his legs and stretching. 'I hate to scour the cramp-rings.'

'Nobody chains my servant,' said Carey ominously, 'except me. So watch it, Barnabus.'

They came out, Carey still carefully not meeting Philadelphia's eyes. Dodd was as straight-faced as he knew how, though he thought that Barnabus was getting undeserved soft treatment.

'Have you fed the other two prisoners, Mr Barker?' he asked.

'Oh ay, sir. They got garrison food, same as Barnabus.'

Poor bastards, thought Dodd. When Janet turns up I'll send her in with some proper vittles.

'Did ye want to talk to 'em, sir?' he asked.

Carey thought about it. 'No, I don't think so, Sergeant,' he said. 'I need more information.'

And where was he proposing to get it if he didn't even want to talk to his prisoners, Dodd wondered sourly, but didn't ask. Philadelphia remained quiet as they walked out of the dungeons and into the silky morning sunlight, all washed clean by the rainstorms of the previous day. She looked about and sighed.

'You called me from checking over the flax harvest, Robin,' she said. 'So I'm going back to it.'

Carey nodded, with the expression of a man who wants to say something comforting but doesn't quite know how. He remembered the report he had written for Scrope and gave it to Philadelphia to pass on to her husband. She tossed her head, took it and marched off across the yard, trying to pull her apron straight as she went. Dodd felt he was not called upon to comment and so he followed Carey silently as he strode down to the Keep gate and past Bessie's into Carlisle town.

# WEDNESDAY, 5TH JULY 1592, MORNING

Dodd was very shocked when he realised Carey was about to go straight into the house with red lattices and the sign of the Rainbow over the door down an alley off Scotch Street.

'Sir,' he protested. 'I dinna…'

'You've got a mucky mind, Sergeant,' said Carey. 'I'm only making sure Barnabus was telling the truth about where he was.'

'Oh.'

From the way Madam Hetherington greeted the Deputy Warden with a curtsey and a kiss, it was obvious he had been there before, which further shocked Dodd's sense of propriety. It wasn't that he didn't know the bawdy house—he'd been there a couple of times himself, when drunk, and prayed Janet would never find out about it—only he felt it was a bad thing for an officer of the Crown to be seen entering the place in daylight. Carey didn't seem to care; no doubt Londoners, courtiers and lunatics had different standards in these things.

'No, mistress,' said Carey courteously to the lady's enquiry. 'I want to talk to you about my servant Barnabus Cooke.'

They were led into her office and wine was brought for both of them. Dodd sipped his cautiously and then found to his surprise that it tasted quite good.

Carey smacked his lips as he put the goblet down.

'I now know who has managed to find the only decent wine in Carlisle.'

Madam Hetherington had sat down on a stool beside a table clear of anything except some embroidery and she smiled modestly.

'I have a special arrangement with my cousin, sir,' she said.

'Hm. You're aware of Barnabus Cooke's arrest.'

'Of course, sir.'

'Can you tell me where he was on Monday night?'

Madam Hetherington took her embroidery and began stitching like any lady of a house. Dodd stared about at her little solar; it was hung with painted cloths and floored with rushmats. When he looked closer at the painted cloths, he stretched his eyes: naked women abounded, were pinkly profuse in all directions. There was a naked woman with a lascivious-looking swan on her lap, and another naked woman riding a bull and a third who seemed to be very happy to receive a lot of gold coins tumbling down a sunbeam. Surely that would hurt, Dodd thought incoherently, all those pennies hitting your bare skin. He was mesmerised by the round pearly shapes and little red touches here and there on lips and nipples…In comparison with Janet's these were rounder and plumper and…

'What do you think, Dodd?' Carey asked.

'Ah,' said Dodd, caught out and he knew it. Carey seemed amused.

'I was saying that Barnabus was certainly here on Monday night after Bessie shut her doors,' repeated Madam Hetherington kindly. 'He left early on Tuesday morning in time to go in at the gate to attend Sir Robert.'

'Oh,' said Dodd.

'Madam Hetherington does not think one of her girls will be believed by a jury either.'

'Er…No, that's right,' Dodd said desperately, staring at Madam Hetherington's embroidery hoop. 'They wouldna. They'd say she was nae fit person to be in front of them and could be bribed and they couldnae place any confidence in her word.'

Madam Hetherington and Carey nodded.

'In fact,' said Madam Hetherington, stitching away at a shape that looked suspiciously like a buttock, 'Barnabus spends much of his free time here. He was here on Sunday night as well, twice.'

'Oh?' said Carey neutrally.

'Yes, he left at a reasonable time and not too drunk and then he returned a little while later with more money to spend, which he spent.'

'Yes,' said Carey. 'I know how that happened. Another thing I would like to know is how someone also managed to get hold of one of Barnabus's knives.'

Madam Hetherington was threading a needle and she said nothing.

'Mr Pennycook owns the freehold of this house, doesn't he?' pressed Carey.

'I'm sure I have no idea what you're talking about, sir,' said Madam Hetherington coldly. 'Will you or your henchman be wishing to take your pleasure with one of the girls now, sir?'

Carey rose to leave. 'I must be on my way, Madam Hetherington,' he said. 'Oh and by the way, Barnabus has the clap.'

She frowned and bit off a piece of thread. 'Not from my house,' she said.

'No?' asked Carey. 'Good day to you, Madam.'

She rose to see them to the door, curtseyed and gave no farewell kiss.

Dodd was quite glad to get out of the place with no more upsetting sight than one of the girls in her petticoat and bodice hurrying through with a bucket of water. He hoped no one had seen them. Janet was likely to be in town soon.

'Right,' said Carey to himself and set off again down Scotch Street with that long bouncy stride of his.

Andy Nixon's landlady was a Goodwife Crawe, widowed a few years back in a raid, who lived precariously by spinning and letting out her loft. Her two tousle-headed young boys were at the football in the alley when Carey and Dodd arrived.

'Tell me what Andy Nixon did on Monday, Goodwife Crawe,' said Carey formally.

'Well,' she said unhappily, 'I dinnae want to get him in any more trouble because he's a good lodger and a nice lad and pays his rent every other Monday and it's a pleasant thing to have a grown man about the house, for the boys, ye ken.'

'Only tell me the truth, Goodwife; that will help him best of all.'

'Hmf. Y'see, I heard he was accused of cutting Mr Atkinson's throat and I dinna see him doing it. In a fight, perhaps; he's a bonny fighter is Andy...'

'I know,' muttered Carey.

'...and sometimes doesnae ken his ain strength, but from behind with a knife—nay, he's not the type.'

'How about his...friendship with Mrs Atkinson?'

'Ay,' said Goodwife Crawe heavily. 'That was it, y'see. I couldnae blame them for it, but the Lord knows it's a sin and a scandal.'

'What happened on Sunday night, Goodwife?'

She sighed as she stepped backwards nimbly over the rushes, her fingers flying as she smoothed the wool into a taut thin thread.

'Some men jumped him in the alley as he came home,' she said. 'Poor lad, he was in a terrible state. He couldnae get up the ladder and his hand was all puffed up. And some dirty thieving bastard

398

had cut his purse as well, which Andy took very hard because it had his rent in it and he knows well how I fare and that I need the money. He knew who it was too, sir, for he said he heard the man's voice and there was nobbut one voice like that in Carlisle.'

Carey nodded. 'Yes,' he said simply. 'It was my servant, Barnabus.' He felt in his belt pouch and brought out some money. 'Here's your rent, Goodwife Crawe,' he said. 'I'm sorry about it. I've told him often enough about footpadding, but some habits die hard.'

Don't give it to her yet, ye soft get, thought Dodd in despair, wait until she's told ye what she knows. Do ye not know anything?

Goody Crawe took the half crown and put it in her bodice looking thunderstruck, as well she might.

'Ay well,' she said. 'Once a reiver, allus a reiver, I say.'

'When did you find Nixon then, Goody?'

'Och, a while before dawn when I came down to milk the goat. He slept down here on the fleeces when he couldnae climb the steps in the night. I gave him milk to gi' him strength and put some cold water on his face and give him a sling for his arm, though he said it annoyed him. Then off he went when the sun was up and that's the last I saw of him that day, for he didnae come back until it was well dark and I was in bed, but I heard him at the door and going up the ladder.'

'That was Monday night.'

'Ay sir. A little before midnight, I hadnae heard the bell yet. And then yesterday, he was up as usual and looking a bit better though he hadnae much stomach to his meat for breakfast, and then he was off to see Mr Pennycook, the man he works for. And then he come home in the afternoon and he was in a terrible state o' fear, and he didnae tell me what it was but I think he heard ye'd gone to arrest Mrs Atkinson, and he packed his bags and promised me the back rent as soon as he could get it, and then he was off out the door as fast as he could go. And that's the last I saw of him, sir, as ye know, for I told ye yesterday.'

Carey smiled at her. 'Thank you, Goodwife. That's very clear.'

'Ah've done him nae good, have I sir?' She had actually stopped her toing and froing to look at Carey.

Ye've about hanged him, woman, Dodd thought but didn't say. Instead he handed her a fresh basket of lambstails for spinning and she gave him a distracted smile of thanks.

'We'll see what happens,' said Carey diplomatically. 'Nothing is certain yet.'

Goodwife Crawe screwed her face up anxiously. 'It'll be a sad thing for the boys if he hangs, for they like him.'

'If he did the murder, Goodwife, it's only right he should hang for it,' said Carey pompously.

She sniffed and started the wheel turning again. 'Ay, well,' she said. 'He's nobbut one man. He's no' rich nor a gentleman nor a gentleman's servant and his father's not strong enough to save him either, so nae doubt he'll hang whether he did it or no'. Poor lad.'

Carey looked annoyed. Why was he so touchy, Dodd wondered. Goodwife Crawe had only stated the obvious.

'I give you my word, Goodwife, if he isn't guilty I'll try and make sure he doesn't hang.'

'Hmf. But ye willna favour him over your ain servant, now will ye, sir?'

'I might.' Carey's voice was cold. He went to the door and opened it. Goodwife Crawe curtseyed as she walked with her spinning. 'Thank you for your help, Goodwife.'

Carey was looking thoughtful as they left the alley. He stopped in the middle of the way and Dodd nearly bumped into him.

'You still there, Dodd?'

'Ay,' said Dodd.

'Why are you following me around?'

'It's no' fitting for the Deputy Warden to be wandering around Carlisle town wi'out any man of his ain to back him,' said Dodd, highly offended at this example of southern ignorance. 'And dangerous, what's more. D'ye think the Grahams willna kill ye if they have the chance?'

Carey had the grace to look embarrassed. 'To be honest, I hadn't thought I was in danger in Carlisle.'

'Ay, well,' said Dodd. 'Would ye go out unattended in London?'

'I might. If I didn't see any need to make a fuss.'

'Ye're not the Deputy Warden in London. Ye're but one o'

thousands of rich courtiers milling about the place, nae doubt.'

'And you weren't trotting after me like a calf with his mother yesterday either.'

'Sir,' said Dodd patiently. 'The way ye flourish around upsetting folk, has it never crossed your mind that somebody might put a price on ye? Wattie Graham for sure; if he didnae after Netherby, he will now, and Sir Richard Lowther as well, I shouldn't wonder.'

'Good Lord,' said Carey, evidently rather taken with the idea. 'Do you really think they have? How much do you suppose it's for?'

Their next visit, Dodd was relieved to see, was to Bessie's alehouse because Dodd for one was parched from all the wool fluff filling the air of Goodwife Crawe's house. Carey asked Nancy if he could speak to Bessie and she came out from her brewing shed with smoke smuts on her face, wiping her hands on her apron, and curtseyed to him. In silence, Carey counted out the ten shillings and seven pence he had run up as his tab while Bessie watched him with an odd expression of mingled satisfaction and alarm on her broad red face. He turned to leave, which Dodd thought was a pity and Bessie called out to him. 'Will ye not take a quart before ye go, sir?'

Carey turned and looked at her with his eyebrows raised.

'I don't usually go back to a place where I'm refused credit,' he said to Dodd's horror. Where else did the silly fool think he was going to get beer as good as Bessie's?

Bessie clearly wasn't thinking straight. She beamed at him as friendly as she knew how. 'Och no,' she said. 'That was all a mistake and a lot of gossip I was fool enough to believe. Sit down sir, and take a drink...on the...on the...' she nearly choked saying it, 'on the house, sir. A quart of my best double-double.'

'What will you have, Dodd?' Carey asked him.

'The same.' Dodd's mouth was watering.

'Two quarts of double-double on the house, Nancy,' cried Bessie with painful gaiety as she bustled back into the yard and Nancy served them in a booth.

'Cheers,' said Carey with a sly grin and lifted his tankard. Unwillingly Dodd found himself tempted to smile back so he drank quickly to hide it.

Carey was the first to break the companionable silence. 'It's all sounding very black for Andy Nixon,' he said.

'Ay sir,' said Dodd regretfully. Lord, how his wife would give him trouble for being part of the process that led to Andy Nixon on the end of a rope. Not to mention Kate Atkinson at the stake. Carey was drawing pictures again with beer spillage on the wooden table between them. The alehouse was almost empty at that time of the morning, but would be full by noon, full and bursting with all the men come in from the haymaking with their money burning holes in their purses.

'This is how I see it,' Carey went on more to himself than to Dodd. 'On Sunday night Long George, Sergeant Ill-Willit Daniel Nixon and two others of Lowther's troop waylay the unfortunate Andy Nixon in the alley and beat him up. They tell him to stay away from Atkinson's wife, because Atkinson paid for it.'

'How d'ye ken that, sir?'

'Long George told me.'

'Ah.' Long George was always a fool, Dodd thought; why did nobody know how to keep his mouth shut? And he had never liked Ill-Willit Daniel.

'Andy Nixon is helped into his doorway by my appalling servant, Barnabus Cooke, who completes Andy's happy evening by cutting his purse.'

'Ay.'

'Next morning, Andy Nixon is full of wrath and vengeance. He comes up with a plan for landing Barnabus in trouble and getting his own back on Atkinson. Probably he asks his master Pennycook for help, and Pennycook agrees to loan him a handcart and get hold of one of Barnabus's knives. Nixon himself comes up to the Keep to get one of my gloves—perhaps at Pennycook's suggestion, who has reason not to like me.'

'Why's that, sir?'

'Oh, I'm interfering with the smooth corrupting of the victualling contracts for Carlisle. He was very upset.'

'Oh.'

'Andy Nixon with Kate Atkinson's help then cuts Jemmy Atkinson's throat in his bedroom; they bundle the body onto the handcart after dark and take it to Frank's vennel, where they dump it along with Barnabus's knife and my glove, and there you are.'

Dodd sipped some more of his beer and thought for a while. 'Hm,' he said.

'Is that all? Hm? I think that's what happened, don't you?'

'Ay, perhaps.'

'Why don't you agree?'

'I didna say I dinnae agree.'

'You don't look as if you do.'

It occurred to Dodd that perhaps one of the things you learnt at Court was bald-headed persistence. Certainly Carey had that. He gave up trying to keep his counsel. After all, the Deputy kept saying he wanted to know Dodd's opinion.

'Ay well, sir, it's in the character. He's no' a clever courtier like yourself, sir, Andy isnae. He's a fine wrestler and a bonny fighter...'

'So everybody keeps telling me.'

'But he's no' a clever man. If he was angered enough to kill Jemmy Atkinson then he wisnae cool enough to think out all yon about gloves and knives.'

'Perhaps Pennycook helped him.'

'Ay. Perhaps. Will ye ask him yet?'

Sighing deeply Dodd finished his quart and followed Carey on his self-imposed mission to prevent the Deputy getting a knife in the ribs before he had a chance to do for Lowther.

\* \* \*

They went straight to Maggie Mulcaster's house, across the road from the shut-up Atkinsons' place, and found Kate's little girl Mary sitting by the door very slowly shelling peas. She had her tongue stuck out and she held her breath every time she pressed open a peapod which made her gasp occasionally when she forgot to breathe again.

Mary looked up at Carey and immediately flinched back. Her face crumpled up and she started to cry. The bowl slipped off her knees and Dodd bent down just in time to catch it from going into the mud.

Dodd squatted in front of her and put the bowl down on the doorstep.

'Mary, Mary,' he said gently, 'd'ye know me?'

She nodded, very big-eyed. 'You're Mrs Dodd's bad-tempered husband.'

Carey, who had looked glum at finding the little maid frightened of him, grinned at this, though Dodd failed to see what was funny.

She nodded and then shook her head. 'She's gone to fetch in Clover. She said it wis soft to leave her in our garden since there's nobody there and she's need of the milk as well for the extra pack of weans the Deputy put to her, the southern bugger, and what was he thinkin' of arresting Kate and her a poor widow and us poor orphans. And I'm shelling peas,' she finished with a sunny smile.

It faded and she shrank back again because the Deputy Warden had sat himself down on the step beside her. He took off his hat, put it beside him and scratched vigorously at his head. There wasn't room for Dodd so he leaned against the wall.

'Is it true you know the Queen, sir?' she asked.

'Yes,' said Carey simply. 'She's my aunt.'

Mary's mouth opened, revealing a gap where she had lost one of her teeth.

'What does she look like?'

Carey took a penny out of his belt-pouch, tossed it up and showed her the head.

'She looks like that only her skin is pink and white and her hair is red.'

'Does she really have a hundred smocks and kirtles and petticoats?'

'More like a thousand.'

Mary's mouth opened wider. 'Why?'

'People give them to her because they know she likes to look pretty.'

'What colours are they?'

'Most of them are black and white with some different coloured trimming, but some of them are cloth of gold or cloth of silver and a lot of them have pearls sewn on them loose enough to drop off when she walks.'

'Why?'

'So people will pick them up and keep them and remember her by them.'

'Will she come here?'

'It's very unlikely. She doesn't travel so much now she's...er...a little older.'

Dodd had learnt enough about the Queen from Carey by now to know that mentioning her age was skimming dangerously close to treason as far as Her Majesty was concerned.

'Is she very old?'

'She was already a grown woman and Queen when I was born. But she's still beautiful,' said Carey diplomatically.

'Will she die soon?'

'It isn't polite to talk about it.'

'How many gowns has she got?'

'A couple of hundred, most of them made of velvet.'

'Like your doublet?'

'Yes.'

'I like your clothes. They're pretty. Do you have lots of pretty clothes like the Queen?'

'Not nearly as many,' said Carey straight-faced. 'And not a tenth as pretty.'

'Why are your hose so fat?'

'Because it's fashionable.'

'Does it no' make it hard to walk?'

Carey grinned. 'A bit. But you get used to it.'

'Do you like pretty clothes?'

'Yes, very much.'

Now there's the truth, thought Dodd.

'What, made of brocade?'

'Yes, only it's purple. Mrs Dodd gave the bits to me mam when she made hers. It's very beautiful.'

'It sounds it. You're a lucky girl.'

For God's sake, Dodd thought to himself, what is the Courtier on about, prattling over clothes with a child?

'And I am learning to sew. I made a purse for money.'

'Excellent.'

Carey made a small choking sound which he turned into a cough and then smiled.

'I'll give you two pennies if you can show me you have a good memory.'

Eh? thought Dodd.

'I have a very good memory,' said Mary. 'Me mam says so. She says she canna speak her mind without I'll repeat it after.' Her face clouded over momentarily as she remembered how the Deputy had come and taken her mam away.

'I thought so. But I bet you can't remember what happened on Monday.'

'That was the day before me dad died?' said Mary anxiously.

'Yes,' said Carey simply. 'And I'm sorry for your dad dying.'

Mary blinked at him for a moment. 'Why? Ye didnae like him, ye sacked him.'

'Er...yes.'

'I didna like him neither,' Mary pronounced. 'Is he no' in heaven now?'

'I...expect so,' said Carey cautiously, who doubted it.

'Well, then, it's no' sad, is it? Because we dinna have to be sae quiet when he's about wi' a sore head and there's no sore heads in heaven. That's happy, is that.' Her face clouded and threatened rain. 'It's me mam I'm sad for,' she whispered.

'Do you think you can remember such a long time ago as the day before yesterday?' Carey prompted hurriedly.

Mary paused, thought for a moment. 'I can so,' she said complacently. 'Will ye gi' me the pennies now?'

'No. Prove it to me. What happened on Monday? Start with when you got up.'

She took a deep breath, frowned, closed her eyes and began. She had come downstairs when her mother called with her kirtle and petticoat already on, but her mother had to do up her laces because she couldn't do bows yet. Did the Deputy Warden think bows were pretty? He did; Her Majesty had a kirtle all covered over with them made in blue satin. What happened next? Well, the boys came down in a hurry and ran off to school with the reverend and she ate her porridge and Julia came in late and she went hurrying up the stairs to find a ribbon she lost and then she came down again and her mother told her to start making the butter before the day got too hot and where had she been and Julia said nowhere and her mother was kneading bread and she said oh ay, then ye'd best be at the butter. So Julia said humph and went to the dairy for the yesterday's cream to pour it in the churn and her mam said...

'What colour was Julia's ribbon?' asked Carey inanely.

'Oh,' said Mary, frowning. 'I dinna remember.'

'Never mind. What happened after you ate your porridge?'

Mary had got out her sewing and started making some stitches and her mam had promised to show her a new one when she came down from taking her dad's porridge and beer up to him and she went up with a full tray.

Mary paused here and frowned. 'She was up a long time,' she said. 'And she came down and she'd forgot all about my sewing and wouldnae teach me the stitch but she sent me with a Message to fetch Andy Nixon.'

Carey nodded. 'What was she wearing?'

'Och, what she allus wears, her blue kirtle and petticoat, with the black bodice, nothing fine.'

'What about her apron.'

'Ay, she allus has her apron?'

'Was it...was there anything different about her when she came down the stairs?'

Mary frowned again and shook her head. 'Nay, only her voice was soft, like a whisper.'

Off went Mary in her memory to fetch Mr Nixon, with a long digression on Susan Talyer and how fine she thought herself because she had black velvet trim on her everyday kirtle, found him in the street with his arm in a sling and brought him back and he almost forgot to give her a penny, but then he did, and he went up the stairs to see her dad.

'What did he say about your dad?'

'Och,' said Mary, frowning again. 'He said he didnae want to see him at all and me mam said it didna matter, he'd see anyway and up he went and I had the buttermilk from Julia in the kitchen while she washed the butter and she asked what was happening and I said I didnae ken. I like Mr Nixon,' she added.

'And then what happened?'

Andy Nixon had come running down the stairs and out the door.

'Ahah,' said Carey grimly. 'What did he look like? Was he dirty?'

Mary gave him a sidelong look of pity. 'A bit. He was in his working clothes, but he doesnae labour, he's a rent collector.'

'Was there anything on them? Like mud or...er...blood?'

Mary shook her head.

'Did you hear anything, a shout or a call?'

'Nay, they was talking quietly.'

'Can you remember seeing blood anywhere around?'

'Oh ay,' said Mary seriously. 'There was blood all over the sheets to me mam's bed, for she said she'd lost a wean in the night, and she was in a state about washing them before it could set worse.'

Carey frowned at this. 'Was the blood dry?'

'Ay, mostly.'

'When did she strip the bed?'

'While I wis running for Mr Nixon, see, she had them in the basket by the door when I come back with him. It took all day to wash them sheets, ye should have seen them, all stiff they were...' The ghoulish child sighed at the thought. 'Me mam gave me a penny for grating the soap for it.'

'And then what happened?'

The day was overwhelmed with sheet and blanket washing and Mary was sent out to play with Susan Talyer which she didn't want to do but went because her mother gave her another penny and they skipped and played at Queens and Princesses and then Susan Talyer wanted to be the mam and have Mary as the child and Mary wanted to be the mam and when Susan Talyer pinched her she only tapped her a very little with her hand, hardly at all, and accidentally pulled a little of her hair and is wisnae fair...

'When did you go to bed?'

She had eaten her bread and milk with the boys when they came back from school and then they had all gone up to bed though it was still light and they had seen Andy Nixon coming out the back wynd from Clover's byre with a handcart with a whole lot of hay on it. And their mam had come in and told them a long story about Tam Lin and how the Queen of the Elves had taken him and Janet and gone to fetch him back—not Janet Dodd, another Janet—and how he changed into all different things by magic... Did the Deputy Warden know the Queen of the Elves too?

'No,' said Carey thoughtfully. 'I've not met that Queen at all. Perhaps I will one day.'

'Ye mustnae eat nothing they give ye in Elfland,' said Mary seriously. 'If ye do ye'll be bound to serve for seven years and when ye come back all your kin will be dead and gone for they'll be seven hundred years here.'

'That's good advice,' said Carey.

'Can I have my pennies now?' said Mary and Carey handed them over. 'I've got five pennies to my dowry,' she said happily.

'Mary Atkinson, what are you doing there?' demanded the voice of Maggie Mulcaster. She was holding a very obstinate-looking cow by a halter and breathing hard. Carey unfolded himself to stand up, put his hat back on.

'We were waiting for you, Mrs Mulcaster,' he said mildly. 'I was telling Mary about the Queen's gowns.'

Maggie Mulcaster snorted and gave a mighty tug at the cow's halter.

'Give me five minutes and I'll have this thrawn beast into our yard. You get on wi' those peas, Mary; we're eating them tonight.'

'Ay, Aunt Maggie.'

'Get *on* wi' ye, Clover! *Will* ye get on...'

'Er...Sergeant,' said Carey with a meaningful look at the cow. Dodd sighed, slapped the beast's bony hindquarters and helped Maggie Mulcaster drive her round by the wynd and shut her up in their own small byre for the night. There was just room for Clover and Maggie Mulcaster's cow to stand in there.

'I dinna like to leave kine on their own at all. You never know what might happen to them,' she confided in him. 'This one's upset. Kate's the only one can do anything with her.' Her eyes narrowed as she remembered the last time she had seen him. 'Well?' she demanded. 'Have ye come to arrest me as well, Sergeant?'

'Nay, Mrs Mulcaster,' he said hurriedly. 'It's all some notion of the Deputy Warden's, none o' mine.'

'Hmf.'

Very pointedly, Maggie Mulcaster did not invite them over the threshold, but stood stalwart in her doorway with her arms folded, and little Mary shaded by her skirts, while Carey asked her what she remembered of the Monday. There wasn't much, a day like any other, in fact. It was the next day that stuck in her memory, she said heavily, what with Mr Atkinson found dead in Frank's vennel in the morning and Kate arrested after. Carey thanked and left her and went to her next-door neighbour.

He painstakingly asked each of them the same question. One had helped Julia and Kate Atkinson with washing the sheets from Mrs Atkinson's miscarriage. She told of that only with much coaxing from Carey, who was starting to look very puzzled indeed.

Mrs Leigh was at home, more enormous and lethargic than ever, and very pale. She pushed at wisps of her hair, shoving them back under her cap in such a way that they immediately came out again and whispered that she hadn't been watching.

Carey started back to the Castle as Dodd's stomach began growling for its dinner.

'What'll we do now sir?' he asked, hoping to hear the name Bessie in the answer.

'Hm?' said Carey, still lost in thought. 'Oh, I think we'll talk to Andy Nixon now.'

Why not before we did all this prancing about the town and spending an hour prattling with little maids about pretty clothes, wondered Dodd. Aloud he said sadly, 'Ay sir.'

# WEDNESDAY, 5TH JULY 1592,

## EARLY AFTERNOON

That was all the conversation they had as they walked back up to
the Castle, while Dodd reflected that Carey wasn't deliberately
keeping him from his meat; it was simply he was too caught up in
thinking to remember food. At this rate Dodd would be reduced
to eating garrison rations in the Keep hall simply to keep body
and soul together.

Carey was frowning as he knocked on Barker's door.

'You know, up until I talked to the child I was quite certain
what had happened,' he told Dodd quietly. 'Now I'm not so sure.'

'Ay, but ye willna put too much faith in what a little maid would
say?' protested Dodd.

Barker unlocked the Keep door and led them into the passage
full of the cool pungent smell of wine and then the throat-scraping
stink of old piss from the dungeons.

'I don't think she was lying and there were a number of things
she said which don't fit.' Carey opened the Judas hole for Andy
Nixon's cell and saw he was lying perched uncomfortably on the
narrow stone ledge.

'Well, she got them mixed up,' said Dodd. 'She's only small.
Ye canna call her as a witness in any case.'

'Of course not.'

Their voices woke Andy Nixon, and he turned and sat up with
a clank.

'Is that ye, Deputy?'

'It is.'

'I want tae confess.'

Carey's mood lightened at once although he was astonished.
He had been wondering how to persuade the man. 'Excellent. Can
you wait until I get witnesses and a clerk?'

'Willna make no odds, will it?'

At last they assembled in Scrope's council chamber, with Scrope behind his desk and Richard Bell taking notes behind him. Just as Andy Nixon was brought shuffling in, Sir Richard Lowther arrived with his usual foul-weather face. There was quite a crowd in there, including Dodd and Archie Give-it-Them who were guarding the white-faced Nixon. Carey told Scrope briskly how he had discovered the name of the man who wanted his glove, gone after him and arrested him.

'What have you to say for yourself?' asked Scrope gravely.

Andy Nixon took a deep breath. 'That I killed Jemmy Atkinson. His missus didnae ken a thing about it until the deed was done.'

Lowther snorted disbelievingly.

'Then what did you do?'

'We hid the body under the bed. I'd asked a...friend what we should do, and he said, best thing was to dump it in an alley. So after nightfall we got it in a handcart covered wi' hay and that's what we did.'

'Explain to me about Barnabus's knife and my glove,' put in Carey.

'Ay, well.' Andy Nixon coughed and continued staring at the floor. 'My...er friend said it wasnae enough to dump the corpse, somebody had to take the blame, and it might as well be ye, sir, since ye hadnae kin here and ye were a gentleman so ye wouldnae swing for it but only go back to London, which would suit Mr Pe...my friend. So he arranged for your man's knife to be got at the bawdy house.'

'My glove?'

'Ay. Well, I thought it weren't enough to catch ye, so I thought I could get something of yourn to add to it, see, and I went by myself and found out which boy was your servant and then bet him he couldnae get me one o' your gloves, and he give it me, and then I put it with Jemmy's body as well. It was me own idea.'

Overegging the pudding, Carey thought; just as well for me you did that, you young fool.

Nixon looked contemplative. 'I'll hang for that glove, will I not?' he said.

'Yes,' said Carey. 'Tell me how you did the murder?'

'What's the point, sir? It's done now.'

'The point is that I want to know.'

Lowther tutted and rolled his eyes and Carey noticed that Long George had come up to the council chamber and was standing at the back, sniffling self-importantly. What's happened now, he wondered.

'Ay well, the murder, sir.' Nixon thought for a while. 'He were killed in bed, in his sleep, sir. I...er...I climbed up from the street and got in at the window, and then I...er...I cut his throat.'

Carey's eyes narrowed. 'How did you climb up from the street?'

'On the Leighs' shop awning and the scaffolding and then onto the eaves. And then back again when I'd done it.'

'And when was the murder done?'

'About dawn on Monday.'

There was a concerted gasp, though of course that had to be right. Scrope interrupted fussily.

'Wait a minute. Are you telling us that Jemmy Atkinson was killed early on Monday morning, not on Monday night?'

'Ay sir, of course. We hid the body through the day, first under the bed and then in Clover's byre and then I put it on a handcart and I...'

'Quite so, quite so. But his throat was slit on Monday morning.'

'Ay sir. Dawn or thereabouts.'

'Hmf,' said Lowther, 'why should we believe you?'

Nixon shrugged. 'It's when he died, sir. I dinna ken how to prove it to ye.'

'After you climbed the awning and got through the upstairs window?' Carey asked again with a frown.

Nixon nodded. Scrope tutted. 'What is the point of repeating it, Sir Robert?'

'I'm not sure,' Carey admitted. 'I'd like...'

'Well then, don't interfere. Very well, Nixon, you can go back down to the cells for the moment and we'll consider what to do with you.'

Dodd and Archie marched him out and Long George came forward to whisper urgently in Carey's ear.

'One moment, my lord,' he said. 'Apparently the woman wishes to confess as well.'

413

Scrope looked pleased. The whole thing was turning out very neatly. With luck his wife would stop giving him trouble over the way he was treating her brother, as if that could be helped.

Her brother, however, was being aggravating, shaking his head and pacing up and down.

'That's not right, that can't be right,' he was saying.

'What on earth is troubling you, Robin?' Scrope demanded. 'Nixon has just exonerated Barnabus Cooke for you.'

Carey blinked at him as if he'd forgotten all about Barnabus.

'But, my lord,' he said in a voice tight with frustration. 'What Andy Nixon has told us makes no sense at all. I have the testimony of his landlady that she was with him from the dark before dawn until the sun was up.'

'Perhaps he mistook the time.'

'Hardly likely, my lord, if he's confessing. And it's hard to make a mistake about something like dawn. Noon perhaps, but not dawn. And in any case, I can't see Andy Nixon climbing any awning or scaffolding to get to a high window, not with his hand the way it still is. He was badly beaten up on Sunday night and his hand trodden on. I doubt he could do it now.'

Lowther was staring at Carey from under his bushy eyebrows, as if at some two-headed wild man of the New World. Carey ignored him and carried on pacing until Kate Atkinson was brought up from the prison by Dodd and Archie. She stood staring round at them and Carey saw she was ghostly white and shaking.

'Tell us what you want, Mrs Atkinson,' said Scrope.

'I...I want to confess to k-killing my husband.'

'In the name of God,' growled Lowther. 'This is a bloody farce.'

'Just a minute, Sir Richard,' said Carey. 'Are you getting this down, Mr Bell?'

'Ay sir.'

'Mrs Atkinson, tell us how you killed your husband?'

'I crept upstairs after I'd given the children their porridge, and he was still asleep, so I took a knife and I...I cut his throat like a pig's.'

'While he was in bed on the Monday morning?'

'Ay sir. And then I sent for Andy Nixon...'

'Your lover,' put in Lowther contemptuously.

'My friend,' said Mrs Atkinson firmly. 'I sent Mary for him and when she brought him, he said he would ask Mr Pennycook, who he works for, what to do.'

'Ahah,' said Carey, one suspicion confirmed.

She looked at the floor as the silence settled around her. Carey had stopped his pacing and was now staring at her with his arms folded and his eyes like chips of ice.

'Are ye satisfied wi' this, Sir Robert?' asked Lowther sarcastically.

'At least it's possible,' he said levelly in return. 'Which Andy Nixon's tale is not.'

Kate Atkinson looked up at that name and then returned to examining the toes of her boots.

'You are a very wicked woman,' said Scrope gravely. 'You have committed a most serious and terrible crime.'

'Ay sir, I know,' muttered Mrs Atkinson.

'Your husband is your rightful lord, according to the Holy Bible and all civilised laws. To murder your husband is more than murder, it is treason.'

'Ay sir, I know.' Tears were falling down Mrs Atkinson's face.

'Why did you commit this evil deed, Mrs Atkinson?' Carey asked her gently.

She stared at him wildly, with the tears still welling. 'Sir?'

'Did he treat you badly? How was he worse than other husbands?'

'Well, he wasna, sir. He beat me sometimes but no worse than any other man.'

'Why did you do it, then? You must have known what could happen.'

'For heaven's sake, Robin,' warbled Scrope. 'I expect she did it so she could marry her lover. She's only a woman, she probably didn't think what would happen to her.'

Mrs Atkinson had bright colour in her cheeks and she took breath to speak, but then let it out and stared at the floor again.

'Ay sir.'

'Is that why?' Carey pursued. 'So you could marry Andy Nixon?'

'Ay sir.'

Lowther let out a long derisory snort but held his peace.

'What were you wearing that morning?'

'Sir?'

'Sir Robert,' said Scrope. 'What is the point of all this?'

'Bear with me, my lord.'

'Oh, very well. But get on with it. I haven't had dinner yet.'

'What were you wearing that day, Mrs Atkinson?'

'What I always wear, except Sundays, sir. My black bodice and my blue kirtle and petticoat and my apron.' She was puzzled at that.

'What you wore when I came to speak to you yesterday.'

'Ay sir.'

'What you're wearing now, in fact?'

'Ay sir.' She looked down at herself and frowned.

'But Mrs Atkinson, your sheets were soaked and so was the mattress, and the rushes. How did you keep the blood off your clothes?'

She shut her eyes. 'I...I was careful, sir.'

Carey stood and stared at her for a moment, mainly with exasperation.

'But...'

'Ye may as well ask,' muttered Lowther in general to the tapestries.

'I think we've had enough of this,' said Scrope. 'Take the woman back to the cells, Sergeant. You'd better chain her, I suppose.'

'Ay sir,' said Dodd stolidly, not looking at Kate. He jerked his head towards the door at her and she went in front of him with her hands clasped rigidly together at her waist, as if they were already manacled.

# WEDNESDAY, 5TH JULY 1592, AFTERNOON

Janet Dodd née Armstrong had ridden into Carlisle all the way from Gilsland that morning, on an errand of assistance. The previous day her father had sent her youngest half-brother with a message for her about the twenty horses from King James's stables that they were looking after for Will the Tod, who was hiding them for some of their disreputable relatives. That had caused her enough trouble, to scatter the horses among their friends the Pringles and Bells. He had added the information that Jemmy Atkinson had been killed, because he knew she and Kate had been friends when Janet was in service with the old Lord Scrope years before. And so once she was sure the Deputy Warden would not be able to find the horses and, if he did, he wouldn't connect them with herself and the Sergeant, she saddled Dodd's old hobby Shilling and brought her half-brother Cuddy Armstrong on Samson their new workhorse with her to Carlisle. To make the ride worthwhile she took some good spring cheeses, a basket of eggs, a basket of gooseberries and another of wild strawberries to sell to Lady Scrope and while she rode she thought of the price of hay and how much they might get for their surplus if she sold direct to the Deputy instead of going through Hetherington or Pennycook as a middleman. Her baskets would have cost her four pence toll at the City gate if she hadn't been married to a garrison man. Bringing in vittles on the Queen's prerogative was one of Dodd's few worthwhile perks.

The first thing she knew about the further disaster of Kate's arrest was when she arrived at the Atkinsons' house to find it locked and empty. A couple of workmen on the scaffolding around the Leighs' roof called down to her that she should try the Leighs' door and they'd do their best to be of service too—with much winking and leering.

She was about to shout something suitable back at them when she saw a tight knot of women in their aprons gathered opposite, talking vigorously. Maggie Mulcaster with the withered arm called her over.

She was enfolded into a whitewater of talk and speculation and disapproval and after a quarter of an hour had the full tale as known to the local women. It passed belief that her own husband could have been so cloddish as to arrest Kate Atkinson for murdering her husband. You expected idiocy from a gentleman, but she had honestly thought Henry would have more sense. She was about to say this when she spotted Julia Coldale, Kate Atkinson's cousin and maidservant, standing at the back of the group, looking as knowing and superior as any sixteen-year-old maid can. She took Julia aside and cross-examined her and fifteen minutes later she mentally took her apron off, rolled up her sleeves and prepared for battle.

'Hush now,' she said to the girl. 'We'll go and see the Deputy Warden.' Julia flinched back in alarm. 'For goodness' sake, ye goose, he willna bite you. Under all his finery, he's only a man.'

'Ay,' said Julia doubtfully.

And an uncommonly nicely made one at that, thought Janet, who had greatly enjoyed watching him in his shirt and fighting hose on top of her own haycart. By God, if Dodd got himself killed in a raid one of these days, leaving her a widow...

Get a grip on yourself, ye silly cow, she told herself sternly; this will not save Kate from burning.

'And that's a foul piece of slander too,' she snapped, having caught the tail end of a sneer from Mrs Leigh.

'Why?' demanded Mrs Leigh, one hand at her back and another at the prow of her belly. 'It *is* God's judgment on her. You may have lower standards, Goodwife Dodd, but she's a dirty bitch for keeping a fancyman as far as I'm concerned.'

Janet considered whether slapping her would bring on the wean and decided it might. 'Ay,' she said caustically. 'I'm sorry to find ye sae full of jealousy and so short of charity, Goodwife. All this virtue wouldnae have aught to do with your lawsuit over her house, now would it?'

'Nothing at all,' said Mrs Leigh with a toss of the head and a satisfactory reddening of her cheeks. 'Some of us know what's right.'

'Well, some of us might do more good looking over the Bible where it talks of judging not that ye be not judged,' said Maggie Mulcaster unexpectedly, who was able to read quite well. She looked significantly over at the next wynd where little Mary Atkinson was skipping with one of her friends.

There was a mutter of agreement. Mrs Leigh was less popular than she thought with the other women of the street.

'*If* you can read, that is,' said Alison Talyer, Kate Atkinson's other neighbour.

'Well, I'm very sure *you* cannot,' said Mrs Leigh snappily.

Alison Talyer heaved her large round shoulders with laughter. 'That's true, but then I dinna give meself so many airs, eh, Mistress Leigh, with three maidservants, and a man and a boy and a fine new roof to me house?'

'*Can* ye read?' pursued Janet. 'I'm learning it when I can find the time and it's no' so very hard, ye ken.' The kindness in her voice would have spitted a suckling pig.

'I'm sure I don't have time to stand gossiping here,' sniffed Mrs Leigh, quite defeated, and waddled back into her house, leaving the women behind to shred her character instead of Kate's. Since it was an emergency and she had always liked Maggie Mulcaster, Janet gave her one of the cheeses, six of the eggs and half the wild strawberries to tide her over with looking after three extra children. She left Cuddy with her as well, in case she could put the lad to some use, rather than have him wandering about the Keep and getting into trouble.

'Come along,' she said to Julia, who had pulled a comb out of her purse, and was giving her long copper hair a good seeing to. 'And ye can pull yer bodice lacings up tight again, you young hussy. What do you think ye're at?' she added flintily as she took Shilling's bridle to lead him on. Julia blushed.

\* \* \*

It was all terribly annoying, thought Scrope, gazing at the two contenders for the post of Deputy Warden of the English West March who were glaring at each other again. If these two fire-eaters could possibly bring themselves to agree, they might clean up the entire March between them and leave him with very little work to do. They would make a perfect team: his brother-in-law had energy and courage and a certain amount of wild ingenuity on his side, whereas Lowther had the local influence and vast experience. It was true that Lowther was deep in corruption and Carey was full of arrogance, but in the Lord's name, it was possible. The Queen had persuaded men more fundamentally at odds than they were to work in harness together. Wistfully, Scrope wondered how she had managed it.

'I don't like your insinuations, Sir Richard,' Carey was saying through his teeth.

Lowther was tapping the fingers of his left hand on his sword-hilt. 'Ay, d'ye not?' he said. 'Well, I dinna ken and I dinna care how ye got the silly woman to confess like that, but it's a poor thing to hide behind a woman, so it is.'

'Now, Sir Richard,' Scrope interrupted quickly before blades could be drawn again. 'You have no evidence for that suggestion at all.'

'Imprimis,' said Lowther, placing a square thumb on a square finger. 'Atkinson's body was found in Frank's vennel, not in his bed...'

'I explained that the mattress was stained with blood...'

'Item, his throat was cut and I've never heard of a woman killing anybody by cutting his throat; they haven't the strength, they haven't the height and forbye they havenae the courage. That's a footpad's trick, is that, and your man Barnabus is a footpad and well ye know it.'

Carey didn't say anything to that, because it was true.

'Item, we've only the woman's word for it his throat was cut on the Monday morning and I dinna believe her. And naebody knows where your man was on the Monday night when Atkinson was likely done to death. It's all a bit pat, is it no', the time she gives is the time when Cooke has an alibi from Solomon Musgrave.'

Carey was breathing hard through his nostrils.

'It's possible to twist the clearest evidence,' he said.

'Clear? I dinna think so. We've no witnesses, no nothing. So what have we got? Your man's knife and your glove by the body which is the next best thing. That'll do. And ye'll have wanted Atkinson out of your way, what's more, so there ye have it. Ye had the will; ye had the tool in Barnabus, and he could ha' done it. It's good enough for a rope.'

'I have explained about how his knife...'

'Och, and a cock and bull story it is too. A boy says Andy wanted yer glove. Ye say Pennycook got Cooke's knife fra the bawdy house. It's all very complicated, verra elaborate, Sir Robert, but it willna wash, for all ye've got a couple of fools in the gaol to swear out their lives for ye.'

'How the devil do you think I got them to do that, eh, Sir Richard? Your own methods of bribery or threats would hardly persuade anyone to die for me.'

'Hmf. It's no' so hard. I heard ye had a long chat wi' little Mary Atkinson, did ye no'?'

It was impossible to miss the implication, even without the heavy sneer across Lowther's jowelly face. Sir Robert's face took on the white masklike appearance of a Carey about to kill someone, and his hand fell on his swordhilt. Scrope leapt to his feet and put himself between them.

'Now, now,' he said. 'This is all complete speculation. And very offensive, Sir Richard, very offensive indeed. You have no call to go making that kind of accusation.'

'Me?' said Lowther. 'I'm not making accusations, my lord. If the boot fits him, let him wear it.'

'Yes, well, you know perfectly well what you're about. I think you should withdraw it.'

There was a moment of tension while Scrope wondered if he would, and then he growled, 'Ay, well, perhaps I let my tongue wander on a bit. I dinna believe the woman, though, and I willna without better reason to.'

'You withdraw your hints about Mary Atkinson?' pursued Scrope.

'Ay, I do,' said Lowther heavily. Carey bowed slightly in acknowledgement, obviously still too angry to speak. 'In fact, I'll go further,' Lowther added. 'I'll say that perhaps—perhaps, mark you—it was all a misunderstanding betwixt yerself, Sir Robert, and your servant. Was there no' a king I heard of once, that said he wanted to be rid of a priest and off his henchmen went and killed the man wi'out asking did he mean it? Now, I could see that happening here, Sir Robert; I could accept that.'

Carey was still silent which encouraged Lowther to expansiveness.

'There's always the risk of misunderstanding when ye've a quick tongue and a short fuse. And you've come up from London where perhaps they do things differently, and perhaps you and your man have made a mistake.'

'And?' enquired Carey very softly.

Lowther smiled as wide as a death's head on a church wall and waved a velvet-clad arm.

'Och. It's only Barnabus Cooke that did the deed, especially if he did it on a misunderstanding. If you take yerself back down to London again, where you belong, we'll hang your little footpad and that'll be the end of it, for me.'

'I'm sure you think that's very generous,' said Scrope quickly. 'But...ah, of course, it's a nonsensical suggestion and I'm certain you had no intention of further insulting Sir Robert, but I have to tell you that I think—quite objectively, mind—that you are wrong. I believe the woman, Mrs Atkinson. I think she did kill her husband, and conscience has very properly prompted her to confess to us at last.'

'Ha!' said Lowther, moving to the door. 'I see blood's thicker than water as usual. Ay well, it willna make no odds in the long run. Your footpad will hang, Sir Robert, and if it's aught to do with me, you'll face the axe on the same day.'

The door banged as he made his exit and Scrope turned nervously to Carey, who was still standing there gazing into space.

Carey gave a little jump and looked at him remotely as if not entirely seeing him there.

'Hm? Oh, Lowther. Yes. He's well dug in, isn't he? I expect he's got the inquest jury packed.'

Scrope sighed at this undeniable truth. 'I've done my best to find gentlemen who hate him too,' he said. 'Unfortunately, the reason why they hate him is generally that they're afraid of him and his Graham allies.'

Carey sighed. 'I suppose that's what I thought would happen. Never mind.' He turned to go, looking tired and depressed.

'You know,' said Scrope, just remembering something important in time. 'My lady wife is...er...very annoyed with me. She says I work you too hard and don't feed you properly; she wants you to have dinner with us this afternoon.'

Carey bowed. 'I am at your lordship's command,' he answered.

'Tell my lady sister I'll be delighted to come. Would you mind if I made some more enquiries into Atkinson's death?'

'Yes, I would,' said Scrope instantly. 'Firstly, I'm quite satisfied that Mrs Atkinson did it as she told us she did. And secondly, there are the letters to write concerning the muster, and the Coroner's jury to empanel, and I simply cannot ask Richard Bell to do all of it so you'll have to.'

Carey's face darkened again, though more with depression than with anger. It didn't take a genius to guess that he hated paperwork, even if he hadn't had some notion about poking around looking for yet another suspect for Atkinson's murderer.

'Yes, my lord,' Carey said meekly enough. 'I must take Thunder out for a run but then I'll deal with it.'

'Of course, of course, my dear fellow,' said Scrope, hugely relieved that he had escaped the whole interview without either blades or blood being drawn. 'I'll see you later then.'

\* \* \*

Despite the sunlight, as soon as he had returned Thunder to the stables and told the head groom to fetch in the farrier for a new set of shoes, Carey conscientiously went to his office to work on the letters organising lodgings for the gentlemen coming in for the muster and the inquest. The simple act of riding Thunder had done a lot to relax him. Unfortunately, as soon as he re-entered the Queen Mary Tower his whole towering thundercloud of worries closed in on him again. Richard Bell was there waiting for him, with a list of people to write to and a couple of form letters to give him the style. It had not occurred to him, when he persuaded the Queen to let him come north, that he would spend so much of his time acting like one of her own blasted secretaries, but he darkly supposed she knew perfectly well and had found it funny. He was a third of the way through the letters when there was a knock on the door to the stairs.

'Enter,' he said automatically, hoping Simon Barnet might have come with the beer, as ordered at least an hour ago. Barnabus was still in the gaol and would stay there at least until the inquest.

He heard the feminine rustle of petticoats in the rushes and looked up to see Janet Dodd, magnificent in her new hat and red gown, followed by a doe-eyed copper-haired creature in a blue-green kirtle who seemed vaguely familiar. Both of them curtseyed to him but Janet Dodd then folded her arms and gazed at him steadily. He looked back with considerable wariness.

'What can I do for you, Mrs Dodd?' he asked, his courtesy a little strained.

'Is it true what I hear about Kate Atkinson burning for killing of her husband?'

'Aahh...Has the Sergeant told you?'

'Nay, I've not seen him. I had word by my father that her husband was dead so I came in to help my old friend Kate. I heard it from her gossips. And why d'ye want to burn her?'

'She murdered her husband.'

'Hmf. Is it right what Julia says, that his throat was cut in his bed before dawn on Monday?'

Carey's eyes had suddenly gone intensely blue. 'That's when Mrs Atkinson confesses to having cut it.'

'Och God, the silly bitch,' said Janet disgustedly. 'She's saying she cut her own man's throat in their own marriage bed?'

'Yes.'

'Did ye have Andy Nixon under lock and key when she told you it?'

Carey smiled a little oddly. 'Yes, and in fact Andy had just finished telling us that it was him cut the man's throat and Mrs Atkinson knew nothing about it. Unfortunately, my Lord Scrope believes Mrs Atkinson.'

'And you?' demanded Janet. 'What do ye believe? Sir?' she added belatedly.

'Please, Mrs Dodd, be seated. And you too...er...'

'Julia,' simpered the girl, who had not in fact done her bodice up again. 'Julia Coldale, sir.'

'Julia.' And what a lovely warm smile the Deputy had for a girl with copper curls tumbling down her back and her bodice half-open, to be sure, even though it was clear he had a lot on his mind. Janet's own expression would have done credit to her husband.

There was only one joint stool in there which Carey was using to pile his completed letters upon. Janet removed them, put them carefully on the chest by the door and sat down. Julia perched herself at the other end of the chest, a little tilted forwards to make the best of herself.

'Well, sir?' Janet said. 'Which do you believe?'

'I don't believe Andy Nixon did the killing because my man Long George Little has confessed to beating him up in an alley along with three other men that very night and furthermore the window would be far too small for him to get in by. I doubt I could get through it myself and I'm narrower built than he is.'

'Just what I was going to say, sir,' said Janet, lightening slightly. 'And Kate?'

'Mrs Atkinson?' Carey looked stern. 'She's confessed to it.' Privately he was worried by Lowther's logic, but couldn't bring himself to admit it.

'And ye believe her?'

'Why shouldn't I?'

'Och God. Nobbut a man would believe she could do a thing like that,' said Janet springing to her feet and advancing on Carey's desk.

'Why?' he demanded. 'I don't believe a woman incapable of murder.'

Janet planted her hands on the desk and leaned towards him.

'Sir Robert,' she said. 'Have you ever washed a full set of sheets and blankets and bed-hangings?'

He was not amused at the suggestion, which he might have been under other circumstances.

'No, Mrs Dodd,' he said. 'I haven't.'

'Then ye dinna ken what backache is.'

Carey rather thought he did know what backache was, having spent up to twelve hours on his feet waiting on the Queen in one of her moods, and he disliked Janet's truculence, but he only lifted his eyebrows. This encouraged her.

'It's a full day's work, is that, on top of all the other—or you'd have to hire a woman and risk her telling the world. Ye'd needs be fighting for yer life or gone Bedlam mad to cut anything's throat in yer bedchamber.'

He looked away and then back at her. 'I admit, I hadn't thought of that.'

'Ay,' she said. 'Now, I'll not deny that a woman's capable of murder, though it's a harder thing for her against a man if he's awake and in his right mind, ye ken.'

'And besides being a crime, it's an appalling and wicked sin,' put in Carey.

'Ay,' agreed Janet unexpectedly. 'It is. There's rarely any need to murder your husband if ye've any men in your family at all.'

Carey coughed. It wasn't what he had meant.

'But...' Janet was sticking her finger under his nose, which annoyed him. '*But* in your ain marriage bed so the blood gets all over the sheets and the blankets ye've woven, and the bed-hangings the price they are—no, never. In the jakes, perhaps, with a lance; or poison in his food; or get him drunk and put a pillow over his head...But cut his throat in the bedroom? It's a man did that, because he wouldnae think of the washing after.'

She finished triumphantly, removed the offensive finger and folded her arms again.

'Mrs Dodd,' said Carey, allowing a little of his annoyance to show through in his voice. 'Please be seated.'

She sat, not abashed.

'Did you know Sir Richard Lowther thinks the same as you?' Carey asked.

She was stunned. 'Does he now?'

'He does. Mainly because he prefers to believe my servant Barnabus did it.' Or so he says, Carey thought, struck anew by an old suspicion.

'Oh.' Her thoughts were plain to be read on her face and typically she gave voice to them. 'Ay, well then, I expect poor Kate's a dead woman.'

Very few things annoyed Carey more about the whole business than everyone's bland assumption that it mattered not at all who had actually done the murder, it only mattered who could be brought to hang for it. They assumed he was as little interested in justice as any of them, and would find the weakest victim he could to blame. At the moment it passed his capacity to think of words to persuade them that if he genuinely thought Barnabus had slit Atkinson's throat, for whatever reason, he would hang the man himself. It was too outlandish a way of thinking for Borderers.

After a moment he said, 'I hear what you say, Mrs Dodd. Perhaps you're right. But the problem is, it's not enough. Andy Nixon, I think, is safe, but there is no denying that Mrs Atkinson was in the house at the time and had the opportunity of doing it. Now I'm not saying she did...' he went on hurriedly as Janet Dodd took breath again, '...I'm only saying that she'll have a hard job convincing the Coroner's jury she didn't even if she does withdraw her confession.'

'Ay,' said Janet thoughtfully. 'I see. The jury will a' be men, of course, and they'll know naught of washing sheets either.'

'Quite. And the confession will weigh heavy with them, unless I can convince them she was a woman distraught and unable to help herself. It weighs heavy with me and not only because I'm Barnabus's master. We did nothing to make her confess, you know, Mrs Dodd, she came to us of her own free will.'

'She was worriting about Andy Nixon, of course, the silly bitch,' said Janet.

'Do you think she should have let Nixon hang for her? He was willing to do it; that's why he lied to us.'

Janet looked at him as if he were mad.

'Ay, of course,' she said. 'He's a good man, is Andy, but she's got her bairns to think of. But then she allus was featherheaded, was Katy Coldale, and allus did think the sun and the moon and the seven stars shone out of Andy Nixon's...er...face.'

She looked over her shoulder at Julia Coldale who seemed mildly shocked at this ruthlessness.

'Well, go on,' she said. 'Tell him about the sheets anyway, Julia.'

Julia wriggled a bit and told the story of the Monday morning in a breathless voice. She had arrived and been set to make the butter while Mrs Atkinson kneaded the bread. Then Mrs Atkinson had fetched some bread and beer for her husband and gone up with it. She came down in a dreadful state and had sent Mary for

427

Nixon, then gone up with a laundry basket. She brought all the sheets and blankets down and they were dirty with blood. They had put the sheets in to soak in cold water in the big brewing bucks they had in the yard sheds, and Mrs Atkinson had gone up to sweep up the rushes and then come back down again saying it was better to do it later, which had puzzled Julia. At the same time, Mrs Atkinson had told her she had had a sudden issue of blood in the night, though it seemed a bit much even for a miscarriage, and Mrs Atkinson didn't look ill enough for a woman who had had a miscarriage although she certainly was pale, and she hadn't sent for the apothecary nor the midwife neither. Then most of the day was taken with scrubbing and soaping and bringing out the triple-strained lye to soak the sheets in again. Julia had been kept busy going to the street conduit with buckets and back again, and once she was sent over to Maggie Mulcaster to borrow another scrubbing brush, but they had done the sheets and blankets by the evening, pretty much, and left them to soak in fair water until the morrow when they had wrung them and hung them out on the hurdles. It had ruined the day completely.

'Ye see,' said Janet significantly. 'Nobbut a man would make so much trouble.'

'Yes,' said Carey thoughtfully. 'Now, Julia, what was it you did at dawn on Monday which you haven't told us about?'

The effect of this simple question was very interesting. Julia gasped and put her hand to her mouth as if the Deputy Warden had struck her. Janet swivelled round and glared at her.

'Eh?' she said.

'You've left something out, haven't you?'

Julia put her hand down again. 'No sir,' she said quite calmly. 'I told you just as it happened.'

'How did you know that Mr Atkinson had his throat cut on Monday morning?'

'It were the sheets,' she said. 'I knew from the sheets.'

Carey gave her a very hard stare which she returned, quite recovered, and then lowered her eyes modestly to the rushes.

'Hm,' he said. 'If you saw anything, Julia, I strongly advise you to tell me.'

'Me, sir?' said Julia. 'I saw nothing, sir, only what I told you. I helped Mrs Atkinson with the bed covers and such.'

Doubt crept into Carey's mind; perhaps he had mistaken her reaction. She certainly seemed scared of him, which was a pity. He sighed, caught Janet Dodd's expression and tried to hide the thoughts and speculations chasing themselves across the surface of his mind. There was a short awkward silence, of which only Julia seemed unconscious, for she picked up a letter she had knocked off the chest, smoothed it and put it back in a very distracting way.

Deputy, the sooner you're safely wed to Lady Widdrington the better for everyone, Janet thought to herself, wondering vaguely why there were soft squeaking noises coming from the curtained four-poster bed; and as for you, Julia, you little hussy...

'We'll be off and out of your way, Sir Robert,' she said briskly, rising and waving at Julia to come with her. 'D'ye know where my husband is?'

Carey shook his head, not really paying attention to Janet at all as Julia went to the door. Janet make an impatient noise and began hustling the girl out, but Carey beckoned her to him.

'Ay sir?' she said suspiciously.

'Send Julia to find your husband,' he murmured. 'I want a word with you alone.'

Janet's expression cleared slightly. 'Ay sir.'

Julia went with a wiggle of her hips and a toss of her red curls while Janet darkly considered what she would do to the little bitch if she aimed her wiles at Henry while she was fetching him. Carey had a thoughtful expression on his face.

'Mrs Dodd,' he said. 'I'm worried about that girl.'

Me too, thought Janet, but she held her peace.

'I think she may have seen something which she isn't telling us because I've heard that she went upstairs at the Atkinsons' house around dawn, to fetch a ribbon, she said, and she hasn't mentioned that although I invited her to.'

'She might have forgotten,' suggested Janet.

'Do you really think so?'

'No, I dinna. Where did you hear that from?'

'From Mary Atkinson, which means I can only wonder.'

'Ye've questioned the little girl?'

'We had a very long conversation. Dodd was there, he can tell you what she said, but she seemed to me to be a bright child and quite truthful.'

Janet examined his face thoughtfully. It surprised her that he could have coaxed Mary to give him anything like a coherent tale after he had arrested her mother.

'Don't look at me like that,' he said defensively. 'I've no need to bully maids to get them to talk to me.'

And isn't that the truth, thought Janet.

'Now, Mrs Dodd, I haven't the time to go enquiring about Jemmy Atkinson's death. My lord Warden considers the matter solved by Mrs Atkinson's confession and he has given me direct orders to get on with organising the muster for Sunday and the inquest for Thursday and as I have no clerk yet, I have to write the letters myself. But Sergeant Dodd is presumably at a loose end...'

That thought made her blood run cold. With money in his pocket and Bangtail in town...She nodded.

'First, I want him to subpoena Pennycook's clerk, Michael Kerr, to appear at the inquest tomorrow. Then I want him to enquire into the matter for me. Poke around a bit and see what he finds. And you too, Mrs Dodd. Mrs Atkinson's gossips will talk differently to you than they would to me.'

Janet's mouth fell open. Carey didn't seem to have noticed what he had said and now he was cocking his head to listen to the funny noises from the bed. Next minute he was on his feet and beckoning her over to it. She followed suspiciously. He drew back one of the faded curtains gently; she peered in and then started to laugh. The yellow bitch lying there with her pups nuzzling up against her flank lifted a lip and gave a low growl.

'Shame on you, Buttercup,' said Carey. 'Mrs Dodd, this is Buttercup and Buttercup this is Janet Dodd. Buttercup,' he said with the first proper smile she had seen from him that day, 'has evicted me from my own bed.'

He let the curtains fall again as Dodd came shambling lankily

430

in, looking injured and sorrowful as usual. At least his long dour face brightened when he saw Janet who came over to kiss him and then he remembered what he had been doing recently and his expression became wary.

'Where's Julia Coldale?' she demanded.

'Och, the maid with the red hair?' he asked.

'Ay.'

'She said she had tae go back to the town again urgently and she didnae want to wait for ye, so I said she could go.'

'By herself?' sniffed Janet.

'Er...no,' admitted her husband. 'Bangtail and Red Sandy went with her to see she was all right.'

'They're both married men.'

'Ay, they'll protect her right enough.'

'*Quis custodiet ipsos custodes*,' said Carey suddenly.

'Eh, sir?' asked Dodd.

'"Who will protect her from the protectors?"' Carey translated, and Janet laughed.

'Now there's a piece of sense,' she said. 'Who said that?'

Carey thought for a moment. 'I can't remember,' he admitted. 'Some Roman or other.'

'Well, it's uncommon good sense for a foreigner,' said Janet patronisingly. 'Good afternoon to ye, sir.'

\* \* \*

She saw Julia Coldale come along the street with two of the garrison men, one on each side, both of them as full of pride and preening as a couple of cock pheasants. The girl had a high colour and seemed to be enjoying herself. She left them outside as she went into the Leighs' own draper's shop.

And then she saw Janet Dodd and her husband, also coming along the street. Janet paused to talk to Alison Talyer who was shelling peas in her door while Dodd came on and disappeared under the scaffolding. She heard creaking and realised he was climbing the ladder, very cautiously, and she heard his voice drone as he spoke to the foreman.

Mrs Leigh put down her work, struggled herself off the window seat and went to the top of the stairs.

'Jock!' she yelled. 'Jock Burn!'

'Ay, mistress,' came the answering shout. 'I'll be with ye in a minute.'

It was quite a bit after a minute that the skinny little man finally came up the stairs and stood lowering at her in his greasy jerkin and the incongruous new blue suit her husband had given him. Julia left at the same time and could be seen through the window chatting and laughing with the garrison men.

'What did Julia Coldale want?' she demanded.

He looked shiftily away from her. 'Och,' he said. 'She was time-wastin', only wantin' to hear the price o' this and that.'

'Oh?'

He gave her the straight stare of the experienced liar.

'Where's the master, Mrs Leigh?' he asked.

'Over at the new warehouse. Why?'

'Ay,' said Jock, taking off his shop apron. 'I need to speak wi' him; will ye excuse me, mistress?'

She nodded, suddenly glad he could lie, and he turned and pattered down the stairs again. That perhaps was why she failed to notice that, when Dodd came creaking down the ladder again some time later, he was carrying a small bundle.


# WEDNESDAY, 5TH JULY 1592,

## LATE AFTERNOON

Carey was deep in the tedium of paperwork again, his mind nibbling frustratedly at the problem of Jemmy Atkinson as he worked, when he had another visitor. After the first flash of fury, he saw it was the Bell headman who had called out his family against Wattie Graham the day before.

'Mr Bell,' he said courteously, wondering when he would be finished with his damned letters. 'What can I do for you?'

Archibald Bell came stumping in through his chamber looking uncomfortably hot in a homespun green suit and a new high-crowned hat.

'Ah've come about the blackrent,' said Bell. 'To pay it, I mean.'

For a moment, Carey didn't understand.

'Er…Lowther's not here,' he said cautiously.

'Ay, I know that. I've come to pay it to ye, sir.'

Carey sat down again, wondering how to handle this. On the one hand he direly needed the money because his winnings from Lowther wouldn't last for ever and he was sure nobody in Carlisle would make the mistake of playing primero for high stakes with him again. On the other hand, blackrent was one of the cankers of the Border, as poor men paid protection money to crooks like Lowther and Richie Graham of Brackenhill to keep their herds and houses safe from reivers. Since no one could live paying rent to two landlords, most of them got their living by reiving and demanding blackrent of their own.

Archibald Bell had his purse in his hand, ready to do the business. He was looking puzzled.

Carey stood again, went and poured two goblets of the diabolical wine which Goodwife Biltock had sent up by Simon Barnet who was, as usual, not around.

'Mr Bell,' he said, handing one to the headman, who looked astonished. 'How much blackrent was Sir Richard demanding?'

'Thirty shillings a quarter,' Bell answered promptly. 'But I havena paid it for a while, so I brung what we owe which is six pounds.'

That was no less than extortionate.

'I give you a toast,' said Carey, while he struggled with temptation. 'I give you, confusion to Richard Lowther and the Grahams.'

Bell lifted his goblet and drank the lot without noticeable strain.

'Ye willna be wanting more, sir?' he said anxiously. 'For we canna pay it.'

'No,' said Carey. 'I'm sure you can't. In fact, I'm not sure I should accept it.'

'Eh?' Bell was flabbergasted.

'Well,' said Carey reasonably, 'you give blackrent in return for protection from reivers, don't you?'

'Ay.'

'To be frank with you, Mr Bell, I'm not sure how much more protection I can offer you. I haven't Lowther's contacts or his family backing. I'm only an officer of the Queen.'

'Ye did well enough keeping my stock fra Wattie's clutches yesterday.'

'I have to admit it wasn't my prime consideration.'

'Nay, I ken that. I know well enough you was protecting Mr Aglionby's packtrain.'

Something in the pit of Carey's stomach gave a lurch of excitement. Now that made sense of a fifty-man raid at hay-making. Carefully he drank more of the sloe-coloured vinegar in his good silver goblet.

'Ah,' he said wisely. 'And how did you find that out?'

'It was one o' the reivers we caught yesterday. He was in such a taking, yelling and shouting about what he'd lost by ye and how he hated ye, and the packtrain the heaviest to go into Carlisle for years and so on. So then I knew why ye were there, which was puzzling me; it was for the packtrain, to keep it fra Wattie Graham,' Bell explained.

Carey stared into space, his mind working furiously. He was remembering the cardgame at the Mayor's house. Suddenly he knew who had killed Jemmy Atkinson.

'I supposed you haven't got the reiver any more?'

'Nay, we ransomed all of them back, the minute Skinabake's man turned up wi' the money.'

'Do you know his name?'

'Ay, it was Fire the Braes Armstrong.'

'And where does he live?'

'The Debateable Land, seeing he's at the horn for murder and arson in two Marches.'

Carey came to a decision.

'Mr Bell,' he said. 'I'll be straight with you. I don't want to take blackrent, which is against the law, but I'll take my rightful

Wardenry fee for protecting your cattle, which is two pounds.'

'Ay,' said Bell. 'But I want yer protection in the future.'

'You have that,' Carey explained. 'It's one of the duties of the office of Deputy Warden to protect you from raiders.' Dammit, thought Carey, really it's the only one. 'You shouldn't have to pay me rent for that; the Queen's supposed to do it.' Not that she did, or not regularly. 'You only pay me a fee for a particular raid.'

Bell was looking deeply suspicious.

'Are ye tellin' me to pay my blackrent to Lowther?'

'No, Mr Bell, I'm telling you to give me two pounds sterling and call it quits. Keep the money. Buy weapons or steel bonnets for your family or even a new plough or whatever. Just give me information when it comes to you and turn out to fight for me when I call and that's all the blackrent I want.'

Bell's mouth was hanging open. Carey was glad neither Dodd nor Barnabus were there to tell him he was mad turning down good cash; he even felt a little mad and reckless doing it. But he was grateful to Bell for solving Atkinson's murder for him and besides, if he himself took blackrent like Lowther, how could he stop anyone else from doing it?

Bell had a broad spreading grin of incredulity on his face.

'Are ye tellin' me ye willna set on anybody to raid me if I dinna pay ye off?'

'Yes,' said Carey, wondering if every Borderer would now think him soft, as well as Dodd, the garrison and Jock of the Peartree. 'I want my Wardenry fee, though. I have to live too.'

'Ay,' said Bell, still grinning. 'Ay, o' course ye do. Ay.'

He took two handfuls of crowns and shillings from his purse and carefully counted them out. Then he spat on the palm of his hand and held it out to Carey.

'Ah'll come out for ye, Deputy,' he said. 'There's ma hand, there's ma heart.'

Carey spat on his own palm and grasped Bell's firmly.

'And mine, Mr Bell,' he said. 'Pass the word, if you will.'

'Ay,' said Bell, still grinning as he put away his purse and moved to the door quickly before Carey could change his mind. 'Ay, I will. By God,' he added, shaking his head and Carey heard him laugh as his hobnails clattered down the stairs.

* * *

Edward Aglionby, Mayor of Carlisle, was expecting a visit from the new Deputy Warden and was ready for it when, belatedly, it came. The Deputy arrived on horseback and seemed to be in a tearing hurry, but he invited the young man into his solar for wine and wafers and even asked him to dinner.

'I'm sorry, Mr Aglionby, I'm bidden to my sister's table and in fact I'm going to be late. But I must talk to you first.'

Edward Aglionby stood with his arms crossed, waiting.

'You know, of course, that there was an attempt made on your packtrain by Wattie Graham...'

'And Skinabake Armstrong. Yes, Sir Robert. I also know that it was you who prevented it, thereby saving me a great deal of gold and trouble.'

Aglionby waited for the new Deputy's demand, but it seemed Carey wanted to shillyshally first, asking irrelevantly about Atkinson's inquest.

'Yes,' he answered the Courtier. 'The case does fall under City jurisdiction. In fact my lord Warden was quite willing for the Carlisle Coroner to hear the inquest, although my lord has empanelled the jury.'

Carey nodded. Given a very tight spot, with Lowther on the one hand badgering him to find Carey or his servant guilty and Philadelphia badgering him on every other hand to find someone else, Scrope would gratefully wriggle out.

'Who is the Coroner?' he asked.

Aglionby smiled. 'I am.'

'Excellent.' Carey beamed back. 'I have a favour to ask of you, Mr Aglionby, which I hope you will...at least consider.'

'Mm,' said the Mayor cautiously.

'We have a multiplicity of suspects for murderer,' said Carey. 'Among them, though I think no longer the most suspected of them, is my servant Barnabus. Now I have no way of being his good lord here—I have no influence with the jury and would not dream of insulting you by attempting to influence you yourself—excepting if I can put my case against the man I think truly did the deed, directly in open Court.'

'Are you a lawyer, Sir Robert?'

Carey coughed, not willing to lie directly. 'I have some small experience of law and lawyers, though I never was a member of an Inn of Court. I would like to act as *amicus curiae*, a friend of the Court, in an unofficial capacity.'

'Mmm.'

'It's the best way I can think of helping my unfortunate servant who was only accused as a way of attacking me. Obviously I can't hire him a barrister since he's accused of a capital crime.'

'Hm. *Amicus curiae.* Is that all?'

Carey's face was guileless, though in fact he was wondering how long Aglionby would take to decide and how furious Philadelphia would be when he was late.

'Yes,' he said.

Aglionby was very suspicious at such a cheap discharge of an obligation. There was no question that the Deputy Warden had saved him large sums of money. On the other hand, why look a gift horse in the mouth?

'I see no reason to deny you, Sir Robert; in fact, I'm happy to be of service in the matter.'

'Thank you very much, Mr Mayor,' said Carey, and then decided that since he was going to be late anyway, he might as well drop a little poison. 'Do you know who it was who passed on word of your packtrain to the Grahams?'

'No,' admitted Aglionby. 'Though I have suspicions.'

'It was Sir Richard Lowther.'

Aglionby did not look surprised. His square smooth-chinned face changed only slightly.

'He was at the cardgame where your lady sister...'

'Was indiscreet. Yes. And one of my men saw him at the Red Bull...er...later. Mick the Crow was certainly there too and I know Mick was the messenger to Wattie that brought in the raid.'

'Ah,' said Aglionby. 'Mick the Crow hasn't named Lowther?'

'Of course not. I deduced it.'

'It isn't enough to accuse him.'

It will be, thought Carey; when I indict him for ordering Atkinson's murder, it will. Aloud he said, 'No. But straws show which way the wind blows.'

It was obvious. Lowther needed money and would have got it as his cut from the packtrain profits. Also he would be undermining Carey in the City of Carlisle with the implication that commerce wasn't safe under his rule. Why had he let Carey take his patrol out? Simple greed, perhaps, coupled with the hope that if Carey came on Skinabake with Sergeant Ill-Willit Daniel Nixon behind him, that was Carey out of his way for ever. And Atkinson was killed to keep him quiet about it.

'Mm,' said Aglionby again.

'Mr Mayor,' Carey said, making for the door. 'I simply must get back to the Castle or my sister will skin me alive. It's arranged for tomorrow?'

'Ay,' said Aglionby. 'You can be *amicus curiae* for the inquest, no bother. Good evening to you, Deputy.'

## WEDNESDAY, 5TH JULY 1592, EARLY EVENING

It was a quiet little supper party, with only Philadelphia, Scrope and Carey himself, eating his way voraciously through five covers of meat and a number of summer sallets, sharp with herbs and nasturtium flowers. Philadelphia forgave him for being so late and exerted herself to keep the conversation going; she was worried by Carey's rather remote politeness. She even asked Carey's advice about her son who was away south at school and perpetually in trouble, but with typical masculine obtuseness all he would say was that she should worry more if the boy didn't get into scrapes now and then.

Eventually, Scrope wandered over to the virginal in the corner. He opened it and began plinking the notes gently, head cocked, listening for sourness, face dreamy. After a moment of struggle, he sat down and began playing.

'My lord,' said Carey tactfully, watching the spider-like hands move. 'What can I do or say that might convince you to release Barnabus...'

'My dear fellow, I know perfectly well that you didn't have anything to do with Atkinson getting his throat slit; it isn't your style at all.'

'Lowther thinks different.'

'Yes, he does, doesn't he? Now isn't that interesting?'

'Interesting, my lord?'

'Fascinating, in fact. At one time I was quite sure Lowther himself had done it, for some reason, or at any rate, paid somebody to do it. When he came to see me yesterday morning he was in such a rage and was so certain it was you, I was almost convinced he was simply overdoing things a bit.'

'My lord,' Carey interrupted. 'Surely you see that whoever actually did the killing, it *must* have been Lowther who ordered it.'

'Must have been?'

Scrope had stopped playing. Carey lifted up one finger. 'Imprimis, he was the last man to see Atkinson the night before he was killed. He was at the Red Bull when Atkinson was paying Long George and his friends for beating up Andy Nixon.'

'Oh.'

'He was also, by the way, the man who sent Mick the Crow to Netherby with the information that not only was my Lady Widdrington on the road, but so was a large packtrain from Newcastle. Unfortunately, I've no way of proving it.'

'How did he know about the packtrain?' put in his sister. Carey looked at her.

'You let it slip at the card party,' he said, careful to keep accusation out of his voice. 'Remember?'

Philadelphia flushed and fell silent.

'Ah,' said Scrope, trying to look wise. 'You know you did have a little too much wine that evening, my dear. I have often said...'

'No doubt Atkinson was threatening to tell Aglionby,' Carey trampled on, hoping to distract the Scropes from a quarrel.

'Perhaps he was no longer so useful since I'd sacked him from the Paymastership. Perhaps they quarrelled. And I'm not at all sure Lowther didn't have a hand in Andy Nixon's attempt to frame Barnabus and me for it. He wanted to get rid of me. A man like Lowther does it the indirect way...'

'Mmm,' said Scrope, unhappily. 'But then there's his offer to you.'

Carey paled and then flushed. 'You mean his suggestion that if I took myself back to London, he would stop with Barnabus?'

'Yes. Very unlike him.' Scrope started playing at venture again, warming his hands up.

'My lord?'

'Sorry, got caught up in the music.'

There was a clattering as Hughie, John Ogle's eldest son, cleared the dirty plates and Philadelphia followed him to supervise their scouring and locking away. Scrope's long fingers were at home and at ease on the rosewood keys; they moved by themselves and gave expression to his thoughts in a tangled elaboration of a haunting tune Scrope had heard sung by one of the local headmen's harpers.

'Where was I?'

'We were speaking about Lowther, my lord.' The smooth voice was thinning with impatience.

'Um...yes. You see, he's not a man to let his prey escape. If all of this was some elaborate trap to catch you, he'd not rest until you were beheaded or at the horn.'

'No doubt that is what he wants.'

'Oh, no doubt at all. But offering you a way out and keeping hold of your servant...I'd almost say he genuinely thinks Barnabus is the killer and will settle for losing his chance of you, if he can have his way with Barnabus.'

'Or he's cleverer than you think him and offering me a way out is a trap as well, a means of getting me to admit my guilt by running away.'

Scrope looked sideways at him. That was the irritating thing about the Careys; sometimes they were sharper than they seemed.

'Yes, that's also a possibility. If so, then you must have disappointed him.'

Carey looked away and swallowed, still clearly furious at Lowther's imputation that he was threatening little Mary Atkinson in order to maker her mother confess to the murder.

Scrope stopped playing, stood and started digging in the casket of sheet music.

'I'm sorry, Robin, I don't believe it. The whole thing is far too elaborate and complicated for Lowther. Oh, he's capable of it, but if he'd been the man behind the killing Jemmy Atkinson would have wound up in your bed with his throat slit, not his own or Frank's vennel or wherever it was. Lowther's simply grabbing at an opportunity he sees to oust you. While I'm not at all surprised about the packtrain, I doubt very much he made that opportunity himself.'

Philadelphia had come back into the room and sat down quietly.

'But that leaves only Mrs Atkinson as the murderer.'

'Quite,' said Scrope complacently. 'I think she did it, just as she confessed.'

Carey held onto his temper.

'My lord, I'm sorry, but I think she was lying to save Andy Nixon's skin, just as Andy Nixon lied to save hers. I have to admit I think Lowther was right about that; cutting someone's throat is not a woman's means of murder. And Mrs Dodd has pointed out to me that doing the deed in her own bedchamber let her in for a great deal of work in washing the sheets.'

Philadelphia nodded vigorously.

'Janet Dodd is talking good sense,' she said. 'And in any case, what on earth could Mrs Atkinson hope to gain by it?'

Scrope smiled at her kindly for her womanly obtuseness. 'She wanted to marry Andy Nixon,' he explained. 'So of course she had to kill her husband.'

Philadelphia glared at him for some reason, then turned and picked up her workbag, delved in it, pulled out some blackwork and began stitching with short vicious movements.

'Let's make up a fairy tale,' she said at large. 'Let's pretend, Robin, that you wanted to marry someone who was married to another man.'

Carey gave her a glare of warning but she wasn't looking at

him, she was squinting at a caterpillar made of black thread, which was eating a delicately worked quince.

'Now let's suppose that you and this other man's wife plot together and you decide to solve your problems by killing the woman's husband. Would you cut his throat?'

Carey harrumphed. 'What are you getting at, Philly?' he asked in a strained voice.

'Robin, I'm not accusing you of anything improper. I'm playing let's pretend. Go on. Would you cut his throat?'

'Probably not.' Carey's voice was wintry in the extreme.

'Do you think Eli…the woman would cut her husband's throat?'

'Er…no.'

'And why not?'

'Well, obviously, you would want to make his death look like an accident so no one would be blamed. If his throat was cut people would look around for the murderer and unless his wife had an excellent alibi, they would think of her.'

'She would be risking a charge of petty treason?'

'Yes.'

'And burning for it?'

'Er…yes.'

'So do you think Mrs Atkinson *wanted* to die at the stake?'

The question was actually intended for Scrope, although it was aimed at her brother. Neither man answered her.

'I mean, burning to death is a very painful way to die,' Philly continued thoughtfully as she elaborated on the caterpillar's markings, 'I'm not sure hanging, drawing and quartering is that much more painful. Think of the Book of Martyrs and Cranmer and Latymer burning for their faith under Queen Mary—half the point is that they faced a much worse death than just hanging or the axe. Isn't it?'

'I was intending to order the executioner to strangle Mrs Atkinson at the stake,' said Scrope gently, 'before the fire was lit.'

Philly didn't look at him. 'Well, she couldn't know you would do that. Nobody bothers with witches, do they? Do you really think Mrs Atkinson is stupid enough to kill her husband by cutting his throat in bed, where the blood alone is likely to accuse her, never mind the corpse? I mean, there's nothing much less accidental than a cut throat, is there?'

'Well, she might not have thought of it...' said Scrope lamely.

Philadelphia found her snips and cut her thread peremptorily.

'Oh, my lord,' she cooed. 'Every woman knows the loyalty she owes her husband as her God-given lord. Every preacher makes it clear, every marriage sermon tells her. It's not a secret. Mrs Atkinson isn't half-witted. Cutting his throat would have been idiocy for her.'

'But Philadelphia,' wailed Scrope. 'Who did it then? If it wasn't Barnabus and it wasn't Andy Nixon and it certainly wasn't Lowther and it wasn't even Kate Atkinson, who did it?'

His wife was stitching a cabbage quite near the caterpillar. She stopped and looked up at Carey.

'Ask the question nobody seems to have thought of yet,' she said to him simply. 'You remember, Robin, Walsingham's question.'

'What's she talking about?' demanded Scrope, his brow furrowed.

It wasn't exactly the light of revelation, more the promise of it, the moment when Alexander the Great drew his sword when faced with the Gordian knot.

'She means the lawyer's question. *Cui bono?* Who benefits?' Carey explained slowly. 'It was what Sir Francis Walsingham always asked when faced with some complicated political puzzle.'

'Ah,' said Scrope, not sounding very enlightened. 'Well, you'd best be quick about it, Robin. The inquest opens at eleven o'clock tomorrow which is the earliest the jury can get here.'

And I've been wasting my time with damn silly letters about lodgings, Carey thought to himself.

'Plenty of time if you get up early enough,' said Philadelphia brightly, reading his mind. 'And my lord gives you leave.'

'Oh, ah, yes, of course,' said Scrope, his attention already diverted back to the music in front of him. He squinted at the close-printed notes and began playing again.

'Thank you, my lord.' Carey said nothing more, blinked past the candles on the virginal lid at the copper sunset light slowly seeping into the bright sky. He shook his head suddenly like a horse with a fly in its ear, as if he had almost fallen into a dream standing up.

Scrope sighed happily and turned a beaming face to him.

'Splendid. What it must be to be able to sing...'

The music had worked some of its accustomed magic; Carey smiled back and dug in the box of music.

'You're sure it wasn't Lowther?' he said, still sounding puzzled.

'Quite sure,' said Scrope. 'For the same reason I was sure it wasn't you either. Character.'

'Character?'

'I loathe the man as much as you do and I don't doubt you're right that he sent Mick to bring in the Grahams and lift Lady Widdrington. That's much more his style. In any case, why duplicate his effort? Presumably he wanted Lady Widdrington kidnapped so as to lure you into some kind of trap.'

'I suppose so.'

'Well, then, what's the point of it if you're in irons for Atkinson's murder and can't risk and break your neck trying to rescue her?'

Carey sighed. That was certainly logical, blast it. So now he had three suspects in gaol and not one of them the right person. He turned back to the sheet music and finally found what he had been looking for.

'This is the one the Queen likes.' He set the music before Scrope.

'Good lord, this is new.'

'All the rage at Court, my lord,' murmured Carey.

Scrope was running through the music, first right hand, then left hand, then both together.

'Here you go, two and one.'

Carey sang the Latin voice part to the end, knowing it quite well. Scrope turned the page, blinked hard at the close-tangled black notes, and carried straight on sight-reading, humming to himself and tapping his foot. It was a delicate pastoral piece, the kind of thing the Queen always liked to play. Carey sat down in Scrope's carved chair to listen until Philadelphia returned again. Despite the somnolence brought on by a heavy meal and the end of the day he was in no hurry to return to his bedchamber, the absence of Barnabus's snores and the ridiculously short truckle bed to which Buttercup and her family had relegated him. If he closed his eyes he could imagine an Arcadia of shepherds, shepherdesses and Elizabeth Widdrington, as constant in his phantasy as the Queen at Court, and quite as formidable, despite being generally mother-naked in the Greek style. He smiled a little.

'Oh, look at him,' said Philadelphia when she returned at last, leaning over her sleeping brother. 'Poor thing.'

Scrope was lost in the lands of music and only said 'Eh?', before carrying on with a complex variation on the notes before him. Philadelphia called John Ogle and his eldest lad. They carried Carey to the guest chamber where Scrope's own bodyservant, Humphrey Rumney, undressed him and put him to bed to the complex strains from the nearby dining room, and through it all Carey smiled.

## THURSDAY, 6TH JULY 1592, BEFORE DAWN

Carey awoke with that feeling of dislocation that comes from sleeping in a different bed than the one expected. At least it was just long enough for him. The curtains drawn around his bed were half-open and the darkness had that faint pearly greyness of false dawn. For a few seconds he blinked and picked his way through fragments of dream and memory. There was snoring in the room, as usual coming from a truckle bed by the door, though on a subtly different note from Barnabus. No, he was not in fact in bed with a woman; unfortunately he was alone. For a moment he dwelled on his unnatural and pitiable womanless state; in Carey's opinion, if God had meant men to live without women, He wouldn't have created Eve.

But Court music was still flowing through his memory. Oh yes. He had been listening to Scrope's playing the night before and had dozed off; they must have put him to bed. Had he been drunk? No, his memories of the evening were too clear; he had simply been tired.

Memories filtered back. At the forefront of them all was Philadelphia's reminder of Walsingham's question: who benefits? If not Lowther, if not Kate Atkinson, who actually benefited from

Jemmy Atkinson's very bloody death?

The answer had come to him from God while he slept: it lay in the fact that by English law, all the murderer's property went to the victim's family. Underneath all the complications, that was a simple beacon. Andy Nixon couldn't have benefited simply because it was so likely he would be accused; as Philly had said, that went double for Mrs Atkinson who was not at all martyr material. No, he was actually looking at an attempt at double or even triple murder, with himself intended as the murder weapon.

He flung back the sheets and counterpane and jumped out of bed. Energy filled him; he loved this time of day and he was impatient to do what he should have done from the start. He knew where he was now, mentally and physically: who could mistake the virulent dragon and St George on the tapestry hangings, and the strangely shaped pointy-hatted women of the last century? He wondered why Philadelphia had not sent for some better hangings from London for her guest chamber, as he used the chamber pot under the bed, found the tinderbox to light a taper, and looked about for his clothes.

In the truckle bed he found Simon Barnet, lying on his back and imitating his noisy uncle.

'Quicker if I dress myself,' said Carey, passed his hand over his chin and decided to shave now. He doubted he would have the time to go to the barber's later and he certainly didn't trust Simon with a razor yet. On the other hand he needed hot water.

He shook the truckle bed vigorously until Simon sat up on his elbow and blinked at him.

'Wha'?' Simon asked.

'Good morning,' Carey said brightly. 'Run and fetch me a pitcher of hot water to shave with and something to eat and drink, there's a good lad, Simon.'

Simon swung his legs over the side of the truckle bed and rubbed his eyes. Like most of the boys in the Castle he hardly ever bothered to take his clothes off. 'Yessir,' he muttered, got up, swayed, hauled his boots on and shambled out of the door.

'I said run,' Carey called after him reproachfully. 'I'm in a hurry.'

'Urrh,' sighed Simon and speeded to a tottering trot.

One of the boys from the kitchen eventually turned up with a pitcher of hot water, saying Simon was on his way. Stuffing his face again, Carey thought, as he worked the soap into a lather and nipped through to Scrope's chamber to borrow his razor; I'll have to get him new livery soon, the rate he's growing. It was a lot of trouble shaving himself, but life at Court had ingrained it into him that he couldn't appear in any official capacity with a chin covered in stubble. And he couldn't regrow his beard until the black dye in his hair had finished growing out, which he hadn't thought of when he did it. The Scropes were still fast asleep, along with their respective maid and manservant, their bedchamber a choir of snores. Amazing how people wasted the best part of the day lying in their beds.

Half an hour later he was in his green velvet suit and shrugging the shoulder strap of his swordbelt over his arm. As usual, Simon Barnet was taking three times as long as Barnabus to do a perfectly simple job and Carey soon got tired of waiting for him. He put his hat on, crept through the intervening chamber and his sister and brother-in-law's bedroom, and clattered down the stairs of the Keep. Nobody was stirring in the hall, where most of the servants still slept wrapped in their cloaks, on benches or in the rushes, and out into the cold morning air. There wasn't anybody about so Carey went across to the Keep gate and had a quick word with Solomon Musgrave. Then he went to his chambers in the Queen Mary Tower, greeted Buttercup, lit a candle and did some hurried paperwork. Finally he went to the new barracks, and knocked on the door of Sergeant Dodd's little chamber next to the harness room.

It took a while but eventually there were thumping sounds inside and Dodd opened the door in his shirt and hose, with his helmet in one hand and his sword in the other.

'What the hell is it…?' he demanded. 'Och, sorry, sir. Is there a raid?'

'Er…no, Sergeant,' said Carey, trying not to look past his shoulder at where Janet Dodd lay in the rumpled little bed. 'Only we have a lot to do and not much time to do it in.'

'Oh. Ah,' said Dodd, slowly catching up with this. 'There's no raid?'

'No.'

'Och God, it's still the middle of the night, sir; it's…'

'Dodd,' said Carey patiently, wondering what on earth was the matter with the man. 'It's a couple of hours before dawn and I want to start rounding up witnesses for the inquest, so I'd be grateful if you would get yourself dressed and come and help me.'

Dodd leaned his sword against the wall and then put his hand across his eyes and moaned like a cow in calf.

'Ay sir,' he said heavily at last. 'I'll be wi' ye.'

Dodd yawned and shut the door. Carey went outside the barracks building and stood in the yard, mentally making lists. Janet came out still lacing her kirtle and hurried past him with an amused expression on her face.

'Have they opened the buttery yet, do ye know sir?' she asked him.

'I don't know, Mrs Dodd.'

'Och,' she shook her head and hurried on.

By the time Dodd was ready, the stable boys were beginning to stir although the gate wasn't due to open for an hour yet. Solomon Musgrave opened the postern gate for them and Carey and Dodd went down past the trees and into Carlisle town. There were a few lights lit in the windows and a night-soil wagon clattered slowly down Castlegate ahead of them, while two men with shovels picked up the least unpleasant piles of manure and tossed them in the back.

'Now,' said Carey. 'Firstly, what did you find out last night, Sergeant?'

Dodd blinked and rubbed his eyes. 'Ay,' he said with great effort. 'Er…well, after I found Michael Kerr, I spoke to the men working on the roof by the Atkinsons' house and asked if any of them had seen aught, and the foreman said they hadnae but they had found a bloody knife stuck deep in the new thatch and they were going to give it to the master.'

'To John Leigh?'

'Ay. So any road, I got them to give it to me and it's in my room now.'

'Excellent, Sergeant, well done. Anything else?'

There were a few women moving about the streets, maidservants who didn't live in going to their work.

'Ah…Janet went to speak to Julia Coldale again, but got nothing but cheek from the girl, so she came away. None o' Mrs Atkinson's gossips saw aught; it was too early in the morning and they were too busy. Janet says none of them save Mrs Leigh thinks Kate Atkinson did the murder. Maggie Mulcaster was wanting to know was there anything they could gi' ye to persuade ye to leave it.'

Carey sighed. 'What did she say?'

'She said she didnae think so and besides ye're a courtier and verra expensive, but in any case she thought ye had enough sense to see she didnae do it, but it was a case of convincing the jury and ye hadnae set that up, Lowther had.'

'Well, that's something. Though Lowther still thinks it was Barnabus. Anything else?'

'Then we went to Bessie's to see if anybody there had heard anything, but they hadnae except that Pennycook's left town and gone back to Scotland.'

'Very wise of him,' said Carey. 'And that was it?'

'Ay sir.' Dodd saw no reason to fill Carey's enquiring pause with the details of their evening in Bessie's. 'Janet says she thinks ye should arrest young Julia and frighten her into…'

'Speak of the devil,' said Carey softly. 'Look there.'

It was hard to miss the girl's wonderful fall of hair, even under her hat, as she walked quickly down the street ahead of them. Carey put his arm out to stop Dodd and then followed her cautiously. The girl went to the door of the Leighs' house and knocked softly. The door opened at once and she stepped in.

'What's she up to?' Carey said to himself, walking about under the spidery growth of poles and planks on the Leighs' house. The workmen had pulled up all their ladders when they left the night before. Carey whistled very softly between his teeth.

'Right, Dodd,' he said. 'Give me a leg up.'

'Eh?'

'Give me a boost. I want to get up the scaffolding.' He was already unbuckling his sword.

Dodd sighed, bent his knee next to one of the poles and Carey climbed from knee to shoulder, to an accompaniment of complaint from Dodd, caught the horizontal pole of the first platform and heaved himself up.

Carey's legs were kicking, so Dodd backed off a bit. It was the Courtier's padded Venetian hose that were causing the trouble; they had caught on the edge of one of the planks. No doubt they were well enough for a life spent parading in front of the Queen, thought Dodd with sour pleasure.

At last Carey was onto the first platform, a bit breathless. He let down one of the ladders and Dodd climbed up after him, bringing the swordbelt, then he pulled the ladder back up to use it for getting to the second platform. Once there, Carey went to the boundary with the Atkinsons' house and called Dodd over. He nodded at the place where Carey was pointing.

'Ay,' he said, suppressing a feeling of sickness at being so high over the street. 'I was wondering about them marks.'

Carey went along the platform again. 'Where did they find the knife?'

'Just about here, sir.'

'Right. Help me make a hole.'

'But sir...'

'Don't argue, Sergeant. I don't need a warrant.'

'But they just had the roof done, sir.'

'So they did, Sergeant.'

Carey had drawn his poignard and was digging away among the rushes. Reluctantly Dodd took out his own knife and helped. The hole was rather large when the Courtier finally hissed softly through his teeth and started pulling something from the thatch.

It was a man's linen shirt, crackling and stiff with brown crumbling stains.

'Och,' said Dodd and then, 'The silly bastard.'

Carey looked at him quizzically and gave him the shirt.

'Why?'

'Should ha' burned it, that's why. What's he want tae keep it for?'

'Couldn't bring himself to waste a shirt. Or was going to but hasn't had the chance yet.'

Dodd shook his head. Carey led the way back along the platform and started down the ladder, but Dodd stopped by the small window and peered in between the shutter slats.

'Sir,' he said softly. 'Come and look at this.'

Carey came back, peered between the shutters as well. It was hard to be sure in the half-light, but there were two people standing in the little room. One was John Leigh, the other the girl with long red curls. They were murmuring too low for Carey to hear. The girl shrugged and spoke sharply. John Leigh nodded and held out what looked like a heavy purse. The girl reached to take it and in that moment, John Leigh dropped the purse, grabbed her wrist and hit her hard on the jaw. She reeled back and slumped. Then John Leigh was on her with his hands round her neck, silently squeezing the life out of her.

Dodd's mouth was open. Carey stepped back, lifted his boot and kicked the shutters hard, kicked again. Dodd remembered something, left him to it, and slid down the ladder to the next level.

It was a horrible shock to John Leigh when a boot suddenly started splintering the wood of his window shutters and then burst apart the lead flushings of the expensive little diamond window panes.

Foolishly he let go of Julia Coldale's neck, and started back, staring wildly. The head and one shoulder of the Deputy Warden shoved through the tattered window, causing glass to fall and shine in the rushes.

'Get away from that girl,' ordered Carey.

He can't get through the window, thought John Leigh; it's too small for him. Without really thinking things through, he reached for Julia Coldale again. There was a loud hammering downstairs. She was making crowing noises and blindly trying to crawl away from him; he grabbed her shoulder, pushed her back, clipped her jaw again and started strangling her once more. Something hard hit his ear painfully, drawing blood. He looked up, saw Carey with two more diamond panes in his hand, taking aim to throw them at him, his dagger in his left hand. He did throw them, John Leigh ducked, but didn't duck fast enough and was hit on the cheek. He let go of Julia to put his hand up to the cut and another piece of glass hit him on the forehead.

There were footsteps on the stairs, but John Leigh had picked up his wife's sewing table and was using it as a shield against the rain of missiles from Carey. The door was booted open and there stood Sergeant Dodd, breathing hard, a drawn sword in each hand.

'Now,' said Dodd sadly between pants. 'Ye'd best do as the Deputy tells ye, Mr Leigh.'

Leigh's teeth showed like a cornered dog's. He drew his own dagger, dropped the sewing table in a mess of pincushions and thread spools, and picked up Julia, turned her about so he could put his blade to her neck. Her legs weren't supporting her and she didn't look as if she was breathing.

'Stay away, Dodd,' he shouted wildly. 'Or I'll cut her throat.'

Dodd stopped, partly because Julia Coldale was between him and Leigh and it was always hard to put a sword through two bodies at once. The girl made a loud snoring noise and then another, started coughing and gagging.

'Matilda,' roared John Leigh. 'Matilda, come and help me. Matildaaa!'

There was no answer. Dodd stood there, a sword in each hand and no way to use either of them while Leigh kept his knife to the girl's neck.

'Get back,' whispered Leigh hoarsely. 'Get back through the door.'

'Now listen,' said Dodd regretfully. 'Ye canna make it work. We both saw ye trying to kill the girl an' I dinna care why and nor does the Deputy. But ye willnae hang if ye dinna kill her, see, so why not let her go and save us all trouble and sweat?'

The girl was gagging and whooping pitifully, still not able to stand. She must be an awful weight on his arm, thought Dodd, taking one considered step back. Leigh followed, facing him, his hand with the knife trembling dangerously.

I wonder what the Deputy's up to, Dodd thought to himself.

'Where will ye go?' he asked Leigh reasonably. 'What will ye do? Ye'll be at the horn for sure and could ye live in the Debateable Land?'

'Other men have,' said Leigh desperately. Julia slipped against him and he hefted her up again, sweat on his face.

Dodd shook his head. 'Fighting men,' he said. 'Wi' all the respect in the world, sir, ye're not a fighting man. Have ye a sword? Harness? A helmet? D'ye have horses? Can ye use a lance? My brother-in-law Skinabake Armstrong has his pick o' men to join his gang, sir, and he'll no' take a Carlisle draper.'

The knife was shaking hard now. 'I can learn,' croaked Leigh.

'Ay, ye could,' said Dodd, consideringly. Behind Leigh something white appeared at the little window. 'But could ye learn fast enough? The prime raiding season starts in August, after Lammastide, and we're well into July already, sir.' He raised his voice. 'Ye'd have a lot to learn, ye ken. Are ye in one of the Carlisle trained bands, or did ye pay another man to take your place? Ay, I see ye had a substitute—and why should ye no', ye're a busy man, a prosperous merchant, an' there's nae reason in the world why ye should waste yer time out on the race course playing about wi' pikes and arquebuses and the like...'

Carey barked his shoulders painfully, easing them through the window, then snagged his shirt on a piece of glass and had to free it. He caught the beam above the windowseat with the tips of his fingers and hefted himself through as quietly as he could, with his knife in his teeth and his tongue and lips as far back from its edge as he could grimace. He sucked his stomach in as far as it would go and prayed devoutly as he hauled his hips through past the points of the broken window panes. And then his knees were in, he could drop to the ground quietly, while Dodd droned impassively on about civic duties and Leigh's own children. Carey was a head taller than Leigh. So with the back of John Leigh's neck and his expensively furred brocade gown only a pace in front of him, Carey took his dagger lefthanded from his mouth, reached over the man's shoulder to clamp Leigh's wrist in his right hand and brought the hilt of the poignard down as hard as he could twice on the back of Leigh's head.

Leigh grunted and collapsed, dropping his knife as well. Julia Coldale fell too, then picked herself back up onto her hands and knees and was sick. She looked up at Carey, past his hairy calves and his bare knees and his now ragged white shirt to his face, made a soft croak and fainted.

Dodd looked at him impassively and handed his sword back.

'I'll go and fetch in yer suit, shall I, sir?' he asked.

'If you would, Sergeant,' said Carey.

# Thursday, 6th July 1592, Dawn

'Wh-what are you doing with my husband?' Mrs Leigh demanded. She was in her smock and dressing gown and her hair in its nighttime plait.

'We're arresting him, Mrs Leigh,' said Dodd. 'Would ye kindly move away?'

'Wh-what for?'

'Trying to kill Julia Coldale,' came Carey's voice from above. 'He nearly succeeded as well.'

'That little whore,' sniffed Mrs Leigh. 'My husband has nothing to do with the bitch.'

That's what you think, mistress, thought Dodd, who could think of one reason why a man would give a woman money. He didn't say that, mainly because he didn't want to bring on Mrs Leigh's labour.

'We only just stopped him throttling the life out of her,' said Carey. 'Please, Mrs Leigh, out of our way.'

She did move back into the doorway of the shop. Jock Burn was standing there as well, licking his lips. As he went past, John Leigh looked desperately at his wife.

'Matilda,' he whispered. 'Do something.'

She looked away.

They had a full escort of small boys and dogs by the time they got back to Carlisle Castle and Carey was beginning to puff and blow a bit with Julia's weight. She had managed to stop whooping by then, so he put her down and she leant very prettily on his arm, trying to give him the occasional trustful smile. Oddly enough he didn't smile back.

They were running out of space for prisoners; there was only the Lickingstone cell left apart from the hole under the Gaoler's floorboards which was reached with a ladder. In the end they decided the hole was the least bad of the two.

'Chain him,' said Carey.

'But sir...' Dodd protested. 'He didnae actually kill her.'

'Only by the Grace of God,' said Carey coldly. 'And besides, haven't you worked out why? Chain him.'

'Ay sir.'

John Leigh sat down on the bench in the Gaoler's room with his head bowed while Dodd locked his feet together in the leg irons. When he had climbed down awkwardly, and the ladder pulled up again, Carey looked at Dodd.

'Fetch at least four men from the barracks and go and arrest Jock Burn. If you can't find him, tell the men on the City gates that they're on no account to let him out. And have the Crier give his name at the marketplace.'

'Ay sir,' said Dodd, wondering what on earth he was at but not inclined to argue with the expression on Carey's face.

Philadelphia had already taken Julia Coldale up to her stillroom, given her a dose of something unpleasant and painted her usual infusion of comfrey on the terrible bruises around her neck.

By the time her brother arrived looking grim and followed by a puzzled Richard Bell, Philadelphia had decided she should be put to bed.

'I have to speak to her first,' said Carey. 'I must know...'

Philadelphia drew him aside and whispered fiercely at him. 'The poor girl can hardly breathe, let alone speak; you can talk to her tomorrow...'

'It must be today,' said Carey implacably. 'Unless Scrope can get the inquest adjourned.'

'What's that got to do with—?'

'That's what I want to find out.'

He gently put her aside and went to stand over Julia who had started weeping quietly into her apron.

'Well?' he said. 'Will you talk to me now?'

'Ay,' she whispered.

By that time the jury for the inquest were assembling at the town hall and Scrope was putting on his black velvet court gown and his gold chain of office, while the prisoners were fetched out of their various cells. Carey sprinted up the stairs of the Queen Mary Tower to his own chamber to change his clothes to his good black velvet suit and found Simon Barnet asleep and snoring on the truckle bed.

Finally ready, Carey ran down the stairs again to join the tail end of the inquest procession, with his hat in his hand. Ahead, guarded by Sergeant Ill-Willit Daniel Nixon and Lowther's men, were all of the prisoners, including John Leigh: Barnabus shambled along looking frowsty and bad-tempered, Kate Atkinson walked with her head bowed and Andy was having trouble with his leg irons. It was a slow march. Dodd fell in behind him at the Keep gate with his four men and no prisoner.

'No sign of him?' Carey asked.

'Nay sir,' said Dodd mournfully. 'We were too late. He must have run as soon as we left. I did the rest of what ye said.'

'Damn, damn, damn,' muttered Carey. 'Why the hell didn't I think of it?'

'Well, sir,' Dodd was comforting. 'Ye couldnae arrest Jock Burn as well as his master wi' only the two of us and a half-dead maid to carry; Jock would ha' made mincemeat of us.'

'I suppose so.'

'And ye've caught the master good and proper, sir.'

'Have you got the shirt?'

'Ay sir, but no' the knife. I'll send Bangtail for it; he's a fast runner.'

Bangtail sprinted off from the end of the procession. Carey saw Janet Dodd among the crowd at the entrance to the town hall, a very formidable sight in red, black and brocade, surrounded by many of Kate Atkinson's gossips, likewise dressed in their Sunday best. There was no sign of Mrs Leigh, which was hardly to be wondered at.

Edward Aglionby looked impressive in his budge-trimmed green velvet gown, black damask doublet and hose and tall hat. He stood on the steps of the hall as the Castle procession arrived and greeted Scrope with suitable respect.

'My lord,' he said in a carrying voice. 'There's nae room in the hall for all the folk that must be seen and examined and all the folk that wish to attend and so I have decided to hear the inquest at the market cross.'

'An excellent idea, Mr Aglionby,' beamed Scrope, who had been secretly dreading the heat and smell of a small town hall full of people in summer. 'Please dispose your inquest as you wish.'

Carey looked about him, wondering if Aglionby had considered security for the inquest. He needn't have worried. The Mayor and Corporation had called out the City trained bands and all three hundred of them stood around the cross, controlling the crowds, capped in steel, bearing halberds and billhooks and delighted to get such prime viewing positions.

Running his eye critically over them for the first time, Carey decided he liked the look of them. They were clean and so were their weapons and while they didn't stand to attention, they were orderly, paying attention and not one was picking his nose.

The Chancellor of the Cathedral came in solemn procession, bearing the large Bible from his lectern. Each of the twelve gentlemen of the jury stepped forward to swear that he would truly judge of the matter before him, so help him God.

Behind Carey the marketplace was packed with people, talking excitedly, held back by their sons, brothers and husbands, stern-faced with office. An inquest was not precisely a trial, but it could be very much more than simply finding what a person had died of. Since the Assize judge and his armed escort would not be coming from Newcastle until Lammastide at the beginning of August, and as there were suspects in the case—too many, in fact—the Coroner had wide powers to establish the identity of the man or woman who actually went before the judge as the accused. At which point, of course, the thing was pretty much a foregone conclusion.

'It is your duty, gentlemen of the jury,' said Aglionby sonorously, 'to decide how, when and why the deceased died and whether he died of natural or unnatural causes, by Act of God or by man's design. To this end you are charged by Almighty God and Her most gracious Majesty the Queen...'

It's still a bloody farce, Carey thought with disgust, looking at the two rows of assorted faces before him. Apart from Thomas Lowther there were Captain Carleton, his brother Lancelot and Captain Musgrave. He recognised another as Archibald Bell. One friend, eleven neutral or enemies. Their general hostility to Londoners was plain. His stomach tightened.

'Does the jury wish to view the body?' asked Aglionby and Thomas Lowther rose to answer him.

'It willna be...'

Archibald Bell pulled on his gown from behind and whispered in his ear. Lowther coughed.

'It seems it will be necessary,' he finished.

The jury filed up the steps to the hall where Atkinson's body, already smelling gamey, was laid out ready for them. They came back down, all of them impassive.

Aglionby asked Sir Richard Lowther to give evidence from the steps of the cross, since he had been called immediately and was the first gentleman to have seen the body. After swearing his oath loudly he gave evidence of where the body lay, in Frank's vennel, on Tuesday morning, with great emphasis. He then added that he had immediately known who must have done the deed, to wit, one Barnabus Cooke, late of London town, footpad, currently pretending to serve Sir Robert Carey. He had hurried back to the Keep, found the said Cooke, and arrested him. Although he, Lowther, had besought the vile Cooke to confess his crime with eloquent words, he, the vile Cooke, had refused with many foul oaths, thereby compounding his offence. Seizing his moment, Carey stepped forward and bowed.

'Your honour...' he said hintingly to Aglionby. Scrope looked at him, puzzled. Aglionby smiled and tilted his head.

'Yes, Sir Robert, please continue.'

'Just a minute,' snorted Sir Richard. 'What's he want?'

'He is acting as *amicus curiae*,' Aglionby told him repressively. 'He will ask supplementary questions to aid the Crown.' Scrope leaned over and whispered urgently, to which the Coroner replied with another smile and half-shut eyes.

'Sir Richard,' he said respectfully. 'Who came to fetch you on Tuesday morning?'

Lowther's face darkened. 'Some clerk or other.'

'Was it one Michael Kerr, factor to Mr James Pennycook?'

'It might have been. Ay, it was. So?'

'Your honour, I trust Mr Kerr is available to give evidence?' Carey said to the Coroner. Aglionby rifled through the papers in front of him and found the list of witnesses.

'Yes, Sir Robert. We can call him next, if you wish.'

'If your honour pleases.'

Aglionby turned aside to whisper to his clerk who transmitted the whisper to one of the trained band. Carey looked at Lowther.

'Sir Richard, can you describe what Frank's vennel looked like when you came to see the body?'

Lowther snorted again and said contemptuously that it had had a body lying in it and a powerful lot of people looking on and one o' the dogs being dragged off.

'Was there blood?'

'I dinna ken. There might have been.'

'But was there in fact any blood?'

'I dinna recall.'

'Did you notice anything else unusual in the alley?'

'No.'

'Er...Sir Richard, what made you think that Barnabus Cooke had killed Mr Atkinson?' put in Scrope helpfully. Dammit, thought Carey, whose side are you on? Aglionby let him get away with it.

'Oh, ay. I found Barnabus's knife and one of Carey's gloves on the body,' said Lowther, looking slightly embarrassed.

Carey smiled kindly at him. 'Where were these incriminating items?' he asked.

Lowther coughed. 'Laid on top o' the body.'

Now isn't that interesting, Carey thought. I did you an injustice, Tom Scrope.

'I'm sorry, Sir Richard,' he said, elaborately obtuse. 'I don't quite understand. Exactly how were they placed?'

'Well, the corpse was on its back, and the knife lay on its chest and the glove by it.'

Carey paused to let this picture sink in. 'Someone had carefully put them there, in other words,' he said.

'I dinna ken.'

'Well, they could hardly have dropped so neatly by accident, could they?'

Lowther shrugged. Carey waited a moment to see if he would say anything else, then continued.

'Now when you found my servant Barnabus Cooke, where was he?'

'In yer chambers.'

'At the Keep?'

'Ay.'

'What did he say when you accused him?'

'I didnae understand because he spake braid London,' said Lowther.

Probably just as well, thought Carey. 'Did he say anything you understood?'

'He lied.'

'What did he actually say?'

'He said he didnae do it. But he...'

'What did you do then?'

'I arrested him.'

'Barnabus, stand forward,' Carey said and Barnabus took a step out of the group of accused. 'Is this the man you arrested?'

'Ay.'

'Tell me, how did his face come to be so battered?'

Lowther shrugged and wouldn't answer. There was a certain amount of muttering among the public, none of whom were naïve.

'Who else was in my chambers?'

Lowther shrugged again. 'A boy,' he said.

'In fact, Simon Barnet, Cooke's nephew.'

'If you say so, Sir Robert.'

'Is it true that you tried to get into my office and Barnet prevented you, so you beat him as well?'

'Nay. He was insolent.'

'Did Lady Scrope then come and order you out of my chambers which you were preparing to search?'

'Ay.'

'Did you, in fact, threaten her as well?'

'Nay,' said Lowther. 'She threatened me.'

Scrope blinked gravely at Lowther. 'You hadn't mentioned this, Sir Richard,' he said reproachfully, which was why Carey had brought it up. Lowther cleared his throat and Aglionby put out a repressive hand. Scrope subsided.

'Now, Sir Richard,' said Carey. 'Apart from a knife and a glove laid carefully on the corpse, did you have any other reason at all for accusing Barnabus Cooke?'

'The man's throat was cut. Yon's a footpad's trick.'

'Is there no other man in Carlisle who can use a knife?' Carey asked, rhetorically.

'It's a footpad's trick,' repeated Lowther doggedly.

'So you actually had no other evidence or reason for thinking that Barnabus Cooke had killed Atkinson?'

Go on, thought Carey, I dare you; I dare you to say you thought I'd told him to do it. For a moment he was sure Lowther would say it, but in fact he did not, he simply stood there with his arms folded and a sour expression on his face.

'Thank you, Sir Richard.'

Carey made a gesture of dismissal and the Coroner nodded that Lowther could go.

Michael Kerr was ready to be examined next. He gave his evidence in a mutter that the jury had to strain to hear. He had happened to go through Frank's vennel that morning. No, he had not been sent. Yes, he did know he was on oath. No, he had not been sent, well, he had wondered if there was anything to find there. He couldn't remember why. Yes, he knew the dead man. Yes, he was Mr James Pennycook's factor and son-in-law. Yes, he

461

understood Mr Pennycook had left town. He had gone to join the Scottish King's Court, he believed. No, he didn't know anything about anything else.

According to the list Carey had provided, the next to be called was Fenwick the undertaker who had come to fetch the body away.

He explained that he had done this but that he had been worried by many things about the body.

'Oh?' said Aglionby with interest. 'What were they?'

Fenwick's grave face was troubled and he put up one finger. 'Considering the man's throat was cut, there should have been blood in the wynd. There was none that I could see. There was blood on his shirt, but not his outer clothes, except the linings. He lay very straight, as if he had been arranged, quite respectfully really, and on his back which is not the way someone falls when they have been attacked from behind.'

'I see, thank you. Sir Robert?'

'Did you notice any tracks in the wynd, Mr Fenwick?'

He hadn't at the time, though now he came to think about it he thought there might have been marks of a handcart in the softer parts.

The next was Barnabus himself, brought forward under guard to stand by the cross. Of course, as one of the accused he was not allowed a lawyer, even if there had been one available. The day was warm and Carey had already started to sweat under his black velvet: Barnabus was unwell and unhappy in the sunlight after so long in semi-darkness, with his battered round brimmed hat crushed in his hands, his bruised ferret-face with its collection of pockmarks and scars making him look an ugly sight even to Carey, who was used to him. The thin film of moisture on his skin didn't help either.

The Coroner looked at the unsavoury little man impassively.

'Barnabus Cooke,' he said after Barnabus had whinged out his oath with his hand on the cathedral Bible. 'Remember you are on oath and at risk of sending your immortal soul to hell if you lie.'

'Yes, yer honour.'

'Did you kill Mr James Atkinson?'

'No, yer honour. I didn't.'

462

'Why does such an important gentleman as Sir Richard Lowther think you did?'

'I dunno, yer honour. Only I didn't.'

'Where were you on Monday night?'

Barnabus's eyes darted from side to side, making him look even shiftier.

'Well, see, yer honour, I was at Bessie's first, because my master was out wiv a patrol. Then I...I went to a house I know. Perhaps one of the girls lifted my knife while I was there. I never went nowhere near Frank's vennel.' Barnabus paused and then smiled slyly. ''Course it's funny in a way and serves me right,' he volunteered, while Carey winced inwardly. 'I've been teaching the girls to do tricks with dice and such, and I expect one of them used 'er lessons on me.'

Half of the people in the marketplace knew exactly where Barnabus had been on Monday night. The other half learnt it from them within a few seconds. They hissed and muttered at each other at the news that Madam Hetherington's girls had been taking lessons in cheating at dice. Carey fought not to laugh. That would teach Madam Hetherington not to betray her customers.

'Do you mean you were committing the sin of fornication on Monday night?' interrupted Scrope pompously.

Barnabus didn't look at him and nor did Carey. 'Yes, my lord,' said Barnabus, turning pointedly to the Coroner. 'I wouldn't say, if I wasn't on my Bible oath, yer honour, but I was. I'm a poor sinner, yer honour, and if I'm sentenced to do penance for the fornication, well, I can't gainsay as I deserve it, but I never murdered Mr Atkinson and that's a fact. I don't deserve to swing for a murder I never did, yer honour.'

Lowther leaned over from his place on the other side of the cross.

'Ye're a footpad, and that's a fact,' he snarled.

'Sir Richard!' snapped Aglionby.

'Well yer honour, 'e's right and 'e isn't, if you follow. It's true I was a footpad down in London, but since Sir Robert Carey took me on as 'is servant, I've left my evil ways behind, sir.'

More or less, thought Carey, smiling inwardly at the strained piety on Barnabus's face.

'Apart from passing on what small skills I have to Madam Hetherington's girls,' he added reflectively, making sure the audience got the point. 'Anyway, no footpad would make the mistake of cutting someone's froat, yer honour.'

Aglionby raised his heavy grey brows.

'Oh? Why?'

''Specially me, because I'm too short. I'm about four inches shorter than Mr Atkinson, yer honour. If I'd wanted 'im dead, which I didn't, I'd have stabbed 'im in the back. In the kidneys. S'much safer and less messy.'

Carey risked a glance over his shoulder to see how the people in the marketplace were taking this. A lot of them were nodding wisely. Even one or two of the jury were nodding. Barnabus, thought Carey, you don't need me at all, do you?

'Yes,' said Aglionby, impressively straight-faced. 'Thank you, Cooke.'

Barnabus stepped back among the other suspects and looked modestly at the cobbles.

Somewhere on the other side of the marketplace, Lady Scrope had arrived with the litter transporting Julia Coldale, who was helped down from it. Carey waited for the stir to die down a little, then nodded at Richard Bell to call the next witness.

That was Mrs Katherine Atkinson. She was shaking and as white as her apron. Compared with the other women watching, tricked out to the nines in their best clothes, she was a doleful hen sparrow, her blue working kirtle and her apron showing the signs of her imprisonment. She wasn't manacled; Carey assumed Dodd had quietly forgotten Scrope's order to chain her.

She swore her oath in a voice that was almost too soft to hear. Edward Aglionby stared at her solemnly and then said, 'Well, Mrs Atkinson, tell us how you killed your husband?'

There was a muttering from the people. Mrs Atkinson gripped her hands tight together, looked straight up at him and said clearly, 'I didna.'

This time there was a distinct gasp. Carey instinctively

swivelled his head round to look at his sister's face and found her very pleased with herself.

'I beg your pardon?' said Scrope.

'I didna kill my husband, my lord.'

'But...but you confessed to it. Yesterday. You stood in front of me and you said you did it.'

Scrope was leaning forward, half-standing, forgetting himself in his outrage. Mr Aglionby had been very patient with him but now leaned towards him and whispered something sharp in his ear. Scrope coughed and sat down again. Carey was starting to like Mr Aglionby.

'Please, Mrs Atkinson,' the Coroner was saying to her. 'Address yourself to the Court.'

'Ay sir,' said Mrs Atkinson, quailing at his annoyance. 'My lord, I did say so. I'm very sorry. But I wasna on my Bible oath then, and I dare not put my soul at risk wi' perjury.'

'What's your story now?'

''Tisn't a story, your honour,' said Mrs Atkinson, two hot spots of colour starting in her cheeks. 'I lied to my lord Warden before, because I'm a poor weak-willed woman and I was frightened. But I've had time to think and pray to God and what I'm saying now is God's own truth, your honour.'

Scrope sniffed eloquently but said nothing.

With the Coroner pumping her with questions, Kate Atkinson told the tale in a stronger voice now Scrope had made her angry. She told the sequence of the morning's events, how she had left her husband sleeping in the dark before dawn and gone down to milk the cow and how Julia had come and finally brought herself to the moment when she took a tray up to her husband and found him dead in his bed.

'Your honour,' said Carey, stepping forward again. 'May I?'

'Yes, Sir Robert.'

'Mrs Atkinson, what did the bedroom look like?'

'Och, it was terrible, sir. It was all covered wi' blood, like a butcher's shambles. It was on the sheets and the blankets and the hangings and the rushes...It made me stomach turn to see.'

'And your husband?'

465

'He was lying on the bed…with…with…'

'With his throat slit.'

She swallowed hard. Her knuckles were like ivory. 'Ay sir,' she said.

'Tell me, when you got up that morning, did you open the shutters?'

She frowned at this sudden swoop away from the awful sight of her husband's corpse. 'I didna,' she said at last. 'I don't usually; Mr Atkinson likes to sleep a little longer and it would wake him.'

'Did you open them on this day?'

'Nay sir, I didna.'

'When you came up to see your husband dead, how did you see him? Was there a candle lit in the room?'

'Nay, sir, it had burned down. I saw by the daylight…Oh.'

'Were the shutters open by that time, then, Mrs Atkinson?'

She nodded at him. 'Ay,' she said in a surprised tone of voice. 'Ay, they were, and swinging free, what's more, not hooked back.'

'Now tell me what happened after you saw your husband.'

She looked at the floor again and mumbled something.

'Please speak up, Mistress,' said Aglionby.

'I said, I fainted, your honour. Then I couldna think what to do, so I went downstairs again and I sent my little girl Mary to fetch…to fetch my friend, Mr Andrew Nixon.'

Her brow was wrinkled now. 'When he came, what did he look like?' Carey asked.

'Oh, he was not well,' said Mrs Atkinson. 'He'd been in a fight, and lost it by the looks of him, and his right hand was in a sling and at first he said he didna want to meet my husband because he was angry.'

'Quite so,' said Carey hurriedly. 'What did you decide to do?'

'Neither of us could think of anything, sir, so Andy…er… Mr Nixon went to his master, Mr Pennycook, to ask his advice, and he took two pieces of silver plate from my chest wi' him, for a present.'

'And what did Mr Pennycook advise?'

'Well, he said we should borrow his handcart and put m-my

husband's body in a wynd and he'd see to it that ye and yer London servant got the blame, not us.'

'How?'

'He said he could get hold of one of Barnabus Cooke's knives wi' a bit of luck, for the week before he'd left it in pledge at Madam Hetherington's, which is a house with a lease he owns. He sent Michael Kerr to Andy with it, as well as the handcart. I was busy at washing the sheets and blankets—it took all day—but I sent Mary out and Julia Coldale too and that's when we brought his body down from the bedroom and into Clover's byre. Clover's my cow,' she added, in case there was any mistake. 'Andy got the glove.'

This recital was causing immense excitement in the crowd and Aglionby banged with his gavel. The noise died down gradually. Carey saw with interest that Michael Kerr had his face in his hands. Mrs Atkinson had fallen silent.

'And then?' he prompted.

'Well, I kept the children from looking out the window by telling them a story while Andy put the body on the cart under some hay and left it in the back so I could milk Clover before sunset, and then when it was dark, Andy took the cart away.'

'Why didn't you send to the Keep for Sir Richard Lowther and tell him what had happened at once, as your duty was?'

Mrs Atkinson licked her lips. 'I was too afraid to think straight. All I could see was he'd been killed; he was my husband, he'd been killed in his bed and I was about the place and so I was…I was afraid.'

'Why?'

'I was afraid…that I would get the blame for it, sir. I know what a terrible sin it is for a wife to kill her husband, sir, and I would never ever do it, but I knew people would say I had. And I was right, sir, they did. You did.'

'So you decided to try and hide the body and lay the blame on me,' said Carey sternly.

'Ay sir. I'm sorry. I've done many wicked things in the past few days, sir, but none of them was murder, as God sees me, sir. I never killed him.'

'One more thing. Exactly when was Mr Atkinson killed?'

'I told you, sir, it must have been around dawn on Monday, between the time when I got up to milk Clover and when I came back wi' his breakfast.'

'Thank you, Mrs Atkinson.'

Thomas Lowther was whispering to the man on his right, shaking his head. Carey could do nothing about that: truthfulness shone from Mrs Atkinson but the jury could refuse to see it if they chose.

To try and make sure that Andy Nixon made up no more foolish stories, Carey called Goodwife Crawe his landlady next. She stood small and stalwart under the cross before all the solemn men and repeated in a high clear voice what she had told Carey: she had found Andy Nixon in a bad state in her living room, when she went in before dawn on the Monday morning. She had nursed him, bound up his hand and given him food and drink and he had left after the gates opened. She didn't know where he had gone after that, only he had come home late that night.

Carey approached Andy Nixon with the feeling he might be a lighted bomb. He took his oath, stood straight and frowned with concentration.

Ay, he had been jumped in the alley on Sunday night by Goodwife Crawe's front door. Ay, they had been four men; he didn't know who they were or why they were there, or he wasna certain, and he had been too sore to climb the ladder to his own bed in her loft, so he had slept on Goodwife Crawe's fleeces. Ay, she had nursed him. Ay, he had gone out and met Mary Atkinson and against his will gone to see Kate Atkinson. He had been appalled when she showed him the body of her husband. After that, it had been as she said, he had gone to see Pennycook, who had recommended blaming Carey and to make sure of him, Andy himself had gone up to the Keep and inveigled one of Carey's own gloves from Simon Barnet his serving lad.

Ay, he had left Atkinson in Frank's vennel. No, he hadnae left him sprawled; he had laid him out proper, as was right.

'Why didn't you go and tell Lowther immediately as your duty was?' Carey asked. 'Instead of trying to get me blamed for it.'

Andy Nixon flushed. 'I wasnae thinking straight. I was afraid Kate...er...Mrs Atkinson would be blamed, and she was afraid too. We're no' important people, sir, we didnae think anyone would listen.'

'It was a disaster that Mr Atkinson's throat was cut, wasn't it?'

'Oh, ay,' said Nixon feelingly. 'It was.'

Scrope had learned the manners to look to the Coroner for permission to ask a question. Wisely Aglionby granted it. 'Mr Nixon, why did you tell me yesterday that you did the murder?'

Andy Nixon stared at the ground, lifted a foot to scrape his toe and was reminded of his leg-irons.

'I thought ye would think Mrs Atkinson did it,' he said. 'I didnae want her to burn, so I said I did it as hanging's an easier death.'

In France Carey had seen how hanged men could jig for twenty minutes if the executioner botched the drop and he doubted it was as easy as all that. There was a feminine buzz of approval from the audience behind him.

'But I'm on oath now and feared for my soul if I perjure myself,' Nixon added with commendable piety. Somebody had been coaching these witnesses and Carey knew it wasn't him. Out of the corner of his eye, he could see his sister nodding approvingly at Andy Nixon. Thomas Lowther snorted in a manner exactly like Sir Richard's.

'If you lied once, you might lie again,' said Scrope irritably.

'No my lord.' Andy Nixon was quite steady, for a miracle. 'Not on oath.'

Aglionby said he could step back now. Carey bowed to him.

'Your honour,' he said. 'May I address the jury?'

Aglionby nodded though it was highly irregular. Carey took a deep breath, paced up to the two benches full of jurymen and removed his hat, bowed to them.

'Gentlemen, you can see what perplexity I was in yesterday,' he said. 'Here were three suspects for a murder and the only one that could in any way have done it was a woman. Now if it had been a less bloody and violent murder, I would have been in less doubt. If Mr Atkinson had died by poison, for instance. But he did not. His throat was cut and in his bed. If you cut a man's throat from behind, you may avoid being soiled, but that was not possible because he was asleep in bed. It must have been done

469

from the front. Now I myself have sliced open a man's throat in battle with a sword, and I may tell you, gentlemen, that I never was more dirty with blood in my life. Is it possible to do it without being sprayed? I doubt it.'

Most of the gentlemen in front of him had fought their own battles, perhaps one or two of the elder ones even with Carey's own father, during the Northern Rising. They were listening gravely, a couple of them nodding.

Their eyes swivelled to where Mrs Atkinson stood and took in the fact that although her clothes were dirty, there were no bloodstains.

'She is a woman, gentlemen. God made woman to serve man and accordingly he made her weaker, more timorous and less apt to violence. Is it believable she could have cut her own husband's throat, a dreadful crime and against all nature, and then gone downstairs immediately, spoken with her daughter, set a tray with breakfast, and gone up again? Of course not. Even if she could have done it, why should she? She is not mad nor melancholy. Even if she was such a wicked Jezebel as to turn against her rightful lord, why should she do it in such a way that she was bound to be suspected?'

Apart from Thomas Lowther, whom Cicero himself could not possibly have convinced, the other gentlemen were looking encouragingly puzzled.

'Well, gentlemen, although I cannot claim to be a learned lawyer, I did finally bring myself to ask the lawyer's question, *cui bono*? Who benefits? Who could possibly benefit from James Atkinson's death? And in particular, who could benefit from the manner of it? The very bloody manner of it which guaranteed that Mrs Atkinson would be accused of the crime of petty treason and would most likely burn.'

He paused impressively to let them think about it and a tiny thought darted through his mind like a silver fish that here was a surprise, the world could be focused down to an intoxicating point of intensity outside a card game or a battlefield. For a second he was intrigued and happy and then he turned his attention back to the jury.

'*Cui bono?*' he said again. 'Well, gentlemen, it's important you know that in a case of proven murder, the murderer's property goes to the victim's family.'

Lancelot Carleton was frowning at him. 'Yes, gentlemen. Mr Atkinson's death would normally mean that Mrs Atkinson inherited his goods and property, including the house where they lived. However, if she was arraigned and burned as his murderer, neither she nor her children could enjoy the gain. Instead, all the property would pass to Mr Atkinson's family. In this case, to Mrs Matilda Leigh, née Atkinson, his half-sister, and of course, her husband Mr John Leigh, draper, and their next-door neighbour.'

It was terribly satisfying to listen to all the gasps around him. Carey swept his glance around the packed marketplace, took in Scrope who had his fingers interlaced and a surprised expression on his face, and Edward Aglionby whose expression was very intent, and then went back to the jury who were staring at him with their mouths open.

'Your honour,' he said to the Coroner. 'May I call first Mr Leigh, then Julia Coldale, maidservant to Mrs Atkinson, and then return to Mr Leigh?'

Aglionby wanted to hear the story too. He nodded immediately.

John Leigh reluctantly took the oath.

'Mr Leigh,' said Carey, pointedly putting his hat back on his head. 'Is it true that you have a long-running lawsuit in Chancery over the ownership of Mr James Atkinson's town house?'

Leigh looked from side to side and nodded.

'Speak up, please.'

'Ay,' he said with an effort. 'It's true.'

'Is it true that the case was costing you a great deal of money you could ill-afford, but you wanted the house in order to expand your business and your family into it?'

'Ay,' muttered Leigh.

'Your wife was estranged from her half-brother; the lawsuit made things worse, especially when the young lawyer the Atkinsons had retained then married the daughter of the judge in the case and might have gained from that a great deal of influence.'

Leigh nodded again, caught himself and said, 'Ay. I cannot deny it, sir.'

'Thank you, that's all for the moment. Mr Bell, will you call Julia Coldale?'

Carey had Julia stand close to the jury so they could hear her, and also see the marks on her throat.

Julia said she was a cousin of Kate Atkinson's and she was serving her to learn houswifery. The sun was high overhead by now and the heat causing sweat to trickle down Carey's spine.

'What happened early on Monday morning, Miss Coldale?' he asked the girl.

Julia coughed, took a deep breath. 'A man stopped me in the street when I was going to Mrs Atkinson's house—I live with my sister in Carlisle, sir—and he asked would I do him a favour for five shillings and I said I wasnae that kind of woman, and he said no, it was only to open a window shutter in the Atkinsons' bedroom, so he could throw a message in.'

She spoke slowly and huskily and leaned a little forward to Carey.

'Who was the man?'

As he asked the question there was a sound behind Carey, tantalisingly familiar and yet out of place, not quite the whip of a bow, more a...

The small crossbow bolt sprouted like an evil weed, a little above and to the side of Julia Coldale's left breast. She jerked, looked down and stared, put her hand up uncertainly to touch the black rod, then slid softly to the cobblestones.

The marketplace erupted. Over the shouting and screaming and the open-mouthed astonishment of the jury, half of whom instinctively had their swords out, Carey caught Aglionby's eye. The man was astonished, swelling with outrage, but he wasn't panicking.

'Mr Mayor, shut the gates,' Carey said to him, quite conversationally under the din, knowing the different pitch would get through to him when a shout would be lost.

Aglionby nodded once, was on his feet and up the steps to the market cross.

There was a thunk! beside him and Carey turned to see a crossbow bolt stuck into the table wood quite close by. Is he shooting at me or the Mayor, he wondered coldly, moving back. Scrope was also on his feet, sword out, looking about him for the sniper as aggressively as a man with no chin could. The trouble with crossbows was that they made very little sound, didn't smoke and didn't flash.

The towncrier's bell jangled from the market cross.

'Trained bands o' Carell city,' boomed the Mayor's voice and some of the noise paused to hear him speak. 'Denham's troop to Caldergate, Beverley's troop to Scotchgate, Blennerhasset's troop to Botchergate, close the gates; we'll shut the City. At the double now, lads, run!'

One of the jurors had already run up the steps and was ringing the townbell. Moments later the Cathedral bell answered it. Three bodies of the men-at-arms around the marketplace peeled off and ran in three different directions.

Another bolt twanged off the stone cross beside Aglionby and he gasped and flinched, but stayed where he was.

'Sir Robert,' he called. 'D'ye ken the name o' the man makin' this outrage?'

'Jock Burn,' said Carey instantly.

Dodd had come up behind Carey who was still trying to calculate where the bolts were coming from. Most of the jurors had taken cover in the hall. The men-at-arms were commendably still surrounding the group of prisoners, though looking nervous.

'Shut the Castle?' he asked.

'Send up to Solomon Musgrave,' Carey began, 'but he's to let him in and...'

The tail of the bolt stuck in the table pointed directly back at the house covered in scaffolding. With a prickle in his neck Carey finally worked it out as a renewed shrieking broke from that direction, people streaming away from it in fear.

The woman with the withered arm—Maggie Mulcaster—came staggering through the crowd, bleeding and crying.

Behind her was a man on horseback, coming cautiously out of a yard-wynd, a crossbow aimed at her back. In front of him on the horse's withers sat Mary Atkinson, crying busily. Jock Burn cuffed her left-handed over the ear and snarled, and she choked back the tears.

'He's taken her,' gasped Maggie. 'He's got Mary. He says he willna kill her if ye let him through the gate.'

Jock had even found the time to raid Mrs Atkinson's platechest, judging by the clanking lumpy bag slung at the back of his saddle, no doubt while he was lying low in the locked house.

In the distance they heard the booms as the Scotchgate and Botchergate were shut and barred. Carey could see the whiteness of Jock Burn's teeth.

'If ye think Ah willna kill the little maid, Ah will,' shouted Jock. 'Ye cannae hang me mair than once.'

The boom was softer from Caldergate because it was furthest away. The lift of Jock's shoulder showed he had heard it.

Carey stepped forwards, his hands held away from his sides, away from his swordhilt.

Jock turned a little, so the bolt was aimed at Carey's chest now. He didn't need to explain what would happen if anyone tried to rush him. At the back of his mind Carey wondered why his stomach muscles were contracted so hard when they couldn't stop a bolt.

'Come nae closer, Deputy,' Jock warned.

Carey stopped. He has one shot, he thought, he can't wind up a crossbow on horseback, but he can break the little girl's neck with one blow. She was staring at Carey with enormous eyes. Somebody was shouting, screaming from the bunch of men-at-arms and suspects behind him, a woman's voice. He wasn't sure what she said; he thought it might be Kate Atkinson's voice.

Then another voice reached him, sharp with London vowels and lost consonants.

'I got a cuttle for the co; you get the kinchin.'

Some part of him which had picked up a smattering of thieves' cant from Barnabus got ready to move, the tension tightening in his chest and back. Jock kicked his horse, one of the jurors' no doubt, and moved sideways away from them, the horse prancing and shifting nervously, as its rider put pressure on ready to gallop to the Scotchgate.

Carey watched, praying Barnabus wouldn't leave it too late,

waiting, changing his mind about what to do.

The horse pecked and at once there was a cry of 'Gip!' from Barnabus and a soft sound in the air.

No time to see where the knife went.

Carey launched himself across the cobbles, heard the metallic twang of the crossbow, no time even to know if he'd been hit because he was at Jock's stirrup, catching Mary's kirtle with his left hand, the stirrup and boot with his right, jerking down with one hand, up with all his strength with the other, Jock going over the horse's back one way, little Mary falling squealing towards him, catching her by his fingertips tangled in her kirtle and hair, putting her behind him, shouting, 'Run to your mam!'

Still squealing, she ran. Jock had hit the ground on the other side of the horse, which swayed back and forwards, panicking, in Carey's way and finally reared and galloped off away from the crowds, nearly kicking him in the face as it did so. Then he saw that Jock was up again, sprinting for the Scotchgate, long knife in one hand, eating knife in the other, a bright splash of blood on his arm, not serious—not like Barnabus to miss, but it had been a fiendishly difficult shot.

Carey was already after him. Jock's short legs were a blur; he had a good nippy speed on him, but Carey had height and was using his greater length of stride now he had got moving. Dodd was on the chase as well, guttural shouts of 'Tynedale!' behind him, and the men at the gate running down towards them yelling 'Carel' in return.

Suppressing the urge to call 'T'il est haut!' as if he was on the hunting field, Carey dodged after Jock down a narrow alley between houses...

And almost charged straight onto Jock's knife, lying in wait. He dodged at the last second, felt cloth part along his ribs, cannoned into a wattle and daub wall which gave alarmingly and then used its spring to launch himself back at Jock who was distracted by Dodd thundering in his wake.

He caught the little man by the shoulder and punched him hard enough in the face to send pain lancing all the way up his own arm. Jock staggered, shook his head and came back at him. Dodd swung with his sword, tearing a long gash down Jock's arm. Jock was snarling, the alley crowded behind them with enthusiastic helpers, especially now Jock was wounded, and a sudden voice said inside Carey, 'No, this one's mine.'

Later he claimed he would have preferred to hang the man but had thought that a living prisoner was always a danger to others who could be made hostage by his family. He might be bought out. He might escape. He might be torn apart by the crowd.

In fact, Carey had a cold white rage in his heart for a man who could shoot a redhead like Julia Coldale and use a little girl as his shield. That coldness carried him past the stabbing knife in Jock's hand, knocking it unconcernedly aside, catching him by the front of his jerkin and pulling hard as he stabbed up leftwards into the man's chest under his breastbone with the poignard he wasn't even aware of drawing.

The blood came from Jock's mouth, not the slender wound caused by the poignard. Carey found himself supporting the man's weight one-handed and let him crumble to the muddy ground, twisting and pulling his blade out with that distinctive sticky sound.

Then the blood came, but mostly on the ground, not him. Carey stood there, hands bloody, lace cuffs bloody, knife bloody, chest heaving, and Dodd came over and watched dispassionately while Jock's heels drummed and his eyes turned to frogspawn.

'Ay,' said Dodd with satisfaction, wiping his sword on a clean bit of Jock's jerkin. Carey bent and did the same, feeling remote from his own hands and very tired, the way a killing rage always left him. He had never before knifed a man in an alley, though.

The Carlislers who had come to help cheered and slapped his back approvingly as he pushed his way out into Scotch Street again. He smiled back, wishing they wouldn't get in his way, picked up his hat which had fallen from his head as he ran and as he did so felt the cold draught and sting on his ribs which told him where Jock's knife had passed and ruined his brand-new (unpaid-for) black velvet suit.

That brought him back to earth a little.

Aglionby had adjourned the inquest for two hours and when the jury reconvened it was in the Mayor's own bedroom, to which Julia Coldale had been moved. The surgeon came, saw, shook his head and went himself to fetch a priest.

The jurors gathered around her along with the Coroner himself, Scrope and Carey, while Philadelphia sat by the bed and looked curiously like a small sphinx in her gravity. It turned out she was the one who had given Barnabus her knife in the confusion when Jock rode out with Mary Atkinson. Now she was holding Julia's hand. Julia's back was arched, her breath bubbled and her red curls were dark with sweat: the surgeon had said he could not get the bolt out without cutting and as it was so close to her heart, he didn't think she had a chance of living if he did.

'Do you want to give your testimony?' asked Philadelphia. 'Are you sure?'

The girl nodded, winced and began to speak breathily.

The next set of gasps for breath pained his ears to listen to them. Carey wondered remotely if there were any sort of death that didn't hurt and then put the thought from him deliberately as undoubtedly leading to madness and melancholy. It occurred to him for the first time that she was a brave lass, for all her foolishness in trying to blackmail John Leigh.

'Ay well,' she whispered. 'I'll get a dove on me grave...'

A dove was the sign of a girl who died still virgin, and it seemed some girls found the thought romantic. Philadelphia had tears in her eyes. Sniffles sounded from a couple of the jurors.

Aglionby faced the jury.

'I doubt she'll say any more, gentlemen,' he rumbled.

They took the hint and left her.

The inquest was reconvened at the market cross again, after Fenwick had come with his litter to collect Jock Burn's body. Julia Coldale had not died yet, but was sure to do so that night or the next day, depending on how strong she was.

The jury filed soberly into their benches. Aglionby declared that the inquest was reopened; Carey faced the jury feeling unutterably weary, and called Mr John Leigh.

He said nothing and would not take the oath. Carey reminded him that the penalty for failing to plead at his trial was pressing to death and then, at the Coroner's nod, began to speak.

'John Leigh wanted the house next door to his own to expand into. Unfortunately, not only had his brother-in-law Jemmy Atkinson inherited it wrongfully, as he thought, he also refused to sell it. The Chancery case, as Chancery cases will, was taking years and costing a fortune. John Leigh was having money problems in other ways and he came up with an idea which was probably inspired by seeing the thatchers working on the scaffolding round his roof.

'Mr Leigh decided to kill Jemmy Atkinson in such a way that Kate Atkinson was sure to be accused and convicted and so he and his wife would get her property. After she burned at the stake. For in fact, this is an attempt at a double murder, with his honour the Coroner and you yourselves, gentlemen, used as the weapon in the second, judicial murder.'

Carey paused and cleared his throat. As he had said to Elizabeth, he could orate if he had to: thank the Lord there was hardly any law involved here.

'At first I misunderstood. I had seen the window to the Atkinsons' bedchamber and I thought it impossible for a man to squeeze through it unless he were very slim. John Leigh is not a small man, though Jock Burn is. Was. On the other hand, Leigh couldn't trust a servant to do the killing for him without laying himself open to blackmail. Another thing you no doubt already know is that the Leighs' house is next door to the Atkinsons' and as alike as two peas. Certainly the upper windows are the same size. You can see them over there and inspect them later, if you wish.

'This morning I climbed the scaffolding on the Leighs' house and dug about in the thatch. My Sergeant had found a knife hidden there the previous afternoon.'

Dodd stepped forwards smartly and held out the knife so the jurymen could see it. Thomas Lowther took it and passed it along, and Archibald Bell rubbed his thumb on the crumbs of brown at the place where the blade met the hilt.

'We found a bloody shirt,' said Carey, gestured. Dodd took the shirt out of a small bag and handed it to Thomas Lowther. He passed it on with the combination of distaste and prurience that seemed right for a bloody shirt. Nobody argued about the identity of the stiff brown stains on it, although Captain Carleton sniffed at them sceptically.

'As you can see,' Carey continued, 'it's a gentleman's shirt, fine linen and well-stitched. There were no other clothes. At first I thought he might have put it over his clothes to protect them from the blood, but I admit I was still puzzled. Then when I saw John Leigh through his own upper window attempting to kill Julia Coldale, I kicked the shutters and glass in and tried to get through. I couldn't, my shoulders wouldn't fit. I was reduced to throwing bits of window glass at him and I don't mind telling you, gentlemen, I was very annoyed.'

The barrel-like Captain Carleton was leaned back and smiling understandingly at him.

'The only problem he had—how to make sure the shutters were open to Jemmy Atkinson's bedchamber—we have just heard how he solved it. At the cost of Julia Coldale's life, she has told us the truth of what she did that morning. And so the mystery is solved. John Leigh waited until he heard Julia opening the shutters and going down the stairs again, and then climbed out of his own window onto the scaffolding and across. There was some risk he would be seen from the street, but it was early in the morning and not light yet. He climbed in through the window, cut Jemmy Atkinson's throat, climbed out again, took off his shirt and hid it with the knife in the thatch, and then climbed back in by his own window. He could have done it in five minutes, washed and dressed and gone downstairs. Then all he had to do was sit back and wait for someone to find the body.

'He must have been worried when Andy Nixon and Mrs Atkinson conspired to move the body and blame the killing on me. In fact, they were trying to pervert the course of justice, which is in itself a crime, although I hope his honour the Coroner will be lenient with them on that score. However, in the end, he must have been sure he would gain all he wished after the Lammastide assizes, when Mrs Atkinson surely would have been convicted of petty treason and executed. Perhaps Andy Nixon would have died with her, as her accomplice, perhaps not. Evidently, he didn't care one way or the other.'

He wondered if he should mention the fact that the Atkinson children would thus be left fatherless, motherless and homeless, but he didn't. The jury could work it out for themselves. Mary herself had been allowed to cling amongst her mother's skirts, sucking her thumb and watching.

'There you have your verdict, gentlemen of the jury: Jemmy Atkinson was murdered most foully; his throat was cut by John Leigh and the reason was only so that John Leigh and his wife could eventually inherit his property as the nearest relatives of the victim. That is what you must find.'

Aglionby summed up briskly and the jurymen went up the steps into the hall in order to deliberate. A few of them went over to look at the houses in question. A short sharp argument between Thomas Lowther and Archibald Bell floated out at the windows which ended in Thomas Lowther's sullen agreement. They filed back down the steps again.

Without looking straight at his brother, Thomas Lowther delivered himself of the jury's majority verdict in a loud chant, like an old Mass priest.

'The jury finds that Jemmy Atkinson was murdered by John Leigh his brother-in-law.'

There was a scattered cheering and an approving buzz of talk from the stoutly watching public. Barnabus, Andy Nixon and Kate Atkinson were released immediately. Carey felt too wrung out to be triumphant, although he shook Barnabus's hand and congratulated him on a fine shot. The next inquest would be for Julia Coldale and Jock Burn. No doubt Jock had been paid to kill her by Mrs Leigh herself, but they could never prove it now unless Mrs Leigh confessed.

The procession formed itself again to travel back to the Castle and some of the crowd booed at John Leigh. Mrs Croser the midwife stood in his doorway to see him. He lifted his head at the muffled sound of shrieking from within, and then shook it despairingly and plodded on.

Relief and fatigue made Carey's perceptions unnaturally sharp, like glass. He had glimpsed Kate Atkinson weeping over the red marks the manacles had left on Andy Nixon's wrists and Nixon stroking her neck awkwardly as they walked. He had also seen Mary Atkinson swept up in her mother's arms and covered with kisses. Barnabus had disappeared in a hurry behind the hall and come out fastening his codpiece and looking green about the gills. John Leigh kept trying to take longer strides than his ankle chains allowed, almost pitching forwards on his nose. Philadelphia Lady Scrope was nowhere to be seen—perhaps she had slipped away to visit Julia Coldale. Carey wondered if he should go, and thought perhaps he shouldn't. It was partly cowardice: he didn't want to see a pretty girl in such suffering.

Lord, what a waste. To Jock Burn he gave no further thought, except a mild regret that the man could not be hanged.

A happy idea suddenly struck him. He had a quick word with Dodd and then strode over to where Andy Nixon was still scandalously entwined with Kate Atkinson by her own front door.

'Andy Nixon,' he said and Nixon let go and looked worried. 'I've a proposition to put to you.'

Nixon looked even more worried. 'Ay sir?' he said warily.

'I need another man for my troop of men in the garrison. Would you be interested in the place?'

'Och,' said Andy, thunderstruck. 'But d'ye not mind the trouble we put ye to, sir?'

'I'm blaming James Pennycook for that.' Carey smiled. 'I hardly think you came up with the idea, did you?'

'Nay sir. Well...'

'I doubt very much if Pennycook will be coming back south of the Border again. He'll certainly not be purveying to the garrison any more.' Why Scrope didn't have his victuals supplied by a powerful local man like Aglionby was a mystery to Carey, which he intended to put right as soon as he could. 'And so you're in need of a new master.'

In his delight at Kate's freedom and his relief at his own, Andy hadn't thought of that and his square face clouded.

'Ay, sir, you're right.'

'Well, then? I want good fighters, which you are, and you've shown yourself faithful, at least to your woman. The pay's one shilling and thruppence a day and perks, including some of what we get in fees for rescuing cattle and such. And it's steady work based in the Castle.'

'But is there not a fee for the place?' Andy asked with puzzlement.

'You can owe it.'

Andy whispered quickly to Kate and then turned back to Carey.

'I'll do it, sir.'

'Excellent. Talk to Sergeant Dodd in the morning.'

He left them wrapping themselves round each other again, and tried to suppress his burning envy of them as he hurried back to the Castle.

## THURSDAY, 6TH JULY 1592, AFTERNOON

'What happened to you?' he asked Young Hutchin.

Young Hutchin grinned. 'It was verra interesting.'

'No doubt.' Carey looked around for Barnabus, remembered he was in the Keep, waiting for Philadelphia to give him a draught of something cleansing and foul from her stillroom. He took his sword belt off and leant it against the wall, opened up the top buttons of his black velvet doublet in the approved melancholy style, so he could at last breathe properly. He gestured at the still-curtained bed.

'Have you seen the pups?' he asked Young Hutchin.

'Ay. The kennelman came and moved Buttercup and all down to the pupping kennel where she should ha' been to start with,' said Hutchin. 'But your counterpane's in a terrible state.'

Carey wandered over, looked at it, and closed the curtains again. He went restlessly to the flagon standing on one of his clothes chests and found that without Barnabus about, nobody had refilled it. Curbing the impulse to throw it at the wall, he sat down on the chest and blinked at Young Hutchin.

'Well?' he asked.

'I couldnae get through to Thirlwall Castle, sir, for my uncle had put too many men about it, and they had dogs forbye. So I slept under a bush and when she came out on the road, I went along wi' her, to the north a bit.'

'I thought you'd been caught by your relatives.'

'Nay sir,' said Hutchin, cheekily. 'Not me, sir.'

At the end of that day's travelling, Lady Widdrington and her small party had come in sight of Hexham without any incident, which had rather surprised Hutchin.

'I stopped your uncle at the Irthing ford,' Carey said shortly. 'Sent him back to Netherby with his tail between his legs.'

'Ay, I thought something like that had happened. So I rode down and joined Lady Widdrington and told her all about it and she went red but she didnae say nothing. Then she had me ride behind, and when she got to Hexham, there was the Middle March Warden and he had...'

'Sir John Forster?'

'Ay sir.'

'How is he?'

'Very old and a mite forgetful, but well enough. Anyway, he was there and so was her husband.'

'What?'

'Ay, Sir Henry Widdrington.'

Carey's mouth had gone dry. 'How did he greet her?'

Young Hutchin shrugged. 'She curtseyed, he nodded at her. They went in. A while later, I was called for and gi'en a letter for ye. Then I come back wi' the dispatch rider from Newcastle. The ordnance carts from Newcastle was there too, sir, and we passed a powerful lot of packtrains by the road. The Newcastle man said that Sir Henry was for Scotland, although he didna ken why.'

Silently Carey put out his hand and Hutchin laid the letter on it. If I don't open it, he found himself thinking, then I won't know what it says and can ignore it.

Meanwhile his fingers were breaking the seal and unfolding the paper. It was Lady Widdrington's handwriting, her spelling as wild as most women's.

*'From Lady Elizabeth Widdrington, to Sir Robert Carey.*

*Sir, I must ask you to have no more dealings with me in any shape or form and what friendship we may have had is now at an end.*

*Please honour my request as a knight of the Queen should.'*

That was simple enough. Impossible to tell whose brain had framed the words: was it Elizabeth herself, or had she written at her husband's dictation? She had made it plain enough she thought his courtship of her was foolish.

Carey looked up unseeingly. He was amazed to find he could not feel anything. Perhaps it wasn't so amazing: after a fight or a football match he often found bruises and grazes he had not felt at the time.

'Sir,' came a boy's alien voice.

'What? You still there, Young Hutchin?'

'Ay sir. She had a verbal message. She whispered it to me when she give me the letter, sir, under cover of straightening my jerkin.'

Young Hutchin shut his eyes tight and frowned. 'It was in foreign, sir. She said to tell ye, ah mow tay, Robin, ah mah bow simper.'

Carey thought hard to rearrange the sounds. *'Amo te*, Robin, *amabo semper?'* he asked.

Young Hutchin nodded vigorously. 'Ay,' he said. 'That was it. Is it French?'

'No. Latin. Please forget it, if you like Lady Widdrington.'

Young Hutchin nodded again, a mixture of cunning and an attempt at forthright honesty on his face.

Simon came back with the small beer and some pieces of ox-tongue pie. Carey had lost his appetite. He told the boys to strip the ruined counterpane off the bed and see if they could find Goodwife Biltock to get another one for him. Then he wandered unseeingly down the stairs again.

By a kind of habit, he found himself in the stable yard where the Head Groom was at evening stables with Scrope.

Carey went to Thunder's stall, went in and started picking up Thunder's feet to see how the farrier had done his work. Not bad. Not bad at all. But Thunder should go back to London. He had no use for a tournament charger here in the West March.

*Amo te*, Robin, *amabo semper*. She didn't know much Latin. Perhaps she had persuaded Young Henry to tell her the words, or a tiny bit of schooling had stuck as it had with him. She had obediently written her letter cutting off their friendship at her husband's dictation and then, being as honest as she was, she had quietly defied him. The words were curt but sufficient.

I love you, Robin, she had said, promising no more than that, risking God knew what kind of persecution, I will love you always.

# A SURFEIT OF GUNS

*To Rosie, with thanks*

# R IS FOR... EXTRAORDINARY

The number of 'R' words that come to mind when describing P.F. Chisholm's rousing Elizabethan detections is remarkable. Filled with rakish, ruthless, reckless, rapacious, rough-riding, ruffianly, rascally, reprobative, roguish, occasionally rueful rapscallions, raiders, and reivers, they are rich, ribald, rowdy, riveting, riotous, robust, rollicking, rambunctious, randy, roistering, racy, and rattling good reads. What makes them so?

It is, of course, their blend of those basic components of fiction—plot, characters, setting—plus content, all washed with the sort of prose that turns such elements into literary gold. Rare is the novel in which the reader finds each building block to be of high quality, rarer still when a real balance is achieved. In my book, the Robert Carey novels, *A Famine of Horses, A Season of Knives* and *A Surfeit of Guns* reach that plateau.

As P.F. Chisholm, *nom de plume* of author Patricia Finney, has previously noted, Carey is a real historical character whose life was itself the stuff of fiction. He's a natural to be the hero of a book, or books, that flesh out the bones of the historical record and embrace not only what we actually know of Carey, but imagine what could have been the truth of his life and character.

Elizabeth Widdrington, too, is a real woman and I think it's especially to Chisholm's credit that she gives us Elizabeth's character and behavior in a manner consistent with her time and not as rendered through the lens of today's sensibility. An Elizabethan woman would not have carelessly abandoned her marriage but endured its vicissitudes, although many took such comfort as there was along the way, nor would she have shown disrespect to her husband in public, nor been heedless of her reputation. Nor would she have risked a breach with the Queen which, in the case of a relationship with Robert, the Queen's blood kin, would have been likely. The rocky course of the Carey/Widdrington romance is, of course, the very stuff of good fiction. Interesting, too, is its unlikely nature, for Elizabeth was no beauteous maiden but a mature woman who'd acceded to an arranged marriage with her elderly husband. She had, thus, family obligation to honor along with personal and political considerations. I think Chisholm captures her dilemma movingly in the closing pages of *A Season of Knives*.

Other historical personages appear such as Philadelphia, Carey's sister, and her ineffectual husband Lord Scrope. But *A Surfeit of Guns* belongs, in great part, to that difficult monarch James VI of Scotland, son of the beheaded Mary, cousin and perhaps heir to Elizabeth, husband of Anne, and progenitor of those unlucky and ill-judging Stuart kings who ruled England and Scotland during the 17th Century. James it is who eventually gave Carey his break in life, and James it is who really rules these pages as the story moves back and forth from Carlisle to Dumfries. With James comes his court, the powerful Earl of Mar, the quarreling and scheming nobles and their henchmen, foreign agents, and the nasty boy, Lord Spynie, who has captured the wayward king's heart. With James, the role of Favorite, usually filled by female forms, went to men, some of whom, like Lord Spynie, played power games of their own.

Chisholm has a dazzling ability to plunge her readers straight into the late 16th Century, straight into the Debateable Lands, the most dangerous part of Elizabeth's kingdom, that border country so porous that blood relations took arms against each other and posses rode back and forth on legitimate hot trods and illegitimate raids. So well transported are we that any interruption becomes unwelcome and we must follow the twists and turns of the plots to the end. In *A Surfeit of Guns* we are led to Dumfries, 'the centre of gunmaking for the whole of Scotland, being placed in the area of highest demand,' and thus onto an enlarged stage.

*A Surfeit of Guns* is arguably the bleakest of the Carey stories, filled with doubts, duplicity, double dealings, and death. It is of the novels the most political, centering around the machinations of the Scottish court, and it is the most venal. While in part a police procedural, consonant with Carey's official post as a sort of Sheriff, the plot is built upon power politics and espionage. Its hook lies in armaments, in the valuable guns shipped into—and out of—the Carlisle garrison. To what purpose? the author asks, and challenges us to work out the answer.

As a plotter, Chisholm is inventive and does not repeat herself. In her third Carey novel she is, I think, more interested in character than in story. And it is somewhat dour. Let's face it, there is less to like in James and his court than in Elizabeth's, and less *joie de vivre*, less electricity. It was, for the Stuart monarch, a waiting time and a waiting game. But, in the overreaching arc of the Carey series—and I, for one, hope for many more novels as we build up to the events of 1603—it's as important to establish the anchor end in Scotland as it is the other anchor in London, though we spend much time on the grounds where Carey filled his post as Deputy Warden. Thus we need to meet up with James and firm the connection between him and Carey.

To me, the real joy of the Careys lies less in the real life figures than in the glorious secondary characters, as ruthless, charming, and complex a bunch of survivors of what Chisholm spares no pains to reveal as a harsh, unforgiving, real minimalist life, as ever you will meet. From stalwart Sergeant Dodd to the randy servant Barnabus to the unfortunate Long George and his Little family to the imp Young Hutchin, you meet them and you know them, just as you learn to wander familiarly among the Grahams and the other Border clans. You could as easily be in our American Wild West, caught up in Tombstone territory with rustlers, outlaws, hired hands, and a few guys sporting badges, the whole bunch operating under the umbrella of shifting alliances or clan loyalties—or just for the paycheck.

I've paid tribute to the characters, the setting, the plot, and the historical content of Chisholm's work. In the end, however, what makes me a True Fan and completes that sense that 'You Are THERE!' —noted by Sharon Kay Penman in her Introduction to *A Famine of Horses* and Dana Stabenow in her Introduction to *A Season of Knives*—is the language. It is through her lively dialogue and unfailingly canny sense of the Right Word that Chisholm conveys the rags and riches of the period and the in and outs of character. There is no question her research has been prodigious, though it is never flaunted nor allowed to take over the narrative. But somehow, perhaps as a consequence, she has simply stepped into a pattern of speech as into a time warp and sucked us right along with her. It is the web of language she weaves that holds us, once transported to Carey's world, and leaves us reluctant to travel back when the end of the tale is reached.

To bolster my recommendation further, let me end with a statement from a reader. 'P.F. Chisholm's strength lies in her ability to write a dialogue which is natural and not preciously "period" and she certainly seems to understand the mind of the borderer. I speak as a borderer myself, albeit from the East, not the West March. I would strongly recommend this book to lovers of both historical and mystery fiction.'

Barbara Peters
The Poisoned Pen Mystery Bookstore
poisonedpen.com
poisonedpenpress.com

# A SURFEIT OF GUNS

# FRIDAY, 7TH JULY 1592, LATE AFTERNOON

Sir Robert Carey woke up to a knock on the door, feeling sticky-mouthed and bad-tempered and uncertain what time of day it was. He was in his clothes with his doublet buttons undone, his boots by the side of the bed. Through the window the diamond mosaic of sky had greyed over. Barnabus Cooke his manservant came stumping in carrying a bowl of cold water, a towel over one arm, a leather bottle of small beer under the other.

'Afternoon, sir,' he said in his familiar adenoidal whine. 'Sergeant Dodd wants to know where you was thinking of patrolling tonight.'

Ah. Night patrol, therefore an afternoon nap.

'I haven't decided yet,' Carey answered.

He sat up and swung his legs over the side of the bed, hearing the elderly strapping creak beneath the mattress. Although the bed had once been honoured by the sleeping body of Her Majesty the Queen of Scots while she was briefly an uneasy guest in Carlisle, that was nearly thirty years before and it had had a hard life since then. He honestly thought a straw pallet on the floor might be more comfortable and certainly less noisy.

While he splashed his face with cold water and drank some of the beer, Carey gathered his thoughts and tried to wake up properly. Barnabus fastened his many buttons, helped him on with his jack. As always there was a depressing moment when the padded, double-layered leather coat, with its metal plates in between, weighed him down like original sin. Then, once it was laced and his belt buckled so the weight was evenly distributed between his shoulders and hips, his body adjusted and he no longer felt it. As armour went, it was very comfortable, much better than his tilting plate that was in pawn down in London. He had his new broadsword, the best the Dumfries armourers could produce, and Barnabus had oiled it well, though the hilt still felt rough and odd against his hand after he had strapped it on. His helmet was a fine piece, a blued-steel morion, with elaborate chasing on its peaks and curves, well padded inside. He knew it made him conspicuous, but that was the idea after all—his men needed to know where he was in a fight.

Fully dressed, he caught sight of himself in the mirror, saw the martial reflection and unconsciously smiled back at it. Barnabus knelt to put his spurs on, tutting at the state of the riding boots which Barnabus's nephew had forgotten to clean. Finally accoutred, Carey clattered down the stairs, his handguns in their case under his arm, weighing perhaps sixty pounds more than he had when he got up.

Sergeant Dodd and the men were waiting with their horses in the courtyard. Carey did a quick headcount, found they were all there and went over to ask Dodd what Long George had to say for himself.

Long George Little was the man standing next to Dodd. He was showing a pistol to him, a new one by the gleam of its powderpan, and Dodd was sighting down the barrel and squeezing the trigger.

'Dumfries work, is it?' Dodd was asking.

'Ay,' said Long George, who was actually no taller than Dodd and an inch or two shorter than Carey himself, but gave the impression of even greater height because he had long bony legs and arms.

'What did ye pay for it?'

Long George coughed. 'Twenty-five shillings, English.'

'Mphm,' said Dodd noncommittally.

'Good evening, gentlemen,' said Carey with some sarcasm. 'I'm delighted to see you, Long George. Where have you been since Wednesday?'

Long George's face was round and his beard a straggling decoration that refused to grow around his mouth but flourished all the way down his neck and into his chest hairs. The face suddenly became childlike in its innocence.

'It were family business, sir,' he said. 'One of the weans was sick and the wife thought it might be the smallpox.'

'Ah. And was it?'

'Was what, sir?'

'Was it smallpox?'

'Nay, it was chickenpox.'

Had he had that, Carey wondered, and decided he had. He remembered his mother putting him in a camomile bath to soothe the itching and cutting his nails down short.

'I might have needed you as a witness at the Atkinson inquest.'

Long George shrugged and wouldn't meet his eye. Clearly he had made himself scarce precisely in order to avoid being a witness. 'I'm here for the patrol, sir, amn't I?' he said truculently. 'That's all ye want, is it not?'

Carey gave him a considering stare. 'It will do for the present,' he said coldly. Long George gazed into space, put a helmet on, knuckled his forehead and went to find his horse.

They were a little late going out, but the watch at the city gates had waited for them. They crossed Eden Bridge and struck north and east, heading for Askerton Castle and Bewcastle beyond that.

As the sun set behind its grey blanket of cloud, and the night closed in, they slowed down, letting their horses feel their way. It was a black night, blacker than mourning velvet, the sky robbed of diamonds and the countryside full of hushed noise. Most of the cattle were still up at the shielings but the small farms announced themselves with the snoring of pigs and occasionally sheep would wander abstractedly across the path they were using. The men were quiet behind him apart from the occasional clatter of a lance against stirrup or the jingle of a bridle.

However, most of the night passed in jingling boredom. And then at last they were passing by an outpost of forest not far from the Border and Carey was about to order them to turn for home, when they heard a crashing and clattering from between the trees. The men immediately began to spread themselves along the path and tighten their helmet laces. Carey put his hand up for caution. Long George was pouring powder into the pan of his new gun. But whatever was coming was four-legged and certainly not horses...

The deer burst from the wood, tightly bunched, a group of young staggards and other rascals from what he could see of their antlers, their nostrils flaring and their white rumps flashing. They came suddenly, blindly, upon a line of men downwind of them and dodged in their panic from place to place. Long George lifted his pistol two-handed, screwed up his face thoughtfully and fired. The boom of the shot caused the deer to leap and double their speed, but one of them was turned into a still-moving fountain of blood, with most of its neck destroyed by the bullet. Gradually catching up with the disaster its legs stopped running and its body slumped into the ground, flopping about until it lay still.

'Good shot!' shouted Carey, delighted at the prospect of fresh venison. Long George grinned with pleasure and blew the remnants of powder off his pan.

Carey and Dodd dismounted, waited for the blood to stop and then inspected the beast. It was nicely fat and at least a stag, so although there was no particular honour in killing it, at least there would be good eating.

'We'll gralloch it and drain it for half an hour,' said Carey. 'The butcher can do the rest when we get it home.'

Dodd nodded. 'We're not poaching, are we?'

Carey thought for a moment. 'I don't think so, we're on English land and anyway, Long George only hit the animal by accident, isn't that right, Long George?'

'Ay, sir. Me gun went off wi'out warning, sir.'

The other men sniggered quietly.

'Exactly. And it would be a pity to waste the meat.'

Carey did not have his set of hunting knives with him, but Dodd passed him a long heavy knife with a wicked edge that was suspiciously apt to the purpose. Stepping around to the back of the beast, Carey leaned over the carcass and made the belly-cut with a flourish, thinking of the many times he had broken a beast with full ceremony to the music of drums and trumpets in front of Queen Elizabeth at one of her various courtly hunts.

'By God, he does it prettily,' one of the men remarked in a mutter to Dodd, who happened to be standing next to him. 'Will ye look at him, not a drop on him?'

'Ah've seen it done faster,' sniffed Dodd.

'Ay well, so've I, but that's with one ear out for the keeper...' He paused, cocking his head thoughtfully. Far in the distance, there was more crashing in the deer's wake through the forest.

'That's a man running,' said Dodd, swinging up onto his horse again and taking his lance back from Red Sandy. Carey looked up, stopped, wiped his hands and blade sketchily on the grass and vaulted up onto his own horse's back just as the sound of feet burst out of the undergrowth and shaped itself into the blur of a human being, head down, arms pumping. He saw them waiting in the darkness and skidded to a halt, mouth open in dismay.

Carey knew prey when he saw it; the man's oddly cut doublet was flapping open and his fine shirt ripped and stained, his hose were in tatters and his boots broken. He had pale hair plastered to his face with sweat, a flushed face, a pale beard and a square jaw.

'Hilfe, hilf mir,' he gasped. 'Freunde, helft mir...' His legs buckled and he went to his knees involuntarily, chest shuddering for air. 'Um Gottes willen.'

'He's a bastard Frenchman,' said Red Sandy excitedly, aiming his lance at the man and riding forward.

'Nay, he's that Spanish agent...' someone else shouted. Long George was reloading his pistol as fast as he could.

'*Nein, nein...*'

'Wait!' roared Carey. 'God damn your eyes, WAIT!'

In the distance, they could hear dogs giving tongue. The man heard it too, his eyes whitened, he tried to stand, but he was utterly spent and he pitched forward on his face, retching drily.

Carey dismounted and went over to the man.

'He's a French foreigner,' said Red Sandy again. 'Did ye no' hear him speaking French, sir? Can I get his tail for a trophy, sir?'

'It wasn't French,' said Carey. 'It was something else, High or Low Dutch, I think. He's a German.'

Red Sandy subsided, mystified at the thought of a foreigner who wasn't French.

'Like one of them foreign miners down by Derwentwater,' put in Sim's Will Croser helpfully. 'Ye mind 'em, Red Sandy? They speak like that, ay, with all splutters and coughs and the like.'

'Qu'est vostre nom, monsieur? Parlez-vous français?' Carey asked as he approached the man who was lifting himself feebly on his elbows. Behind him he could hear the men muttering between themselves. They were arguing over whether the German miners had tails like Frenchmen.

'Hans Schmidt, mein Herr, aus Augsburg. Ich spreche ein bischen...je parle un peu de Français.'

'Well, that's French, any road,' said Dodd dubiously as the hounds in the distance gave tongue again, musical and haunting. The German winced at the sound and tried to climb to his feet, but his knees gave way. His fear was pitiful.

'I know, Sergeant,' said Carey, coming to a decision. 'Have the men move off the road into the undergrowth over there, spread them out. Not much we can do about the venison seeing they've got dogs, so leave it. Red Sandy, you set the men and don't move until we know what's coming after this man. If I shoot, hit them hard. Dodd, you stay here with me.'

Dodd loosened his sword, took a grip on his lance and slouched down in the saddle, sighing in a martyred fashion as he stayed out in plain view to back up his Deputy Warden. Heart beating hard, Carey could hear the other horses now, crashing through the undergrowth behind the hounds.

The German, Hans Schmidt, had got to his feet, swaying with exhaustion, jabbering away desperately in High Dutch, not one word of which Carey could make out. He could talk to a whore or an innkeeper in Low Dutch, but that was the size of his ability. French came easier to him.

'Nicht verstehe,' he said. 'Je ne comprends pas. Plus lentement, s'il vous plaist.'

For answer the man put his face in his hands and moaned. There was no time left, the hoofbeats were too close. The German began wobbling away, across the field. Carey shook his head, remounted his horse and pulled both his dags out of their cases. They were already shotted and he wound them up ready to fire, but from the sound of it two shots would not be enough.

'Off, off. Allez!' shouted Carey, riding over to protect his kill, looking around for the huntsmen.

For a moment it was hounds only, the horses heralded by sound. Then, like the elven-folk from a poet's imagination, they cantered out of the tree shadows, three, four, eight, twelve of them, and more behind, some carrying torches, their white leather jacks pristine and lace complicating the hems of their falling bands and cuffs, flowing beards and glittering jewelled fingers, with the plump flash of brocade above their long boots. Carey was surprised: he had expected one of the Border headmen and his kin, like Scott of Buccleuch or Kerr of Ferniehurst, perhaps even Lord Maxwell. Certainly not these fine courtiers.

The Master of the Hunt whipped the hounds off, and the highest-ranking among them rode forward on a horse far too good for the rough ground. Carey recognised him immediately.

'My lord Earl of Mar,' he said in astonishment, looking from the dishevelled panting German to the King of Scotland's most trusted advisor.

'Eh?' said the earl, squinting through the mirk. 'Who's that?'

'Sir Robert Carey, my lord, Deputy Warden of the English West March.'

'Eh? Speak oot, mon.'

Carey repeated himself in Scots. Behind him he could feel Dodd sitting quiet and watchful, his lance pointed upwards, managing expertly to project a combination of relaxation and menace without actually doing anything.

The Earl of Mar was glaring at Carey's dags. Rather pointedly, he did not put them away. Out of the corners of his eyes he could see a further six or eight riders milling about in the forest, rounding up stray dogs, while three of the other huntsmen tried to reassert discipline over the hounds who felt they had a right to the deer's innards after their run.

'What are ye doing here?'

'Well, my lord, I could ask you the same question since we're on English land.'

'We're on a lawful hot trod.'

'Oh?' said Carey neutrally.

'Ay, we are. My lord Spynie, where the devil's that bit of turf?'

A young round-faced man with a velvet bonnet tipped over his ear rode forward. Some crumbs of turf still stuck to the point of his lance, and he was frowning at it in irritation. He was a handsome young man, of whom Carey had heard but had never met, known variously as Alexander Lindsay, Lord Spynie, King James's favourite and the King's bloody bum-boy.

'I see,' said Carey, relaxing slightly and putting his dags away but leaving the case open. 'Well, my lord, in that case, as Deputy Warden of the English West March, I am a proper person for you to tell the cause of the trod to, and if necessary, I will render you what assistance I can.'

The Earl of Mar glared at him. Two of his men had dismounted and were lifting the German to his feet, not very gently.

Knowing he was well within his rights, but feeling a bit of oil might be appropriate in the circumstances, Carey bowed lavishly in the saddle and added, 'If my lord will be so very kind.'

The Earl of Mar harrumphed. He either ignored or did not understand the edge to Carey's obsequity. 'Ay, well,' he said. 'Ye've already assisted me, by stopping this traitor here, so I'll thank ye kindly and we'll be awa' again.'

'Ich bin nicht...' the German began yelling. His arm slipped out of one of his helpers' hands, he swung a wild punch at the other which connected by sheer chance. Hands plucking at the empty scabbard on his belt, he shouldered past another would-be helper, running at a desperate stagger for the forest, only to be knocked off his feet by a kick in the face from one of the other horsemen. He was hefted up again and his hands tied briskly behind him. Carey had tensed when he made his break, every instinct telling him to help one against so many, but intelligence and self-preservation ordering him not to be such a fool. He had eight men—the Scottish courtiers had at least thirty plus the law of the Borders on their side. And the man was a foreigner.

'I see,' he said, looking away as the German was hauled to a riderless horse, still half-stunned and bleeding from the nose, and slung across it like dead game. 'May I ask what form his treason took? Is there anything likely to be a threat to Her Majesty the Queen?'

'Nay,' said the Earl of Mar, backing his horse with a rather showy curvette. ''Tis a private matter between yon loon and our King. We'll be off now.'

With great difficulty the hounds were whipped off the stag, some of them still trailing bits of entrail from their mouths as they lolloped unwillingly away. The whole cavalcade plunged back into the forest, heading north again, with the unfortunate German occasionally visible, like a feebly struggling sack of flour across his horse's back. Cheekily the Earl of Mar winded his horn as they disappeared from sight.

\* \* \*

Dodd said nothing as Carey dismounted and went back to the stag to see what could be salvaged. The stag was quite a bit the worse for wear but much of the gralloching had been done. The skin would not be useable though. The men reappeared and, unasked, hung the stag up on a tree branch by its back legs to drain.

They waited by the tree while the most part of the deer's remaining blood trickled out. With suspicious efficiency the men constructed a travois out of hazel branches and argued quietly over whose horse should pull it.

Dodd was still saying nothing, and cocking his head northwards occasionally with an abstracted expression.

'What's the problem, Sergeant?' asked Carey.

Dodd coughed. 'It's the trod, sir.'

'The Earl of Mar's taken his captive back into Scotland by now, I should think.'

'Ay, sir.'

'So?'

'Sir, did ye never follow on behind a hot trod so ye could claim the beasts ye took were part of it?'

'You mean there might be a Scots raiding party following the Earl of Mar's trail so they can claim they're legally coming into England as part of the pursuit?' Carey asked carefully.

Dodd clearly wondered why he was belabouring something so obvious. 'Ay, after about an hour or so,' he agreed. 'To let the... excitement die down, see.'

'I do see, Sergeant. Do you think they'll come by here?'

Dodd's wooden expression told Carey he had asked another stupid question.

'Only, ye can mix the trails about, sir.'

'Fine. What would you suggest, Sergeant?'

Dodd's suggestion took shape: they took the deer carcass down from the tree and lashed it to its travois, which Long George and Croser hauled into the branches of an oak to keep it away from foxes.

'We can't actually stop them coming south,' Carey said while the others cleared the ground of their own tracks. 'They haven't committed any crime and they're following a lawful hot trod, so...'

Dodd and his brother Red Sandy exchanged patient glances.

'No, see, sir, if we stop them before they've lifted aught, then we'll get nae fee for it, will we? We'll stop 'em after.'

'I see. Very interesting. Do you ever...*arrange* for raids, so you can stop them and get the fees for them?'

'Ay, sir,' said Sandy. 'Why, last year the Sergeant and...'

Dodd coughed loudly.

'...ay, well, Lowther's done it,' his brother finished, managing to look virtuously indignant. 'But *we* wouldnae, would we, Sergeant?'

Even in the darkness, Dodd's glare could have withered a field of wheat.

'One of us must track them on foot,' he said judiciously. 'Sandy's the best man for that job, seeing he's the fastest runner and he knows the land.' Red Sandy made a wry face. 'Then when he's seen them find the beasts they're after, he comes back to us and we stop them on their way home, red-handed.'

'What if they take a different route?'

Dodd rubbed his chin with his thumb. 'They might,' he allowed. 'But I doubt it. They'll keep to the trail the Earl of Mar made with a' his fine men to confuse us from following.'

Carey nodded.

'I rely on your judgement, Sergeant. Shall we take cover now?'

'Ay, sir, it'd be best. Though it might be a long wait.'

Dodd and Red Sandy had a quiet conversation as all of them carefully pushed in among the undergrowth. Carey watched in fascination as each man of his troop then took his horse's head and forced the animal to lie down with great rustling surges in the bracken and leaves. Long George swore because he'd found a patch of nettles, a couple of the horses snorted and resisted. Carey found that the right pressure on his own animal's neck and head laid the rough body down with a great lurch and grunting and splaying of legs. They were completely out of sight. He copied Dodd, lying down as well, with one arm over his horse's head, the other arm supporting his own head.

Red Sandy was nowhere to be seen. Carey realised then that he was already outside the woodland, where it met the rough pasture of the hillside, and inspecting them all for concealment.

'There's a man wi' a shiny helmet moving,' Red Sandy said accusingly. Carey turned his head to see who was revealing them. 'Ay, there he goes again.'

Luckily the dark hid his flush as he realised that he was the guilty man. Dodd reached over with some leafy twigs and stuck them in Carey's plume-tube.

'Tha's better,' called Red Sandy. 'Tell the silly get to stay still, Henry.'

Dodd grunted softly and didn't look at Carey. Red Sandy hardly rustled the bushes as he took cover himself.

The silence clamped down around them, like the forest and the night. Not even the horses moved, though Carey could see the wide eyes of his own mount, alert but very well trained and not moving a hoof.

Time passed. The damp coolness of the earth began working its way through the layers of leather and cloth to his stomach, the warmth of a sultry summer night was weight on his back. Little trickles of sweat began seeking water's own level down the muscles of his shoulders. There was an ants' nest under his knee. Perhaps the ants wouldn't mind.

Strain his ears though he might, he could hear absolutely nothing of the eight other men hiding only a few feet away from him. Not a snort, not a rustle. He could swear they were even breathing quieter than him.

The back of his head was itching where the leather padding of his helmet was making his scalp sweat. Also he was convinced there were ants running up his legs. Also he had a cramp starting in one foot. Where the hell were these theoretical raiders?

There was a loud rustling and crunching sound. For a moment Carey wondered which idiot could be making it, when he saw a small bundle of spines wander into his field of vision. It stopped short, stared at him out of little black eyes. He stared back. Never before in his life had he been nose to nose with a hedgehog, though he had once eaten one, baked in clay.

The hedgehog snuffled out a slug and began eating it noisily with every sign of enjoyment. Carey was irresistibly reminded of one of the Queen's councillors eating a bag pudding and had to swallow hard not to laugh. He swallowed too loudly. Disdainfully, the hedgehog finished the slug and trundled off into the leaves like a small battering ram.

The cramp in his foot was getting worse. And the ants were exploring dangerously high up his thigh. And he desperately wanted to scratch his scalp. Where were the raiders?

Without moving his head, Carey looked for Dodd. Between the leaves the Sergeant seemed quite at ease, his long limbs sprawled and relaxed, peering over his horse's neck. He wasn't like a statue, more along the lines of a bolster on a bed. Blast him.

Nothing happened. Carey wondered what a German from Augsburg was doing in the Scottish Borders and why King James wanted him and what for: he wove several wonderful webs of possibility, but the facts would have to wait until he got back to Carlisle and even then he might never know unless he went into Scotland. The ants seemed to be excited about the discovery of his boot-top. Perhaps they were planning a new nest. Would they have time to build it? Probably the itch in his hair was a louse. Perhaps the ants would form an alliance with whatever other vermin he had picked up in Carlisle...

He thought of the Latin poem he had recited for her a few days before, one of the muckier ones by Catullus that every schoolboy found easy to remember.

His tutor had translated it, disapprovingly, 'Give me a thousand kisses, then a hundred, then another thousand...' It was pleasant to imagine kissing Elizabeth Widdrington, breaking through all her honourable propriety, her entirely misguided faithfulness to her elderly husband, lifting her skirts and petticoat and the hoops of her farthingale and her smock and...

No, it wasn't only his heartbeat. Hooves pointed the metre:

soft unshod hooves on the turf. Carey peered through leaves cautiously and saw horses pass like shadows nearby. There was a pause and another shadow departed, on foot, loping like a wolf in their tracks.

'Sir!' That was Dodd's scandalised hiss. 'Sir, wake up!'

'I wasn't asleep,' he hissed back quickly. 'I was thinking.'

'Oh aye. Well, they've come and gone whilst ye was thinking and Red Sandy's gone off after them. Ye can let your hobby up to stamp about a bit now.'

Knowing he was bright red and still hindered by the effects of thinking about Elizabeth, not to mention the cramp in his instep, Carey staggered to his feet. The horse lurched up and shook out its mane, Carey brushed astonished ants off his boots and got bitten half a dozen times.

They stayed in the bushes, for what seemed like another hour while Carey tried to keep his mind on his job and off his fantasies. Girls he had known at Court flitted irritatingly to and fro before his mind's eye—he surely was in desperate need of a woman. Sorrel nuzzled at him with his broad low-bred nose, and Carey patted him absently.

At last they heard pelting feet, a single man, sprinting down the hill towards them. Dodd cocked his head, led his horse out of the bushes.

Red Sandy himself arrived, breathing hard.

'Bastard Elliots, about seven of them, all mounted,' he whispered triumphantly. 'Wee Colin Elliot's wi' them. They've taken twelve sheep off one of the Routledges an' they're on their way.'

In the distance the sound of protesting baas floated to them, and horses.

'Keep the light hidden,' Carey said and got a protesting 'Ah know that, sir.'

His heart settling to a steady fast thumping, Carey came up close to Dodd.

'This wasn't done by any arrangement, was it?'

'With Elliots, sir?' Dodd was scandalised and Carey remembered that the Sergeant's surname had a fifty-year-old blood-feud running with the Elliots.

'No, obviously not. Well then, let's see if we can catch a few to hang.'

Dodd nodded dourly. Clearly, taking the trouble to capture Elliots was not his highest priority. Carey grinned at him, the prospect of a fight raising his spirits as always.

'One or two will do,' he amended.

Was that the faintest flicker of an answering smile at the edge of Dodd's mouth? Probably not.

The sheep arrived first, milling about confusedly and baaing. Dodd and he rode between them, straight at the reivers, while the rest came around from both sides of the flock. For a moment there was confused shouting; the reivers weren't sure what was happening: Carey fired both his dags, missed both times. A couple of arrows whipped into the ground, Sim's Will rode past with his lance in rest and his horse tripped over a sheep.

'A Tynedale, a Tynedale, Out, Out!' roared Dodd happily, barrelling lance first at the widest mounted shadow.

Carey hauled his sword out, felt rather than saw something coming at him through the night, turned his horse and struck sideways. The sword went into something, there was a splash of hot blood and the blade stuck. He twisted and wrenched it out. Then a horse cantered past on his other side, its rider jumped onto his back and hauled him to the ground, giving him a headful of spinning lights and a nasty twinge from the ribs he had cracked two weeks before. A snarling face was lit up briefly by a bright red flash; dimly somewhere in the distance he heard a very loud bang and a sound of shrieking, but he was too busy to wonder who had been hit.

He elbowed his enemy in the face while neither of them had any nightsight, rolled to loosen the man's grip and brought his sword hilt down on the white patch of face he could just see under the helmet. He tried to get to his feet, there was a blow on his side, the man was trying to grapple his neck, he managed to pull his dagger free with his left hand as he twisted away and stabbed under the man's arm, heard the grating of metal and a gasp. This time he could get his legs under him, he raised his broadsword up and swung down, there was a satisfying meaty thunk and the man's head came off. He hopped backwards quickly to be away from the blood.

Somebody still mounted came riding towards him with a lance, black shadow on a bigger shadow, the shadow of a lance. Carey's world focused down to its point and time slowed. He waited until the last possible minute, then threw himself sideways into the horse's path. The hobby reared, frightened of the movement, one of the hooves caught him a glancing blow on the helmet, he caught the nearest stirrup, reached up, hefted the man out of the saddle and onto the ground. They both tangled in the lance-haft and fell down together and just as Carey got on top of the man, and was preparing to stab him lefthanded in the throat, he realised it was Sim's Will Croser.

For a moment he simply knelt there stupidly as his sight cleared. Then he got up.

'Are you hurt?' he demanded.

'Nay,' said Sim's Will. 'Sorry, sir, Ah mistook ye.'

Both of them were on their feet. Carey picked his sword off the turf, looking around for enemies but none was left. Hooves thudded off in the distance. He wiped his blade down with handfuls of grass and sheathed it. The body of the man Carey had killed was still bleeding into the ground, four horses were trotting around shaking their heads. Further off the shrieking was fading to gasps. Carey went over to the source of the sounds where two others of his men were standing by helplessly. Dodd cantered up and dismounted.

'They've run,' he snarled. 'We got two of them, I think, but it seems my brother canna count. There were at least ten. And Long George is hurt bad.'

That was an understatement. Long George Little was kneeling on the ground, hunched over and making short gasping moans. He looked up at Carey like a wounded dog, his face spattered with black mud. With a lurch under his breastbone of sympathy, Carey saw George was cradling the rags of his right hand against his chest. All the fingers were gone, the thumb hanging by a piece of flesh with the splintered bone sticking out of the meat. Long George had his other hand gripped round the wrist, trying to slow his bleeding.

'Anybody else hurt?' Carey asked.

'Nay,' they all answered.

'Who's got the bandages?'

All of them shrugged. Carey suppressed a sigh. 'There's a dead man over there,' he snapped, pointing. 'Go and cut long strips from his shirt.'

Red Sandy trotted off with his dagger and came back a few minutes later with some strips of grey canvas in his hand. Carey tied up what was left of Long George's hand and made a tourniquet with the rest of the strips. Long George gasped and whimpered as he did it, but managed to hold still with his eyes shut, while Dodd patted his shoulder. A trickle of blood came from his mouth.

'Well, we rescued the sheep,' said Red Sandy brightly. 'That's something.'

'Thank you, Red Sandy,' said Carey repressively. 'Can you ride your horse, Long George?'

'Ay, sir, if ye give me a leg up,' whispered George.

Red Sandy and Dodd helped him over to his horse, lifted him on, while the rest caught the other loose horses and linked them together. Long George was already starting to shiver, something Carey had seen before: when large quantities of the sanguine humour were lost, a Jewish Court physician had told him once, then the furnace of the heart began to cool and might cool to death. Warmth and wine were a good answer, but they could give him neither until they got to Carlisle.

Carey rode up close to the shaking Long George. His face was badly hurt too, he realised now: what he had taken for mud on the right side of it was a mess of cuts and burns that had laid his face open to the gleaming white bone.

'Can you ride as far as Carlisle?'

'Nay, sir, take me home. My farm's by the Wall, not far fra Lanercost.'

'Of course. Red Sandy, do you know where?'

'I know,' he said sombrely.

'Good. Red Sandy, you take the Elliots' horses and help Long George get to his home.'

'Ah wantae go home, sir.' George didn't seem able to register anything except his injury. Tears were running down his face as he spoke.

'Of course you do.'

'Only, there'll be the harvest to get in and all...'

'Don't worry about it. Here.' Carey found his flask of mixed wine and water and helped Long George to drink it. He choked and his teeth rattled on the bottlemouth. 'Red Sandy, a word with you.'

'Ay, sir.'

Carey drew him a little aside. 'If his wife's got her hands full with sick children, stay and help. When it's getting on for morning, take the horses into Carlisle Castle, find the surgeon and send him back to George's place. Tell him I'll pay his fee.'

Red Sandy looked alarmed at that but only nodded.

'You're in charge.'

Something very cynical crossed Red Sandy's face and disappeared, though he nodded again.

'Ay, sir. Dinna be concerned, I'll see him right. I'll bring my own wife to nurse him if need be.'

'Good man.'

They rode off at a sedate pace southwards. Carey noted that the other men were letting the deer down from its tree. Dodd had seen to the rounding up of the sheep and, no doubt, the stripping of the two dead bodies. Carey had no intention of burying them: let Wee Colin Elliot see to it, if he wanted.

## SATURDAY, 8TH JULY 1592, EARLY MORNING

It was an enraging business, taking the sheep back to the Routledge farm they had been raided from. Carey was an innocent about sheep and was astonished at how stupid they were, wiry and rough-coated creatures though these were, in contrast to the smug rotund animals that milled their way through London to Smithfield market every week. Dodd and the others worked around them making odd yipping and barking noises, like sheepdogs, and the whole process took hours. It was past dawn when the sheep poured over another hill and began baaing excitedly at the smell of home and at last moved sensibly in a flock in one direction.

The farmer, who owned his own small rough two-storey peletower, already had a group of men around him, all talking excitedly, while the women saddled the horses.

Carey, who had left the experts to their business, said to Dodd, 'Looks like we're just in time to stop a reprisal raid.'

'Ay,' grunted Dodd. 'It's a pity.'

'Not if you have to deal with the resulting paperwork, it isn't. This is simpler.'

It was, but not much. Jock Routledge seemed very offended that Carey had caught his sheep for him, no doubt because he had been planning to lift a few extra when he retrieved his own from the Elliots. He was also scandalised at the thought of paying the Wardenry fee.

'Ye canna take one sheep in twelve, ye'll ruin me,' he shouted.

'I can in fact take one sheep for every ten, so you owe me an extra lamb,' Carey said. 'I might remit the lamb if I get my rights quickly.'

'Oh ay, yer rights,' sneered Routledge. 'Why did ye not stop them at the Border then, eh? Dinnae trouble to tell me, I know well enough. Well, ye'll not...'

'Sir,' called Dodd from a few paces away. Carey looked round and saw he was slouching on his horse which was eating its way methodically through the pea-vines of a vegetable garden. In his hand was a lit torch. 'Will I fire the thatch?'

Carey held up his hand in acknowledgement.

'The fat four-year ewe, ay, sir,' said Sim's Will riding over stolidly and nipping a nearby animal from the herd, although not the one Carey had pointed to. It bleated piteously at being separated from its mates.

'Ye bastard,' growled Jock Routledge. Carey heard a crackling and saw that there were flames licking through the thatch of the house. He glared at Dodd who looked blankly back at him and moved away from the roof he had just set fire to. Luckily it was still too damp to burn well.

Carey growled and turned his horse, led his men away from the farmstead, followed by shouts of anger and the hissing of water on the flames.

As they continued south, following the course of the Eden towards Carlisle, Carey rode beside Dodd.

'Sergeant, why did you fire their thatch before I asked you to?'

Dodd blinked at him. 'I thought that was what ye wanted.'

'I was trying to get what I wanted without burning first.'

Dodd was a picture of blank incomprehension. 'Whatever for, sir?' he asked. 'He's only Jock Routledge. He pays blackrent to everybody, he might as well pay a bit to you.'

'That was our fee for the night's work.'

'Ay, sir, like I said. And he'll be more civil next time.'

Carey growled but decided not to pursue the matter. While he rode he examined his side cautiously and found that something must have hit him there. He had a mark on his jack the width of his hand, but the metal plates inside had turned the blow. Unfortunately that was just where the knife slash was and from the tenderness he thought it was bleeding. It was only shallow, but it was scabbing into the bandages Philadelphia had wrapped round it and it pulled whenever he turned.

Their fee was unwilling to be taken from kith and kin and was as much trouble to drive as the full twelve had been. It was well into the morning before they came to Long George's small farm. As expected, Red Sandy was gone but the barber-surgeon's pony was cropping the grass outside. Four children were sitting in a row on the wall, and not one of them had any kind of rash or fever. The three boys were muttering together, and the littlest, a fair-haired girl, had her hands clamped tight over her ears.

'Now then, Cuddy,' called Dodd as they rode up.

'Good morning, Sergeant,' said the eldest boy, politely, sliding down off the wall. His breeches were filthy and his feet were bare, his shirt had a long rip in it and his cap was over one ear. 'Who's that?'

'The new Deputy Warden,' said Dodd sternly. 'So mind your manners.'

Cuddy pulled his cap off and made something of a bow.

A strangulated howl broke from the farmhouse. The little girl winced, hunched and stuck her fingers deeper in her ears. Her eyes were red from crying.

'They're cutting me dad's arm off,' said Cuddy matter-of-factly.

'Will it grow back?' asked the youngest boy, fascinated.

The howling rose to a shriek, bubbled down again. Cuddy unwillingly stole a glance over his shoulder, looked back at Carey who was staring at the farmhouse, waiting.

Another scream which at last faded down to a sequence of gasps.

'It's over now,' he said, mostly to the little girl.

She shook her head, screwed up her face and dug her fingers in deeper. Her bare feet under her muddy homespun kirtle twisted together.

All of them listened but there was no more noise.

'How did ye know, sir?' asked Cuddy.

Carey coughed, looked at the ground. Somehow he felt the boy should know, that imagination would be worse than the facts.

'The first cry is when the surgeon begins to cut. Then you can't get your breath for a bit, but just as he finishes you can get out another yell, and then the final one is when they put pitch on the end.'

'Oh,' said the boy, inspecting him for missing limbs. 'Ye've watched before then?'

'Yes,' said Carey.

'Who was it? Did he live?'

'Oh yes. He's got a hook instead of a hand now.'

'Will it no' grow back?' asked the smallest boy anxiously. 'Will it no' get better again?'

'Ye're soft,' sneered the middle boy. 'It's no' like a cut.'

'It will get better, but it won't grow again,' Carey explained. The little girl had taken one finger out of her ear and was blinking at him with the tears still wet on her cheeks. 'He should be well enough by harvest time, there's no need to cry.'

'If he doesnae die of the rot,' said Cuddy brutally.

The girl nodded. 'Ay, that's what me mam said.'

'Anyway,' Cuddy added, 'she's only crying because mam wouldna let her watch.'

'Me mam said it's your fault, if ye're the Deputy,' accused the middle boy.

'Call him sir,' snarled Dodd.

'Is it yer fault, *sir*?'

Carey took a deep breath and began to stride to the house.

'Nay, ye soft bairns,' Dodd said. 'It were the Elliots, that's who we were fighting.'

Cuddy nodded fiercely. 'When I'm big enough I'll find the man that did it and cut his hand off.'

'That's the spirit lad,' said Dodd approvingly.

\* \* \*

Long George's farmhouse was one of those built quickly after a raid, out of wattle and daub, with turves for a roof and pounded dirt bound with oxblood and eggwhite for a floor. George was lying in a corner on a straw pallet covered over with bracken, gasping for breath and moaning. One man who looked like his brother and another older one who seemed to be his father, were standing next to him talking in low voices, while Long George's wife tended the fire on the hearth in the middle of the floor to keep the broth boiling. Smoke shimmered upwards into the hooded hole in the roof. She stood up and wiped her hands on her apron and blinked at Carey as he stood hesitating in the doorway, his morion making a monster out of him.

The father stepped forward protectively, while Long George's brother moved unobtrusively for an axe hanging on the wall.

'Who're ye?'

'I'm the Deputy Warden.'

There was a sequence of grunts from the men and a sniff from the wife. Carey saw that the barber-surgeon was squatting beside his patient, tending the stump. Finally he wrapped the remains of George's hand in a bloody cloth and rinsed his arms in water from one of the three buckets. George's tightly bandaged stump was partly hidden by a cage of withies that the surgeon had bound around it. It lay stiffly inert beside George, not seeming to be part of him.

'Did ye kill the man that did it?' demanded George's father with his eyes narrowed. 'What family was he, sir?'

'I killed one Elliot myself, I don't know who killed the other.'

'Did ye not hang the rest?'

'They escaped.'

George's brother spat eloquently into the bucket of blood by the bed. The surgeon stood up, nodded to Carey, handed the gory package to George's wife.

'Bury that with a live rat tied to it to draw out any morbidus,' he prescribed reassuringly. 'Give him as much to drink of small beer as he'll take but no food till tomorrow and I'll come the day after to see to him. My fee...'

Carey caught the man's eye and shook his head. The man looked puzzled, then caught on, and nodded happily, no doubt tripling his fee on the instant. He began wiping, oiling and packing his tools away in his leather satchel, whistling between his teeth.

Long George's family stared at him and Carey went over to the bed, squatted down beside it. Carey had visited wounded men of his before; he knew there was not much he could say that would make anything better, but he was very curious about the cause of Long George's maiming.

'Long George,' he said softly. 'Can you hear me?'

'Ay, Courtier.' The voice was down to a croak and Long George's face had the grey inward-turned look of someone in too much pain to think of anything else. He was panting softly like an overheated hound. It was a pity he had been too tough to faint while the surgeon did his work.

'I'm sorry to see you like this, Long George,' Carey said inadequately.

'Ay.' Long George tried to lick his grey lips. 'What about ma place?'

For a moment, Carey was nonplussed.

'Ah canna fight now, see ye.'

'Oh for God's sake, don't worry about it. I'll look into a pension for you.'

'Ay.' Long George sounded unconvinced.

'What happened to your new pistol?'

A long long pause for thought. 'I dinna ken.'

'Did it blow up in your hand? Is that what happened?'

One of the men behind him sucked in a breath suddenly, but said nothing.

Another long pause. 'Ay. Must've.'

'Did you load it twice?'

Long George couldn't understand this, the unbandaged bits of his face drew together in a puzzled frown.

'Why would he do that?' demanded his father. 'He wouldnae waste the powder.'

'It might happen, in the excitement.'

'Nay,' whispered Long George. 'Once.'

Carey sighed. 'Where did you get the pistol?'

No answer.

'He canna talk,' said the woman sharply. 'He's sick and hurt, sir. Can ye no' wait till he's better?'

Carey straightened up, nearly hitting his head on a roofbeam, and turned to her.

'Do you know where Long George got his pistol, goodwife?' he asked.

Her thin lips tightened and she folded her arms. 'Nay, sir, it's nae business of mine.'

'Or either of you?' Both the other men shook their heads, faces impenetrably blank.

Carey sighed again. Almost certainly the pistol was stolen goods from somewhere and completely untraceable now it was in bits on the Scottish border. Trying to swallow the coughing caused by woodsmoke and a foul mosaic of other smells, Carey moved to the doorway, bent ready to duck under the half-tanned cowhide they had pegged up out of the way so that the surgeon could see to cut.

On an afterthought he felt in his belt pouch and found a couple of shillings which he put into the hard dirty hand of Goodwife Little. From the smell of it, the pot on the fire had nothing in it except oatmeal.

'I'll ask the surgeon if he has any laudanum,' he said. 'If he hasn't, I'll talk to my sister about it.'

Oppressed by the hostility of their stares and the smells of blood and sickness in the little hut, Carey went out to where the surgeon was waiting and told him to come for his fee to the castle in Carlisle, and come to him personally. The surgeon did not carry laudanum, since that was verra expensive, and an apothecary's trade foreby. Carey returned to Dodd, mounted and they continued wearily back to Carlisle. Behind them the children stood in a hesitant row outside their hut, arguing over whether they should ask to be let back in again.

\* \* \*

They went into Carlisle Castle by the sally-port in the north-east wall and led their horses between the buttery and the Queen Mary Tower to the castle yard which was bare save for two empty wagons parked in the corner. Carey handed Sorrel's bridle to Red Sandy and told Dodd to see to the horses and put their rebellious fee in the pen by the kitchens and then try and make sure all of them got some sleep and food before evening. There was no chance any of his men would go prudently to bed early that night, when the taverns would be full of their friends and relatives come in for the Sunday muster. In the meantime, if he could get his report to Lord Burghley written and ciphered quickly he might catch the regular Newcastle courier before he left at noon.

He climbed the stairs to his chambers in the Queen Mary Tower, found nobody there at all. Damn it, where were the two servants he paid exorbitantly to look after him? Feeling hard done by, he stripped off his filthy helmet and jack and left them on the stand. He opened his doublet buttons to take the pressure off his side, then answered the heavy door himself to a timid knock.

Surgeon's fee paid, he decided he could stay awake until the evening. Sleeping during the day always made him feel frowsty and ill-tempered, and he was surprised to find himself so soggy and weary after only one night's lost sleep. He stamped into his office, rubbing his itchy face, his head aching but the memory of the night's doings clear. One of the many things he had learned when he attended Sir Francis Walsingham on an embassy to

Scotland in the early eighties had been the vital importance of timeliness in intelligence. Burghley was not the spymaster that Sir Francis had been, but he needed to know about James VI's mysterious German as soon as possible—which meant by Tuesday, with luck. Carey took a sheet of paper, dipped his pen and began to write, hoping that what he was writing was reasonably comprehensible.

An hour later Philadelphia came hurrying up the stairs, knocked and entered her brother's bedchamber and found it empty. She heard snoring from the office, went through and found Carey with his head on his arms fast asleep at his desk.

'Oh, for goodness' sake,' she sniffed, and shook his shoulder gently. 'Robin, if that's a letter to Lord Burghley, you'll drool on it and smear the ink...'

Robin grunted. Philly saw his doublet was open, pulled it back and saw blood on his shirt. Her lips tightened.

Moments later she was in the castle courtyard, sending every available boy scurrying to find Barnabus. The small ferret-faced London servant eventually arrived looking hungover and even uglier than usual.

'Good day, Barnabus,' she said with freezing civility. 'Did you have a pleasant evening?'

'Er...' said Barnabus.

'I'm delighted to hear it. Are you free to do your job now?'

'I didn't know 'e was...'

'When I want to hear your excuses, I'll ask for them. Now get up there and help me put your master to bed, you lazy, idle, good-for-nothing...'

'What's wrong with him?' muttered Barnabus resentfully as they climbed the stairs. ''E drunk then...?'

A tremendous backhanded buffet over his ears from Philadelphia almost knocked him over. Barnabus shook his ringing head and blinked at her in astonishment. Seeing her fury, and remembering whose sister she was, he decided not to say the various things he thought of, and carried on up the stairs.

Carey was extremely unwilling to be woken, but finally came groaning to consciousness and let his doublet and shirt be taken off him so that Philadelphia could attack the reopened cut with rosewater, aqua vitae and hot water. She peeled the bandages off, making him wince.

'God damn it, Philly...'

'Don't swear, and hold still. You've another bad lump on your head, what did that?'

Carey thought for a moment. 'Sim's Will Croser's horse kicked me,' he said. 'My helmet's dented.'

'I'm not surprised. What was he thinking of?'

Carey blinked and said with dignity, 'Insofar as Sim's Will is capable of thought, I should think he was thinking I was an Elliot.'

'Hmf. I wish you wouldn't get into fights.'

Carey began laughing. 'Philadelphia, my sweet, it's my job.'

'Hah! Hold still while I...'

'Ouch!'

'I told you to hold still. Barnabus, where are you going?'

'I was only getting a fresh shirt from the laundry.'

'Bring bandages and the St John's wort ointment from the stillroom and small beer and some bread and cheese too.'

'I'm not hungry, Philly.' She bit her lip worriedly and felt his forehead, her gesture exactly like their mother. 'No, I'm not sickening. I'm not as delicate as you think me. It's Long George. He had to have his right hand cut off this morning. His pistol exploded and took most of the fingers from it.'

'I don't see what Long George's hand has got to do with you not eating,' said Philly, with deliberate obtuseness, getting out her hussif from the pouch hanging on her belt and cutting a length of silk. 'Are you feeling dizzy, seeing double?'

'No, no,' said Carey. 'I'm perfectly all right, Philadelphia.' She stepped back and stared at him consideringly. In truth he looked mainly embarrassed at having fallen asleep over his work, like some night-owl schoolboy. 'Can you send out some laudanum to Long George's farm? And some food?'

Her face softened a little. 'Of course.' Carey nodded, not looking at her and she frowned again.

'I think you should be in bed so your cut can heal,' she said.

'Don't be ridiculous.'

520

'Well, anyway, I'm going to sew the edges up and then bandage it again to try and stop it from taking sick and don't argue with me. Don't you know you can die from a little cut on your finger, if it goes bad, never mind a great long slash like that? Go on. Sit on the bed and lean over sideways so I can get at it.'

She looked a great deal like her mother when she was determined, despite her inevitable crooked ruff. Sighing, her brother did what he was told. Barnabus shambled back with supplies from the stillroom and then went away again to fetch food. Philadelphia threaded her needle and put an imperious hand on his ribcage.

'Now stay still. This is going to hurt, which is no more than you deserve.'

It did, a peculiarly sore and irritating sharp prickle and pull as the needle passed through. Carey tried to think of something else to stop himself from flinching, but wasn't given the chance.

'You couldn't have picked a worse time to get yourself hurt, you know,' Philadelphia said accusingly as she stitched. 'What with the muster tomorrow and King James coming to Dumfries and all. Don't twitch.'

Before he could protest at this unfairness, Barnabus came limping back with a tray and a fresh shirt. Philadelphia knotted and snipped.

'About time,' she sniffed, putting her needle carefully away and picking up the pot of ointment and the bandages. 'Up with your arms, Robin.'

Trying not to wince while she dabbed the cut with more green ointment, Carey asked, 'What did you come to see me about, Philly?'

For answer she tapped irritably at a scar on his shoulder. 'When did this happen?'

'In France. A musketball grazed me. It got better by itself.'

'You were lucky. Why didn't you tell me?'

'What for? So that you and Mother could worry about it?'

'Hah. Hold this.'

Holding the end of the bandage with his elbow raised and his other arm up, Carey said again, patiently, 'What did you want me for?'

521

She blinked at him for a moment and then her face cleared with recall, and switched instantly to an expression of thunder. 'I assume you know that my lord Scrope has appointed an acting armoury clerk to replace Atkinson?'

'WHAT?'

'And the guns from London came in at dawn this morning while you were prancing about poaching deer on the Border and they've been unpacked and stored already and Lowther's changed the lock on the armoury door again...*Will* you stay still or must I slap you?'

'God's blood, what the Devil does your God-damned husband think he's playing at...?'

'Don't swear.'

'But Philly...OUCH.'

'Stay still then.'

'But what's Scrope up to? Does he want me out? What is he *doing*?'

'You weren't here when the guns came in. Lowther was. Scrope was panicking about who was going to keep the armoury books and Lowther said his cousin could do it for the moment and Scrope agreed. He must have forgotten that the office should be one of the Deputy Warden's perks.'

'The man's a complete half-witted...'

'And as far as I know, Lowther's cousin didn't even pay anything.'

Carey was now tucking his shirt tails into the tops of his trunkhose and he winced when he moved incautiously. 'Atkinson paid fifty pounds for it, damn it.'

'I know. And the armoury clerkship has always been in the gift of the Deputy Warden. I checked with Richard Bell and he agreed with me, but when I talked to my lord Scrope all he would say was that the appointment was only temporary and you could have the sale of it later.'

Carey shrugged into his old green doublet and snapped his fingers impatiently at Barnabus to do up the points to his hose at the back.

'God damn it,' he muttered. 'I was relying on selling the clerkship to pay the men next month.'

For once Philadelphia did not tell him off for swearing. Her small heartshaped face was bunched into a worried frown. 'It's worse that Lowther has the keys to the new lock and you haven't,' she pointed out. 'I'm sure he'll find reasons not to let you have any of the new weapons.'

Carey went into his little office and sat down at his desk again, ignoring the bread and cheese Barnabus had laid out for him. He propped his chin on his fist and stared into space.

'Has the Newcastle courier gone yet?'

Philadelphia looked blank at the sudden change of subject. Barnabus coughed modestly. 'No, sir,' he said. 'He was in Bessie's, last I saw.'

'And where the Devil were you, Barnabus?'

'Well, I...'

'I don't ask much of my servants, just that they occasionally be present to serve me. Nothing elaborate.'

'Yes, sir. Sorry, sir. Shall I fetch the courier for you, sir?'

'If it isn't too much trouble, Barnabus.'

Barnabus limped out the door muttering under his breath about his water being sore and his master being sarcastic and life in the north being even worse than he expected. Carey continued to stare into space for a moment and then shrugged, took a fresh sheet of paper and a small leather notebook out of a locked drawer in his desk.

'What are you going to do, Robin?'

'Finish writing to London. I'll ask Burghley to try and persuade the Queen to pay my salary direct to me, and to do it quickly, and try to find me some funds for paying informers as well. I'm deaf and blind round here at the moment.'

'Are you going to tell him about my lord Scrope and the clerkship?'

Carey looked at her seriously. 'Do you want me to?' he asked. 'The Queen thinks little enough of your husband as it is, and she hasn't sent his warrant yet. He's not even officially Lord Warden. Do you want to give her excuse for delay?'

Philadelphia scowled and shook her head. She watched as Carey's long fingers took up the pen and began the tedious business of ciphering his letter.

'Will you go to bed when the courier's gone?' she asked after a few minutes.

'Well, I...'

'Only I want you fresh for this evening.' Carey stopped writing and glanced at her warily.

'Why?'

'I want you to come to the dinner party I'm giving for Sir Simon Musgrave, who brought the convoy in, and some of the other local gentlemen who have come for the muster.'

'Must I?'

'Yes. If the Deputy Warden isn't there, people will begin to wonder if my lord is planning to take your office away, especially when they hear about the armoury clerkship.'

'Damn.'

'And besides everyone in the country wants to meet the dashing knight who solved Atkinson's murder, never mind what he was up to the week before last—of which I have heard at least five different versions, and none of them as ridiculous as the truth.'

Carey rolled his eyes at the sarcasm in her voice.

'I have nothing fit to wear.'

Philly looked withering. 'This isn't London, you know. The only people who dress fine around here are the headmen of the big blackrenting surnames, like Richie Graham of Brackenhill. I'll make sure Barnabus has mended your velvet suit by then; but your cramoisie would do well enough.'

Carey grunted and continued counting letters under his breath. Philly came and kissed him on the ear.

'Do say you'll come, Robin.'

'Oh, very well. So long as you don't expect me to do anything except feed my face and smile sweetly at people.'

'That would be perfect.'

* * *

The boom of gunfire woke him up. Carey found himself halfway to the window with a dagger in his hand before he was fully awake. He peered out into the castle yard and saw a small crowd of garrison folk gathered around a cleared space. He smiled at himself, thinking back to his time in France the year before when he had been similarly on a hairtrigger. As he watched, a thickset middle-aged man in a worn velvet suit and Scottish hat lined up a caliver with a well-earthed target and squeezed the trigger. Carey nodded. Typical. Not only had they unloaded the weapons without him, now they were testing them while he had a much-needed rest.

Muttering to himself he went back to bed, drew the curtains and tried to go back to sleep in the stuffy dimness. Eventually he did.

Awakened once more by Barnabus, Carey decided to dress early and go and talk some sense into Lord Scrope.

The Lord Warden of the English West March was nowhere to be found, however, until Carey thought to go round to the stables to see how Thunder his black tournament horse was faring. There he ran Scrope to earth, deep in conference with four local gentlemen.

'Ahah,' said Scrope, raising a bony arm in salute as Carey wandered round the dungheap which was being raked and trimmed by three of the garrison boys. 'Here he is. Sir Robert, come and give us some advice, would you?'

Carey coughed and with difficulty, managed a politic smile at his brother-in-law.

The gentlemen were debating horse-races. Specifically, they were insistent that a muster of the West March could not possibly be held without a horse race or three and were even willing to chip in for the prize money. They had already decided on one race for three-year-olds and two for any age, and a ten-pound prize for each.

'No,' said Carey in answer to one of the gentlemen. 'Thunder's not a racehorse, he's a tournament charger.'

'Might be useful in the finish,' said the gentleman. 'Twice the leg length of a hobby and good bones. Be interesting to see how he ran. How does he do in the rough country hereabouts?'

Carey raised eyebrows at that. 'I never use him on patrol, he's too valuable.'

'Oh quite so, quite so,' said the gentleman. 'Still. Got a mare might come into season, you know.'

'I wouldn't put Thunder to a hobby,' Carey said. 'The foal might be too big.'

'Well, she's a bit of a mixture, not a hobby really, got hobby blood so does well on rough ground, but still...'

'Sir Robert couldn't ride him in the race,' put in Scrope. 'He's the Deputy Warden, he has to maintain order at the muster. Can't have him breaking his neck in the race as well.'

'Put someone else up,' suggested another gentleman with a florid face, who had been feeding the horses carrots.

'That's an idea,' said Carey, warming to the notion. If Thunder won a race, it would at least put the stallion's covering fees up. 'Who would you suggest? He's not an easy animal to ride.'

'Find one of the local lads,' said a third gentleman. 'Little bastards can ride anything with four legs, practically born in the saddle.'

There was a flurry on the top of the dungheap, fists swung and then a sweaty mucky boy scrambled down to land in front of Carey.

'Me, sir!' he was shouting. 'I'll ride him, let me ride him, I'll bear the bell away for ye, sir!'

Carey squinted at the boy, and finally recognised Young Hutchin Graham under the dung.

Another boy, one of the steward's many sons, leaned down from the top of the heap, holding a puffy lip and sneered, 'Ay, ye'll bear it away on yer bier, ye bastard, ye canna ride better than a Scotch pig wi' piles...'

Young Hutchin ignored this with some dignity, and stood up, brushing at himself ineffectually.

'I can so,' he said to Carey. 'I've rid him at exercise and he...'

Carey stared fixedly at the boy as the gentlemen listened with interest.

'...he's a strong nag, an' willing,' Hutchin finished after an imperceptible change of course. 'And I'd be willing, sir, it'd be good practice.'

'I wouldn't want you to be disappointed if he proved slower than you expected,' said Carey gravely.

'Och, nay, sir, I wouldnae expect him to win, not wi' Mr Salkeld's bonny mare in the race and all,' said Young Hutchin, all wide blue eyes and innocence.

Mr Salkeld was standing beside Carey and gave a modest snort.

'Well, she shapes prettily enough,' he admitted. 'Prettily enough, certainly.'

'Hm,' temporised Carey artfully. 'I'm not sure it would be worth it.'

Mr Salkeld took out his purse.

'Sir Robert,' he said with a friendly smile, 'I can see ye're too modest for your own good. How about a little bet to make it worth your while?'

'Well...'

'I'll do better than that. I'll give ye odds of two to one that my pretty little mare can beat your great Thunder.'

'Now I think *you're* being modest, Mr Salkeld.'

'Three to one, and my hand on it. Shall we say five pounds?'

They shook gravely while Carey wondered where he could find five pounds at short notice if he had to.

After that nothing would do but that Scrope must show the gentlemen his lymer bitch who had pupped on the Deputy Warden's bed at the beginning of the week. There was little to see at the back of the pupping kennel, beyond yellow fur and an occasional sprawling paw, while the bitch lifted her lip at them and growled softly. Carey waited while the rest of them went off to examine some sleuth-dog puppies, then put his hand near her muzzle. She sniffed, whined, thumped her tail and let him pat her head.

'I should think so,' said Carey, pleased. 'Where's your gratitude, eh? I want that big son of yours, my girl, and don't forget it.'

'Sir Robert,' hissed a young voice behind him and Carey turned to see Young Hutchin slouching there. He smiled at the boy who smiled back and transformed his truculent face into something much younger and more pleasant.

'Now then,' Carey said warily.

Hutchin drew a deep breath. 'When I take Thunder out for his evening run, will I let anybody see him?'

'Certainly,' said Carey. 'Let them see he's no miracle.'

Young Hutchin nodded and grinned in perfect understanding.

Scrope and his party returned and Carey tagged along while they wandered down to the Captain's Gate to look at the alterations and refurbishments being done to the Warden's Lodgings in the gate-house. Finally the gentlemen went off into Carlisle town which was already getting noisy and Carey at last had Scrope to himself.

Scrope, however, did not want to talk about the armoury clerkship or the weapons. He chatted about horses, he held forth on Buttercup the lymer bitch's ancestry and talents, he spoke hopefully that some of the falcons might be out of moult soon, he congratulated Carey on the venison his patrol had brought in and the sheep which was being butchered even now, and he regretted at length the sad news about Long George.

At last Carey's patience cracked. 'My lord,' he said, breaking into a long reminiscence about a tiercel bird Scrope had hunted with five years before. 'Will you be issuing the new weapons for the muster?'

'Oh ah, no, no, Robin, not at all, never done for a muster, you know.'

'But for God's sake, my lord, even the Graham women have bloody pistols and my men are only armed with longbows.'

'Never done, my dear chap, simply never done. Now don't huff at me...'

'I would have taken it very kindly if you had waited to consult me over the temporary clerk to the...'

'Quite so, quite so, I'm sure you would.' Scrope beamed densely. 'Very patient of you, bit of a mix-up over the armoury clerkship, and once it's all sorted out, we'll look into the matter, of course, but in the meantime, if you could...ah...be kind enough to leave it with me? Eh?'

Carey took breath to say that he was not patient and was in fact highly displeased, but Scrope beamed again, patted his shoulder with irritating familiarity and said, 'I would love to carry on chatting, Robin, but I simply must go up to the keep and change or Philadelphia will skin me, bless her heart.'

Carey could do no more than growl at the Lord Warden's departing back.

'Ay,' said a doleful voice behind him and Carey turned to see Sergeant Dodd standing there. 'Valuable things, guns. So I heard.'

Carey's lips tightened with frustration. 'Well, Sergeant, thanks to my Lord Warden, I've lost the sale of a fifty-pound office and you've lost about ten pounds in bribes from hopeful candidates trying to get you to put in a good word for them.'

It hardly seemed possible but Dodd's face became even longer and more mournful, which gave Carey some satisfaction.

'Och,' said Dodd, sounding stricken, 'I hadnae thought of that.'

Carey snorted and turned to go back to the Queen Mary Tower to see how much money he could raise for backing Thunder the next day. Dodd fell into step beside him.

'Lowther'll gi' us none of them,' Dodd predicted.

Carey snorted again.

'If they're there at all,' added Dodd thoughtfully.

'What?'

'If they're there...'

'Are you saying the guns might not have been delivered?'

'Och, I heard tell there were barrels full o' something heavy delivered this morning and barrels of gunpowder and all, but I never heard anyone had seen the guns broken out of the barrels.'

There was a short thoughtful silence.

'I saw Sir Simon Musgrave testing a caliver in the yard.'

'I heard him too, the bastard.'

Strictly speaking Carey should have reprimanded Dodd for talking about one of the Queen's knights so rudely, but he didn't like Musgrave either.

'You know he's one o' Sir Henry Widdrington's best allies,' Dodd added.

'Hmm.'

'And I know he proved two calivers, but naebody saw any of the other guns save Sir Richard Lowther and his cousin, the new armoury clerk. And they was mighty quick to change the locks again, so ye couldnae see them yourself, sir.'

'Hmm.'

Carey said nothing more because he was thinking. At the foot of the Queen Mary Tower he turned and smiled at Dodd.

'Could you manage to stay moderately sober tonight, Sergeant?'

'I might.' Dodd was watching him cautiously.

'Good. Meet me by the armoury an hour after the midnight guard-change.'

'Sir, I didnae mean...'

'Excellent. I'll see you there, then.'

Dodd shut his mouth since Carey had already trotted up the spiral stairs and out of sight. 'Och, Jesus,' Dodd said to himself sadly. 'What the Devil's he up to now?'

## SATURDAY, 8TH JULY 1592, EVENING

Philadelphia sat at her table in the dining room that presently doubled as a council chamber and stewed with mixed rage and hilarity. This supper party was clearly not going to be an unqualified success. All down the table were ranged the higher ranking of the local gentlemen who had come in for the muster, and some of the hardier wives and women-folk. They were talking well, their faces flushed with spiced wine and the joys of gossip, hardly tasting their food as they thrashed out the two most recent excitements: the inquest into the previous armoury clerk's death and the raid on Falkland Palace the previous week. Seated with infinite care according to rank and known blood-feuds between them, they were settled in and looked like being no trouble.

However there was trouble brewing right next to her where her husband sat, his long bony face struggling to appear politely interested. At his right sat Sir Simon Musgrave, and facing Sir Simon was Scrope's younger brother Harry, who had brought his young wife. The silly girl was tricked out to the nines in Edinburgh fashion, halfway between the German and the French styles, bright green satin stomacher clashing horribly with tawny velvet bodice and a yellow-starched ruff. She was also flirting outrageously with Robin who was next to her and courteously swallowing a yawn.

Sir Simon was booming away to Scrope about some tedious argument between the Marshal of Berwick and the Berwick town council. Sir Simon was firmly on the side of the town council. This was tactless of him because the Marshal of Berwick was Sir John Carey, elder brother of Robin and herself.

'It's ridiculous,' opined Sir Simon for the fourth time. 'You cannot let your garrison troops run wild in the town and then expect the mayor and corporation to pay for them...'

Scrope nodded sagely, while young Harry Scrope, who was even less bright than his brother, but had the sense to know it, kept his mouth shut.

Meanwhile Harry's wife Mary cooed at Philly's favourite brother, 'Oh, Sir Robert, tell me more, it must be so exciting to serve the Queen at Court.'

'It certainly can be,' said Robin, being courageously polite. Philadelphia felt sorry for him. It was essential that he be seen there, but he looked more than ready for his bed and there was the cut in his side which must be hurting. Perhaps she could think of some excuse for him to leave. Then she saw him smile and lost all sympathy. Weary or not, he simply could not help being scandalously conspiratorial with Mary Scrope, who clearly thrilled to it. 'It's particularly exciting when the Queen takes against something you've done and throws her slippers at you,' he said.

Mary Scrope gasped and her breasts threatened to pop loose. She tilted a little so Robin could get the full benefit of them.

'Oh! What do you do then, Sir Robert?'

'Duck,' said Carey, picking up his goblet and drinking.

Philly noticed he had eaten practically nothing but that the page had refilled his drink three times. The continuing drone from beside her caught her ear briefly.

'...Sir John's never been any good as Marshal, you know, my lord, he hasn't got the grasp of Border affairs. I'd niver say nothing against his father, mind, but the...'

Mary Scrope batted her eyelashes: she was a sandy sort of girl, Philly thought unkindly, sandy hair, sandy eyebrows, sandy complexion and whoever had recommended tawny had done her no favours.

'I can't think what *you* could do to offend her.'

Carey smiled with a slightly sardonic turn. 'It depends on your sex and your activities,' he said, letting his gaze wander all over

Mary's willing chest. His voice dropped. 'A woman might offend her by dressing too well or misplacing a gem.'

Good God, Robin, thought Philadelphia, you're not going to allow yourself to be seduced by Mary Scrope of all people, are you?

Robin cut a choice piece from the dish of mutton in front of him, placed it delicately on Mary Scrope's plate with the tip of his knife, smiled winningly again with his eyes half-hooded.

'And a man might offend her by marrying or sed...'

Philly kicked her brother.

'Or not knowing what he was talking about,' she said brightly with a warm smile at Mary. 'That sort of thing offends her seriously.'

'Oh,' said Mary Scrope coolly. 'Have you been at Court, Lady Scrope?'

'She's one of Her Majesty's favourite ladies in waiting,' said Robin, a reproachful glance on the oblique to Philly. 'So much so that the Queen even forgave her when she married my lord Scrope.'

'So it's true Her Majesty doesn't like her courtiers to marry,' breathed Mary Scrope, with her breasts in desperate danger now as she leaned sideways. 'Have *you* ever had that trouble, Sir Robert?'

Robin swallowed and smiled. 'Not yet.'

On impulse Philly dropped her napkin and took a peep under the table: Robin had now tucked his long elegant legs awkwardly to the side, while Mary had one foot at full stretch trying to find his knee to touch. Philadelphia wondered where the various limbs had been before she kicked him. Honestly, men were impossible creatures. Imagine flirting with Scrope's sister-in-law, as if his position weren't delicate enough as it was. There was also a small lapdog, who had crept in somehow and was snuffling about on the rushmat for droppages.

Pink with suppressed emotion, Philadelphia took her seat again. Carey gave her a knowing look, but Mary Scrope hadn't noticed, still being intent upon her prey.

'What else do you do at Court, Sir Robert?' she was asking.

'Oh, we dance and we stand around in antechambers playing cards and waiting to be sent on errands and we...'

'Seduce the maids of honour,' boomed Sir Simon who had finally noticed that nobody except Lord Scrope was listening to his stories about the politics of Berwick. 'Isn't that right, Sir Robert?'

Nobody could escape the edge of hostility in his voice. It was also the first time he had actually spoken directly to Carey.

'Not all of us, Sir Simon,' said Robin mildly. 'Some of us have better things to do.'

Lord, thought Philly admiringly, that was a good barefaced lie, Robin.

'Ay,' sniffed Sir Simon. 'I'll be bound. Run around Netherby tower in disguise and borrow horses from other people's wives, eh? That have no business lending 'em, poor silly woman.'

'You've heard about Robin's little adventure, then?' said Lord Scrope, reedily trying to deflect Sir Simon.

'Oh, ay. Widdrington's not best pleased by it, I can tell you. The nags were exhausted by the time she got them back to Hexham, and one of them gone lame. The fool woman'll no' make that mistake again if I know Sir Henry.'

Interesting, thought Philadelphia, feeling sorry for Elizabeth and the nape of her neck prickling at the sudden sense of boiling rage coming from her brother. Robin's gone white. He has got it badly, I wonder what he'll do?

To everyone's astonishment, the unregarded Harry Scrope spoke up.

'But in the process didn't Sir Robert manage to persuade the Borderers on Bothwell's raid to steal the King's horses at Falkland Palace, rather than kidnap the King himself?' he said nervously. 'That's what I heard.'

'Maybe,' grunted Sir Simon. 'But that's not *all* that I heard, eh, Sir Robert?'

Robin sat for half a heartbeat, as if considering something very seriously. Then he finished his wine, stood up and made his most courtierly bow to Lord and Lady Scrope.

'I can't imagine what you're talking about, Sir Simon,' he said with freezing civility in a voice loud enough for the rest of the table to hear, 'but I'm afraid I'm thick-headed at the moment. I was fighting reivers most of yesterday night and so if you will forgive me, my lord, my dear sister, I'll go to my bed.' Philadelphia managed a gracious nod and a bright smile. 'Good night, Mr Scrope, Mrs Scrope. God speed you back to Berwick, Sir Simon.'

Mary watched him stalk out of the council chamber with regret written all over her face: it was perfectly true, Philly thought affectionately, her brother was a fine figure of a man in his (as yet unpaid-for) black velvet suit, though his hair was presently shaded between black and dark red from the dye he had used for his Netherby disguise. Who could blame Mary Scrope if she wanted a spot of dash and romance to liven her life in the dull and practical north?

## SATURDAY, 8TH JULY 1592, NIGHT

It was Sir Richard Lowther's turn to patrol and he had long gone. Once again the night was sultry and dark with cloud, though the rain still refused to fall. Solomon the gate guard was sitting and knitting a sock with his one arm, one needle thrust into a case on his belt to hold it steady, a second ticking away hypnotically between his fingers and the other two dangling. He was away from his usual lookout on the Captain's Gate, sitting quietly by the north-western sally-port where he could see into the castle yard. There was a stealthy sound to his left and he turned to look.

Two men crept out of the Queen Mary Tower, one tall and leggy, the other short and squat. The tall one was carrying a dark lantern, fully shuttered so only occasional sparkles of light escaped. His face made a patch of white against darkness as he looked up at Solomon, who lifted his shortened upper arm and nodded.

Carey hadn't felt it necessary to explain why he had paid Solomon to keep watch, but it was no surprise that he and his short henchman padded quietly to the armoury door. Carey was trying a key in the lock, but it seemingly no longer fitted. He stepped aside and the smaller man took something in his hand and jiggled it into the keyhole. Shortly afterwards there was a stealthy sequence of clicks and the door opened.

There was a sound from the barracks. The taller man tensed, touched his companion on the shoulder. Out of the barracks door came the unmistakable slouching rangy form of Sergeant Dodd. He padded across the courtyard, there was a low conversation and then they all disappeared inside the armoury.

Solomon nodded to himself. He had served under the new Deputy's father, Lord Hunsdon, during the revolt of the Northern Earls, and he remembered Carey as a boy of about nine, perpetually in trouble, normally hanging about the stables and kennels while his tutor searched for him. The boy was father to the man there, no doubt about it. He grinned reminiscently. On a famous occasion, the young Robin had decided to try reiving for himself, along with his half-brother Daniel. The thing had ended unhappily, with Lord Hunsdon having to pay for the beast and the boys eating their dinners standing up for days afterwards.

Down in the armoury, Carey carefully unshuttered the horn-paned lantern and looked about at the racks.

'Well, they're here at least,' he said to Dodd softly, as dull greased metal gleamed back at him from all around.

'Ay, sir,' whispered Dodd. 'Shall we go now?'

'Not yet, Sergeant.'

Carey nodded at Barnabus who carefully took down the nearest caliver and handed it to him. 'We're going to mark them, carve a cross at the base of the stocks.'

'All of them, sir?'

'That's right.'

'But it'll take a' night...'

'Not if we get started now.'

'Ay, sir,' said Dodd with a sigh.

There was quiet for a while, with the occasional clatter of a dropped weapon and a curse when somebody's hand slipped. At the end of an hour and a half, Dodd put his knife away.

'Will that be all, sir?'

'Hm? Yes, I think so. Barnabus, did you bring those calivers I gave you?'

'Yes, sir.'

'Give them here then.'

Carey took two guns at random from the middle of the rack and replaced them with Barnabus's weapons. He held up the lantern and although the replacements had darker-coloured stocks, they would likely not be noticed by someone who was simply counting weapons.

From outside came a low significant sound of an owl hooting. Carey shuttered the lantern immediately, put his fingers to his lips. Feet crunched past the armoury in the yard, someone yawned loudly outside. They stood like statues.

There was the sound of muttered conversation, a scraping and clattering of firewood bundles and then the heavier, laden footsteps walking away again. Moments later came another owl hoot.

'The baker, of course,' said Carey to himself and yawned. 'We're finished here, gentlemen.' Dodd surreptitiously mopped some sweat off his forehead while Carey slipped the lantern shutters closed and went to the door, peered out cautiously. A cat was sitting in the middle of the empty yard, watching something invisible. It too yawned and trotted away as the three men slipped out of the armoury.

'I'll meet you an hour before dawn, then, Sergeant.'

'Ay, sir,' said Dodd on another martyred sigh.

Solomon was turning the heel of his sock when he heard the lock snick shut, and then one set of soft footsteps approaching. The once amateur reiver turned Deputy Warden loomed over him in the darkness, smelling of black velvet, metal and gunoil.

A small purse made a pleasant chink on the ground beside him.

'Are ye satisfied, sir?' asked Solomon when he was safely past the tricky bit in his knitting.

'Hm? Yes, for the moment. Will you be at the muster tomorrow?'

'Ay, sir, I'm on the strength after all. Garrison, non-combatant.'

'Anything or anyone I should watch out for?'

Solomon's sniff was eloquent. 'Where should I start?'

Carey laughed softly. 'I know I'm not popular.'

'Ay. Ye can say that. What was ye at wi' the guns, sir?'

There was a long silence while Carey considered this. After a moment Solomon realised why and chuckled again.

'Och, sir, ye've no need to fear my tongue. Who was it opened the gate for ye when ye and yer half-brother brought back that cow?'

Carey coughed. 'Lord,' he said, 'I'd forgotten that.'

'Had ye? Yer dad failed his purpose then, which wouldnae be like him.'

Apart from a reminiscent snort, Carey didn't say anything for a moment. 'I've marked the guns so that if I ever capture a reiver carrying one of them, I'll know where it came from.'

Solomon almost dropped a stitch as he choked with laughter.

'Ay,' he said. 'Ay, ye'll know.'

Carey thought this was tribute to his ingenuity. There was smugness in his voice as he went back to the ladder.

'Good night, Solomon.'

'Ay, sir,' wheezed the gate guard, shaking his head.


## SUNDAY, 9TH JULY 1562, BEFORE DAWN

Dodd found Carey was either up before him, or more likely hadn't bothered to try and snatch an extra two hours' sleep at all. Probably very sensible of him, Dodd thought sadly to himself as he tottered over to the well to slake his thirst in the dark blue predawn. He hated drinking water in the morning, especially from a bucket, but it was too early for the buttery in the Keep to be open and he was desperate. One of the stable lads was waiting in the courtyard, holding two of the horses from the stables, who were stamping and shaking their heads unco-operatively. The boy was yawning enough to split his face.

'Now then,' croaked Dodd.

'Morning, Sergeant,' said the boy with a cheeky grin.

Dodd grunted and washed his face, shivering at the coldness and slimy taste of the water, dried himself on his shirt-tails. He had slept in his hose after their midnight raid on the armoury, which always left him feeling ugly, quite apart from his sorely missed rest.

'Ahah,' said Carey, appearing at the door of the Queen Mary Tower with his dags in their case and Barnabus behind him with a heavy bag no doubt containing the borrowed calivers. 'Good morning, Dodd. If you can get yourself dressed in time, you can come with us.'

He strapped the firearms onto the hobby in front of the saddle, and checked the girth. There were already ten leather flasks of gunpowder slung over the pony's back. Dodd went back into the new barracks for his clothes, wondering what demon it was that got into the Courtier early in the morning and how he could kill it. Carey jumped into the saddle, just as Dodd slouched out of the barracks once more with his blue woollen statute cap pulled down to protect his eyes, lacing up his jerkin and hating people who were happy at dawn.

'How long will this take, sir?' moaned Dodd.

'Only an hour or so,' Carey explained, blowing on the glowing end of the coil of slowmatch he had slung over his shoulder. 'I'm doing some target shooting. Are you coming or not?'

Dodd supposed he had to now. 'Ay, sir.'

'Well, hurry up, I don't want a mob going with me.'

They went out through the sally-port to which Carey had the key and rode round to the fenced-off racecourse. Dodd had lost more money there than he cared to think about.

They left their horses at the other end of the course, securely tied. Then they went down to the end where the archery butts and the new shooting range were set up.

It turned out that what Carey really wanted was to see how well Dodd could shoot with the Courtier's own wheel-lock dags. Dodd thoroughly disliked firearms, and once he had warmed a little to the argument was a stout defender of longbows.

'See ye, sir,' he said, as Carey demonstrated how to wind up the lock which spun a wheel against the iron pyrites in the clamp, making the sparks that supposedly lit the fine powder in the pan and thus fired the gun. 'See ye, an arrow kills ye just as deid as a bullet and I can put a dozen in the air while ye're fiddling about with yer keys and all, sir.'

'Well, try it anyway, Sergeant.'

'Och, God,' said Dodd under his breath, who hated loud noises in the morning. He took the dag, sighted along the barrel to the target and fired. The kick was not as brutal as a caliver, but the boom and the smell of gunpowder made his eyes water. Carey had the armoury caliver and was loading it briskly, lit the match in the lock, put the stock on his shoulder, took a sideways stance and aimed the gun. The roar nearly blew the top of Dodd's head off and a hole appeared in the target, irritatingly close to the bull. Dodd's bullet had puffed sand and sawdust a yard below the target.

Behind them the market traders from the city were setting up their stalls ready for the muster, being chivvied into their proper pitches by harassed aldermen's servants. They had looked up at the sound of guns, but turned back to their own affairs once they saw that nobody was attacking.

'Firearms are the future, Sergeant,' said Carey didactically, while Dodd carefully swabbed, charged, loaded and wound up the dag again. 'Anyone who's fought on the Continent knows that.'

'The future?' repeated Dodd, thoroughly confused.

'It takes five years to make a longbowman and six weeks to make an arquebusier, it's as simple as that. This time remember it isn't a bow, you don't need to aim low at this distance. Think of a straight line from the muzzle to the bull.'

While he talked he was reloading the caliver, each movement precise, identical and rhythmic. Dodd watched, recognising something new in the way he did it. Carey smiled.

'Dutch drill,' he explained as he finished. 'I'm planning to teach it to you and the men once we get hold of the guns.' He stood square to the target, lifted and lowered the caliver to his shoulder and squinted as he aimed.

'*Christ!*' yelled Dodd and made a wild swipe with his arm which knocked the weapon out of Carey's hands. It clattered to the ground and the match fizzed on the spilled powder.

'What the Devil do you think you're doing...?' Carey demanded, cold and furious.

Dodd stamped on the match end with the toe of his boot and then picked up the caliver gingerly. He could feel his knees shaking and his stomach turning.

'Look, sir,' he said, trying not to stammer. 'There's a crack in the barrel.'

Carey looked and his face went white. He took the caliver out of Dodd's hands, and turned it, traced the death-dealing weakness all along the underside of the gun.

'Thank you, Henry,' he said at last, in the whisper of someone whose mouth has gone completely dry. 'I see it.'

Dodd turned, aimed the dag he was still holding and discharged it, this time at least hitting the target now he wasn't trying. Carey was staring at the caliver which had nearly blown his hands and face to shreds. It was still charged. Dodd put the dags back in their case on Carey's horse, as Carey began very carefully using the ramrod to scrape out the wad and bullet and shake the gunpowder onto the ground. When it was empty he blew out his breath gustily and small blame to him if he had been holding it in.

'And that's something else ye have nae fear of wi' longbows,' Dodd added, unable to resist making the point.

'True,' admitted Carey very softly. 'True enough.'

Dodd met the piercing blue eyes and knew that both of them were thinking of Long George and his mysterious pistol.

They rode back to the castle in silence. Carey went straight up to the Queen Mary Tower, still holding the caliver and also taking the one that hadn't been fired. When Dodd came up to fetch him, ready for duty at the muster, he found the Deputy Warden still in his doublet and bent over his desk.

'What are ye doing, sir?' asked Dodd cautiously, wondering if Carey had gone mad. The desk was covered over with bits of metal and various tools.

Carey was muttering to himself. 'Look at this,' he said eventually. 'The barrel metal's not thick enough and it's not been hammered out straight. And the forge-welding of the underseam is appalling. Look, it's got a hairline crack along its length, see, where the wood can hide it.'

'Is that the one that was faulty, sir?'

'No. This has never been fired.'

Never mind Carey, Henry Dodd himself might have pulled its trigger and ended up worse off than Long George. He felt queasy again.

'Ay.'

Carey was peering squint-eyed at another piece of metal. 'This is very cheap and nasty,' he said, prodding it with one of his little tools. 'See how it scratches. I doubt it was case-hardened at all. I can't believe they ever came from the Tower. Nor even Newcastle.'

'Nor Dumfries, sir,' added Dodd, puzzling his poor aching head.

'Eh?' said Carey.

'Dumfries,' Dodd repeated for him. 'Where the best guns in all Scotland are made, though ye'll pay through the nose for them.'

Carey was staring into the middle distance, at the painted hanging of a siege which warmed the stone wall of his chambers.

'Interesting,' was all he said as he piled the bits into a cloth and wrapped it up, put it in a drawer of the desk.

'Are ye coming to the muster at all, sir?' asked Dodd hintingly.

'Hm? Oh yes. *Barnabus!*'

Dodd went to wait at the foot of the tower while Carey speedily changed out of his black velvet and into his second best cramoisie suit, plus his newly cleaned jack and straightened morion helmet. He came down the stairs two at a time and Dodd fell in beside him as he strode across the yard to where their troop was lining up.

'Do ye think they're all alike, sir?' Dodd asked in a mutter.

'Almost certainly. I didn't even look at which calivers I was taking.'

'The pistols too?'

'I think so.'

'But who could have done it?'

'I've no idea. Never my brother, nor anyone at court. Maybe not Lowther either.'

'Why not, sir, seeing how he'd laugh if ye was maimed?'

'Because he was so quick to put his man in as acting armoury clerk. If it was him got at the guns, he would have made sure I appointed the clerk.'

'Your man might have spotted the difference.'

'I doubt it. I didn't. On the outside they look fine.'

'What shall we do?'

'Nothing for the moment, since we'll be late for church if we don't move ourselves.'

Most of the men were hungover but relatively clean, their horses groomed and their lances and helmets polished. Dodd still didn't see what the connection was between good soldiering and the state of your jack, providing it kept off swords, but had to admit it pleased him to see that his troop easily outshone Lowther's and Carleton's men who were dingy by comparison. Carey had them line up, checked them over, told one that his tack was a disgrace and so were his boots, complimented their latest recruit on the fact that he already had a morion and a jack and led them down early to the cathedral for Sunday service.

## SUNDAY, 9TH JULY 1592, MORNING

The young King of Scotland rode into the West March town of Dumfries by the Lochmaben Gate at about eight in the morning, to be met by the old Warden, the mayor, the corporation and both major local headmen, Lord Maxwell and young James Johnstone. There was tension in the air between the headmen that would have given good resistance to a battleaxe, mainly because their two families had been at feud for generations and both their fathers had been murdered by the other's relatives. At the moment, the Maxwells were ahead in the feud, the most powerful and wealthy surname in the West March of Scotland. For this reason, the Maxwell was wearing a brocade doublet slashed with bright red taffeta, a lace-trimmed falling band and a shining back-and-breast-plate, chased with gold. Behind him were a hundred of his largest men, in their jacks, mounted in two rows of fifty, their highly businesslike lances tricked out with blue pennants.

The young laird of Johnstone was wearing a pale buff jack, a plain red woollen suit, and an anxious expression on his face, mainly because he had only fifty men behind him. The white pennants on their lances fluttered merrily enough, but fifty against a hundred is poor odds at the best of times, never mind what

Maxwell could call on from his friends and followers in Dumfries, a town that he owned. At least, thought the Johnstone, most of my lads have good handguns and balls and powder to go with them. And surely even a Maxwell will not plan trickery when he's to be made March Warden and the King is about, though God help us when the King is gone back to Edinburgh.

Naturally, neither of the two surname-headmen had admitted to knowing anything about the Earl of Bothwell's raid on Falkland Palace which was the main reason for their sovereign's sudden arrival with three thousand soldiers behind him. However, both had come in and composed with him, promising in writing to behave themselves, not raid, not feud and not intrigue. Both of them were hoping very much that King James would not find out what they had really been up to.

Trumpets rang out a fanfare for the third time as the cavalcade came up to the gate, led by five hundred footmen from Edinburgh. Behind them on a prime white French-bred horse, came the King. As to his dress, he was not at all a martial sight, wearing a high-crowned black hat with a feather and a multiply slashed and embroidered purple doublet. His linen was somewhat grey. Hats and caps came off raggedly as he passed, a few sorry souls actually bent their knees as if he were the Queen of England. Most bowed dourly.

James Stuart, sixth of that name, was twenty-nine years old, a small man the shape of a tadpole, with powerful shoulders and short, very bandy legs. Luckily he was an excellent horseman. His face had never looked anything other than cautious, canny and slightly self-satisfied. He was the son of Mary Queen of Scots, but had last seen his mother when he was a baby. Certainly he had not remembered her well enough to intervene when Queen Elizabeth of England had decided to execute her five years back. Having been a king since babyhood he was accustomed to deference; having been a king of Scotland, he was well-inured to powerlessness, poverty, kidnapping, ferocious court faction fights and the suicidal lunacy of many of his most prominent nobles.

Everyone in the cavalcade was sweating freely into their fine linen, since the day was dull and heavy with moisture. Ever since the king's harbingers had arrived in Dumfries in search of lodging, provisioning and entertainment for the King, his court and the three thousand men, the town had been in a ferment, wagons and packtrains of provisions arriving every day, barns being cleared, pretty sons, daughters and cattle being driven up into the hills round about. Food prices had become farcical, what with the bad harvest weather and the press of people into the area.

The desperate trumpeters excelled themselves as the King stopped at the Lochmaben gate, escorted by the outgoing Warden, Sir John Carmichael. The King was feeling the heat as well, the sweat making runnels down the grease on his face. All his clothes were heavily padded because he was, rightly, afraid of daggers. Behind him his courtiers affected the same portly, soft-edged style, not because they themselves were in the least afraid of daggers, but because he was the King.

The King's heavy-lidded eyes flickered from the Johnstone to the Maxwell and back again. He was waiting, very patiently, for something.

Lord Maxwell came to himself with a start, dismounted, stepped to the King's stirrup and kissed the long heavily-ringed hand that was stretched down to him.

'Welcome to the West March, Your Highness,' he said.

King James suppressed a sigh. No doubt it was foolish to wish that his subjects would address their monarch with the more respectful 'Your Majesty' introduced by the Tudors in England. 'Your Highness' would have to do.

'Ay,' said the King. 'My lord Maxwell, have ye heard anything of the outlaw Hepburn?'

This was the erratic Earl of Bothwell, nephew of that dashing Border earl who had raped the King's mother (according to her story) in the tumultuous year after James's birth. The younger Bothwell had been an outlaw for over a year, but his latest outrage had taken place only a week before when he had raided the King's hunting lodge three hundred miles away at Falkland, trying to kidnap James.

'No, Your highness,' said Lord Maxwell. 'Naebody kens where he is.'

'Playing at the football on the Esk in England, last I heard,' said the King drily. 'Well, let's go in.'

## SUNDAY, 9TH JULY 1592, MORNING

Standing at the back of the cathedral while the Bishop of Carlisle battered his way through the Communion service before the serried rows of gentlemen and their attendants, Dodd watched the Courtier out of the corner of his eye. Somewhat to his surprise, he realised Carey was paying full attention to the words he was following in a little black-bound prayerbook.

Dodd was shocked. He hadn't taken Carey for a religious man and yet here he was, clearly praying. Then obscurely he found the thing reassuring.

After all, if the Courtier had some pull in heaven, that might be no bad thing. And there was no question he was a lucky man, the way he kept giving death the slip: he should have been hanged by the Grahams two weeks before, never mind the knife fight at the inquest and the caliver that morning.

The Bishop began to preach on the text 'Vengeance is mine, saith the Lord, I will repay.' Dodd listened for a few words in case the Bishop had any new ideas on how to take revenge and then lost track amongst the Latin and Hebrew.

They slipped out early to be ahead of the rush to mount up. The people of Carlisle were streaming towards the Rickersgate, lines of packponies shouldering through the bedlam with barrels and parcels on their backs, storeholders with handcarts shouting at each other and the women with their baskets worse than the rest of them put together.

Scrope had ordered the garrison and townbands to muster in the open space before the Keep, by the orchard. They were first there, and lined up by the fence. Carey watched critically as the rest of the men who were supposed to keep the peace arrived and settled themselves. When Lowther arrived, high coloured and wearing a serviceable back-and-breast-plate, Carey actually put his heels to his horse's flank and rode over before Dodd could stop him. For all Carey's elegant bow, Lowther cut him dead and after a couple of attempts Carey rode back again, his lips compressed.

'I could have told ye he wouldnae speak to ye,' said Dodd in an undertone. 'What did ye want him for? Ye could likely talk to Carleton just as well.'

'I wanted to discuss firearms with him.'

Dodd's mouth fell open. 'Ye werenae hoping to tell Lowther the guns are rotten, were ye, sir?'

Carey raised his eyebrows. 'Why not?'

'Well, but if it's right he doesnae ken about the guns, all ye need to do is keep your gob shut about it and ye could get yer ain back on Lowther and a' the trouble he's caused you...'

Something about Carey's look made a dew pop out on Dodd's forehead.

'I'll pretend I didn't hear that witless suggestion, Sergeant.'

It was such a lovely opportunity, it was awful to see the Courtier missing a way of paying back Lowther that was neater than anything Dodd had ever seen.

'But, sir...'

Carey turned in the saddle. 'Dodd, shut up. I'm not making more cripples like Long George for the sake of scoring off Lowther,' he said.

Offended, Dodd fell sullenly silent. That's what religion did for you, he thought, made you sentimental. Who the hell cared if Lowther or any one of his kin had his hand blown off? Serve him right for being a bastard.

A group of wives from the castle hurried past them, carrying bundles and baskets, surrounded by squealing running flocks of children. Everyone was in their finery with even the babes in arms wearing ribbons on their swaddling clothes, all trekking out to the muster, ready to watch the fine gentlemen and horses in hopes of some major disaster.

'It looks like a fair,' Carey commented to Dodd. He was being pleasant again: Lord, the man's moods were like a weathercock.

'Ay, sir,' growled Dodd.

'Poor old Barnabus won't be coming, says he's too sore and he'd rather have the day off in bed.'

Dodd, who knew that Barnabus had picked up a dose at the bawdyhouse, grunted. That was what venery and immorality got you, he thought, and tried not to speculate on which of the six whores in Carlisle Barnabus had been bedding. It must have been Maria, she was the youngest and juiciest and...

There was the sound of a single trumpet from the Keep and the two drums following. Scrope appeared, Philadelphia behind him, mounted and followed by her women. Carey's sister looked well on a horse, Dodd had to admit, in black satin and pink velvet, with a pretty beaver hat set perkily on her cap and finished with a long curled feather. Behind them came the Keep servants, all in their best liveries, and at the end an excited-looking Young Hutchin Graham in the suit he had been given for the old Lord's funeral, leading Thunder, Carey's tournament charger. So it was true the Courtier was entering him in a race to show off his paces. Dodd narrowed his eyes and looked carefully at the gleaming black animal.

Scrope himself was resplendent in his shining back-and-breast, with a plumed morion and a brocade cloak—he had attended church in the Keep chapel. He trotted down under the Queen's banner and took up position facing the lines of garrison men.

Carey spurred his horse across the green, made his bow lavishly from the saddle and spoke quickly under his breath to Scrope. Scrope smiled reassuringly, patted Carey's shoulder and shook his head. Carey's eyebrows did their usual dubious dance, but he bowed again and trotted back elegantly across the cobbles.

'If ye'd asked me, sir,' droned Dodd. 'I would ha' tellt ye we dinnae take the armoury guns out on a muster.'

'Just making sure,' said Carey. 'Though isn't that what a muster's for, to reckon up the strength of the countryside?'

'Ay, sir,' said Dodd, still as tonelessly as a preacher at a bier. 'But we ken very well how many guns is in the armoury, sir, we want tae know what's out in the countryside, and we dinnae want any of our guns...'

'Going absent without leave,' said Carey.

'Ay, sir.'

Carey nodded in silence. 'I keep forgetting to use the peculiar logic of the Borders,' he said to no one in particular.

Scrope was making the remarks his father had made last year and the year before that: they were to watch for outlaws but only to take note of their associates; they were to be tactful and alert to stop any trouble before it got out of hand. They were not to get drunk, on pain of the pillory.

He called Carey to go behind him with his men and led the way down Castle Street and out through the eastern gate. There were still a few people in town, holding packponies or leaning on lances giving desultory cheers as they went by.

The racecourse was heaving with men, already sorting themselves out into long lines, ready to be called. Carey had seen far more chaotic musters in the Armada summer, when numbers of excited peasants had turned out in their clogs with a touching faith that their billhooks, English blood and love for the Queen would shortly see them trampling down the veteran Spanish tercieros and scattering them like chaff. At the time he had agreed with them, but that was before he had done any serious fighting himself and found it to be as addictive as hunting, but much more dangerous for the undisciplined.

These, as he looked up and down straggling lines of footmen and bunches of mounted men, were better furnished than he had expected. Scrope's father had always given miserable accounts of the musters, as his predecessor had done before him: there were no horses, there were no swords, nobody had proper armour...

Carey started to laugh. 'You cunning old devils,' he said under his breath. 'Look at them.' It was true that none but the richest headmen and gentry had back-and-breast-plates; almost everybody was in the pale elaborately quilted leather of their traditional jacks. But everybody had something hard on their head, even if it was only a clumsy cap of iron hidden under a hat. Not a single man there was without a weapon of some sort, a lance at the least, and often a sword as well, though few of them had firearms.

Dodd was watching him suspiciously and Carey swallowed his hilarity. So much for his oath faithfully to report to his Queen:

Carey knew he would infallibly lie as much as any of the Wardens and no doubt his own father and brother in Berwick had done before him. If anyone had presumed to report the true level of general battleworthiness on the Marches to the Queen, two things would have happened: she would instantly have stopped sending arms and munitions north to Berwick and Carlisle; worse, she would have become suspicious of the power wielded by her three March Wardens and started moving them in and out of office as her cousin monarch, King James, did with his.

The morning was taken up with the main business of the muster, a very tedious matter. In the centre of the racecourse sat Scrope on his horse and in front of him Richard Bell with the muster books laid out on a folding table. There were two sets, Carey noted, and grinned.

Every half hour or so, a trumpet would sound and Richard Bell would call out a headman or a gentleman's name. The Carlisle town crier repeated it at three times the volume, the cry was carried back through the crowd. After some confusion the worthy who had been called paraded before the March Warden with all his tenants or the men of his surname. Then each of the men came up to the table, repeated his name, landholding and his weapons for marking in the book, then stepped back among his kin. There was a considerable skill even to the business of calling the surnames, because it would be a sad mistake to call out two headmen who were at feud, especially when they had their riders behind them.

Once each surname had been mustered, the headman dismissed them and they fell to the real business of the day of eating, drinking, gossiping, listening to the educated among them reading out the handbills of the horses running in the races, argument and ferocious betting.

As the day wore on, the alewives and piesellers made stunning profits and the crowd grew ever less orderly and more genial. There would be occasional sporadic outbreaks of shouting and confused running about. At that moment, Carey, Dodd and his men rode over and physically pushed the combatants apart, leaving them to glare at each other and call names, but giving them a face-saving way out.

Later, when all but a few unimportant families had been called, the crowds drifted over to the racecourse fences and the stewards began lining up the horses that had been brought for the races. Carey was over in the paddock, patting Thunder's neck and giving Young Hutchin Graham advice at length while the boy grinned piratically up at him.

Dodd saved his money in the first race, which was won by a Carleton filly, just as a long line of pack ponies trailed into Carlisle by the Rickersgate. The second race took a while to start because there was argument over who should be by the rail. Dodd had two shillings riding on a likely-looking unshod gelding which trailed in at the end, second to last, puffing, blowing and looking ashamed of itself, as well it might.

For the third race, Carey came over to him munching on a meat pie, having finally finished advising Young Hutchin. At the line up Thunder looked like a crow among starlings, towering over the mixed rough-coated hobbies and in particular an ugly little mare with a roman nose. Carey shouldered his way to the rail with a ruthlessness that belied his courtly nickname, with Dodd in his wake.

The gun fired, the horses charged forwards and bedlam broke out, Carey no different from any other man watching his horse run, bellowing and pounding the rail with his fist.

The first time the horses swept past, Thunder was up at the front, Young Hutchin's tow head bobbing away above all the other riders. The second time he was still there and Dodd started yelling as well, in hopes of mending his fortunes a little. The big animal looked too big to be fast, but length of leg does no harm and he was pounding away willingly. By the third lap, many of the other horses had fallen behind and there was only Thunder, a brown gelding and the ugly little mare who swarmed along the ground like a caterpillar and yet stayed up at the front. They were close packed as they swept past, the riders laying on with their whips for the finish.

The disaster happened between there and the finishing line, with Young Hutchin's head down close by Thunder's neck. The brown gelding moved in close, there was a flurry of arms and legs and then Young Hutchin was pitched off over Thunder's shoulder, hit the ground and rolled fast away from the other horses' hooves, while the ugly little mare ran past the finish to ecstatic cheers from the Salkelds.

'God damn it to hell!' roared Carey and kicked a hole in the fencing beside him. 'Did you see what that bastard did, did you see it, Dodd?'

'Ay,' said Dodd mournfully, thinking of all the garrison food he would be eating until whenever his next payday happened to be. 'I saw.'

Carey was cursing as he vaulted the fence and went over to where Young Hutchin was picking himself up, flushed with fury and a knife in his hand. It took some argument from the Courtier to bring the lad over to Dodd, instead of going to wreak vengeance on the brown gelding's rider and Dodd had every sympathy. It didn't surprise him at all to see Sir Richard Lowther in the distance patting the brown gelding and its rider on the back and shaking Mr Salkeld's hand. Carey saw it too and his eyes narrowed to wintry blue slits.

'Hell's teeth,' he muttered. 'I've been had.'

'Ay, sir,' said Dodd.

'Let me go, Deputy, I willnae kill the bastard until this evening, Ah swear it. There'll be nae witnesses, or none that'll make trouble...'

'Will you hold your tongue, Young Hutchin Graham?'

Ay, lad, thought Dodd, but didn't say, do it quietly and keep your mouth shut.

'Ah wisnae expecting to be shoved like that, Ah wisnae, sir, if...'

'Be quiet. Did you take any hurt when you fell?'

'Nay, sir, but I cannae let that Lowther bastard...'

'He's a Lowther, is he?'

'Ay, sir, he's a cousin or similar, will ye no' let me go and talk to him, just? Please, sir?'

'Absolutely not. Stay away from him.'

'But I lost the race because of him, for Christ's sake, sir, will ye no' let me...hurt him, at least, sir?'

'It was only a horserace,' said Carey, distantly, clearly doing some mental arithmetic of his own. 'I'm sorry, but you don't murder or assault people over a horserace.'

Hutchin's young face was miserable with disappointment and uncomprehending resentment.

'But, sir...'

'And besides, he's bigger than you are and he'll be ready for you. I wouldn't be surprised if he had some others of his kin waiting for you, so you stay by me.'

Young Hutchin's face took on an evil look of cunning at this and he calmed at once.

'Ay,' he said thoughtfully. 'Ay, ye've the right of it, sir, he will. Ay. Me dad allus says there's time to take yer vengeance, all the time in the world.' Carey either wasn't listening or tactfully pretended not to hear.

'Whit about Thunder, sir?' Hutchin asked after a moment.

'One of the boys has already caught him, don't worry about it. You should have won and it wasn't your fault you didn't; just don't get yourself hanged over it, understand?'

'Ay, sir,' said Young Hutchin ominously.

Carey smiled faintly. 'Keep an eye on him, Dodd.'

He sighed, squared his shoulders and marched briskly over to the triumphantly grinning knot of Salkelds, taking his purse out from under his jack and doublet.

Even Dodd had to admit that there was more style in bowing graciously to Salkeld as he patted his mare's nose and personally led her up and down to cool her off. Carey paid his losses with a negligent flourish, smiling and laughing good-humouredly with Salkeld and ignoring Lowther. You could see that it took the edge off the bastards' pleasure that the Courtier didn't seem to care about his losses.

Philadelphia Scrope was less suave as she presented the silver bells for prizes. She glowered ferociously at Mr Salkeld as well as at Sir Richard Lowther, from which Dodd guessed she was hurting in her purse as well. It couldn't have helped that Sir Simon Musgrave had been sitting beside her and was looking as happy as Lowther. Dodd saw her hand a small fat purse to him and sighed. God damn it, if Carey and his sister had lost their shirts on the race, where were Dodd's wages to come from?

The savour had gone out of the day for him, and it only confirmed his mood when his wife caught up with him and demanded briskly to know exactly how much he had lost on the Courtier's big charger and didn't he know better than to think a Salkeld would lose so easily?

He heard his name called and turned eagerly to see who it was. Red Sandy was standing on one of the marker stones of the race track gesturing over by the rail, where a crowd swirled around a knot of shouting men.

Dodd mumbled an excuse to his wife and arrived at the outskirts in time to see two Lowthers piling into a Salkeld with their fists. The Salkeld bucked and heaved and slipped away, started shouting for his kin, three more Salkelds attacked the Lowthers and then it seemed half the crowd was at it, swinging fists, shouting and roaring and pulling up hurdles from the fencing to use as weapons.

Dodd had more sense than to dive into that lot, even if Carey had not given them strict orders on no account to get into any fights on their own. He blew the horn he had on his baldric, dodged somebody with a club and heard hoofbeats behind him. Carey was riding up with four of the men, leading a horse for Dodd which the Sergeant took gratefully and vaulted into the saddle.

'Reverse lances,' Carey called. 'Don't stick them.'

In the early moments of a fight they could push the combatants apart; once it had got to this stage, the only thing they could do was stop it from spreading by using their horses as barriers and try and push the fighters over and away from the main crowd. The shouting swirled and spread, more of the garrison horse came over, Carleton with his troop and the rest of their own. There were knives flashing now, ugly and bright, someone was puking his guts up by the fence and the horses were whinnying as they objected to being used as mobile fences. Then Sir Richard Lowther rode over with Mr Salkeld behind him and instead of joining the line of garrison men, he rode straight into the middle of the mêlée and began laying about him with the flat of his sword. Evidently, thought Dodd, he had gone mad. There he was, bellowing that as God was his witness, he would shoot one of them—ay, Ritchie's Clem, you too—if the fighting didn't stop.

Astonishingly, it did. Men who had been at each other's throats let go of each other, the knives disappeared, the fence posts were dropped. A few seconds later all of them had dispersed into the crowd.

Lowther sheathed his sword and rode over to where Carey was sitting with his fist on his hip, looking contemplative.

'That's how ye keep order at a muster,' said Sir Richard, swelling like a turkey. 'Ye know the men because ye've been ruling 'em for years and ye call them by name.'

Carey ignored him pointedly.

Lowther's jowls purpled above the tight ruff while Dodd gazed busily into the distance. Away in the hills to the north was a long line of animals, small as ants, no doubt heading for Dumfries where King James would be in need of supplies. Eventually Lowther rode away.

The muster of the West March didn't come to an end so much as tail off. Those who lived less than ten miles away went home, those who lived further out went to their exorbitantly priced, shared beds in the inns and taverns of Carlisle, or lit camp fires and prepared to doss down for the night, each surname forming its own small armed camp in the meadows and gardens around Carlisle. The competing smells of bacon pottage and salt fish rose here and there.

Carey caught up with Scrope at last and found him deep in conference with Sir Simon. He waited politely for a while and finding himself to be somehow invisible, turned his horse away to go and seek out Thunder and give him some carrots. You couldn't blame the horse: he had been doing his best to win and it wasn't his fault that he had mislaid his rider.

Carey had got as far as the paddock when he heard a shrill cry behind him.

'Deputy, Deputy!'

He realised that a woman had been chasing after him and shouting for some time, so he turned his horse to look down at her. It was a skinny whippet of a woman, with her blue homespun kirtle held up and her feet bare.

'Goodwife Little,' Carey said courteously. 'What can I do for you?'

She came up to him, skidded to a halt and dropped a sketchy curtsey which he acknowledged.

'Deputy, I want Long George's back wages and a pension.'

'I'm sorry?'

'How am I to look after his bairns? We havenae land of our own, he was a younger son, and now I must pay the blackrent we owe the Graham and...'

'Goodwife, wait a minute.' Carey dismounted and stepped towards her. 'Are you saying Long George is dead?'

She blinked up at him, bewildered that he didn't yet know of her world-shattering disaster.

'He died in the night,' she said bleakly. 'The surgeon said if he saw the dawn, he'd likely be well enough. But he didnae. He went to sleep and he died. He were stiff as a board this morning.'

Carey shut his eyes briefly. 'I'm very sorry to hear of it,' he said. 'My condolences, goodwife.'

'Whit about his wages?'

'I haven't the money on me now.'

'Well, what do I do about getting it?'

Carey struggled to make his thoughts behave themselves. He kept thinking how the little girl's feet had twisted themselves together under her kirtle.

'I'm not sure I can help you myself at the moment,' he said. 'Do you need shroud-money for the burial?'

Goodwife Little sniffed. 'He's in the ground already, his dad did it this morning. I need the money for the blackrent to Richie Graham of Brackenhill, or they'll burn us out again.'

For a moment Carey stood still, thinking of Long George being buried in unconsecrated ground like a dog or a suicide, wondering if his ghost would walk. He shook himself, felt inside his doublet and shirt and found his purse which had a couple of shillings in it, his entire fortune.

'That's all I have, goodwife,' he said, handing it to her. 'I've troubles of my own at the moment, but I'll try and see what I can do for you.'

She curtseyed again, muttered her thanks as she took the purse and ran off into the crowd. Hitching Sorrel to the fence and ducking under the poles, Carey found Thunder in the middle of an admiring circle of boys and men, mainly English Grahams, with Young Hutchin holding his bridle and enlarging on the wickedness of that poxed pig of a Lowther that tipped him out of the saddle. Thunder whickered and nuzzled Carey. There was no question that Hutchin had kept him in beautiful condition, his coat gleamed and felt like warm damask, and he hardly seemed tired by his race. Nor was it Hutchin's fault that his uncle was one of the worst gangsters on the Border. Carey gave him the rest of the day off.

It was soothing to Carey to ride Thunder back to the castle at the head of his troop, patting his withers while the big animal shook his head and pranced a little. Dodd, who had drunk enough at the end of the day to be imaginative, could have sworn the animal looked embarrassed and puzzled not to be wearing the victor's bell. Dodd himself was weary and miserable and his stomach queasy with the after-effects of four meat pies, a strawberry turnover and a gallon or two of beer.

However there was no rest in prospect once they got back to the Keep. Something was happening in the courtyard when they rode in through the golden evening. It was full of shouting men carrying lanterns and torches, with Lord Scrope standing wringing his hands in the middle.

Carey frowned and looked in the same direction as the Lord Warden. Then he checked his horse and sat completely still, his lips parted as if he was about to say something and had forgotten what.

Dodd followed his gaze and thought, that armoury door is a mess, will ye look at it, bust apart and off its hinges...Je-esus Christ!

Somebody had raided the armoury while the Carlisle garrison was at the muster. In broad daylight, under the noses of the Warden, Deputy Warden and all the defensible men of the March, they had raided it and emptied it of every single caliver and pistol that it contained.

## SUNDAY, 9TH JULY 1592, EVENING

The meeting took place in the Council Room that doubled as a dining room, Scrope presiding, Lowther, Carleton, Richard Bell and Carey all present. Carleton's best jack was still dirty from his hurried ride out with his men to try and catch up with the guns or at least find some kind of trail. He had returned empty-handed, complaining that the number of feet that had trampled round the area made it completely impossible to find a trace.

Barnabus Cooke was holding the floor, answering Scrope's questions.

'I was asleep, my lord,' he whined. 'I'm sick wiv a fever and I was in my bed in Sir Robert's chambers, sleeping. I din't see nothing, din't hear nothing.' That was all he would say with such monotonous regret that it was hard not to believe him.

There had only been six people in the Keep altogether, two of whom had been drunk and still were. The other two had been prisoners in the dungeon who hadn't seen daylight for days and certainly couldn't be suspected. And Barnabus had been asleep.

Scrope dismissed Barnabus and turned to his wife who was standing at his right hand.

'Walter Ridley?'

Walter Ridley was Lowther's cousin, the acting armoury clerk whom Carey had never met and now probably never would. He had been found at the back of one of the stables, knocked out cold.

'He's more deeply asleep than anyone I've ever seen in my life,' Philadelphia answered rather quietly. 'He's snoring and his colour's bad. There's a dent in his skull: I think he's going to die, my lord, so if you will excuse me I'll go back to him now.'

She shut the door behind her softly.

'Why would they kill him if he was helping them?' asked Scrope in a frustrated voice.

'To stop him telling who paid him?' said Thomas Carleton significantly, swivelling his barrel body to look at Sir Richard Lowther.

'There's no reason to suppose he was helping them,' Lowther sniffed. 'No doubt they hit him on the head to prevent him raising the alarm.'

'What was he doing up at the Keep in any case?' asked Scrope.

'Perhaps counting the weapons to be sure naebody had got at them.'

'Of course, it's possible the thieves didn't intend to kill him,' said Carey. 'Perhaps they just wanted to give him an alibi.'

All of them knew they were avoiding the main issue. Scrope had pressed his fingers very tightly together.

'I need hardly tell you that this is a very serious matter,' he said pedantically. 'All of the new weapons in the armoury have disappeared while we were mustering. And most of the ammunition and most of the fine-grain priming powder. How it could have happened is of less importance than finding and returning them... If the Queen got to hear of it...' His voice trailed off.

There was a moment of dispirited silence while Lowther and Carleton, who had never met her, wondered if all they had heard was true. Carey and Scrope, who knew that the legend was only the half of it, tried not to think of her rage.

'She simply must not be allowed...she must not be troubled with this,' said Scrope at last. 'We must retrieve the weapons and that's all there is to it. In any case, we can't possibly ask for more weapons and munitions, so we must get them back. And we must also not let it be generally known what has happened, how weak we are. Or we shall have every reiver in the Scots West March riding south to take advantage.'

Scrope was looking upset, thought Carey, which was understandable. Carleton seemed quietly amused by the whole thing and Lowther...Now Lowther's attitude was odd.

Carey coughed behind his hand. Scrope turned to him.

'Do you have something to say, Sir Robert?' he demanded rather pettishly.

'No,' Carey said blandly. 'Although I think it's going to be difficult to keep quiet. I also think there's more to all these goings-on in the armoury than meets the eye.'

It seemed that Scrope didn't want to hear it. He made an abstracted smile and spoke at large.

'We are agreed then that the Queen must not be allowed to hear of this and we must therefore make sure that our ambassador in Edinburgh doesn't hear of it either. We will have to make very discreet enquiries as to what exactly happened and who stole the weapons...'

Carey continued to look bland. 'My lord,' he said smoothly, 'I shall of course bend every effort to finding the guns. But in the meantime—have you informed His Majesty of Scotland?'

'What?' Scrope looked more obtuse than seemed possible.

'Why the Devil should he do that?' demanded Lowther.

'King James is in Dumfries with an army to catch the Earl of Bothwell. That was the reason for the muster, if you recall, Sir Richard.' Carey lifted his eyebrows insolently at Lowther.

'I recall it, ay.'

'Surely the likeliest thief of the weapons is Bothwell or one of his friends, since they'd have need of them. They could be planning another attack on the King while he's in the area.'

'I thought you said that Bothwell had gone to the Highlands,' Scrope protested.

Carey spread his hands. 'I heard that, my lord. I don't know if it's true. He could be in the Hermitage in Liddesdale, raising an army to meet King James.'

There was a short silence while they all considered what could be done to the delicate balance of chaos on the Border and in the Debateable Lands by a couple of hundred handguns and barrels of gunpowder. Scrope rubbed his eyes with his fingers and then knitted his knuckles again.

'I must say, I hadn't considered that,' Scrope admitted. 'Puts a different complexion on the raid, rather. High treason and so on.'

'Precisely, my lord,' murmured Carey deferentially.

'Perhaps we had better tell the King, better to keep...ah...to show him respect.'

Very carefully, Carey did not smile. Scrope was as interested in keeping sweet the King of Scotland and likely future King of England as the Cecils or anyone else for that matter. As was Carey himself. King James in Dumfries, only a day's ride over the Border, was an opportunity not to be missed, even if he had certain personal reasons for caution at the Scottish court.

'What? Send a messenger into Scotland wi' news of the guns being reived?' demanded Lowther with a sneer. 'Why not print it up in a pamphlet and sell it at the Edinburgh Tolbooth—it would have more chance of keeping quiet?'

Scrope was looking round the room in the way he had, his fingers fluttering on the table unconsciously as his gaze roamed past the covered virginal in the corner. Carey forced himself to sit still and keep his mouth shut. Would Scrope do it? It was an obvious course of action, but Carey had a strong suspicion that if he showed himself too eager, Scrope would shy away from the idea.

'We should send someone to the King with a verbal message for him alone,' Scrope pronounced at last. 'Someone discreet that the King would be certain to receive.' His restless froggy eyes rested on Carey. 'Whom the King already knows, perhaps?'

Lowther frowned. 'My lord, I see no necessity...'

'Then you do know who stole the weapons, Sir Richard?' Carey snapped at him.

'No, I do not.'

'Enough, gentlemen,' put in Scrope with unwonted firmness. 'I will have no...no disputes. Sir Robert, would you be willing to ride to Dumfries and speak to the King?'

Carey inclined his head. 'Of course, my lord.'

Even Scrope's face was cynical. 'You could start tonight...'

'No, my lord,' Carey said. 'Not tonight. I don't know the area and I might be mistaken for a reiving party crossing into Scotland. I would want to take three men with me...'

'What for?' sneered Lowther. 'To protect ye?'

'Yes, Sir Richard,' said Carey sneering back. 'I know the Scottish court and a man with no followers there is of no account at all. Three men is enough for respect.'

'You could take your whole troop.'

'No need, my lord, and in any case, I doubt I could find them anywhere to sleep. Also we will need to take supplies for us and the horses...'

'Ye sound like ye're going on campaign,' Lowther put in again.

Carey sighed. 'Clearly,' he said, 'Sir Richard has never seen a Royal court on progress, as I have, many times.' Scrope nodded anxiously.

'I might have known ye'd be drooling after the chance to meet the King,' said Lowther. Carey stared at him and wished he could find an honourable excuse to punch the man. The words were bad enough but Lowther's tone twisted them into an implication of sodomy.

'I have met the King of Scotland,' Carey said with cold patience. 'Nearly ten years ago on Walsingham's embassy.' Lowther sniffed.

'What about the weapons?' Scrope asked, swerving back to the problem at hand. 'If you leave tonight you could be sure of telling the King before they can be used against him.'

'Either they are on packponies or they have been moved to wagons. Ponies, I would imagine, they move faster in this part of the world. But the quickest a pony train could go so heavily laden would be about fifteen miles a day, and it's thirty-five at least to Dumfries. I can get a good night's sleep and still talk to the King before the guns are likely to get near him.'

'It's not nearly so far to the Debateable Land.'

'True. But if that's where they're going, they're there already and nothing we can do about it.' Scrope nodded. 'I'll need some kind of excuse for going to the Scottish court as well.'

'Hm? Oh, no problem, Sir Robert. You can take a letter of congratulations to my lord Maxwell on his forthcoming appointment as Warden of the West March of Scotland. It would be polite of me to send one and I want to ask for a Day of Truce, do some justice. That will do, won't it?'

'Perfectly, my lord.'

'I'll send the water-bailiff with you, he's a Graham and he knows the way.'

Lowther scraped his chair back as he stood up. 'Ay, it's a pretty sight,' he sneered heavily. 'Ye'll keep it from Her Majesty the Queen what happened to her own weapons, but ye'll tell it to the Scotch King to keep him sweet.'

Scrope coughed and tapped his fingers on the table as Lowther marched out. 'And now, unless any of you has any useful suggestion on retrieving our weapons...'

There was a pregnant silence. Not even Carey spoke.

'...I think we will end this meeting. No, Mr Bell, I do not require a record of it. Good evening, gentlemen.'

Carey was the last to leave, rapidly totting up what he would need to take with him by way of clothes and supplies and money.

He drew Scrope aside once the others had clattered down the stairs and told him that Long George was dead.

'Dear me,' said Scrope, looking concerned. 'Was that the man who lost his hand when you ambushed Wee Colin Elliot?'

'Yes. He leaves a wife and four children and they need a pension.'

'Er...well, I'm not at all sure if...'

'My lord, without one they will either starve or turn to theft.'

'Well, yes, but there's no obligation for us to provide a pension to...'

Carey looked around at the hangings, the wax candles, the softly shining rosewood of the virginal and the silver flagon of wine in the corner. Bad wine, true, but wine.

'Not only an obligation, my lord, but a necessity,' he said through his teeth, something old-fashioned and feudal rising in him at Scrope's modern stinginess. 'If other men see that their families might starve should they be killed in the Queen's service, how the Devil do you think we shall find men to garrison the Keep?'

'Er...yes. True.'

'Whereas if Goody Little receives a pension, even a small one, the word will get round that we look after our own at least as well as the Grahams.'

That was a hit. Scrope flushed slightly and his jaw set. 'Well... if you put it like that, Robin...Yes. Of course, Goody Little must have a pension.'

'Thank you, my lord. I'll talk to Richard Bell before I go. There is also the matter of money that I need to take with me into Scotland. I shall need a minimum of ten pounds for bribes, possibly more, some good silver plate and another five pounds sterling for rooms and stabling.'

'Haven't you got it?'

'No, my lord. To be bald, I haven't a penny at the moment.'

Scrope blinked at him. 'But you brought a large loan from the Queen with you. And you won a considerable amount from Lowther only last week.'

Carey coughed self-deprecatingly. 'And I've spent it, my lord,' he said. 'And...er...lost it.'

'On the horse-racing? On Thunder?'

Carey shrugged. 'Not having the sale of the armoury clerkship in prospect, my lord, I felt I needed to raise cash to pay the men next month.'

Scrope wandered over to his beloved virginal, sat down in front of it and began stroking the lid. 'Well, er...Robin, I'm very sorry, but I'm in a few difficulties that way myself.'

'But, my lord, your estates yield...'

'Oh, to be sure, to be sure, theoretically. Do you have any idea how much it costs to be March Warden? Especially if I'm to pay pensions to the families of men killed in my service? Let alone burying my father properly? The funeral cost me more than two thousand pounds, most of it cash which I had to borrow. And the Queen has not yet seen fit to send my warrant, nor any of my fees.'

Carey stared at his brother-in-law, half-thinking of Long George being put in the ground by his father as cheaply as a dead dog. Though a peer of the realm was not to be compared with a Border tenant farmer, of course, still the worms would find them equally tasty...

'But, my lord, can you not at least advance me something against my own fees, for travelling expenses?'

Scrope began playing with a faraway expression on his face, something pretty and tinkling, making Carey want to slam the virginal lid shut on his spidery fingers. He shook his head.

'Your sister was...ah...as hopeful of Thunder's prospects as you were yourself. I'm afraid I have no actual money at all at the moment.'

The perky little tune tweedled up the keyboard and down again and Scrope's attention was gone with it, far into the realms of music where grubby King Mammon held no sway. Carey bit his tongue on several unwise retorts and strode to the door.

'Um...Robin?'

'Yes, my lord?'

'Ah...Thomas the Merchant Hetherington is reliable and not too...um...exorbitant. A penny in the shilling, mainly.'

'Per month?' Carey's tone was undeniably sarcastic, but Scrope only coughed.

'Er...no. Per quarter.'

Carey shut the heavy door behind him with exaggerated care and the gossamer notes faded into the darkness of the spiral staircase.

'Did ye tell him of the guns?' Dodd asked in the dusky courtyard, after Carey had ordered him curtly to make ready for a journey to Dumfries.

'Good God, no. How on earth could I explain how I knew?'

'We're going into Scotland.' Dodd stared into the middle distance, looking gloomy. 'Ay. Tonight?'

'No, no. Tomorrow. There's a couple of things I need to do first and I need a good night's sleep.'

'We're going into Scotland in braid daylight?' Dodd was shocked and horrified.

Despite his money-worries, Carey grinned at him. 'Yes,' he said. 'Why not? We're not planning to lift any livestock, are we?'

'Nay, sir, but...'

'Not that you've ever done any reiving in that area yourself, have you, Sergeant?' Dodd's neck reddened immediately. I really shouldn't tease him, Carey thought to himself, it's not fair.

'Er...nay, sir, but...'

'So there wouldn't be any fear of you meeting any enemies, would there?'

'Well, there would, sir, if ye follow me. There's the Johnstones for one, and what'll we do if we meet up with Wee Colin Elliot again?'

Carey gave him a cold blue stare. 'Smile sweetly and bid him good day. We're going to Court, not to a God-damned battle. Make sure you're in your best jack and your helmet is polished.'

Dodd nodded sadly and went to check on his tack. It was clear he would infinitely have preferred a battle.

## MONDAY, 10TH JULY 1592, EARLY MORNING

Carey's sister refused to let Barnabus travel with them, which was deeply annoying since it meant Carey would have to do without a manservant at the Scottish court. Still, Barnabus was clearly very unwell, looking yellow, feverish and tightlipped. Philadelphia had put him back to bed in the little sickroom next to her stillroom with a brazier burning sweet herbs and a pile of blankets to help the fever. Carey, who had miraculously avoided ever catching a dose himself, hoped devoutly that he would stay lucky: Barnabus had been adenoidally eloquent on the trouble he had passing water and a number of intimate medical details that Carey could have done without. Philadelphia had also been firm on the subject of money.

'I haven't a penny,' she sighed, busily stirring a steaming little pot over a dish of hot coals on her stillroom table. Putty-coloured and unnaturally still in the sickroom's other bed, Walter Ridley snored heavily in the background. 'I can't even afford to buy embroidery silks, thanks to you and that big lolloping horse of yours,' she added accusingly. 'And my lord's no help; he says I should have known better than to wager on anything with Sir Simon Musgrave, let alone horse-races. Why don't you take Thunder with you and sell him at the Scottish court? King James likes good horseflesh, and he's probably a bit short at the moment, what with the raid on Falkland Palace and everything.'

Carey looked at her with annoyance, because he hadn't thought of that himself.

'Isn't it illegal to trade horses into Scotland?'

Philadelphia sniffed. 'Don't be silly, Robin, that law's for peasants and their hobbies, not proper tournament chargers.'

It would be a wrench to sell Thunder. George, Earl of Cumberland had offered him forty pounds for the animal before he left London, and he had been too sentimental to take it. Besides, at the time he had just wheedled a loan out of the Queen and was feeling rich. But there was no denying that Thunder was eating his head off in Carlisle, was too big-boned and heavy for Border-riding and was very unlikely to win him any tournaments at the moment. He might make something in covering fees but not enough to earn his keep.

'Hm,' Carey said, thinking it over. 'Perhaps it would be worth taking him. But in any case, I need travelling money now and some for bribing the Scots courtiers as well.'

Philadelphia shrugged and stopped mixing the tisane she was making for Barnabus. 'Well then, you'll have to hock some rings, Robin, I'm sorry.' She cautiously sipped the brown liquid in the pot over her chafing dish with a silver spoon and shuddered. She began carefully decanting it into a silver goblet through a muslin strainer.

'What's in that?'

'Hm? Oh, wild lettuce, camomile, dried rosehips. That kind of thing. It should make him a bit less sore, but I'm afraid if Barnabus is going to go on catching the clap every year, he'll need to see a surgeon. Have a word with him about it when he's better.'

And so Carey delayed their departure for an hour while he did his business with Hetherington. This gave Dodd time to find his brother and tell him he was going into Scotland with them. Both Dodds were appalled at the thought of only themselves and Sim's Will Croser crossing the land between Carlisle and Dumfries with the Courtier, who was plainly insane and tired of life, and the Graham water-bailiff who was not to be trusted.

'It's no' the going there I'm so worried about,' Red Sandy said, chewing a bit off his fingernail. 'It's the coming back. D'ye mind that raid a few years ago where the Johnstones jumped us by Gretna?'

'Ay,' said Dodd, who had a scar on his leg for a souvenir. 'We could take every man in the garrison wi' us and still not be more than halfway safe.'

'He's mad,' said Red Sandy, positively. 'Run woodwild.'

'Are ye coming or no'?'

Red Sandy sighed heavily and bit down on his thumbnail. 'Ay, of course I am, brother. God help us.'

Sim's Will Croser was a stocky and phlegmatic man who saddled up without complaint as if he were doing no more than taking a dispatch to Newcastle. Carey had left orders that they were to bring a week's supply of hard-tack and horse fodder with them, and so they also had to load up four packponies with food and a fifth with blankets and a bag that clanked when shaken.

Carey chose that moment to come striding into the yard, followed by the English Graham water-bailiff. Dodd noticed that the Courtier was broader by the thickness of a money belt around his middle under his jack and black velvet doublet and that he had two rings fewer on his long fingers. 'Are we running a raid intae the fair Highlands?' Red Sandy wondered, shaking his head at the preparations. Carey smiled at him.

'Plagues of locusts and looting Tartar hordes have nothing on a Court for stripping a place bare,' he said. 'And that's only the English court I'm thinking about; God alone knows what King James's gentle followers are doing to Dumfries.'

He went over to the stables and led out Thunder, who was already tacked up, hitched him to the big horse called Sorrel that was Carey's normal Border mount. Thunder whickered in protest at the indignity of being led, and pulled at the reins as Carey swung into the saddle.

He led them at a brisk pace out of the crowded town, nodding to some of the local gentry he had met at the old Lord's funeral, and headed north towards the Border. They would have about five miles of the southern end of the Debateable Land to cross in order to go over the Border and Carey obviously needed to do it as quickly as possible, before word could get to any broken men about Thunder and their packponies.

He was in a hurry but to Dodd's surprise, Carey did not immediately take the route across the Esk and past Solway Field that led mostly directly to the Dumfries road. Instead, after a conversation with the Graham water-bailiff, he turned aside to Lanercost, until he came to the little huddle of huts where Long George's family lived. The half-tanned hide across the entrance of the living hut still hung down unwelcomingly, although there was movement within. There was also a fresh grave a little way from the place, under an apple tree. Dodd looked at it and wondered nervously about ghosts.

Carey dismounted, went over and knocked on the wattle wall and poked his head around the leather, immediately to start coughing at the smell of woodsmoke and porridge. All the four children he had seen before were piled up asleep like puppies in the bundle of bracken and skins and blankets where Long George had died and Goodwife Little was stirring at the pot hanging over the central fire.

To Goody Little the Deputy's sudden appearance like that was a nightmare come true again, and she shrieked softly at the horned appearance of his morion before recognising the face.

'Cuddy,' she shouted. 'Get up and stir the pot.'

The boy fell blinking out of bed, scratching himself under his shirt and shambled obediently over to the pot. Goodwife Little wiped her hands on her apron and came to the Deputy, where she curtseyed.

'Ay, sir?' she said, looking up at him, her hard thin face steely with hope firmly squashed and sat upon so it could not sour on disappointment.

'May I come in, Goodwife?'

She gestured and Carey stepped around the hide.

'Long George was owed sixty shillings and sevenpence back pay, of which I have fifteen shillings and sevenpence here.' Goody Little took breath to speak but subsided when Carey raised his hand, palm towards her. 'I have also arranged a pension which is only threepence a day, but which I have the word of the Lord Warden will be paid on any day of the month that you choose to collect it. You may collect the rest of his back pay at the same time, in instalments, or as a lump sum, and you must present yourself in person with this paper here at the Carlisle Keep.'

Goody Little had gone pale and put her hand against the wall. She smelled sourly female and as well-smoked as a bacon haunch, and as far as Carey could make out she had no breasts and no hips to speak of.

Was she going to faint, blast her? 'Goodwife? Are you well?'

'Yes, sir,' she whispered. 'Only I was...I was relieved. I can pay Richie Graham what we owe him now, ye follow. I hadnae expected to see ye again, sir.'

Carey said nothing for a moment. He took her scrawny rough hand between his two long-fingered hard ones.

'Goodwife, this will not affect your pension, but I greatly desire to know the answer. It could help avenge your husband.'

She looked at him warily.

'What were Long George and his kin up to on the Wednesday before he was hurt? Don't tell me lies: if it's over dangerous for you to tell me, then I won't press it, but please, it would help me. What was he doing?'

'Why, sir?' she asked shrewdly. 'Why is it so important to you to know?'

'He got a gun in payment for it, right? A pistol?'

After a moment she nodded at him.

'Well, Goodwife, whoever it was gave him the weapon was the man that killed him. That pistol was faulty: it burst in his hand when he fired it the second time, and that was how he came to lose his life.'

Her mouth opened slightly and her eyes narrowed. She was not a fool, Carey could see, only very wary and weary also.

'Are all of the guns bad?' she asked. 'All the guns that was in the armoury?'

Carefully, not revealing what she had let slip, Carey nodded.

Goodwife Little thought for a moment longer while Carey held his breath because he desperately wanted to cough. 'My man was out wi' his uncle and cousins,' she said finally. 'Taking a load of guns from carts and loading them on a string of packponies.'

'And, I suppose,' said Carey quietly, 'putting another load of guns into the carts that went on to Carlisle?'

Goodwife Little nodded.

'Where did the exchange take place?'

'East of here, in the Middle March, at a meeting place. I dinna ken where.'

'Please, Goody, I will not say where I got the information, but where did the guns come from?'

She laughed a little. 'Where all trouble comes, fra ower the Border, where else?'

Carey nodded, released her hand, gave her the purse he was carrying and the paper, then bowed in return to her curtsey and pushed his way out of the tiny smoky little hellhole. He was coughing and wheezing as he got back on his horse and when he wiped his face with his handkerchief he found a pale brown dinge on it.

'Christ,' he remarked to no one in particular. 'How can anyone live in a place like that?'

'It's no' sae bad, sir,' sniffed Dodd, offended once again. 'Ye stop crying and coughing in a week and then they're snugger than a tower, believe me.'

'Thank you, Dodd,' said Carey, hawking and spitting mightily. 'I'll try and remember it.' He put in his heels and led them at a fast trot back to the path, without looking back.

* * *

'So tell me about the guns,' the Courtier said conversationally to Henry Dodd as they turned their horses' heads west and northwards.

'The guns, sir?'

'Yes, Sergeant. The guns in the armoury. What is it that everybody else knows about them and I don't?'

Dodd's face had taken on a stolidly stupid expression.

'I'm sorry, sir...'

'What I'd really like to know is what makes the armoury clerkship worth fifty pounds, since it seems that's what Lowther and his cousin Ridley managed to bilk me out of. It can't simply be a matter of selling all the guns as quickly as you can: even on the Border someone would notice, surely.'

There was the faintest flicker of Dodd's eyelid.

'For Christ's sake, Dodd, have pity.'

Dodd coughed.

'Well, sir, ye see, ye can loan the handguns out for a regular fee with a little care—and a deposit, of course—and get more in the long run than ye would by selling them.'

Carey greeted this with a shout of laughter. 'By God, that's ingenious. I hope the clerks at the Tower never get to hear of it, the Spaniards would end up better armed with our ordnance than we are. So generally when there was an inspection, the guns would all be there?'

'Ay, sir. It fair queered Atkinson's pitch, you rousting the place out without warning like that.'

'Did Scrope get a cut?'

'I dinna ken, sir,' said Dodd carefully. 'But ye see, it had the benefit that the surnames would kill more of each other's men wi' the guns and save us the bother.'

'I wonder if that sort of thing goes on in Berwick. I must tell my brother.'

'I dinna ken, sir,' said Dodd again, having heard some of the stories about Sir John Carey.

Carey caught his tone. 'Oh, I see,' he said cynically. 'So I'm the only innocent who doesn't know about it.'

Dodd grunted and thought it more tactful not to answer.

'What about the risk that the surnames would be better armed in a fight than the garrison?'

'Wi' Lowther leading the trods, sir?'

'No. Plainly the situation wouldn't arise. I tell you, Sergeant, I'm not bloody surprised this March is gone to rack and ruin and there's been no justice out of Liddesdale for sixteen years.'

'Rack and ruin, sir?'

Carey turned his horse and waved an arm expansively.

'Look at it, Sergeant. Look at that.'

It was only a huddle of burned cottages and a broken-down pele-tower, plus some overgrown fields. Hardly surprising, so close to the predatory Grahams of Esk and the assorted wild men of the Debateable Land. Dodd thought the place might have been Routledge lands once.

'Ay, sir?'

'It's tragic. This is beautiful country, rich, fertile, wonderful for livestock, and there's more waste ground than field, more forest than pasture. And what do you see? Pele-towers and such for the robbers to live in, or burned-out places like that. How can anyone till the ground or plant hedges or orchards or anything useful if they never know from one day to the next if they're going to be burned out of house and home?'

Dodd looked at the burned huts. Like Long George's children, he had lived in places like that in his youth, they weren't so bad, usually warm and dry if you built them right. And why would anyone want to plant an orchard, with all the trouble that was, when a cow would give you milk inside three years and mainly feed herself?

'And this thing about blackrent, it's a scandal and a disgrace.'

Dodd stared at him. Blackrent was traditional. Carey made an impatient gesture.

'You're only supposed to pay one lot of rent, Dodd, to your actual landlord, plus tithes to the church, of course,' he said. 'You shouldn't be paying another lot of rents to a bunch of thieving ruffians to stop them raiding you.'

'Well, it's worth it if they protect you,' protested Dodd.

'Do you pay blackrent, Dodd?'

'Ay, of course I do. I dinna need to pay off the Armstrongs and I willna pay the bloody Elliots nor Lowther neither, but I pay Graham of Brackenhill like everyone else and I pay a bit to the Nixons and the Kerrs to keep them sweet.'

'Did you know it's against the law to pay it? Did you know you could hang for paying it?'

Dodd was speechless. His jaw dropped.

'Who in the hell made that law?' he demanded when he could speak again. 'Some bloody Southerner, I'll be bound.'

'So who pays you blackrent in turn, Dodd?'

'Naebody.'

Carey's eyebrows did their little leap.

'It's no crime to take blackrent,' he said sourly. 'Only pay it. And yes, it was a bloody Southerner made that law, and he was an idiot.'

'Well, it's no' precisely blackrent, see ye,' Dodd began to explain. 'But some of the Routledges give me a bit and what the wife collects on my behalf I dinna ken and...'

'Oh, never mind. Look over there. Do those look like hobbies to you?'

Dodd looked and saw to his relief that the horses were on English Graham land. The water-bailiff was at the back of their small party and hadn't noticed Carey's interest.

'Nay, sir, they do not.' Let Bangtail's dad talk his way out of this.

'Six of them, and very nice they are too, if a little short of food.'

'Och, them fancy French horses eat their heads off...' Dodd began and stopped. '...Or so I've heard.'

'Hmm.' Carey looked sideways at him and Dodd wondered what it was about Carey that caused Dodd's own tongue to become so loose. He made his face go blank and stared severely at the foreign horses trotting about in the field ahead of them.

Carey did nothing much about the horses: simply pulled out a leather notebook and a pen and little bottle of ink and scribbled down the descriptions of each one of the horses in the field, resting the book on his saddle bow. They carried on, noting eight more horses of suspiciously fine breeding in lands owned by Musgraves and Carletons.

At last, to Henry Dodd's relief, Carey picked up his heels a bit as they approached the Border country itself. They crossed at the Longtown ford and then covered the five miles of Debateable Land at a good clip. They took the horse-smugglers' path by the old battlefield and followed it into the Johnstone lands north of Gretna, where Carey had them slow down to bate the horses.

We have thirty-five miles to ride to Dumfries before night, Dodd thought sourly, through some of the wildest robber country in the world, and hardly a man with us, just a bloody Graham water-bailiff and a Deputy Warden who thinks he's immune to bullets.

To Dodd's mind, Carey rode like a man going to a wedding with a cess of two hundred behind him. He took his time, never doing more than a canter, and stared around with interest at what he called the lie of the land, which looked like rocks and hills to Dodd, asked the few people in the villages they passed through what surname they were and generally behaved as if he was somewhere in soft and silly Yorkshire, where no one was likely to attack him at all.

When Dodd tactfully tried to reason with him, he got nowhere.

'Dodd, Dodd,' Carey said with that tinge of tolerant amusement in his voice that Dodd found intensely irritating, 'nobody is going to attack us at this time of all times. King James is on the Border with three thousand men and he would just love to suck up to the Queen by hanging anyone who attacked me.'

Ye think ye're very important, Courtier, thought Dodd, but heroically didn't say. Has it crossed your mind that there are broken men all over the place here and not a one of them that gives a year-old cowpat for King James and all his men? He glanced across at the leathery water-bailiff, with the telltale long bony Graham face and cold grey eyes. He was riding along on his tough little pony looking as if he was half-asleep. No help from there.

'Ay, sir,' said Dodd, still trying to rotate his head on his neck like an owl. 'I'm verra glad to hear it. Will we be there by nightfall at this pace, sir?'

He paused, stark horror chilling his blood like winter. 'And what's that, sir?'

There was movement in the distance, the characteristic purposeful movement of a man riding towards them at speed. They sat and watched for a few seconds and then Carey was quietly loading his dags, and Red Sandy and Sim's Will Croser drawing their swords. Dodd spun his horse about, staring suspiciously at the farmlands and waste ground about them. Nothing. The land was empty save for the inevitable women weeding gardens and harvesting peas. Only there was the lone horseman riding like the clappers.

Man? He seemed small and light, and there was a smear of gold above his face, beneath his dark woollen cap.

'Och,' said the Graham water-bailiff, visibly relaxing. 'I ken who that is.' He shook his head and tutted.

'Well?' said Carey impatiently.

'That wild boy, Young Hutchin.'

It was. As the figure came closer he resolved into Young Hutchin, wearing the black livery he had worn for Scrope's funeral, bending low over his hobby's neck and riding like one demented.

As he came up to them at last, he reined in and grinned. 'Do you have a message for me?' Carey demanded, tension showing in his voice. Young Hutchin looked surprised.

'Nay, sir. Your lady sister said I wis to serve ye for page if I could catch up to ye, sir. That's why I'm here.'

The boy had a very guileless blue stare and for a moment even Dodd believed him.

'You're lying,' said Carey with emphasis. 'My sister would no more send you to be my page at King James's court than parade ten naked virgins mounted on milk-white mares through the Debateable Land at night.'

Hutchin's face fell slightly. 'She did so,' he muttered. 'I'm to be yer page.'

'She did not. Go back to Carlisle.'

'Ah willna.'

'Young Hutchin,' said Carey through his teeth. 'I have enough to do without nursemaiding you through the Scotch court. Go back to Carlisle.'

'Ye canna make me.'

'I can tan your impudent arse for you, if you don't do as you're damned well told!' roared Carey.

The water-bailiff tutted and rode forward. 'Sir,' he murmured modestly. 'A word wi' ye.'

'Yes, what is it, Mr Graham?'

'The lad's my cousin's child and he's three parts gone to the bad already.'

'Do you want King James's court to complete the job?'

'Ye canna make him go back if he doesnae want to. He'll only ride out o' sight and then trail us intae Dumfries alone.'

Carey growled under his breath. 'Are you telling me I have to take him as my page and under my protection or risk him coming to Dumfries on his own anyway?'

'Ay, sir. That's the size of it.'

'God damn it to hell and perdition. What the Devil possessed you, Young Hutchin? I don't need a bloody page.'

'Ye do sir, at court. Ye canna be at court without a servant to attend ye. What would the Scottish lords think?'

'Who gives a damn what the Scottish lords think? And anyway, that's not why you came.'

Hutchin grinned knowingly. 'Nay, sir. I had a fancy to see the Scotch court for maself.'

Carey stared at him narrow-eyed for a moment, as if trying to size up exactly how much he understood of the world. Eventually he shrugged.

'On your own head be it,' he said. 'I don't want you and if you've a particle of sense you'll turn around and head back to Carlisle.'

Young Hutchin sat and waited Carey out. Carefully, the Courtier discharged his dags into the air, causing Young Hutchin's horse to pirouette and rear. If Carey thought that would make Young Hutchin think twice, he was mistaken: the lad was a Borderer born and bred and had heard gunfire since babyhood. He waited until Carey had gestured his small party onwards with an impatient hand, and fell in at the back looking as meek and prim as a maiden. Although if what Dodd had heard about the Scottish court was true, one of Carey's fanciful virgins on horseback would have been safer there.

They ate late of the food they had brought with them by the side of the track in Annan, after being refused point blank when they offered to buy anything the womenfolk happened to have around. The women claimed bitterly that there was not a scrap of food left anywhere since the King's harbingers had been through and they had seen nothing but forest berries and fresh peas for two days. The water-bailiff was known there and got some guarded nods.

The afternoon passed wearily for Dodd in the long complex climb up and through low hills and bogs to Dumfries. Carey was enjoying himself again. Some of the way he was whistling one of the repetitive complicated ditties he and his brother-in-law seemed to set such store by, to Dodd's mystification. What was the point of a song that had no story? Finally Dodd rode a little ahead, to get away from the wheedling little tune. The countryside gave him a bad feeling in his gut all the way: true, he was legal this time, and riding with the water-bailiff. It didn't help. Every time previously that he had passed into Scotland, except for the occasional message to Edinburgh when he was a lad, had been at dead of night and very very quietly. He did know the area somewhat, different though it looked in daylight, although the Johnstones and the Maxwells were both a little spry to be stealing cows off too regularly. A few years back there had been some pickings when the two surnames had been at each other's throats. They were quiet at the moment and Dodd wondered gloomily what they were brewing. There were plentiful signs of devastation about: broken walls, burnt cottages, even a roofless pele-tower here and there, many fields going out of cultivation. The Courtier seemed less morally outraged by it, though, presumably because the sufferers were only Scots.

Nearer Dumfries there was less waste, more fertile farmed land, but still it looked bad. Some of the farmers had taken their harvest in early, no doubt to take advantage of the King's Court.

But that meant the oats and wheat that was left over would be subject to rot later on. Oh, there was a famine brewing for next year and no mistake: first Bothwell and his men and then this, the Court and the Scottish army. Nowhere in the world could hope to feed so many people so suddenly and not suffer. Not to mention the horses. Dodd thought he would mention it to his wife, so she would keep any surplus from their harvest and not sell it.

## MONDAY, 10TH JULY 1592, EVENING

They came into Dumfries at the south-westernmost end of the town, on the path from Bankend that splashed through the Goosedub bogs by the Catstrand burn, past the evil green of the Watslacks on their right before passing into the town itself at the Kirkgate Port. Dumfries had no walls. It was amply defended by being built on a soggy bend of the River Nith with river on two sides and bog on the other two.

To Dodd and Young Hutchin the town was a howling maze of chaos, full of people with strange ways of speaking and strange cuts and patterns to their jacks. The water-bailiff said he would go and stay with a woman of the town that he happened to know and disappeared among the beer-drinking crowds before either Carey or Dodd could find out where. Carey shrugged and began threading through the eternal evening twilight of July, patiently asking in his fluent Scots at the three inns and five alehouses if anyone had room for them. Mostly the Dumfries citizens laughed in his face and Dodd began to wonder if cobbles were as bad to sleep on as they looked. Typically, as the sky darkened a roof of cloud formed and it was coming on to rain a fine mizzle. Tents had ominously mushroomed in the Market Place itself, huddles of pavilions pitched between the Tolbooth and the Fish Cross, and rows of better quality, some of them painted and coloured with badges, behind the Mercat Cross. Crowds of men streamed in and out of the best house they had seen in Dumfries, a large solid stone building with pillared arches at its ground-floor entrance, and more were sheltering under them, richly dressed and leaning against the stone or playing dice like men who were used to waiting.

Carey dismounted and led his horse to one group, spoke softly and handed over some coins. The Dodd brothers, Sim's Will Croser and Young Hutchin watched hopefully until they saw the sneers.

Carey came back to them shaking his head.

'Sir?' asked Dodd, mentally girding his loins for a night in the open.

'I am reliably informed that the lad might have some chance of lodging,' Carey replied drily, 'but none of us do.' If Young Hutchin understood what the Courtier meant by that, he gave no sign of it.

'If we go out of town a little way there might be a dry place we could light a fire...' Dodd said, preparing to make the best of it and hoping Carey would not sleep a wink on the hard cold ground.

Carey smiled. 'One more place to try.'

They trailed back through the crowds and tents and horses, picking their way over the dung that already lay in heaps at street corners, to one of the smaller inns at the corner of Cavart's Vennel.

Again Carey dismounted and spoke to one of the men lolling by the door picking his teeth, handed over some more money. They waited while the ponies behind stamped their feet tiredly, and ugly-looking men in jacks passed by eyeing the supplies and livestock. Dodd eyed them right back.

At last the servingman came back, shrugged and gestured. Carey smiled, led them forwards under the low arch, where men were already settled down for the night, bundled up in their cloaks with a little fire in a corner, and into the inn's tiny yard. It was clogged with horses, tethered in rows and looked after by harassed grooms.

'Red Sandy, Sim's Will and Hutchin, take care of the horses,' Carey ordered. 'Unload the packs, pile them up and have a man guarding them at all times, no matter what happens. I'm going to see the old Warden.'

Sir John Carmichael was finishing a late supper in the tiny common room, seated at the head of one of the trestle tables, with his followers packed tight on the benches. He had his court clothes on which made him look incongruously gaudy in gold and red brocade, and a broad smile on his face.

'God's blood,' he boomed as Carey walked in, followed by Dodd. 'It's Mr Carey.'

Carey smiled and made his bow, which Sir John returned.

'I'm Sir Robert now, my lord Warden,' he said. 'And my father sends his best regards.'

'Ay, and how is he? How's his gout? Och, sit ye down, and Jimmy, will ye go ben and fetch vittles for the Deputy. Ay, that's fine, shove up, lads, make room.'

Dodd had never been so close to so many Scots in his life unless he was killing them, and certainly not in their own land. He sat down gingerly on the bench where a space appeared and wondered if there was any hope at all of getting out if they turned nasty. Carey perched on the end next to Carmichael and smiled.

'And also either his congratulations or his commiserations, depending on your mood, at your resignation from the Office of West March Warden,' Carey continued in the complicated way he could command without a tremor.

'Congratulations?' shouted Carmichael, his round red face beaming. 'I wis never sae glad to get shot of an office in my life. D'ye ken what the King pays? Ain hundred pound Scots, that's all, and I spend more than that on horsefeed in a season.'

Carmichael had a vigorous tufting of white hair all over his head, and broad capable hands, and his face had an almost childlike straightforwardness about it.

Carey winced sympathetically. 'I had heard tell the place was ruination for anyone but a magnate,' he said.

'Ay, it's the truth. And not a hope of justice fra the scurvy English either,' Carmichael added with a fake glower. 'Ye're Deputy Warden now under Scrope, I hear. How d'ye find it?'

'More complex than I expected,' Carey answered. 'And harder work.'

'They do say peddling gie's a man a terrible thirst,' said Carmichael with a grin. Carey had the grace to grin back and accept a horn mug filled with beer. To his surprise, Dodd was given one as well. The beer was sour. 'By God, that was a good tale I heard about you at Netherby. Jock o' the Peartree held prisoner in his own brother's tower...Nae doubt that's when Bothwell's ruffians found out about the horses at Falkland.'

'It was. I can't think how I let it slip out.'

Carmichael barked a laugh. 'Ye did me an ill turn there, ye ken, lad. My cousin Willie Carmichael of Reidmire at Gretna's in an awful taking about a black horse that was stolen that night and he reckons Willie Johnstone of Kirkhill's got it.' Carey raised his brows and said nothing. 'See, the horse is the devil of a fine racer, though he's only a two-year-old, he'll bear away the bells at every meet he goes to next year if Cousin Willie can get him back and he's writing me letters every week giving me grief about it like an auld Edinburgh wifie. I've written to Scrope about it, but can ye do aught for me?'

'I'll try,' said Carey. 'You know what it's like with horses.'

'Och, ye canna tell me anything about it. I mind the time some Dodds hit us for our stables, once, stripped out the lot of them.'

'Did they?' said Carey neutrally, not looking at the Sergeant. 'What did they get?'

'Och, it was a while back, a fair few years now, but they were nice horses—there was Penny, and Crown, and Farthing and Shilling...'

Dodd buried his nose in his beer. Was the old Warden teasing him?

'Dodds and English Armstrongs it was, a nice clean job of it too. We never got them back nor a penny of compensation.'

Carey coughed. 'I'm very sorry to hear of it, Sir John. I'm afraid I can't help you with them, but I'll see what I can do about your cousin Willie's black horse. What's it called?'

'Blackie, I expect,' said Carmichael. 'The man's got nae imagination.' He tossed a chicken leg at a pile of dogs in the corner which promptly dissolved into a growling fight. 'Meantime, what can I do for ye, Sir Robert?'

'Tell me about your successor as Warden.'

'Lord Maxwell.' Carmichael nodded and smoothed out his white moustache. 'He's clever and he's got something in the wind.'

'Against the Johnstones?'

'Of course. Who else? He was uncommon willing to be made Warden, which means he'll use his Wardenry against Johnstone, and he's rich and he's cunning. I dinna like the man myself, ye ken, but he's a good soldier.'

'Catholic too, I understand.'

'Ay, and that's another matter. Ye may mind the trouble he caused hereabouts in the Armada year?'

'Didn't the King arrest him for backing the Spanish?'

'Ay, and executed a couple of dozen of his kin.'

Carey whistled. 'And he's going to be made the new Lord Warden?'

Carmichael shrugged. 'The King's a very forgiving prince when he wants.'

'Must be.'

'Ay, well, Maxwell's been in Spain and France and all over, brought home some fancy foreign tastes. A while back he had his ain personal wine merchant fra foreign parts, and his ain personal wine merchant's wifie as well.' Carey raised his eyebrows quizzically and Carmichael barked with laughter. 'Ye wait till ye see her, lad. She's moved on fra the Maxwell now, dropped him like an auld glove once the Earl of Mar showed an interest in her. Even the King tolerates her and God knows, he's no love o' women nor foreigners.'

'Spanish?' asked Carey.

Carmichael shook his head. 'Italians.'

'How very cosmopolitan of the Maxwell.' Carmichael snorted and finished his beer. 'Tell me, my lord Warden,' Carey went on, 'any Germans about the Court at the moment?'

This produced an interesting result. Carmichael drew back and went still.

'What d'ye know of him?'

'I saw him arrested by the Earl of Mar.' Carey described the sinister encounter, which had been coloured over for Dodd and almost obscured by the wounding of Long George.

'Well, I dinna ken meself, because I've not been in Edinburgh inside a year, but I think he was an alchemist. I think he was going to make the King a Philosopher's Stone or gold or some such, in

Jedburgh, and it all went wrong. He made an enemy of the King and that's an ill thing to do, mark my words.'

'What happened to him?'

'I heard, he got the Boot to learn him better manners and then the King handed him over to some Hanse merchanters from Lubeck who hanged him for some bill he'd fouled over in Germany.'

Carey sighed. 'Damn,' he said. 'I wanted to talk to him.'

Carmichael shrugged.

'How about his Majesty the King, God bless him?' Carey continued after a moment. 'Do you know what he's planning to do with his army?'

'Hit Liddesdale and burn a lot of towers, nae doubt,' said Carmichael comfortably. 'He's got blood in his eye for the Grahams and nae mistake, he blames them entirely for the raid and he says they're all enchanters and witches like the Earl of Bothwell for the way they could carry off so many horses from so far away.'

'They're highly experienced raiders...' said Carey.

Carmichael smiled. 'Don't tell him,' he said. 'Ye'll make him worse.'

'And the Italians?'

'Who knows?' Carmichael belched softly into his napkin and wiped his moustache. 'Now then, Sir Robert, how're ye for a place to lay your head the night?'

Carey shook his head. 'Worse than the Holy Family on tax night in Bethlehem.'

'How many have ye got?'

'Myself, Sergeant Dodd here, two men and a boy.'

Carmichael's eyebrows drew together. 'A boy?'

Carey spread his hands helplessly. 'The bloody child followed me half way here on some half-witted whim of his own, and rather than have him come into Dumfries by himself and take his chances, I let him join me.'

Carmichael harrumphed and shook his head. 'Ay, well.'

'We've our own supplies though.'

'Hmn. Let's take a look at them.'

Carmichael came to his feet, followed politely by Carey and picked his way round the benches and men, went through into the yard. There Sim's Will and Red Sandy had found a clear patch of ground where they had hobbled the ponies in a circle and put Thunder and the packs in the middle. Hutchin had his doublet off and was rubbing the animals down at a frenetic speed.

Carmichael spotted Thunder instantly, and was naturally transfixed. Other horsemen in the yard, some of them worryingly well-dressed and armed, were standing eyeing the animal too. Carmichael smiled with the pure childlike pleasure of a Borderer faced with prime stock.

'Now there's a handsome beast,' he said to Carey. Carey nodded noncommittally.

'My tournament charger, Thunder. I brought him in case there was any tilting.'

Carmichael evidently didn't believe this. 'Ay,' he said knowingly, pushing between the hobbies to pat Thunder's nose and feel his legs. Dodd instantly bristled at the sight of a Scot sizing up one of their horses, but Carey seemed relaxed. Carmichael slapped the high arched neck lovingly.

'By God, this one puts Blackie in his place. Would ye be interested in selling him?'

Carey looked indifferent. 'I hadn't considered it, my lord Warden,' he lied. 'I wouldn't have thought anyone at this Court could afford him.'

Carmichael's smile stiffened slightly. 'Och, I don't know about that,' he said. 'It's only we dinna choose to throw our money awa'. Would ye be open to offers?'

Carey examined his fingernails. 'That would depend on what they were,' he said.

Carmichael's smile relaxed to naturalness again. 'Ay,' he said. 'Nae doubt. Well, Sir Robert, if ye'll have yer men bring the packs intae the inn we can all budge up and find space for ye this night at least. Would ye mind a pallet on the floor, if I put ye in wi' my steward?'

'Not in the least, my lord. Half an hour ago I was bracing myself for cobbles.'

'Och,' said Carmichael. 'They'd be soft enough by now, what wi' all the animals in town. Would ye credit the place?'

'Oh, I've seen worse, my lord. Far far worse.'

'Ay, the Queen's progresses are said to be a marvel to behold.'

'That's one way of putting it.'

## TUESDAY, 11TH JULY 1592, DAWN

Dodd slept extremely badly that night, his head on one of the packs, a knife in his hand and one of the horse-tethers in the other, under a canvas awning. The night was warm enough but the noise of drinking and fighting in the town never stopped and it seemed that every time he shut his eyes he was in the middle of some horrible nightmare in which he was a mouse in a den of cats, all speaking broad Scots. The Courtier was inside on a straw pallet, bundled into his cloak and no doubt giving grief to Carmichael's steward with his snores. That was some satisfaction.

Bleary-eyed and itchy with ferocious Scotch vermin at dawn, Dodd relieved his brother to try and snatch an extra hour, and began feeding and watering the horses. Young Hutchin was curled up among the packs still asleep; Dodd had excused him standing a watch on the grounds that he was one of the valuables they were guarding.

Noises and lights inside the inn announced that Carmichael was no stranger to brutally early rising. The Courtier appeared in the doorway, also scratching like an old hound, and went to wash his face in a bucket of water.

'Morning, Sergeant,' he said cheerily as he went past combing his hair, and Dodd grunted at him.

They ate a good breakfast of bread and ale and then left Red Sandy and Sim's Will with the packs to go and visit Lord Maxwell in his town house at the other end of Dumfries. Carey took Thunder as his mount, which seemed a further piece of complacent lunacy to Dodd, and Young Hutchin rode one of the packponies.

The marketplace was heaving like a ten-day-old corpse. The reason was easy to see: drawn up in a circle around the Mercat

Cross were wagons and handcarts full of food, round loaves of rye and oat bread, round cheeses of varying levels of decrepitude and serving men crowding up to buy from the barkers sitting on the wagons. Dodd recognised a JP stamped on the cheeses and pointed it out to Carey who seemed to find it funny. If King James's court was eating rations originally intended for the Carlisle garrison (and rejected on grounds of age), that was fine by Dodd.

The press of people was so tight, it was hard to get their horses to push through, so Dodd and Young Hutchin dismounted and led them forward. Carey stayed mounted for the better vantage point. Then, just as they came to the schoolhouse on the corner of Friar's Vennel, empty of schoolboys but filled with men, Carey saw something that made him stop and turn his horse's head away and to the right.

Dodd followed his stare and saw the tall severely dressed woman in her grey riding habit and white lacy falling band, riding pillion behind a groom among the crowds by one of the wagons. He struggled to keep up with Carey who was shouldering Thunder through the close-packed obdurate Scotsmen. Just as Carey almost reached her, she touched the groom's shoulder, their horse stopped, and the groom dismounted to hand her down. Dodd wondered if she was pregnant, because there was something oddly stiff in the way she moved.

'Lady Widdrington, Lady Widdrington,' called out Carey with a boyish laugh of excitement, sliding from his horse and ducking around the animal to follow her. 'My lady, I...'

She paused just long enough to look over her shoulder at him. The long grave face coloured up and the grey eyes sparkled, but she shook her head severely and turned her back on him. Carey stopped in mid-bow with a guilty expression.

'Bugger,' said Dodd.

Facing Carey now was a wide balding Englishman in a magnificent black velvet suit and furred gown. He had corrugated ears and a long sharp nose. Carey straightened up quickly.

'What business do you have with my wife, Sir Robert?' demanded Sir Henry Widdrington in a very ugly tone of voice.

For once in his life it was clear Carey couldn't think of anything to say. Dodd loosened his sword and pushed through the crowd: in his experience, elderly English headmen with the gout never went anywhere without their men and they were in lawless Scotland now. Carey seemed to have remembered it too: his hand was also on his swordhilt.

Sir Henry Widdrington limped up close to Carey and pushed him in the chest with a knobbly finger. Instinctively the crowd widened around them.

'I have forbidden my wife—*my wife*, Sir Robert—to have any further conversation with you under any circumstances at all.'

Yes, thought Dodd, he does have backing: there's that spotty Widdrington boy over by the inn gate and four more I don't like the look of in the crowd behind the Deputy, and what about those two over by the horses...Why the hell didn't we bring the patrol, at least, poor silly men though they are, we're almost naked in this pack of Scotsmen and thieves. He began to sweat and look for good ways out of the marketplace.

Carey was still silent which seemed to enrage Widdrington.

'I know, ye see,' he hissed, still poking Carey in the chest. 'I know what ye were at when I made the mistake of letting her go to London in the Armada year, you and your pandering sister between ye.'

Och God, groaned Dodd inwardly, knowing how Carey loved his sister and spotting another knot of six men at their ease just within the courtyard. Carey however gave the impression of being struck to stone, with only his eyes too bright a blue for a statue.

'...and as for Netherby...' Rage made Widdrington quiver and gulp air. 'What did ye give her for the loan of my horses, eh, Carey? How did ye persuade the bitch, eh?' Poke, poke went the finger. 'Eh? *Eh?*'

Carey's face was a mask of contempt.

'You know your lady wife very little, Sir Henry,' he said, in a soft icy voice. 'She has too much honour for your grubby suspicious little mind. As Christ is my witness, there has never been anything improper between us.'

Sir Henry Widdrington spat copiously on Carey's boots.

Dodd was directly behind Carey when this happened. Knowingly risking his life, he held Carey's right elbow and whispered urgently, 'Dinna hit him, sir, he's got backing.'

Carey's face was masklike and remote. Sir Henry seemed to be waiting for something, watching them both closely.

'Hit him?' Carey repeated coldly and clearly. 'I only hit my equals or my superiors, Dodd. I would never strike a poor senile gouty old man, that has the breeding of a London trull and the manners of a Dutch pig.'

Well, it was nice to see the way he turned his back on Widdrington, insolence in every line of him, and remount Thunder. Perhaps having Thunder prance a showy curvette was taking defiance a little far, but it at least cleared the area around them slightly so that Dodd and Young Hutchin could mount as well. Carey led the way to the Town Head where Maxwell's house was. Dodd showed his teeth at Widdrington who was bright red and gobbling with fury, and followed him. Still, his back itched ferociously right up to the gate of the magnificent stone-built fortified town house that the Dumfries men called Maxwell's Castle. It continued to itch while Carey talked to the men standing guard at the gate and passed over the usual bribes, and went on itching even as they passed through into the small courtyard. That too was packed tight, though here all the men were either in livery or wearing Maxwell or Herries jacks and no lack of family resemblance either. As usual Thunder drew a chorus of covetous looks and some quietly appraising talk. Carey beckoned that Dodd was to follow him.

Back still pricking like a hedgehog's, Dodd gave Young Hutchin his horn with orders to wind it if one of the scurvy Scots so much as laid a finger on anything of theirs. Young Hutchin grinned and touched his forelock.

The servingman was leading them through the crowded hall and out the back past the kitchens into a long low modern building tethered to the castle like a barge. Dodd followed Carey in through the door and blinked in the morning light coming through the high windows.

The shock of the caliver blast almost by his ear nearly caused Dodd to leap under the table. Even Carey jumped like a skittish horse, whisked round and half drew his sword.

Loud laughter made Dodd's ears burn and he turned to snarl at whoever had frightened them. A blurred glimpse of an elaborate padded black and red slashed doublet and a wonderfully feathered velvet hat made him bite back his indignation. It was the tall man who had fired a caliver at a target surrounded by sandbags at the other end of the bowling alley. The barrel was smoking as he blew away the powder remnants from the pan.

'Whae's after ye and what did ye reive?' asked the man, still laughing. 'Ye baith jumped like frogs at a cat.'

Carey took in the magnificent clothes, dropped his sword back in its scabbard and managed a fairly good laugh and shallow bow in return.

'We did, sir,' he said in Scots. 'Ye have the better of us. I am Sir Robert Carey, Deputy Warden of Carlisle, and I am in search of the honourable Lord Maxwell, newly made Lord Warden of this March. Would ye ken where we could find him?'

'Ay, ye're looking at him.'

Carey did a further, splendid court bow, the gradations of which Dodd was just beginning to appreciate, and took out of his belt pouch the exquisitely penned and sealed letter that Scrope had dictated and Richard Bell written the night before.

'I am sent to bring congratulations to you, my lord, from my Lord Scrope, Warden of the English West March, with the hopes of a meeting soon to discuss justice upon the Border and in Liddesdale.'

Maxwell was a tall well-made man with dark straight hair and beard and hazel eyes under a pair of eyebrows that ran right across his face like a scrivener's mark.

'Well,' said Maxwell, handing the letter to a smaller, subfusc man behind him in a plain blue stuff gown. 'I'm honoured at the rank of the messenger, Sir Robert.' He tilted a finger at the clerk.

The clerk coughed hard, unrolled the paper and began to read in a nasal drone that Scrope greeted his brother officer of the peace right lovingly and made no doubt that now justice would be done impartially and immediately upon the Borders and out of Liddesdale with such an excellent and noble lord...And so on and so forth. Dodd understood about half of it, despite it being seemingly written in English, but no doubt that was the lawyers' part in the writing of it.

Meanwhile Maxwell was cleaning and reloading his caliver. Carey watched, looked at the target which already had a hole in it not far from the bull's eye. Then as Maxwell settled the stock into his shoulder, squinted along the barrel and prepared to squeeze the trigger and bring the match down into the powderpan, he suddenly stepped forward with a cry and pinched out the glowing slowmatch end with his gloved hand. There was a flurry as Maxwell pulled away from him and Carey cursed, flapping his hand as the leather smouldered.

'What the hell d'ye think ye're playing at?' thundered Maxwell, outraged. Carey reached over to one of the wine goblets standing on the table behind Maxwell and doused his fingers in the wine.

'I'm very sorry, my lord,' he said, swirling them about and wincing. 'But that caliver's faulty.'

'It is no',' roared Maxwell. 'It's brand new.'

'If you fire it again, it will burst in your hand,' Carey said stolidly, stripping off his gloves and examining his fingers.

'It willna.'

'It will. I'll bet a hundred pounds on it.'

'It's a new weapon fra...Ain hundred pounds?'

The Courtier hasn't got a hundred pounds, Dodd thought; as far as I know he hasn't got ten pounds at the moment, bar the travelling money.

Maxwell's eyes had lit up at the thought of the bet.

'On the next firing?'

'The next firing. If you've fired it once already.'

'Ay, that's what had ye jumping about and pulling out yer blade.'

'True. Nevertheless.'

'Ain hundred pounds? English or Scots?'

Carey shrugged. 'English, of course,' he said, with the irritatingly self-satisfied air that Dodd had noticed he also wore when he was playing primero. Betting in English money had just raised the stakes by a factor of ten. Each Scots pound was worth only two shillings thanks to repeated debauchings of his money's silver content by the impoverished Scottish King. 'If you've got it, my lord,' he added, sealing his fate as far as Dodd was concerned.

Maxwell drew himself up and beckoned a servant over. Unlike Sir John Carmichael, he was a powerful magnate with ample funds from legal rents, blackrent and various other criminal activities. The servant went scurrying off and came back with a bulging leather purse. Maxwell counted out the money in good English silver.

'What about ye?' he asked insolently. 'Have ye got it?'

Carey took off his largest ring, the one with a ruby the size of his finger nail in the middle of it and thumped it down on the table.

'I think that's worth about a hundred and fifty pounds, English,' he said with fine courtierly negligence. 'The Queen of England gave it to me.'

Maxwell smiled wolfishly, picked up the ring and examined it closely. Like most noblemen he was a good judge of jewels. He smiled again and put Carey's ring back on the table where Dodd mentally bade it farewell.

They tied the caliver to one of the benches with rope, cleared the bowling alley of all hangers-on, servingmen and children. Lord Maxwell refilled the caliver with a full charge—though Carey offered to permit a two-thirds charge, so confident was he. At last Maxwell leaned over from behind the upturned table to put the slowmatch to the pan.

Dodd was already squatting down behind the table with his fingers in his ears. There was a different timbre to the cracking boom of the gun and the patter of metal hitting the wood in front of him. He thought he saw a bit of the stock go sailing up onto the roof. It had a cross scratched in it, which finally made sense of the Courtier's actions.

Maxwell stood up to look at the remains of the caliver and the hollow it had made in the bench, with a face gone paper white.

'Holy Mother Mary,' he whispered. 'Will ye look at it.'

Carey stood, picked up his ring. 'My lord?' His hand hovered over the Maxwell side of the bet.

Maxwell was still examining the remains of his new gun, while servingmen went running for stronger drink than early-morning beer and like Lord Maxwell some of them crossed themselves. Their lord looked up at Carey abstractedly. Maxwell was still pale as a winding sheet, a sheen of sweat on his nose as his imagination caught up with him, and small blame to him, thought Dodd. Carey had just saved at least his arm, perhaps his eyes and probably his life.

'Ay,' he said in a shaky voice. 'Ay, take it, it's yours, Sir Robert. Jesus Christ. Will ye look at it. Jesus.'

Carey swept up the money with a happy grin, poured it back in the purse and hung it on a thong round his neck under his shirt. He waved over one of the servingmen who had been peering bulging-eyed at the remains of the gun. One piece of barrel was stuck firmly in a beam, gone as deep as an arrow.

'Aqua vitae for my Lord Maxwell,' he ordered. He had found the goblet of wine and was swirling his scorched fingers in it again.

A servant in Maxwell livery brought the aqua vitae which Maxwell and Carey both tossed off like water. The Maxwell then came over to Carey and solemnly gave him his right hand.

They shook on it, and Maxwell clapped Carey on the shoulder. 'That's one in the eye for the Johnstones,' he said triumphantly. 'Cunning bastards.'

'My lord?' asked Carey cautiously.

'Ye'll eat wi' us, of course. And yer Sergeant and yer men?'

'I've only got a boy who's with the horses at the moment. The others are with Sir John Carmichael,' Carey explained innocently, to Dodd's horror.

'Ye brought nae men wi' ye?' asked Maxwell, puzzled at the idea of riding anywhere with fewer than twenty men behind him, and quite right too, thought Dodd, it was indecent.

'The bare minimum, my lord. Short of an English army complete with horse and ordnance it seemed safer to rely on good faith. Sir John has been most hospitable.'

'Och, no,' said Maxwell. 'He's resigning the day and I'm Warden now. Ye're my guest, Sir Robert, my friend and guest. Ye'll sleep here tonight, by God. That was well done wi' the slowmatch, man. Is yer hand sore? Will I get the surgeon to it?'

Carey was examining the blisters and blowing on them before dipping them back into the wine to cool them.

'No, it's only scorched.'

'How did ye ken sae fair the gun was bad?'

'I have a feel for weapons, my lord,' lied Carey gravely. 'And there are a number of faulty firearms somewhere around the Border at the moment.'

'Where from?' Maxwell demanded, his eyes narrowed suspiciously again.

Carey shrugged. 'I'd give a good deal to know that myself. They're not English make, nor Scots I think. One of my men was killed by one a couple of days ago.'

Maxwell was staring at Carey. 'Killed?'

'Blew his hand off and he died of it.'

The Maxwell's jaw set. Carey was looking at the blisters on his fingers again while Dodd stared at the painted walls of the bowling alley and thought of Long George showing him the gun when they waited to go out on patrol, and how he had been envious at the man's good luck. Carey smiled at Lord Maxwell.

'Perhaps the Italians know something about it?' he ventured.

'Nay...I doubt it. Jesus,' swore Maxwell again. 'Jesus Christ. I wonder...'

Carey sauntered to the silver plates of tidbits laid out on the table for Maxwell's refreshment, took a small flaky pie and bit into it.

'A number of them?' repeated Maxwell.

'Yes, my lord.'

'All bad like that?'

'Some of them worse. Some burst on the first firing.'

'How d'ye know?'

Carey swallowed, drank some wine, winced and coughed. 'A couple of them came into my...er...possession and Sergeant Dodd did the same good deed for me that I did for you, my lord. I took another apart and there's no doubt of it: the forge-welding's faulty.'

'Jesus Christ,' said Maxwell monotonously. He was twiddling his moustache around his fingers and tapping his fingers nervously on his empty cup. 'But they've the Tower mark on them?'

Dodd was having difficulty keeping a straight face and by the grave impassivity of his demeanour, so was Carey. He shrugged.

'It's a famous mark and I'm sure it's no more difficult to forge than any other.'

'A number of them?'

'A couple of hundred, my lord. I hope you've not been persuaded to buy any weapons for which you do not know the provenance.'

The unctuous concern in Carey's voice almost had Dodd exploding like a gun. So that was the way, was it? The Maxwell and Lowther between them had raided the Carlisle armoury at some trouble and expense and were now the proud possessors of a heap of scrap iron. Now that was poetical, if you liked. That could restore a man's faith in God's impartial providence.

Suddenly the Maxwell waved to one of his liverymen and when the servant ran over, spoke low and urgently into the man's ear. The servant whitened, and sprinted off in the direction of the stables.

There was something indefinably different about Carey as he allowed one of the Maxwell women to salve his fingers, a deference that Dodd had not seen before. He smiled a lot and peppered his conversation with 'my lords', owned himself greatly impressed with the size and appointments of the new bowling alley, and asked flattering questions about the way Maxwell had had his fortified house made strong. Ay, thought Dodd, finally enlightened, this is the Courtier we're seeing. He didn't like it. Frankly he found it embarrassing, watching Carey lavishly butter up a Scotch nobleman, and dull, which was worse.

Dodd finally caught Carey's eye, who raised his brows at him. Dodd coughed.

'Only I was thinkin' of going and seeing how Young Hutchin was getting along wi' the horses and all, sir,' he said awkwardly.

'Good idea, Sergeant,' said Carey easily. 'See if you can get yourselves some refreshments while you're at it.'

Dodd nodded his head, trying to hide his fury at being treated like some servant, turned on his heel and marched out.

The horses, Thunder in particular, were not in the courtyard. One of the men hanging around finally told Dodd that they'd been taken to the stables. Dodd hurried to the stables, checked every stall and found his horse and Hutchin's pony, but no sign of the black charger and no sign of Hutchin either.

Dodd caught a groom as he rushed past with a bucket of feed in each hand.

'The big black stallion that was here with the blond lad,' he said. 'Where are they?'

The groom shrugged. 'I dinna ken.'

Dodd didn't let go. 'I think ye do,' he hissed. 'Or I think ye'd better guess.'

The groom looked at Dodd's hand on his arm. 'And who the hell are ye?' he wanted to know.

For a moment Dodd was on the brink of saying he was Sergeant Henry Dodd of Gilsland, which in those parts would have put the fat well and truly in the fire, but thought better of it. 'I'm with the Deputy Warden of the English West March. The beast's his own, and he's presently sitting at my lord Maxwell's table and talking about guns. D'ye want me to fetch him and say ye've let his tournament charger be reived under the neb of my lord Maxwell? Eh?'

The groom paused. 'A courtier came to the blond lad and asked him if he'd show the animal to my lord Spynie.'

Dodd's eyes narrowed. 'And he went? Just like that? I dinna think so. Ye come wi' me and we'll talk to yer headman...'

The groom coughed. 'Well, the courtier gave the lad some money for it, not to make a fuss.'

'Och, God. Put the buckets down, man, and come wi' me.'

Reluctantly, the groom obeyed.

Carey, Maxwell and some of Maxwell's cousins were in the great hall of the Castle, at table under the war banners, eating a haggis with bashed neeps, some baked pheasants and a boiled chicken.

'What's the matter, Dodd?' asked Carey, catching Dodd's expression and then seeing the struggling groom.

Dodd glowered with satisfaction at being proved right so quickly. 'According to this man, Young Hutchin's gone off with one of Lord Spynie's men and taken Thunder to show him. Little bastard. Nae doubt of it, the lad's planning to sell Thunder for ye, pocket the cash and run for it to the Debateable Land. That one wants his hide tanned for him.'

Carey put down his spoon with a worried frown.

'Gone off? When?'

Dodd shrugged again.

'Damn.' Carey was up off the bench and reaching for his swordbelt.

'Ay,' Dodd said with mournful satisfaction. 'Put a Graham in charge of a prime piece of horseflesh like your bonny Thunder and what d'ye expect, it's putting the wolf in charge of the sheepfold, that's what it is for sure...'

'For God's sake, Dodd, stop blethering; it's not the bloody horse I'm worried about, it's the boy.'

'What does he look like?' asked Maxwell.

'Blond, blue eyes.'

Maxwell laughed coarsely. 'Well, he'll thank ye for it once his arse heals up. They'll pay him well enough.'

'Can I borrow a few of your men, my lord?'

Maxwell's face became serious. 'Och, why bother? He's only a boy and a Graham to boot.'

Carey didn't seem particularly surprised at this rebuff. He smiled sweetly at Maxwell. 'Never mind the men, my lord. Where do you think they might have gone with him?'

'Och, wherever. Spynie's with the King, down by the market-place in the Mayor's bonny house with the arches. I heard tell his friends were lodging in the Red Boar beside it, that has the hole in the wall, but what's the hurry...'

Carey was already striding through the hall. Over his shoulder he called, 'My lord, if you want to borrow one of my dags for the shooting competition, I'll have to find Thunder first because they're in a case on his back.'

Maxwell had his mouth full and was still chewing, with a comical expression of annoyance.

Dodd followed Carey through the crowds as he marched down the muddy street to the Red Boar, looking uncommonly grim. With some effort Dodd caught up with him just under the painted sign and asked, 'Will I fetch Red Sandy and Sim's Will, sir?'

Carey paused, opened his mouth to answer and stopped.

There was the sound of shouting and a boy's shrieking of insults, suddenly muffled, from the upstairs private room. Carey put his head back and listened. Dodd heard a soprano yell of 'Liddesdale!' followed by a couple of dull thuds, a crash as furniture went over, a deep-voiced cry of pain and more thuds and crashes.

'No time, damn it,' said Carey. Some large lads were sitting stolidly by the inn door, playing dice and ignoring the commotion. Carey passed by them boldly, set his foot into the lattices on the wall, tested it for strength and before the lads could do more than stare, was climbing up to the first floor like a monkey on a stick. Dodd watched with his mouth open, as did the diceplayers. Carey kicked open the double window that the sounds were coming from, and disappeared inside. His broad Scots roar echoed down the street.

'Get away from that boy, you God-rotted sodomites!'

There was a confused babble of voices, followed by the crack of a fist on somebody's flesh and a dull thud, no doubt of a boot landing somewhere soft.

Dodd was already amongst the diceplayers, sword in one hand, dagger in the other. The lad who was just scooping up dice unwisely tried to draw his sword and Dodd booted him in the face. The only other one who seemed interested in a fight became suddenly less interested when Dodd put the point of his sword against his neck and grinned.

There was some nasty work going on upstairs as crashes and the clattering of plate reverberated, but there was nothing Dodd could do about it except what he was doing. If Carey got himself killed in a sordid brawl over a pageboy, it would do no more than serve him right for not bringing enough henchmen with him to Dumfries. Still holding the diceplayers at bay with sword and dagger, Dodd cautiously toed open the inn door. The commonroom was full of men, caught in mid-move, staring at him and beyond him. Dodd wondered what they could see at his back but didn't dare take his eyes off the diceplayers long enough to look.

Almost to Dodd's disappointment, there was the crash of an upstairs door flung open and footsteps. Carey appeared at the top of the stairs with a scarlet and dishevelled Young Hutchin in front of him. He came down sideways, with his sword holding a brightly dressed young man at bay. Young Hutchin had his dagger in his hand as well and had the squint-eyed look of a Graham about to kill something.

'Out to me, Hutchin,' Dodd called. It seemed Carey had managed to avoid bloodying his sword and seeing this was King James's court and these were some of King James's best-liked hangers-on from the glamour of their clothes, that might be a good thing to continue. Hutchin stumbled forwards, ducked by the staring diceplayer still on the verge of death from Dodd's sword, and stood behind Dodd with his chest heaving and his mouth working.

Carey backed out to the door, silently daring the company to attack him. It wasn't at all that the young courtiers following him down the stairs or the liverymen in the commonroom were cowards; it was only that Carey looked as if he positively hoped they'd try an attack so that he could kill them. Nobody wanted to be the first to take on a lunatic Englishman, they were all waiting for someone else to try it first. It showed you the sad corruption of the court, Dodd felt; most Scotsmen he had ever met would have taken the both of them without even thinking about it. Dodd kicked the nearest diceplayer's kneecaps hard enough so he fell backwards and they both came away and into the street.

Maxwell was standing there with fifteen of his men, shaking his head and grinning. For the first time in his life Dodd found himself warming to a Scot. Another Maxwell came hurrying out of the little vennel by the side of the inn, leading the big black horse almost as wide as the passage. Carey caught sight of this all in the one moment and started to laugh.

'Ay, it's true what I heard,' said Maxwell. 'Ye're an education and an entertainment, Sir Robert.'

Carey bowed with a flourishing salute of his sword.

A handsome young man in gorgeous padded purple and green brocade was leaning out of the window with spittle on his lips.

'King James'll hear of this, ye bastard Englishman! I'll hae ye strung up for treason...'

Both Carey's knuckles were grazed. He sucked the left one and looked up at this and his face darkened with instant rage.

'Come anywhere near me or mine again, my lord Spynie,' he bellowed, 'and I'll cut off your miserable little prick and stuff it down your neck.'

A gaggle of women were tutting behind Dodd, an interested crowd was forming.

'Ye dinna sceer me...' sneered the young man, although he had recoiled a little, no doubt from the sheer volume of noise.

'And then I'll stick you on a pole and shoot at you like a popinjay,' finished Carey, calming down enough to be witty.

'King James will...'

'Isn't the King's bed enough for you, my lord?' Carey asked in a voice that drawled insinuatingly. 'Do you want fresher meat than His Majesty's? I'm sure he'd be very interested to hear it.' With a theatrical turn, Carey tutted and shook his head sadly. Lord Spynie flushed and he pulled his head back in again.

The crowd laughed knowingly and some of them began haranguing the young men about the door for the court's sinfulness in the sight of the Lord. Some of them were well-educated enough to begin quoting Leviticus at length. Carey sheathed his sword, turned and strode back in the direction of Maxwell's Castle, with the Lord Maxwell on his left, Thunder being led by Young Hutchin on his right and Maxwell henchmen in an almost reassuring bunch around them. Dodd tagged along, still keeping a weather eye open for Scotch ambushes and wondering whether it would still be possible to get out of town unscathed now Carey had put the King's favourite against him. Probably not. Which would be better? Rejoin Red Sandy and Sim's Will with Sir John Carmichael, or send for them both to come and take refuge with the new Lord Warden? Better stick with the new, now Carmichael had no official power. On the other hand, could Maxwell be trusted?

They had no trouble coming to Maxwell's Castle, overflowing with Maxwell's cousins and Herries kin as well. In the courtyard, Maxwell exclaimed over the beauty of Thunder and felt his legs and looked in his mouth, all the while Carey solemnly denied that he was interested in selling the beast at all.

Hutchin held the horse's bridle as if it was a mooring in a storm and said nothing. When Maxwell had gone back into the hall, Carey looked at the boy and raised his eyebrows.

'The man said he was fra the King and give me a shilling to come and show Thunder for him,' Hutchin answered in a sullen mutter. 'How should I ken what they wanted?'

Dodd waited for Carey to shout at Hutchin, tell him what a fool he was for believing any man with a tale like that, perhaps give him a beating for being so gullible. Hutchin's face was still working with rage and humiliation. He had gripped his dagger so tight in his hand, Dodd could see blood on his palms, coming in half-moons from where his nails had bitten.

'Scum,' said Carey to Young Hutchin gravely. 'They're scum. There's dregs like that at every court but there are more here because the King...The King is soft on his followers.'

Tactfully put, Dodd thought.

'They try it with every unprotected boy they find and they'll do the same with every girl and the reason why is that they're evil bastard scum and they think they'll get away with it.'

Hutchin was still shaking with rage.

'I'll mind them,' he managed to whisper. 'I'll mind every one o' their faces.'

'You do that, Young Hutchin,' said Carey. 'I'll look forward to hearing the tale of how you kill them all when you're grown.'

'I marked one of them this time,' said Hutchin fiercely. 'I hope he dies screamin' o' the rot.'

'So do I,' said Carey. 'Go and see what's to eat in the kitchens and then stay close to us. If you have trouble again, give your family warcry...What is it?'

'L-Liddesdale.'

Carey smiled wryly. 'I'll come to it and so will Dodd. Off you go now.'

Dodd's mouth was open with outrage. When Hutchin had trotted off, he gasped, 'But sir, will ye no' thump him for nearly losing ye the horse?'

Carey laughed softly. 'Lord, Dodd, what could I do to him that would be worse?'

'But he'll no' respect ye...'

599

'Oh, the hell with the bloody horse, Dodd, there's no chance Spynie could keep Thunder, any more than Maxwell could. And I think the boy will be more careful now.'

'Sir, how did ye guess so fine what they were after?'

'Come on, Dodd, you know I've been at King James's court before? Though I have to say it wasn't this bad then.'

Dodd shut his gaping mouth before he said something he would regret. Wild speculation and surmise began to crowd through his mind. He managed to nod stolidly.

'Ay,' he said. 'Will I go and fetch Sim's Will and my brother now?'

Carey considered this. 'No,' he answered. 'Not on your own, not yet. I'll get my lord Warden to send one of his servants with a letter to Carmichael and a couple of his men as backup.'

Dodd nodded approvingly at this. The two of them took Thunder round to the stables and settled him in the best stall which had been cleared by Maxwell's head groom. Carey unstrapped the dag-cases and slung them on his shoulder.

'More shooting, sir?' Dodd asked sadly.

'My lord wants to win the shooting match and I promised him the loan of my dags for it, though I think he'd be better off with a longer barrel. Come on. You can have a few shots too, if you like.'

'No thank ye, sir,' said Dodd with dignity. 'I dinna care for firearms.'

* * *

They sat down again to eat with Lord Maxwell who had polished off much of the haggis and half the chicken, Carey waving Dodd to a seat on the bench next to him. Mollified as to his dignity, Dodd took the rest of the haggis, though it wasn't as good as the ones his wife made when they had done some successful raiding.

'Boy keep his maidenhead then?' asked Maxwell casually.

'Just about.'

'I could have warned you not to bring a lad that pretty here.'

Carey sighed. 'I know, my lord.'

Maxwell swilled down some more of the terrible wine. 'Ye ken what it's like,' he said. 'Lord Spynie's friends and relations reckon they can do as they please, and mainly they can...'

'On her last progress, the Queen hanged a man that was caught raping a girl—after a fair trial, of course.'

Maxwell nodded. 'The King should do it too, but Spynie begs him and the King always gives in. Any road, who knows; most of the time, the girls are willing enough for a ring or a couple of shillings. It's the boys I feel sorry for.'

The talk wandered on in a desultory way until it came back, remarkably enough, to the topic of the mysterious German.

'No one knows,' said Maxwell flatly. 'I heard he was a mining engineer from the Black Forest and he was to find the King a rich gold mine at Jedburgh and work it for him, by a new and Hermetic system for seeking out metals in the earth, but the mine collapsed and the King hanged him for lying about his knowledge.'

Carey nodded wisely at this.

'I heard he was from Augsburg,' he said.

'Nay, the Black Forest, I'm certain of it.'

'What was his name?'

Maxwell made a small moue of ignorance and shook his head. 'I never saw him, only heard tell of him.' He poured himself some more of the wine, sipped, seemed to notice the taste for the first time and spat it out into the rushes. 'Jesus Christ, this stuff is shite.'

Carey looked sympathetic again. 'I had heard that you had found a decent wine merchant to supply you with...'

Maxwell's face darkened with anger. 'I found a slimy bastard of an Italian catamite, that's what I found, Sir Robert, him and his wife together.'

The depth of sympathy in Carey's face was masterly.

'Oh?' he said.

Maxwell grunted. 'Brought them into Scotland, introduced them to the Court and what thanks do I get for it? None. Bonnetti's bringing in French and Italian wine by the tun for His Highness and do I get a drop of it? I do not. As for his whore of a wife...' Maxwell spat into the rushes again. 'If I didnae ken very well it's not likely, I'd say she was in the King's bed and Queen Anne should watch out.' He drank some more of his inferior wine and made a face. 'Mind, she's nothing so special there either, for all her looks.'

'You've...er...'

Maxwell shrugged elaborately. 'Ye ken what these Southern bitches are like, Sir Robert. Allus on heat. But I dinna care to eat another man's leavings, if ye understand me.'

Carey nodded, completely straight-faced, while Dodd hurriedly buried his nose in his beer mug.

'She might be slipping out of favour wi' the King as well,' Maxwell added, 'seeing she came making up to me a couple o' days since. I soon settled her, though. Bitch.'

He stared up at his family's battle trophies with an expression of gloomy reminiscence. There was a short awkward silence. Carey broke it.

'And how is the King finding Dumfries?' he asked.

Maxwell shrugged. 'His Highness says he likes roughing it in the best house in town, after mine, but he wouldna stay here with me for all the assurances I gave him. He said he doesnae like castles much, for all he wouldnae be surprised by Bothwell here with me as he was at Falkland and Holyrood as well.'

'No,' agreed Carey in a tactful voice.

'At least he said he's coming to my banquet tomorrow, though, after he's been hunting.'

'Mm. Where is he hunting?'

'Five miles west of Dumfries, over by Craigmore Hill. My gamekeepers and huntsmen have been finding game for him all week, and we'll beat the drive tomorrow.'

'Mm.'

'Of course, we canna use guns in the hunting, the King doesnae like them.'

'Of course. Will this be a private hunt or...'

Maxwell laughed at Carey's tact. 'Och, God, ye can come along if ye want, everyone else will. The King's always in a good mood after a hunt, ye canna pick a better time to ask him for something.'

Carey smiled back. 'Splendid,' he said. 'I wonder if he'll remember me.'

'And then there's my banquet. It's a masked ball and he said last time I spoke to him, he'll be here incognito and seduce all the ladies. Good God,' Maxwell added with distaste, 'who does he think he's fooling?'

Carey said nothing to that. He spent an hour after the meal showing Maxwell how to wind up the fancy lock of one of his dags and arguing with him over the right charge and how much it threw to the left. Maxwell was enchanted by a firearm not completely crippled by rain and further one where you did not have the bother of hiding the bright end of a slowmatch if you were lying in wait in some covert. Carey and he had a long technical discussion on the rival merits of wheel-locks and snaphaunces compared with matchlocks, but as the Maxwell pointed out, when you were talking about a fight, the key was numbers and anything more complicated than a matchlock was fiendishly expensive. The thought of the Maxwell clan armed with weapons like that made Dodd shudder, but Carey didn't seem to see it. On the other hand, the Courtier's fancy dags missed fire often enough for Dodd to feel that if you had to use the infernal things, perhaps you were better off with ones you were more sure might work in a tight spot.

The bowling alley reverberated to the booms from the gun while Maxwell got its measure, and then all of them went out to the pasture on the other side of the river where the earthbank and targets had been set up. The King was not there, though an awning with a cloth of estate and carven chair had been set up ready for him. He was only a little less frightened of guns than he was of knives and would not come out until the contest was over and the football match ready to begin. The legend was that his unnatural fear of weapons had come about while he was still in his mother's belly: Mary Queen of Scots had been six months pregnant with him when her husband Lord Darnley and the Scottish barons of the day had dragged her advisor and musician David Riccio from her presence at gunpoint and stabbed him to death in the next room. Or it could have been the shock of seeing his foster father bleed to death from stab wounds when the King was five years of age. Whatever the reason, King James was seriously handicapped as King of Scotland by being probably the least martial man in his entire kingdom. On the other hand he was at least still alive after twenty-seven years on the throne, a rare boast for a Stuart.

Dodd stood with Carey as the various lords who had come out with their followers to provide James with his army, stood forward one at a time to show off their prowess at shooting. For the archery they shot at a popinjay: not a real parrot, being too expensive for the burghers of Dumfries, but a bunch of feathers on a high stick, that wobbled in the soft wind. It was a far harder mark than the targets set up against an earthbank ready for the musketry competition.

Carey watched with attention and then said to Dodd quietly, 'If you want to recoup your horse-racing losses...'

'I cannae,' said Dodd gloomily. 'The wife has all that was left.'

'I thought you managed to give her the slip at the muster?'

'Her brothers found me afterwards in Bessie's once we'd gone back up to the Keep and she wouldna take no for an answer.'

Carey tutted sympathetically.

'Ay,' said Dodd. 'She even took the money I had back for my new helmet and said she'd pay it herself or we'd end up in debt to the armourer.'

'Very disrespectful of her.'

'Ay,' moaned Dodd. 'And I'll be getting an earful of it every time I see her no matter what I do. I'd beat her for it, I surely would, sir, but the trouble is it wouldnae make her any better and there'd be some disaster come of it after.'

The last time Dodd had tried to assert his authority with his wife he had wound up in ward at Jedburgh as a pledge for one of her brothers' good behaviour and spent three months in the gaol there because the bastard had seen fit to disappear immediately after. Dodd still wasn't sure how it had come about, but he had no intention of making the experiment to find the connection. Besides she was fully capable of putting a pillow over his face while he slept if he offended her badly enough and she'd never burn for the crime of petty treason because Kinmont Willie would take her in as his favourite niece, no matter what she did. That thought alone had kept Dodd remarkably chaste while he did his duty at Carlisle and his wife spent most of her time running Gilsland.

Still no bairn though, which was a pity. There was no wealth like a string of sons.

Applause and ironical cheers distracted him from his normal worries. The archery contest had been won by a Gowrie. Now the gun shooting contest began and it seemed as if Carey had been busy laying bets. The laird Johnstone shot first and did reasonably well; Maxwell stepped forward and managed to put his first shot in the bull. Then a tall broad-shouldered young Englishman with a face as spotty as a plum pudding stepped out. Carey groaned.

'Damnation,' he said to Dodd. 'It's Henry Widdrington the younger. I hadn't realised he was in it or I'd have put all my money on him.'

'Good, is he?' asked Dodd with gloomy satisfaction that Carey was going to get a set down. Of course, Carey was craning his neck, looking about in the crowd: no sign of Lady Widdrington or her husband, thank God, thought Dodd, though Carey was disappointed.

'Too good, and he has a decent gun as well.'

'Who's the lad standing by him?'

'His brother Roger, I think.'

They watched the competition in an atmosphere of deepening dismay, shared by the rest of the crowd who disliked watching an Englishman beat a Scot at any martial exercise. To scattered applause and some booing, young Henry Widdrington easily bore away the bell which was presented by the King's foster-brother and erstwhile guardian, the Earl of Mar.

Carey sighed deeply, counted about twenty pounds out of his purse and went off to pay his debts. He wound up in the knot of men congratulating Widdrington on his shooting, and when Dodd wandered over nosily to find out what they were about, discovered that Carey was being persuaded to come into the football match and steadfastly refusing.

The King arrived at that point, announced by appalling trumpet playing, surrounded by a crowd of brilliantly dressed men and riding on a white horse from which he dismounted ungracefully and stumped to his chair. Lord Spynie was there, a little back from the main bunch about the King, talking intently with the wide balding figure of Sir Henry Widdrington. Elizabeth paced stately at her husband's side, curtseyed poker-backed to the King and took up a place nearby. Spynie laughed at some comment of Widdrington's, then went and stood by a stool beside the carven chair.

Dodd stole a look at Carey's face as he watched Lady Widdrington. Unguarded by charm or mockery, for a moment the Courtier's heart was nakedly visible there as his eyes burned the air between him and the woman. It was the face of a starving man gazing at a banquet.

Dodd elbowed the Courtier gently. 'Sir,' he growled. 'If I was Sir Henry, I'd shoot ye for no more than the look of your face.'

Carey blinked at him, evidently not all there. Dodd tried again.

'Sir Robert,' he said, gruff with annoyance at feeling sorry for the silly man. 'Ye'll do her more harm if ye stare like that.'

For a moment the blue glare was ferociously hostile and then Carey coloured up and looked at the ground. He cleared his throat.

'Er...yes, you're right. Quite right.'

Watching the way he settled himself, it was exactly like watching a mummer put on a mask. Dear Lord, thought Dodd, he's caught a midsummer madness to be sure. Carey was moving again, to the background noise of the Dumfries town crier announcing the King's pleasure at the football match to be held and making a hash of it.

When the sheep-like bleating had finished, Carey moved up to the awning, swept his hat off, muttered quickly to the town crier and genuflected on one knee to the King. Sweat shining on his face the town crier shouted something incomprehensible about Sir Ronald Starey, Deputy Warden of the English West March.

King James squinted his eyes suspiciously for a moment as he looked down on the Courtier and then his face cleared and lightened with a surprisingly pleasant smile as he spoke. Against his will, Dodd was impressed: it seemed the King of Scots did know Carey and was willing to acknowledge him. Carey held out the other letter he had brought from Carlisle. The King took it and read it with heavy-lidded boredom and let Carey stay there with one knee in the damp grass for a considerable time while he sat and talked to Lord Spynie and the Earl of Mar on his other side about the contents. Eventually the King nodded his head affably and said a few words. Carey rose to his feet, backed away, bowed again.

This time Dodd watched Lady Widdrington. She looked once at Carey, when his attention was on the King, and for a moment, if Dodd had been Sir Henry, he would have shot her too. Then her lips compressed and she stared into the middle distance instead.

Carey arrived, busy undoing the many buttons and points of his fine black velvet doublet. He unbuckled his belts and shrugged it off his shoulders, handing it to Young Hutchin.

'I wouldn't lay any bets on this match,' he said conversationally to Dodd as he rebelted his hose, rolled up his shirtsleeves and undid the ties of his small ruff, which ended coiled in his hat. 'Not with the number of Johnstones on the one side and Maxwells on the other.'

'Ye're not going to play at the football, are you, sir?' asked Dodd, appalled at this further evidence of the Deputy's insanity.

'Well, I can hardly refuse when the King asked me to, now can I? Even if he told me to play for the Johnstones, since they're a man short.'

'Have ye played at the football?'

Carey's eyes were cold and surprised. 'What do you take me for, Dodd? Of course I have, and in Scotland too. The King likes watching football. He has a notion that it promotes friendliness and reconciliation.'

'Friendliness and reconciliation?' Dodd repeated hollowly, remembering some football games he had played.

'That's right.'

'Och, God.'

Carey nonchalantly handed over to Dodd what was left of his winnings from Maxwell, which felt as if it amounted to some eighty pounds or so and was much more money than Dodd had ever met in one place in his life before. Wild thoughts came to him of slipping away from the match and riding like hell for Gilsland to give it to his wife and calm her down, but Dodd was not daft. He slung the purse round his own neck and felt martyred.

Dodd looked across at the young laird Johnstone who was disaccoutring with his men. The Lord Maxwell was stripping off as well. Silks, velvets and brocades piled one on top of the other, producing two anonymous herds of men in shirts, hose and boots, who glowered at each other across a grassy chasm of competitive rivalry and family ill-feeling. Carey spoke briefly to Maxwell, who laughed and shrugged. Then he sauntered over and joined the other lot.

Dodd shook his head and stepped back with the crowd. Young Hutchin was sitting up on a fence. The Earl of Mar stood on a small hillock in the middle of the field and announced that the holes dug at each end of the pasture were the goals and no man was to touch the ball with his hands or run with it under his arm. And further no weapons of any kind were to be used or even brought on the pitch.

King James smiled kindly from his carved seat, said a few words about playing in a Godly and respectable way, raised a white handkerchief. Lord Spynie threw the ball into the middle of the crowd of men, the handkerchief dropped and the game began.

\*\*\*

Elizabeth Widdrington stood beside her husband near Lord Spynie and stared at the field full of desperately struggling football players, trying not to squint in order to focus on one particular man among them. She could feel her husband simmering with spleen beside her, waiting for her to make some slip he could punish her for. She prayed automatically for strength, but could not help thinking that it was very unfair of God to put Robin Carey across her path so persistently when it hurt her heart to look at him and know she could never speak to him again. Her husband had decreed it and backed his orders with the threat, which she had no doubt he was capable of carrying out, that he would personally geld Carey if she disobeyed. She would have obeyed him in any case, naturally, since that was her duty, or she thought she would, but...She trembled for Robin's impetuosity, his odd contradictory nature: he could plan and organise as wisely as an old soldier or the Queen of England herself, and then suddenly he would take some wild notion and throw himself into the middle of hair-raising risks with blithe self-confidence and trust in his luck. She loved him for it but she was certain that Sir Henry could use his daring to outmanoeuvre and destroy him very easily. And even though she felt as if a stone was hanging from her heartstrings in the middle of her chest at the thought of never talking to him or smiling at him, there was some comfort at least in his still being alive, whole, running like a deer over the rough grass with the ball at his feet, his elbows flying and his face alight with laughter at the pack of Maxwells behind him.

Christ have mercy, she could not take her eyes off him.

Sir Henry's fingers bit into her arm. 'Enjoying the match, wife?'

She could feel her cheeks reddening, but she managed to look gravely down at her grizzled husband. Remotely she wondered if her life would have been easier if she had been of a more womanly height: it had been the source of the first contention between them, the simple fact that she was taller.

'No, my lord,' she said evenly. 'It has always seemed to me much like watching a herd of noisy cows lumbering from one end of the field to the other.'

Sir Henry snorted and peered at her, looking for deceit. There was none; how could she enjoy the match? What if Robin was hurt or killed?

'Do you want to go back to our lodgings?'

She thought for a moment, what her answer should be. The words were kind and solicitous, but the tone of voice was ugly. She ducked her head humbly.

'Whatever you wish, my lord,' she said eventually, taking refuge in pliancy. It didn't mollify him. His fingers bit deeper, hurting her. He might be short, but her husband was very strong for all his ill-health and his gout.

'Ye can stay,' he hissed. 'Stay and watch. And keep your countenance, bitch.'

She curtseyed to him and said, 'Yes, my lord.' The stone hanging from her heart swayed and chilled. He was planning something ugly, and he wanted her to see. Oh, my God, Robin, take care, be careful...Lord Jesus, look after him, guard him...

The courtiers were enjoying themselves, cheering on either the Johnstones or the Maxwells, depending on their affinities and their wagers. There was a blurring in Elizabeth's eyes and she stared at the field in a general way, trying not to focus on Carey. The herd of two-legged cattle thundered past them again, shouting confusedly. Occasionally a faster runner than the others would burst from the ruck and run in one direction or the other with the ball bobbing at his feet and then generally two or three of the other side would launch themselves at him, punch him or wrestle him down, the ball would run free and a yelling shouting heap of men would struggle for possession until somebody else burst from the ruck and the process began again, leaving the occasional body prone on the broken sod behind them. She couldn't help but catch sight of Carey every so often, generally kicking the ball away from him to James Johnstone and on one occasion leaping in, fists flying, to a more than usually vicious contention for the ball near one of the goal-holes.

She couldn't warn him. She could only watch helplessly and pray.

When it did happen the thing was so confused she had no clear idea how. One moment the ball was in the air and Carey was in the centre of a pyramid of men all trying to leap and head it one way or the other. The next moment, the ball was in play down the other end of the field and Carey was lying on his side with his knees up to his chest, writhing silently. She saw Sergeant Dodd and the rather beautiful fair-haired Graham boy run out from the crowd and bend over him solicitously, then help him off slung between their shoulders, his face still working and his legs not seeming able to support him.

Sir Henry trod heavily on her foot and combined both a satisfied grin and a scowl.

'I said, keep your countenance, wife.'

Elizabeth looked down at him and for a moment felt strangely remote from him and herself, as if she was staring down at an ugly squat creature from some mountain peak. If she had had any kind of weapon in her hand at the time, she would have killed him and burned for it gladly. Sir Henry seemed to recognise her hatred, paused, perhaps even recoiled a little.

She could no longer see Carey, who seemed to be sitting by the fence with people round him. She had seen no blood when he was helped off the field, but she knew enough not to put reliance on that. Please God, let him not be hurt badly.

'Did ye hear me, bitch?'

She looked back at her husband, the man she had been so determined to serve dutifully as a good wife when the match had been arranged ten years before, the man she had tried so very hard to please because God required it of her. Quite suddenly, like a lute string tuned too far, her loathing broke and transmuted itself into cold, indifferent distaste.

'Yes, my lord,' she said, not bothering to hide her weariness of him and his posturing.

'I paid one o' the Johnstones to grab his bollocks,' said Sir Henry. 'That'll learn him to keep his gun in its case.'

'Did you, my lord?' she said tonelessly. Sir Henry's eyes narrowed. 'I suppose you got Lord Spynie to convince the King to have him play?'

'What are friends for?'

'Yes, my lord.' She turned slightly away and swallowed a yawn—from nervousness, not boredom, but Sir Henry didn't know that and she could feel the anger vibrate in him again. He told her to keep her countenance, but in fact he wanted her to break down and weep and beg him to have mercy. She had even tried it years before, but she never made the mistake of repeating experiments that failed. He sneered at her sometimes for being as stiff-necked as a man, and she thought bitterly that no man would stand for what she stood for, no, not a galley slave in the French navy. No man would have to.

He will beat me again tonight, she thought, still distant from herself, her body gathering and shrinking inside her clothes with well-learned fear, her mind strangely unmoved. Perhaps she was at last getting used to it.

Instead of bowing her head as she usually did, consciously trying to placate him, she turned and looked in Carey's direction though she couldn't see him since he was still sitting on a rock. What was the point of trying to placate someone who enjoyed beating her? She carried on looking, ignoring the fingers bruising her arm and shifting her feet to avoid Sir Henry's, until she saw

Carey standing, still pale, still coughing, but not obviously dying. He was shaking his head.

This is a stupid thing to do, she thought to herself; I don't even like football.

'My lord, I am feeling a little faint with the heat,' she said to her husband in a voice loud enough to be heard by the other courtiers nearby. 'By your leave, I'll go back to our lodgings now as you so kindly suggested.'

She knew the King would have no interest at all in the few women attending him, unlike Queen Elizabeth. She also knew that now she had seen what Sir Henry had brought her to see, he would be less insistent.

Sir Henry looked briefly pleased at having made an impression and then hissed, 'Ye can stay and watch till the end.'

She curtseyed gravely to him, as if he had said yes. 'My lord is very kind.'

Without pausing, she turned and curtseyed to the King in his carven chair and then walked away over the Brig Port and back into Dumfries. Obedience to Sir Henry had never made any difference as far as she could see, so she would try pleasing herself for a change. Besides, she wanted to get some sleep before the evening. Behind her the football match continued with much shouting.

## WEDNESDAY, 12TH JULY 1592, DAWN

Carey had slept very badly, partly because his balls were sore. In the long run, though, he had been well out of the football match which had descended into a pitched brawl at the end amid such confusion that nobody could tell which side had won. The King had been very displeased. The other reason for wakefulness was the fact that the truckle bed Lord Maxwell's servants had found him was alive with fleas and six inches too short for his legs which dangled off the end even though he lay diagonally. On waking up he found that one of Maxwell's enormous Irish wolfhounds had curled up next to him at some time during the night and could thus explain the strange hairiness of the dream women he had met in his sleep.

'Good morning, bedfellow,' he said politely. The wolfhound panted, yawned and slobbered a vast tongue lovingly over his face. There was shouting in the next room, something about a surgeon.

It seemed Lord Maxwell was already awake. He came in, drinking his morning beer while he put on his jack.

'The King's gone fra the town for the hunt already,' he said without preamble as Carey swung his legs over the bed and sat up scratching and wiping dog drool off with his shirtsleeve. 'I'm riding out to join him, if ye care to come?'

'I said I would, my lord,' Carey answered after a moment as he put on his hose.

Dodd appeared in his usual foul dawn mood, Red Sandy and Sim's Will at his back, but there was no sign of Young Hutchin.

'Not again,' said Carey. 'Did you see anything that...?'

'He slipped off when he woke, said he wanted to find his cousins and to tell ye not to be afeared for him, he willnae fall for it twice.'

'Bloody Grahams,' muttered Carey as he put on his doublet and began buttoning the front. 'Will it be safe to leave our packponies and remounts here, my Lord Maxwell?'

Lord Maxwell was already on his way down the stairs, irritable about something. He gestured.

'They'll be as safe as mine own. Are ye coming?'

Carey hurried to pull his boots on and follow the new lord Warden down to the courtyard, still rubbing his face and wishing he could shave. The wolfhound came padding softly after him, shaking herself occasionally. There was no doubt about it, Maxwell was in a temper and was looking at him with suspicion under those sooty eyebrows of his. What had Carey heard when he woke, something about a surgeon? Ah. Inspiration suddenly flowered.

'The guns,' he said aloud.

'Guns?' asked Maxwell, eyes like slits.

'The two hundred-odd mixed calivers and pistols you have in Lochmaben, along with ammunition and priming powder,' Carey enlarged coolly. 'If you like, I'll inspect them for you and tell you if they're bad or not.'

It wasn't how he had planned to find out for certain whether Maxwell had the guns from the Carlisle armoury, but springing it on him that way certainly got an answer. Maxwell was bug-eyed with surprise.

'How did ye ken...?'

Carey sighed. 'Somebody bought them,' he said. 'And you have the money.'

Maxwell leaned over the trestle table set up to feed the men, and cut a piece of cheese. 'Why should I want so many guns?' he asked with a failed attempt at being casual.

Carey laughed. 'To wipe out the Johnstones, of course, my lord, once King James has gone back to Edinburgh.'

Maxwell sniffed and examined his fingernails elaborately. His other hand drummed a beat on the table.

'How do ye know?'

'I didn't know for sure, my lord,' Carey admitted, breaking open a penny loaf and throwing some crumbs to the doves from the cote on the roof who had come out cautiously in hopes of food. 'Only, any man would like to end a feud in his favour if he could.'

Maxwell started examining the other fingernails now, while his right hand began stroking at his dagger hilt. Oh, not again, Dodd groaned inwardly. He had been too outraged at Carey's question to speak, why can the bloody Courtier never let be? We're in the Maxwell's own townhouse and he's March Warden forbye...

But Carey was grinning, sitting carefully down on a bench, leaning back and plunking his boots on the table with a heavy double thud.

'I don't care what you do to the Johnstones, my lord,' he said, waving his bread. 'It's none of my concern, because it's Scottish West March business entirely and the Johnstones are a thorn in our side as well. I'm only interested in guns.'

'And ye'd know if ye saw them whether they were faulty or not?'

'Yes,' said Carey simply. 'And if somebody's already been hurt by one, don't you think that would be wise, before you take on the Johnstones?'

Maxwell stared at him for a moment longer, calculating. 'My cousin,' he answered obliquely, 'was blinded last night and may not live the week. When can you check them?'

'At your lordship's convenience, after I've seen the King.'

* * *

The King of Scotland was hunting the deer. In the distance, he could hear the hounds at full cry and the beaters behind them with their drums and trumpets and clappers and in between the beating of hooves on the ground as the game the foresters had found in the days preceding were driven inexorably down through the valley to where the court waited, bows strung at the ready. Occasionally the King liked to stalk a single noble beast, perhaps a hart of twelve points, the King of the Forest, with only the help of a couple of lymer-dogs and foresters, spending perhaps a day or more to waylay the animal and take his life personally with a crossbow. Certainly that was the hunting which gave him the greatest personal satisfaction and he knew he was good at it, being as patient and cunning as a ghillie, but this was business. His court needed venison in quantity, which unfortunately eliminated finesse.

Their hides had been well-built and disguised with brush. Each of the nobles had their best-liked weapon, whether longbow, crossbow or lance. Some had boar spears in case some wild boar should have been put up. None had firearms, mainly because of the damage they did to the skins and also to reduce wastage in beaters. And it was well known King James didn't like them.

The dawn was exquisite: pale peach and gold at the eastern horizon shading to royal blue overhead, and the nearer forest was quiet with anticipation, a breeze blowing which carried all the scents of greenery and earth, unreproduceable no matter how many perfumes you mixed. Only the sounds of the drive coming nearer gave tension, the lift and overhang of a wave before it broke...

The game burst milling from the forest: red deer and roe and fallow, all ages and sexes. The King took aim at the best animal: a stag of ten, shot it with a bolt through the neck, reached out his hand and was given another loaded crossbow in exchange for the discharged one and shot it again directly under the chin. The whup and twang of longbows and crossbows filled the air with a music that delighted the King's ear, and beasts lurched and fell as they slowed and turned, leaped about in panic. King James laughed with pleasure at the sight: here was a true glory—to meet the bounty of the wild and conquer it.

With two men behind him rewinding his bows, the King had shot four of the deer by the time the forest's harvest was lying down and flopping about, save a couple of wiser or luckier does who had jumped past the hides and disappeared into the undergrowth behind.

Sweating foresters began the work of turning the carcases on their sides. King James stepped from behind his hide and marched up to the stag he had killed first. He took the long heavy hunting knife from the gamewarden, who had been warned to be on bended knee, and waited impatiently for the musicians who were hidden off to one side to begin playing. He had heard that the Queen of England always unmade the first deer to the sweet strains of music.

One of the musicians popped his head up from the foliage, ruining the effect of faery music that had been planned. The musician's velvet cap was askew.

'Your Highness, one of the deer fell on George Beaton's viol.'

King James waved the hunting knife. 'Get on with it,' he growled.

'Ay, sire.'

After a couple more moments, frenetic sawing began from the bushes, with pipes and drums at variance and the strings all at venture. King James sighed deeply, bent to make the first cut. Although he stabbed at the furry throat gingerly, a red tide burst out of the animal's nostrils and washed over his boots, ruining his red pompoms.

King James dropped the knife in the mud and stepped stickily away from the small lake of blood. He sighed again. What was the saying? Make a silk purse of a sow's ear? God knew it sometimes seemed to him that he had a better chance of making a lady's veil of a sow's pigbed than imitating the English court, but they had to learn ceremony, these mad battle-crazy nobles of his, or they would humiliate him when the old bitch in London died and he came into his own.

While the butchery was carried out in front of the hides and some of the professional huntsmen took lymers and crossbows to track down the deer that had been wounded but not killed in the confusion, King James remounted his white horse. It had been a successful drive and the court was now supplied with much of the meat it needed in Dumfries. He smiled and waved his hand at dear Alexander Lord Spynie's compliments and then, for all his good temper, became grave again. A long fellow with odd hair in a nicely London-cut black velvet doublet was approaching, limping slightly as he threaded between the horses and the boasting nobles. He was carrying a goblet and a white towel. Well, were they learning at last?

The long fellow doffed his hat, genuflected gracefully twice and then after ceremoniously tasting the wine in the King's sight and wiping the goblet's lip with the towel, held it up to him so he only had to bend down and take it.

King James did so and finally recognised the man properly.

'Sir Robert Carey again, is it not?' he said as he drank. Spices hid the fact that the wine was as bad as all the wine in Godforsaken Dumfries, except for what he himself had brought. Yes, Carey was at Court, he remembered now, though as always his memory of the previous afternoon was somewhat wine-blurred. Carey had played well in the football match until the eye-watering foul that put him out of it. Even James had felt the urge to cross his legs.

'Are ye quite recovered now, Sir Robert?' he asked solicitously. 'No ill-effects, I hope.'

'No, Your Majesty. I don't think so.'

'I think the best remedy would be a piece of steak,' James went on ruminatively. 'Externally rather than internally, ye follow. And an infusion of comfrey with perhaps a few ounces of blood from the arm.'

'Your Majesty is most kind in your concern. I tried the steak last night and it certainly...helped.'

James smiled at Carey. Lacking it conspicuously himself, he had always found a strange fascination about male beauty: a wonder and a miracle in the way big bones and hard muscles produced something powerful and cleanly exciting, utterly different from the cloying softness and vapidity of women. Carey, at the age of twenty-three when King James had first seen him in Walsingham's ambassadorial train, had truly been beautiful, with sophistication and fluent French from his recent stay in Paris, and the glorious arrogance of youth. James had been a few years younger in years, a few centuries older in experience and had delighted in him. Poor d'Aubigny would have approved James's tall base-born cousin as well, but by that time poor d'Aubigny had been thrown out of Scotland by the Ruthven Raiders and was dead. After Walsingham went south again, King James had sent several warm letters and spent considerable time trying to persuade the Queen of England and Carey's father, Lord Hunsdon, to let Carey come back to the Scottish court for a longer stay. Unfortunately, the old lord had blocked him for some reason and James had turned to find other friends for his loneliness. Carey had carried some messages to Edinburgh for the Queen of England, had even been the man rash enough to bring the news of Mary Queen of Scots' execution— not that James had let him set foot in Scotland that time. Now, many years after their first meeting, Carey was back once more. His shoulders had broadened as you would expect of the son of one of King Henry VIII's byblows. But he had lost none of his charm and, from the look of him, none of his arrogance either.

King James felt the heat rising in him again, decided to prolong the conversation.

'And what did ye think to the sport, Sir Robert?'

'I marked a kingly shot at the highest-ranked deer present,' said Sir Robert smoothly. 'Was it Your Majesty's?'

Ay, it was lovely the way the English could flatter. Carey had been at Queen Elizabeth's court for ten years, the best school of courtesy in the world. Still, it *had* been a good shot. King James allowed himself to preen a little.

'I think it was. I had the benefit of a clean view.'

'In the best run of hunts, a man may always miss if his hand be not steady,' said Sir Robert. 'I saw Your Majesty kill at least five.'

'Is a King but a man?' James asked, wondering if philosophy would make the Englishman sweat at all. No; he was smiling.

'In the sight of God we are all but men,' said he. 'But in the sight of men, I believe that a king must be, as it were, a god.'

James was enjoying this immensely. He finished the wine. 'Did ye have a particular god in mind, Sir Robert?'

Carey hesitated not at all, which confirmed King James's suspicion that he was rerunning a good workmanlike arselick that had already seen service up Queen Elizabeth's metaphorical petticoats.

'Apollo sprang to mind, Your Majesty.'

'Not Diana, mistress of the hunt?'

Carey almost grinned, but not quite. 'No, Your Majesty, saving your grace's pardon, I would reserve the figure of the pale virgin of the moon for my liege and Queen, Your Majesty's good cousin.'

'And so I should hope. Well, Apollo will do for the present.' It was nice that Carey remembered the courtly games and masques they had played years ago, with King James taking the role of Apollo the Sun God and much ribaldry on the subject of that Virgin Moon as well.

Having emptied the goblet, King James made a move to hand it back, but Carey stepped away and spread his hands gracefully.

'How dare mere mortal lips touch that which has refreshed the Sun God?' he said with a fine rhetoric. Over behind his left shoulder in the pressing knot of courtiers, James heard someone mutter that if every fucking Englishman was as prosy as this one, it was no fucking wonder their Queen could never be brought to decide on anything.

King James sighed again, and examined the silver goblet, which was nicely chased and inlaid with enamel and a couple of reasonable garnets. There was no question but that his court could do with some polish.

'Ay,' he said. 'It's a mite melted round about the rim. I'll keep it and have my silversmith mend it for me.'

'Your Majesty, may I ask a boon?' added Carey, once more with his knee crunching in the leaf-litter. No doubt all the fucking Englishmen would have terrible rheumatism of the kneejoints with all the bending and scraping they must do at the Queen's court, continued the commentary behind the King.

'Ay, what can I do for ye, Sir Robert?'

'Would Your Majesty favour me with a few minutes of your time?'

So he wanted audience and knew how to ask for it prettily. Lord, it was a lot easier on the nerves than some of the earls about the King who tended to march up to him and begin haranguing him at the least opportunity. And perhaps...who knew? Perhaps they could be friends? Or more? King James positively beamed at his cousin.

'Ay, of course, Sir Robert. It would be a pleasure. This afternoon, I think, when I have refreshed myself after the hunting.'

'Your Majesty does me the greatest conceivable honour.'

'Ay, nae doubt of it. Farewell, Sir Robert.'

King James rode off with his goblet tucked into his saddlebag, chuckling to himself and wondering idly was Carey still as much of an innocent as he had been? Surely not. Lord Spynie was riding close by, but casting looks like daggers over his shoulder at Carey. Well, it was always a pleasure to see a well-looking man with a bit of polish and a nice smooth tongue on him, it reminded him of poor d'Aubigny in a way that none of the ruffianly heathens and sour-faced Godlovers that generally surrounded him could ever do. Certainly not Spynie, whose polish was thinly applied and increasingly gimcrack.

The King began to look forward to the afternoon's audience.

\* \* \*

Young Hutchin had spent the morning finding the house of the Graham water-bailiff's woman, in the unhealthy part of town near the Kirk Gate. His curiosity to see the court had completely left him, but he had a more urgent desire now. In the little wooden house he had discovered the water-bailiff, well settled in and dandling a baby on his knee while a plump girl laughed and stirred a pottage on the fire. Round the table were two other cousins of his, and his Uncle Jimmy.

There was some ribald cheering when he came in and his cousin Robert asked if he was planning to join the court and if he thought King James would like him too. Uncle Jimmy cuffed his son's ear and asked if it was true what he had heard, that the Deputy Warden had gone after him alone with his sword.

Beetroot at the thought of the story getting back to his father, Young Hutchin nodded.

'He shouldnae have let ye come here,' opined cousin John, who was the elder and took his responsibilities seriously.

An innate sense of fairness forced Hutchin to explain. 'I came after him meself and I wouldnae go back to Carlisle though he told me to,' he said. 'Ye cannae blame the Deputy for the mither.'

Uncle Jimmy grunted. 'D'ye want us to do anything?' he asked.

Hutchin thought about this for a while. It was a serious matter. If he said the word, he could be sure that every man in the room at the Red Boar would have a price on his head and the whole Graham surname after his blood. It was a warming thought, that, but would it be as satisfying as seeing them die himself?

'Nay,' he said at last. 'I'll kill them all meself when I'm grown. I can wait.'

Uncle Jimmy exchanged looks with the water-bailiff who nodded approvingly.

'That's right, lad,' said Uncle Jimmy. 'Allus do the job yerself if ye can, and be sure it's done the way ye want it. And what's the Deputy doing here anyway?'

'He's looking for the guns that were reived out of Carlisle Keep on Sunday, for one thing,' Young Hutchin told him. Uncle Jimmy laughed shortly. Everyone knew what had happened to them, except the Deputy of course. 'And he keeps asking after a German he saw arrested on the Border the Saturday as well, wants to talk to him.'

'Why?' asked Uncle Jimmy.

Young Hutchin frowned. 'How would I know?' he said. 'He might want to make friends. Can ye keep an eye out for him?'

The other Grahams sighed deeply. 'That's ticklish, Young Hutchin,' said his other cousin. 'What if this German doesnae want to meet the Deputy?'

Young Hutchin shrugged. 'I think he'll be as bitten by curiosity as any other man,' he said. 'Would ye not at least go to gawk, Cousin Robert, if ye were not at the horn, that is?'

Cousin Robert snorted.

Not one of the Grahams, other than Young Hutchin and the water-bailiff, was legally there, because at least one of the stated reasons for the King being in Dumfries was to harry the evil clan of Graham, that had lifted so many of his best horses, off the face of the earth. The evil clan knew this perfectly well and were anxious to hear about it when the King finally decided what to do with his army.

So there were the Johnstones who were old friends and with the town as packed as it was, a few extra louring ruffians in worn jacks were hardly noticeable. Uncle Jimmy and his sons promised to look out for the German, and gave Hutchin news of his father and his Uncle Richard of Brackenhill, who were finding that people were even slower with their blackrent payments than usual. According to Uncle Jimmy, Richie of Brackenhill blamed the new Deputy Warden who was shaking everything up so well, and wanted Hutchin's estimate of what it would cost to pay him off and how he should be approached.

Hutchin blew out his cheeks and drank some of the mild ale poured by the water bailiff's woman. She had pretty brown hair and a lovely pair of tits to her; Hutchin found his attention wandered every time she passed, and when she sat herself down on a stool to feed the babe, it was all he could do not to stare. God knew, it was older men and weans had all the fun. None of the maids he met would let him so much as squeeze their paps.

'Young Hutchin?' pressed Uncle Jimmy, looking amused. 'How much for the Deputy's bribe?'

'It's hard to tell,' Hutchin said slowly. 'I dinnae think he thinks like other men.'

'Och nonsense,' growled Uncle Jimmy. 'Every man has his price.'

'Ay, but I dinna think it's money he wants.'

'What d'ye mean?' demanded cousin Robert. 'O' course he wants money, what man doesnae?'

'Land? Cattle? Women?'

'Nothing so simple, see ye, Uncle Jimmy,' said Hutchin. 'Ay, he wants something, but I dinna ken for sure what it is.'

'When ye find out, will ye pass the word to your Uncle Richie, Hutchin? God knows, it's why we paid to put ye in the Keep in the first place.'

'Of course.' Hutchin was offended. 'I know that. But it's no' so simple as I thought. It's...well, he doesnae treat me like ye'd expect, and he doesnae think like a Borderer. I'm no relation of his at all, but there it was, he came after me.'

Surprisingly, Uncle Jimmy nodded. 'Your Uncle Jock o' the Peartree was saying something alike the other day. He's as puzzled as ye are. But dinna forget, Carey's got his price, same as any man. All ye need to do is find out what it is and we'll do the rest.'

Hutchin smiled. 'Whatever it is, it'll be high. Have ye seen the velvets and silks he wears and the way he treats 'em?'

Uncle Jimmy laughed. 'Och, we'll even pay his tailor's bills for him, if he wants. Uncle Richie's a businessman, no' a headcase like Kinmont Willie.'

Belly packed tight with a hot pottage and more ale Young Hutchin said goodbye to his relatives and started back up the Soutergate towards the Townhead and Maxwell's Castle. He felt very proud of himself for never mentioning the water-bailiff's rather older wife that he had left in Carlisle.

As he picked his way between the heaps of dung and the men playing dice and drinking at every corner, he realised that someone was keeping pace with him. Narrow-eyed with new suspicion, he looked sideways as he drew his dagger, saw a stocky youth a little older than himself, but well-dressed in a wool suit and wearing a sword, though not obviously a courtier. His face seemed a little familiar, but Hutchin couldn't place it.

'Good afternoon,' said the youth cheerfully. 'Are you Hutchin Graham?'

'Who wants to know?' demanded Hutchin, backing to the wall and looking around for ambushes.

The youth took his cap off politely. 'Roger Widdrington, second son of Sir Henry,' he said, and then added, 'Lady Widdrington sent me.'

Young Hutchin relaxed slightly. He could hear easily enough that this Roger Widdrington was no Scot, but did indeed come from the East March.

'Ay,' he said. 'I'm Hutchin Graham.'

'Sir Robert Carey's pageboy?'

'Ay. What about it?'

Roger Widdrington moved closer, ignoring Hutchin's dagger,

623

so that they were under the overhang of an armourer's shop. 'Ye know that my Lady Elizabeth has been forbidden to speak to the Deputy?'

Hutchin nodded. He had carried the letter, but had not been able to read it. However, it was easy enough to guess what it said from the Deputy's reaction to it.

'Well,' said Roger Widdrington with a knowing grin, 'my stepmother still likes to hear about him. Will ye tell me anything you can about him while he's in Dumfries?'

'The Deputy doesnae take me into his confidence much.'

Roger Widdrington nodded wisely. 'Whatever you can tell me,' he said. 'And my lady will pay you of course, sixpence for each item of information.'

Hutchin nodded cannily. That made sense and Lady Widdrington was a sensible woman. God knew, he sometimes thought the Deputy needed a nursemaid to keep him out of trouble.

'Ay,' he said. 'I can do that.'

'What can you tell me now?'

'Not much. I havenae seen him since last night, for I left the Castle before him this morning.'

'How are his balls?'

Hutchin suppressed a grin. 'Not bad, not bad at all, considering some bastard tried to swing on them, though he doesnae ken who, it being too close and too quick. He didnae need the surgeon, though Dodd was all for sending for one, but the Deputy said most of the surgeons he knew were ainly interested in what they could cut off, and that wasnae what he had in mind.'

Roger Widdrington laughed. 'I'll tell her he's better,' he said, and handed Hutchin a silver English sixpence as proof of his integrity.

'Meet me here tomorrow at noon,' said Roger Widdrington. 'Can you do that?'

'I reckon I can.'

'Excellent. Oh, and don't tell the Deputy about this—Lady Widdington doesn't want him worrying about what might happen to her if Sir Henry finds out.'

'Ay,' said Young Hutchin, well pleased with himself, pulled at his cap and went on up to Maxwell's Castle.

King James had finished his repast, mainly of brutally tough venison, and was well into the Tuscan wine when the English Deputy Warden was announced. Beaming happily he rose to greet the man and found him down on one knee again.

'Up, up,' cried King James. 'By God, I had rather look ye in the eye, than down on ye, Sir Robert. Will ye sit by me and take some wine? Good. Rob, my dear, fetch up some of the white Rhenish and some cakes for my good friend here.'

King James watched his page trot off dutifully and sighed a little. At that age they were delightful; so fresh-faced and rounded, but King James was a man of principle and had promised himself he would have nothing to do with children. Poor d'Aubigny had been clear in his contempt for those who did and besides, as he had also said in his delightful trilling French voice, how could one tell that they would not suddenly erupt with spots or become gangling and bony? Beauty was all to d'Aubigny, beauty and elegance, things in precious short supply in Scotland.

King James turned back to Carey and smiled. 'It's such a pleasure to meet someone newly from the English court,' he said. 'Can ye tell me aught of my esteemed cousin, Her Majesty Queen Elizabeth?'

Carey, who was extremely tall once off his knees, had sat down at once when invited to, tactfully upon a low folding stool by the King's great carven armchair. He spoke at length about the Queen, from which King James gathered that the old bitch was still as pawky and impossible as ever; that she was spending money like water upon the war in the Netherlands and the miserable fighting against the Wild Irish led by O'Neill in the bogs of Ireland; that if James's annual subsidy was actually delivered he should be grateful for it, since there was no chance whatever of an increase—a sad piece of news to King James, but not unexpected.

'Och, it's a fact, Sir Robert,' he said sadly. 'There is nothing more stupid than a war. If I have a hope for the...for the future, it is that I may one day become a means of peace between England and Spain.'

Sir Robert took this extraordinary sentiment like a man. Not a flicker of surprise did his face betray; instead he managed to bow from a sitting position and say 'Her Majesty is often heard to say the same thing: that the war was never of her making and that she fought against it with all she had and for as long as she could, but that at the last you cannot make peace with one who is determined to fight.'

'Ay,' said the King. 'That's true as well and well I know it.'

'What Her Majesty deplores most of all is the waste of gold to pay for weapons. She says it is like a great bottomless pit, and if you tip in cartloads of gold, still you never hear them so much as tinkle.'

King James smiled at the figure, but felt he could improve it. 'Or the mouth of an ever hungry monster, a cockatrice or a basilisk, perhaps.'

'It's not surprising,' continued Carey. 'For weapons are expensive, above all firearms.'

'So they are, so they are,' agreed King James affably as the young Robert came trotting back with a silver flagon and two silver goblets. The wine was better than most of the stuff swilling around Dumfries, but still not up to its surroundings, and Carey had some work to swallow it. King James was more used to the rotgut that the Hanseatic merchants had been unloading on thirsty Scotland until the Bonnettis arrived, and knocked his own drink back easily.

'We had a strange accident in Carlisle upon the Sunday,' said Carey after a moment's pause. 'A number of newly delivered firearms were stolen out of our very armoury while we were at muster in readiness to assist you.'

'Never?' said King James. 'Well, I am sorry to hear it, Sir Robert, sorry indeed. Such dishonesty...'

'It was thought that they might have come to Scotland, perhaps brought by an ill-affected noble?'

'Och no, to be sure, they'll have been auctioned all over the Debateable Land by now,' said King James. 'The surnames might well be a wee bit concerned with myself in the district to do justice and the hanging trees all ready with ropes. It's not to be wondered at that they might try a thing like that to arm themselves better against me. Not that it will do any good.'

'And then there was the rumour of a Spanish agent at Your Majesty's court.'

'Never,' said King James very positively. 'Now why would we do a silly thing like that, harbouring an enemy of England, considering the manifold kindnesses and generosities to us of our most beloved cousin, the Queen of England.'

'Not, of course, with Your Majesty's knowledge,' said Carey, managing to sound very shocked, slipping from his stool to go on one knee again. 'Such a thought had never crossed my mind. It struck me, however, that some among your nobles might have... designs and desires to change the religion of this land, or something worse, and the Spanish agent might be a part of it.'

'Och, never look so sad, man, and get off yer poor worn-out knee again. That's better. Have some more wine. Nay, any Spaniard at the court, and I'd have had word of him from my lords here all at daggers drawn, quarrelling for his gold.' He smiled wisely at Carey who smiled back.

'Of course, Your Majesty, I was a poor fool to think otherwise.'

'Ay, well, we'll say no more on it. And when I go into the Debateable Land to winkle out Bothwell, that black-hearted witch of a man, I'll keep a good eye out for your weapons, never fear.'

'Yes, Your Majesty. If I might venture a little more on the subject: for God's sake, do not try any that you might capture, for they are all faulty and burst on firing. You may tell one of the faulty guns by a cross scratched on the underside of the stock.'

King James nodded. 'I shall bear it in mind,' he said. 'But personally I do not care for the crack and report of firearms no more than for the clash of knives or swords. Ye may have noted how most of the beasts we hunted this morning were slain by arrows or bolts or the action of dogs. So I'll be in no danger from yer badly welded pistols, have nae fear.'

'I am very happy to hear it,' said Carey after a tiny pause. 'Your Majesty's life is, of course, infinitely precious, not only in Scotland, but also in England.'

Hm, thought King James, is this some message from the Cecils, I wonder? Do they see danger somewhere? I wonder where?

Gently he probed Carey, but thought that in fact the man was as he seemed: concerned at the lost guns from Carlisle and with the rumoured Spanish agent, but he had left London in the middle of June and was already a little behind with the court news. Also it transpired that he was one of the Earl of Essex's faction, rather than with the Cecils, which showed he was disappointingly short-sighted.

Surely it couldn't be much longer to wait, thought James as they discussed the merits of hunting par force de chiens as opposed to using beaters; surely the old battle axe would die soon. But it seemed that she was like the Sphinx: full of riddles and immortal, her health depressingly good apart from being occasionally troubled by a sore on her leg.

King James was sinking the wine as quickly as he usually did, with Rob already gone down to the butler for a refill. One of the clerks would be in soon with administrative papers for him to sign and letters to write: he knew he was getting a little tipsy when he slopped some of the wine down his doublet and laughed. Ever the courtier, Sir Robert fetched one of the linen towels off the rack by the fireplace and proffered the end to wipe up the spillage—something that would never even have occurred to Rob or the Earl of Mar or any one of his overdressed hangers-on.

James was full of goodwill and caught Carey's wrist with his hand as he came close.

'Will ye speak French to me?' he asked. 'I dinna speak it well mesen, but the sound of it always thrills my heart.'

'Avec grand plaisir. Alas, Your Majesty, my accent is not what it once was and I have forgotten much,' said Carey in that language. On an affectionate impulse, James kissed his cheek which was so near and so inviting. Only a kiss.

It was a mistake. Carey permitted the familiarity but no more. James felt the tension in him: damn the cold-hearted bloody English, they all bridled at a touch from him as if he was diseased.

'Ye used to remind me so much of d'Aubigny, ye know,' James said thickly, hoping as he looked into Carey's handsome face that the man was either easily overawed or as sophisticated as he seemed. 'Ye still have very much his style, Robin.'

Carey smiled carefully. 'Perhaps from the French court,' he said, in Scottish this time. 'My father wanted me to learn Latin as well as French, but alas I was a bad student and spent most of my time pursuing sinful women.' Yes, there was a distinct, if tactful accent on the 'women'. Another man still in thrall to the she-serpent then. 'My ignorance is entirely my own fault.'

James let go of Carey's arm and drank down what was left of his wine. 'My tutor George Buchanan warned me that the wages of sin is death,' he said, wondering whether to be angry at the rebuff or simply sad, and also whether it would be worth having Carey to supper privately and filling him full of aqua vitae. He had known it work sometimes, with the ambitious, although that of course also contained the seed of heartache, in that the love could never be pure. How he longed for the clarity of the love and partnership between Achilles and Patroclus, or Alexander and Hephaistion. And David and Jonathan: it had been a revelation to him when he read how their love surpassed that of women, for how could the ancestor of Christ be guilty? Their love was never condemned in the Bible as was David's adultery with Bathsheba.

'Mr Buchanan was right, of course,' said Carey softly, not looking at James, his face impossible to read. 'We are all sinners and all of us die.'

'Even godlike kings?' sneered King James.

'Your Majesty knows the answer to that better than I do.'

'And queens? What about queens, eh? When do they die?' I am getting drunk, thought King James. That was a tactless question. Carey bridled only a little.

'When Death comes for them.'

'Has she bribed him, or what?'

Carey smiled, the blue eyes intense as chips of aquamarine. 'If that were possible, she surely would, but as you know, she would prefer to hold him rather with the promise of a bribe and a flood of sweet words.'

King James laughed at the satire. Carey was sitting down on his stool again, meekly, as if James had never touched his hand, nor kissed his face. It was a pity, a pity: he had lovely shoulders and although his hair was odd, most of the curls black but the roots reddish brown, he had the long Boleyn face and the Tudor hooded bright blue eyes, and he had the smoothness and culture that d'Aubigny had shown King James when he was a raw lad of sixteen. The King's face clouded: affection and sophistication had been heady things to discover for the first time in his hard-driven scholarly life. He looked on the time he had spent with d'Aubigny as a brief respite in Paradise, before the bastard nobles had kidnapped their King in the Ruthven Raid, with their usual lack of respect, and forced him to send d'Aubigny away. Not content with that they had then almost certainly poisoned the Frenchman. One day, thought King James, one day I'll have satisfaction on all of them for it.

'Speak some French to me again,' he said, watching Rob refill his goblet and Carey's. But it wasn't boys he wanted, unlike Spynie and his friends, it was men with good bodies and good minds: true companions as the Greeks had been, without the mucky dim-witted clinginess and greedy softness of women. Lord God, how Queen Anne his wife bored him with her pawing and treble complaints.

'Je parle tres mal la belle langue,' said Carey, the brand of his Englishness striking through all the music of French. It was like hearing a spinet played by someone in gauntlets and King James sighed again. What was it about the French language that had the power to bewitch him so? The first time he had heard d'Aubigny speak with the rolled rrs so different in Scots and the lilting cadences, he had been moved almost to tears with longing. Perhaps it had been witchcraft...No, the witches were all Scottish like the Earl of Bothwell. D'Aubigny had simply been...d'Aubigny, and this large, proud and beautiful Englishman was nothing of the kind.

There had been a knock at the door some time before and now the secretary and the clerk stood there waiting with sour impatience. Carey had opened the door for them: well, it wasn't James's fault if Carey couldn't see what Buchanan had beaten into the boy-King so well: that, like the wicked French mermaid Queen Mary his mother, women were darkness and dirt combined, the true root of sin, and an ever-present danger to every man's soul, the invariable tools of the Devil. Poor Carey, to be in thrall to such creatures...Never mind. Perhaps a quiet supper some other time, perhaps the promise of advancement when King James came into his own: the English were the greediest nation on earth, everyone knew that.

King James gestured imperiously to dismiss Sir Robert, who once more genuflected and kissed the royal hand, the contact of skins dry and without content. The clerk and the secretary exchanged glances when they saw their king's squint-eyed look, and the secretary reordered the papers he was holding. Dammit, he could drink if he wanted to, he was the King.

Carey backed off, bowed at the door, stepped back another three paces out of sight and then turned and left. King James sighed, tears of self-pity pricking at his eyes: one day he would find someone like d'Aubigny again, one day it would happen. He was the King, and he tried to be a good king and bring peace and justice to his thrawn dangerous uncharming people; surely God would relent again and let him taste love.

Dodd came on Carey washing his hands and face in well-water and drinking aqua vitae by the gulp. He was already a little drunk, Dodd saw, which was no surprise if he had just had audience with the King of Scots, and he was also wound up tight, almost quivering with tension.

'Did the King have anything to say about the guns?' asked Dodd, who knew what Carey had been hoping for.

Carey grunted, shook his head, looked about for a towel, saw that the courtyard of Maxwell's town house had no such things, and wiped his hands on his hose.

'Any luck with the German or the Italians?' he demanded harshly.

Dodd shook his head in turn. 'I dinnae think the German can still be alive,' he said positively, wishing he knew why the foreigners were important. 'I've been up and down this bloody nest of Scots and not a hide nor a hair of him is there anywhere. Signor Bonnetti is supplying His Majesty with wine, but ye knew that already. How's the King?'

At least I didn't nearly puke in his lap this time, thought Carey gloomily, but Jesus, it was close. What is it about me that makes him like me so? I don't look anything like Lord Spynie, thank God. The aqua vitae burned pleasantly in his throat and he poured Dodd some, as well as more for himself. Dodd, he saw, was full of morbid curiosity about his audience and clearly fighting the impulse to ask nosy questions.

'Drunk when I left him, drunk and maudlin,' snapped Carey. 'Come on, let's go out and ask some more questions.'

They spent the rest of the afternoon on Irish Street, starting at one end and going into every armourer's and gunsmith they could see.

As it turned out, the first one was typical. 'Nay, sir, I canna undertake yer order,' said the master gunsmith, with his broad hands folded behind his leather apron and a bedlam of bellows, furnace, hammering and screeling metal behind him.

'Not even if I pay you forty shillings sterling for each pistol and fifty shillings for the calivers?' pressed Carey, holding one of the sample wares from the front of the shop and looking at it narrowly.

'Nay, sir, it's impossible,' said the master gunsmith firmly. 'Not if ye was to pay double the amount, I couldnae do it. Not before Lammastide next.'

'How about by Michaelmas?'

The master gunsmith sucked his teeth. 'I tellt ye, it's impossible,' he said, 'I'm no' dickering for a price, sir, I could get what I asked, but I canna make enough guns for the orders on my books as it is.'

'What's the problem?'

'See ye, sir, we allus have full order books, because in Dumfries we make the best weapons in the world, and my shop here makes the best, the finest weapons in a' of Dumfries. I have none but journeymen makers, here, not a part of yer gun will be made by a 'prentice, and the lock will be made by meself or my son-in-law that's a master gunsmith as well. My guns shoot true, they dinna misfire, and they never blow up in yer hand. I've turned down bigger orders than yourn fra the Papists, because I canna fill them.'

'Could you not take on extra men?' Carey asked.

The master gunsmith's red face took on a purple hue. 'What? Untrained? Cack-handed fools that canna tell one end of the stock fra the other? No, sir. And ye'll not thank me if I did, for the weapons they made would be as like to kill ye as yer enemy. We make the finest weapons in the world here and...'

'I thought Augsburg had good weaponsmiths,' said Carey provocatively.

The master gunsmith spat magnificently. 'Sir,' he said. 'I'll thank ye to leave my shop. I'll have nae talk of German mountebanks in this place, ye might sour the metal. Go to Jedburgh for yer weapons if ye've a mind to, but begone from here. Out.'

Carey went meekly enough, rubbing his lower lip with his thumb and looking pleased. He tried two more shops, the second of which was full of the choking indescribable stench of the flesh being burnt off horse hooves in a dry cauldron, so that the hooves themselves could be used to case-harden the gun-parts. They retreated from the place in some disorder and stopped at a small alehouse to drink aqua vitae to clean their throats. Carey sent Red Sandy Dodd on with Sim's Will Croser to carry on the questioning. Dodd stayed with him.

'Sir,' he said tactfully. 'What do ye plan to pay for the new weapons with?'

Carey spread his hands. 'Consider the lilies of the field,' he orated. 'They toil not, neither do they spin.'

'Sir?'

'I only want to know if the Dumfries armourers could fill an order like that and it seems they can't. Which is interesting.'

'Oh?'

'Interesting but not surprising.'

'Ay, sir.'

'Do you know what I'm talking about, Dodd?'

'Ay, sir. Ye've the Maxwells and the Johnstones glowering at each other, all wanting guns. Ye've the Armstrongs, the Bells, the Carlisles and the Irvines wanting to protect themselves fra the Maxwells and the Johnstones, and each other, not to mention the Douglases and the Crichtons hereabouts. Ye've Bothwell buying armaments, and ye've King James's army in town, also wanting armaments and ye've the Irish rebels over the water and they want guns too.'

'And us,' added Carey softly. 'One lot of good Tower-made weapons lost on the road from Newcastle, swapped for deathtraps, and one lot of deathtraps reived out of the Carlisle armoury under our noses. And where did they go, Dodd? Answer me that.'

'I thought Maxwell had 'em.'

'He's got the deathtraps, Sergeant, not the good weapons. Two hundred mixed calivers and pistols don't disappear into thin air; somebody has them.'

'Bothwell?' wondered Dodd.

'God forbid. But whoever it was made the exchange is the man who murdered poor Long George.'

'Ay,' said Dodd. 'That's a fact.'

'Besides, I want them back. Some of them had snaphaunce locks and I want them back.'

'Can the King not help ye, sir?' Dodd knew he was pushing it a little, seeing how upset the Deputy had been ever since his audience. Carey's face darkened instantly, and he finished his aqua vitae in a single gulp.

'Oh, bugger the King.'

'Ay, sir.' Dodd kept his face absolutely straight, which was just as well for Carey glared at him suspiciously.

Luckily Red Sandy and Sim's Will returned at that point to tell them that for all the multitude of gunsmiths in Dumfries, there was not a single one that could fill their order. They went back to Maxwell's Castle in awkward silence, Carey striding ahead with an expression of thunder on his face.

Hutchin turned out to be in Maxwell's stables, assiduously turning Thunder's black coat to damask.

'I should have brung some ribbons to plait his mane with, sir,' said the boy sorrowfully. 'I couldnae find a haberdasher's that had any the day, so I cannae make him as fine as the ither horses that'll be in the masqueing.'

Carey grunted and ordered Hutchin to wash his hands and come and brush his doublet and hose with rosepowder. Hutchin looked surprised but went meekly enough to the pump. Dodd followed him to wash his own hands and face. He had never before seen the Deputy in such an ill temper.

'What the Devil's got intae the Deputy?' Hutchin wanted to know.

Dodd shrugged. 'The King must have said something to upset him.'

'What could it be?'

'Well, I...'

'None of your bloody business, Dodd,' snapped Carey's voice behind them. 'I don't suppose either of you knows how to shave a man?'

They shook their heads.

'Hutchin, run down to the kitchens and fetch me some hot water. Boiling, mind. Dodd, did you bring your best suit as I told you?'

'I'm wearing it, sir,' said Dodd with some dignity.

'Jesus Christ, it's homespun.'

'Ay, sir. My wife's finest.'

'You're the Land Sergeant of Gilsland. Can't you afford anything better?'

He's drunk, Dodd reminded himself at this insult. 'Happen I could, sir,' Dodd said coldly. 'But it's no' what I choose to spend my money on.'

Carey's blue eyes examined him minutely for a moment. 'Get it brushed down and I'll lend you my smallest ruff.'

'Am I to attend ye at this Court masque, sir?'

'All of you are. Red Sandy and Sim's Will can stay outside with the horses, but I want you and Hutchin attending me inside.'

'Ye'll have to forgive me, sir,' said Dodd, still very much on his dignity, 'I've no' been to Court, like yourself, sir.'

'You can learn. If Barnabus could, you can.'

'Ay, sir,' said Dodd, blank-faced. 'Will I take my sword?'

Carey got the message at last, that Dodd was no servingman to order about, but a freeholder and a land-sergeant with as much right to bear a sword as Carey or Lord Scrope. He paused and his face relaxed slightly.

'Yes, dammit, take your sword and try to look respectable.'

'I shall look like what I am, sir,' said Dodd, with frigid dignity.

For an hour there was a whirlwind of shaving and combing hair, powdering and brushing of velvet, checking of ruffs and polishing of boots and blades. It finally dawned on Dodd, as Carey stood in a clean shirt, critically examining his black velvet suit, that one of the things eating the Courtier was the fact that he wasn't able to dress fine enough for a Court feast. For a moment Dodd almost laughed to see a man as put out by his lack of brocade and gold embroidery as any maid short of ribbons. He swallowed his amusement hastily, quite certain the Courtier wouldn't see it that way.

By the time they were ready strains of music were coming up from Maxwell's hall and Maxwell and Herries horsemen were assembling in the courtyard with torches. Looking down on it from the turret room next to Maxwell's solar, where Carey had a truckle bed, you could tell that this was no raid from the ribbons and ornaments on the horses and the splendour of some of the clothes. You could also tell from the way they lined up and sorted themselves out that raiding was more usual to them than masqueing.

He followed Carey down the winding stairs and found Red Sandy, Sim's Will and Hutchin Graham waiting with the horses, polished and smart and shining so he was quite proud of them, really. The Courtier inspected them with narrow eyes and nodded curtly, before going off to talk about precedence with the Lord Maxwell. He came back wearing a black velvet mask on his face which did nothing to disguise him but did make him look ridiculous, in Dodd's opinion.

The masked cavalcade streamed out of the gate of Maxwell's Castle and down through the marketplace of Dumfries where the townsfolk stood shading their eyes from the golden evening to see them.

They waited outside the townhouse where the King was staying for half an hour before the cavalcade of Scottish courtiers and lords and ladies came glittering from the gate to mount the horses waiting in rows. For the first time, Dodd saw womenfolk among them and was shocked: they were wearing the height of French fashion, most of them, their hair shining with jewels and their silken bodices begging for lungfever with the acreage they left bare, their faces decorated into birds of paradise with their own delicate jewelled and feathered masks. Even Lord Spynie helped a woman to her horse, which must have been his wife, and amongst the crowd,

Dodd spotted Sir Henry and Lady Elizabeth Widdrington, though she was wearing English fashion that made her more decent. Both of them were masked, Sir Henry expansive with bonhomie and solicitously helping her to her pillion seat behind him. She did not look well, Dodd thought, her face pale and tired under the velvet, with her lips clamped in a tight disapproving line. He stole a glance at Carey but Carey was busy keeping a skittish Thunder under control in his reasonably honourable place behind and to the right of the Lord Maxwell.

They rode in stately fashion down from the Mercat Cross, past the town lock-up and the Tolbooth, past the Fish Cross until they could hear the watermill on the Millburn. Then they turned right and came back again up Irish Street to the Townhead while speeches were made at intervals and the musicians in a wagon clattering and squelching along behind, played music from the French court.

By the time they got back to Maxwell's Castle the long summer evening was worn away and the sky in the west gone to purple satin. The horses lined up stamping in the courtyard, far too many of them with all the attendants as well, and the higher folk separated themselves to go into Maxwell's hall.

Carey beckoned Dodd and Hutchin to him and they went in to the feast after Lord Maxwell and his attendants.

Dodd had seen feasting before but not on this scale, and not with this kind of food, most of which he did not recognise at all. Dodd found a seneschal placing him well below the salt with distant Maxwell cousins, while Hutchin was ordered to stand behind Carey like the other pageboys, to fill his goblet, pass his napkin and hold the water for him to wash his hands between courses. Carey was on the top table, not far from the King, exerting himself to be pleasant and taking very little from the silver- and gold-plated dishes that passed him. He had a plump, comfortable woman on his right to whom he spoke gravely; she seemed to enjoy the conversation well enough. Sir Henry wasn't as close to the salt as Carey, not being there in any official capacity and not having any tincture of royalty in his veins either. He looked irritable now, under his velvet mask, as if he found Carey's higher placing than himself a calculated insult, rather than the normal effect of precedence.

The noise was bedlamite, for no one stopped to listen to the musicians and the King under his cloth of estate was visibly rolling drunk. Dodd watched with disapproval.

Even below the salt the bread was white and the meats soused in sauces full of herbs and wine and garlic, stuffed with strange mixtures heavy with spices. Dodd ate very little, and only what he could identify with certainty, but the beer was good enough and he drank that.

At last trumpets blasted out. The King stood, the company at the top table stood and moved out of the hall, filtering through the passageway towards Maxwell's bowling alley.

'Where are we going?' Dodd asked himself and was answered by the Herries man that had been on his left.

'There's more food there.'

'More?' He was shocked. 'Good God, is the King no' full yet?'

And it was true; at one end of the bowling alley were more tables covered in white cloths and strangely carved and glittering glass dishes, with creams and jellies and brightly coloured and gilded gingerbreads gleaming like jewels under the high banks of candles. Amongst them went the womenfolk and courtiers, with little dishes made of sugar plate, picking and selecting from the red and green and pink jellies and comfits, like butterflies among flowers.

Dodd stood by the tapestry-covered wall and watched with the other henchmen. Somewhere they seemed to have lost the King and some of the courtiers and he supposed they were having their own even more extravagant sweetmeats somewhere else.

But then there came a blasting of trumpets and a strumming of harps so loud Dodd jumped and put his hand on his sword. Into the bowling alley came a kind of chariot, painted and gilded, pulled by men clad in strange clothes, and in it, with a gilded wreath on his head and some kind of gold breastplate on his chest, was King James. He was laughing and nearly fell out when the chariot jerked to a stop. One of the attending lords, wearing an extraordinary helmet with plumes on the top, made a speech in rhyme which seemed to be talking about Alexander the Great and some magical fountain. Dodd noticed that King James had his arm wrapped round Lord Spynie who was in the chariot with him, also decked out in a fake silver breastplate.

The chariot paraded up and down the bowling alley, stopping every so often for another of the courtiers to make a speech in rhyming Scots, or for the womenfolk to dance in a way which somehow combined the stately and the lewd. No doubt it was all very cultured and courteous, though Dodd had rarely been so bored in his life: why could they not listen to a gleeman singing the old tale of Chevy Chase or making the backs of their necks prickle with the song of the Twa Corbies? What was the point of all the prosing about Alexander the Great, whoever the hell he was? Or have the women dance a little more: that was good to look on, though King James seemed more interested in cuddling up to Lord Spynie, God forgive him. Carey seemed to enjoy it greatly: he laughed with the other courtiers at some of the verses and clapped when the King replied. Hutchin, who was still standing behind him, seemed on the point of falling asleep.

At last the King got down from his chariot, which was wheeled away again, and helped himself to jellies and creams from a separate table. And then, just as Dodd was beginning to hope the thing was finished and they could go home to their beds, all the bright company followed the King back through the passageways into Maxwell's hall.

His servants had been busy clearing the tables and benches away, leaving the newly swept boards lit by torches and candles hanging from the great carved black beams of the roof. The musicians were up in the gallery and when the King waved his hand, they began to play a strenuous galliard.

Dodd had no intention of making a fool of himself by dancing measures he had never learned, which was a pity because at last the women came into their own. They formed up, talking and laughing, and flapping their fans in the stunning heat from the lights, while the men paraded in front of them like cock pheasants.

And there was Carey, a long streak of melancholy in black velvet slashed with taffeta, bouncing and kicking in the men's

639

volta, gallant and attentive to his partner in the galliard, stately as a bishop in the pavane. By some subtle method invisible to Dodd he managed to dance several times with the peach of the ladies' company, a dark woman with alabaster skin, black hair in ringlets snooded with garnets, a perky little mask made of crimson feathers and a crimson velvet gown to match, whose bodice must surely have been stuck on with glue, because otherwise, Dodd could not understand how it stayed where it was.

Carey was talking to her all the time as he danced and whatever he was saying seemed to please her, because she laughed and tapped him playfully with her fan. When the dance ended, she allowed him to escort her to a bench at the side of the room. Carey looked around impatiently for Hutchin, but his expression softened when he saw the boy on a stool by the door, fast asleep. He beckoned Dodd over.

'Sergeant,' he said quietly. 'Will you do me the favour of fetching a plate of sweetmeats for Signora Bonnetti, and some wine?'

For a moment Dodd bridled at being treated like a servant again, but then he thought that if he was making up to a pretty woman like the Signora, he might not want to leave her alone for someone else to find either.

Coming back with a sugar plate piled with suckets and a goblet of wine, he gave it to Carey and then stood nearby, trying to eavesdrop on how you talked to a court-woman.

He grew no wiser because Carey was speaking French at a great rate and in a caressing tone of voice. The Signora answered him with little inclinations of her head and popped suckets in her mouth greedily. Smiling she pulled Carey's head down near hers and fed him a sweetmeat and they both laughed in a way which was instantly comprehensible in any language in the world.

How does he do it, Dodd wondered enviously; how the hell does he draw the womenfolk like that?

He looked about the hall for the Widdringtons and found them, Elizabeth sitting wearily on one of the benches although she had not danced, and Sir Henry standing, rocking on his toes with his hands behind his back. Carey's performance with the Italian woman was easy for him to see, although it didn't seem to be pleasing him. Sir Henry bent down to Elizabeth and spoke to her, nodded in their direction. Elizabeth looked briefly, shut her eyes and said nothing. Sir Henry's fist bunched, but his son came back from dancing a pavane and sat beside Elizabeth. He had the painfully careful movements of a boy who had broken a lot of furniture before he got used to his size, and it was touching how protectively he sat between his stepmother and his father. When he saw what Carey was up to, his spotted features frowned heavily.

Carey had more than one audience for his courtship of Signora Bonnetti. The King himself seemed interested in it, which surprised Dodd, for between kissing Lord Spynie on the cheek and applauding the dancers, occasional regal glances would come in Carey's direction and then sweep away again. If Carey noticed all the attention, he didn't show it.

I wonder where the Signora's husband is, Dodd thought, but he saw nobody else among all the courtiers in Maxwell's hall who seemed foreign.

As it happened, Carey was asking the Signora precisely that, to be rewarded by an arch look from under the crimson feathers on her face and a wrinkling of her nose.

'He has a flux,' explained Signora Bonnetti in her lilting Italianate French. 'He was much too ill to come feasting for he cannot be more than five steps away from a close stool.'

'Poor gentleman,' said Carey with fake concern. 'But how generous to allow his wife to come dancing and gladden this northern fastness with the fire of her beauty.'

Signora Bonnetti giggled. 'He has a woman to attend him,' she said. 'And I am the worst of nurses.'

'I can't believe it.'

Signora Bonnetti tapped Carey's arm with her fan. 'But I am, sir. I am angry and furious with anyone who is sick.'

'And when you are sick?'

'I am never sick, save when with child. And then I am angry and furious with myself. To be sick is to be dull and squalid, isn't it? And full of sorrow and self-pity; oh, Lord God, the pain, oh, my dear, my guts, oh God, fetch the pot...arrgh.'

Carey laughed. 'And I cannot believe you are a mother?'

'But I am, and two of them still live, thank the Virgin. They are at home with my family in my beautiful Rome.'

'Such devotion to follow your husband to the cold and barbaric north, Signora.'

'Sir, you are the first Scot I have met who admits to being a barbarian.'

'I am not a Scot, Signora; I am English and we are a little less barbaric because more southerly.'

'English. Well! I would never have guessed. Why are you here?'

Carey told her and watched a fleeting instant of calculation cross her face under the feathers. Her manner instantly changed from a pleasurable flirtation into something much more focused and intent. He smiled in response, a smile which was an invitation to conspiracy, and she smiled back, slowly, the feathers nodding and tapping her smooth pale cheeks, a light dusting of glitter in the valley between her breasts catching the torchlight in the roofbeams.

She tapped him with her jewelled fan again. 'Shall we dance again, Monsieur le Deputé?' she said, and he bowed and led her into the rows of lords and ladies waiting for the first chord in the music.

To dance with the Signora was a delight: she was small and her feet in their crimson silk slippers moved like thistledown. Briefly, like a man feeling a sore tooth with his tongue, Carey wished he could dance with Elizabeth Widdrington instead, but that was utterly impossible with her jealous bastard of a husband standing guard over her. He had never before known the obsession with a woman that he felt for Elizabeth and he disliked it thoroughly. He felt perpetually confused and at war with himself, wanting to take the simplest route, march over to where she sat, pale, composed and frankly dowdy in her high-necked velvet gown, punch her loathsome consort in the nose and sweep her away with him. What he would do with her then made the material of all the sleeping and waking dreams that pestered him and frayed his temper. But none of it was possible. Elizabeth herself, with her stern sense of propriety, could and would prevent him. He could hardly see her without creating elaborate internal flights of fancy in which he tore off her clothes and took her gasping against a wall, and yet he also knew that he could not bear to hurt her and would stop if she so much as frowned. It was all too complicated for him.

If I press my suit to the Italian lady, thought the calculating courtier within him, it may ease Sir Henry's suspicions. It might even convince the King I am not what he thinks me and perhaps... perhaps, who knows?—Signora Bonnetti might not be quite so staunch in defence of her honour?

The music of the pavane stopped and he realised he had gone through all its figures without even registering them. Signora Bonnetti curtseyed low to him and he bowed and they waited for the next dance.

Another volta, and Carey found himself grinning impudently at her. There were ways and ways to find out. He pranced and spun through the opening jig, and held her hand lightly while she responded with the women's footwork. With his index finger he gently stroked the hollow of her palm as she danced. She laughed and spun, her skirts billowing, came neatly into his arms and in the beat and a half when he was placing his hands to lift, he made his move. In the volta the man was supposed to grip the bottom edges of the woman's stays, front and back, to lift and spin her as she leaped. His hands disguised by crimson satin, Carey put them in two quite different places, causing the Signora to gasp and flush. He lifted her anyway as she jumped, and she spun neatly and came back to him again. He was braced for her to slap him, or stand on his toe or even accidentally on purpose dig her fan handle into his privates—all of them counter-moves he had known court-ladies make before. She didn't, only leaned against him as he caught her, and whispered, 'Gently, my dear, I am not made of marble.'

'Nor am I,' he whispered back, as he placed his hands exactly where they had been before. 'See what you do to me.'

She jumped as he lifted, spun, jumped again and laughed when he steadied her in an equally scandalous manner.

The dance separated them into their own figures and Carey concentrated on lifting the solidly built lady who came into his arms as the partners changed without rupturing himself or hurting his back. His whole body was alive with the dance and the music, he felt like thistledown himself and his feet flung themselves through the complicated steps without any need for his conscious direction. He could look across the expanse of whirling courtiers and find Signora Bonnetti watching him. Perhaps? Please God, he prayed profanely, thinking about Catholic countries where the possibilities were so pleasingly endless and forgiveable.

At last the dance brought her back, whirling breathlessly into his arms and once again he held her delectably tight arse instead of her stays and flipped her up. Although he believed he had done it properly, he thought he must have mistaken the balance. She came down heavily and seemed to twist her ankle. Immediately contrite he held her up and as the measure finished, he supported her to the bench at the side of the hall.

'Signora, I am sorry,' he said. 'How embarrassing for you to have such a clumsy partner...'

'Yes,' she said, not looking at all annoyed with him. 'My ankle is sore and I am very hot indeed. Please take me into the garden to cool myself.'

He held his arm out to her and she wove her hand into the crook of the elbow and squeezed eloquently. 'Monsieur le Deputé, you are very gallant.'

'Signora Bonnetti, you are very beautiful, but too formal. Will you not call me Robin, as the Queen of England does?'

Another squeeze and the brush of her hip against his told him she was pleased.

'Why then, Robin, you may call me Emilia as my husband does—though he is no longer so gallant, alas.'

Carey bowed his head. 'How can I help paying court to Emilia, the fairest jewel in Scotland?' Hackneyed, he knew; whatever had happened to his tongue?

She tossed her head and limped assiduously as he led her out towards the bowling alley, past the crowd of lords and ladies predating on the delicacies of the banquet, and through the door into the garden, where their feet crunched on gravel paths between herb beds and her ankle seemed much better already. She led him through hedges into a rose garden, from the scent, and sat them both down on a stone bench.

'For the crime of hurting my ankle with your wickedness,' said Emilia Bonnetti in a whisper, 'you must now forfeit a kiss.' She proffered her cheek and shut her eyes.

Just for a moment, uncharacteristically, Carey hesitated. Somewhere inside him came a plaintive cry, protesting that this was the wrong woman, that what he needed to do was go back into the hall, kill Sir Henry Widdrington and bring Elizabeth out to the rose garden instead...And then the unregenerate old Adam arose and pointed out that wrong or not, this was *a* woman and an extremely juicy one at that and...God knew, he needed a woman.

She was still holding up her cheek to be kissed. He bent towards her, touched her very gently with his lips below the feather fringe of her mask, then took her shoulders and turned her so that her mouth came under his. Then he kissed her properly.

After that there was another, more ancient dance than the volta, only marginally complicated by her farthingale and his padded hose, which ended inevitably with her sitting astride his lap giggling as he bucked and gasped into the white-hot little death and bit her quite carefully on her creamy shoulder, just below the line of her gown.

She squeaked, nibbled his ear and lifted the hand that was under his doublet and shirt to tweak his nipple. They stayed like that for a while.

'We should go back,' she whispered, and sighed.

'Just a minute, Emilia my heart,' he temporised, happier than he had been in months, sliding his hands under her thighs again. God, they were beautiful to feel; why did women hide their beautiful plump smooth arses under acres of silk and linen, it was a miraculous treasure that they kept there and he wanted more...

She squeaked again, differently, and laughed. 'Mon Dieu,' she said flatteringly. 'I had heard Englishmen were cold-hearted.'

'Not me,' he managed to pant, his heart building up to a gallop once more, Jesus God, it had been so long... 'Kiss me.'

'Tut tut. At least it's true that Englishmen are greedy...' She was thoughtful, or her top half was, while her rump rocked gently to and fro and made him feel he was going to burst again.

'I admit it,' he muttered. 'I admit it, I'm greedy, only kiss me again.'

She slid her arms out of the front of his doublet and held him round the neck so he could do it more thoroughly. She twisted her fingers in his hair and grasped in a way that would normally have hurt him while he directed her honeypot and let himself quite slowly drown in it. This time both of them cried out dangerously in the empty rose garden, and Carey crushed her against his chest as her faced relaxed like a baby's.

The night had darkened while they were dancing, and now the first few spots of rain began to fall. Emilia Bonnetti gasped with dismay as the specks of cold touched her neck and shoulders and lifted her head.

'Blessed Virgin, my gown will be ruined,' she cried in Italian, hopping off him to his own near ruin and rummaging under the silks to rearrange her underskirts. Carey thought wistfully about taking a nap, but he didn't want his black velvet to spot and run either. He stood with a few creaks and winces as the hardness of the bench told on him at last, and made himself decent. She used the edge of a petticoat to wipe her facepaint off his face, an intimacy that made them both smile, and they trotted down the path back to the bowling alley and the torches.

A few steps from the door, Emilia began limping again.

'Am I respectable?' she asked, looking him over critically before they joined the surprising throng of dalliers in the garden.

Carey bowed with more than usual extravagance. 'Positively virginal,' he said, naughtily. 'But you were limping on the other foot before.'

She wrinkled her nose at him. '*You* have done your doublet buttons up unevenly,' she told him, turning to go in.

'Wait. When can we meet again?'

'I am lodging with my husband at the sign of the Thistle near the Fish Cross, very expensive and not at all clean. Will you come and attend me there tomorrow morning, Robin, and entertain me? I shall be very bored and in a bad mood, I'm afraid.'

'With the greatest possible pleasure, ma belle.'

She went in ahead of him, looking plump and pleased with

herself, straightening her mask. He waited for a count of thirty and followed her, still happily glowing.

The King was on the point of going to bed, barely held up by Lord Spynie who was not much better off, hiccupping and laughing at the invisible jokes of alcohol. It was an odd thing to see a monarch so drunk he could hardly stand, Carey thought. The mere idea of the Queen of England so unguarded smacked of sacrilege. The company stood and bowed or curtseyed as the trumpets blew discordantly, while King James with his surrounding company withdrew to take horse back to the Mayor's house.

The Signora went with the courtiers, studiously and cautiously ignoring him. He took care not to do more than glance at her, thinking fondly about stroking the secret places between her thighs and...

Elizabeth Widdrington was staring at him, looking as if she was reading his mind. Guilt and a schoolboy sullenness brought the blood into his face involuntarily. Black velvet masks made for an exciting and illusory anonymity, but it was also harder to read people's expressions. He hoped she couldn't see him flush, he couldn't work out what she was thinking at all, if she could tell, if she minded (of course she minded). She linked hands distantly with her rightful husband, turned and left, young Henry yawning at her other shoulder.

Just for a moment he felt truculent. Am I supposed to spend my life yearning after her like some goddamned troubadour, he thought rebelliously. I'll marry her the instant Sir Henry's safely buried, but until then, what am I supposed to do? Live like a goddamned Papist monk? It didn't matter. Sadness and weariness set in and more than ever he wished it had been Elizabeth straddling his crotch in the rose garden, Elizabeth moaning and collapsing against him at last, Elizabeth telling him to do his doublet buttons up straight...He sighed and went over to where Dodd was sitting on a bench near the curled-up and sleeping Hutchin, nibbling at some shards of sugar plate.

Dodd's miserable face cheered him up a little, it was so full of the plainest envy.

'What now, sir?' asked Dodd, dolefully.

'Bed. Let's wake the boy, I'm not carrying him up those stairs.'

Hutchin was not easy to wake and smelled of wine fumes. He was a fast learner, Carey thought with amusement; he had already learned the pageboy's trick of toping a quick mouthful out of every drink he poured for his master. Carey himself was much less drunk than he had been earlier and Dodd looked exactly the same as always.

'Did you enjoy the feast, Sergeant?' he asked.

Dodd shook his head. 'Is that what ye do at court, sir?' he asked. 'All the time?'

'Pretty much.' Though it was interesting to contemplate what King James's court at Westminster would be like if the King was habitually drunk in the evenings.

'It wouldna suit me, sir.'

'You can get used to it.'

'Ay, sir,' said Dodd, disapproving and noncommittal. 'Nae doubt.'

## THURSDAY, 13TH JULY 1592, MORNING

Dodd was still in a bad mood the next morning, along with every single man in Maxwell's entire cess. Finding the hall where he had slept before so packed with men rolled in their cloaks that it was hard to pick your way among them, he, his brother and Sim's Will had dossed down in the stable next to Thunder. He neither knew nor cared where the Deputy Warden had slept since he thought the man deserved to sleep on the floor, and Young Hutchin had curled up by the hall fire in a pile of pageboys all sleeping like puppies. It was very different from what he had imagined about court life. And what were they doing, still there anyway?

Carey came striding into the stable the next morning, a whole hideous hour before sunrise, looking fresh and not at all hungover. He was wearing his jack and morion. Behind him was a red-eyed silent Hutchin and outside in the courtyard there was a brisk feeding and watering and saddling of horses.

'What now?' moaned Dodd, leaning up on his elbow and picking straw out of his hair. Beyond the stable door he could see that it was spitting a fine mizzle.

'My lord Maxwell is very anxious for us to ride out to Lochmaben and inspect his guns,' said Carey cheerfully. 'Good God, what's wrong with you, Dodd? You didn't drink much yesterday.'

'Och,' said Red Sandy, sitting up and scratching, 'he's allus like this, he hates mornings. Always has. Will ye be wanting us too, sir?'

'No. I want you and Sim's Will to go and do some drinking on my behalf.'

Red Sandy brightened up at that.

'Ay, sir.'

'I want you to spend time with the men around town, buy a few drinks, and see if you can catch any hint of a sudden influx of good firearms anywhere. Just listen for rumours, or envious complaints and take good note of who's talking and who they're talking about. That clear?'

Red Sandy was on his feet and so was Sim's Will, both looking much encouraged. Sim's Will nodded and went out to see who had taken their feed bucket, while Red Sandy brushed down two of the hobbies and put their saddles on.

Carey handed over several pounds in assorted Scots money to Red Sandy while Dodd sat up and fumbled for his boots.

'Do you think you could do that work for me without getting roaring drunk or into any fights with the Scots?' Carey asked. Red Sandy was offended.

'Ay, o' course, sir.'

'Young Hutchin, you have to stay either with me or Red Sandy. Which do you prefer?'

Young Hutchin swallowed stickily and looked at the ground.

'I'd prefer to stay with Red Sandy, sir,' he said. 'Ah...the Maxwells are at feud wi' the Grahams, sir; Dumfries is well enough with the King here and all but it might be better for me not to go to Lochmaben.'

Carey lifted his eyebrows at the boy. 'Is there any Border family your relations are not at feud with?' he asked.

Hutchin looked offended. 'Ay, sir, we're no' feuding with the Armstrongs or the Johnstones, nor never have.'

'And that's all? Has it never occurred to your uncles that merrily feuding with every surname that offends you in any way might not be a good long-term policy, especially if you have the King of Scotland after your blood as well?'

Hutchin looked blank. 'What else can we do, sir?' he asked. 'Be like the Routledges, every man's prey?'

Carey sighed. 'Stay with Red Sandy and Sim's Will and try to keep out of trouble.'

'Ay, sir.'

\* \* \*

Lord Maxwell looked no happier than any of his relatives or attendants, and seemed to have cooled towards Carey as well. They broke their fast hurriedly on stale manchet bread and ale, and then followed him out of the Lochmaben Gate of Dumfries and north east along the road to his castle. They struck off the road after about four miles, into a tangle of hills and burns, until they met with a number of angry-looking Maxwells, gathered about three battered wagons whose wheels bit deep into the soft forest track. Lord Maxwell's steward came forward and spoke urgently into his ear, at which Lord Maxwell's face became even grimmer.

He waved at the wagons.

'There ye are, Sir Robert,' he said. 'See what ye can make of them.'

'Are we not going into the castle?' Dodd questioned under his breath.

'It seems my lord Warden wants to be able to deny the weapons are anything to do with him,' Carey answered softly. 'Count your blessings, he's not going to be a happy man.'

Carey slid from his horse, squelched over to the nearest wagon and climbed onto the board next to the driver. He pulled out a caliver or two, turned them upside down, grunted and threw them back. The last one he examined more carefully and then shook his head.

'Well?' demanded Maxwell impatiently.

'They're all faulty,' said Carey simply. 'The barrels are all badly welded, the lock parts have not been case-hardened and some of them are cracked already. If you use these in battle, my lord, your enemies will laugh themselves silly.'

'One of my cousins has been blinded by one and another man had his hand hurt.'

'There you are then, my lord. If you like we could prove a couple.'

'Ay,' said Maxwell, rubbing his thumb on the clenched muscles in his cheek. 'Do so.'

Although he knew as well as Dodd that it was unnecessary, Carey went through the motions, rigged a caliver to a tree stump and spattered it all over the clearing.

There was a kind of contented sigh from the Maxwells standing about. Carey left the wagon, came back to his horse and mounted up again in tactful silence. They waited, finding the paths all blocked by Maxwells.

The tension rose, broken by wood-doves currling at each other through the trees and anxious alarm calls from the jackdaws.

Finally Maxwell flung down his tall-crowned hat and roared, 'God damn it! Bastard Englishmen, bastards and traitors every one, by God...'

He swung suddenly on Carey and at the motion the Maxwell lances seemed to lean inward towards the Deputy Warden and Sergeant Dodd. 'And what d'ye ken of this, eh, Sir Robert? Sitting there so smarmy and clever and telling me I canna do what I plan because the guns are nae good...'

'Would you have preferred me to keep silent and let you use them against the Johnstones, my lord?' asked Carey levelly. 'I could have done that.'

Ay, thought Dodd viciously, wondering how many of the lances were aimed at his back, and why didn't you, you interfering fool?

'Ye're in it wi' Scrope and Lowther and the Johnstones, aren't ye, aren't ye?' yelled Maxwell, forcing his horse over close to Carey and leaning in his face. 'And a clever plot it was too, to gi' the advantage to the pack of muirthering Johnstones.'

'Nothing to do with me, my lord,' said Carey steadily.

'Lord Scrope's yer warden, ye'd do what he tellt ye.'

'I might,' allowed Carey. 'If he had mentioned this to me, of course. In which case I would hardly have come here with you, would I? But I don't think it was him.'

'And who was it then?'

'From whom did you buy the guns, my lord? Ask yourself that and then ask who did you the favour of stopping you firing one of them.'

Oh, thought Dodd as a great light dawned on him. So that's what the interfering fool's about, is he? Well, well. It took most of his self-control not to let a wicked grin spread itself all over his face. That night spent tediously marking all the guns in the armoury with an x before we even knew there was anything wrong with them, it was time well-spent. And now we've found them again and we can go home.

Maxwell's face was working. He seemed to be thinking and calming down.

'Ye came to find these, did ye no'?' he said at last.

Carey shrugged. 'I knew we had lost the guns during the muster on Sunday, and I knew someone must have put a big enough price on them for...someone to want to take the money and embarrass Scrope at the same time.' Noticeably he did not mention the previous theft on the road from Newcastle, when the Tower-made guns had been swapped for the deathtraps now owned by Maxwell.

'The bastard,' breathed Maxwell repetitiously. 'God damn his guts.'

'Amen,' answered Carey piously.

'I paid good money for this pile of scrap iron.'

Carey tutted. 'Who to, my lord?' he asked casually.

Maxwell's lowering face suddenly became cunning. 'I canna tell ye that, Sir Robert.'

Carey sighed at this sudden niceness. 'No, of course not,' he agreed. 'Will you say what you paid?'

'Twenty-five shillings a gun, English, and we were to send them back once we'd had the use of them.'

Up went Carey's eyebrows at this unexpected titbit. 'Really?' he said slowly. 'Is that so?'

'The usual arrangement, ye ken, only we wanted more of them. And for longer. Sir Ri...He was to find them at Lammastide in an old pele-tower near Langholm, ye follow.'

'Ah yes, I understand. And take the credit for it. Hmm. Well, what will you do with them now, my lord?'

'Throw 'em in a bog.'

'Don't do that, my lord.'

'Will ye take them back then?'

Carey smiled thinly. 'I don't think so, my lord. But will you keep them here for a couple of days?'

'Why?'

Carey looked opaque and tapped his fingers on his saddle horn. 'Just in case, my lord, just in case. You never know what might happen.'

Maxwell grunted sullenly. 'What am I to dae about the Johnstones?' he demanded to know.

'Entirely your affair, my lord. But if I were you, I'd let them sweat until you're ready.'

'And stay bloody Warden all that time?'

Carey made a self-deprecating half-bow from the saddle. 'It might not be so bad,' he suggested. 'Perhaps you and my lord Scrope could even agree on a Day of Truce and clear up some of the bills that have been accumulating for the past sixteen years.'

Maxwell glowered at him. 'Good God, whatever for?'

'For peace, my lord. For the rule of law.'

The sneer on Maxwell's handsome features was magnificently comprehensive. 'While I've my men at my back, I'll make my ain laws and my ain peace.'

Carey said nothing. Maxwell was silent for a time which seemed very long to Dodd's stretched nerves. Carey sat patiently, seeming intent on the stitching of his riding gloves, the growth of the nearest tree.

Maxwell jerked his horse round and came close to him.

'Well?' he demanded.

'What can I do for you, my lord?' said Carey softly.

'I want my money back.'

'What?'

'Ay.' Maxwell leaned on his saddle horn and spat words. 'The Deputy Warden of Carlisle sold me a pile of scrap-iron that half-killed my cousin, and I want my money back.'

'Not this Deputy Warden,' said Carey.

Maxwell shrugged. 'Who cares. Ye get me my money back. I want it and it's mine.'

'From Lowther?'

'I never said that. From whoever. D'ye understand me?'

There was something almost amusing about one of the richest lords in the Scottish West March demanding his money back like an Edinburgh wife waving a bad fish at a stallholder, almost but not quite. The fact that the whole thing was ludicrously irrational and unjust hardly mattered when they were surrounded by Maxwell's kinsmen and Maxwell himself looked like a primed caliver ready to go off at any minute. Dodd began praying fervently. Please God, let the Courtier keep a civil tongue in his head, please God...

'I'll do my best, my lord,' Carey said, prim as a maiden.

'Ye'd better.'

Maxwell turned his horse foaming back towards the wagon and shouted orders, then whipped the beast to a canter in the direction of the road to Dumfries. Perforce, Carey and Dodd rode with them, less escorted than guarded now.

\* \* \*

They returned quickly to Maxwell's townhouse, recipients of a double-edged hospitality. Carey strode into the stall where Thunder stood stamping and tossing his head impatiently and found Hutchin there already.

When the boy turned to greet him, they saw a magnificent black eye, a bust lip and pure rage.

'Oh, Lord,' said Carey, wearily stripping off his gloves. 'What happened? Did Lord Spynie...'

The boy spat. 'Red Sandy and Sim's Will got intae a fight.'

'How?'

'Wee Colin Elliot was in the Black Bear wi' some of his kin and when Red Sandy come in, Wee Colin asked him if he'd lost any sheep lately and Red Sandy went for him. An' they're both in the town lock-up now. It wasnae my fault,' finished Hutchin self-righteously.

'Who's in the lock-up? Wee Colin as well?'

'Nay, sir. Just Red Sandy and Sim's Will, of course.'

Carey glared at Dodd as if it was his fault his brother was an idiot.

'That's all I bloody need,' said Carey. 'Come on, we'll go and see them.'

They were stopped at the gate to Maxwell's Castle by a stern-faced Herries.

'Ye canna all go out,' he said to Carey. 'My lord Maxwell says one of ye must stay here.'

'As a hostage,' said the Courtier, coldly.

'Ay, if ye wantae put it that way.'

Carey looked at Dodd and Hutchin, calculating. 'Then it's you, Dodd, I'm sorry. I'll see what I can do to bail your brother.'

Dodd wanted to protest at being left in the middle of a heaving mass of Maxwells, but could see there was no point. It was better for Carey to have freedom of action since he at least had some friends among the Scots. Hutchin was a bit young to play the hostage and a Graham furthermore. It had to be him. He nodded gloomily.

'Ay,' he said. 'I'll be wi' the horses.'

Carey hurried down the street, Hutchin trotting at his heels, until he came to the small round lock-up by the Tolbooth. As expected, it was packed full of brawlers, half of them still drunk, and it took a while for Sim's Will to struggle out of the crowd and peer through the little barred window.

'Well?' said Carey, furious at this complication.

'Ah...Sorry, sir,' said Sim's Will, looking very sheepish. He was battered, though not too badly, considering the idiocy of taking on a pack of Elliots on their own ground.

'How's Red Sandy?'

'No' so bad. He lost a tooth but he found it again, and he's put it back now and his nose stopped bleeding a while ago,' Sim's Will said.

'Tell me how the fight started.'

Sim's Will recounted a very pathetic tale in which Wee Colin Elliot had snarled scandalous and wounding insults about Red Sandy and Sim's Will, impugning their birth, breeding, courage and wives. To this unprovoked attack Sim's Will and Red Sandy had responded with mild reproach, until the evil Wee Colin had sunk so low as to attack the sacred honour of the Deputy Warden, at which point, driven beyond endurance, Red Sandy had tapped him lightly, almost playfully, on the nose and...

Carey rolled his eyes. 'Red Sandy hit Wee Colin Elliot first.'

In a manner of speaking, allowed Sim's Will, you could say that, although the way Wee Colin Elliot had been ranting you could see it was only a matter of seconds before...

'I don't suppose you found out anything of use before that, did you?' Carey asked.

Sim's Will Croser's face was blank for a moment before, rather guiltily, recollection returned. 'Ah. No, sir,' he said.

'No rumour of somebody suddenly having quite a lot of guns where before they had none?'

'Nay, sir. Nothing like that. And we did ask before we met...'

'Wee Colin Elliot. God's truth. Well, you can tell Red Sandy I'll do what I can to bail you out of there, but since the matter's ultimately a decision for the Lord Warden of this March, I don't know how long it will take.'

'Ay, but is that not Lord Maxwell?' said Sim's Will. 'Red Sandy said ye're friends wi' him.'

'Well, I was. I'll see what I can do.'

An attempt to talk to the King at the Mayor's house produced the information that His Majesty was out inspecting some of his cavalry and likely to go hunting after that.

And so Carey found himself heading for the alehouse known as The Thistle, as crowded as any of the others with the King's attendants and minor lords. The common room was a bedlam of arguing, dicing and drinking and as no one stopped him, he and Hutchin quietly went and climbed the stairs to the next floor. Four doors off a narrow landing faced him and after listening for a moment, he tried the one on his right. No answer, so he tried the next one and heard Signora Bonnetti's voice answer, 'Chi é? Who is?'

'C'est moi, Emilia,' said Carey, trying the latch and finding the door bolted.

A moment later it opened a crack and Carey stepped through, firmly stopping Hutchin with a hand on the chest.

'Sit at the top of the stairs and shout if someone tries to come in,' said Carey and Young Hutchin grinned with understanding beyond his years. 'And if I catch you listening or peeping at the latch-hole, I'll leather you, understand?'

'Ay, sir,' said Hutchin.

In fact, Hutchin managed to restrain his curiosity for nearly twenty minutes until the muffled noises coming through the door told him he was safe enough. He put his eye to the latch-hole and was rewarded by the sight of two pairs of legs on a bed playing the old game of the two-backed beast. For all his efforts at squinting and seeing through wood, he could see nothing else and had to use his imagination. Fortunately he had more than most.

The red feather mask had flattered Signora Emilia Bonnetti because it had hidden the fine tracery of lines around her magnificent dark eyes. Carey no longer doubted that she had borne children, for she had the marks of it on her belly and her deliciously dark and pointed nipples. He didn't care. He had always preferred older married women for dalliance and not simply because, at the Queen's Court in London, to meddle with the virgin Maids of Honour was to risk the Queen's fury and a ruinous stay in the Tower. His first woman had been a much older and more experienced French lady in Paris, and he had never got over his awed pleasure at finding the truth in the saying that women burned hotter the older they got.

Now he lay full length in the little half-curtained bed and watched sleepy-eyed as Emilia, full of vigour and mischief, poured him wine and chatted to him in French and Italian mixed.

It seemed he could do her some great service, if he chose. Ah, he thought, we're coming to the point at last now. Ten years before he might have been disappointed that sheer desire for him had not been Emilia's motive after all. No more. He had long ago decided that women rarely had fewer than four different motives for anything they did.

He took the goblet of wine and drank as Emilia pulled a white smock over her head and disappeared briefly, still talking.

At first he wasn't certain he had heard right. 'I beg your pardon?'

'I want to buy firearms,' repeated the Signora. 'You know, guns.' She said the word in English to be sure he could understand.

Mind working furiously, he watched her and waited for her to explain herself.

'Signor Bonnetti has a commission to buy at least twelve dozen calivers and twelve dozen pistols, with perhaps more later. It has been very difficult, we came to Dumfries full of hope to buy them here where so many are made, but now we find that so many are used here as well the gunsmiths are fat and lazy, and they will not sell to us.'

'Who are the guns for?'

She shrugged her creamy shoulders and made a moue of disdain. 'I do not know; for the Netherlanders perhaps, or the Swedes. Even the French Huguenots might want them; Signor Bonnetti has not told me.'

She's lying, Carey thought to himself, every one of those people have better sources nearer home than Dumfries.

'Have you any money to pay for them?'

'We have gold and bankers' drafts,' she said. 'But none will take them. Or they will take them, but they will give us nothing but promises in exchange. Where can I find guns to buy, Robin chéri, so that I may leave this cold and uncivilised place and go back to my beautiful Roma?' She sat next to him on the bed and put her head down on his chest. 'We have sold all the wine, but we cannot leave without the guns, and we are both miserable.'

'Why are you asking me?' Carey wondered, twiddling his fingers in her black ringlets. 'Why do you think I have guns?'

'Well, the Scots all say it. If you canna get guns here, they say, try the Deputy Warden of Carlisle. And then they laugh.'

Carey smiled and stroked her cheek. 'Hmm,' he said. 'And why do they laugh?'

She shrugged and sat up, tidying her hair with a busy pulling out and pushing in of hairpins. 'Because many of them have very beautiful firearms from Carlisle and are proud of it. The laird Johnstone has many of the finest Tower-made, which is why my lord Maxwell is so worried.'

'Have you tried asking Maxwell?'

Her face screwed up with distaste. 'He was the first one I tried and he said he might be able to help me in a little while, but he is untrue and a liar and he will not speak to me any more. The laird Johnstone says he needs his guns against the Maxwells. The Earl of Mar has been very kind...'

'Lucky Earl of Mar.'

She sniffed. 'But he is only trying to delay me because I think he takes money from the English. And the King, of course, is not very approachable and the Queen has no influence with him. Huntly is in too much disgrace and poor beautiful Moray is dead. I have no one to turn to.'

'Poor darling,' said Carey not entirely listening to her sad tale. He gave her an inquiring squeeze. She disentwined his arms and frowned at him.

'You must get up and dress,' she scolded. 'You have already been here a very long time.'

'But if I find you some guns, I will never see you again,' Carey protested, putting his hand to his brow sorrowfully. Emilia prodded him in a sensitive spot without warning and made him gasp.

'You might. But if I have not guns in the next few weeks, the Signor and I shall be ruined and so you will never see us more at all.'

'And if I can find you a few guns?'

'We will pay you perhaps forty shillings each for them.'

Carey stared hard at her as she busied herself pulling on her stays. He was thinking and calculating and wondering how far he could trust his luck this time. Imperiously she ordered him to help her with her backlaces, and he obediently did the office of a lady's maid, with a few additions of his own invention. Unfortunately, she was no longer in the mood and they didn't work. The complex layers went over her inexorably, one after the other, and when she was fully dressed and pinning on her cap, she turned on him and frowned again.

'And you are still disgraceful, why will you not put your shirt on?'

'Hope,' he said with mock despair and a lewd gesture.

She gave him his shirt and hose crushingly. 'No, Monsieur le Deputé, I think not.'

'And if I can find you some guns?'

Now she smiled. 'Who knows?'

He laughed. 'If I get you the guns you need, I'll want more than kisses in recompense.'

'A ten per centum finder's fee?'

'Twenty.'

'Fifteen.'

'Done,' Carey said happily, drinking to it.

'Now you must meet my husband.'

\* \* \*

Giovanni Bonnetti was in a sorrowful state as he sat casting up his accounts. He was a small lightly built, swarthy man with a curled up waxed beard and moustache and very dark bright eyes. Three shirts and a knitted waistcoat under his fashionable orange and black taffeta doublet could not keep out the dank cold of the miserable joke that the Scots called summer. His legs were a perpetual mass of goose-pimples under his elegant black hose and, while the uproar in his bowels had calmed somewhat, he was not a well man. Cursed inefficient northerners, none of them knew what proper plumbing was.

And furthermore he had a stifling head-cold which caused his nose to drip all the time and a sore throat and hardly any of the illiterate savages of Scotland could speak Italian and many of them only spoke halting French with a nasal drawl that would have disgraced a Fleming. A generation ago they had been better cultured, when their alliance with France was strong and they had the wisdom of Mother Church to guide them. The foul heresy of Protestantism had sealed them up in their poor little country to stew in their own juices. And the King was no better than his nobles, though he at least had Italian and French.

But the worst of it, the absolute worst, was that here he was in Dumfries, the centre of gunmaking for the whole of Scotland, being placed in the area of highest demand, and nobody would sell him any handguns, not pistols, nor calivers, nor arquebuses. He might as well have been in London trying to buy munitions from the Tower. The locals looked at him and denied point blank that they owned any guns, ever had owned any guns, even knew what guns were. The gunsmiths he could persuade to talk to him in the first place said their order books were full for the next six months and they could barely keep up with demand. It had seemed such a fine idea from Antwerp. He would make use of his wife's scandalous liaison with the Lord Maxwell to make contact with the Scottish Court. They would both travel to Scotland with Maxwell and there buy weapons and ammunition to ship on to the Irish rebels and thus help to destroy the Earl of Essex, Elizabeth's general in Ireland. Perhaps with good weapons for the Irish thrown in the balance, he might be the means of dislodging the heretical English grip on Ireland completely. And Ireland, as the Queen of England and the King of Spain both knew very well, was the back door into England. His elaborate and painfully written proposal had gone through the many layers of Spanish bureaucrats and officials and finally returned with the tiny mincing script of the King of Spain in the top righthand corner: fiat, let this be done.

Their children had not exactly been taken in ward, only the officials had made it clear that they would come to Antwerp and remain there, as security for Philip II's investment. Giovanni had triumphantly taken his Medici bank drafts and converted some into gold to defray his expenses and buy wine as samples. He had taken ship with his minx of a wife and her noble Scottish bandit of a lover, closing his eyes firmly to her antics and solacing himself with one of his maids, all within the last few months.

And now here he was, on the verge of the biggest coup of his life, and nobody would sell him guns. The King was no help, insisted that he hadn't enough firearms himself, though he bought and drank every drop of the wine Bonnetti had brought as his cover-story: the powder he had been promised at a swingeing price would, no doubt, be bad and his time was running out before the autumn gales closed the seas between Scotland and Ireland. Also the wine that the Scottish nobility drank was appalling. If he could only pull off his coup, he might indeed set up as a vintner, supplying the barbarians with something a little better. He drank some more, the cloves and nutmeg completely failing to hide the fact that it had been pressed from the last sweepings of third-rate Gascony vineyards, watered, adulterated and brought in foul leaky barrels.

There was a knock at the door of the miserable back room of the alehouse he had rented as a makeshift office to take orders for wine.

'Prego,' said Bonnetti, gulping down the rest of his vinegar.

His wife appeared at the door with a man behind her, though not, unfortunately, the Lord Maxwell. He had been furious with her when she had quarrelled with her Scottish lover; her wilfulness had brought their whole enterprise in danger. He had known what she was doing to find another contact and it made him no happier.

This one was a new barbarian, elegantly dressed in black, with dyed hair. Extremely tall, even for the Scots, and with the national tendency to loom menacingly.

'Bonjour, monsieur,' said the barbarian in excellent French, making the merest fraction of a bow. 'I'm very pleased to make your acquaintance.'

'Votre nom, monsieur?'

'Sir Robert Carey, Deputy Warden of Carlisle.'

Every ounce of self-control Bonnetti possessed was needed to stop him from leaping out of his seat and jumping from the window. He stared and croaked for a moment with his heart thumping and his hand behind the table, stroking the hilt of the little knife he had strapped to his wrist for emergencies. Meanwhile his wife smiled sweetly and triumphantly at him, and modestly withdrew. The Englishman stood at ease with his left hand tilting the pommel of his sword and his right propped on his fashionable paned hose. He said nothing, simply smiled and waited for Bonnetti to recover. As Bonnetti became capable of thought again, he realised he had actually heard something of the Careys from his brother in London: the nearest thing to Princes of the Blood Royal that the feeble Tudor line possessed, much favoured cousins of the Queen. This particular one he had not come across by name, but the fact that he was Deputy Warden of the English West March was bad enough. Nothing of their mission could possibly be accomplished if the infernal English knew about it: they might not have been able to stop him buying weapons in Scotland, but they could and would send ships to prevent him transporting them to Ireland.

'Please, don't be afraid,' continued the Englishman softly. 'I came because I heard you were interested in buying firearms.'

Deny it? No, the man was too sure of himself. No doubt his little whore of a wife had been blabbing.

'I might be,' Bonnetti admitted cagily. 'Please sit down.'

The Englishman sat on the chair for potential customers, stretched out his long legs and crossed them at the ankle.

'Excellent,' said Carey. 'I have eighteen dozen handguns, mainly calivers with some pistols, that I might be willing to sell to you. If you happen to be buying.'

It must be a trap. This was too extraordinary. An English official selling him weapons to fight the English in Ireland? It was certainly a trap.

'I am not buying weapons,' said Bonnetti. 'I am not even interested in weapons. I am here to negotiate for the sale of Italian wine with the Scottish court.'

'Oh,' said the Englishman, without a trace of discomfiture. 'Have you any samples? I might be interested in buying some myself.'

'The Scottish court has drunk them all.'

Carey grinned. 'Isn't that a surprise? Well, Signor Bonnetti, I'm sorry to hear you aren't interested in my suggestion, since the Signora was quite sure you would be. You must know that nobody in Dumfries or anywhere in Scotland will sell weapons to you because you are a Papist and a foreigner. The King of Scotland will very soon lose patience with you, take your money anyway and probably you will end up with a dagger in your back. Never mind. Not my affair. Good day to you.'

'One moment,' said Bonnetti. 'You are an English official. What you are doing is therefore treason.'

'Treason?' said the man blankly. 'I understood the weapons are to take into Sweden. Why would selling you weapons meant for the Swedes be treason?'

Bonnetti's head was spinning, but at least it was clear that his wife had not gossiped about where the weapons were intended to go. He heard the threat in what Carey said about the King; no doubt the English Deputy had men who could put daggers into backbones, just as much as the King of Scots.

And the English were the most avaricious and unprincipled nation on earth, everyone knew that. Perhaps the offer was a genuine one. Perhaps the Englishman would take his money one way or the other. Perhaps there was even something in what he said.

Bonnetti coughed, blew his nose. 'What kind of weapons would these be?' he asked. 'And how much would you want for them?'

The price was outrageous. Carey wanted sixty shillings each for the weapons. Argue as he might, Bonnetti could not get him below fifty, in gold and bankers' drafts, half in advance and half on delivery, plus a sum of money he delicately referred to as a finder's fee. On the other hand, now Bonnetti had had time to get his breath back, there might be a great benefit in buying the weapons off a Carey, even at an inflated price. By blood, he was close to the Queen; blackmail might well make him very useful. In fact, as a coup for gaining control of one of the Queen's closest relatives, this weapons dealing could be only the beginning of a glorious new career for Bonnetti. His brother had dabbled a little in espionage: Giovanni was not at all sure precisely what had happened, but he suspected that Walsingham, the Queen's spymaster, had caught him and turned him. This would be a much greater triumph, a fitting revenge. And he did have the money for it.

With typical barbarian lack of finesse, Carey insisted on half his fifteen per cent bribe in advance, in gold, as well as a banker's draft for half the price of the guns. If he had not been desperate, Bonnetti would never have agreed, but he had no choice, as the Englishman blandly pointed out. Without some good faith from him, Carey had no reason to take any risks to help him.

## THURSDAY, 13TH JULY 1592, NOON

Roger Widdrington had been sitting at the crowded alehouse waiting for the tow-headed Graham boy to meet him for at least an hour and a half. The boy finally appeared, at the trot, looking flushed and excited and in a tearing hurry.

'I canna stay long, Sir Robert sent me out for a pie and I must be back. Ye can tell her ladyship that Sir Robert's got to make friends with my lord Maxwell again, to fetch Red Sandy and Sim's Will out of gaol, and so he's gonnae buy a big load of guns off him. He's going out to Lochmaben to get them.'

'Where is he getting the money from?' Roger Widdrington asked.

'I wouldnae ken that,' said Hutchin.

'Did he bring it with him?'

'Nay, he couldn't have, he had to pawn some rings for travelling money, or so Red Sandy said. He's got it here in Dumfries but who knows how?'

'Anything to do with the Italian woman he's been paying court to?'

Hutchin's face became so craftily noncommittal, Roger almost laughed.

'I wouldnae ken. Any road, I must go. Will ye tell my lady that she mustnae put too much on the Italian woman, he couldnae help it for she all but flung herself at his head.'

Roger nodded gravely, not trusting himself to speak, and paid the boy a shilling. He had heard different but there was no reason to argue. He watched Hutchin Graham hurry away to find a pie-seller and as soon as he was safely out of sight, he went back to report to his father.

* * *

Signor Bonnetti fully expected the Deputy Warden never to reappear again, but to his astonishment he was back within the hour, slightly flushed and looking very pleased with himself.

'They are in wagons in the forest, five miles north east of Dumfries,' he explained. 'Would you like to come and inspect them, Signor Bonnetti?'

Bonnetti had the feeling of being watched as he rode on the mean little soft-footed long-coated mare behind Carey and his young golden-haired pageboy. His heart had not yet stilled its thumping: the Englishman could simply be inveigling him out to the forest the better to put a knife in him, though the King's protection might possibly help him...No, not in a forest. But if what this cousin of the Queen of England said was right, then Giovanni Bonnetti had done what he had set out to do and might even see Rome again by the end of the year. Assuming the shipment to Ireland went well...

The wagons full of armaments were in a clearing under guard by some Scots wearing their native padded jacks—miserably poor as they were, they could not afford breastplates. Carey was in a jocular mood: he made some incomprehensible comment as he handed over a letter and a ring as identification to one of the thugs who greeted them and the man laughed shortly.

Giovanni examined the guns. They seemed well enough, but then you never knew unless you fired one.

'Fire this one for me, monsieur,' he said to Carey in French.

'What about the noise?'

Giovanni shrugged. 'I will certainly not buy any weapons without seeing at least one of them fired first.'

Carey bowed, loaded and primed the caliver with long fingers that seemed slightly clumsy about it, borrowed slowmatch from one of the men and lit the gun's match. It hissed, lighting his face eerily from below.

'What shall I shoot?' he asked.

'The knot in the middle of that oak over there.'

Carey smiled a little tightly, raised the caliver to his shoulder, brought it down and fired.

Giovanni went to inspect the hole left by the bullet while Carey cleaned the gun. The long fingers were shaking again, which reassured Giovanni: it was right and proper for a man probably committing high treason out of greed to be nervous.

'Good,' he said, coming back. 'It fires a little to the left, I see.'

'Perhaps my aim was off.'

'You are modest, monsieur.'

Giovanni took the caliver, which was still hot, examined the pan and the barrel and then nodded.

'The shape of the stock is unusual,' he said. 'Almost a German fashion.'

'I understand that some Germans work for the Dumfries armourers,' said Carey.

'And this is from Dumfries?'

'Indirectly.'

Giovanni waited for further explanation on the guns' provenance and got none.

'Well, monsieur,' said Carey politely. 'Are you satisfied, or shall I fire another?'

Giovanni went over to the wagon, pulled out a pistol, looked it over and put it back. He did the same with a number of the other weapons. They seemed well enough.

'No,' he said. 'I am satisfied.'

In fact, although he was pulling out guns and looking at them, flicking the locks and squinting down the barrels, in his relief Bonnetti was thinking far ahead, about the next stage. He would have the weapons greased and packed in winebarrels for the journey on barges down the River Nith to Glencaple where he had a small ship lying ready. Given God's grace (which surely would be forthcoming for such a noble cause) he would cross the narrow sea to Ireland in two stages, stopping off at the Isle of Man. Providing he met no English or Irish or Scots pirates, and the weather was calm and the ship sprang no leaks, he might be back in a month or so, God willing.

Carey confirmed the legendary reputation of the English for avarice in the way he dickered over the hiring fee for the wagons to take the guns into Dumfries. The Lord Maxwell was even willing to furnish guards and men to help load the weapons on barges, again for a fee. It would have to be done that night, Carey said, for there were no guarantees and the King himself might well decide to confiscate the weapons if he heard what was happening, since he had need of them too. At last it was all agreed and Giovanni was the proud possessor of eighteen dozen assorted guns which he could now send to the O'Neill in Ireland. He felt quite light-headed with the relief of it. And he also had a valuable lever to use against the noble English official who had sold him the weapons: as the Englishman mounted up and rode away, Giovanni was already framing the letters he would send to his brother in London and to the King of Spain in his palace at San Lorenzo and thinking about how he would return to this miserable northern country next year and begin to apply a little pressure.

Dodd was still awake in a corner of Maxwell's hall when Carey finally returned, although it was well past sunset and he was yawning fit to crack his jaw. He had spent an uncomfortable and tense day cooped up in the crowded house, finding that whatever he did and wherever he went, two large Maxwell cousins went with him. At any moment he expected an order to be given and himself hustled into some small cell and the door locked. It would almost be a relief, he tried to convince himself, because then at least he would know where he stood. But he knew too much about the accidents that could happen to any man held hostage by a Border lord, and he knew as well that there was nothing he could do to help himself. He had to rely on Carey finding some way to mollify Lord Maxwell and pay him off, and for the life of him he didn't see how that was possible.

In the end, he had taken refuge from being followed and watched by sitting in a corner of the hall, next to Maxwell's plateboard set with gold and silver dishes, put his feet up on the bench and started whittling a toy out of a piece of firewood.

As it happened, Carey came in with Lord Maxwell himself, both of them laughing uproariously over some joke and Maxwell at least quite drunk. There was much backslapping and bonhomie: Dodd wondered if the Courtier could tell how false it sounded, but he looked drunk as well. Maxwell disappeared through the door into his parlour, shouting for meat and drink.

Dodd examined the little fighting bear he had nearly finished and kept his feet on the bench. Carey came over to him, humming a court tune, while Hutchin trailed yawning over to the fire, kicked himself a space amongst the pageboys and curled up into sleep like a puppy.

'Well?' asked Dodd grimly.

'My lord Maxwell is quite happy now,' said Carey with a bright smile, checking the silver jugs next to Dodd. He found some aqua vitae in one and drank it straight down.

'Whit about Red Sandy and Sim's Will?'

'They can stay the night in the lock-up to teach them sense but my lord Maxwell says he'll bail them tomorrow morning and we can leave whenever we want.'

Well, it sounded promising, if you could trust a Scottish baron, which personally Dodd didn't believe possible.

'How did ye do it, sir?'

'Acted as an honest broker and found a buyer for Maxwell's scrap iron.'

'Who?'

Carey smiled and tapped his nose like a southern coney-catcher. 'Ahah.'

By God, he's full of himself, thought Dodd, and what poor unfortunate bastard did he persuade to buy the damned things? The Johnstones? The King?

'Ye didnae sell them to the Johnstones?' Dodd asked in dismay. They had to pass through Johnstone land to get home and he could imagine the vengefulness of that clan if a few of their number had had their hands blown off.

Carey tutted at him and sat down beside him on the bench. 'No, of course not. In any case, I think it's the laird Johnstone that made the original swap for the Tower weapons. I've heard he's well-armed which is what panicked Maxwell into stripping Carlisle bare.'

'Nay, I dinnae think so, sir.' Dodd was shaking his head as he thought it through. 'The Johnstones have been well-armed for a month or more. That's why Maxwell hasnae taken them on yet.'

'It's what I heard, anyway. You can rest easy, the guns won't be staying in Scotland or England to plague us.' He laughed and drank some more Scottish aqua vitae. 'They've gone to the best people for them and I've made enough on the deal to pay you and the men next month.'

What the hell did he mean by that? Who could he...The Italian lady? He'd sold wagonloads of firearms to a Papist? Good God, he couldn't be such a fool. Surely? Yes, he could, came the despairing thought, because when you put Carey under pressure, there was no telling what he might suddenly decide to do.

'Are ye drunk, sir?' asked Dodd pointedly. 'Because if ye arenae, ye're plainly tired of life and it'd be a kindness to put a dagger in ye.'

'Lord, Sergeant, what's your problem? You've come over all prim.'

'Prim, sir, is it? Ye've just sold the entire load of Carlisle's weapons tae the Italian wine merchant that any fool can see must be working for the King of Spain and...'

'What the hell do you think we were going to do with them? Take them back to Carlisle? Use them?'

It was disgraceful. 'And which poor creature did ye get to fire one of the bloody things?'

'Me.'

Dodd shook his head and finished the last of the beer. 'Ye're mad, sir,' he told Carey flatly. 'Ye think ye're being ower clever, but ye're no'. Ye cannae deal weapons wi' a foreigner like that, especially not a Papist, it's treason. And why did my lord Maxwell not deal with 'em direct, eh?'

'Didn't have time to think of it. He only knew the weapons were bad this morning.'

'Time enough, I'd say. He was the one brung the foreigners here to Scotland, he could have done the deal hisself and not lost any of the gold to ye. Did ye think he's too stupid? Nay, he's too clever...'

'I don't remember asking your opinion, Sergeant.' Carey's voice was cold, perhaps a little slurred. How much booze had he put down his throat in the twenty-four hours or more since his interview with the King of Scotland? It wasn't that he was reeling or even unsteady, only he must be more affected by it than he seemed, to have pulled a mad dangerous trick like this one, full of the ugly scent of treason and trickery.

'Ay, sir,' said Dodd. 'Nor ye didnae, but if I see a man riding full pelt for a cliff edge, I wouldnae be human if I didnae call out to him.'

Carey was rechecking the jugs, and doomed to disappointment. 'Oh, rubbish, Sergeant. I thought you'd be more grateful to me for rescuing your idiot brother from gaol and you from being a hostage. Where else was I going to get the money to calm Lord Maxwell down? Rob the King's bloody treasury?' Carey grinned again. He was irrepressibly and ludicrously pleased with his own cleverness. 'Mind you,' he added. 'That's a thought, isn't it? I'll bet His Majesty's got his funds in a chest under his bed at the Mayor's house guarded by naught bar a couple of bumboys.'

Dodd for one did not see why he had to sit there and watch the Courtier preen. With sudden decision he removed his boots from the bench, put away his nearly formed chunk of firewood and stood up. 'I'm for my bed,' he said. 'I cannae keep court hours. Goodnight to ye, sir.'

'Goodnight, Sergeant,' said Carey.

'Are we tae go back to Carlisle the morrow?'

'No, Sergeant, we haven't finished yet.'

'And why the hell not?'

'Don't take that tone with me, Sergeant. I appreciate you disapprove of what I've done and frankly I don't care. But you can talk to me civilly or not at all.'

Dodd grunted. He struggled for self-control because as often happened, the loquacious little devil inside him was in a good mind to give the Courtier a mouthful and see how he liked it. But Dodd had paid thirty pounds English for the Sergeantship and he knew his wife wanted the investment back: the truth was, he was more afraid of his woman than he was inclined to give the Deputy a punch in the mouth, a fact which made him feel even more tired than he already was.

'Why have we no' finished, sir?' Dodd said after a moment, with heavy politeness.

'We haven't retrieved the true Carlisle handguns from the Johnstones yet, Sergeant, the ones the Queen really sent us from the Tower armouries, and we're not going until we do. Goodnight to you.'

## FRIDAY, 14TH JULY 1592, BEFORE DAWN

If Sir Henry Widdrington had ever been priest-hunting with one of Sir Francis Walsingham's men, things would have gone very differently, Carey often thought afterwards. Unlike the priest-finders, the Widdringtons had not properly scouted their target nor forewarned their helpers.

It was the shouting and ruddy light of torches in the black of the night that propelled Young Hutchin Graham out of his sleep by the fire. He ran to the window and squinted through stained glass to look out into the yard. The Maxwell guards were arguing with a square-shaped gentleman, hatted and ruffed and standing outlined in the open postern gate. There was a flash of white paper; the ominous phrase *In the King's name* floated to Hutchin's ears. Lord Maxwell himself and two of his cousins hurried through the dim hall, fully dressed and armed, to meet the men at the gate.

It suddenly occurred to Hutchin that he might have been a little too trusting of Roger Widdrington.

'Och, God, no,' he moaned, turned and sprinted through the parlour and up the spiral stairs to Lord Maxwell's solar and through from there into the anteroom that had been given to Carey. The two enormous wolfhounds that he was sharing it with woke up and growled at him, and Carey himself sat up, blinking.

'What is it?'

'Sir, sir, I'm sorry, I thought it was Lady Widdrington, not Sir Henry.'

'What? What are you blabbering about? And what the Devil's that noise?'

Hutchin swallowed hard and fought for control. 'It's Sir Henry Widdrington, Deputy. He's got a Royal Warrant to arrest someone.'

There was the sound of the gate bolts being opened.

Noticeably, Carey didn't ask who the warrant was for. His eyes narrowed to chips of ice.

'You've been passing information about my doings.'

'Ay, sir,' Hutchin confessed miserably. 'To Roger Widdrington. I thought it was for my lady. That's what he said.'

Carey was out of bed now, peering through the narrow window into the yard where Sir Henry and a large number of men were marching across between the horses and men camping out there, towards the hall door.

'You halfwitted romantic twat,' said Carey, feeling under his shirt and unbuckling a moneybelt. 'Pull up your doublet and shirt.'

Mouth open, Hutchin did as he was told. Carey strapped it onto him, where it went round twice.

'Och, it's heavy, sir,' said Young Hutchin Graham, waking up rather more and now beginning to take on a canny expression.

'It's gold and a banker's draft.'

'Christ.'

'Don't swear. Come with me.'

Carey led the boy out into Maxwell's solar where there was a trapdoor let into the ceiling. He hauled a linen chest underneath, stood on it, opened the bolts, shoved back the trapdoor and then boosted Young Hutchin up into the dark spaces above.

'What's happening, sir?' Young Hutchin asked, kneeling at the edge of the hole. 'Where does this go?'

'There'll be an escape route via the roof, no doubt. I never heard of a Border lord yet that didn't have one. Use it.'

'What about ye, sir?'

'Thanks to you, I think I'm about to be arrested by the King of Scotland.'

'But can ye not come with me?'

'Use your head, Hutchin. This is Maxwell's bolthole. It's me they're after, and if I'm not here, his lordship will know where I've gone and they'll catch both of us. Whereas nobody's interested in you.'

'Och, Jesus, sir. Will they hang ye?'

'Certainly not. Being of noble blood, I've a right to ask for beheading. Here, catch this ring.'

'Whit d'ye want me tae do, sir?'

'You've a choice, haven't you? You could go to Dodd if he's still at liberty, or try and see Lady Elizabeth Widdrington, herself, in person this time and not through intermediaries. Show her the ring and ask for her help. She might even give it.'

'Or?'

'Or you could pelt off to your cousins and run for the Debateable Land with the gold that's in that belt. Which might be safer for you in the short term.'

Young Hutchin said nothing.

* * *

Young Hutchin silently scrabbled at the heavy trap and put it back in its hole. Carey scrubbed the fingermarks off with his shirtsleeve, jumped down, pushed the chest back against the wall, kicked the rucked-up rushes about a bit and ran back to his anteroom, shutting and bolting the door behind him while the dogs milled around him looking puzzled, and the tramp of boots echoed on the spiral stair. First one and then both of the wolfhounds began to bark and growl menacingly, standing to face the door with their hackles up and their teeth bared. Carey patted them both affectionately. If he had wanted to make a fight of it, they would have given their lives for him, but he saw no point in that.

There's nothing like a bolted door to please a searcher, old Mr Phelippes had told him once, it is so exactly the kind of thing one is looking for. Also the bolt gave Carey time to pull on his hose and boots, before the end of it cracked out of the doorjamb to the multiple kicking. He faced Sir Henry Widdrington and about five other Widdringtons with his sword in his hand. The wolfhounds began baying like the Wild Hunt.

'What in the name of God is going on?' he demanded over the noise.

Sir Henry Widdrington had a loaded wheellock dag in one hand and an official-looking paper in the other. He hobbled forwards a few paces on his swollen gouty feet, his face turned to a gargoyle's by the torches and deep personal satisfaction. Like a town crier he read out the terms of the warrant in a booming tone.

From behind him Lord Maxwell called his dogs to him and they stopped barking, looked very puzzled, whined sadly at Carey and padded out to their master. Maxwell then, rather pointedly, left.

All was perfectly legal: the King of Scotland had made out a warrant for the arrest on a charge of high treason and trafficking with enemies of the realms of both Scotland and England (nice touch) of one Sir Robert Carey.

'Let me see the seal,' said Carey.

'You're not suggesting, I hope, that I would forge the King's Warrant?' said Sir Henry.

'Lord above, Sir Henry, I wouldn't put anything past you.' Carey was still holding out his left hand for the warrant, his sword en garde between them. Sir Henry reddened and swelled like a frog, then shrugged and gave it to him, the dag's muzzle not moving an inch from the direction of Carey's heart. Carey wondered how much insolence it would take from him for the weapon to go off unexpectedly and shoot him dead. Also the seal was genuine.

Carey handed back the warrant and laid his sword down on the truckle bed. He was immediately grabbed by four of Widdrington's henchmen and his arms twisted painfully up behind his back, which started to make him angry as well as afraid.

'I've surrendered to you, Sir Henry,' he managed to say through his teeth. 'There's no need for this.'

Sir Henry answered with a punch in Carey's belly which almost had him spewing up the sour remains of the aqua vitae he had drunk earlier.

'Ye chose the wrong man to put the horns on, boy,' hissed Sir Henry in his ear as he tried to straighten up. 'Any more lip from ye an' I'll send ye to the King with your tackle mashed to pulp.'

Carey didn't answer because he hadn't got the breath. Somebody was putting wooden manacles on his wrists behind him, some kind of primitive portable stocks.

They propelled him downstairs and through the parlour where Maxwell was standing with his men, watching impassively. Over his shoulder, Carey called to him, 'I don't know what I've done to deserve this from you, my lord Warden.'

Maxwell shrugged and looked away, which was not worth the further fist in the gut administered by Sir Henry.

Widdrington's keeping away from my face, Carey thought, when he could think again, which means he's been ordered to bring me in unharmed. That's good. Or is it? Perhaps King James just wants a fresh field for his interrogators to start work on. No, they're not that subtle.

It was hard to keep his feet as they shoved him along, through the hall, through the courtyard now filled with sleepy watchers, and out into the Town Head. One of the Widdringtons held him up when he missed his footing on the cobbles and would have sprawled full length. Carey caught a glimpse of looming breadth and heroic spottiness and recognised young Henry, Widdrington's eldest son. Henry was wearing a steady flush and a sullen expression and kept his head turned away from Carey's as he helped him.

They were hustling him on foot down towards the Mercat Cross and the town lock-up, but that was not where they were going. Instead, before they reached it, Sir Henry and his men turned and went under the arcades of the Mayor's house, through the side door and into the broad kitchen. There a baker was firing his oven and woodmen beginning the work of relighting the fires on the hearths for cooking, while the older scullery boys still slept near the heat and the flagstones gleamed from washing by the yawning younger ones.

Next to the massive table in the centre, under the hams and strings of onions dangling from the roof, Carey tried to slow down, turn, demand to know what the hell was going on here. Somebody, not young Henry, grabbed his shirt and shoved him forwards, causing him to skid on the wet stones and land on his side, which winded him once more. Until his eyes unblurred it was confusing: a whirl of flames from the main hearth and the bread-oven, and men with hard faces, but at least nobody had kicked him while he was on the ground. He got his feet under him and stood up with some difficulty.

'Keep yer mouth shut,' hissed Sir Henry Widdrington, dag at the ready once more.

And yet, Carey still had the feeling that this was cautious handling: certainly they had not been so gentle with the German. Once more he was grabbed by the shoulders and hurried across the kitchen and into a dark passageway. Yes, there was a sense of furtiveness and hurry, definitely. Surely this was far less official than it appeared? Or why use an English gentleman for the dirty work? King James might be short of loyal soldiers, but any one of his nobles would have been highly delighted to arrest and ill-treat an English official.

They went down stairs echoing with the clatter of boots and his own heavy breathing, into another narrow corridor that smelled headily of wine. A massive iron-bound door was unlocked, swung briefly open and somebody, Sir Henry no doubt, booted him into the opening. He stumbled on the slippery bits of straw on the floor and barked his shoulder as he rammed into the opposite wall. The door slammed shut immediately to a clashing of keys and bolts, leaving him in a darkness that put him in doubt whether his eyes were open or shut. The smell of wine permeated everything, so strong it made his head reel almost at once, though there was another less pleasant smell mixed in with it.

Carey set his back against the wall he had hit and caught his breath. For a while all he could hear was the beating of his own heart and the air in his own throat. Then gradually his nose told him what the other smell was: there was someone else in the wine cellar, someone who had been there for some time. For a moment he was afraid it was a corpse and then he made out the other man's harsh breathing.

'Who's there?' he asked tentatively.

A kind of moan, nothing more.

'Well, where are you?'

This time, a kind of grunt. How badly injured was he? Had the other man been tortured? Or was he a plant of the kind that

Walsingham had used to get information from Catholics in prison?

Wishing he had the use of his hands, Carey began shuffling cautiously across the wine cellar from one wall to the other, trying to learn its geography. The huge wine tuns were in a row by the furthest wall, with smaller barrels set at random on the floor, lying in wait so he could stub his toes and bark his shins on them. Sawdust and straw on the floor to soak up spillage, cool dampness and that maddening Dionysian smell. At last his feet struck something soft and he squatted down. More incomprehensible muttering. What the Devil was wrong with the man?

On impulse Carey tried the few words of High Dutch that he knew: 'Wie sind sie?'

Silence and then the sound of soft sobbing. 'Oh, Christ,' said Carey, suddenly understanding almost everything. 'You're the German—what was it—you're Hans Schmidt? Das ist Ihre Name, ja?'

'Jawohl.'

'What the hell did they do to you?'

A high whining, choked with sobs.

For a while, Carey was too sickened and depressed to do more than sit uncomfortably on the damp straw beside the German. Somewhere at the back of his mind a large and complicated structure was forming to explain all that had been going on, but what he was mainly conscious of was the fact that the chill of the wine cellar was cutting through his shirt and giving him goosepimples, he was already dizzy from the fumes, his stomach hurt and so did his shoulder, and that whatever was left of the man beside him was weeping its heart out.

'All right,' said Carey awkwardly at last, as if talking to a horse gone lame. 'All right now. Ich...er...ich help sie.'

Sniffling, coughing, thick swallowing, well, there was at least enough of the German's pride for him to try and get a grip on himself. And this was no plant: none of that kind of crew were good enough actors. Carey deliberately pulled his thoughts away from what might have happened to the unfortunate foreigner. He couldn't find out anyway, with his hands bolted behind him. The rough wooden shackle hanging on his wristbones was already causing his fingers to prickle and tingle painfully.

'All right,' he said pointlessly again. 'I'm Sir Robert Carey, Deputy Warden of Carlisle. It seems we share an enemy. I want to talk to you. Ich will mit sie sprache.'

There was something a little like a bitter laugh. 'Nonsense,' Carey snapped. 'If it's too hard to talk, just grunt. Give one grunt for yes, two grunts for no and three for I don't know. Eins fur ja, swei fur nein, drei fur ich kenne nicht. Ja?'

'Ja.'

So far, so good, thought Carey, shifting his back up against the wall again and trying to get his legs comfortable. He wished with all his heart he spoke more German, or the German more English. Though from the mushy sounds next to him he suspected the man was having to talk out of a mouthful of broken teeth. 'Now, do you understand French? Sprechen sie Franzosich?'

'Oui. Meilleur qu'anglais.'

'Thank God,' said Carey, mentally switching gears into that language. 'Alors, parlons nous.'

* * *

Young Hutchin sat in Maxwell's loft with his arms wrapped round his knees and watched the rats watching him in the light squeezing up through the ceiling boards from the candles and lanterns below. The cold heavy belt wrapped round his waist was warming up. In his imagination he saw the gold there, thick heavy roundels of it, straight from Spain, stamped with letters he could not read and, no doubt, a few with bite marks in them. He had seen gold when his father had had a good raid, he knew what it looked like and what it could buy.

Below him and to the right there were bangs and thumps and talk. Sir Henry and his men were searching Carey's sleeping place for the gold, but although Hutchin could feel his heart beating hard and slow, he was less afraid than excited. Hiding from searchers was something he had done many times after thieving; it was only a matter of staying still and silent. He had already taken the precaution of putting one of the main roof beams between himself and the trapdoor, in case someone should come up for a look, treading softly and carefully over the narrow boards while Carey argued with Sir Henry below. He could see an escape route where the slates were loose on one side. Picturing the building in his mind, he thought it was at a point on the roof where there was a way down to the roof of the bowling alley and from there to the ground. Or he could go down through the trapdoor when the men below had given up and gone. After that, once out of Maxwell's Castle—there were horses aplenty in the town, or he could find his cousins on foot, an unremarked boy among dozens in Dumfries. And then...

Young Hutchin shook his head with exasperation. The Courtier had somehow caught him neatly in a trap of words and loyalty. What had he said, after outlining precisely the things Hutchin could do? He had said the choice was Hutchin's. No hint there of which he should choose, only the bald stating of it. And yet, Young Hutchin knew perfectly well that the Deputy Warden would be hoping he would find Dodd or Lady Widdrington and get him out of whatever dungeon the Scottish King had thrown him in. What could they do? Ransom him perhaps with the gold around Hutchin's middle. Jesus, what a waste of a fortune.

Hutchin bit his lip, weighing up his choices. If he ran off, he was as good as killing the Deputy, or worse. He had heard the words of the warrant through the ceiling boards, the ugly frightening phrase 'high treason'. Sir Henry Widdrington had read it out loudly enough. They did worse than hang you for high treason, he knew, though he had never seen it done. They hanged you first, then they took you down while you were still alive, cut off your cods and burned them in your face and slit your belly and pulled out your guts and then cut you in four bits like a woman making a chicken stew. He had heard tell that if the hangman wasn't bribed beforehand, he'd let you down before you were more than a little blue and then...Hutchin had seen hangings and more than his share of men dying, but his imagination balked at this. It was true, he had a morbid curiosity to see it done at least once, and envied the apprentice boys in Edinburgh who had more of a chance, but not to the Courtier. He liked the Courtier, soft southerner though he was, and after all, Carey had come after Hutchin when he had been inveigled away from the stables by the young man in tawny taffeta. Carey had appeared at the upstairs window like an avenging angel, while Hutchin was fighting and dodging for his life, had climbed through, punched one of the men and kicked another, giving Hutchin the chance to bite the other man holding him and head-butt a fourth. That had been a good fight, though Hutchin personally would have liked to see Carey's sword bloodied instead of merely used as a threat.

Never mind, the fact was he had been there as if he were an uncle or an elder brother or something, not just a southern courtier. And Young Hutchin had repaid him by spying for his enemy, Sir Henry Widdrington. That annoyed Hutchin profoundly. He had been taken like a wean by Roger Widdrington, he had naïvely believed the tale about Lady Widdrington, *him*—Hutchin Graham, most promising son of the canniest surname on the Border. It was infuriating and shaming. And hardly a word had Carey said to curse him for it, though he was facing arrest by the very man he had no doubt horned, and plainly due to Hutchin's treason. And now Young Hutchin had the means of freeing him. Or not.

God damn it, thought Hutchin, they were still turning over Carey's room, what the Devil's taking them so long? Do they not know how to find good loot in a room? Stupid bastards. He started to pick his teeth with his fingernail. Perhaps he'd be here all night. Perhaps by the time they had finished, the King's men would have broken Carey's long legs in the Boot and put him out of hope of ever walking again. Perhaps after a session with Scottish torturers, he would prefer to die, even by hanging, drawing and quartering?

Young Hutchin was getting tired of thinking. He realised that at last the thumps and bangs had stopped. Still moving cautiously, he picked his way through rat droppings and ancient clothes chests to the loose slates and pulled a few out. There was a gutter that seemed firm enough. The curve of the roof hid him from the yard where Widdrington's men were gathering. With painful slowness he eeled his way out through the small hole and lay full length on the roof, gripping with the toes of his boots and his fingers. He inched his way down until his foot met the edge of the leads, and he could rest his weight on it a little and go sideways to the place where the roof of the bowling alley joined the main building. Although this was a fortified town house, there was no roof platform here for standing siege, only some crenellations and elaborate chimneys, more for show than for use, and a nuisance to climb over.

The bowling alley roof was newer and had no crenellations. At least it was at a flatter pitch and by lying full length and gripping the ridge with his arms at full stretch he could inch himself along and so gain the change from shingle to thatch where the stables began. Arm muscles bulging at the extra weight round his middle, Hutchin let himself down off the bowling alley roof by means of the gutter, watching the pinnings creak and pop. He dropped onto the thatch before the whole lot could come away. The thatch was rotten and he actually went part way through, his feet dangling sickeningly in space, his hands grabbing at one of the cross-ties. A couple of horses whinnied and snorted below.

'Och, the hell with it,' Young Hutchin said to himself, knowing the stables were only one storey high, and he let go of the cross-tie and let himself slide through and rolled into the thick straw between two alarmed horses. Brushing straw and reeds off himself he calmed the animals down, patting them and swearing at them gently under his breath, until he felt the iron prod of a sword in his back and stopped dead.

'Stealing horses again, eh, Young Hutchin?'

'Sergeant Dodd,' said Young Hutchin, his stomach lurching back from his throat with relief.

'Ay. And ye woke me up, ye little bastard.'

The sound of a yawn followed this, so Hutchin cautiously turned about. Sergeant Dodd had bits of straw in his hair and his eyes full of sleep. The hand not holding a sword was scratching fleabites on his stomach and his foul temper in the mornings was legendary.

'It's a pity the men in the yard didnae do the like then,' Hutchin said in a triumphant hiss. 'Sir Henry Widdrington just came with a Royal Warrant and arrested the Deputy Warden.'

The sword didn't move, but Dodd blinked slightly. He moved to one of the half doors, still keeping his sword pointed at Hutchin, opened it a fraction and looked out. He was just in time to see the

682

last Widdringtons leave the yard and the Maxwells on guard shut the gate behind them.

'What was the charge?' asked Dodd after a moment's pause.

'High treason and...er...trafficking with enemies.'

Dodd whitened and looked out into the empty yard again.

'I told him,' he muttered. 'I told the fool.'

'Ye mean it's true?' asked Hutchin, impressed. 'Is the bill foul then?'

'Near enough.'

'Jesus. What shall we do, Sergeant?'

Dodd appeared to be thinking while he stared at Hutchin. Hutchin hoped very much that the Sergeant wouldn't notice the thickening round his middle.

'Well, we canna rescue the Courtier this time by calling out the Dodds or even the Grahams,' he said with finality. 'This is official business. Who was it came to arrest him?'

'Sir Henry Widdrington and his kin.'

'Was it now? That's odd.'

Hutchin Graham nodded. 'And they were in an awful hurry and it didn't sound like they knocked him about much.'

'How did you get away?'

'The Courtier put me up under the roof through the trapdoor when he heard them and gave me this to take to Lady Widdrington.' Hutchin showed him the ring on his thumb which he had been admiring for the size of its red stone and the letters of some kind carved in it. 'Is it a ruby, d'ye think?'

'Ay, no doubt.'

'What are the letters?'

'RC for Robert Carey,' answered Dodd at once, impressing Young Hutchin for the first time with his clerkly knowledge. 'Did he give ye anything else?' Dodd asked casually. Hutchin shook his head. 'They've got it then,' he said sadly.

'Got what?' asked Hutchin with artful ignorance.

'Nothing to concern ye, lad. Come on.'

'Where to?'

'Out of here first, and out of the town too. I dinna want to end up in the Dumfries hole with the Courtier.'

683

Hutchin shook his head. 'I'm for going to Lady Widdrington,' he heard himself say. 'That's what the Courtier wanted me to do, and that's what I'll do.'

'Ye'll come with me, lad.'

'Where are you going?'

Dodd thought for a moment. 'If the Maxwells are agin ye, who's most like to back ye?' he asked rhetorically. Hutchin nodded. It made sense to try the Johnstones. 'Do you know a good way out of this place? Is there a garden gate?'

Hutchin thought about this professionally. 'I heard tell from one of the other boys there's a way by the new bowling alley, that Maxwell had built from the old monastery stone. The wall there's nobbut the monastery wall and they werenae too choosy how they treated it.'

Dodd nodded. 'If I can make it back to Carlisle, we'll get the Warden to write to the King and see if we can ransom him out of there.'

Hutchin's face twisted. 'That's nae good,' he said. 'Once it goes to the Warden, then he's done for one way or the other, for the Queen will hear of it.'

Dodd had put on his jack and his helmet, giving him the familiar comforting silhouette of a fighting man, though the quilting on the leather was different from the Graham pattern. Now he was busy bundling up the shape of a man in the corner where he had been sleeping, out of straw and his cloak.

'Lad,' said Dodd gravely, almost kindly, 'we cannae spring the Courtier out of the King's prison.'

'Why not? Ye saved him from my uncle when he was trapped on Netherby tower.'

'That was different. Your uncle's one thing, the King's another.'

'I dinnae see why,' said Hutchin stubbornly. 'They're both men that have other men to do their bidding, only the King's got more.'

'That's enough, Young Hutchin. We canna rescue the Courtier again because...Anyway, what can a woman do about it?'

'He wanted me to take the ring to Lady Widdrington, so he must think she can do something. And that...' said Hutchin virtuously, the decision somehow made for him by Dodd's opposition, '…is what I'll do, come ye or any man agin me.'

He slipped under the horse's belly and whisked to the rear door that led to the midden heap. Sword still in his hand, Dodd didn't try to stop him, so Hutchin checked that the backyard was clear and the Maxwells were watching outwards, and then turned again to the Sergeant with an impish grin.

'He gets in a powerful lot of trouble, doesn't he?' he said. 'For a Deputy Warden.'

'Ay.'

## FRIDAY, 14TH JULY 1592, DAWN

Elizabeth Widdrington always woke well before dawn to rise in the darkness and say her prayers. In the tiny Dumfries alehouse where they were lodging, it was easier for her to do it: firstly her husband had been out much of the night and had not been there to disturb her sleep with his snoring and moaning and occasional ineffectual fumbling. Secondly the new belting he had given her on top of the old ones the night before had kept her from sleeping very well in any case.

Fastening her stays was always the hardest part, as she pulled the laces up tight and the whalebone bit into the welts and bruises, but once that was done they paradoxically gave her support and armour. None of her clothes fastened fashionably at the back, since she did not like to be dependent on a lady's maid, and so it was the work of a few minutes to tie on her bumroll, step into her kirtle and hook up the side of her bodice. She had changed the sleeves the night before and half-pinned her best embroidered stomacher to it and so once her cap was on her head she was respectable enough to meet the King if necessary.

She knelt to pray, composing her mind, firmly putting out of it her swallowed fury at her husband since it was, after all, according to all authority, his right to beat her if she displeased him, just as he could beat his horses. She worked to concentrate on the love and mercy of Our Lord Jesus Christ.

After a few minutes she said the Lord's Prayer and stood up: it was hopeless and always happened. She couldn't keep her mind on anything higher than the top of Robert Carey's head. Since the age of seventeen she had been married to Sir Henry, happy as the fourth, gawky and dowryless Trevannion daughter to travel on the promise of marriage from the lushness of Cornwall to the bare bones of the north. Everything had been arranged through the Lord Chamberlain, Lord Hunsdon, as a kindness to one of his wife's many kin. She had gone knowing perfectly well that her husband-to-be was gouty and in his fifties but determined to do her best to be a good wife to him, as God required of her. She had tried, failed and kept trying because there was no alternative. And then, seven miserable years later in 1587 the youngest son of that same Lord Hunsdon had spent weeks at Widdrington, waiting to be allowed to enter Scotland with his letter from the Queen of England which tried to explain to King James how Mary Queen of Scots had so unfortunately come to be executed. Robin had ridden south again at last, the message delivered by proxy, and she had wept bitter tears in her wet larder, where she could blame it on brine and onions. And then there had been the nervous plotting with her friend, his sister Philadelphia Scrope, so she could travel down to London the next year, the Armada year of 1588, and the year that shone golden in her memory, with Robert Carey the bright alarming jewel at its centre. But she had kept her honour, just. Only by the narrowest squeak of scruples on several occasions, true, but she had kept it.

Four years later she was still as much of a fool as ever, still burned to her core by nothing more than a glimpse of him caught as she dismounted in the street. She had accepted punishment from her husband for her loan to Robin of his horses the previous month, accepted it because ordained by God. But to be beaten for no more than a look, accused unjustly of cuckolding her husband and nothing she said believed...

I am wasting my time, she thought, trying to be firm. Besides, Robin has very properly abandoned his suit to me, look at how he was paying court to Signora Bonnetti...

Her stomach suddenly knotted up with bile and misery. How could he so publicly abandon me, he did not even try to speak to me at the dance the day before yesterday? (Ridiculous, of course he wouldn't, Sir Henry was standing guard over me.) How could he dance with the vulgar little Italian in her whore's crimson gown? (Whyever should he not, since he could not dance with me?) How could he disappear into the garden with her and what had he done there...(What business is it of mine, what he did, and do I really want to know?) How *could* he, the bastard, *how could he*...?

I will go for a walk outside, Elizabeth Widdrington said to herself, and escape this ridiculous vapouring. Anyone would think I was a maid of fifteen. I will not allow myself to hate Robin Carey for doing exactly as I told him to in my letter (*bastard!*).

She slipped her pattens on her feet and ducked out of the little alehouse. It had been very crowded with her husband's kin, various cousins and tenants but now the place seemed half-empty. Her stepson Henry was lying asleep on one of the tables with his cloak huddled up round his ears, his pebbled face endearingly relaxed. He seemed to get broader every time she looked at him: his father's squareness reproduced but almost doubled in size. Roger was nowhere to be seen. Because she was looking for sadness, she found more there. She had brought them up as well as she could and now they were growing away from her, abandoning her for their father's influence.

Stop that, she commanded herself and walked briskly down the wynd that led behind the alehouse, past a couple of tents filled with more of King James's soldiers, past three drunks lying clutching each other in the gutter, whether in affection or some half-hearted battle, past the jakes and the chickens and the pigpen and the shed where the goat was being milked, into the other wynd and back down the other side of the alehouse. Inside she still found no sign of her husband or half his men and climbed the stairs.

A boy was sitting swinging his legs on the sagging trucklebed she had been using, a rather handsome boy with cornflower-blue eyes and a tangled greasy mop of straight blond hair, the beginnings of adult bone lengthening his jaw already. Despite his magnificent black eye, she recognised him at once.

'Is it Young...Young Hutchin?'

The boy stood up, made a sketchy bow and handed over a small piece of jewellery. It was a man's signet ring with a great red stone in the centre, carved...Robert Carey had shown it to her at court.

The scene burst into her mind's eye, the Queen's Privy Garden at Westminster in 1588, the clipped box hedges and the wooden seat under the walnut tree, Robin peacock-bright in turquoise taffeta and black velvet, the day before he rode south with George Cumberland to sneak aboard the English fleet and go to fight the Spanish. 'If ever you see this away from my hand,' he had said in the overly dramatic style of the court, 'then I am in trouble and need your help. Do not fail, my lady, I will need you to storm and take the Tower of London, for the Queen will have thrown me into gaol for loving you better than I love her.' She had laughed at him, but she had also shown him the small handfasting ring with the diamond in the middle that had been her sole legacy from her mother, and told him the same thing. That had been one of her narrower escapes from dishonour; she had rashly let him kiss her that time.

So she took the ring, her heart beating slow and hard. She examined it carefully for blood or any other sign of having been cut from a dead hand, sat down on the bed with it clasped over her thumb and looked at Young Hutchin.

'What's happened to him?' she asked as calmly as she could.

He told her the tale quite well, with not too many diversions and only a small amount of exaggeration about how he had climbed from a roof. So that was what her husband had been up to all night. She made Young Hutchin go through the whole thing again, listening carefully for alterations. Young Hutchin mentioned handguns; she made him tell her about them and more of her husband's activities became clear to her. The rage she had stopped up for so long, which had killed her appetite and kept her dry-eyed through all her husband's accusations and brutality, suddenly flowered forth in a cold torrent. She sat silent, letting it take possession of her, using it to form a plan.

'Sir Henry and Lord Spynie are old allies,' she said at last. 'Sir Henry knew Alexander Lindsay's father years before he was born.

Take it from me, Young Hutchin, King James knew nothing of this outrage.'

She dug in her chest and found paper and a pencase, which she opened and scrabbled out pens and ink. She waited for a moment for her hands to stop shaking and her thoughts to settle. Although she was only a woman, she had influence if she chose to use it. Her husband was not the only one with friends at the Scottish court. She began with a letter begging urgent audience with the King.

'Take this to the Earl of Mar,' she said, folding the first letter and sealing it with wax from the candle. 'Where is Sergeant Dodd?'

Young Hutchin spat expressively. 'Run fra the town, mistress, I hope. He said he'd try the Johnstones.'

'Good. When you have delivered the first letter, come back to me here. Don't speak to any of the Widdringtons except me, do you understand?'

'Ay, mistress. Will all this writing free the Deputy?'

'It might. Off you go.'

The lad whisked out of the door and pelted down the stairs. Elizabeth took up her pen again, though her hand was starting to ache, and wrote another letter to Melville, King James's chancellor, who had stayed in Edinburgh. They were old friends for she had fostered his son at Widdrington for a year, at a time when Scotland was too hot for him and he had been afraid of his child being used against him. In it she set down a precise account of what she guessed or knew about her husband and his activities, which she folded up, sealed and put crackling under her stays. Then she went downstairs again, face calm as she could make it. The few other men who had been sleeping there had woken and gone out to see to the horses. Her stepson had also woken up at last, and was sitting on his table, scratching and yawning and gloomily fingering yet another spectacular spot that had flowered on his nose in the night.

'Good morning, Henry,' she said sedately.

Henry coughed and winced: blood-shot eyes told her the rest of the tale.

'Who gave you so much to drink?'

The young jaw stuck out and the adam's apple bobbed. 'Nobody,' he said truculently. 'Sir Henry's still at the Red Boar.'

Elizabeth's eyes narrowed. 'What do you know about the arrest of Sir Robert Carey?'

He looked away sullenly, his ears red and his feet twining together as they dangled off the table. Elizabeth went to the almost empty beer barrel, pushed aside the scrawny creature trying pathetically to clean up spillages with a revolting mop and tilted it to get the last of the beer out into a leather mug.

'Drink that,' commanded Elizabeth.

'I'll puke.'

'You will not,' said his stepmother drily. 'You'll find it has a miraculous effect. Go on.'

With an effort Henry drank, coughed again, wiped his mouth where the incipient fur on his top lip caught the drops and put the mug down.

'Go on, tell me.'

'Well, I had to do it, didn't I? He's my father, isn't he?'

Elizabeth said nothing. Henry sighed.

'Sir Henry rousted us all out about midnight or one o'clock, said he had clear evidence Sir Robert was trafficking guns with the Italian wine merchant.'

'And how did he find out?'

'Roger got the tale from his pageboy.'

'On the pretext that I wanted to know?'

Henry nodded.

'Go on. I shall speak to Roger later.'

'And Sir Henry said Lord Maxwell had confirmed it and was very annoyed because he said Carey had cheated him on the deal. So we went up to the Mayor's house with him, with Father I mean, and waited about a bit and then Father came down again with my Lord Spynie and the warrant. We went back to Maxwell's Castle and Lord Maxwell let us in and we kicked Sir Robert's door down and there he was with his sword in his hand and his hose and boots on, wanting to know what we wanted.'

'Did he fight?'

'No. Once he'd seen the Privy Seal on the warrant and the signature, he surrendered.'

'What did he say about it? Did he say he was innocent?'

'He didn't get the chance.'

'How badly was he beaten?'

Henry coughed and looked away again. 'Not badly,' he muttered. 'I've had worse.'

Elizabeth nodded thoughtfully. 'And where is he now?'

'We took him back to the Mayor's house again, to the wine cellar. Aside from the Dumfries gaol, which is full, it's the only lock-up they've got here.'

'Where did your father go?'

'He's off with Lord Spynie and his friends.'

'So you came here and drank yourself asleep, instead of telling me.'

'Father made me swear not to tell you.'

'Oh, *did* he?'

Clearly Henry did not understand the significance of that, but it lightened Elizabeth's heart. If Sir Henry didn't want her to know something that he knew would cause her pain, then there was an excellent reason for it. She could think of only one good enough.

'Smarten yourself up, Henry,' she said with a wintry smile. 'Or at least comb your hair. Then find the steward. When I've talked to him we're going to see the King.'

\* \* \*

Walking alone at dawn into the rough encampment of Johnstones in the part of Dumfries south of Fish Cross, Dodd had not been recognised at once. This was a relief to him since he still had a number of kine and sheep at Gilsland that had once belonged to various Johnstone families. When he insisted that he had important information about the Maxwells that he would give to the laird only, they brought him through the tents to the best one, which had been brightly painted and carried two flags.

The laird was breaking his fast on bread and beer. He was a bony gangling young man with a shock of wiry brown hair and his face prematurely lined with responsibility. His great grandfather, the famous Johnny Johnstone, had been able to put two thousand fighting men in the saddle on the hour's notice, but the King of those days had taken exception to such power being wielded by a subject. Johnny Johnstone had been inveigled into the King's presence on a promise of safeconduct and summarily hanged. Now the power of the Johnstones was much less and their bitter enemies the Maxwells were stronger than them.

'Your name?' asked the laird.

Dodd took a deep breath and folded his arms. 'Henry Dodd, Land-Sergeant of Gilsland.'

Johnstone's brown eyes narrowed and his jaw set.

'Ay.'

'I'm here with Sir Robert Carey, Deputy Warden of the English West March.'

'Mphm. Last I heard, ye were staying with the Maxwell.'

'That's why I've come to ye, sir,' said Dodd. 'Maxwell's got the Deputy Warden arrested on a trumped-up charge.'

'Well, ye shouldnae've trusted him, should ye?'

'You're right, sir,' said Dodd bitterly. 'But Sir Robert wouldnae listen to me.'

There was a very brief cynical smile. The Johnstone finished his beer.

'And?'

'Did ye know that the Maxwell recently bought at least two hundred firearms, powder and ammunition off Sir Richard Lowther in Carlisle?'

Johnstone wiped his mouth fastidiously. 'I had heard something about it. What of it?'

'Would it interest ye to know more about the guns?'

'It might.'

Dodd stood there with his arms folded and his whole spine prickling, and waited.

Johnstone smiled briefly again. 'What d'ye want for the information?'

'Your support, sir. Your protection against Maxwell for myself and Sir Robert. Your counsel.'

Johnstone took his time thinking about this, looking Dodd up and down. He had a fair amount to consider, to be fair to him. What Dodd was offering, unauthorised and unstated, was a possible alliance between the Johnstones and the Wardenry of Carlisle. It wasn't merely a matter of information.

'Hm.'

It all depended on whether the laird had any of the daring of his great grandfather. He would be taking a chance on Dodd's faith, and the faith of Sir Robert, although Dodd thought he would also be quite grateful for the information as well, once he had it. But there again, the laird could then discard Dodd and Sir Robert if he chose: they were both taking a chance on faith.

Johnstone stared into space for a moment. 'Very well,' he said without preamble. 'Ye have my backing agin the Maxwells for you and your Deputy Warden, and my counsel for what that's worth.'

So easily? Dodd was still suspicious. But there was nothing else he could do: he simply had to hope that the laird was a man of his word, unlike Lord Maxwell.

He coughed. 'The Maxwell's weapons are all bad, worse than useless. They explode on the second firing. Maxwell knows this now and he's got rid of them, but his men have practically no guns as a result.'

Johnstone was sitting utterly still. 'Ye're sure of this?'

'On my honour, sir.'

Johnstone held his gaze for a long moment more. Then he banged his folding table with the flat of his hand and jumped to his feet. 'By God,' he laughed. 'Let's have them.'

After that, Dodd was almost forgotten as Johnstone strode from his tent trailing a flurry of orders and the camp began to stir and buzz like a kicked beeskep. Dodd knew he had just broken the strained peace between the two surnames and rekindled what amounted to open civil war in the Scottish West March. It was extremely satisfactory.

\* \* \*

Carey had been in prison before. Paris had been expensive and in the end his creditors had caught him and thrown him in gaol until his father could send him funds and a scorching letter through the English ambassador. At the time he had been in the depths of misery, cooped up in a filthy crowded communal cell and away from his fascinating Duchesse (who, he found out later, had tired of him in any case). But it had only lasted a couple of weeks and he had not been chained nor in darkness.

He tried to do something about his hands, flexing them and trying to shift the wooden manacles, which made his shoulders cramp and his fingers buzz with pins and needles. He had found out all he needed to know from the German, whatever he was really called—Hans Schmidt was clearly not his name—through a painful process of question and answer, guesswork and elimination. He had been merciless in his quest for hard facts and the exhausted man now slept, moaning softly every so often. Perhaps it would have been sensible to sleep as well, but he couldn't, not with the stink of wine and pain in his nostrils, and the overwhelming pit of fear in his bowels.

He thought back to what he had done, wondering if he had made a mistake. Perhaps...perhaps he had acted hastily, dealing on his own initiative with the Italian. Perhaps he should have talked to the King first. But the King had either lied about the guns or genuinely not known what was going on. And the opportunity had been there to be seized, with no time for careful letters to London. Naturally he would file a report back to Burghley when it was all over, but...He had not expected to be arrested. He had not expected Young Hutchin to be so willing to spy for the Widdringtons. Perhaps his greatest mistake had been prancing back to Maxwell's Castle so blithely, trusting Maxwell at all. But he had done what the Maxwell wanted, he had gotten the man his money back and Lord Maxwell had been full of gratitude and favour. Seemingly. Damn him to hell.

He had been caught rather easily. Perhaps he should have fought: but that would have given Sir Henry the excuse he needed to shoot. And what was his legal position anyway—arrested on a false warrant for a crime of which he was in fact guilty? Technically.

Gloomily he thought it would make no difference anyway: possession was nine-tenths of the law and King James would no doubt wink at the fact that he had probably not actually seen the warrant himself.

Carey tried hard to stop his mind from running on to the further consequences: the grave letters back and forth from Edinburgh to London while he and the German rotted in Dumfries. Almost certainly, the Queen would insist on his extradition for questioning by Sir Robert Cecil's experts, like Topcliffe. Oh, Jesus Christ.

Carey swallowed hard, terror taking on a new and even uglier dimension. Queen Elizabeth was a Tudor and took any hint of betrayal extremely seriously indeed. She also took it personally. The fact that she had liked him would make that worse, not better.

He simply could not stay still and his backside was freezing and numb from the stone-flagged floor anyway. He struggled to his feet, causing the German to groan protestingly, stamped and swayed on the spot in the darkness, like a horse in its stall, hunching his shoulders and ducking his head and trying to get some feeling back in his hands.

Another appalling thought hit him. Perhaps Hutchin had not been coney-catched by Roger Widdrington. Perhaps Lady Widdrington had indeed been the one paying him for information; perhaps Carey's chasing after the pretty little Signora had turned Elizabeth utterly against him. Perhaps she had bought back her husband's favour by giving her would-be lover up to the wolves. No. Surely not. She would never...She might. Who could tell how any woman's mind worked? Even though it had been nothing but a light-hearted dalliance he could hardly be expected to turn down, she might be unreasonably jealous, she might be angry enough. In which case his sending Hutchin to her was worse than useless...

He was standing like that, quite close to mindless panic, vaguely wondering how it was possible for him to be sweating while he was also shivering, when the door rattled and creaked open. He had to blink and squint from the light of lanterns. The German didn't because his eyes were too swollen. In fact his whole face was a horrible foreboding, like an obscene cushion, pounded until it was barely human. No wonder the poor bastard had had difficulty speaking. His arms had been chained to a bolt above his head, his fingers were also grotesquely swollen and black, as was his right foot and ankle. Carey looked away from him.

Sir Henry again, three henchmen at his back, Lord Spynie at his side. Lord Spynie was at the head of a different group of three men, luridly brocaded and padded as were all King James's courtiers. Had none of them heard of good taste?

Spynie looked extremely pleased with himself, but also a little furtive. Carey wondered again if he had really been arrested by the King's warrant, or did Spynie have access to some legally trained clerks and the Privy Seal of the Kingdom? Given James's sloppiness with his favourites, surely it was possible? Lord Spynie came up close to him, sneered something he couldn't quite catch in Scots and spat messily in his face. Rage boiled in Carey, it was all he could do to keep from childishly spitting back.

Two Widdringtons gripped him under the arms while one of Spynie's men dragged a little stool into the middle of the wine cellar floor, next to a barrel on its end. On the barrel top, as on a table, another courtier with a puffy eye ceremoniously placed a bunch of small things made of metal.

Carey recognised the courtiers. Two of them still bore the marks of his fist, and one had Hutchin's toothprints in his arm. They all crowded the little space of the wine cellar and fogged it with their breath and heat, and the smoke from their torches and lanterns.

'Good morning, gentlemen,' said Carey, his mouth completely dry and his stomach gone into a hard knot of recognition. Those were thumbscrews lying on the barrel top.

'Why are his legs free?' demanded Lord Spynie.

'We havenae brought leg-irons,' said a courtier. 'Shall I fetch some?'

'No,' said Spynie. 'Use his.' He pointed at the German still slumped against the wall. A key was produced, and the chains holding him to the ring in the wall were unlocked, allowing him to crumble down into a lying position at last. He lay still as a corpse, hardly breathing.

One of the Widdringtons who had brought him here took the irons and knelt to lock them round Carey's ankles.

'Sit down, traitor,' said Lord Spynie.

Carey looked at him, knowing dozens like him at the Queen's court. Alexander Lindsay, Lord Spynie was a young man, around twenty years old, and already beginning to lose the freshness of his beauty. He had a young man's cockiness and sensitivity to slights, and he had acquired a taste for power as the King's minion. Now he knew he was losing it, although he was not intelligent enough to know why. But he was hiding his uncertainty. Carey could read it there, in the way he stood, the way his hand gripped his swordhilt, just as if Spynie was bidding up his cards in a primero game. Instinctively Carey felt it was true: this was unofficial, a favourite taking revenge, not King's men about the King's business.

'I appeal to Caesar,' Carey said softly, pointedly not sitting.

'What?'

'I want to see the King.'

Sir Henry backhanded him across the mouth, having to reach up to do it.

'I'll want satisfaction for that, Widdrington,' Carey said to him, anger at last beginning to fill up the cold terrified spaces inside.

Sir Henry sneered at him. 'Satisfaction? You're getting above yourself, boy. Tell us what we want to know and we might recommend a merciful beheading to the King.'

'If your warrant came from my cousin the King, then he is the one I will talk to,' Carey said coldly and distinctly, hoping they could not hear how his tongue had turned to wool. 'If it did not, then you have no right to hold me and I demand to be released.'

Spynie stepped up close. 'Do you know who I am?' he demanded rhetorically.

Carey smiled. 'Your fame is legendary even at the Queen's Court,' he said, sucking blood from the split in his lip. 'You are the King's catamite.'

Spynie drew his dagger and brought it up slowly under Carey's chin, pricking him slightly.

'Sit down,' whispered Spynie.

'I can't,' Carey said reasonably. 'Your dagger's in the way.'

Spynie took the dagger away, pointed it at Carey's eye.

'Sit down.'

'Why? You can talk to me just as well if I'm standing. Take me to the King.'

'Where's the Spaniard gone?' demanded Sir Henry suddenly.

Carey shrugged. 'I've no idea,' he said. 'And as my lord Spynie knows perfectly well, he's an Italian.'

'You admit talking to him then?'

'Of course. One of my functions as Deputy Warden is to discover what foreign plots are being made against Her Majesty the Queen.'

'How much did ye sell him the guns for?'

'What guns?'

Spynie lost patience and grabbed the front of his shirt. 'Where's the gold?'

'What gold?'

'The gold Bonnetti gave you for the guns?'

'It surprises me,' Carey said looking down at Spynie's grip, 'that you think he had any money left at all, after being at the Scottish court for as long as he had. The bribes to all of you gentlemen must have been costing him a fortune. Take me to the King.'

'What were you doing in the forest this afternoon?' gravelled Sir Henry.

'Hunting. Take me to the King.'

'Where's the fucking gold?' shouted Lord Spynie. 'You got it from him, I ken very well ye did, so what did ye do with it?'

'Take me to the King and I'll tell him.'

Spynie finally lost control and started hitting him across the face with the jewelled pommel of the dagger. As if that were the signal for all pretence at civilisation to disappear, there was a flurry of blows and hands grabbing him, his arms were twisted up behind his back until he thought they would break. By sheer weight of numbers they made him sit on the stool and they forced his head down until his cheek rested on the barrel-top. It smelled of aqua vitae. Cold metal slipped down over the thumb and first two fingers of his left hand behind him and tightened. He went on struggling uselessly, blind with panic, not feeling it when they hit him.

Then somebody was tightening the things on his hands until shooting pains ran up his arms, until he knew beyond doubt that his fingers would break if they tightened any further and then they did and more pain scudded through his hand. It was astonishing how much pressure it took to break a bone. There was more metal slipping onto the fingers and thumb of his right hand, tightening, biting, until his palms contracted reflexively and he shut his eyes and gasped.

'Now,' hissed Lord Spynie. 'Ye've one more chance. Half a turn more and your fingers will break and ye'll never hold a sword nor shoot a gun again. Where's the gold?'

'Take me to...my cousin the King.'

Spynie banged Carey's head down on the table, bruising the place where Jock of the Peartree had cracked his cheekbone the month before.

'The King doesnae ken ye're here. It's me and my friends, naebody else. I'll give ye ten minutes to think about it.'

Carey had stopped struggling. He did think about it, despite the shrieking from the trapped nerves in his fingers, and he decided he had nothing whatever to lose by keeping silent until he had to talk. If Young Hutchin had indeed gone to Lady Widdrington it would give her time to act, if she wished, and if he had not, it would give the boy a chance to get into the Debateable Land, away from Spynie and his friends, which would be some satisfaction at least. God help me, thought Carey, how long can I hold out?

He turned his head so his forehead was resting on the table and tried to marshal his strength for the next step. It came sooner than he expected, which was no doubt intentional. The half turn was made on the forefinger of his left hand, with a vicious sideways jerk, and the bone broke. He couldn't help it, he cried out. The next finger took a full turn before it went. He jerked and gasped again but there were too many people holding him down. Saliva flooded his mouth, his stomach was too empty to puke. No wonder Long George had wept when his pistol burst.

'Where's the gold?'

'Fuck off.'

They were going to break the fingers of his right hand. Never to hold a sword again, never to fight...

He closed his eyes and took a deep breath, held it, so he wouldn't scream when the next finger broke, he was on the edge of screaming already...

For a moment he thought he had, a long drawn-out roar of despair and rage. The men holding him let go momentarily and he caught a glimpse of someone charging at Lord Spynie, a shambling hobbling creature with a monstrous face, flailing his way through the courtiers, launching himself at Lord Spynie with a magnificent headbutt, blood flowering on Spynie's astonished, affronted face. Carey half-stood, cheering the German on and had his feet swept from under him so he slammed over onto his side, causing a stabbing pain through his ribs, and lost himself in whitehot agony when his hands hit the floor. Someone trod on him, he was helpless with his feet tangled in chains, somebody else kicked him and then the mêlée opened out and he saw the German falling, threshing like a gaffed fish with a dagger in his throat.

Spynie was dabbing at his nose with a lace-edged handkerchief and breathing hard. He stepped back from the kill and the German's body was rolled over, out of the way, next to the wine barrels. Mentally Carey saluted the man.

'Pick him up,' Spynie hissed.

Carey was hauled upright again, forced to sit on the stool again, his head shoved down again. It didn't seem possible, they were going to do it and his gorge rose. Once more he held his breath and tried to get ready.

There was a clatter and a creak behind him which he couldn't identify.

'Lord Spynie,' came a new voice, wintry and measured. 'Sir Henry Widdrington, release that man.'

It was the voice of King James's foster-brother, the Earl of Mar. A pause, then the men holding Carey down let go. Very very carefully he let out his breath, lifted his head off the barrel-end and looked straight up at the Earl. For the moment he couldn't stand, he wasn't sure of his legs. The Earl's face was hieratic and stern, but neither sympathetic nor surprised.

'I want to see my cousin the King,' Carey whispered.

'Ay,' said the Earl of Mar and jerked his chin at one of the courtiers in unspoken and imperious command.

After a moment's hesitation, and with no gentleness, the man unlocked the wooden manacles from Carey's wrists so he could

700

bring his hands round and rest the agony of metal on his lap.

He was not surprised to find he was shaking, astonished that there was no blood. The Earl of Mar was bending in front of him, unscrewing the thumbscrews which made his swollen fingers hurt worse than they had before, leaving livid pressure marks behind. He had to bow his head and stop breathing again while Mar took them off the broken ones. Mar saw the swelling and bruising, the unnatural bend, and took time to glare at Spynie, before taking out his handkerchief.

'I'll bind these two to the third for the moment,' he said. 'Can ye hold still while I do it?'

'Yes,' said Carey remembering Long George. When Mar had finished he stood up, cautiously. He was lightheaded, the pain in all but his broken fingers was beginning to change to a dull throbbing and for some reason, he was desperately thirsty.

'You'll come wi' me,' said the Earl of Mar. 'The King wants to see ye.'

He couldn't help it: he gave a triumphant grin to Lord Spynie and Sir Henry Widdrington, both of whom were looking stunned and afraid. His sudden joy wasn't only because he had kept the use of his right hand; it was because of what the Earl of Mar's intervention told him about Elizabeth.

He came joltingly back down to earth when he moved to follow Mar and the chains on his ankles almost tripped him up.

'Like this, my lord Earl?' he asked falteringly.

Mar looked him consideringly up and down. 'Ay,' he said.

'But...'

'The King said he wanted tae see ye. Naebody said anything about releasing ye.'

Carey was about to argue, but then stopped himself. He rested his broken hand carefully on the better one and told himself worse things could easily be happening to him than having to clank in chains through the Scottish court in nothing but his filthy shirt and hose, with a bloody face and no hat on his head. It was no good. The humiliation of it on top of everything else made him feel sick with rage, until he could hardly lift his feet enough to follow the Earl.

Lord Spynie moved to follow them out, but the Earl of Mar stopped him.

'You and Sir Henry are under arrest, my lord,' said the Earl. 'Ye can bide here together until His Highness is ready for ye.' And he shut and locked the wine cellar door in their faces.

That Carey was also still under arrest was made clear by the Earl of Mar's men in their morions and jacks, carrying polearms like the Yeomen of the Guard at the Tower, who were waiting to surround him at the top of the stairs. He went with them, for the first time in his life wishing he were not so tall. He wanted to hunch down so they could hide him, but forced himself to stand up straight and concentrate on moving his feet so the chain didn't trip him up. The stairs were hard to manage, he had to pause every so often to get his balance and his breath back. Once he did trip, but the guards waited for him and although he saw faces he had known, they didn't seem to recognise him, perhaps because of the blood and dirt he was wearing.

At the door to the King's Presence chamber, Carey stopped, balking completely. The Earl of Mar turned and glared at him.

'What is it?'

'Let me wipe my face, at least,' begged Carey. 'I cannot see His Majesty like...'

There was a dour look of amusement around Mar's mouth. 'Och, never ye mind what ye look like,' he said gruffly. 'He's no' sae pernickity as yer ain mistress.'

'But, my lord...'

The Earl of Mar tutted like an old nurse and banged on the door. A young page with one oddly ragged ear opened it to them and blinked at the apparition without expression. The guards left him at the door and stood there, not to attention, but simply waiting in case they were needed.

In they tramped, Carey more acutely embarrassed than he could have imagined: every minute of training during his ten years' service at Queen Elizabeth's court told him that it was not far off blasphemy to appear in front of royalty in such a bedraggled state. Without the assured armour of well-cut clothes and a good turn-out he felt as tongue-tied and confused as any country lummox.

Her Majesty would have been throwing slippers and vases at the smell of him by now.

Something deeper inside him suddenly rebelled at his own ridiculous shyness, anger rising at his craven fear of disapproval by someone who was, whatever God had made him, still only a man.

The man in question, who could sentence him to a number of different unpleasant deaths, was standing by a table, stripping off his gloves, with wine stains down one side of his padded black and gold brocade doublet. He was watching Carey gravely, consideringly.

Realising he was standing there like a post, Carey made to genuflect, remembered in the nick of time that he had chains on his ankles and went down clumsily on both knees in the rushes, jarring his hands.

'Sir Robert, I'm sorry to see ye like this.'

He was expected to respond. How? What would work with Queen Elizabeth might annoy King James and vice versa. On the other hand he would never ever have been brought so easily into the Queen's presence after a charge of treason had been made. Even in a letter, abject contrition would have been the only course. But this was not a brilliant, nervy, vain and elderly woman, this was a King three years younger than himself, who would almost certainly be King of England one day. King James might be unaccountable, with odd tastes, but he was at least a man.

'Your Majesty, I'm sorry to *be* like this,' Carey said, trying for a glint of wry humour.

'Ay,' said King James. 'No doubt ye are. What the Devil's happened to your hands?'

Carey looked down at them. The Earl of Mar's handkerchief splint hid his broken fingers which had settled down to a steady drumbeat throbbing, but the others were swollen and the ones that had felt the thumbscrews were going purple. His last remaining gold ring on his little finger was almost hidden by puffed flesh.

'My Lord Spynie was impatient to hear his tale,' explained the Earl of Mar.

King James's eyes narrowed. 'He's nae right to torture one of the Queen's appointed officials, let alone my ain cousin, does he no' ken that? Why did ye let them take ye, Sir Robert, I had ye down for a man of parts?'

'My Lord Spynie and Sir Henry Widdrington said they had a Royal Warrant. It had your signature on it. Naturally, in Your Majesty's own realm I had no choice but to surrender.' He omitted the detail of being outnumbered and outgunned.

King James made an odd sniff and snort through his nostrils. 'A Warrant?' he said. 'With the Privy Seal?'

Carey nodded. 'Yes, Your Majesty. And your signature.'

The King turned to the Earl of Mar.

'He's no' to have access to the Seal nor the signing stamp any more,' he said, 'if this is how he uses it.'

The Earl of Mar's face took on a patient expression.

'Ay, Your Highness.'

'And take the gyves off the man's legs. He's never going to attack me with his hands in that condition.'

Mar beckoned to one of the guards, who came over and took the chains off Carey's ankles. He was not invited to stand, and so he didn't. No matter, he had knelt for hours at a time while attending on the Queen in one of her moods.

King James went to the carved chair placed under the embroidered cloth of estate and sat down, ignoring the large goblet of wine standing on a table by his hand. His face had somehow become sharper, more canny.

'Now then, Sir Robert. What was it ye were so determined to keep fra my lord Spynie?'

'Your Majesty, may I begin the tale at its right beginning?'

The King nodded. 'Take your time.'

Where the hell to start? Carey took a deep breath, and began with the German in the forest and Long George's pistol exploding.

An hour later he had finished, his throat beginning to get infernally dry and croaky. King James had interrupted only to ask an occasional sharp question. Running out of voice, his knees beginning to ache and his left hand turned into a pulsing mass of misery, Carey finally brought himself into Lord Spynie's clutches and left the tale there.

'Ye say the German's down in the wine cellar now?'

'His corpse is, Your Majesty.'

'Hmm. And ye say the false guns ye sold to Signor Bonnetti explode at the second firing?'

'Yes, Your Majesty.'

King James started to laugh. He laughed immoderately, leaning back in his chair, hanging one leg over the arm and hooting.

'Och,' he said, coming to an end at last. 'Och, that's beautiful, Sir Robert, it's a work of artistry, it surely is. Ay. Well, my lord Earl, what d'ye think?'

The Earl of Mar was stroking his beard. 'I think we can believe him, Your Highness.'

King James leaned forward, suddenly serious. 'What did ye get for them and where did ye put it?'

Carey's gut congealed again. 'That was what my Lord Spynie was so anxious to know.'

'Ay. So am I.'

Carey coughed, smiled apologetically, spread his throbbing hands. 'I gave it to a friend of mine, but I don't know where he's gone.'

The atmosphere had cooled considerably. 'When did ye give it?'

'When I heard Sir Henry coming and realised he had a warrant.'

'Mf. This friend o' yourn, did he ken it was gold he was carrying?'

'Yes, Your Majesty.'

King James looked regretful. 'Ay well, nae doubt of it, he's ower the Border by now.'

'He might be.'

'And ye say ye're still in search of the right guns for Carlisle, the ones that came fra the Tower o' London?'

'If I can find where Spynie's got them hidden, Your Majesty.'

The King was still half-astraddle the chair, gazing out of the portable glazed window, occasionally sipping from his wine goblet. Carey stayed where he was, his face itchily stiff with dried blood, weariness weighting every limb, and his throat cracked down to a whisper. God, for some beer and a bowl of water to wash in.

After what seemed a very long time, King James seemed to come to a decision. He swung his short bandy legs to the floor and stood up.

'My lord Earl,' he said, 'have Sir Robert taken to the tapestried chamber upstairs, give him the means to clean himself and a surgeon brought to him, and find him some clothes. When he's eaten and drunk his fill, bring him back to us.'

'Your Majesty is most merciful,' said Carey humbly, wondering if this would give the King's men time to comb the streets for Young Hutchin. King James's eyes narrowed.

'Ay,' he snapped. 'Merciful maybe, but I'm no' daft and if I find out any of this is a lie, ye'll be begging me to gie ye back to Lord Spynie before the day is out.'

Carey bowed his head. None of it was a lie, he had told strictly the truth, but he had certainly not included any of the things he had learned or guessed from what the German told him. He wasn't daft either.

He got himself to his feet after the King had rolled from the room, looked at the Earl of Mar and waited. The procession re-formed itself. He needed all his concentration to stay on his feet since his brain was spinning with weariness and tension, and he had to keep his head high in case anyone he knew should recognise him.

\* \* \*

Elizabeth Widdrington was waiting with Young Hutchin Graham and her stepson Henry in an anteroom when they saw the Earl of Mar and the guards go by. She recognised Robin only by his height and the way he moved: his face was a mask of blood with an unhealthy grey tinge underneath. Her first emotion was sheer breathtaking joy that he was alive and could still walk. She stood and followed quietly behind, no longer caring what happened to her afterwards. It was not beyond the bounds of possibility that Sir Henry would kill her if he got out of this. The King had told her he would be arrested along with Lord Spynie. It was more than likely that he would try to take her down to destruction with him, if he could.

They took Carey to one of the upper rooms, and the key turned in the lock, she could hear it clearly. She waited on one of the narrow landings until the Earl of Mar came by and then she stepped in front of him and curtseyed. He blinked down at her.

'Ay,' he said. 'Lady Widdrington.'

'My lord,' she said. Her voice stopped in her throat. What was she going to ask him? To see Carey? For what reason that wasn't concerned with her unruly heart? And if he let her? What price her honour then? Would she make all Sir Henry's accusations and suspicions true?

'Hrmhrm,' said the Earl of Mar, old enough to read her sudden dumbness. 'If it's Carey ye're after, he's still under arrest, but the King's more pleased wi' him than angry, and I'm to call the surgeon.'

Her heart thundered stupidly; she had seen him walking, why panic? But still her voice shook.

'Is...he...is he badly hurt?'

'Nay,' said the Earl kindly enough. 'He'll need splints on a couple of his fingers for a few weeks and his thumbs will be sore enough for a while, but he's no' half so bad as he looks.'

She nodded silently, enraged with her husband for hurting Robin, perversely also furious with Robin for making it so easy for him. She wanted even more to see him, was hoping the Earl of Mar would ask a question that made it possible for her to ask, and also hoping that he would not.

Her second prayer was answered, he did not. He made a courteous bow to her, which she returned, and when she had stood aside he carried on down the stairs, leaving two of his men on guard by the door.

She went back to where Henry was waiting at the foot of the stairs.

'Well?' he asked. 'Did you see him?'

If she spoke she would certainly weep. What was wrong with her? His hands would get better, given the chance. She shook her head, tilting her face so that the unshed tears would stay in her eyes, led the way brusquely back to the anteroom, where she waited to find out what would become of her husband and if she would have another audience with the King.

'Was he...' Henry began, stopped himself and began again as he hulked along beside her. 'Did they...er...'

'Torture him?' Her voice came out metallic in her determination not to break down. 'I think they had started but the Earl of Mar reached them in time.'

Henry clearly had many more questions to ask, but couldn't bring himself to ask any of them. Instead he nodded, dropped his hand from her arm.

'Lady Widdrington.' It was the Earl of Mar's voice again, austere and somehow colder than it had been.

She turned and curtseyed.

'His Highness the King asks if you will consent to tend to Sir Robert Carey,' said the Earl, 'since it appears the surgeon is drunk.'

For a moment she stood there stupidly. Should she risk it? But what the King asked, even in Scotland, was a command. She could hardly say no.

'Of course, my lord,' she said gravely.

'Your stepson and page must stay here.'

Henry stepped back beside Young Hutchin, looking nervous. He was still too gawky to be entirely happy at being on his own, surrounded by the nobility of Scotland. She must send him to London soon, so he could get some polish. The roguish Young Hutchin Graham looked far more poised and at home than he did.

Once more she followed the Earl of Mar, through the over-crowded rooms of the best house in Dumfries, full of nobles dressed in French fashions or sober dark suits, and their multiple armed hangers-on, up the stairs, between the guards in the narrow second-storey passage lined with rooms, and the Earl unlocked the door again.

'My lord,' she said. 'I may need bandages and salves and the like.'

'Knock on the door and call through what you need,' said the Earl stiffly. 'It will be brought.'

The door opened: it was an irregularly shaped room, very small, with a bed in it and a table, and unexpectedly bright tapestries on all the walls, full of complex erotic doings of the Olympian gods, swans and bulls and cupbearers and the like. The light streamed in through a small window. Carey was standing by the table, trying ineffectually to wash his face in a bowl of water. He straightened up at the first sound of their coming in, and he stood there now, a comical expression of horror and dismay under the water and blood on his face. Lord Above, he was embarrassed, his face was flushed. Elizabeth swallowed the tender smile that would have offended him mortally. Why were men so vain?

She stood and looked at him for a moment until she could speak without a tremor and then turned sharply to the Earl.

'My lord, I want two bowls of water, one hot, one cold with comfrey or lovage in it, and at least four clean white linen cloths. I want any comfrey ointment you might have in the place, I want a good store of clean bandages and a clean shirt and hose for him and...'

'I'll see it done, my lady,' said the Earl of Mar, his face masklike.

'I may also need splints: send in at least four withies, about this thick and so long and a knife to cut them with.'

'No knife.'

'My lord, please don't be ridiculous. I will be responsible for the knife.'

'Hrmhrm.'

'Do you have laudanum in the house?'

'I dinna ken.'

'If you have, I would like some. You say the bonesetter's drunk?'

'The surgeon. Ay.'

'Well, I shall do my best, my lord.'

She marched into the room, heard the door shut and lock behind her and could have kicked herself for forgetting to ask for an older lady to act as chaperone. Well, no matter, she had done enough already to enrage her husband: merely confirming all his suspicions might even cheer him up.

The silly goose had tucked his hands behind his back. His shirt, which was one of Philadelphia's making, she saw, was in a revolting mess, stained to ruination with mud, blood, sweat, and something pink, and torn in several places. His hose were black and so less obviously disgraceful, but still disgusting. He smiled crookedly at her because his mouth had swollen, though much of the blood had come from his nose and some cuts on his forehead and cheeks.

'Have mercy, my lady,' he said trying for rueful charm. 'Don't be angry with me.'

She simply could not think what to say to him, since what she wanted to do was run to him and hold him tight and kiss him and then slap him as hard as she could. Instead she walked to the bowl of water, looked at it for a moment, carried it to the tiny window and carefully tipped it out. Dirty water splattered its way down the roofs below. The silence between them was very awkward.

Somebody knocked on the door: one of the guards opened it, and two boys came in, each carrying a bowl of water and a man followed them with his arms piled high.

'The hot water on the table,' she snapped. 'Cold water on the floor. Where is the comfrey that should be in the water?'

'The Earl says we havenae got none.'

'Very sloppy. Do you have splints?'

The man produced several withies, some too wide, and a very small but sharp knife and put it on the table. Elizabeth took the clothes, cloths and bandages from him and laid them out on the bed.

'Out,' she snapped. 'And tell the Earl I want a woman to come in here with me, to protect my reputation.'

'Ay, my lady,' said the man, hiding a grin. If she had been at home, Elizabeth would have cuffed his ears for the knowingness of it.

'You, wait,' she said imperiously as the boys trotted out again. 'So I do not get my hands dirty, would you please take Sir Robert's boots off him? Take them away and get them cleaned.'

For a moment the man looked mutinous, then as Carey sat still smiling on the bed and stuck out a foot, he did as he was told, walking out with them held well away from his smart cramoisy suit. The door locked behind him.

'Stay there,' Elizabeth ordered Carey, who made a wry face and also did as he was told, sitting meekly on the edge of the bed with its half-tester above him.

She took one of the white cloths and wrapped it round her waist for an apron so as not to spoil the expensive grey wool of her kirtle, took another cloth, dipped it in the hot water and began dabbing carefully at his face in silence. When that was clean at last, she came close and examined the cuts on his head.

'Where's Hutchin?' he whispered at once.

'Downstairs with Young Henry. I thought it better to keep an eye on him.'

Carey smiled in obvious relief, making her wonder what was so important about the boy.

'That's good. Where's Dodd?'

'I believe he's gone to the Johnstones.'

'Hm.'

'And what made these cuts?' she demanded.

'A dagger's jewelled pommel, wielded by an enraged minion.'

She sniffed. 'None of them are bad, I'll leave them as they are. There's blood on the side of your shirt,' she added. 'What happened there?'

Carey looked down in surprise. 'Oh,' he said. 'I took a cut there a week ago and I suppose it must have opened again. I'd forgotten all about it.'

'Did Philadelphia bandage it?'

'Yes, after she sewed it up.'

'Have you changed the bandage since then or had the stitches out?'

'Er...no.'

She put her fists on her hips. 'Is it hurting, throbbing?'

'Not much. Mostly it itches.'

'Show me your hands.'

He didn't want to, he put them further behind his back. Elizabeth tapped her foot and glared at him and so he brought them out again and let them rest on his thighs, palms up.

'Thumbscrews?'

'Yes.'

'Turn them over.'

He did, wincing slightly. At the moment, they were no longer such beautiful hands, Elizabeth thought, forcing herself to be dispassionate; they looked as if they had been slammed in several doors. Very gently she examined the right hand.

'I think you'll lose the thumbnail anyway, and perhaps the two fingernails as well, although there is something I can do about that. Are they broken?'

Carey was looking at them as well as if seeing them properly for the first time.

'I don't think so,' he said absently. 'I think they're just bruised. I can move them.'

Elizabeth pointed at the fingers still splinted together. 'These two are broken.'

'Yes.'

'My husband, no doubt.'

'And Lord Spynie.'

'I expect despicable behaviour from Lord Spynie.'

Carey looked up at her woefully, the expression in his blue eyes exactly like a little boy who has fallen out of a tree he was forbidden to climb. Damn him, she wanted to kiss him again.

'Are you very angry with me, sweetheart?'

Honestly, why was it he could melt her so easily? She took a deep breath and told him the truth.

'I am extremely angry,' she said. 'With my husband, with Spynie and with you.'

She straightened up and went to look around the various bottles that the boy had brought. There was an elderly bottle marked 'Comfrey bonesetting ointment' half full of something that smelled just about useable. The bottle marked laudanum had some sticky substance at the bottom and nothing else.

'There's no laudanum,' she said to herself in dismay.

'Oh.'

'Can you take your own shirt off, or will I do it for you?'

'If you undo the ties, my lady.'

She did so, not looking in his face, nursing her anger so she could be cold enough to help him properly. He struggled the shirt over his head and dropped it on the floor, and she kicked it into a corner. It was not the first time she had seen him stripped to the waist. She remembered nursing him alongside Philadelphia when he came back from Tilbury in a litter after fighting the Armada, not wounded, but completely off his head with a raging gaol-fever caught aboard ship. Against all the advice of the doctors they had fought to cool him down. That had been easier than this was going to be, because it was comforting for him to be sponged, even in

712

his delirium. Still, she tried not to look at him too much because it unsettled her, and made her long to run her hands down the muscles of his shoulders and back...

She put the bowl of hot water on the floor by the bed and cold water on the table.

'Put your hands in the cold water,' she said.

'Why?'

'To bring down the swelling.'

She went to the door and shouted through it: 'Bring me a crewel needle, embroidery snips and eyebrow tweezers and aqua vitae. And food and mild ale.' There was an answering shout. Carey was looking distinctly nervous when she came back to him, but he had his hands in the water.

The bandage around his side was stained and smelled. She used the small knife to cut it off him and hot water to soak it away from his wound. The wound itself was not bad at all, mostly healed, only one end had opened again and exuded a trickle of blood and white fluid. The skin around Philadelphia's neat silk stitches was red and angry and Elizabeth tightened her lips with annoyance at the congenital carelessness of men.

There was a knock at the door again, and a page slid round it. He was carrying a small hussif and a leather bottle. He scooted across the floor, put them down on the table by the bowl and scooted out again. Elizabeth wondered what was scaring everyone so much and sat down beside Carey.

With the eyebrow tweezers and embroidery snips she took out the stitches that were actually causing trouble now the rest of the wound had healed. She cleaned the part that had bled and bandaged it all carefully again.

Carey sat in silence, not even wincing. He seemed to be far away, in a kind of daze. She took the withies, measured them, trimmed and cut them to size.

'Now,' she said, mentally girding her loins, 'I'm going to cut off that bit of rag holding your fingers together.'

'It's the Earl of Mar's handkerchief.'

'I'll buy him a new one. Take your left hand out of the water, and put it on my lap.' After a moment's hesitation, he did. Very carefully she cut the cloth with the small knife. As the fingers came free, Carey sucked in his breath and held it.

The splints and bandages were beside her on the bed. She started by patting his swollen hand dry and examining the thumb, which was bruised, but not broken. There were marks and bruises around his wrists but nothing that needed attention.

'Let me tell you a story,' she said, taking his forefinger and feeling it carefully. The swelling was down a little and she could feel the greenstick fracture inside the flesh. It would have needed no more than a splint only someone had twisted it sideways. 'About two weeks ago, while I was still in Carlisle, my husband called out most of his kin at Widdrington and rode due west to the Border.' She knew Carey was watching her face intently, trying to ignore what she was doing to his hand. 'Probably at Reidswire in the Middle March he met his friends from the Scottish court, come south from Jedburgh, and took command of a string of heavy-laden packponies, carrying handguns. Then he rode south and east again and, according to my steward, he met Sir Simon Musgrave and the arms convoy on the Newcastle Road at night. Sir Simon is an old friend of my husband's, they collect blackrent off each other's tenants. There they exchanged one set of guns for another.'

He was interested now, listening properly. She held his forearm tightly under her arm, took his forefinger, pulled and stretched it straight, ignoring the jerk and his startled 'Aahh', until she felt the ends of bone grate into place. Quickly, she put the splint up against it and bandaged it on.

'How do you feel?' she asked. 'Dizzy?'

His face had gone paper white, but he shook his head.

'Warn me next time,' he said, panting a little.

'Very well.' The next one would be harder, being the long middle finger. She took it and started stroking it again. This was more of a crushing fracture, badly out of place. Well, all she could do was her best.

'Try not to clench your hand,' she said. 'Ready?'

He nodded, watching anxiously.

'Robin,' she said. 'Look over at the tapestry, over there.'

He did, fixing his eyes on a place where the heavy folds swung gently as if in an invisible breeze. She took the finger, gripped his arm tight against her stays and set the bone into place. It took longer this time to get it to her satisfaction and splint it to the other withy, and at the end she had sweat running down under her smock and stinging the grazes there. Carey was green and clammy, eyes tight shut. She smeared ointment on, splinted the three fingers together, took the little bottle off the table, tasted it to make sure of what it was, and gave it to him.

'Not too much,' she warned, watching his adam's apple bob. 'I haven't finished yet.'

'What the hell else is there to do?'

'I can make your other fingers feel better if I release the pressure of the blood under the nails.'

He was cradling his left hand against his chest and swaying slightly.

'How?' he asked, not looking at her.

'By making a hole in the nails.'

'Oh, Christ. Are you working for Lord Spynie?'

He meant it as a joke, though it was a very poor one. She tried to smile and failed. She was not enjoying this, although she might have thought she would, given the stupid man's cavortings with Signora Bonnetti.

'It doesn't hurt so much,' she managed to say. 'My mother did it for me when I caught my hand in a linen chest lid.'

Now he was offended for some reason. 'Get on with it then,' he growled.

She got the strongest needle out of the hussif case, sharpened it on the carborundum and slipped the cobbler's handstall on. There was a candle and tinderbox by the little fireplace. She lit the candle and heated up the end of the needle. The blood that came out from under his thumbs was sullen and dark, so she thought he would keep those nails, but when she drilled through into the nailbed of his right forefinger, the blood spurted up into her face and Carey yelped.

She mopped herself with her makeshift apron, pressed to make sure it was all out and attacked the final one, leaning well away.

There was pressure under that one as well. She cleaned them both up, once more fighting the distraction of his body. At last she bade him put just his right hand in the cold water again and wrapped a compress round the thumb of his left hand.

'Are you finished?' he asked.

'Yes,' she said. 'I'll make you a sling when you're dressed, but I see no point in bandaging your right hand when the bruising doesn't need it. You can take it out of the water when it stops throbbing. What you need now is to sleep.'

He shook his head, as much to clear it as to dismiss the notion. 'What's the rest of your tale? Who helped make the transfer on the Border? Was it the Littles? And why did they give guns in payment to the Littles who helped them?'

'I don't know what you're talking about.'

Carey explained about Long George and his new pistol and Elizabeth shrugged cynically. 'I have no doubt that Long George simply stole one. What else do you expect?'

'All right. So the Scottish weapons are now on the Newcastle wagons and coming into Carlisle with Sir Simon. What happened to the English weapons?'

'Apparently my husband took them north again to Reidswire where he handed them over to Lord Spynie's men.'

Carey sighed and tilted his head back. 'Of course, where else? Put like that, it's bloody obvious.'

'What is?'

'Everything. Who has our guns, where the bad ones came from, why they were swapped, who killed Long George.'

'Well, I'm glad somebody understands what's been happening,' said Elizabeth tartly.

He grinned at her, ridiculously pleased with himself again, and kissed her smackingly on the lips.

'You are a woman beyond pearls and beyond price,' he told her, putting his arms around her with great care. 'I love you and I will never never chase Italian seductresses again.'

She tried to hang onto her anger, but she couldn't. 'Don't make promises you can't keep,' she muttered and he laughed softly.

'Was that tale about your husband what you told the King,

to get me out? About the swapping of the firearms?'

'I told him more than that,' she snapped, still unwilling to be mollified. 'I told him what you did last month to stop Bothwell's attempt at kidnapping him. Anyway, all I needed to do was tell him what Spynie was up to. You know the King likes you.'

Carey shrugged, then grinned, tightened his arms around her bearlike. She could feel his heart beating against hers.

'Magnificent, beautiful, capable woman,' he whispered. 'Come back to Carlisle with me. Leave your old pig of a husband, come live with me and be my love.'

For a moment she struggled with temptation, more amused than offended by his rapid recovery. He found her mouth, began kissing her intently. Why not, she thought, why not? I've taken my punishment for it, why shouldn't I take the pleasure? She was letting him overwhelm her, she didn't care that she had the taste of the blood from his lip in her mouth, that he smelled of blood and sweat and surprisingly of wine...And then one of the splints on his fingers jarred on one of the raw places on her back and they both winced away together. He was puzzled, she was suddenly enraged with herself and him.

'No, no, no,' she snapped, jumping up and straightening her cap with shaking fingers. 'How can you want me to break my marriage vows that I made in the sight of God?' The words sounded pompous and false because they were false; she knew she would have broken any vow in the world if she could have done it without destroying him.

His face was nakedly distressed. 'Because I am so afraid,' he said, quite softly. 'I'm...I'm afraid that Sir Henry will kill you or break you before he dies. And I love you.'

Infuriatingly, the door unlocked, opened and two boys and a manservant processed in carrying food: a cockaleekie soup, bread, cheese and some heels of pies, plus a large flagon of mild ale. The manservant stretched his eyes a little, to see her standing beside a half-naked man, even if she was fully dressed.

'Now,' she said, turning to the Scot as businesslike as she could manage, considering that she was trembling and close to tears. 'What's your name?'

'Archie Hamilton, ma'am.'

'Well, Archie, do you think you could act as Sir Robert's valet de chambre?'

A short pause and then, 'Ay, ma'am, I could.'

'Excellent. Clear the table, lay the food. I shall leave while you help him to dress. Be very careful of his hands.'

She walked out with the boys carrying the bowls of dirty water, waited in the little passageway and fought to get control of herself. At last Archie re-emerged and she went in again, quickly made a sling for his arm. They had laid the table for two and she sat herself down again at the other end of the bed, so the table was between them, and dipped some bread in the soup.

Carey was in a plain black wool suit of good quality though a little small for him, with a plain shirt and falling band, a short-crowned black felt hat on his head. He was still pale and moved his left arm as little as possible, but somehow, despite it all, he was in good spirits. He ate and drank as if he were not facing another dangerous interview with the King of Scotland. Elizabeth could only nibble and sip.

'What's wrong, my lady?' he said. 'This is good; it's from the King's table, I think. Are you very offended with me?'

She shook her head, but she could see he had thought up something amorous and courtly to say by way of apology and further invitation.

'If I burn with love...' he began and she interrupted him brusquely.

'You're still a prisoner,' she said. 'I can't think how to get you out.'

He smiled, winced and touched his lip, drank his ale very carefully. Sometimes he was so easy to read: there went the courtly phrases back into the cupboard in his mind marked 'For soothing offended females (young)'.

'Never you worry about it,' he said, switching to irritating cheeriness. 'I know the King and he's a decent man. It's hardly treason to sell your enemy eighteen dozen booby traps.'

'Who were they for?'

'The Wild Irish, I expect, poor sods.'

'Don't you feel sorry for them?'

'Yes. I also feel sorry for Bonnetti if he hangs around in Ireland long enough for them to find out what he's brought. I'll ask the King to make sure he gets away with them.'

'And the real guns?'

Carey's eyes were dancing, though he was careful not to smile again.

'We'll see what we can do.'

They finished their meal, talking amiably and distantly about young Henry and his awkwardness, and the Grahams. Robin said nothing more about Elizabeth leaving her husband and coming to live with him. It was impossible anyway, and always had been. If news of any such behaviour came to the Queen's ears, which it would, she would strip Carey of his office and call in all the loans she had made him. He would be bankrupt, on the run from his creditors and with no prospect of ever being able to satisfy them because the Queen would never allow him back at court again. Frankly, unless he turned raider, they would starve.

When they had finished, Carey wandered to the locked door, kicked it and shouted out for the Earl of Mar. It opened and the Earl was standing there, his face as austere as before.

'Ye'll be wanting to see His Highness again.'

'If he wants to see me, my lord.'

'Ay, he's cleared an hour for ye.'

'Excellent. And thank him for sending Lady Widdrington to tend to me, she is unparalleled as a nurse and far better than any drunken surgeon.'

'Hmf. Ay.'

'My lord Earl,' said Elizabeth. 'May I ask what's happening to my husband?'

The Earl sniffed. 'That's for the King to decide, seeing he's under arrest.'

'And Lord Spynie?'

Another much longer sniff. 'Ay, well,' said the Earl. 'The King's verra fond of him, ye ken.'

'Yes,' she said with freezing politeness. 'So it seems. Sir Robert, what would you suggest I do now? May I serve you further or should I tend to my husband?'

'Tend to your husband by all means, my lady,' Carey said very gravely. 'I am greatly beholden to you.'

She curtseyed, he bowed. She walked away from him, refusing to look back, refusing to think of anything but dealing with her husband.

'Lady Widdrington.' She stopped and turned, felt a touch from him on her shoulder where it was most tender and automatically shied away. Carey was there, smiling at her.

'May I have my ring back?'

She blushed, embarrassed to have forgotten, wondering at the sudden hardness in his eyes. She fished the ring out of her purse under her kirtle and put it into his hand. He fumbled it onto his undamaged little finger, bowed once more and turned back to the patiently waiting Earl and his escort.

\* \* \*

The King of Scotland had often enjoyed the use of the secret watching places he had ordered built into many of his castles. Through holes cunningly hidden by the swirling patterns of tapestries brought from France, he found the truth of many who swore they loved him and learned many things to his advantage about his nobles. It was something of a quest for him: he never stopped hoping for one man who could genuinely love him as d'Aubigny had, in despite of his Kingship, not because of it. And like a boy picking at a scab, he generally got more pain than satisfaction from his curiosity.

At the Mayor's house in Dumfries he had lacked such conveniences. But in the little rooms on the third storey there had been a few with interconnecting doors and it had not been difficult to set up some with tapestries hung to hide those doors. Thus he need only leave his room quietly, nip up the back stairs and into the next-door chamber to the one where he had told Mar to put Carey. Sitting at his ease, with the connecting door open, he had quietly eavesdropped on Carey and his ladylove, as he had before on Lord Spynie and on some of his pages and others of the Border nobility. Some might have found it undignified in a monarch: James held that nothing a monarch did could be undignified, since his dignity came from God's appointment.

This time, as he descended the narrow backstairs and stepped to his own suite of rooms, he wasn't sure whether to be disappointed or pleased. That Carey turned out to be a lecherous sinner was not a surprise to him; that Lady Widdrington was a virtuous wife astounded him. He was saddened that Carey was clearly a hopeless prospect for his own bed, but he did not want to make the mistake with him that he had as a younger and more impatient King with the Earl of Bothwell. And Carey had called him 'a decent man'. It was a casual appraisal, something James had been taught to think of almost as blasphemous, but the accolade pleased him oddly because it was spoken innocently, in private and could not be self-interested. And further, it seemed that both of them were honest. Yes, there was disappointment that his suspicions were wrong; but on the other hand, honest men and women were not common in his life, they had all the charm of rarity.

He was sitting at the head of a long table, reading tedious papers, when Carey at last made his appearance in the chamber, having been kept waiting for a while outside. He paced in, genuflected twice and then the third time stayed down on one knee looking up at the King and waiting for him to speak. King James watched him for a while, searching for signs of guilt or uneasiness. He was nervous and paler than was natural for him, his arm in a sling, but he was vastly more self-possessed than the bedraggled battered creature that the King had seen in the morning.

'Well, Sir Robert, how are ye now?' he asked jovially.

'Very much better, thank you, Your Majesty.'

'We have made sundry investigations into your case,' the King pronounced, 'and we are quite satisfied that there was no treason by you, either committed or intended, to this realm or that of our dear cousin of England. And we are further of the opinion that ye should be congratulated and no' condemned for your dealings with the Spanish agent in the guise of an Italian wine merchant that some of our nobles were harbouring unknown to us.'

Carey's head was bowed.

'We have therefore ordered that all charges be dropped and your good self released from the Warrant.'

Carey cleared his throat, looked up. 'I am exceedingly grateful to Your Majesty for your mercy and justice.' Was there still a hint of wariness in the voice? Did the Englishman think there might be a price for it? Well, there would be, though not the one he feared. King James smiled.

'Well now, so that's out o' the way. Off your knees, man, I'm tired of looking down on ye. This isnae the English court here.' Carey stood, watching him.

King James tipped his chair back and put his boots comfortably on the tedious papers in front of him.

'Oh, Sir Robert,' he said, 'would ye fetch me the wine on the sideboard there?'

Carey did so gracefully, though with some difficulty, without the offended hunch of the shoulders that King James often got from one of his own subjects. On occasion he was even read a lecture by one of the more Calvinistically inclined about the evils of drink. It would be so much more restful to rule the English; he was looking forward to it greatly, if the Queen would only oblige him by dying soon and if the Cecils could bring off a smooth succession for him.

Carey was standing still again after refilling his goblet, silently, a couple of paces from him. On the other hand, it was very hard to know what the English were thinking. Sometimes James suspected that with them, the greater the flattery, the worse the contempt. Buchanan had said that the lot of them were dyed in the wool hypocrites, as well as being greedy and ambitious. Well, well, it would be interesting at least.

'It's a question of armaments, is it no'?' he said affably. 'Ye canna tell the Queen that ye lost the weapons she sent ye and ye canna do without them.' He paused. 'It seems,' he said slowly, 'that I have a fair quantity of armament myself, more than I had thought. Lord Spynie was in charge of purveying my army's handguns, and it seems he did a better job than I expected.'

Carey's eyes were narrowed down to bright blue slits. 'Indeed, Your Majesty.'

'Bonnetti is in the midst of lading his...ah...his purchases into his ship. He is still not aware of any...problems.' King James beamed. 'I gave him some gunpowder I'd no use for.'

'Your Majesty is most kind.'

King James let out a shout of laughter. 'I am that. Now,' he said again. 'I'm no' an unreasonable man. I see ye're in a difficult position with the armaments and I would like to put a proposal to ye.'

Carey's eyebrows went up.

'Oh?' he said.

'Ay, I would. I...we would like to sell ye our...spare weapons for the price of twenty shillings a gun, it being wholesale, as it were.'

Carey's face was completely unreadable. There was a short silence.

'I should hate to make a similar mistake to Lord Maxwell's,' he said cautiously at last.

King James nodded vigorously. 'Of course ye can check them over, fire them off a few times, take them apart if ye like. Ye'll find they're right enough: most of them have the Tower maker's mark on them which was a surprise to me.'

Carey nodded, face completely straight. 'Of course,' he murmured. 'May I ask if Your Majesty has sufficient weapons to defend yourself against Bothwell?'

'It's kind o' ye to be concerned for us, Sir Robert,' said the King. 'But we have decided there is no need to burn Liddesdale since the headmen there have come in and composed with us so loyally. Richie Graham of Brackenhill has made a handsome payment, for instance. And we have it on excellent authority that Bothwell has gone to the Highlands. We had always rather make peace than war, as ye know. Besides, it often strikes us that when ye give a man a weapon ye dinna always ken what he'll use it for.'

If Carey disapproved of this reversal of policy, there was no sign of it in his face. He tilted his head politely, though he seemed very depressed about something.

'Now,' said King James, who hated to see any man so sad. 'I would have wanted to talk to ye in any case, Sir Robert, even without all this trouble.'

'Your Majesty does me too much honour,' said Carey, mechanically, as if he were thinking about something else.

'Not a bit of it,' said King James, leaning forward to pat the man's shoulder. 'It's the horse.'

'The horse?'

'Ay. That big black beast o' yours.'

'Thunder?'

'That's the one. Now it seems to me ye'll hardly be doing much tilting whilst ye're Deputy Warden, and he's the finest charger I've seen in a long weary while, myself. What would you say to selling him to me for, say, half the gold finder's fee ye got from the Italian, at the same time as you sign over to me all the bank drafts in payment for the guns. Eh?'

Carey paused and then spoke carefully. 'Let me be sure I've understood Your Majesty. You will give me the guns Lord Spynie reived from the Newcastle convoy to Carlisle...'

'I never said they were the same, only that they were originally from the Tower of London.'

'Of course, Your Majesty. You will give me your spare guns, release my men Red Sandy Dodd and Sim's Will Croser from the Dumfries lock-up, give me all my gear back including my pair of dags...'

'They're waiting for ye downstairs,' put in the King helpfully.

'...in exchange for Thunder, several hundred pounds English of bankers' drafts and half my liquid cash.'

'Only half.'

'Your Majesty, I am overwhelmed.'

'Is it a done deal?' asked King James.

'If the weapons have not been tampered with by...any ill-affected persons, then yes, Your Majesty, it is a deal.'

'Excellent,' beamed King James. 'Have some wine, Sir Robert. Oh, and what would ye like me to do with Sir Henry Widdrington?'

Carey compressed his lips together and looked down.

'May I think about it, Your Majesty?'

'Ye can, but not for long. He's an Englishman, given leave to enter the realm, I must charge him and have him extradited or let him go. An' I'm no' so certain what the charge should be, neither.'

In fact this was another of King James's games. He liked to tempt people; as usual he had already decided to release Sir Henry since it would save him a mountain of tedious letter-writing to the Marshal of Berwick, but he was interested to see what kind of revenge Carey would want.

He met the bright blue eyes and wondered uneasily if Carey had somehow penetrated his game. Carey still had his lips tight shut. At last he spoke.

'If you still have him here, Your Majesty, I want to talk to him in private.'

'Why?'

'I am afraid for his wife. I know she was the one who came to you with the information on her husband's doings, and he may... be angry with her for her betrayal.'

And small blame to him, thought King James, a typical woman to do such a thing.

'Is she your mistress?' King James asked nosily.

Carey's face went red like a little boy's. At first the King thought it was embarrassment, but then he realised that Carey was pale-skinned enough to go red with anger as well. Perhaps he had been a little tactless.

'No, Your Majesty,' Carey said quietly enough, and then smiled tightly. 'Though not for want of my trying.'

'Ay well,' said the King comfortably. 'They're odd creatures, sure enough. I dinna understand my Queen at all and it's not as if she's been over-educated and addled her poor brains, she seems naturally perverse.'

Carey coughed and smiled more naturally. 'Lady Widdrington is a woman of very strong character,' he said. 'If I could make her my wife, I would be the happiest man in the Kingdom.'

'Oh ay?' said the King, sorry to hear it and wondering if Carey was about to ask him to do away with his rival somehow.

'Although to be honest,' Carey continued, 'what I would like is to petition Your Gracious Majesty to string her husband up and make an end of him, unfortunately I am completely certain that if I did, she would marry any man in the world except me.'

King James shook his head sympathetically. 'There's no pleasing them, is there?' he said. 'Ay well, I'm glad ye didna ask me to do it because I canna string him up in any case, our cousin the Queen would be highly offended if I took such liberties with any of her subjects.'

He caught Carey's narrow look: that was as close as a King could come to an apology and he was glad that Carey had taken the hint.

'It would be a shame,' Carey said obligingly, 'if Her Majesty were to be disturbed with any of these...er...problems.'

'It would,' agreed the King heartily.

'Such a thing would only be necessary if there was a further... er...problem with the guns. Or if my Lady Widdrington were to die unexpectedly for any reason whatever.'

King James sniffed in irritation at this piece of barefaced cheek, justified though it was. 'We are quite sure that the guns are as they should be.'

'Lady Widdrington?'

'*I'll* speak with Sir Henry, if ye like. He'll understand where his true interests lie.'

'Of course, Your Majesty. There is also the practical problem of getting the guns back to Carlisle, since I brought hardly any men with me. And as I said, two of them are in the Dumfries lock-up for fighting.'

The King waved a hand. 'Speak to the Earl of Mar and we'll bail your men and find ye an escort. Can ye lay your hands on the money?'

'I think so, Your Majesty,' said Carey resignedly, no doubt thinking of what the funds could have bought him if he had managed to keep them. 'I hope so.' Still, you've no cause for complaint, Sir Robert, thought the King comfortably; I could have taken the lot of it for all the trouble you've caused me.

'Speak to the Earl of Mar to fetch your gear. Ye can make the exchange today if ye move quickly.'

# Friday, 14th July 1592, afternoon

Sir John Carmichael had only just heard the latest gossip about the doings at the King's court when the subject of it breezed into the alehouse in the late afternoon, free, armed and with his left hand bandaged and in a sling. At his heels trotted his Graham pageboy. Sir John was not quite sure how to treat the hero of such melodramatic stories but, for the sake of his father, led him into a private room and sent for wine.

It turned out that all Carey wanted to do was borrow the services of a trustworthy clerk and dictate an exact account of what had been going on in Dumfries and Carlisle over the past couple of weeks, particularly in relation to no less than two loads of mixed calivers and pistols which seemed to have had the most exciting time of all.

By the end of it, Sir John was calling for more wine and damning Lord Spynie's eyes and limbs impartially. He was particularly shocked at the idea of a gentleman and cousin of the Queen being tortured by some jumped-up lad of a favourite as if he were a bloody peasant. Carey agreed with him, read over the fair copy and then took a pen in his purple fingers and painfully wrote a further paragraph in a numerical cipher, topping and tailing the whole with the conventional phrases of a son to his father. Sir John privately doubted that Sir Robert was in fact as humbly obedient to Lord Hunsdon, the absentee Warden of the East March, as he professed to be or indeed should have been.

'My father's in London,' Carey said. 'Would you make sure this reaches him without going near either Lord Scrope or Sir John Forster, nor even my brother in Berwick?'

Sir John Carmichael nodded sympathetically.

'Will he show it to the Queen?'

'Only if I die...er...unexpectedly in office, or that's what I told him to do.'

'Mphm. Ye'll stay the night here, of course, since ye can hardly go back to Maxwell.'

Carey coughed. 'Hardly. Thank you. Now, Sir John, I wonder if I could ask you another favour?'

'Ye can always ask and I can always listen.'

'I talked to Sir Henry Widdrington before I left the Court and the King promised to hold him for me until tomorrow evening, but I have a packtrain of armaments to get back to Carlisle. Even if I leave before dawn that won't give me much of a start.'

'Ay,' agreed Carmichael, having got there long before him. 'I canna lend you men, but I can give ye some information. Someone stirred up the Johnstones this morning: the laird and his kin moved out of Dumfries in a body. My esteemed successor went hammering out of town in the direction of Lochmaben shortly after, wi' every one of his men.'

Carey frowned.

'The Maxwells and Johnstones are massing for battle?'

Sir John tipped his head. 'Maxwell blames you.'

'Oh, Christ. What the hell has he got against me?' demanded Carey, clearly not feeling as blithely confident as he looked. 'I saved his life.'

'Och, but that was days ago,' said Carmichael. 'Wi' the like of him, it's a hundred years back. And he wants your guns.'

'To wipe out the Johnstones?'

'Ay. See ye, the Johnstones had just taken delivery of a surprising number of guns fra Carlisle, through the usual...er... system, ye ken, when ye arrived in the north and made yer surprise inspection of the Armoury. After that, they got to keep them and that had Maxwell awfy worried, so he put in a large bid to Thomas the Merchant Hetherington to get some for himself, which went, I believe, through your ain predecessor in office, Sir Richard Lowther.'

'Why can't any of these idiots buy guns in Dumfries?' asked Carey wearily. 'Why does Carlisle have to supply their every want?'

Carmichael shrugged. 'It's cheaper, mostly, the Dumfries armourers are very pricey men, and slow if ye want a lot in a hurry, and o' course it's more fun that way. Now, ye may have saved Maxwell's life, but ye also diddled him out of a fortune and spoiled his plan for catching the Johnstones unawares, which he resents and so...'

Carey knuckled at his eyes and then shook his head.

'And I haven't even kept the bloody money. What about the King? I've got twenty lancers from him already to see me through the Debateable Land. Would he give me more troops as protection, do you think?'

'Ay, the King,' said Carmichael carefully. 'They do say he kens an awful lot more than he lets on.'

Carey looked straight at him, considering. 'Yes,' he said. 'That's what I thought.'


## Saturday, 15th July 1592, dawn


When dawn came up the next day Carey and his packtrain were already heading eastwards into its bronze light, with a royal escort of twenty lancers and a Royal Warrant in Carey's belt pouch commanding safeconduct for him to the Border. Young Hutchin was not at his side, having been sent ahead with an urgent message on the fastest pony Carey could find.

He was not at all his usual self that morning. He already felt weary and a night of poor sleep made fitful by the throbbing pain in his hands had not helped. He was nervous because he knew perfectly well he could not even hold a sword, let alone wield it, and if he tried to shoot one of his dags, he would drop it. It was hateful to be so weak and defenceless, and the knowledge of his incapacity shortened his temper even further and filled him with ugly suspicions. He was quite sure that many of the lancers escorting his convoy were privately wondering just how annoyed their King would be if they simply stole some of the weapons and slipped back to their families. He very much doubted if they would lift a finger for him if the Maxwells showed up.

*When* the Maxwells showed up, he corrected himself, because they were guaranteed to do so. Lord Maxwell was a Border baron, descended from a long line of successful robbers; what he wanted, generally speaking, he took. And Carey was alone apart from the battered and subdued Red Sandy and Sim's Will, and made very nearly helpless by Lord Spynie.

He kicked his horse to a canter alongside the line of patiently plodding ponies, up to their leader which was being ridden by a dour-faced Scottish drover.

'Is this the fastest pace you can take?' he demanded of the man.

The drover stared at him for a moment, then spat into a tussock of grass.

'Ay,' he said. 'There's thirty-five mile to cover. Ye canna do it in less than two days and if ye have no fresh beasts waiting at Annan, ye canna do it at all wi'out care, the way they're laden.'

That was unanswerable. Carey harrumphed impatiently and rode a little ahead where he had put the least villainous-looking of King James's inadequate troops. No wonder the King didn't want to take them into Liddesdale on a foray. Then he rode back to the rear of the train to take a look at the others there. He was wasting time and effort, he knew. The ponies plodded on in their infuriatingly patient way and all he had to do was look at their tails and pray silently.

It was almost a relief to him as they climbed on what passed for a path along the sides of the hills, when he began to see armed men notching the skyline to their left and heard the plovers being put up in the distance.

'Here they come, sir,' said Red Sandy, loosening his sword and taking a firm grip on his lance.

'Do you know who they are?' he demanded.

'Ay,' said Sim's Will. 'By the look of their jacks, they're Maxwells.'

'God damn it,' muttered Carey. 'Where the hell is Dodd?'

'Ah'm here, sir.'

'Not you, Red Sandy; your brother.'

Red Sandy looked puzzled and Carey stood in his stirrups and looked around. Ahead of them on the road was the golden flash of sun on a polished breastplate and the flourish of feathers in a hat.

Carey pressed his horse to a canter again. 'Keep going no matter what happens,' he snarled at the chief drover as he passed.

Lord Maxwell's saturnine face was aggravatingly relaxed as Carey approached.

'Good day to ye, Sir Robert,' he called out.

'Good day, my lord,' said Carey, tipping his hat with the very barest minimum of civility.

'We'll escort ye to Lochmaben now.'

For a moment Carey thought of a variety of responses, ranging from the reproachful to the courteous. In the end he ditched them all in favour of honesty.

'In a pig's arse, my lord.'

This was not how Maxwell was accustomed to being addressed. He blinked and his heavy eyebrows came down.

'What?'

'I said, in a pig's arse, my lord,' repeated Carey with the distinctness usually reserved for the imbecilic or deaf.

'I'll have my guns one way or the other, Carey.'

'To begin with, my lord, they are not your guns, they are guns belonging to the Queen's Majesty of England.'

'They're mine now,' said Maxwell with a shrug.

'No,' said Carey. 'They're not.'

'Ye're not in yer ain March now, Carey. If ye give me no trouble, I'll let you and yer men go free without even asking ransom.'

The sound of a single gun firing boomed out like the crack of doom in the quiet hills and danced between them. Carey looked over to his right and saw the distant lanky figure of Sergeant Dodd standing on a low ridge to the south of the road, with a smoking caliver. He lowered it, handed it to the Johnstone standing beside him who began the process of swabbing and reloading, and took another caliver that also had its match lit, blew carefully on the end to make it hot and took painstaking aim at Lord Maxwell.

Maxwell knew that breastplates do not stop bullets and that where one Johnstone was visible there were likely to be plenty more. He darkened with fury.

Carey worked hard to keep his relief from showing on his face. He had known that Dodd and the laird Johnstone were both too experienced to show themselves before their enemies had done so, but he hadn't been sure they would be there at all.

'Now, my lord, unless you want a fight with the Johnstones over the packtrain in which the Johnstones have guns and you have not you'll let us go on to Carlisle in peace.'

Maxwell's face twisted. 'Is that what ye think? D'ye believe the laird Johnstone will let your precious packtrain into Annan and ever let it out again?'

'Nobody in Scotland is getting possession of these weapons,' said Carey through his teeth, 'though at the moment I am more inclined to trust the laird Johnstone whom I have never met than I am to trust you, my lord.'

Maxwell sneered.

'But,' Carey continued, 'in the interests of peace on the Border and the amicable co-operation of the two Wardenries, I am willing to allow this arrangement. You and the laird Johnstone may accompany me to the Border itself along with your men to be sure that neither one of you lays hands on the guns.'

'Ye're in no condition to dictate terms.'

'I believe I am, my lord. Think where I must have got these guns from. Think who's sitting in Dumfries with an army.'

'The King couldnae take Lochmaben.'

'He could if we lent him our cannon from Carlisle.'

'Well, ye've the Johnstones and the King to protect ye. Are ye not man enough to protect yourself?'

Perhaps it was just as well Carey couldn't hold a sword at that moment. Maxwell's gesture made his imputation clear enough.

'Take it or leave it,' said Carey when he could trust himself to speak, settled down in the saddle and stared at Maxwell.

He was never sure afterwards why Maxwell blinked first. Perhaps it was the ominous distant hiss of slowmatches from the hillside where the Johnstones were watching, or perhaps it was the drovers bringing the ponies up and past them as if neither side were there. Maxwell had not been Warden of the Scottish West March very long, perhaps he was uncertain enough of what King James might really do to be willing to wait for a better time to take on the Johnstones.

Never did a packtrain have a more puissant escort. All the long road into Annan, all the long night while Carey, Dodd and the King's lancers stood guard in watches over the guns, and all the next day, the Johnstones and Maxwells watched balefully over the weapons that could tip the balance so lethally between them.

As they watched the ponies splash over the Longtown ford into England at last and start south on the old Roman road, Carey growled at Hutchin.

'If your relatives turn up now, I'm taking you hostage.'

Young Hutchin grinned at him. 'Ay, my Uncle Jimmy thought about it,' he said disarmingly. 'It's very tempting after all.'

'And?'

'I persuaded them not to.'

'Indeed.'

'We've the King after us wi' blood in his eye for the Falkland raid, after all. We dinna want mither wi' the Queen as well.'

'Oh? That sounds very statesmanlike.'

'Ay. And our friends the Johnstones shared the guns they got to keep after ye turned over the Armoury, and besides we wouldnae want to mix it with the Maxwells without all our men here.'

'Astonishing. Borderers thinking before they fight.'

'Ay, sir. We're learning.'

The two surnames watched glowering from the other side of the Esk to be sure that neither one of them made a sudden attack. The ponies passed the ford and plodded on for the last eight miles of their journey, leaving them far behind. For the first time in his life, Carey felt quite weak with relief that there was not going to be a fight.

## SUNDAY, 16TH JULY 1592, EVENING

Lord Scrope, Warden of the English West March, was of course delighted to see Carey return from his trip to Scotland at the head of a packtrain laden with guns, all of Tower-make, all of precisely the pattern that the Queen issued to the north, with only about ten missing. It was worrying to see he had somehow injured his left hand, which was bandaged and in a sling, and also from the evidence of his face he had been in at least one fistfight. Sergeant Dodd, Red Sandy and Sim's Will Croser were looking uncharacteristically subdued, while a lad who had been missing from Carlisle had evidently tagged along with Carey unasked, and got into a fight as well. Heroically, Scrope suppressed his questions until they had dealt with the weapons. Those were stowed in the Armoury again while Richard Bell took a record of exactly what was there, Carey locked the door with a flourish and a suppressed wince and then turned to Scrope.

'Um...' said Scrope, bursting with curiosity to know what had happened to him. 'Your report?'

'To you, verbally, my lord,' said Carey. 'Now.'

That was worrying. They returned to Scrope's dining-room cum council chamber and Carey sat down in one of the chairs with a sigh and blinked at him.

'Will you call for beer, my lord?'

'Of course.'

They waited, Carey tipping his head back against the chair and shutting his eyes. When the beer came, Carey reached out to take the nearest tankard and noticed he still had his gauntlet on. With his teeth he stripped the glove off. Scrope stared at his hand which was mottled purple and red, and missing two fingernails.

'Good God, man, what happened to your...?'

'Thumbscrews,' said Carey shortly and drank most of his beer. 'I'll give you my interpretation of events as I go along, shall I, my lord?'

Scrope nodded, clearly finding it hard to look at his damaged fingers. Carey didn't blame him. The empurpled nailbeds made him feel queasy in a way that a much worse wound would not.

Carey blinked again at the florid hunters on the tapestry hanging behind Scrope's head, marshalling his thoughts with great effort. At last he spoke again in a flat tired voice.

'Well, my lord, in my humble opinion we were dealing not only with two loads of firearms, but also with two separate plots. One load of firearms came from the Tower of London and was stolen on the road from Newcastle. The second load was swapped for them to hide the theft. They were the ones that ended up in our Armoury and every single weapon was faulty.

'The first plot concerns Lord Spynie. He had been given the power to procure the King of Scotland's handguns, but like most army contractors he spent much of the money on other things and was then in a quandary to buy the weapons he needed. Luckily there was a German in Edinburgh, newly arrived from Augsburg where they also make weapons, who offered to supply him the guns at a cut price. All would have been well if the German had in fact been a master gunsmith as he claimed, because to be honest, my lord, the German weapons are usually better than ours. Unfortunately he was not a master, nor even a journeyman. He had been expelled from a Hanseatic gunsmithing guild for shoddy workmanship and fraud. Spynie didn't know this, or didn't care, and accepted the deal happily.

'The German, going by the name of Hans Schmidt, set up a gun foundry in Jedburgh where he simply turned out the guns as quickly as he could with untrained labour. I don't believe he bothered to caseharden the lock parts and the forge-welding and beating out of the barrels was so badly done, they were bound to crack at the first firing and explode at the second.

'Spynie had paid for them, taken delivery of them, when he found out—no doubt, the same way we did—that they were no better than scrap metal. Also the German had disappeared, the King's procurement money was spent, and Spynie couldn't make the weapons useable. The problem became more acute after Bothwell's raid on Falkland Palace, when the King called out his levies for a justice raid.'

'But didn't he find his runaway German? You told me you had witnessed his arrest...'

'Yes. Schmidt was hiding with a woman who sold him to Spynie once he ran out of money—I'm afraid he was as bad a fraudster as he was a gunsmith.'

'Bloody man deserves to hang, for the maiming and deaths he caused.'

Carey shut his eyes again. 'He's dead,' he said shortly. After a moment he carried on.

'So then Spynie gets wind of our new delivery of weapons from London and with a little help from his English friends—most notably Sir Simon Musgrave, Sir Henry Widdrington and his kin, and the family of Littles—he carries out a daring swap a day or two out of Carlisle. He gets the good Tower weapons; we get the ones the German sold him and put them into our Armoury. Purely incidentally, while helping to swap the weapons over, Long George Little steals himself a new pistol. Which explodes in his hand when he's on night patrol with me.'

Scrope had steepled his fingers and was looking through them like a child at a frightening sight.

'Clear so far?' prompted Carey.

'Eh? Oh, yes, very clear. A model of clarity, my dear Robin. Would you prefer to continue with this tomorrow, after you've had some sleep? You can have had none at all last night—you must be exhausted.'

'I am tired,' Carey admitted in a wintry voice. 'But I prefer to make my report while it's fresh in my mind.'

Scrope inclined his head politely.

'Now we must switch to another plot. Quite separately, Lord Maxwell was very anxious to lay hands on a good supply of firearms to continue and, he hoped, finish his feud with the Johnstones. He needed them because the Johnstones appear to be very well armed, again with guns corruptly acquired from the Carlisle Armoury.'

'I wish one lot or the other would win,' interrupted Scrope wistfully. 'It would cut in half the amount of trouble from the West.'

'Maxwell made contact with Sir Richard Lowther and asked for the longterm hire of the weapons in the Armoury, on the usual illegal and damnably corrupt terms. Not in any way realising that the guns were faulty—in fact they hadn't arrived at this point—Sir Richard agreed.'

Scrope nodded.

'But with me around and his pet Armoury clerk, Jemmy Atkinson, dead, he realised the old system could no longer work. At the same time, he wanted Maxwell's money. And so Lowther arranged to break into the Armoury while we were at the muster and steal the guns out of Carlisle. The plan was he would eventually "find" them again once Maxwell had finished off the last Johnstone and no longer needed them. While he was about it, I wouldn't be at all surprised if he had found clear evidence that it was I stole 'em.'

Scrope let out a humourless little 'Heh, heh, heh.' Then he added anxiously, 'Unfortunately you have no proof it was Lowther who organised the theft.'

'No, my lord, I haven't. There's nothing you could call proof for any of this.'

Scrope tutted.

Carey paused, editing his story. Would it be wise to tell Scrope he had broken into the Armoury the night before the guns were stolen, marked them and borrowed two for target practice? Scrope would quite probably be finicky about that and also about why Carey hadn't told him. No, there was no point.

'At any rate, the bad guns went to Lord Maxwell and nobody knew there was anything wrong with them.' Carey's expression changed to disgust. 'That man has the luck of the Devil. If I hadn't happened to be in Dumfries and saw that the gun he was using looked like Long George's, we'd be shot of one major Border nuisance.'

Scrope nodded, poured aqua vitae into his tankard and sipped. 'Never mind,' he said comfortingly. 'You weren't to know, after all.'

Matters were getting a bit delicate here. Carey decided to skate over some of the details.

'The long and the short of it is, my lord, that Maxwell was highly offended with me when I told him his new guns were all faulty. As a result of his treachery and Sir Henry Widdrington's, I was arrested by Lord Spynie on a trumped-up charge of treason.'

'Ah,' said Scrope sympathetically. 'The thumbscrews.'

'Yes. Fortunately, I have friends at the Scottish court who told the King what had happened and His Majesty was pleased to release me as soon as I had explained myself.'

'How very lucky for you,' said Scrope neutrally. Carey did not respond to his unspoken question.

'Yes. His Majesty was also munificent enough to return to me in recompense the guns that Spynie had stolen from our arms convoy and provide me with an escort to bring them to Carlisle.'

'How extremely...er...munificent. And that's the story, is it?'

'Yes, my lord,' said Carey.

'The full story?'

All of it that I'm prepared to tell you, Tom Scrope, Carey thought to himself. Too tired to talk, he simply nodded.

'How much of this should we pass on to the Queen?'

'None,' Carey answered instantly.

Scrope's face broke into a childlike smile of pure relief.

'Absolutely. I quite agree, my dear Robin, Her Majesty shouldn't be troubled with any of these little difficulties at all.'

'That's what I said to King James.'

'Splendid, splendid,' said Scrope, leaning over to pat Carey's arm and then, after thinking better of it, his knee. 'His Majesty's very wise and so are you. Discretion, clearly, is in order here.'

'Yes.'

'Right. Well. You'll be wanting to get to your bed, I expect. Barnabus is waiting for you in your chamber. We'll house and feed your escort and the ponies and send them back in a couple of days. Where's Thunder, by the way?'

'Oh,' said Carey distantly, stumbling over another reason to feel depressed, 'I sold him to the King.'

'Excellent,' beamed his inane brother-in-law. 'Dreadfully expensive to feed and far too good for this part of the world. He'll be much happier in the King's stables. Did you...er...get enough for him?'

'Yes, my lord, I can pay the men next month.' He hoped Dodd still had his winnings from the bet with Maxwell that he had given him to look after. Even without that, he thought he could make shift.

Scrope leaned over and aggravatingly patted his knee again. 'You're a miracle-worker, Robin,' he said. 'Absolutely extraordinary.'

\* \* \*

Never had the spiral stair up to his chambers at the top of the Queen Mary Tower seemed so long. He actually had to stop halfway up with his better hand on the stone central spine to catch his breath and wait for his head to stop spinning.

The door of his chamber was open wide with Barnabus getting the fire going and Philadelphia standing there, hands on hips, imperiously overseeing. Carey paused again on the threshold, wondering how much more he could deal with before he fell over.

Philadelphia turned, saw him and ran to him, then skidded to a halt and frowned severely at him. With uncharacteristic gentleness, she folded her arms around him. God, thought Carey, I must look bloody terrible.

However bad he looked, he felt worse. He went and sat on the bed, which had yet another new counterpane on it. Philadelphia sent Barnabus away and then sat down next to him.

'I heard,' she whispered. 'I heard it all from Hutchin and Dodd. Let me see.'

'For God's sake, Philly, I...'

'Oh, shut up.' She picked up his right hand, examined it with her lip caught in her teeth, then took his splinted left hand. 'This is Elizabeth Widdrington's work.'

'Yes,' said Carey, trying to remove it from her grasp. 'And it hurt like hell when she did it, so don't undo it...*Aagh!* Christ *Jesus*, woman, what the hell do you think you're...'

'I only pressed the ends of your fingers to make sure you still have feeling in them.'

'Well, I do.'

'Don't growl at me like Father; numbness is the first sign of gangrene.'

'Philly, I've had about as much nursing as I can take.'

'Then you won't want the spiced wine I brought you with laudanum in it to help you sleep.'

'No, I...'

'And you won't want to hear what I found out about my lord Scrope.'

Pure curiosity helped to clear his bleary head. He blinked at her questioningly.

'Scrope knew all about it, about swapping our proper guns for the faulty ones on the Newcastle road. And I'll bet he knew of

Lowther's little scheme to steal the faulty ones out of our Armoury too.'

'How do you know that?' he asked. 'When did you find out?'

Philadelphia sniffed eloquently.

'When I read King James's letter about it to Scrope, the night after you left for Scotland. He had it in that stupid secret drawer in his desk which I check every so often to make sure he isn't doing anything idiotic like dealing with Spanish agents and the like.'

She looked at him with kittenish satisfaction at knowing something he didn't, and her face fell. 'Oh,' she said. 'You knew?'

Carey shook his head. 'I suspected,' he said. 'Who arranges the bearfight?' he said. 'The bear or the bearwarden? No, it had to be King James operating through Lord Spynie. I remember the Earl of Mar said that the King wanted the German, that night when we saw them capture him in the forest.'

Philly nodded vigorously. 'They had it all cooked up between them. Scrope kept quiet about the guns being swapped, King James could use our firearms to settle matters with the Debateable Land, and then he would return the guns to us. They only used the bad guns as dummies because you were about, causing trouble. It wasn't exactly official, but the King did pay my lord a consideration.'

'A consideration,' said Carey bleakly. 'Philly, Scrope's lands yield three thousand pounds a year.'

'Oh they do, but we spend an awful lot.'

'So then what about Lowther...'

'I expect Scrope thought he had nothing to lose and plenty to gain by letting Lowther steal the bad guns. Maxwell might be badly weakened by the guns exploding in people's hands, he might even lose a big battle with the Johnstones as a result, which would sort him out and even up the balance in the Scottish West March.'

'He might have died himself.'

'Yes, true. And of course, if he didn't, he would be very annoyed with Lowther for selling him bad weapons, so Lowther would be weakened as well.'

'So why in God's name did Scrope send me into Scotland

without telling me any of this so I could protect myself?'

Philly smiled crookedly at him. 'The silly idiot doesn't trust anyone and he didn't think you'd work it out. And I couldn't send Young Hutchin to you because the silly boy had disappeared. Scrope knew you'd want to go. You were the mechanism for King James to return the good guns to us in the end.'

Carey laughed a little hollowly. 'So I've been rooked,' he said.

'You knew all this, didn't you?' Philly said intently. 'Or you guessed?'

Carey nodded and rubbed the heel of his right palm into his eyes, yawning mightily. 'I guessed,' he said. 'I guessed because of the way Scrope kept me away from the firearms; not at the time, unfortunately, but later, on the way back. Oh God, Philly, why does everything have to be so complicated?'

'Well,' said Philly judiciously, 'I suppose to Scrope it wasn't a lot different from King James borrowing our cannon to reduce some noble's fortress, which he does occasionally; it was just on a private basis, instead of officially.'

'Yes. That wasn't what I meant.'

'He didn't know Lord Spynie would do that to you.'

'No. Did he know Sir Henry Widdrington would be there, trying to curry favour with King James in readiness for when the Queen dies?'

Philadelphia shrugged. 'I don't think so. And you were eager enough to go and curry favour too.'

'So I was.'

'How's Elizabeth?'

'Her husband beat her black and blue for lending me his horses last month, and I think he beat her again after she dared to look at me across a street in Dumfries,' said Carey bleakly.

Philadelphia nodded, unsurprised. 'She told me she thought he might,' she said. 'About the horses, I mean. I'm not surprised he did it again either. For all his gout, he's very jealous of her.'

'How long does it take an old man to die of the gout?'

'Too long.'

Neither of them said anything for a while. At last, mercifully without a word, she undid his doublet buttons and laces for him, gave him the goblet of spiced wine and kissed him on the cheek when he had drunk some.

'I'll send Barnabus in to see to you,' she said.

'Philly.' Carey's voice was remote. 'You don't think he'll kill her, do you?'

She considered gravely. 'He might. But there's no point challenging him to a duel because he'd be bound to appoint a champion, so the whole thing would be a waste of time.'

Carey smiled wanly. 'I thought of that. When I talked to him in Dumfries, after King James had arrested him, I told him that whatever way he hurt his wife, I would infallibly do the same to him twice over and be damned to my honour.'

'Well, you'd have to catch him first and beat off his surname, but I don't think he will kill her. He's old and he's sick and he needs her to nurse him when he's having an attack. In a way, I feel sorry for him despite what he does to Elizabeth.'

'I don't,' said Carey.

Philly smiled. 'Sleep well, my dear,' she said and shut the door softly.

By the time Barnabus went in to help him undress, he was snoring.

# Author's Note

Anyone who wants to know the true history of the Anglo-Scottish Borders in the sixteenth century should read George MacDonald Fraser's superbly lucid and entertaining account: *The Steel Bonnets* (1971). Those who wish to meet the real Sir Robert Carey can read his memoirs, *The Memoirs of Robert Carey* (edited by F.H. Mares, 1972) and some of his letters in the Calendar of Border Papers.